T0373326

LOEB CLASSICAL LIBRARY

FOUNDED BY JAMES LOEB 1911

EDITED BY

JEFFREY HENDERSON

BARLAAM AND IOASAPH

LCL 34

[JOHN DAMASCENE]

BARLAAM AND IOASAPH

WITH AN ENGLISH TRANSLATION BY

G. R. WOODWARD

AND

H. MATTINGLY

INTRODUCTION BY D. M. LANG

HARVARD UNIVERSITY PRESS
CAMBRIDGE, MASSACHUSETTS
LONDON, ENGLAND

First published 1914
Reprinted with new Introduction 1967

ISBN 978-0-674-99038-8

Printed on acid-free paper and bound by The Maple-Vail Book Manufacturing Group

CONTENTS

PREFACE
to 1967 Printing

Since *Barlaam and Ioasaph* first appeared in the Loeb Classical Library in 1914, a number of discoveries have been made, relating especially to the Indian Buddhist origins of the tale and its transmission to the West. Ancient fragments in vanished languages of Central Asia have been recovered at Turfan in Chinese Turkestan; Arabic and Persian recensions have become available for study; and the researches of N. Y. Marr, Paul Peeters and R. L. Wolff on the Georgian text, of which a new and more complete manuscript was found in Jerusalem in 1956, have cast fresh light on the origins of the familiar Greek redaction, from which all the European versions trace their descent. The effect of these discoveries has been to undermine the former attribution of the work to St. John Damascene, and to render necessary new assessment of the evolution of this remarkable hybrid Buddhist–Christian document.

These facts in no way affect the excellence of Woodward and Mattingly's edition, the Greek text of which is in fact that originally established by J. F. Boissonade, occurring in vol. IV, pp. 1–365, of his *Anecdota Graeca*, Paris, 1832. Boissonade's text has yet to be superseded. The value and originality of Woodward and Mattingly's work, however, lies in the splendid English translation, with its rich Biblical and slightly Gothic flavour, which makes it a delight to

read. This translation, along with the numerous Biblical and Patristic references, and the copious index, have been reprinted without change.

I take this opportunity of expressing my special gratitude to Professor Ilia Abuladze, Director of the Institute of Manuscripts of the Georgian Academy of Sciences, Tbilisi, who has made available to me the results of his authoritative researches on the manuscripts of the Georgian recension, of which our Greek Barlaam and Ioasaph is itself an adaptation.

D. M. Lang

School of Oriental and African Studies,
University of London,
London, W.C.1

INTRODUCTION

There are few medieval Christian worthies whose renown exceeds that of Barlaam and Josaphat, who were credited with the second conversion of India to Christianity, after the country had relapsed into paganism following the mission of the Apostle Thomas. Barlaam and Josaphat were numbered in the roll of saints recognized by the Roman Catholic Church, their festival day being 27 November. In the Greek Church, Ioasaph (Josaphat) was commemorated on 26 August, while the Russians remember both Barlaam and Ioasaph, together with the latter's father, King Abenner, on 19 November (2 December Old Style). Sir Henry Yule once visited a church at Palermo dedicated to 'Divo Josaphat'. In 1571 the Doge Luigi Mocenigo presented to King Sebastian of Portugal a bone and part of the spine of St. Josaphat. When Spain seized Portugal in 1580, these sacred treasures were removed by Antonio, the Pretender to the Portuguese crown, and ultimately found their way to Antwerp, where they were preserved in the cloister of St. Salvator.

After the European settlement of India, and the arrival there of Roman Catholic missionaries, certain enquiring spirits were struck by similarities between features of the life of St. Josaphat, and corresponding episodes in the life of the Buddha. Early in the

seventeenth century, the Portuguese writer Diogo do Couto remarked that Josaphat ' is represented in his legend as the son of a great king in India, who had just the same upbringing, with all the same particulars that we have recounted in the life of the Buddha . . . and as it informs us that he was the son of a great king in India, it may well be . . . that *he* was the Buddha of whom they relate such marvels.' Diogo do Couto was on the right track, though it was not until the 1850s that scholars in Western Europe embarked on a systematic comparison between the Christian legend of Barlaam and Ioasaph, and the traditional life of Gautama Buddha, and came to the startling conclusion that for almost a thousand years, the Buddha in the guise of the holy Josaphat, had been revered as a saint of the principal Churches of Christendom.

The Buddhist Background

The parallels between the book of Barlaam and Ioasaph and the life and ministry of Gautama Buddha fall into two categories: first, many identical features of incident and biographical detail; and second, doctrinal and philosophical resemblances, where Christian apologetic is seen to stem ultimately from Buddhist ethical teaching.

The relevant features of the life of the Buddha, as contained in the ancient Indian traditions and later reflected in the Barlaam and Ioasaph romance, include the following: The Bodhisattva or Buddha-elect is born in miraculous fashion to Queen Maya, consort of King Suddhodana, who ruled over the

Sakyas of Kapilavastu on the Nepal border. The king consults his advisers and astrologers to find out the boy's future destiny. According to the *Jataka Tales*, a Brahmin named Kondanna foretold that the prince would forsake the world after witnessing Four Omens, that is to say, a man worn out by age, a sick man, a dead body and a monk. To prevent this, the king tries to shelter the boy from all contact with worldly misery. Whenever the prince is taken to the temple, the streets are cleaned and decorated beforehand, trumpets are blown and bells rung, and all cripples and blind or deformed beggars cleared out of the road.

King Suddhodana has a dream in which he sees his son leaving the palace and putting on the ochre-coloured garb of an ascetic. He takes stringent precautions against his son's escape, providing him with three palaces in which all forms of pleasure and recreation are provided. On one occasion, however, the young prince sets out with his faithful charioteer Chandaka to visit a garden by the eastern gate, and catches sight of a broken-down, toothless and grey-haired old man leaning on a stick. Chandaka tells him that none can escape this fate if they attain old age. On later trips, the Bodhisattva prince sees a sick man, a corpse and mendicant. The charioteer explains their condition to the prince, who is downcast by this revelation of human decay and mortality. In the *Mahavastu*, the Bodhisattva's encounter with the mendicant foreshadows the appearance of the hermit Barlaam to Ioasaph. To quote the rendering of the late J. J. Jones, the *devas* ' conjured up to stand before the prince a wanderer who wore the

yellow robe, whose faculties were under control, who had mastered the four postures, who did not look before him farther than a plough's length in the crowded royal street of Kapilavastu. . . . When he had seen him, the prince asked the wanderer, "Noble sir, with what object did you become a wanderer?" The wanderer replied, "O prince, I became a wanderer for the sake of winning self-control, calm, and utter release."' Shortly after this encounter, the Bodhisattva, like St. Ioasaph in the Christian context of the Barlaam romance, 'grew calm with the thought of Nirvana . . . and aspired after it.'

King Suddhodana tackles this crisis in the royal family by distracting the prince with dancing girls and similar allurements, but the Buddha-elect is adamant. He begs his father for permission to depart from the court, though offering to remain if Suddhodana can promise him immunity from decay, disease and death. Since these things exceed the king's powers, he is obliged to give his son leave to go. Riding out at dead of night on his horse Kanthaka, the Bodhisattva prince gallops till dawn, when, dismissing his horse and groom, he changes clothes with a wandering hunter, cuts off his hair and goes to seek the truth.

The Bodhisattva prince studied under two Brahman philosophers, and practised such extremes of asceticism that he almost died. At length, meditating under a pipal tree (*ficus religiosa*), he received illumination and was arrayed in the perfect intelligence of a Buddha. He then repaired to the sacred city of Benares, and in the deer park 'set the wheel

of the law rolling' by preaching his first sermon. Forty-three years of wandering and preaching followed. He died at the age of eighty at Kusinagara near his old home in Nepal, in the arms of his faithful disciple Ananda, who crops up in the Arabic version of Barlaam and Ioasaph under the name of Ababid. His last words to his disciples were: 'Behold now, brethren, decay is inherent in all component things! Work out your salvation with diligence! Be a light unto yourselves, for there is no other light!' After this, the Buddha died and attained to Nirvana, his body being cremated and the ashes distributed among eight tribes, who deposited them beneath burial mounds or *stupas*.

On the doctrinal and metaphysical plane, the resemblance between the ethical system of the book of Barlaam and Ioasaph and the teachings of the Buddha is not complete in every respect, particularly since the Manichaeans of Central Asia, the Arabs of Baghdad, and then the Christian translators, all worked over the text in their turn, and adapted it to fit the dogma of their particular faith. When it is said that Barlaam and Ioasaph is largely 'Buddhistic', what is meant is that a good deal of the subject matter came originally from a Buddhist book, or rather books; but the result was a new work, containing relatively little that is peculiar to the creed or doctrines of Buddhism. For example, the Barlaam romance contains no hint of atheism or even agnosticism, no denial of human personality and no explicit hint of *karma* and metempsychosis. The peace of Nirvana is, naturally, exchanged in the Christian Barlaam for the concept of heavenly bliss.

On the other hand, any doctrine or practice that had a common basis in Christianity or in Christian human nature, and in Buddhism and Buddhistic human nature is emphasized and exaggerated, such as the presence of suffering in the world, the impermanency of earthly things, their unsatisfying character, the unending round of changes that go on for ever, the strength of temptation and the necessity to guard against it, the evils of the world, the flesh and the devil, of all self-seeking, and the duty of penance, endurance and celibacy. All these are stressed in the Christian Barlaam to a disproportionate degree and their validity, in fact, is virtually taken for granted, to the extent that the contrary viewpoint, summed up in the exhortation, 'Eat, drink and be merry, for tomorrow we die!' is not even given a hearing.

It is interesting to note that the holy Barlaam, for all his Christian eloquence, retains many traits of the Buddhist monk, whose rules of conduct were to abstain from: (1) destruction of life; (2) theft; (3) falsehood; (4) sexual intercourse; (5) intoxicants; (6) meals after midday; (7) dancing and gaiety; (8) personal adornment; (9) comfortable beds; and (10) the use of money. Possessions could be held only by the order as a whole. There was originally no hierarchy of rank in the confraternity, only respect for seniority of membership. These particulars agree closely with the description given by Barlaam of his own life and that of his comrades in the desert. Certainly, the seventeen inoffensive monks whom King Abenner tortures to death (see pp. 333–343 below) are portrayed as more like

wandering Indian holy men than as members of any monastic order known to medieval Christendom.

Manichaean Influences

During the early centuries of our era, Buddhism spread rapidly northwards into Tibet, where it remained the official religion until our own times, and also north-westwards into Central Asia, including the region nowadays called Chinese Turkestan. From here, its influence spread into adjacent areas, notable Sogdiana and Bactria. According to Clement of Alexandria, Buddhist holy men were active in Bactria during the second century after Christ. They were said to have deified the founder of their religion, and to pay homage to relics of their god buried beneath a pyramid, that is to say, a Buddhist *stupa*.

In this region, Buddhism came into contact with Manichaeism, the dualistic faith founded by the prophet Mani (216–274). Manichaeism was an eclectic faith, assimilating and adapting elements of older local creeds wherever it spread in Asia, Europe and North Africa. Mani himself declared:

'Wisdom and deeds have always from time to time been brought to mankind by the messengers of God. So in one age they have been brought by the messenger called Buddha to India, in another by Zoroaster to Persia, in another by Jesus to the West. Thereupon this present revelation has come down, this prophecy in this last age, through me, Mani, messenger of the God of Truth to Babylonia.'

Professor R. C. Zaehner has reminded us that

'Manichaeism equates evil with matter, good with spirit, and is therefore particularly suitable as a doctrinal basis for every form of asceticism and many forms of mysticism.' From the Manichaean viewpoint, 'the body is composed of the substance of evil . . . it is a prison and a carcase.'[1] It is precisely this idea which underlies much of Barlaam's teaching in the Christian Barlaam and Ioasaph; it has well-established authority in many Buddhist texts, as for instance the well-known *Questions of King Milinda*, in which the human body is referred to as:

> 'Covered with moist skin, the nine doored thing, a great sore, [which] oozes evil-smelling bodily secretions all round.'[2]

If one examines the course of conduct laid down for the 'Elect' Manichee, as distinct from the lay adherent or 'Hearer', one finds precepts recalling the life of the Buddhist monk, on the one hand, and the Christian ascetic on the other, but most peculiarly similar to the austerities practised by Barlaam, Ioasaph's mentor. Thus, while all Manichaeans were vegetarians, the Elect abstained from wine, from marriage and from property. They were supposed to possess no more than food for one day and clothes for one year. Their obligation not to produce fresh life or to take it extended even into the vegetable kingdom: they might neither sow nor reap, nor

[1] R. C. Zaehner, *The Teachings of the Magi*, London, 1956, pp. 53–4.

[2] *Milinda's Questions*, trans. I. B. Horner, London, 1963, Vol. I, p. 101.

even break their bread themselves, 'lest they pain the Light which was mixed with it.' So they went about, as Indian holy men do, with a disciple who prepared their food for them. It would be hard to think of anyone who fulfilled these prescriptions more faithfully than the hermit Barlaam, with his single tattered hair garment, wandering in the desert and existing on a diet of herbs.

Internal textual evidence does much to confirm the assumption that the Christian Barlaam romance originated in Central Asia as a Manichaean religious tract. An Old Turkish fragment brought back by A. von Le Coq from Turfan in Chinese Turkestan contains the episode of the encounter of the Bodisav (Bodhisattva) prince with a decrepit old man, and his consequent disillusionment with the life of this world.[1] A second Turfan fragment contains a Manichaean Turkish version of an unsavoury tale which later occurs in an Arabic adaptation of the Barlaam story made by a certain Ibn Babuya of Qum in Persia (*d.* 991). This anecdote relates how a certain prince became so intoxicated that he falls into an open grave and mistakes a corpse for a desirable maiden. After attempting sexual intercourse, he awakes in the dead body's embrace, and is horrified at his own depravity. This anecdote, illustrating the Manichaean aversion to sexual pleasure, is omitted from all the Christian recensions. Particularly significant, in view of the eclectic character of Mani's doctrine and writings, is the insertion into the early versions of the Barlaam romance of the Parable of

[1] References in D. M. Lang, *The Wisdom of Balahvar*, London, 1957, p. 27.

the Sower from the New Testament. Professor W. B. Henning has drawn attention to the Manichaean character of an important part of the 'wisdom' of the book, as it appears in the Arabic texts, in spite of superficial Islamicisation.[1]

Certainly, the early Muslim theologians had no doubt that Budhasaf, or the Bodhisattva, was one of a number of dangerous heretics in vogue among the Persians. In a work on Muslim schisms and sects composed by a Baghdad divine around A.D. 1000, we read that the Orthodox 'approve of considering a heretic everyone who falsely claims to be a prophet, whether he lived before the days of Islam, like Zoroaster, Yudasaf (i.e. Budhasaf), Mani, Bardaisan, Marcion and Mazdak . . . and the others after them who falsely claimed prophecy.' In a very different context, the alacrity with which the Cathars or Albigensians of southern France—themselves a late offshoot of the Manichaean world movement—adopted the Christian Barlaam romance as one of their own favourite tracts in the twelfth and thirteenth centuries provides further testimony to the work's affinities with Mani's own authentic teachings.

Arabic and Persian Texts

According to the historian Mas'udi, the reign of Harun al-Rashid's father the Caliph Mahdi (775–785) in Baghdad was marked by an upsurge not only

[1] W. B. Henning, 'Persian manuscripts from the time of Rudaki,' in *A Locust's Leg: Studies in honour of S. H. Taqizadeh*, London, 1962, p. 93.

of Iranian cultural influences generally but of Manichaean propaganda in particular. Baghdad was flooded, it is alleged, with translations of works by heretics and false prophets such as Mani, Bardaisan and Marcion. From a bibliographical treatise called the *Kitab al-Fihrist*, written in A.D. 987–988, we learn that these foreign books circulating in Baghdad included no less than three works about the Buddha (al-Budd), also known as Budhasaf (i.e. the Bodhisattva prince). One of these books was called *Kitab Bilawhar wa-Yudasaf* (corruption of Budhasaf), and this is the direct ancestor of our Greek Barlaam.[1] It is interesting to note that this work is cited in the ' Philosophical Treatises ' of the Brothers of Purity (*Rasa'il Ikhwan al-Safa* '); this was an esoteric philosophical sect which flourished in Basra towards the end of the tenth century. From the Arabic was made a Hebrew paraphrase by the Spanish rabbi Abraham ibn Chisdai (*d.* about 1220).

Also going back to the Middle Iranian Manichaean tradition is an early tenth century Persian metrical version, fragments of which were identified by Dr. E. M. Boyce and Professor W. B. Henning in the Berlin collection.[2] This verse rendering ranks as the most ancient poem known in Classical Persian. Another Persian adaptation was made later on from the Arabic recension of Ibn Babuya of Qum.

The importance of the Arabic versions in the transmission of the Buddha's life story to the West

[1] I have discussed these Arabic versions at length in *The Wisdom of Balahvar*, pp. 30–39, also the article ' Bilawhar wa-Yudasaf ' in the *Encyclopaedia of Islam*, new edition.

[2] Henning, op. cit., pp. 89–98.

is very great. They contain a number of parables later omitted in the Christian versions, as being inappropriate or out of harmony with Christian theology and ideals. Furthermore, the vagaries of Arabic orthography, which relies heavily on diacritical marks in the form of groups and combinations of dots to distinguish between one letter and another make it possible to trace variations in the spelling of the names of the principal actors in the drama. Thus, confusion between Arabic 'i' and 'b' results in the transition from Budhasaf (Bodhisattva) to Yudasaf (Ioasaph); Ioasaph's father, the pagan king of India, features as Janaisar in the Arabic, then as Habeneser or Abenes in the Georgian and finally as Abenner in the Greek. Ioasaph's teacher, the ascetic Barlaam, first appears in the Arabic under the name of Bilawhar, which becomes Balahvar in the Georgian, and is finally Hellenized into the more familiar form Barlaam.

The First Christian Version: the Georgian *Balavariani*

So far we have been discussing the recensions of the Bodhisattva's life story and Great Renunciation which were current between A.D. 500 and 1000 among peoples such as the Sogdians of Central Asia, and the Arabs and Persians, who owed no allegiance to Christianity. It remains to determine how and where the Buddha became admitted into the ranks of Christian saints through the medium of the Christian versions of the Barlaam and Ioasaph romance.

The Greek Barlaam first appears as a separate

work in the eleventh century, being simultaneously incorporated in collections of lives of saints edited and compiled by Simeon Metaphrastes and his school. No mention of Barlaam or of Ioasaph occurs in Greek literature in any form prior to this time.

Most of the Greek manuscripts describe the tale rather enigmatically as ' an edifying story from the Inner Land of the Ethiopians, called the Land of the Indians, thence brought to the Holy City, by John the Monk, an honourable man and a virtuous, of the Monastery of Saint Sabas ' (pp. 2–3, below). Certain later copyists add a gloss, identifying this John the Monk with Saint John Damascene (*c.* 676–749), an identification revived by Professor Franz Dölger as recently as 1953.[1] The *lemma* itself is in any case rather incongruous, in so far as it confuses Ethiopia with India, and points to ' John the Monk ' merely as the carrier of the book, not as its translator.

Professor Dölger's explanation, which has the merit of simplicity, is that some band of Indian holy men came mysteriously to Palestine to the Monastery of Saint Sabas, and there recited the Buddha's life story and ethical doctrine to St. John of Damascus, presumably in Classical Sanskrit, and through the good offices of some obliging dragoman. The great Damascene, we are to believe, was so pleased with this narrative that he set to work to rewrite it in Greek as a Christian morality, and thereby to foist the Bodhisattva prince upon the Church as a holy man of Christendom. All this seems highly speculative, especially since nothing is heard of the Greek

[1] Franz Dölger, *Der griechische Barlaam-Roman, ein Werk des H. Johannes von Damaskos*, Ettal, 1953.

Barlaam for nearly three centuries after St. John Damascene's death; nor does such a theory account for the fact that early, non-Christian prototypes of the Barlaam romance had been current for centuries among the Sogdians, Persians and Arabs, who were far closer to Byzantium than the Buddhist holy men of India and Nepal.

Fortunately we have for some years now been in possession of a more tangible link between the Oriental Muslim and Manichaean versions, and the Greek Christian Barlaam romance, in the shape of an early Christian prototype in the language of the Georgians, a martial people inhabiting the Caucasus, the present-day Georgian Soviet Socialist Republic, who had adopted the Christian faith during the reign of Constantine the Great, about A.D. 330. Fragments of a short, abbreviated recension were published by N. Y. Marr as long ago as 1889. The subsequent discovery at Jerusalem of a far more complete and authentic text, copied in the eleventh century (Greek Patriarchal Library, Georgian No. 140), published at Tbilisi by Professor Ilia V. Abuladze in 1957, shows that here indeed is the missing link in the chain connecting the Oriental Buddhist legends with the Christian morality tale, of which the Greek Barlaam is the central exemplar.[1]

Earlier scholars, accustomed to thinking of Syriac

[1] Short Georgian version trans. with commentary in D. M. Lang, *The Wisdom of Balahvar: A Christian Legend of the Buddha*, London, New York, 1957; longer version in Lang, *The Balavariani: A Tale from the Christian East*, London: Allen & Unwin; Berkeley and Los Angeles: California University Press, 1966.

and Armenian as the sole channels through which Byzantine literature could have been enriched by the treasures of Oriental philosophy and lore, found it strange that Georgian should have preserved and transmitted a work like the Barlaam romance, which is unknown in Syriac and comes into Armenian relatively late, and then through the medium of the Greek version. However, the Georgians were eminently suitable for the role of literary middlemen between the Muslim and the Byzantine worlds. From 655 onwards, their capital of Tbilisi (Tiflis) was governed by an *amir* or viceroy sent by the caliph of Baghdad. The Georgians for their part were well established in monasteries throughout the Near East. As early as 440, Peter the Iberian had founded cloisters and pilgrim hostels at Jerusalem and near Bethlehem, where the most ancient Georgian mosaic inscriptions have been discovered. Before the eighth century, a school of Georgian translators and copyists was operating at the Lavra of St. Sabas in the Kedron gorge, where they celebrated prayers in their native tongue and occupied special quarters, known as the Grotto of the Georgians. There was an active Georgian community in St. Catharine's Monastery on Mount Sinai; of the large manuscript collection there, one Georgian codex is dated A.D. 864. In Syria, round about Antioch and notably on the Black Mountain, the Georgians had many hermitages. There were sixty Georgian monks at St. Simeon's monastery on Mons Mirabilis, and others at the cloisters of St. Romanus, St. Procopius, St. Barlaam of Mount Casios, St. Calliopius and Castana. At such centres as these the Georgians were in constant

touch with Muslim and Christian Arab populations, as well as with representatives of other Eastern nations.

The Georgian alphabet dates from the fifth century, being invented almost simultaneously with the Armenian, which it strongly resembles. The Gospels and Psalms were translated into Georgian almost immediately, to be followed by most of the principal biblical and patristic works current in Syriac, Armenian, Greek and Christian Arabic. These Georgian versions frequently preserve texts which have long since perished in their original guise, as may be seen by reference to relevant volumes in the *Patrologia Orientalis*, the *Corpus Scriptorum Christianorum Orientalium* and to the articles of Professor Gérard Garitte and the late Father Paul Peeters in *Le Muséon* and *Analecta Bollandiana*.

The longer, complete version of the Georgian Barlaam romance, or *Balavariani*, is preserved in codex No. 140 of the collection formerly belonging to the Georgian Monastery of the Cross at Jerusalem, and now incorporated in the Library of the Greek Patriarchate; it is a strongly Christianized adaptation of the Arabic *Kitab Bilawhar wa-Yudasaf* current in eighth-century Baghdad, and was evidently composed about the ninth century. Its antiquity and authenticity are confirmed by the existence of an ancient Georgian hymn to the Blessed Iodasaph, based on the text of this Georgian *Balavariani* romance, and already in circulation prior to the time of St. George the Hagiorite (1009–1065), who himself revised and modernized this hymn for use in the Georgian liturgy.[1]

[1] Lang, *The Balavariani*, pp. 43–50.

The derivation of the Georgian version from the Arabic is betrayed by countless textual and syntactical features, not the least significant being the names of the protagonists in the story, and the few geographical terms mentioned, all of which are clearly modelled on the Arabic, to the point of reproducing a few characteristic misreadings of Arabic script. Thus, the ascetic Barlaam appears in Georgian as 'Balahvar', after the Arabic 'Bilawhar'; Ioasaph in Georgian is 'Iodasaph' with a 'd', reproducing the form 'Yudasaf' ('Budhasaf', i.e. the Bodhisattva) of the Arabic texts; his father, King Abenner, is in Georgian 'Habeneser' or 'Abenes', from Arabic 'Janaisar', while the king's confidant Araches is called 'Rakis' in both Georgian and Arabic. It is particularly revealing that Barlaam's hermitage retreat is situated by both the Georgian and the Arabic versions in Sarandib, this being the Arabic name for Ceylon, whereas the Greek places it in Senaar, presumably the Shinar in Mesopotamia where the Book of Genesis locates the Tower of Babel, or else a region of the same name between Ethiopia and Egypt, situated in the modern Sudan. It is interesting to see that the royal city of the Buddha's father, the historical Kapilavastu in Nepal, occurs quite recognizably in the Arabic as 'Shawilabat' or 'Sulabat', which becomes 'Sholait' or 'Bolait' in Georgian; all this was too much for the Greek redactor, who omitted the place name altogether.

This unique codex, Jerusalem 140, containing the complete version of the Georgian *Balavariani*, was copied between 1060 and 1070. One of its marginal

notes mentions St. Prochorus the Georgian, founder of the Monastery of the Cross, and a disciple of Euthymius the Athonite. It is this Euthymius whose name is connected with the translation of the story of Barlaam and Ioasaph from Georgian into Greek.

The Greek Barlaam Romance

When the Greek Barlaam romance sprang fully fledged upon the literary world of eleventh-century Constantinople it created a sensation by its exotic setting, the novelty of its subject matter, and its effectiveness as a piece of propaganda for the Christian faith in its most severe ascetic form. Evidence of its lively appeal is given in the earliest Latin translation of the Greek version, preserved in Ms. VIII, B. 10 of the National Library at Naples, and entitled 'The Story of Barlaam and Iosaphat, brought to Jerusalem from inmost Ethiopia by John, a venerable monk of the monastery of St. Sabas, and translated into Greek by the holy man Eufinius (sic.).' In the preface to this anonymous Latin rendering, the translator writes:

'In the sixth year of Constantine Monomachus, Augustus, the most holy, the lord Triumphator (i.e. A.D. 1048–1049), I was ensnared within the curving walls of the mistress of cities by Imperial duties; and my eager desire for intensive research led my intention among Greek books, that I might set down something worthy of remembrance, taking it, like a bee, from the various flowers of the Achivi. This I was driven to do by the continual contemplation of my solitude, so far from home, pondering the present,

and fearing the future. With my troubles as incentive, while my mind was fluttering hither and thither, a certain man named Leo handed me a book.

'He begged me, for the sake of an offering to God, and for the memory of the Holy Barlaam, that I translate from the Greek into Latin, in simple language, this unknown work from the Ancients, never before translated, and up to my time completely buried in oblivion. Then anxiety for work and brotherly love urged me on, so that eagerness for activity spurred me to undertake a task of whose performance literary inertia was disapproving. And strengthened by the prayers of my brother, I bound myself to translate word for word and sense for sense, after the manner of the Ancients, and also undertook to make the sense clearer in the proper places, or in part to change it, so that my editing would at once render it delightful reading for the diligent, and stop for ever the mouth of the carpingly critical.'[1]

Just before the end of his translation the anonymous Latin writer adds a passage further explaining the circumstances in which he undertook the work. He says here that the first person to translate the story from the 'Indian' idiom into Greek was a monk called Eufimius (i.e. Euthymius), by nationality an Abasgian or West Georgian. Following in the footsteps of this Euthymius, the translator had been persuaded to render the book into Latin through the encouragement of a certain noble man named

[1] Paul Peeters, 'La première traduction latine de " Barlaam et Joasaph " et son original grec,' in *Analecta Bollandiana*, XLIX, 1931, pp. 276–312. The English translation of the passage cited by Peeters is by R. L. Wolff.

Leo, son of John; this took place in the year 1048, when the writer was in his sixtieth year, and the thirty-first of his residence in Constantinople.[1] This Euthymius the Georgian is also mentioned in the *lemma* to a fourteenth-century copy of the Greek Barlaam and Ioasaph romance preserved in Paris, Gr. 1771, which mentions that Euthymius the Georgian, *kathegetes* or administrator of the Great Lavra of St. Athanasius on Mount Athos, had rendered the story from Ethiopic (!) into Greek. The eleventh-century MS. Venice, Marc. Gr. VII, 26, describes the work as having been brought back from Ethiopia to Jerusalem by the monk of St. Sabas, and then translated from the Iberian or Georgian tongue into Greek through the agency of Euthymius the Georgian, ' a worthy and virtuous man.'

Euthymius the Georgian is, of course, a well-known historical figure, whose biography has been handed down in Georgian,[2] as well as in so far inedited Greek recensions (Nos. 4467 and 4573 of the Lampros catalogue of Greek Manuscripts on Mount Athos). The father of Euthymius, John Varazvache, was a Georgian nobleman who became a monk and went to live on Mount Olympus, leaving his young son Euthymius, born about 955, with relatives in Georgia. These kinsmen perfidiously handed the child over to the Greeks, to be held as a hostage for the Georgians' fidelity to the Byzantine emperors. Euthymius lived for some years in court circles at Constantinople,

[1] R. L. Wolff, ' Barlaam and Ioasaph ', in *Harvard Theological Review*, XXXII, 1939, pp. 133–137.

[2] D. M. Lang, *Lives and Legends of the Georgian Saints*, London, New York, 1956, pp. 154–163.

becoming deeply imbued with Greek culture. Eventually Euthymius rejoined his father on Mount Olympus, where the young man took holy orders and was entrusted with revising and completing the Georgian New Testament. and translating many key works of the Greek Fathers, including those of St. John of Damascus, quotations from whose writings are numerous in the Barlaam and Ioasaph romance.

In 979 the Georgian soldier-monk John Tornik rendered a great service to the Byzantine court by recruiting an army of Georgian cavalry and defeating the dangerous insurgent Bardas Scleros. As a reward, Tornik was granted handsome rewards and endowments, with which the Georgians built the Iviron monastery on Mount Athos. Euthymius eventually became its abbot, as well as holding an official position in the Great Lavra of St. Athanasius, as correctly stated in the Paris manuscript Gr. 1771. He was offered, but declined, the archbishopric of Cyprus. In 1028 Euthymius was killed in a street accident while on a visit to the Imperial court. Though relations between the Greek and the Georgian monks were not always cordial, nevertheless the memory of Euthymius was kept alive by an annual memorial service or *acolouthia* (Greek text listed in Lampros, Athos catalogue, No. 4650).

Long residence in Byzantium rendered Euthymius practically bilingual in Georgian and Greek. Manuscripts still preserved on Mount Athos, and at Jerusalem, Tbilisi and other libraries, showed that he rendered about 160 biblical and patristic works from Greek into Georgian, as well as composing several religious treatises in Georgian. Several of his

translations still exist in the saint's own autograph. As the Georgian biographer of Euthymius, St. George the Hagiorite, expresses it, 'the blessed Euthymius went on translating without respite and gave himself no repose; day and night he distilled the sweet honey of the books of God, with which he adorned our language and our Church. He translated so many divine works that nobody could enumerate them, since he worked at his translations not only on Mount Olympus and Mount Athos (which works we can list in detail), but also in Constantinople, and while travelling, and in all kinds of other places.' St. George the Hagiorite adds further, and most pertinently in connection with the Barlaam romance, that 'the sweetness of the books he translated permeates the entire land, not only of Georgia but of Greece also, for he rendered from Georgian into Greek the *Balahvari* (i.e. the Georgian Barlaam romance) . . . and a number of other works.' [1]

We thus have independent, virtually contemporary testimony in three different languages—Latin, Greek and Georgian—that it was Euthymius the Georgian, abbot of the Iviron monastery on Mount Athos, who was responsible for rendering the Barlaam and Ioasaph romance from Georgian into Greek. This combined evidence seems decisive, especially as a number of phrases and passages in the Greek can, through stylistic and linguistic peculiarities, be traced to a Georgian prototype.[2]

[1] Lang, *Lives and Legends of the Georgian Saints*, pp. 161–162, 155.

[2] S. G. Qaukhchishvili, *Bizantiuri literaturis istoria* ('History of Byzantine literature'), Tbilisi, 1963, pp. 206–237.

This is not to say that the Greek text presented in this volume in the edition and translation of G. R. Woodward and Harold Mattingly is a literal translation from Old Georgian. It has undergone intensive remodelling and 'improvement,' in the light of the rhetorical principles characteristic of the era of Simeon Metaphrastes, the Logothete, himself a contemporary of St. Euthymius the Athonite, and his school. The Greek Barlaam has also benefited notably from the insertion of the effective defence of Christianity known as the *Apology of Aristides*, attributed to a second-century Athenian philosopher of that name. This discourse, when placed in the mouth of the heathen ascetic Nachor, who is masquerading as Barlaam in a mock debate on the faith organized by King Abenner (pp. 396–425, below), results in the effectual worsting of the idolaters.[1]

It is hard to say whether St. Euthymius the Athonite personally carried out both the work of translation from Georgian into Greek and also the extensive polishing and metaphrastic embellishment which the text underwent before it was presented to the sophisticated Byzantine reading public. A point to remember is that Euthymius died in 1028, whereas it was only in 1048 that the finished product was laid before our anonymous Latin translator living in Constantinople, as 'an unknown work from the Ancients, never before translated,' and up to that time 'completely buried in oblivion.' The earliest dated copies of the Greek Barlaam recorded are evidently

[1] J. Rendel Harris and J. Armitage Robinson, *The Apology of Aristides*, Cambridge, 1891. (Texts and Studies, Vol. I, No. 1.)

Escurial No. 163 of A.D. 1057 and Magdalen College, Oxford, Greek No. 4 of 1064. This suggests that there was a period of at least a quarter of a century during which a literal rendering of the Georgian *Balavariani* could have circulated on Mount Athos and in Constantinople. There was ample opportunity for a copy to fall into the workshop of Simeon Metaphrastes and his disciples, who will have regarded it as welcome grist to their literary mill. It may even be, as the late Professor K. S. Kekelidze suggested, that Euthymius the Athonite and Simeon Metaphrastes were personally acquainted, and that Euthymius translated the Barlaam romance especially for Simeon's use.[1]

THE LATER DIFFUSION OF BARLAAM AND IOASAPH

From the middle of the eleventh century the Barlaam and Ioasaph story spread rapidly into virtually all the countries of Christendom. It was translated from Greek into Old Slavonic, giving rise to Russian, White Russian and Serbian versions. As late as the nineteenth century, it had a great effect on the novelist Leo Tolstoy, who records in his *A Confession* that it played a decisive part in determining him to renounce all worldly pleasures. From Greek also the story was rendered into Armenian and into Christian Arabic, from which a curious Ethiopic version was made (translated and edited in 1923 by the late Sir Ernest Wallis Budge). In Western

[1] K. S. Kekelidze, *Etiudebi dzveli kartuli literaturis istoriidan* ('Studies in the history of Old Georgian literature'), Vol. VI, Tbilisi, 1960, pp. 66–67.

Europe the story was diffused through the medium of no less than three separate and distinct Latin versions. Vincent of Beauvais (*c.* 1190–1264) included an abbreviated version in his *Speculum Historiale*, while Jacobus de Voragine (1230–1298) incorporated the story in his *Legenda Aurea* or *The Golden Legend*, the English version of which was printed by William Caxton at Westminster in 1483. It is from Caxton's edition that Shakespeare evidently borrowed the Fable of the Caskets for effective use in *The Merchant of Venice*.

Of the medieval French and Anglo-Norman versions, the most celebrated is the verse rendering by Guy de Cambrai. The work was translated into Provençal, and became a favourite ascetic manual of the Albigensian heretics, who found its Manichaean overtones very congenial. Around 1220, Rudolf von Ems made a Middle High German verse translation; thirty years later, King Haakon IV of Norway whiled away the long winter evenings by superintending the work's translation into Norse. Barlaam and Josaphat provided the subject for several fifteenth-century French and Italian miracle plays. Both Lope de Vega and Calderon wrote dramas on the theme, and these were emulated by Jesuit composers of morality plays.

Thus it was that after capturing the imagination of the Manichaeans of Central Asia, the Arabs of Baghdad and the Georgians of the Caucasus, the Bodhisattva prince attained a fresh incarnation as a saintly figure of European Christendom. Even though the Middle Ages lacked direct access to the Buddha's teachings, yet his legendary life story

contributed in this way to the spiritual formation of the age. The fact that Gautama Buddha was venerated for centuries in the guise of a Christian saint, far from providing a stumbling block to the Faithful, may be regarded as yet another proof of the vitality and universal appeal of the teaching and example of the founder of the Buddhist faith, the great Sakyamuni of Kapilavastu.

Select Bibliography

Armstrong, E. C. *The French metrical versions of Barlaam and Josaphat*, Princeton, 1922.

Bolton, W. F. ' Parable, Allegory and Romance in the Legend of Barlaam and Josaphat,' in *Traditio*, Vol. XIV, 1958, pp. 359–366.

Budge, Sir E. A. Wallis, edit. and trans., *Baralâm and Yĕwâsĕf* (Ethiopic text and trans.), 2 vols., Cambridge, 1923.

Der Nersessian, Sirarpie, *L'Illustration du Roman de Barlaam et Joasaph*, Paris, 1937.

Dölger, Franz. *Der griechische Barlaam-Roman, ein Werk des H. Johannes von Damaskos*, Ettal, 1953.

Harris, J. Rendel, and J. Armitage Robinson, *The Apology of Aristides*, Cambridge, 1891. (Texts and Studies, Vol. I, No. 1.)

Henning, W. B. ' Persian poetical manuscripts from the time of Rūdakī,' in *A Locust's Leg: Studies in Honour of S. H. Taqizadeh*, London, 1962, pp. 89–104.

Jacobs, Joseph. *Barlaam and Josaphat*, London, 1896.

LANG, David Marshall. *The Balavariani: A Tale from the Christian East*, London: Allen & Unwin; Berkeley and Los Angeles: California University Press, 1966.

—— *The Wisdom of Balahvar: A Christian Legend of the Buddha,* London: Allen & Unwin; New York: Macmillan, 1957.

LEROY, Jules. 'Un nouveau manuscrit arabe-chrétien illustré du Roman de Barlaam et Joasaph,' in *Syria*, Vol. XXXII, 1955, pp. 101–22.

MANSELLI, Raoul. 'The Legend of Barlaam and Joasaph in Byzantium and in the Romance Europe,' in *East and West*, Vol. VII, No. 4, Rome, 1957, pp. 331–40.

PEETERS, Paul. 'La première traduction latine de "Barlaam et Joasaph" et son original grec,' in *Analecta Bollandiana*, Vol. XLIX, 1931, pp. 276–312.

PERI (PFLAUM), Hiram. *Der Religionsdisput der Barlaam-Legende, ein Motif abendländischer Dichtung*, Salamanca, 1959.

QAUKHCHISHVILI, S. G. *Bizantiuri literaturis istoria* ('History of Byzantine literature'), Tbilisi, 1963.

SONET, J. *Le Roman de Barlaam et Josaphat*, 3 pt., Louvain, Namur, Paris, 1949–1952.

WOLFF, Robert Lee. 'The Apology of Aristides—A Re-examination', in *Harvard Theological Review*, Vol. XXX, 1937, pp. 233–247.

—— 'Barlaam and Ioasaph,' in *Harvard Theological Review*, Vol. XXXII, 1939, pp. 131–139.

BARLAAM AND IOASAPH

ΒΑΡΛΑΑΜ ΚΑΙ ΙΩΑΣΑΦ

ΙΣΤΟΡΙΑ ΨΥΧΩΦΕΛΗΣ ΕΚ ΤΗΣ ΕΝΔΟΤΕΡΑΣ ΤΩΝ ΑΙΘΙΟΠΩΝ ΧΩΡΑΣ, ΤΗΣ ΙΝΔΩΝ ΛΕΓΟΜΕΝΗΣ, ΠΡΟΣ ΤΗΝ ΑΓΙΑΝ ΠΟΛΙΝ ΜΕΤΕΝΕΧΘΕΙΣΑ ΔΙΑ ΙΩΑΝΝΟΥ ΜΟΝΑΧΟΥ, ΑΝΔΡΟΣ ΤΙΜΙΟΥ ΚΑΙ ΕΝΑΡΕΤΟΥ ΜΟΝΗΣ ΤΟΥ ΑΓΙΟΥ ΣΑΒΑ· ΕΝ ΗΙ Ο ΒΙΟΣ ΒΑΡΛΑΑΜ ΚΑΙ ΙΩΑΣΑΦ ΤΩΝ ΑΟΙΔΙΜΩΝ ΚΑΙ ΜΑΚΑΡΙΩΝ.

ΠΡΟΟΙΜΙΟΝ

Rom. viii. 14 "Οσοι Πνεύματι Θεοῦ ἄγονται, οὗτοί εἰσιν 1
υἱοὶ Θεοῦ, φησὶν ὁ θεῖος Ἀπόστολος· τὸ δὲ Πνεύματος ἁγίου ἀξιωθῆναι καὶ υἱοὺς Θεοῦ γενέσθαι
Nazianz. Orat. de Athanas., 386, 34 τῶν ὀρεκτῶν ὑπάρχει τὸ ἔσχατον, καὶ οὗ γενο-
μένοις πάσης θεωρίας ἀνάπαυσις, καθὼς γέγρα-
πται. τῆς οὖν ὑπερφυοῦς ταύτης καὶ τῶν ἐφετῶν
ἀκροτάτης μακαριότητος ἠξιώθησαν ἐπιτυχεῖν οἱ
ἀπ' αἰῶνος ἅγιοι διὰ τῆς τῶν ἀρετῶν ἐργασίας· οἱ
Heb. xii. 4 μὲν μαρτυρικῶς ἀθλήσαντες καὶ μέχρις αἵματος
πρὸς τὴν ἁμαρτίαν ἀντικαταστάντες, οἱ δὲ ἀσκητικῶς ἀγωνισάμενοι, καὶ τὴν στενὴν βαδίσαντες
Mat. vii. 14 ὁδόν, καὶ μάρτυρες τῇ προαιρέσει γενόμενοι. ὧν
τὰς ἀριστείας καὶ τὰ κατορθώματα, τῶν τε δι' 2
Luke xiii. 32 αἵματος τελειωθέντων καὶ τῶν δι' ἀσκήσεως
τὴν ἀγγελικὴν πολιτείαν μιμησαμένων, γραφῇ
παραδιδόναι, καὶ ἀρετῆς ὑπόδειγμα ταῖς μετέπειτα

BARLAAM AND IOASAPH

AN EDIFYING STORY FROM THE INNER LAND OF THE ETHIOPIANS, CALLED THE LAND OF THE INDIANS, THENCE BROUGHT TO THE HOLY CITY, BY JOHN THE MONK (AN HONOURABLE MAN AND A VIRTUOUS, OF THE MONASTERY OF SAINT SABAS); WHEREIN ARE THE LIVES OF THE FAMOUS AND BLESSED BARLAAM AND IOASAPH.

INTRODUCTION

The author setteth forth the purpose of his history

'As many as are led by the Spirit of God they are sons of God' saith the inspired Apostle. Now to have been accounted worthy of the Holy Spirit and to have become sons of God is of all things most to be coveted; and, as it is written, 'They that have become his sons find rest from all enquiry.' This marvellous, and above all else desirable, blessedness have the Saints from the beginning won by the practice of the virtues, some having striven as Martyrs, and resisted sin unto blood, and others having struggled in self-discipline, and having trodden the narrow way, proving Martyrs in will. Now, that one should hand down to memory the prowess and virtuous deeds of these, both of them that were made perfect by blood, and of them that by self-denial did emulate the conversation of Angels, and should deliver to the generations that follow a pattern of virtue, this

παραπέμπειν γενεαῖς, ἐκ τῶν θεηγόρων Ἀποστόλων καὶ μακαρίων Πατέρων ἡ τοῦ Χριστοῦ παρεί-
ληφεν Ἐκκλησία, ἐπὶ σωτηρίᾳ τοῦ γένους ἡμῶν
τοῦτο νομοθετησάντων. ἡ γὰρ πρὸς ἀρετὴν
φέρουσα ὁδὸς τραχεῖά τίς ἐστι καὶ ἀνάντης καὶ
μάλιστα τοῖς μήπω μεταθεμένοις ὅλους ἑαυτοὺς
ἐπὶ τὸν Κύριον, ἀλλ' ἐκ τῆς τῶν παθῶν τυραννίδος ἔτι πολεμουμένοις. διὰ τοῦτο καὶ πολλῶν
δεόμεθα τῶν πρὸς αὐτὴν παρακαλούντων ἡμᾶς,
τοῦτο μὲν παραινέσεων, τοῦτο δὲ καὶ βίων ἱστο-
ρίας τῶν ἐκείνην προωδευκότων, ὃ καὶ μᾶλλον
ἀλύπως ἐφέλκεται πρὸς αὐτὴν καὶ μὴ ἀπογινώσκειν παρασκευάζει τῆς πορείας τὸ δύσκολον.
ἐπεὶ καὶ τῷ μέλλοντι βαδίζειν ὁδὸν δύσπορον καὶ
τραχεῖαν παραινῶν μέν τις καὶ προτρεπόμενος
ἧττον πείσειεν· ὑποδεικνύων δὲ πολλοὺς αὐτὴν
ἤδη διελθόντας, εἶτα κἀν τῷ τέλει καλῶς κατα-
λύσαντας, οὕτω πείσειε μᾶλλον καὶ αὐτὸν ἂν τῆς
Gal. vi. 16; Phil. iii. 16 πορείας ἅψασθαι. τούτῳ οὖν ἐγὼ στοιχῶν τῷ
κανόνι, ἄλλως δὲ καὶ τὸν ἐπηρτημένον τῷ δούλῳ
κίνδυνον ὑφορώμενος, ὅς, λαβὼν παρὰ τοῦ δεσπό-
Mat. xxv. 24 του τὸ τάλαντον, εἰς γῆν ἐκεῖνο κατώρυξε καὶ τὸ
δοθὲν πρὸς ἐργασίαν ἔκρυψεν ἀπραγμάτευτον, 3
ἐξήγησιν ψυχωφελῆ ἕως ἐμοῦ καταντήσασαν οὐδαμῶς σιωπήσομαι· ἥνπερ μοι ἀφηγήσαντο ἄνδρες
εὐλαβεῖς τῆς ἐνδοτέρας τῶν Αἰθιόπων χώρας,
οὕστινας Ἰνδοὺς οἶδεν ὁ λόγος καλεῖν, ἐξ ὑπομνη-
μάτων ταύτην ἀψευδῶν μεταφράσαντες, ἔχει δὲ
οὕτως.

hath the Church of Christ received as a tradition from the inspired Apostles, and the blessed Fathers, who did thus enact for the salvation of our race. For the pathway to virtue is rough and steep, especially for such as have not yet wholly turned unto the Lord, but are still at warfare, through the tyranny of their passions. For this reason also we need many encouragements thereto, whether it be exhortations, or the record of the lives of them that have travelled on the road before us; which latter draweth us towards it the less painfully, and doth accustom us not to despair on account of the difficulty of the journey. For even as with a man that would tread a hard and difficult path; by exhortation and encouragement one may scarce win him to essay it, but rather by pointing to the many who have already completed the course, and at the last have arrived safely. So I too, 'walking by this rule,' and heedful of the danger hanging over that servant who, having received of his lord the talent, buried it in the earth, and hid out of use that which was given him to trade withal, will in no wise pass over in silence the edifying story that hath come to me, the which devout men from the inner land of the Ethiopians, whom our tale calleth Indians, delivered unto me, translated from trustworthy records. It readeth thus.

I

Ἡ τῶν Ἰνδῶν λεγομένη χώρα πόρρω μὲν διά-
κειται τῆς Αἰγύπτου, μεγάλη οὖσα καὶ πολυ-
άνθρωπος· περικλύζεται δὲ θαλάσσαις καὶ ναυσι-
πόροις πελάγεσι τῷ κατ' Αἴγυπτον μέρει· ἐκ δὲ
τῆς ἠπείρου προσεγγίζει τοῖς ὁρίοις Περσίδος,
ἥτις πάλαι μὲν τῷ τῆς εἰδωλομανίας ἐμελαίνετο
ζόφῳ, εἰς ἄκρον ἐκβεβαρβαρωμένη καὶ ταῖς ἀθέ-
σμοις ἐκδεδιῃτημένη τῶν πράξεων. ὅτε δὲ ὁ
μονογενὴς τοῦ Θεοῦ Υἱός, ὁ ὢν εἰς τὸν κόλπον
John i. 18 τοῦ Πατρός, τὸ ἑαυτοῦ πλάσμα μὴ φέρων ὁρᾶν
ἁμαρτίᾳ δουλούμενον, τοῖς οἰκείοις περὶ τοῦτο
σπλάγχνοις ἐπικαμφθείς, ὤφθη καθ' ἡμᾶς ἁμαρ-
Baruch iii. 37; John i. 14; Heb. iv. 15; Luke i. 27, 42 τίας χωρίς, καί, τὸν τοῦ Πατρὸς θρόνον μὴ
ἀπολιπών, Παρθένον ᾤκησε δι' ἡμᾶς, ἵν' ἡμεῖς
κατοικήσωμεν τοὺς οὐρανούς, τοῦ τε παλαιοῦ
πτώματος ἀνακληθῶμεν, καὶ τῆς ἁμαρτίας ἀπαλ-
λαγῶμεν, τὴν προτέραν υἱοθεσίαν ἀπολαβόντες,
καί, πᾶσαν μὲν τὴν διὰ σαρκὸς ὑπὲρ ἡμῶν 4
τελέσας οἰκονομίαν, σταυρόν τε καὶ θάνατον
καταδεξάμενος καὶ τοῖς ἐπουρανίοις παραδόξως
ἑνοποιήσας τὰ ἐπίγεια, ἀναστὰς δὲ ἐκ νεκρῶν καὶ
Mk. xvi. 19 μετὰ δόξης εἰς οὐρανοὺς ἀναληφθεὶς καὶ ἐν δεξιᾷ
Heb. i. 3 τῆς τοῦ Πατρὸς μεγαλωσύνης καθίσας, τὸ παράκλητον Πνεῦμα τοῖς αὐτόπταις αὐτοῦ καὶ μύσταις,
κατὰ τὴν ἐπαγγελίαν, ἐν εἴδει γλωσσῶν πυρίνων
Acts ii. 3 ἐξαπέστειλε, καὶ ἔπεμψεν αὐτοὺς εἰς πάντα τὰ
Mat. iv. 16 ἔθνη φωτίσαι τοὺς ἐν σκότει τῆς ἀγνοίας καθη-
Mat. xxviii; Mk. xvi μένους, καὶ βαπτίζειν αὐτοὺς εἰς τὸ ὄνομα τοῦ
Πατρὸς καὶ τοῦ Υἱοῦ καὶ τοῦ Ἁγίου Πνεύματος,

I

How the Apostle Thomas preached the Gospel to the Indians

THE country of the Indians, as it is called, is vast and populous, lying far beyond Egypt. On the side of Egypt it is washed by seas and navigable gulphs, but on the mainland it marcheth with the borders of Persia, a land formerly darkened with the gloom of idolatry, barbarous to the last degree, and wholly given up to unlawful practices. But when 'the only-begotten Son of God, which is in the bosom of the Father,' being grieved to see his own handiwork in bondage unto sin, was moved with compassion for the same, and shewed himself amongst us without sin, and, without leaving his Father's throne, dwelt for a season in the Virgin's womb for our sakes, that we might dwell in heaven, and be re-claimed from the ancient fall, and freed from sin by receiving again the adoption of sons; when he had fulfilled every stage of his life in the flesh for our sake, and endured the death of the Cross, and marvellously united earth and heaven; when he had risen again from the dead, and had been received up into heaven, and was seated at the right hand of the majesty of the Father, whence, according to his promise, he sent down the Comforter, the Holy Ghost, unto his eye-witnesses and disciples, in the shape of fiery tongues, and despatched them unto all nations, for to give light to them that sat in the darkness of ignorance, and to baptize them in the Name of the Father, and of the Son, and of the Holy Ghost—whereby it fell to the

ὡς ἐντεῦθεν τοὺς μὲν αὐτῶν τὰς ἑῴας λήξεις, τοὺς
δὲ τὰς ἑσπερίους λαχόντας περιέρχεσθαι, βόρειά
τε καὶ νότια διαθέειν κλίματα, τὸ προστεταγμένον
αὐτοῖς πληροῦντας, διάγγελμα τότε καὶ ὁ ἱερώ-
τατος Θωμᾶς, εἷς ὑπάρχων τῆς δωδεκαρίθμου
Acts i. 13 φάλαγγος τῶν μαθητῶν τοῦ Χριστοῦ, πρὸς τὴν
τῶν Ἰνδῶν ἐξεπέμπετο, κηρύττων αὐτοῖς τὸ σω-
Mk. xvi. 20 τήριον κήρυγμα. τοῦ Κυρίου δὲ συνεργοῦντος 5
καὶ τὸν λόγον βεβαιοῦντος διὰ τῶν ἐπακολου-
Eus. H.E., i. 13; iii. 1 θούντων σημείων, τὸ μὲν τῆς δεισιδαιμονίας ἀπη-
λάθη σκότος καί, τῶν εἰδωλικῶν σπονδῶν τε καὶ
Socr. H.E., i. 19; iv. 18 βδελυγμάτων ἀπαλλαγέντες, τῇ ἀπλανεῖ προσετέθησαν πίστει, καί, οὕτω ταῖς ἀποστολικαῖς μετα-
πλασθέντες χερσί, Χριστῷ διὰ τοῦ βαπτίσματος
ᾠκειώθησαν, καί, ταῖς κατὰ μέρος προσθήκαις
αὐξανόμενοι, προέκοπτον ἐν τῇ ἀμωμήτῳ πίστει,
ἐκκλησίας τε ἀνὰ πάσας ᾠκοδόμουν τὰς χώρας.
Ἐπεὶ δὲ καὶ ἐν Αἰγύπτῳ ἤρξατο μοναστήρια
συνίστασθαι καὶ τὰ τῶν μοναχῶν ἀθροίζεσθαι
πλήθη, καὶ τῆς ἐκείνων ἀρετῆς καὶ ἀγγελομιμήτου
Ps. xix. 4 διαγωγῆς ἡ φήμη τὰ πέρατα διελάμβανε τῆς
οἰκουμένης, καὶ εἰς Ἰνδοὺς ἧκε, πρὸς τὸν ὅμοιον
ζῆλον καὶ τούτους διήγειρεν, ὡς πολλοὺς αὐτῶν,
πάντα καταλιπόντας, καταλαβεῖν τὰς ἐρήμους
καὶ ἐν σώματι θνητῷ τὴν πολιτείαν ἀνειληφέναι
τῶν ἀσωμάτων. οὕτω καλῶς ἐχόντων τῶν 6
πραγμάτων, καὶ χρυσαῖς πτέρυξι, τὸ δὴ λεγόμενον,
εἰς οὐρανοὺς πολλῶν ἀνιπταμένων, ἀνίσταταί τις
βασιλεὺς ἐν τῇ αὐτῇ χώρᾳ, Ἀβεννὴρ τοὔνομα,
μέγας μὲν γενόμενος πλούτῳ καὶ δυναστείᾳ καὶ
τῇ κατὰ τῶν ἀντικειμένων νίκῃ, γενναῖός τε ἐν

lot of some of the Apostles to travel to the far-off East and to some to journey to the West-ward, while others traversed the regions North and South, fulfilling their appointed tasks—then it was, I say, that one of the company of Christ's Twelve Apostles, most holy Thomas, was sent out to the land of the Indians, preaching the Gospel of Salvation. 'The Lord working with him and confirming the word with signs following,' the darkness of superstition was banished; and men were delivered from idolatrous sacrifices and abominations, and added to the true Faith, and being thus transformed by the hands of the Apostle, were made members of Christ's household by Baptism, and, waxing ever with fresh increase, made advancement in the blameless Faith and built churches in all their lands.

Of Abenner the king and his idolatry

Now when monasteries began to be formed in Egypt, and numbers of monks banded themselves together, and when the fame of their virtues and Angelic conversation 'was gone out into all the ends of the world' and came to the Indians, it stirred them up also to the like zeal, insomuch that many of them forsook everything and withdrew to the deserts; and, though but men in mortal bodies, adopted the spiritual life of Angels. While matters were thus prospering and many were soaring upward to heaven on wings of gold, as the saying is, there arose in that country a king named Abenner, mighty in riches and power, and in victory over his enemies,

πολέμοις, καὶ μεγέθει σώματος ἅμα δὲ καὶ προσώπου ὡραιότητι σεμνυνόμενος, πᾶσί τε τοῖς κοσμικοῖς καὶ θᾶττον μαραινομένοις προτερήμασιν ἐγκαυχώμενος· κατὰ ψυχὴν δὲ ἐσχάτῃ πιεζόμενος πτωχείᾳ καὶ πολλοῖς κακοῖς συμπνιγόμενος, τῆς ἑλληνικῆς ὑπάρχων μοίρας, καὶ σφόδρα περὶ τὴν δεισιδαίμονα πλάνην τῶν εἰδώλων ἐπτοημένος. πολλῇ δὲ συζῶν οὗτος τρυφῇ καὶ ἀπολαύσει τῶν ἡδέων καὶ τερπνῶν τοῦ βίου, καὶ ἐν οὐδενὶ τῶν θελημάτων καὶ ἐπιθυμιῶν αὐτοῦ ἀποστερούμενος, ἓν εἶχε τὸ τὴν εὐφροσύνην αὐτῷ ἐγκόπτον καὶ μερίμναις αὐτοῦ βάλλον τὴν ψυχήν, τὸ τῆς ἀτεκνίας κακόν. ἔρημος γὰρ ὑπάρχων παίδων, διὰ φροντίδος εἶχε πολλῆς ὅπως, τοῦ τοιούτου λυθεὶς δεσμοῦ, τέκνων κληθείη πατήρ, πρᾶγμα τοῖς πολλοῖς εὐκταιότατον. τοιοῦτος μὲν ὁ βασιλεύς, καὶ οὕτως ἔχων τῆς γνώμης.

Τὸ δὲ εὐκλεέστατον γένος τῶν χριστιανῶν καὶ
τὰ τῶν μοναχῶν πλήθη παρ' οὐδὲν θέμενοι τὸ τοῦ
βασιλέως σέβας, καὶ τὴν αὐτοῦ μὴ δεδοικότες
ὅλως ἀπειλήν, προέκοπτον τῇ τοῦ Χριστοῦ χάριτι,
εἰς λόγου κρείττονα πληθὺν ἐπιδιδόντες, καὶ
βραχὺν μὲν ποιούμενοι τοῦ βασιλέως λόγον, τῶν
δὲ πρὸς θεραπείαν φερόντων Θεοῦ διαφερόντως 7
ἐχόμενοι. καὶ διὰ τοῦτο πολλοὶ τῶν τὴν μονα-
δικὴν ἐπανῃρημένων τάξιν, πάντα μὲν ἐπίσης τὰ
ἐνταῦθα τερπνὰ διέπτυον, πρὸς ἓν δὲ μόνον τοῦτο
εἶχον ἐρωτικῶς, τὴν εὐσέβειαν, καὶ τὸν ὑπὲρ
Χριστοῦ θάνατον ἐδίψων, καὶ τῆς ἐκεῖθεν ὠρέ-
γοντο μακαριότητος. ἐκήρυττον οὖν, οὐ φόβῳ
τινὶ καὶ ὑποστολῇ, ἀλλὰ καὶ λίαν εὐπαρρησιά-
στως τὸ τοῦ Θεοῦ σωτήριον ὄνομα, καὶ οὐδὲν ὅ τι

brave in warfare, vain of his splendid stature and comeliness of face, and boastful of all worldly honours, that pass so soon away. But his soul was utterly crushed by poverty, and choked with many vices, for he was of the Greek way, and sore distraught by the superstitious error of his idol-worship. But, although he lived in luxury, and in the enjoyment of the sweet and pleasant things of life, and was never baulked of any of his wishes and desires, yet one thing there was that marred his happiness, and pierced his soul with care, the curse of childlessness. For being without issue, he took ceaseless thought how he might be rid of this hobble, and be called the father of children, a name greatly coveted by most people. Such was the king, and such his mind.

How, maugre the threats of Abenner, the Christians grew and prospered

Meanwhile the glorious band of Christians and the companies of monks, paying no regard to the king's majesty, and in no wise terrified by his threats, advanced in the grace of Christ, and grew in number beyond measure, making short account of the king's words, but cleaving closely to everything that led to the service of God. For this reason many, who had adopted the monastic rule, abhorred alike all the sweets of this world, and were enamoured of one thing only, namely godliness, thirsting to lay down their lives for Christ his sake, and yearning for the happiness beyond. Wherefore they preached, not with fear and trembling, but rather even with excess of boldness, the saving Name of God, and naught but Christ

μὴ Χριστὸς αὐτοῖς διὰ στόματος ἦν, τήν τε ῥευστὴν καὶ εὐμάραντον φύσιν τῶν παρόντων καὶ τὸ πάγιον καὶ ἄφθαρτον τῆς μελλούσης ζωῆς φανερῶς πᾶσιν ὑπεδείκνυον, καὶ οἱονεὶ ἀφορμὰς παρεῖχον καὶ σπέρματα πρὸς τὸ οἰκείους γενέσθαι
Col. iii. 3 Θεῷ καὶ τῆς ἐν Χριστῷ κρυπτομένης ἀξιωθῆναι ζωῆς. ἐντεῦθεν πολλοί, τῆς ἡδίστης ἐκείνης διδασκαλίας ἀπολαύοντες, τοῦ μὲν πικροῦ τῆς ἀπάτης ἀφίσταντο σκότους, τῷ δὲ γλυκεῖ τῆς ἀληθείας φωτὶ προσετίθεντο· ὡς καί τινας τῶν ἐνδόξων καὶ τῆς συγκλήτου βουλῆς πάντα ἀποτίθεσθαι τὰ τοῦ βίου βάρη καὶ λοιπὸν γίνεσθαι μοναχούς.

Ὁ δὲ βασιλεύς, ὡς ἤκουσε ταῦτα, ὀργῆς ὅτι πλείστης πληρωθεὶς καὶ τῷ θυμῷ ὑπερζέσας, δόγμα αὐτίκα ἐξέθετο, πάντα Χριστιανὸν βιάζεσθαι τοῦ ἐξόμνυσθαι τὴν εὐσέβειαν. ὅθεν καινὰ μὲν κατ᾽ αὐτῶν εἴδη βασάνων ἐπενόει καὶ ἐπετήδευε, καινοὺς δὲ τρόπους θανάτων ἠπείλει. καὶ γράμματα κατὰ πᾶσαν τὴν ὑποτελῆ αὐτῷ
χώραν ἐπέμπετο ἄρχουσι καὶ ἡγεμόσι, τιμωρίας 8
κατὰ τῶν εὐσεβῶν καὶ σφαγὰς ἀδίκους ἀποφαινόμενα. ἐξαιρέτως δὲ κατὰ τῶν τοῦ μοναδικοῦ σχήματος λογάδων θυμομαχῶν, ἄσπονδον ἤγειρε τὸν πρὸς αὐτοὺς καὶ ἀκήρυκτον πόλεμον. ταύτῃ τοι καὶ πολλοὶ μὲν τῶν πιστῶν τὴν διάνοιαν ἀνεσαλεύοντο, ἄλλοι δέ, τὰς βασάνους μὴ δυνηθέντες ὑπενεγκεῖν, τῷ ἀθεμίτῳ αὐτοῦ εἶκον προστάγματι. οἱ δὲ τοῦ μοναχικοῦ τάγματος ἡγεμόνες καὶ ἀρχηγοί, οἱ μέν, ἐλέγχοντες αὐτοῦ τὴν ἀνομίαν, τὸ διὰ μαρτυρίου ὑπήνεγκαν τέλος καὶ τῆς ἀλήκτου ἐπέτυχον μακαριότητος· οἱ δὲ ἐν

was on their lips, as they plainly proclaimed to all men the transitory and fading nature of this present time, and the fixedness and incorruptibility of the life to come, and sowed in men the first seeds, as it were, towards their becoming of the household of God, and winning that life which is hid in Christ. Wherefore many, profiting by this most pleasant teaching, turned away from the bitter darkness of error, and approached the sweet light of Truth; insomuch that certain of their noblemen and senators laid aside all the burthens of life, and thenceforth became monks.

How the king waxed wroth thereat and persecuted the Faithful

But when the king heard thereof, he was filled with wrath, and, boiling over with indignation, passed a decree forthwith, compelling all Christians to renounce their religion. Thereupon he planned and practised new kinds of torture against them, and threatened new forms of death. So throughout all his dominions he sent letters to his rulers and governors ordering penalties against the righteous, and unlawful massacres. But chiefly was his displeasure turned against the ranks of the monastic orders, and against them he waged a truceless and unrelenting warfare. Hence, of a truth, many of the Faithful were shaken in spirit, and others, unable to endure torture, yielded to his ungodly decrees. But of the chiefs and rulers of the monastic order some in rebuking his wickedness ended their lives by suffering martyrdom, and thus attained to everlasting felicity; while others hid themselves

ἐρημίαις καὶ ὄρεσιν ἀπεκρύπτοντο, οὐ δέει τῶν
Mat. x. 23 ἠπειλημένων βασάνων, ἀλλ' οἰκονομίᾳ τινὶ θειοτέρᾳ.

II

Τῆς τοιαύτης οὖν σκοτομήνης τὴν τῶν Ἰνδῶν καταλαβούσης, καὶ τῶν μὲν πιστῶν πάντοθεν ἐλαυνομένων, τῶν δὲ τῆς ἀσεβείας ὑπασπιστῶν κρατυνομένων, αἵμασί τε καὶ κνίσαις τῶν θυσιῶν καὶ αὐτοῦ δὴ τοῦ ἀέρος μολυνομένου, εἷς τῶν τοῦ βασιλέως, ἀρχισατράπης τὴν ἀξίαν, ψυχῆς παραστήματι, μεγέθει τε καὶ κάλλει, καὶ πᾶσιν ἄλλοις, οἷς ὥρα σώματος καὶ γενναιότης ψυχῆς ἀνδρείας χαρακτηρίζεσθαι πέφυκε, τῶν ἄλλων ἐτύγχανε διαφέρων. τὸ ἀσεβὲς οὖν ἐκεῖνο πρόσταγμα ἀκούσας οὗτος, χαίρειν εἰπὼν τῇ ματαίᾳ ταύτῃ καὶ κάτω συρομένῃ δόξῃ τε καὶ τρυφῇ, ταῖς τῶν μοναχῶν λογάσιν ἑαυτὸν ἐγκατέμιξεν, ὑπερόριος γενόμενος ἐν ἐρήμοις τόποις, νηστείαις τε καὶ ἀγρυπνίαις καὶ τῇ τῶν θείων λογίων ἐπιμελεῖ μελέτῃ τὰς αἰσθήσεις ἄριστα ἐκκαθάρας, καὶ τὴν ψυχήν, πάσης ἀπαλλάξας ἐμπαθοῦς σχέσεως, τῷ
τῆς ἀπαθείας φωτὶ κατελάμπρυνεν. ὁ δὲ βασι- 9
λεύς, πάνυ τοῦτον φιλῶν καὶ διὰ τιμῆς ἄγων, ὡς ἤκουσε ταῦτα, ἤλγησε μὲν τὴν ψυχὴν ἐπὶ τῇ τοῦ φίλου στερήσει, ἐξεκαύθη δὲ πλέον τῇ κατὰ τῶν μοναζόντων ὀργῇ. καὶ δὴ κατὰ ζήτησιν αὐτοῦ πανταχοῦ ἀποστείλας, καὶ πάντα λίθον κινήσας, τὸ τοῦ λόγου, ὥστε τοῦτον ἐφευρεῖν, μετὰ οὖν χρόνον ἱκανὸν οἱ εἰς ἐπιζήτησιν αὐτοῦ πεμφθέντες, ὡς ἤσθοντο ἐν ἐρήμοις αὐτὸν τὰς οἰκήσεις ἔχοντα,

in deserts and mountains, not from dread of the threatened tortures, but by a more divine dispensation.

II

Of the chief satrap and how he became a Christian

Now while the land of the Indians lay under the shroud of this moonless night, and while the Faithful were harried on every side, and the champions of ungodliness prospered, the very air reeking with the smell of bloody sacrifices, a certain man of the royal household, chief satrap in rank, in courage, stature, comeliness, and in all those qualities which mark beauty of body and nobility of soul, far above all his fellows, hearing of this iniquitous decree, bade farewell to all the grovelling pomps and vanities of the world, joined the ranks of the monks, and retired across the border into the desert. There, by fastings and vigils, and by diligent study of the divine oracles, he throughly purged his senses, and illumined a soul, set free from every passion, with the glorious light of a perfect calm.

How King Abenner sent for to apprehend him

But when the king, who loved and esteemed him highly, heard thereof, he was grieved in spirit at the loss of his friend, but his anger was the more hotly kindled against the monks. And so he sent everywhere in search of him, leaving 'no stone unturned,' as the saying is, to find him. After a long while, they that were sent in quest of him, having learnt that he abode in the desert, after

διερευνήσαντες καὶ συλλαβόμενοι, τῷ τοῦ βασιλέως παρέστησαν βήματι. ἰδὼν δὲ αὐτὸν ἐν οὕτω πενιχρᾷ καὶ τραχυτάτῃ ἐσθῆτι τὸν λαμπροῖς ποτε ἱματίοις ἠμφιεσμένον, καὶ τὸν πολλῇ συζῶντα τρυφῇ τεταριχευμένον τῇ σκληρᾷ τῆς ἀσκήσεως ἀγωγῇ, καὶ τοῦ ἐρημικοῦ βίου ἐναργῶς περικείμενον τὰ γνωρίσματα, λύπης ὁμοῦ καὶ ὀργῆς ἐπεπλήρωτο, καί, ἐξ ἀμφοῖν τὸν λόγον κεράσας, ἔφη πρὸς αὐτόν·

Ὦ ἀνόητε καὶ φρενοβλαβές, τίνος χάριν ἀντηλλάξω τῆς τιμῆς αἰσχύνην, καὶ τῆς λαμπρᾶς δόξης τὴν ἀσχήμονα ταύτην ἰδέαν; ὁ πρόεδρος τῆς ἐμῆς βασιλείας καὶ ἀρχιστράτηγος τῆς ἐμῆς δυναστείας, παίγνιον μειρακίων σεαυτὸν καταστήσας, οὐ μόνον τῆς ἡμετέρας φιλίας καὶ παρρησίας μακρὰν λήθην πεποιηκώς, ἀλλὰ καὶ αὐτῆς κατεξαναστὰς τῆς φύσεως, καὶ μηδὲ τῶν ἰδίων τέκνων οἶκτον λαβών, πλοῦτόν τε καὶ πᾶσαν τὴν τοῦ βίου περιφάνειαν εἰς οὐδὲν λογισάμενος, τὴν τοσαύτην ἀδοξίαν τῆς περιβλέπτου προέκρινας δόξης, ἵνα τί σοι γένηται; καὶ τί ἐντεῦθεν κερδήσεις, ὅτι πάντων θεῶν τε καὶ ἀνθρώπων τὸν λεγόμενον προτετίμηκας Ἰησοῦν, καὶ τὴν σκληρὰν ταύτην καὶ δυσείμονα ἀγωγὴν τῶν ἡδέων καὶ ἀπολαυστικῶν τοῦ γλυκυτάτου βίου;

Τούτων ἀκούσας ὁ τοῦ Θεοῦ ἄνθρωπος ἐκεῖνος, χαριέντως ἅμα καὶ ὁμαλῶς ἀπεκρίνατο· Εἰ λόγον πρός με συνᾶραι θέλεις, ὦ βασιλεῦ, τοὺς ἐχθρούς σου ἐκ μέσου τοῦ δικαστηρίου ποίησον, καὶ τηνικαῦτα ἀποκρινοῦμαί σοι περὶ ὧν ἂν ζητήσῃς μαθεῖν· ἐκείνων γὰρ συμπαρόντων σοι, οὐδεὶς ἐμοὶ πρός σε λόγος. ἐκτὸς δὲ λόγου τιμώρει, σφάττε,

diligent search, apprehended him and brought him before the king's judgement seat. When the king saw him in such vile and coarse raiment who before had been clad in rich apparel,—saw him, who had lived in the lap of luxury, shrunken and wasted by the severe practice of discipline, and bearing about in his body outward and visible signs of his hermit-life, he was filled with mingled grief and fury, and, in speech blended of these two passions, he spake unto him thus:

The king upbraideth him with his folly

'O thou dullard and mad man, wherefore hast thou exchanged thine honour for shame, and thy glorious estate for this unseemly show? To what end hath the president of my kingdom, and chief commander of my realm made himself the laughing-stock of boys, and not only forgotten utterly our friendship and fellowship, but revolted against nature herself, and had no pity on his own children, and cared naught for riches and all the splendour of the world, and chosen ignominy such as this rather than the glory that men covet? And what shall it profit thee to have chosen above all gods and men him whom they call Jesus, and to have preferred this rough life of sackcloth to the pleasures and delights of a life of bliss.

The chief satrap prayeth the king to put Anger and Desire out of court

When the man of God heard these words, he made reply, at once courteous and unruffled: 'If it be thy pleasure, O king, to converse with me, remove thine enemies out of mid court; which done, I will answer thee concerning whatsoever thou mayest desire to learn; for while these are here, I cannot speak with thee. But, without speech,

ποίει ὃ θέλεις· ἐμοὶ γὰρ ὁ κόσμος ἐσταύρωται,
Gal. vi. 14 κἀγὼ τῷ κόσμῳ, φησὶν ὁ θεῖος καὶ ἐμὸς διδάσκαλος. τοῦ δὲ βασιλέως εἰπόντος, Καὶ τίνες οἱ
ἐχθροὶ οὗτοι, οὓς ἐκ μέσου ποιῆσαί με προστάσσεις; φησὶν ὁ θεῖος ἀνήρ· Ὁ θυμὸς καὶ ἡ ἐπιθυμία·
ταῦτα γὰρ ἐξ ἀρχῆς μὲν συνεργοὶ τῆς φύσεως ὑπὸ
τοῦ δημιουργοῦ παρήχθησαν, καὶ νῦν ὡσαύτως
Rom. viii. 4 ἔχουσι τοῖς μὴ κατὰ σάρκα πολιτευομένοις, ἀλλὰ
κατὰ πνεῦμα· ἐν ὑμῖν δέ, οἵτινες τὸ ὅλον ἐστὲ
σάρκες, μηδὲν ἔχοντες τοῦ πνεύματος, ἀντίδικοι
γεγόνασι, καὶ τὰ τῶν ἐχθρῶν καὶ πολεμίων δια-
πράττονται. ἡ γὰρ ἐπιθυμία ἐν ὑμῖν, ἐνεργουμένη
μέν, ἡδονὴν ἐγείρει, καταργουμένη δέ, θυμόν. 11
ἀπέστω οὖν ταῦτα σήμερον ἀπὸ σοῦ, προκαθε-
ζέσθωσαν δὲ εἰς ἀκρόασιν τῶν λεγομένων καὶ κρίσιν ἡ φρόνησις καὶ ἡ δικαιοσύνη. εἰ γὰρ τὸν θυμὸν
καὶ τὴν ἐπιθυμίαν ἐκ μέσου ποιήσεις, ἀντεισάξεις
δὲ τὴν φρόνησιν καὶ τὴν δικαιοσύνην, φιλαλήθως
πάντα λέξω σοι. πρὸς ταῦτα ὁ βασιλεὺς ἔφη·
Ἰδού, εἶξας σου τῇ ἀξιώσει, ἐκβαλῶ τοῦ συνεδρίου
τήν τε ἐπιθυμίαν καὶ τὸν θυμόν, μεσάζειν δὲ τὴν
φρόνησιν καὶ τὴν δικαιοσύνην ποιήσω. λέγε μοι
λοιπὸν ἀδεῶς πόθεν σοι ἡ τοσαύτη ἐγένετο πλάνη,
καὶ τὸ προτιμᾶν τὰ ἐν κεναῖς ἐλπίσι τῶν ἐν χερσὶ
βλεπομένων.

Ἀποκριθεὶς δὲ ὁ ἐρημίτης εἶπεν· Εἰ τὴν ἀρχὴν ζητεῖς, ὦ βασιλεῦ, πόθεν μοι γέγονε τῶν προσκαίρων μὲν ὑπεριδεῖν, ὅλον δὲ ἐμαυτὸν ταῖς αἰωνίοις ἐπιδοῦναι ἐλπίσιν, ἄκουσον. ἐν ἡμέραις ἀρχαίαις, ἔτι κομιδῇ νέος ὑπάρχων, ἤκουσά τι ῥῆμα ἀγαθὸν καὶ σωτήριον, καί με κατ᾽ ἄκρας ἡ τούτου δύναμις εἷλε, καί, ὥσπερ

torment me, kill me, do as thou wilt, for "the world is crucified unto me, and I unto the world," as saith my divine teacher.' The king said, 'And who are these enemies whom thou biddest me turn out of court?' The saintly man answered and said, 'Anger and Desire. For at the beginning these twain were brought into being by the Creator to be fellow-workers with nature; and such they still are to those "who walk not after the flesh but after the Spirit." But in you who are altogether carnal, having nothing of the Spirit, they are adversaries, and play the part of enemies and foemen. For Desire, working in you, stirreth up pleasure, but, when made of none effect, Anger. To-day therefore let these be banished from thee, and let Wisdom and Righteousness sit to hear and judge that which we say. For if thou put Anger and Desire out of court, and in their room bring in Wisdom and Righteousness, I will truthfully tell thee all.' Then spake the king, 'Lo I yield to thy request, and will banish out of the assembly both Desire and Anger, and make Wisdom and Righteousness to sit between us. So now, tell me without fear, how wast thou so greatly taken with this error, to prefer the bird in the bush to the bird already in the hand?'

He excuseth himself unto the king by telling of a wholesome saying that wrought in him,

The hermit answered and said, 'O king, if thou askest the cause how I came to despise things temporal, and to devote my whole self to the hope of things eternal, hearken unto me. In former days, when I was still but a stripling, I heard a certain good and wholesome saying, which, by its force took my soul by storm; and the remembrance

τις θεῖος σπόρος, ἡ τούτου μνήμη, τῇ ἐμῇ φυτευ-
θεῖσα καρδίᾳ, ἀχώριστος εἰς ἀεὶ διετηρήθη ὡς
καὶ ῥιζωθῆναι, καὶ ἐκβλαστῆσαι, καὶ ὃν ὁρᾷς
καρπὸν ἐνεγκεῖν ἐν ἐμοί. ἡ δὲ τοῦ ῥήματος
1 Cor. i. 28 δύναμις τοιαύτη τις ἦν· Ἔδοξε, φησί, τοῖς ἀνοή-
τοις τῶν ὄντων μὲν καταφρονεῖν ὡς μὴ ὄντων,
τῶν μὴ ὄντων δὲ ὡς ὄντων ἀντέχεσθαί τε καὶ
περιέχεσθαι· ὁ μὴ γευσάμενος οὖν τῆς τῶν
ὄντων γλυκύτητος, οὐ δυνήσεται τῶν μὴ ὄντων 12
καταμαθεῖν τὴν φύσιν· μὴ καταμαθὼν δέ, πῶς
αὐτῶν ὑπερόψεται; ὄντα μὲν οὖν ἐκάλεσεν ὁ
λόγος τὰ αἰώνια καὶ μὴ σαλευόμενα μὴ ὄντα δὲ
τὸν ἐνταῦθα βίον καὶ τὴν τρυφὴν καὶ τὴν
ψευδομένην εὐημερίαν· οἷς, ὦ βασιλεῦ, κακῶς
φεῦ, ἡ σὴ προσήλωται καρδία. κἀγὼ δέ ποτε
τούτων ἀντειχόμην· ἀλλ' ἡ τοῦ ῥήματος δύναμις,
νύττουσά μου τὴν ψυχὴν ἀδιαλείπτως, ἐξήγειρε
τὸν ἡγεμόνα νοῦν εἰς ἐκλογὴν τοῦ κρείττονος·
Rom. vii. 25 ὁ δὲ νόμος τῆς ἁμαρτίας, ἀντιστρατευόμενος
τῷ νόμῳ τοῦ νοός μου, καὶ ὥς τισι σιδηροπέδαις
δεσμῶν με, τῇ προσπαθείᾳ τῶν παρόντων αἰχμάλωτον κατεῖχεν.

Tit. iii. 4 Ὅτε δὲ εὐδόκησεν ἡ χρηστότης καὶ ἀγαθοσύνη
τοῦ Σωτῆρος ἡμῶν Θεοῦ ἐξελέσθαι με τῆς χαλεπῆς ἐκείνης αἰχμαλωσίας, ἐνίσχυσέ μου τὸν
νοῦν περιγενέσθαι τοῦ νόμου τῆς ἁμαρτίας, καὶ
διήνοιξέ μου τοὺς ὀφθαλμοὺς διακρίνειν τὸ φαῦλον ἀπὸ τοῦ κρείττονος. τότε δή, τότε κατενό-
Eccles. i. 14 ησα καὶ εἶδον, καὶ ἰδοὺ πάντα τὰ παρόντα
ματαιότης καὶ προαίρεσις πνεύματος, καθά που
καὶ Σολομῶν ὁ σοφώτατος ἐν τοῖς αὐτοῦ ἔφη
2 Cor. iii. 15 συγγράμμασι· τότε περιῃρέθη τῆς καρδίας μου

of it, like some divine seed, being planted in my heart, unmoved, was preserved ever until it took root, blossomed, and bare that fruit which thou seest in me. Now the meaning of that sentence was this: "It seemed good to the foolish to despise the things that are, as though they were not, and to cleave and cling to the things that are not, as though they were. So he, that hath never tasted the sweetness of the things that are, will not be able to understand the nature of the things that are not. And never having understood them, how shall he despise them?" Now that saying meant by "things that are" the things eternal and fixed, but by "things that are not" earthly life, luxury, the prosperity that deceives, whereon, O king, thine heart alas! is fixed amiss. Time was when I also clung thereto myself. But the force of that sentence continually goading my heart, stirred my governing power, my mind, to make the better choice. But "the law of sin, warring against the law of my mind," and binding me, as with iron chains, held me captive to the love of things present.

and of his deliverance from the law of sin

'But "after that the kindness and love of God our Saviour" was pleased to deliver me from that harsh captivity, he enabled my mind to overcome the law of sin, and opened mine eyes to discern good from evil. Thereupon I perceived and looked, and behold! all things present are vanity and vexation of spirit, as somewhere in his writings saith Solomon the wise. Then was the veil of sin lifted from mine heart, and the dullness, proceeding from the grossness of my body, which pressed

τὸ κάλυμμα τῆς ἁμαρτίας, καὶ ἡ ἐκ σωματικῆς
παχύτητος ἐπικειμένη τῇ ψυχῇ μου ἀμαύρωσις 13
διεσκεδάσθη, καὶ ἔγνων εἰς ὃ γέγονα καὶ ὅτι
δεῖ με πρὸς τὸν δημιουργὸν ἀναβῆναι, διὰ τῆς
τῶν ἐντολῶν ἐργασίας. ὅθεν, πάντα καταλιπών,
αὐτῷ ἠκολούθησα καὶ εὐχαριστῶ τῷ Θεῷ διὰ
Ἰησοῦ Χριστοῦ τοῦ Κυρίου ἡμῶν, ὅτι ἐρύσατό
Ex. i. 14 με τοῦ πηλοῦ καὶ τῆς πλινθείας, καὶ τοῦ ἀπηνοῦς
Eph. vi. 12 καὶ ὀλεθρίου ἄρχοντος τοῦ σκότους τοῦ αἰῶνος
τούτου, καὶ ἔδειξέ μοι ὁδὸν σύντομον καὶ ῥᾳδίαν,
2 Cor. iv. 7 δι᾽ ἧς δυνήσομαι ἐν τῷ ὀστρακίνῳ τούτῳ σώματι
τὴν ἀγγελικὴν ἀσπάσασθαι πολιτείαν, ἥνπερ
Mat. vii. 14 φθάσαι ζητῶν, τὴν στενὴν καὶ τεθλιμμένην εἰλό-
μην βαδίζειν ὁδόν, πάνυ καταγνοὺς τῆς τῶν
παρόντων ματαιότητος καὶ τῆς ἀστάτου φορᾶς
Eccles. ii. 2 τούτων καὶ περιφορᾶς, καὶ μὴ πειθόμενος ἄλλο τι
καλὸν ὀνομάζειν πρὸ τοῦ ὄντος καλοῦ, οὗπερ σὺ
ἐλεεινῶς, ὦ βασιλεῦ, διερράγης τε καὶ διέστης.
ὅθεν καὶ ἡμεῖς διέστημέν σου καὶ διῃρέθημεν,
διὰ τὸ εἰς σαφῆ καὶ ὡμολογημένην σέ τε κατα-
πίπτειν ἀπώλειαν καὶ πρὸς ἴσον κατενεχθῆναι 14
καὶ ἡμᾶς κίνδυνον ἀναγκάζειν. ἕως μὲν γὰρ περὶ
μόνην τὴν κοσμικὴν στρατείαν ἐξηταζόμεθα,
οὐδὲν τῶν δεόντων ἡμεῖς ἐνελίπομεν· μαρτυρήσεις
μοι καὶ αὐτὸς ὅτιπερ οὐδὲ ῥᾳθυμίαν τινὰ οὐδὲ
ἀμέλειάν ποτε ἐνεκλήθημεν.

Ἐπεὶ δὲ καὶ αὐτὸ τῶν καλῶν τὸ κεφάλαιον ἀφελέσθαι ἐφιλονείκησας ἡμᾶς, τὴν εὐσέβειαν, καὶ τὸν Θεὸν ζημιῶσαι τὴν ἐσχάτην ταύτην ζημίαν, τιμῶν τε διὰ τοῦτο καὶ φιλοτιμίας ἀναμιμνήσκεις, πῶς οὐκ ἀμαθῶς ἔχειν σε τοῦ καλοῦ δικαίως ἂν εἴποιμι, ὅτι καὶ παραβάλλεις ὅλως

upon my soul, was scattered, and I perceived the end for which I was created, and how that it behoved me to move upward to my Creator by the keeping of his commandments. Wherefore I left all and followed him, and I thank God through Jesus Christ our Lord that he delivered me out of the mire, and from the making of bricks, and from the harsh and deadly ruler of the darkness of this world, and that he showed me the short and easy road whereby I shall be able, in this earthen body, eagerly to embrace the Angelic life. Seeking to attain to it the sooner, I chose to walk the strait and narrow way, renouncing the vanity of things present and the unstable changes and chances thereof, and refusing to call anything good except the true good, from which thou, O king, art miserably sundered and alienated. Wherefore also we ourselves were alienated and separated from thee, because thou wert falling into plain and manifest destruction, and wouldst constrain us also to descend into like peril. But as long as we were tried in the warfare of this world, we failed in no point of duty. Thou thyself wilt bear me witness that we were never charged with sloth or heedlessness.

'But when thou hast endeavoured to rob us of the chiefest of all blessings, our religion, and to deprive us of God, the worst of deprivations, and, in this intent, dost remind us of past honours and preferments, how should I not rightly tax thee with ignorance of good, seeing that thou dost at all com-

He convicteth the king of error and putteth him in mind of the infinite goodness of God

αὐτὰ πρὸς ἄλληλα, εὐσέβειάν φημι πρὸς τὸν Θεὸν
καὶ φιλίαν ἀνθρωπίνην καὶ δόξαν τὴν ἴσα παραρ-
ρέουσαν ὕδατι; πῶς δέ σοι καὶ κοινωνοὶ ἐσόμεθα
ἐπὶ τούτῳ, καὶ οὐχί, τοὐναντίον, καὶ φιλίαν, καὶ
τιμήν, και στοργὴν τέκνων καὶ εἴ τι ἄλλο μεῖζον
ἦν, ἀρνησόμεθα; ὁρῶντές σε μᾶλλον, ὦ βασιλεῦ,
ἀγνωμονοῦντα πρὸς τὸν Θεόν, τὸν καὶ αὐτό σοι
τὸ εἶναι καὶ τὸ ἀναπνεῖν παρεχόμενον, ὅς ἐστι
Χριστὸς Ἰησοῦς, ὁ Κύριος τῶν ἁπάντων, ὃς
συνάναρχος ὢν καὶ συναΐδιος τῷ Πατρὶ καὶ τοὺς
οὐρανοὺς τῷ λόγῳ καὶ τὴν γῆν ὑποστήσας, τὸν
Ps. cxix. 73 ἄνθρωπόν τε χερσὶν οἰκείαις ἐδημιούργησε καὶ
ἀθανασίᾳ τοῦτον ἐτίμησε, καὶ βασιλέα τῶν ἐπὶ
γῆς κατεστήσατο, καθάπερ τινὰ βασίλεια τὸ
κάλλιστον ἁπάντων ἀποτάξας αὐτῷ, τὸν παρά-
Wisd. ii. 24 δεισον. ὁ δέ, φθόνῳ κλαπεὶς καὶ ἡδονῇ (φεῦ μοι)
δελεασθείς, ἀθλίως τούτων ἐξέπεσε πάντων· καὶ
ὁ πρὶν ζηλωτὸς ἐλεεινὸς ὡρᾶτο καὶ δακρύων διὰ
John i. 1–3 τὴν συμφορὰν ἄξιος. ὁ πλάσας τοίνυν ἡμᾶς καὶ
δημιουργήσας φιλανθρώποις πάλιν ἰδὼν ὀφθαλμοῖς τὸ τῶν οἰκείων χειρῶν ἔργον, τὸ Θεὸς εἶναι
μὴ μεταβαλών, ὅπερ ἦν ἀπ᾽ ἀρχῆς, ἐγένετο δι᾽
Cp. Heb. iv. 15 ἡμᾶς ἀναμαρτήτως ὅπερ ἡμεῖς, καὶ σταυρὸν ἑκουσίως καὶ θάνατον ὑπομείνας, τὸν ἄνωθεν τῷ
ἡμετέρῳ γένει βασκαίνοντα κατέβαλε πολέμιον,
καί, ἡμᾶς τῆς πικρᾶς ἐκείνης αἰχμαλωσίας ἀνα-
σωσάμενος, τὴν προτέραν ἀπέδωκε φιλαγάθως
ἐλευθερίαν, καί, ὅθεν διὰ τὴν παρακοὴν ἐκπεπτώ-
καμεν, ἐκεῖ πάλιν διὰ φιλανθρωπίαν ἡμᾶς ἐπανή-
γαγε, μείζονος ἡμᾶς ἢ πρότερον τιμῆς ἀξιώσας.

Τὸν δὴ τοιαῦτα δι᾽ ἡμᾶς παθόντα καὶ τοιούτων
ἡμᾶς πάλιν καταξιώσαντα, τοῦτον αὐτὸς ἀθετεῖς

pare these two things, righteousness toward God, and human friendship, and glory, that runneth away like water? And how, in such case, may we have fellowship with thee, and not the rather deny ourselves friendship and honours and love of children, and if there be any other tie greater than these? When we see thee, O king, the rather forgetting thy reverence toward that God, who giveth thee the power to live and breathe, Christ Jesus, the Lord of all; who, being alike without beginning, and coeternal with the Father, and having created the heavens and the earth by his word, made man with his own hands and endowed him with immortality, and set him king of all on earth and assigned him Paradise, the fairest place of all, as his royal dwelling. But man, beguiled by envy, and (wo is me!) caught by the bait of pleasure, miserably fell from all these blessings. So he that once was enviable became a piteous spectacle, and by his misfortune deserving of tears. Wherefore he, that had made and fashioned us, looked again with eyes of compassion upon the work of his own hands. He, not laying aside his God-head, which he had from the beginning, was made man for our sakes, like ourselves, but without sin, and was content to suffer death upon the Cross. He overthrew the foeman that from the beginning had looked with malice on our race; he rescued us from that bitter captivity; he, of his goodness, restored to us our former freedom, and, of his tender love towards mankind, raised us up again to that place from whence by our disobedience we had fallen, granting us even greater honour than at the first.

'Him therefore, who endured such sufferings for our sakes, and again bestowed such blessings upon

and of the vanity of this world

καὶ εἰς τὸν ἐκείνου σταυρὸν ἀποσκώπτεις; ὅλος
δὲ τῇ τρυφῇ τοῦ σώματος καὶ τοῖς ὀλεθρίοις
προσηλωμένος πάθεσι, θεοὺς ἀναγορεύεις τὰ τῆς
ἀτιμίας καὶ αἰσχύνης εἴδωλα; οὐ μόνον σεαυτὸν
τῆς τῶν οὐρανίων ἀγαθῶν συναφείας ἀλλότριον
κατεσκεύασας, ἀλλὰ καὶ πάντας τοὺς πειθομένους
τοῖς σοῖς προστάγμασι ταύτης ἤδη ἀπέρρηξας, 16
καὶ ψυχικῷ κινδύνῳ παρέδωκας. ἴσθι τοίνυν ὡς
ἔγωγε οὐ πεισθήσομαί σοι, οὔτε μὴν κοινωνήσω
σοι τῆς τοιαύτης εἰς τὸν Θεὸν ἀχαριστίας, οὐδὲ
τὸν ἐμὸν εὐεργέτην καὶ Σωτῆρα ἀρνήσομαι, εἰ καὶ
θηρίοις ἀναλώσεις, εἰ ξίφει καὶ πυρὶ παραδώσεις
με, ἃ τῆς σῆς ἐξουσίας ἐστίν. οὔτε γὰρ θάνατον
δέδοικα, οὔτε ποθῶ τὰ παρόντα, πολλὴν αὐτῶν
καταγνοὺς τὴν ἀσθένειαν καὶ ματαιότητα. τί
γὰρ αὐτῶν χρήσιμον, ἢ μόνιμον, ἢ διαρκές; καὶ
οὐ τοῦτο μόνον, ἀλλὰ καὶ ἐν αὐτῷ τῷ εἶναι πολλὴ
συνυπάρχει αὐτοῖς ἡ ταλαιπωρία, πολλὴ ἡ λύπη,
πολλὴ καὶ ἀδιάσπαστος ἡ μέριμνα. τῇ γὰρ εὐ-
φροσύνῃ αὐτῶν καὶ ἀπολαύσει πᾶσα συνέζευκται
κατήφεια καὶ ὀδύνη· ὁ πλοῦτος αὐτῶν πτωχεία
ἐστί, καὶ τὸ ὕψος αὐτῶν ταπείνωσις ἐσχάτη. καὶ
τίς ἐξαριθμήσει τὰ τούτων κακά; ἅπερ δι' ὀλίγων
ῥημάτων ὑπέδειξέ μοι ὁ ἐμὸς θεολόγος. φησὶ
1 John v. 19; ii. 15–17 γάρ· Ὁ κόσμος ὅλος ἐν τῷ πονηρῷ κεῖται· καί,
Μὴ ἀγαπᾶτε τὸν κόσμον, μηδὲ τὰ ἐν τῷ κόσμῳ ὅτι
πᾶν τὸ ἐν τῷ κόσμῳ ἡ ἐπιθυμία τῆς σαρκὸς καὶ
ἡ ἐπιθυμία τῶν ὀφθαλμῶν, καὶ ἡ ἀλαζονία τοῦ
βίου· καί, ὁ κόσμος παράγεται καὶ ἡ ἐπιθυμία
αὐτοῦ· ὁ δὲ ποιῶν τὸ θέλημα τοῦ Θεοῦ μένει εἰς
τὸν αἰῶνα. τοῦτο ἐγὼ ζητῶν τὸ θέλημα τοῦ Θεοῦ
τὸ ἀγαθόν, ἀφῆκα πάντα, καὶ ἐκολλήθην τοῖς τὸν

us, him dost thou reject and scoff at his Cross? And, thyself wholly riveted to carnal delights and deadly passions, dost thou proclaim the idols of shame and dishonour gods? Not only hast thou alienated thyself from the commonwealth of heavenly felicity but thou hast also severed from the same all others who obey thy commands, to the peril of their souls. Know therefore that I will not obey thee, nor join thee in such ingratitude to God-ward; neither will I deny my benefactor and Saviour, though thou slay me by wild beasts, or give me to the fire and sword, as thou hast the power. For I neither fear death, nor desire the present world, having passed judgement on the frailty and vanity thereof. For what is there profitable, abiding or stable therein? Nay, in very existence, great is the misery, great the pain, great and ceaseless the attendant care. Of its gladness and enjoyment the yoke-fellows are dejection and pain. Its riches is poverty; its loftiness the lowest humiliation; and who shall tell the full tale of its miseries, which Saint John the Divine hath shown me in few words? For he saith, "The whole world lieth in wickedness"; and, "Love not the world, neither the things that are in the world. For all that is in the world is the lust of the flesh, and the lust of the eyes, and the pride of life. And the world passeth away, and the lust thereof, but he that doeth the will of God abideth for ever." Seeking, then, this good will of God, I have forsaken everything, and joined myself to those who possess the

from which he himself hath been delivered

αὐτὸν κεκτημένοις πόθον καὶ τὸν αὐτὸν ἐκζητοῦσι
Ps. liii. 2 Phil. i. 15 Θεόν· ἐν οἷς οὐκ ἔστιν ἔρις ἢ φθόνος, λῦπαι τε 17
καὶ μέριμναι, ἀλλὰ πάντες τὸν ἴσον τρέχουσι
Luke xvi. 9 δρόμον, ἵνα καταλάβωσι τὰς αἰωνίας μονάς, ἃς
Jas. i. 17 ἡτοίμασεν ὁ Πατὴρ τῶν φώτων τοῖς ἀγαπῶσιν
1 Cor. ii. 8 αὐτόν. τούτους ἐγὼ γεννήτορας, τούτους ἀδελφούς, τούτους φίλους καὶ γνωστοὺς ἐκτησάμην·
Ps. lv. 8 τῶν δέ ποτέ μου φίλων καὶ ἀδελφῶν Ἐμάκρυνα
φυγαδεύων, καὶ ηὐλίσθην ἐν τῇ ἐρήμῳ προσδεχό-
μενος τὸν Θεόν, τὸν σώζοντά με ἀπὸ ὀλιγοψυχίας
καὶ ἀπὸ καταιγίδος.

Τούτων εὐκαίρως οὕτω καὶ ἡδέως τῷ τοῦ Θεοῦ ἀνθρώπῳ ὑπαγορευθέντων, ὁ βασιλεὺς ἐκινεῖτο μὲν ὑπὸ τοῦ θυμοῦ, καὶ πικρῶς αἰκίζειν τὸν ἅγιον ἠβούλετο, ὤκνει δὲ πάλιν καὶ ἀνεβάλλετο, τὸ αἰδέσιμον αὐτοῦ καὶ περιφανὲς εὐλαβούμενος. ὑπολαβὼν δὲ ἔφη πρὸς αὐτόν.

Πανταχόθεν, ἄθλιε, τὴν σεαυτοῦ ἐκμελετήσας ἀπώλειαν, πρὸς ταύτην, ὡς ἔοικεν, ὑπὸ τῆς τύχης συνελαυνόμενος, ἠκόνησας τὸν νοῦν ἅμα καὶ τὴν γλῶτταν· ὅθεν ἀσαφῆ τινα καὶ ματαίαν βαττολογίαν διεξῆλθες. καὶ εἰ μὴ κατ᾽ ἀρχὰς τοῦ λόγου ἐπηγγειλάμην σοι ἐκ μέσου τοῦ συνεδρίου τὸν θυμὸν ποιήσασθαι, νῦν ἂν πυρί σου τὰς σάρκας παρέδωκα. ἐπεὶ δὲ προλαβὼν τοιούτοις με κατησφαλίσω τοῖς ῥήμασιν, ἀνέχομαί σου τοῦ θράσους, τῆς προτέρας μου ἕνεκεν πρός σε φιλίας. ἀναστὰς οὖν, λοιπὸν φεῦγε ἐξ ὀφθαλμῶν μου, μηκέτι σε ὄψομαι καὶ κακῶς ἀπολέσω.

Καὶ ἐξελθὼν ὁ τοῦ Θεοῦ ἄνθρωπος ἀνεχώρησεν
εἰς τὴν ἔρημον, λυπούμενος μὲν ὅτι οὐ μεμαρ-
2 Cor. i. 11 τύρηκε, μαρτυρῶν δὲ καθ᾽ ἡμέραν τῇ συνειδήσει 18

same desire, and seek after the same God. Amongst these there is no strife or envy, sorrow or care, but all run the like race that they may obtain those everlasting habitations which the Father of lights hath prepared for them that love him. Them have I gained for my fathers, my brothers, my friends and mine acquaintances. But from my former friends and brethren "I have got me away far off, and lodged in the wilderness" waiting for the God, who saveth me from faintness of spirit, and from the stormy tempest.'

How the king was wroth, and bade the chief satrap depart from his sight,

When the man of God had made answer thus gently and in good reason, the king was stirred by anger, and was minded cruelly to torment the saint; but again he hesitated and delayed, regarding his venerable and noble mien. So he answered and said:

'Unhappy man, that hast contrived thine own utter ruin, driven thereto, I ween, by fate, surely thou hast made thy tongue as sharp as thy wits. Hence thou hast uttered these vain and ambiguous babblings. Had I not promised, at the beginning of our converse, to banish Anger from mid court, I had now given thy body to be burned. But since thou hast prevented and tied me down fast by my words, I bear with thine effrontery, by reason of my former friendship with thee. Now, arise, and flee for ever from my sight, lest I see thee again and miserably destroy thee.'

and persecuted the monks the more fiercely

So the man of God went out and withdrew to the desert, grieved to have lost the crown of martyrdom, but daily a martyr in his conscience, and 'wrestling

καὶ ἀντιπαλαίων πρὸς τὰς ἀρχὰς καὶ ἐξουσίας,
Eph. vi. 12 πρὸς τοὺς κοσμοκράτορας τοῦ σκότους τοῦ αἰῶνος
τούτου, πρὸς τὰ πνευματικὰ τῆς πονηρίας, ὡς
φησὶν ὁ μακάριος Παῦλος. ἐκείνου μὲν οὖν ἀπο-
δημήσαντος, πλέον ὁ βασιλεὺς ὀργισθεὶς διωγμὸν
σφοδρότερον κατὰ τοῦ μοναχικοῦ ἐκμελετᾷ τάγματος, πλείονος δὲ τιμῆς τοὺς τῶν εἰδώλων ἀξιοῖ
Acts xix. 35 θεραπευτάς τε καὶ νεωκόρους.
Ἐν τοιαύτῃ δὲ ὄντος τοῦ βασιλέως πλάνῃ δεινῇ
καὶ ἀπάτῃ, γεννᾶται αὐτῷ παιδίον, πάνυ εὐμορ-
φότατον, καὶ ἐξ αὐτῆς τῆς ἐπανθούσης αὐτῷ
ὡραιότητος τὸ μέλλον προσημαῖνον. ἐλέγετο γὰρ
μηδαμοῦ ἐν τῇ γῇ ἐκείνῃ τοιοῦτόν ποτε φανῆναι
χαριέστατον καὶ περικαλλὲς παιδίον. χαρᾶς δὲ
μεγίστης ἐπὶ τῇ γεννήσει τοῦ παιδὸς ὁ βασιλεὺς
πλησθείς, τοῦτον μὲν Ἰωάσαφ ἐκάλεσεν, αὐτὸς δὲ
πρὸς τοὺς εἰδωλικοὺς ναοὺς ἀνοήτως ἀπῄει τοῖς
ἀνοητοτέροις αὐτῶν θεοῖς θύσων καὶ εὐχαριστη-
ρίους ὕμνους ἀποδώσων, ἀγνοῶν τίς ὁ τῶν καλῶν
ἁπάντων ἀληθῶς αἴτιος, πρὸς ὃν ἔδει τὴν πνευματικὴν ἀναφέρειν θυσίαν. ἐκεῖνος οὖν, τοῖς ἀψύχοις καὶ κωφοῖς τὴν αἰτίαν τῆς τοῦ παιδὸς
γεννήσεως ἀνατιθείς, πανταχοῦ διέπεμπε συναγαγεῖν τὰ πλήθη εἰς τὰ τούτου γενέθλια· καὶ ἦν
ἰδεῖν πάντας συρρέοντας τῷ φόβῳ τοῦ βασιλέως,
ἐπαγομένους τε τὰ πρὸς τὴν θυσίαν εὐτρεπισμένα,
ὡς ἑκάστῳ ἡ χεὶρ εὐπόρει καὶ ἡ πρὸς τὸν βασιλέα
εὔνοια εἶχε. μάλιστα δὲ αὐτοὺς ἠρέθιζε πρὸς
φιλοτιμίαν αὐτός, ταύρους καταθῦσαι φέρων ὅτι 19
πλείστους καὶ εὐμεγέθεις, καὶ οὕτω πάνδημον
ἑορτὴν τελέσας, πάντας ἐφιλοτιμεῖτο δώροις ὅσοι

against principalities and powers, against the rulers of the darkness of this world, against spiritual wickedness'; as saith Blessed Paul. But after his departure, the king waxed yet more wroth, and devised a yet fiercer persecution of the monastic order, while treating with greater honour the ministers and temple-keepers of his idols.

Of the birth of the prince Ioasaph, and of his birth feast

While the king was under this terrible delusion and error, there was born unto him a son, a right goodly child, whose beauty from his very birth was prophetic of his future fortunes. Nowhere in that land, they said, had there ever been seen so charming and lovely a babe. Full of the keenest joy at the birth of the child, the king called him Ioasaph,[1] and in his folly went in person to the temples of his idols, for to do sacrifice and offer hymns of praise to his still more foolish gods, unaware of the real giver of all good things, to whom he should have offered the spiritual sacrifice. He then, ascribing the cause of his son's birth to things lifeless and dumb, sent out into all quarters to gather the people together to celebrate his son's birth-day: and thou mightest have seen all the folk running together for fear of the king, and bringing their offerings ready for the sacrifice, according to the store at each man's hand, and his favour toward his lord. But chiefly the king stirred them up to emulation. He brought full many oxen, of goodly size, for sacrifice, and thus, making a feast for all his people, he bestowed

[1] *i.e.* The Lord gathers.

τε τῆς βουλῆς ἦσαν καὶ τῶν ἐν τέλει, καὶ ὅσοι περὶ τὸ στρατιωτικόν, ὅσοι τε τῶν εὐτελῶν καὶ ἀσήμων.

III

Ἐν αὐτῇ δὲ τῇ τῶν γενεθλίων τοῦ παιδὸς ἑορτῇ συνῆλθον πρὸς τὸν βασιλέα ἐξ ἐπιλογῆς ἄνδρες ὡσεὶ πεντηκονταπέντε, περὶ τὴν ἀστροθεάμονα τῶν Χαλδαίων ἐσχολακότες σοφίαν. καὶ τούτους ἐγγυτάτω παραστησάμενος ὁ βασιλεὺς ἀνηρώτα ἐξειπεῖν ἕκαστον τί μέλλει ἔσεσθαι τὸ γεννηθὲν αὐτῷ παιδίον. οἱ δέ, πολλὰ διασκεψάμενοι, ἔλεγον μέγαν αὐτὸν ἔσεσθαι ἔν τε πλούτῳ καὶ δυναστείᾳ, καὶ ὑπερβάλλειν πάντας τοὺς πρὸ αὐτοῦ βεβασιλευκότας. εἷς δὲ τῶν ἀστρολόγων, ὁ τῶν σὺν αὐτῷ πάντων διαφορώτατος, εἶπεν ὡς, Ἐξ ὧν με διδάσκουσιν οἱ τῶν ἀστέρων δρόμοι, ὦ βασιλεῦ, ἡ προκοπὴ τοῦ νυνὶ γεννηθέντος σοι παιδὸς οὐκ ἐν τῇ σῇ ἔσται βασιλείᾳ, ἀλλ' ἐν ἑτέρᾳ κρείττονι καὶ ἀσυγκρίτως ὑπερβαλλούσῃ. δοκῶ δὲ καὶ τῆς παρὰ σοῦ διωκομένης αὐτὸν ἐπιλαβέσθαι τῶν Χριστιανῶν θρησκείας, καὶ οὐκ ἔγωγε οἶμαι τοῦ σκοποῦ ἐκεῖνον καὶ τῆς ἐλπίδος ψευσθήσεσθαι. ταῦτα μὲν εἶπεν ὁ ἀστρολόγος, ὥσπερ ὁ πάλαι (Num. xxii.-xxiv.) Βαλαάμ, οὐ τῆς ἀστρολογίας ἀληθευούσης, ἀλλὰ τοῦ Θεοῦ διὰ τῶν ἐναντίων τὰ τῆς ἀληθείας παραδεικνύντος, ὥστε πᾶσαν τοῖς ἀσεβέσι πρόφασιν περιαιρεθῆναι.

Ὁ δὲ βασιλεύς, ὡς ἤκουσε ταῦτα, βαρέως τὴν ἀγγελίαν ἐδέξατο, λύπη δὲ τὴν εὐφροσύνην αὐτῷ διέκοπτεν. ἐν πόλει δὲ ὅμως ἰδιαζούσῃ

largesses on all his counsellors and officers, and on all his soldiers, and all the poor, and men of low degree.

III

Of the prophecy of the astrologers

Now on his son's birth-day feast there came unto the king some five and fifty chosen men, schooled in the star-lore of the Chaldæans. These the king called into his presence, and asked them, severally, to tell him the future of the new-born babe. After long counsel held, they said that he should be mighty in riches and power, and should surpass all that had reigned before him. But one of the astrologers, the most learned of all his fellows, spake thus:—'From that which I learn from the courses of the stars, O king, the advancement of the child, now born unto thee, will not be in thy kingdom, but in another, a better and a greater one beyond compare. Methinketh also that he will embrace the Christian religion, which thou persecutest, and I trow that he will not be disappointed of his aim and hope.' Thus spake the astrologer, like Balaam of old, not that his star-lore told him true, but because God signifieth the truth by the mouth of his enemies, that all excuse may be taken from the ungodly.

How the king set his son in a palace apart

But when the king heard thereof, he received the tidings with a heavy heart, and sorrow cut short his joy. Howsomever he built, in a city set

παλάτιον δειμάμενος περικαλλὲς καὶ λαμπρὰς οἰκίας φιλοτεχνήσας, ἐκεῖ τὸν παῖδα ἔθετο κατοικεῖν, μετὰ τὴν συμπλήρωσιν τῆς πρώτης αὐτῷ ἡλικίας, ἀπρόϊτόν τε εἶναι παρεκελεύσατο, παιδαγωγοὺς αὐτῷ καὶ ὑπηρέτας καταστήσας, νέους τῇ ἡλικίᾳ καὶ τῇ ὁράσει ὡραιοτάτους, ἐπισκήψας αὐτοῖς μηδὲν τῶν τοῦ βίου ἀνιαρῶν κατάδηλον αὐτῷ ποιήσασθαι, μὴ θάνατον, μὴ γῆρας, μὴ νόσον, μὴ πενίαν, μὴ ἄλλο τι λυπηρὸν καὶ δυνάμενον τὴν εὐφροσύνην αὐτῷ διακόπτειν, ἀλλὰ πάντα τὰ τερπνὰ καὶ ἀπολαυστικὰ προτιθέναι, ἵνα τούτοις ὁ νοῦς αὐτοῦ τερπόμενος καὶ ἐντρυφῶν μηδὲν ὅλως περὶ τῶν μελλόντων διαλογίζεσθαι ἰσχύσειε, μήτε μέχρι ψιλοῦ ῥήματος τὰ περὶ τοῦ Χριστοῦ καὶ τῶν αὐτοῦ δογμάτων ἀκούσειεν. τοῦτο γὰρ μάλιστα πάντων ἀποκρύψαι αὐτῷ διενοεῖτο, τὴν τοῦ ἀστρολόγου προαγόρευσιν ὑφορώμενος. εἴ τινα δὲ τῶν ὑπηρετούντων αὐτῷ νοσῆσαι συνέβη, τοῦτον μὲν θᾶττον ἐκβαλεῖν ἐκεῖθεν παρεκελεύετο, ἕτερον δὲ ἀντ' αὐτοῦ σφριγῶντα καὶ εὐεκτοῦντα ἐδίδου, ἵνα μηδὲν ὅλως ἀνώμαλον οἱ τοῦ παιδὸς ὀφθαλμοὶ θεάσαιντο. ὁ μὲν οὖν βασιλεὺς οὕτω ταῦτα διενοεῖτό τε καὶ
Is. vi. 9; Mat. xiii. 18 ἐποίει· βλέπων γὰρ οὐχ ἑώρα, καὶ ἀκούων οὐ συνίει.

Μαθὼν δέ τινας τῶν μοναζόντων ἔτι περισώ- 21
ζεσθαι, ὧν μηδὲ ἴχνος ὑπολελεῖφθαι ἐδόκει, θυμοῦ ὑπερεπίμπλατο καὶ ὀξύτατα κατ' αὐτῶν ἐκινεῖτο, κήρυκάς τε ἀνὰ πᾶσαν τὴν πόλιν καὶ τὴν χώραν ἐκέλευε διαθέειν, ἐκβοῶντας μηδαμοῦ τινὰ τὸ παράπαν μετὰ τρεῖς ἡμέρας τοῦ τῶν μοναζόντων τάγματος εὑρεθῆναι. εἰ δέ τινες εὑρεθεῖεν μετὰ

apart, an exceeding beautiful palace, with cunningly devised gorgeous chambers, and there set his son to dwell, after he had ended his first infancy; and he forbade any to approach him, appointing, for instructors and servants, youths right seemly to behold. These he charged to reveal to him none of the annoys of life, neither death, nor old age, nor disease, nor poverty, nor anything else grievous that might break his happiness: but to place before him everything pleasant and enjoyable, that his heart, revelling in these delights, might not gain strength to consider the future, nor ever hear the bare mention of the tale of Christ and his doctrines. For he was heedful of the astrologer's warning, and it was this most that he was minded to conceal from his son. And if any of the attendants chanced to fall sick, he commanded to have him speedily removed, and put another plump and well-favoured servant in his place, that the boy's eyes might never once behold anything to disquiet them. Such then was the intent and doing of the king, for, 'seeing, he did not see, and hearing, he did not understand.'

where none of the annoys of life might come nigh him,

But, learning that some monks still remained, of whom he fondly imagined that not a trace was left, he became angry above measure, and his fury was hotly kindled against them. And he commanded heralds to scour all the city and all the country, proclaiming that after three days no monk whatsoever should be found therein. But and if any were

and how he harried the Christians yet the more

τὰς διωρισμένας ἡμέρας, τῷ διὰ πυρὸς καὶ ξίφους ὀλέθρῳ παραδοθήτωσαν· Οὗτοι γὰρ (φησίν) ἀναπείθουσι τὸν λαὸν ὡς Θεῷ προσέχειν τῷ ἐσταυρωμένῳ. ἐν δὲ τῷ μεταξὺ συνέβη καί τι τοιοῦτον, ἐφ' ᾧ ἐπὶ πλέον χαλεπαίνων ἦν ὁ βασιλεὺς καὶ κατὰ τῶν μοναζόντων ὀργιζόμενος.

IV

'Ανὴρ γάρ τις, τῶν ἐν τέλει τὰ πρῶτα φέρων, ἐν τοῖς βασιλείοις ἐτύγχανε, τὸν μὲν βίον ἐπιεικής, εὐσεβὴς δὲ τὴν πίστιν· καί, τὴν ἑαυτοῦ σωτηρίαν, ὡς οἷόν τε, ἐμπορευόμενος, λανθάνων ἦν διὰ τὸν φόβον τοῦ βασιλέως. ὅθεν τινές, τῆς εἰς τὸν βασιλέα παρρησίας τούτῳ βασκήναντες, διαβάλλειν αὐτὸν ἐμελέτων, καὶ τοῦτο αὐτοῖς διὰ φροντίδος ἦν. καὶ δή ποτε πρὸς θήραν ἐξελθόντι τῷ βασιλεῖ μετὰ τῆς συνήθους αὐτῷ δορυφορίας, εἷς ἦν τῶν συνθηρευτῶν καὶ ὁ ἀγαθὸς ἐκεῖνος ἀνήρ. περιπατοῦντι δὲ αὐτῷ κατὰ μόνας, ἐκ θείας τοῦτο συμβάν, ὡς οἶμαι, οἰκονομίας, εὑρίσκει ἄνθρωπον ἐν λόχμῃ τινὶ κατὰ γῆς ἐρριμμένον, καὶ δεινῶς τὸν πόδα ὑπὸ θηρίου συντετριμ- 22
μένον, ὅς, ἰδὼν αὐτὸν παριόντα, ἐδυσώπει μὴ παραδραμεῖν, ἀλλ' οἰκτεῖραι αὐτὸν τῆς συμφορᾶς, καὶ εἰς τὸν ἴδιον ἀπαγαγεῖν οἶκον, ἅμα καὶ τοῦτο προστιθείς, ὡς Οὐκ ἀνόνητός σοι καὶ παντελῶς ἀνενέργητος, φησίν, εὑρεθείην ἐγώ. ὁ δὲ λαμπρὸς ἐκεῖνος ἀνὴρ λέγει αὐτῷ· 'Εγὼ μὲν δι' αὐτοῦ τοῦ καλοῦ τὴν φύσιν προσλήψομαί σε καὶ θεραπείας, ὅση δύναμις, ἀξιώσω· ἀλλὰ τίς ἡ ὄνησις, ἣν παρὰ

discovered after the set time, they should be delivered to destruction by fire and sword. 'For,' said he, 'these be they that persuade the people to worship the Crucified as God.' Meanwhile a thing befell, that made the king still more angry and bitter against the monks.

IV

Of a certain virtuous senator and a beggar-man

There was at court a man pre-eminent among the rulers, of virtuous life and devout in religion. But while working out his own salvation, as best he might, he kept it secret for fear of the king. Wherefore certain men, looking enviously on his free converse with the king, studied how they might slander him; and this was all their thought. On a day, when the king went forth a-hunting with his bodyguard, as was his wont, this good man was of the hunting party. While he was walking alone, by divine providence, as I believe, he found a man in a covert, cast to the ground, his foot grievously crushed by a wild-beast. Seeing him passing by, the wounded man importuned him not to go his way, but to pity his misfortune, and take him to his own home, adding thereto: 'I hope that I shall not be found unprofitable, nor altogether useless unto thee.' Our nobleman said unto him, 'For very charity I will take thee up, and render thee such service as I may. But what is this profit which thou saidest that

How certain malignant persons slandered

σοῦ μοι ἔσεσθαι ἔφησας; ὁ δὲ πένης ἐκεῖνος καὶ ἀσθενής, Ἐγώ, φησίν, ἄνθρωπός εἰμι θεραπευτὴς ῥημάτων· εἰ γάρ ποτε ἐν ῥήμασιν ἢ ὁμιλίαις πληγή τις ἢ κάκωσις εὑρεθείη, καταλλήλοις φαρμάκοις ταῦτα θεραπεύσω, τοῦ μὴ περαιτέρω τὸ κακὸν χωρῆσαι· ὁ μὲν οὖν εὐσεβὴς ἀνὴρ ἐκεῖνος τὸ λεχθὲν ἀντ' οὐδενὸς ἡγήσατο, ἐκεῖνον δὲ διὰ τὴν ἐντολὴν ἀπαγαγεῖν οἴκαδε παρεκελεύσατο, καὶ τῆς προσηκούσης ἐπιμελείας οὐκ ἀπεστέρησεν. οἱ δὲ προμνημονευθέντες φθονεροὶ ἐκεῖνοι καὶ βάσκανοι, ἣν πάλαι ὤδινον κακίαν εἰς φῶς προενεγκόντες, διαβάλλουσι τὸν ἄνδρα πρὸς τὸν βασιλέα, ὡς, οὐ μόνον τῆς αὐτοῦ φιλίας ἐπιλαθόμενος, ἠλόγησε τῆς πρὸς τοὺς θεοὺς θεραπείας καὶ πρὸς Χριστιανισμὸν ἀπέκλινεν, ἀλλὰ καὶ δεινὰ κατὰ τῆς αὐτοῦ μελετᾷ βασιλείας, τὸν ὄχλον διαστρέφων καὶ ἑαυτῷ πάντας οἰκειούμενος. Ἀλλ', εἰ βούλει, φασί, βεβαιωθῆναι μηδὲν ἡμᾶς πεπλασμένον λέγειν, καλέσας αὐτὸν ἰδίως, εἰπὲ πειράζων βούλεσθαί σε, καταλιπόντα τὴν πάτριον θρησκείαν καὶ τὴν δόξαν τῆς βασιλείας, Χριστιανὸν γενέσθαι, καὶ τὸ μοναχικὸν περιβαλέσθαι σχῆμα, ὃ πάλαι ἐδίωξας, ὡς οὐ καλῶς δῆθεν τούτου
γεγενημένου. οἱ γὰρ ταῦτα δεινῶς κατὰ τοῦ 23
ἀνδρὸς σκηπτόμενοι ᾔδεισαν τῆς αὐτοῦ γνώμης τὴν εὐκατάνυκτον προαίρεσιν, ὡς, εἰ τοιαῦτα παρὰ τοῦ βασιλέως ἀκούσειεν, ἐκείνῳ μὲν τὰ κρείττονα βουλευσαμένῳ γνώμην δώσειε μὴ ἀναβαλέσθαι πρὸς τὰ καλῶς βεβουλευμένα, καὶ ἐκ τούτου ἀληθῆ λέγοντες ἐκεῖνοι εὑρεθεῖεν.

Ὁ δὲ βασιλεύς, τὴν τοῦ ἀνδρὸς πρὸς αὐτὸν εὔνοιαν ὁπόση μὴ ἀγνοῶν, ἀπίθανά τε ἡγεῖτο

I should receive of thee?' The poor sick man answered, 'I am a physician of words. If ever in speech or converse any wound or damage be found, I will heal it with befitting medicines, that so the evil spread no further.' The devout man gave no heed to his word, but on account of the commandment, ordered him to be carried home, and grudged him not that tending which he required. But the aforesaid envious and malignant persons, bringing forth to light that ungodliness with which they had long been in travail, slandered this good man to the king; that not only did he forget his friendship with the king, and neglect the worship of the gods, and incline to Christianity, but more, that he was grievously intriguing against the kingly power, and was turning aside the common people, and stealing all hearts for himself. 'But,' said they, 'if thou wilt prove that our charge is not ungrounded, call him to thee privately; and, to try him, say that thou desirest to leave thy fathers' religion, and the glory of thy kingship, and to become a Christian, and to put on the monkish habit which formerly thou didst persecute, having, thou shalt tell him, found thine old course evil.' The authors of this villainous charge against the Christian knew the tenderness of his heart, how that, if he heard such speech from the king, he would advise him, who had made this better choice, not to put off his good determinations, and so they would be found just accusers.

the senator to the king

But the king, not forgetful of his friend's great kindness toward him, thought these accusations in-

How the king made trial of him

καὶ ψευδῆ τὰ λεγόμενα, καὶ ὅτι μὴ ἀβασανίστως
ταῦτα προσδέχεσθαι δεῖ, δοκιμάσαι τὸ πρᾶγμα
καὶ τὴν διαβολὴν διεσκέψατο. καί, προσκαλεσάμενος αὐτὸν κατ' ἰδίαν, ἔφη πειράζων· Οἶδας, ὦ
φίλε, ὅσα ἐνεδειξάμην τοῖς τε λεγομένοις μονά-
ζουσι καὶ πᾶσι τοῖς Χριστιανοῖς. νυνὶ δέ, μετάμελος ἐπὶ τούτῳ γενόμενος καὶ καταγνοὺς τῶν
παρόντων, ἐκείνων βούλομαι γενέσθαι τῶν ἐλπί-
δων ὧν λεγόντων αὐτῶν ἀκήκοα, ἀθανάτου τινὸς
βασιλείας εἰς ἄλλην βιοτὴν μελλούσης ἔσεσθαι·
ἡ γὰρ παροῦσα θανάτῳ πάντως διακόπτεται.
οὐκ ἂν ἄλλως δὲ τοῦτο κατορθωθῆναί μοι δοκῶ
καὶ μὴ διαμαρτεῖν τοῦ σκοποῦ, εἰ μὴ Χριστιανός
τε γένωμαι, καὶ χαίρειν εἰπὼν τῇ δόξῃ τῆς ἐμῆς
βασιλείας καὶ τοῖς λοιποῖς ἡδέσι καὶ τερπνοῖς
τοῦ βίου, τοὺς ἀσκητὰς ἐκείνους καὶ μονάζοντας
ζητήσας ὅπου ποτ' ἂν εἶεν, οὓς ἀδίκως ἀπήλασα,
ἐκείνοις ἑαυτὸν ἐγκαταμίξω. πρὸς ταῦτα τί φὴς
αὐτός, καὶ ὁποίαν δίδως βουλήν; εἰπέ, πρὸς
αὐτῆς τῆς ἀληθείας. οἶδα γὰρ ἀληθῆ καὶ εὐγνώ-
μονα εἶναί σε ὑπὲρ πάντας. ὁ δὲ ἀγαθὸς ἀνὴρ
ἐκεῖνος, ὡς ταῦτα ἤκουσε, μηδόλως τὸν ἐγκεκρυμ-
μένον ἐπιγνοὺς δόλον, κατενύγη τὴν ψυχήν, καὶ 24
δάκρυσι συγκεχυμένος ἁπλοϊκῶς ἀπεκρίνατο·
Dan. vi. 21 Βασιλεῦ, εἰς τοὺς αἰῶνας ζῆθι· βουλὴν γὰρ
ἀγαθὴν καὶ σωτήριον ἐβουλεύσω, ὅτι, κἂν δυσ-
εύρετος ἡ τῶν οὐρανῶν βασιλεία, ἀλλ' ὅμως δεῖ
Luke xi. 10; Mat. vii. 8 ταύτην πάσῃ δυνάμει ζητεῖν· Ὁ ζητῶν γάρ, φησίν,
εὑρήσει αὐτήν. ἡ δὲ τῶν παρόντων ἀπόλαυσις,
κἂν τῷ φαινομένῳ τέρπῃ καὶ ἡδύνῃ, ἀλλὰ καλὸν
αὐτὴν ἀπώσασθαι· ἐν αὐτῷ γὰρ τῷ εἶναι οὐκ
ἔστι, καὶ οὓς εὐφραίνει ἑπταπλασίως αὖθις

credible and false; and because he might not accept them without proof, he resolved to try the fact and the charge. So he called the man apart and said, to prove him, 'Friend, thou knowest of all my past dealings with them that are called monks and with all the Christians. But now, I have repented in this matter, and, lightly esteeming the present world, would fain become partaker of those hopes whereof I have heard them speak, of some immortal kingdom in the life to come; for the present is of a surety cut short by death. And in none other way, methinks, can I succeed herein and not miss the mark except I become a Christian, and, bidding farewell to the glory of my kingdom and all the pleasures and joys of life, go seek those hermits and monks, wheresoever they be, whom I have banished, and join myself to their number. Now what sayest thou thereto, and what is thine advice? Say on; I adjure thee in the name of truth; for I know thee to be true and wise above all men.'

How the senator was taken in a snare

The worthy man, hearing this, but never guessing the hidden pitfall, was pricked in spirit, and, melting into tears, answered in his simplicity, 'O king, live for ever! Good and sound is the determination that thou hast determined; for though the kingdom of heaven be difficult to find, yet must a man seek it with all his might, for it is written, "He that seeketh shall find it." The enjoyment of the present life, though in seeming it give delight and sweetness, is well thrust from us. At the very moment of its being it ceaseth to be, and for our joy repayeth us

λυπεῖ. τά τε γὰρ ἀγαθὰ αὐτῆς τά τε λυπηρὰ σκιᾶς ἐστιν ἀσθενέστερα, καί, ὡς ἴχνη νηὸς ποντοπορούσης ἢ ὀρνέου τὸν ἀέρα διερχομένου, θᾶττον ἀφανίζονται. ἡ δὲ τῶν μελλόντων ἐλπίς, ἣν κηρύττουσιν οἱ Χριστιανοί, βεβαία ἐστὶ καὶ ἀσφαλεστάτη· θλῖψιν δὲ ἔχει ἐν τῷ κόσμῳ. ἀλλὰ τὰ μὲν ἡμέτερα νῦν ἡδέα ὀλιγοχρόνια, ἐκεῖ δὲ ὅλως οὐδὲν ἢ κόλασιν μόνον προξενοῦντα καὶ τιμωρίαν εἰς αἰῶνας μὴ λυομένην· τὸ γὰρ ἡδὺ τούτων πρόσκαιρον, τὸ δὲ ὀδυνηρὸν διηνεκές· τῶν δὲ Χριστιανῶν τὸ μὲν ἐπίπονον πρόσκαιρον, τὸ δὲ ἡδὺ καὶ χρήσιμον ἀθάνατον. κατευθυνθείη οὖν ἡ ἀγαθὴ τοῦ βασιλέως βουλή· καλὸν γάρ, σφόδρα καλὸν τῶν φθαρτῶν τὰ αἰώνια ἀνταλλάξασθαι.

Cp. Wisd. v. 9–11

Ἤκουσε ταῦτα ὁ βασιλεὺς καὶ λίαν ἐδυσχέραινε, κατέσχε δὲ ὅμως τὴν ὀργήν, καὶ οὐδὲν τέως τῷ ἀνδρὶ λελάληκεν. ὁ δέ, συνετὸς ὢν καὶ ἀγχίνους, ἐπέγνω βαρέως δέξασθαι τὸν βασιλέα τὰ ῥήματα αὐτοῦ καὶ ὅτι δόλῳ ἦν αὐτὸν ἐκπειράζων. ὑποστρέψας δὲ οἴκαδε ἠνιᾶτο καὶ ἐδυσφόρει, ἀπορῶν τίνι τρόπῳ θεραπεύσει τὸν βασιλέα καὶ ἐκφύγῃ τὸν ἐπηρτημένον αὐτῷ κίνδυνον. ἀΰπνῳ δὲ ὅλην τὴν νύκτα διατελοῦντι ἐπὶ μνήμης ἦλθεν αὐτῷ ὁ τὸν πόδα συντετριμμένος, καί, τοῦτον πρὸς ἑαυτὸν ἀγαγών, ἔφη· Μέμνημαί σου εἰρηκότος θεραπευτὴν ῥημάτων κεκακωμένων ὑπάρχειν σε. ὁ δέ, Ναί, φησί· καί, εἰ χρῄζεις, ἐπιδείξομαι τὰ τῆς ἐπιστήμης. ὑπολαβὼν δὲ ὁ συγκλητικὸς ἀφηγήσατο αὐτῷ τήν τε ἐξ ἀρχῆς πρὸς τὸν βασιλέα εὔνοιαν αὐτοῦ, καὶ ἣν ἐκέκτητο παρρησίαν, καὶ τὴν ἔναγχος προτε-

with sorrow sevenfold. Its happiness and its sorrow are more frail than a shadow, and, like the traces of a ship passing over the sea, or of a bird flying through the air, quickly disappear. But the hope of the life to come which the Christians preach is certain, and as surety sure; howbeit in this world it hath tribulation, whereas our pleasures now are short-lived, and in the beyond they only win us correction and everlasting punishment without release. For the pleasures of such life are temporary, but its pains eternal; while the Christians' labours are temporary, but their pleasure and gain immortal. Therefore well befall this good determination of the king! for right good it is to exchange the corruptible for the eternal.'

How the senator marked the king's displeasure and was sad thereat,

The king heard these words and waxed exceeding wroth: nevertheless he restrained his anger, and for the season let no word fall. But the other, being shrewd and quick of wit, perceived that the king took his word ill, and was craftily sounding him. So, on his coming home, he fell into much grief and distress in his perplexity how to conciliate the king and to escape the peril hanging over his own head. But as he lay awake all the night long, there came to his remembrance the man with the crushed foot; so he had him brought before him, and said, 'I remember thy saying that thou wert an healer of injured speech.' 'Yea,' quoth he, 'and if thou wilt I will give thee proof of my skill.' The senator answered and told him of his aforetime friendship with the king, and of the confidence which he had enjoyed, and of the snare laid for him in his late converse

θεῖσαν αὐτῷ δολερὰν ὁμιλίαν, καὶ ὅπως αὐτὸς
μὲν ἀγαθὰ ἀπεκρίνατο, ἐκεῖνος δὲ δυσχερῶς δεξάμενος τὸν λόγον, τῇ τοῦ προσώπου ἀλλοιώσει τὴν
ἐνδομυχοῦσαν αὐτῷ ὀργὴν ἐνεδείξατο.

Ὁ δὲ πένης ἐκεῖνος καὶ ἀσθενὴς διασκεψάμενος
Dan. iii. 10; Acts ii. 14 ἔφη· Γνωστὸν ἔστω σοι, ἐνδοξότατε, πονηρὰν
ἔχειν πρὸς σὲ ὑπόληψιν τὸν βασιλέα, ὡς ὅτι
κατασχεῖν αὐτοῦ τὴν βασιλείαν ζητεῖς, καὶ πειράζων σε εἶπεν ἅπερ εἶπεν. ἀναστὰς οὖν, καὶ
κείρας σου τὴν κόμην, καὶ ἐκβαλὼν τὰ λαμπρὰ
ἱμάτια ταῦτα, τρίχινα δὲ ἀμφιεσάμενος, ἅμα 26
πρωῒ πρόσελθε τῷ βασιλεῖ. τοῦ δὲ πυνθανομένου, Τί σοι τὸ σχῆμα τοῦτο βούλεται; ἀποκρί-
θητι· Περὶ ὧν μοι χθὲς ὡμίλησας, ὦ βασιλεῦ,
ἰδοὺ πάρειμι ἐν ἑτοίμῳ τοῦ ἀκολουθῆσαί σοι τὴν
ὁδὸν ἣν προεθυμήθης ὁδεῦσαι· εἰ γὰρ καὶ ποθεινή
ἐστιν ἡ τρυφὴ καὶ ἡδίστη, ἀλλὰ μή μοι γένοιτο
μετὰ σὲ ταύτην ἀναδέξασθαι· ἡ δὲ τῆς ἀρετῆς
ὁδός, ἣν μέλλεις βαδίζειν, κἂν δύσκολός ἐστι καὶ
τραχεῖα, ἀλλὰ μετὰ σοῦ ὄντι ῥᾳδία μοι αὕτη καὶ
εὔκολος καὶ ποθεινή· ὡς γὰρ κοινωνόν με ἔσχες
τῶν ἐνταῦθα καλῶν, οὕτω καὶ τῶν λυπηρῶν ἕξεις,
ἵνα καὶ τῶν μελλόντων συγκοινωνήσω σοι. ὁ δὲ
λαμπρὸς ἐκεῖνος ἀνήρ, ἀποδεξάμενος τὰ ῥήματα
τοῦ ἀσθενοῦς, ἐποίησε καθὰ δὴ καὶ αὐτῷ λελάλη-
κεν· ὃν ἰδὼν ὁ βασιλεὺς καὶ ἀκούσας, ἥσθη μὲν
ἐπὶ τούτῳ, ἀγάμενος λίαν τὴν εἰς αὐτὸν εὔνοιαν,
ψευδῆ δὲ τὰ κατ' αὐτοῦ λαληθέντα γνούς, πλείονος αὐτὸν τιμῆς καὶ τῆς εἰς αὐτὸν παρρησίας
ἀπολαύειν πεποίηκεν· κατὰ δὲ τῶν μοναζόντων
ὀργῆς αὖθις ὑπερεπίμπλατο, ἐκείνων εἶναι ταῦτα
λέγων τὰ διδάγματα, τὸ ἀπέχεσθαι τοὺς ἀνθρώ-

with the king; how he had given a good answer, but the king had taken his words amiss, and by his change of countenance betrayed the anger lurking within his heart.

and how by aid of the beggar-man's counsel he regained the king's favour

The sick beggar-man considered and said, 'Be it known unto thee, most noble sir, that the king harboureth against thee the suspicion, that thou wouldest usurp his kingdom, and he spake, as he spake, to sound thee. Arise therefore, and crop thy hair. Doff these thy fine garments, and don an hair-shirt, and at daybreak present thyself before the king. And when he asketh thee, What meaneth this apparel? answer him, "It hath to do with thy communing with me yesterday, O king. Behold, I am ready to follow thee along the road that thou art eager to travel; for though luxury be desirable and passing sweet, God forbid that I embrace it after thou art gone! Though the path of virtue, which thou art about to tread, be difficult and rough, yet in thy company I shall find it easy and pleasant, for as I have shared with thee this thy prosperity so now will I share thy distresses, that in the future, as in the past, I may be thy fellow."' Our nobleman, approving of the sick man's saying, did as he said. When the king saw and heard him, he was delighted, and beyond measure gratified by his devotion towards him. He saw that the accusations against his senator were false, and promoted him to more honour and to a greater enjoyment of his confidence. But against the monks he again raged above measure, declaring that this was of their teaching,

πους τῶν τοῦ βίου ἡδέων καὶ ἀδήλοις ὀνειρο-
πολεῖσθαι ἐλπίσιν.
Ἐξερχόμενος δὲ αὖθις εἰς θήραν, ὁρᾷ δύο μοναχοὺς κατὰ τὴν ἔρημον διερχομένους, οὓς κρατηθῆναι καὶ τῷ αὐτοῦ προσαχθῆναι ὀχήματι κελεύσας,
ὀργίλως τε αὐτοῖς ἐνιδών, καὶ πῦρ, τὸ τοῦ λόγου, 27
πνεύσας, ἔφη· Οὐκ ἠκούσατε, ὦ πλάνοι καὶ ἀπατεῶνες, τῶν κηρύκων διαρρήδην βοώντων μή τινα
τῆς ὑμῶν κακοδαιμονίας μετὰ τρεῖς ἡμέρας ἐν
πόλει ἢ χώρᾳ τῆς ἐμῆς εὑρεθῆναι ἐξουσίας, ἢ
πάντως πυρίκαυστος ἔσται; οἱ δὲ μοναχοί· Ἰδοὺ
(φασὶ) καθὰ δὴ καὶ προσέταξας, ἐξερχόμεθά σου
τῶν πόλεων καὶ τῶν χωρῶν· μακρᾶς δὲ ἡμῖν τῆς
ὁδοῦ προκειμένης τοῦ ἀπελθεῖν πρὸς τοὺς ἡμετέρους ἀδελφούς, ἐνδεῶς ἔχοντες τροφῆς, ταύτην
ἐποριζόμεθα, τοῦ ἔχειν τὰ ἐφόδια καὶ μὴ λιμοῦ
παρανάλωμα γενέσθαι. ὁ δὲ βασιλεὺς ἔφη· Ὁ
θανάτου δεδοικὼς ἀπειλὴν οὐκ ἀσχολεῖται εἰς πο-
ρισμὸν βρωμάτων. λέγουσιν οἱ μονασταί· Καλῶς
εἶπας, ὦ βασιλεῦ· οἱ θάνατον δεδοικότες διὰ φροντίδος ἔχουσι πῶς αὐτὸν ἐκφύγωσι. τίνες δέ εἰσιν
οὗτοι, ἀλλ' ἢ οἱ τοῖς ῥευστοῖς προστετηκότες καὶ
τούτοις ἐπτοημένοι, οἵτινες, μηδὲν ἀγαθὸν ἐλπί-
ζοντες εὑρεῖν ἐκεῖθεν, δυσαποσπάστως ἔχουσι
τῶν παρόντων, καὶ διὰ τοῦτο δεδοίκασι θάνατον;
ἡμεῖς δὲ οἱ πάλαι μισήσαντες κόσμον καὶ τὰ ἐν
Mat. vii. 14; κόσμῳ, καὶ τὴν στενὴν καὶ τεθλιμμένην διὰ
Luke xiii. 24 Χριστὸν βαδίζοντες ὁδόν, οὔτε θάνατον δεδοίκαμεν, οὔτε τὰ παρόντα ποθοῦμεν, ἀλλὰ τῶν μελλόντων ἐφιέμεθα μόνον. ἐπεὶ οὖν ὁ παρ' ὑμῶν
ἐπαγόμενος ἡμῖν θάνατος διαβατήριον γίνεται τῆς 28

that men should abstain from the pleasures of life, and rock themselves in visionary hopes.

How the king met two monks in the desert, and debated with them,

Another day, when he was gone a-hunting, he espied two monks crossing the desert. These he ordered to be apprehended and brought to his chariot. Looking angrily upon them, and breathing fire, as they say, 'Ye vagabonds and deceivers,' he cried, 'have ye not heard the plain proclamation of the heralds, that if any of your execrable religion were found, after three days, in any city or country within my realm, he should be burned with fire?' The monks answered, 'Lo! obedient to thine order, we be coming out of thy cities and coasts. But as the journey before us is long, to get us away to our brethren, being in want of victuals, we were making provision for the way, that we perish not with hunger.' Said the king, 'He that dreadeth menace of death busieth not himself with the purveyance of victuals.' 'Well spoken, O king,' cried the monks. 'They that dread death have concern how to escape it. And who are these but such as cling to things temporary and are enamoured of them, who, having no good hopes yonder, find it hard to be wrenched from this present world, and therefore dread death? But we, who have long since hated the world and the things of the world, and are walking along the narrow and strait road, for Christ his sake, neither dread death, nor desire the present world, but only long for the world to come. Therefore, forasmuch the death that thou art bringing upon us proveth

ἀϊδίου ζωῆς καὶ κρείττονος, ποθητὸς ἡμῖν μᾶλλον ἢ φοβερός ἐστιν οὗτος.

Ἐφ' οἷς ἐξ ἀγχινοίας δῆθεν ὁ βασιλεὺς ἐπιλαβέσθαι τῶν μοναχῶν βουλόμενος, ἔφη· Τί δέ; οὐ πρὸ μικροῦ εἴπατε ὑποχωρεῖν ὑμᾶς, καθὰ δὴ καὶ προσέταξα; καί, εἰ οὐ δεδοίκατε τὸν θάνατον, πῶς φυγῇ ἐχρήσασθε; ἰδοὺ καὶ ταῦτα μάτην κομπάζοντες διεψεύσασθε. ἀπεκρίθησαν οἱ μοναχοί· Οὐ τὸν παρὰ σοῦ ἀπειλούμενον θάνατον δεδοικότες φεύγομεν, ἀλλ' ἐλεοῦντές σε, ἵνα μὴ περισσοτέρας κατακρίσεως αἴτιοί σοι γενώμεθα, προεθυμήθημεν ὑποχωρεῖν· ἐπεί, τό γε εἰς ἡμᾶς ἧκον, οὐδόλως σου τὰς ἀπειλάς ποτε δειλιῶμεν. πρὸς ταῦτα ὁ βασιλεὺς ὀργισθεὶς ἐκέλευσεν αὐτοὺς πυρικαύστους γενέσθαι· καὶ ἐτελειώθησαν οἱ τοῦ Χριστοῦ θεράποντες διὰ πυρός, τῶν μαρτυρικῶν τυχόντες στεφάνων. δόγμα τε ἐξέθετο, εἴ πού τις εὑρεθῇ μονάζων, ἀνεξετάστως φονεύεσθαι. καὶ οὐδεὶς ὑπελείφθη ἐν ἐκείνῃ τῇ χώρᾳ τοῦ τοιούτου τάγματος, εἰ μὴ οἱ ἐν ὄρεσι καὶ σπηλαίοις καὶ ταῖς ὀπαῖς τῆς γῆς ἑαυτοὺς κατακρύψαντες. ταῦτα μὲν οὖν δὴ τοιαῦτα.

V

Ὁ δὲ τοῦ βασιλέως υἱός, περὶ οὗ ὁ λόγος ἀπ' ἀρχῆς εἰπεῖν ὥρμηται, ἐν τῷ κατασκευασθέντι
αὐτῷ παλατίῳ ἀπρόϊτος ὤν, τῆς ἐφήβου ἥψατο 29
ἡλικίας, πᾶσαν τὴν Αἰθιόπων καὶ Περσῶν μετελθὼν παιδείαν, οὐκ ἔλαττον τὴν ψυχὴν ἢ τὸ σῶμα εὐφυὴς ὢν καὶ ὡραῖος, νουνεχής τε καὶ

but the passage to that everlasting and better life, it is rather to be desired of us than feared.'

Hereupon the king, wishing to entrap the monks, as I ween, shrewdly said, 'How now? Said ye not but this instant, that ye were withdrawing even as I commanded you? And, if ye fear not death, how came ye to be fleeing? Lo! this is but another of your idle boasts and lies.' The monks answered, ''Tis not because we dread the death wherewith thou dost threaten us that we flee, but because we pity thee. 'Twas in order that we might not bring on thee greater condemnation, that we were eager to escape. Else for ourselves we are never a whit terrified by thy threats.' At this the king waxed wroth and bade burn them with fire. So by fire were these servants of God made perfect, and received the Martyr's crown. And the king published a decree that, should any be found leading a monk's life, he should be put to death without trial. Thus was there left in that country none of the monastic order, save those that had hid them in mountains and caverns and holes of the earth. So much then concerning this matter.

and waxing angry bade burn them with fire

V

But meanwhile, the king's son, of whom our tale began to tell, never departing from the palace prepared for him, attained to the age of manhood. He had pursued all the learning of the Ethiopians and Persians, and was as fair and well favoured in mind as in body, intelligent and prudent,

How Ioasaph, grown to manhood, desired to know the cause of his imprisonment

φρόνιμος καὶ πᾶσι διαλάμπων ἀγαθοῖς πλεονεκτήμασι, ζητήματά τε φυσικὰ πρὸς τοὺς διδάσκοντας αὐτὸν προβαλλόμενος, ὡς κἀκείνους θαυμάζειν ἐπὶ τῇ τοῦ παιδὸς ἀγχινοίᾳ καὶ συνέσει, ἐκπλήττεσθαι δὲ καὶ τὸν βασιλέα τό τε χαριέστατον τοῦ προσώπου καὶ τὸ τῆς ψυχῆς κατάστημα. ἐντολάς τε ἐδίδου τοῖς συνοῦσιν αὐτῷ, μηδὲν τὸ παράπαν τῶν τοῦ βίου ἀνιαρῶν αὐτῷ γνώριμον θεῖναι, μηδ᾿ ὅτι ὅλως θάνατος τὰ παρόντα τερπνὰ διαδέχεται. κεναῖς δὲ ἐπηρείδετο ἐλπίσι, καί, τοῦτο δὴ τὸ τοῦ λόγου, εἰς οὐρανὸν τοξεύειν ἐπιχειρῶν. πῶς γὰρ ἂν καὶ διέλαθεν ἀνθρωπίνῃ φύσει ὁ θάνατος; οὐ μέντοι οὐδὲ τῷ παιδὶ διέλαθε. πάσῃ γὰρ συνέσει κατάκομον ἔχων ἐκεῖνος τὸν λογισμόν, ἐσκόπει καθ᾿ ἑαυτὸν τίνι λόγῳ αὐτόν τε ἀπρόϊτον εἶναι ὁ πατὴρ κατεδίκασε καὶ παντὶ τῷ βουλομένῳ τὴν εἰς αὐτὸν οὐ συγχωρεῖ εἴσοδον. ἔγνω γὰρ καθ᾿ ἑαυτὸν μὴ ἄνευ τῆς τοῦ πατρὸς προσταγῆς τοῦτο εἶναι. ὅμως ᾐδεῖτο ἐρωτῆσαι αὐτόν· τοῦτο μὲν ἀπίθανον εἶναι λέγων, μὴ τὰ συμφέροντα αὐτῷ τὸν πατέρα διανοεῖσθαι, τοῦτο δὲ σκοπῶν, ὡς, εἰ κατὰ γνώμην τοῦ πατρός ἐστι τὸ πρᾶγμα, κἂν ἐρωτήσῃ, οὐκ ἂν αὐτῷ τὰ τῆς ἀληθείας γνωριεῖ. ὅθεν παρ᾿ ἄλλων, καὶ μὴ παρὰ τοῦ πατρός, ταῦτα μαθεῖν διέγνω. ἕνα δὲ τῶν παιδαγωγῶν προσφιλέστατον καὶ οἰκειότατον τῶν λοιπῶν κεκτημένος, ἐπὶ πλεῖον οἰκειωσάμενος καὶ δωρεαῖς φιλοτίμοις δεξιωσάμενος, ἐπυνθάνετο παρ᾿ αὐτοῦ τί ἂν βούλοιτο τῷ βασιλεῖ ἡ ἐν τῷ περιτειχίσματι ἐκείνῳ τούτου κάθειρξις, καὶ ὡς Εἰ τοῦτο, φησί, σαφῶς διδάξεις με, πρόκριτος πάντων ἔσῃ μοι, καὶ διαθήκην φιλίας διηνεκοῦς

and shining in all excellencies. To his teachers he would propound such questions of natural history that even they marvelled at the boy's quickness and understanding, while the king was astounded at the charm of his countenance and the disposition of his soul. He charged the attendants of the young prince on no account to make known unto him any of the annoys of life, least of all to tell him that death ensueth on the pleasures of this world. But vain was the hope whereon he stayed, and he was like the archer in the tale that would shoot at the sky. For how could death have remained unknown to any human creature? Nor did it to this boy; for his mind was fertile of wit, and he would reason within himself, why his father had condemned him never to go abroad, and had forbidden access to all. He knew, without hearing it, that this was his father's express command. Nevertheless he feared to ask him; it was not to be believed that his father intended aught but his good; and again, if it were so by his father's will, his father would not reveal the true reason, for all his asking. Wherefore he determined to learn the secret from some other source. There was one of his tutors nearer and dearer to him than the rest, whose devotion he won even further by handsome gifts. To him he put the question what his father might mean by thus enclosing him within those walls, adding, 'If thou wilt plainly tell me this, of all thou shalt stand first in my favour, and I will make with thee a covenant of everlasting

How he questioned one of his tutors,

διαθήσομαί σοι. ὁ δὲ παιδαγωγός, ἐχέφρων καὶ αὐτὸς ὑπάρχων, καὶ εἰδὼς τὴν τοῦ παιδὸς συνετὴν καὶ τελείαν φρόνησιν, καὶ ὡς οὐκ ἂν αὐτῷ γένοιτο κινδύνου πρόξενος, πάντα αὐτῷ κατὰ μέρος διηγήσατο, τὸν κατὰ τῶν Χριστιανῶν τεθέντα παρὰ τοῦ βασιλέως διωγμὸν καὶ ἐξαιρέτως κατὰ τῶν ἀσκητῶν, ὅπως τε ἀπηλάθησαν καὶ ἐξεβλήθησαν τῆς περιχώρου ἐκείνης, οἷά τε γεννηθέντος αὐτοῦ οἱ ἀστρολόγοι προηγόρευσαν. Ἵν' οὖν, φησί, μή, ἀκούσας τῆς ἐκείνων διδαχῆς, ταύτην προκρίνῃς τῆς ἡμετέρας θρησκείας, μὴ προσομιλεῖν σοι πολλούς, ἀλλ' εὐαριθμήτους, ὁ βασιλεὺς ἐπετηδεύσατο, ἐντολάς ἡμῖν δοὺς μηδέν σοι τῶν τοῦ βίου ἀνιαρῶν γνωρίσαι. Ταῦτα ὡς ἤκουσεν ὁ νεανίας οὐδὲν ἕτερον προσέθετο λαλῆσαι· ἥψατο δὲ τῆς καρδίας αὐτοῦ λόγος σωτήριος, καὶ ἡ τοῦ Παρακλήτου χάρις τοὺς νοητοὺς αὐτοῦ ὀφθαλμοὺς διανοίγειν ἐπεχείρησε, πρὸς τὸν ἀψευδῆ χειραγωγοῦσα Θεόν, ὡς προϊὼν ὁ λόγος δηλώσειε. 31

Συχνῶς δὲ τοῦ πατρὸς αὐτοῦ καὶ βασιλέως κατὰ θέαν τοῦ παιδὸς ἐρχομένου (ἀγάπῃ γὰρ ὑπερβαλλούσῃ ἐφίλει αὐτόν), ἐν μιᾷ λεγει αὐτῷ ὁ υἱός· Μαθεῖν τι ἐπεθύμησα παρὰ σοῦ, ὦ δέσποτα καὶ βασιλεῦ, ἐφ' ᾧ λύπη διηνεκὴς καὶ μέριμνα ἀδιάπαυστος κατεσθίει μου τὴν ψυχήν. ὁ δὲ πατήρ, ἐξ αὐτῶν τῶν ῥημάτων ἀλγήσας τὰ σπλάγχνα, ἔφη· Λέγε μοι, τέκνον ποθεινότατον, τίς ἡ συνέχουσά σε λύπη, καὶ θᾶττον αὐτὴν εἰς χαρὰν μεταμεῖψαι σπουδάσω. καὶ φησὶν ὁ παῖς· Τίς ὁ τρόπος τῆς ἐμῆς ἐνθάδε καθείρξεως, ὅτι ἐντὸς τειχέων καὶ πυλῶν συνέκλεισάς με, ἀπρόϊτον πάντῃ καὶ ἀθέατον πᾶσί

friendship.' The tutor, himself a prudent man, knowing how bright and mature was the boy's wit and that he would not betray him, to his peril, discovered to him the whole matter—the persecution of the Christians and especially of the anchorets decreed by the king, and how they were driven forth and banished from the country round about; also the prophecies of the astrologers at his birth. ''Twas in order,' said he, 'that thou mightest never hear of their teaching, and choose it before our religion, that the king hath thus devised that none but a small company should dwell with thee, and hath commanded us to acquaint thee with none of the woes of life.' When the young prince heard this he said never a word more, but the word of salvation took hold of his heart, and the grace of the Comforter began to open wide the eyes of his understanding, leading him by the hand to the true God, as our tale in its course shall tell.

and learnt all from him

Now the king his father came oftentimes to see his boy, for he loved him passing well. On a day his son said unto him, 'There is something that I long to learn from thee, my lord the king, by reason of which continual grief and unceasing care consumeth my soul.' His father was grieved at heart at the very word, and said, 'Tell me, darling child, what is the sadness that constraineth thee, and straightway I will do my diligence to turn it into gladness.' The boy said, 'What is the reason of mine imprisonment here? Why hast thou barred me within walls and doors, never going forth and

How Ioasaph besought his father to release him

με καταστήσας; καὶ ὁ πατὴρ ἔφη· Οὐ βούλομαι, ὦ τέκνον, ἰδεῖν σέ τι τῶν ἀηδιζόντων τὴν καρδίαν σου καὶ ἐγκοπτόντων σοι τὴν εὐφροσύνην. ἐν τρυφῇ γὰρ διηνεκεῖ καὶ χαρᾷ πάσῃ καὶ θυμηδίᾳ ζῆσαί σε τὸν ἅπαντα διανοοῦμαι αἰῶνα. Ἀλλ' εὖ ἴσθι, ὦ δέσποτα, φησὶν ὁ υἱὸς τῷ πατρί, τῷ τρόπῳ τούτῳ οὐκ ἐν χαρᾷ καὶ θυμηδίᾳ ζῶ, ἐν θλίψει δὲ μᾶλλον καὶ στενοχωρίᾳ πολλῇ, ὡς καὶ αὐτὴν τὴν βρῶσίν τε καὶ πόσιν ἀηδῆ μοι καταφαίνεσθαι καὶ πικράν. ποθῶ γὰρ ὁρᾶν πάντα τὰ ἔξω τῶν πυλῶν τούτων. εἰ οὖν βούλει ἐν ὀδύνῃ μὴ ζῆν με, κέλευσον προέρχεσθαι καθὼς βούλομαι, καὶ τέρπεσθαι τὴν ψυχὴν τῇ θέᾳ τῶν γενομένων τέως ἀθεάτων μοι.

Ἐλυπήθη ὁ βασιλεὺς ὡς ἤκουσε ταῦτα, καὶ 32
διεσκόπει ὡς, εἰ κωλύσει τῆς αἰτήσεως, πλείονος αὐτῷ ἀνίας καὶ μερίμνης πρόξενος ἔσται. καὶ Ἐγώ σου, τέκνον, εἰπών, τὰ καταθύμια ποιήσω. ἵππους αὐτίκα ἐκλεκτοὺς καὶ δορυφορίαν τὴν βασιλεῖ πρέπουσαν εὐτρεπισθῆναι κελεύσας, προέρχεσθαι αὐτὸν ὅτε βούλοιτο διωρίσατο, ἐπισκήψας τοῖς συνοῦσιν αὐτῷ μηδὲν ἀηδὲς εἰς συνάντησιν αὐτῷ ἄγειν, ἀλλὰ πᾶν ὅ τι καλὸν καὶ τέρψιν ἐμποιοῦν, τοῦτο ὑποδεικνύειν τῷ παιδί, χορούς τε συγκροτεῖν ἐν ταῖς ὁδοῖς παναρμονίους κροτούντων ᾠδὰς καὶ ποικίλα θέατρα συνιστώντων, ὥστε τούτοις τὸν νοῦν αὐτοῦ ἀπασχολεῖσθαι καὶ ἐνηδύνεσθαι.

Ἀμέλει οὑτωσὶ συχνάζων ἐν ταῖς προόδοις ὁ τοῦ βασιλέως υἱὸς εἶδεν ἐν μιᾷ τῶν ἡμερῶν, κατὰ λήθην τῶν ὑπηρετῶν, ἄνδρας δύο, ὧν ὁ μὲν λελωβημένος, τυφλὸς δὲ ὁ ἕτερος ἦν· οὓς ἰδών, καὶ ἀηδισθεὶς τὴν ψυχήν, λέγει τοῖς μετ' αὐτοῦ·

seen of none?' His father replied, 'Because I will not, my son, that thou shouldest behold anything to embitter thy heart or mar thy happiness. I intend that thou shalt spend all thy days in luxury unbroken, and in all manner joy and pleasaunce.' 'But,' said the son unto his father, 'know well, Sir, that thus I live not in joy and pleasaunce, but rather in affliction and great straits, so that my very meat and drink seem distasteful unto me and bitter. I yearn to see all that lieth without these gates. If then thou wouldest not have me live in anguish of mind, bid me go abroad as I desire, and let me rejoice my soul with sights hitherto unseen by mine eyes.'

How the king granted his desire

Grieved was the king to hear these words, but, perceiving that to deny this request would but increase his boy's pain and grief, he answered, 'My son, I will grant thee thy heart's desire.' And immediately he ordered that choice steeds, and an escort fit for a king, be made ready, and gave him license to go abroad whensoever he would, charging his companions to suffer nothing unpleasant to come in his way, but to show him all that was beautiful and gladsome. He bade them muster in the way troops of folk intuning melodies in every mode, and presenting divers mimic shows, that these might occupy and delight his mind.

How Ioasaph in his goings out, saw two men, one maimed, and one blind,

So thus it came to pass that the king's son often went abroad. One day, through the negligence of his attendants, he descried two men, the one maimed, and the other blind. In abhorrence of the sight, he cried to his esquires, 'Who are these, and what is

Τίνες οὗτοι, καὶ ποταπὴ ἡ δυσχερὴς αὐτῶν θέα;
οἱ δέ, μὴ δυνάμενοι τὸ εἰς ὅρασιν αὐτοῦ ἐλθὸν
ἀποκρύψαι, ἔφησαν· Πάθη ταῦτά εἰσιν ἀνθρώπινα, ἅτινα ἐξ ὕλης διεφθαρμένης καὶ σώματος
κακοχύμου τοῖς βροτοῖς συμβαίνειν εἴωθε. καί
φησιν ὁ παῖς· Πᾶσι τοῖς ἀνθρώποις ταῦτα εἴθι-
σται συμβαίνειν; λέγουσιν ἐκεῖνοι· Οὐ πᾶσιν, ἀλλ'
οἷς ἂν ἐκτραπείη τὸ ὑγιεινὸν ἐκ τῆς τῶν χυμῶν
μοχθηρίας. αὖθις οὖν ἐπυνθάνετο ὁ παῖς Εἰ οὐ
πᾶσι, φησί, τοῦτο τοῖς ἀνθρώποις συμβαίνειν
εἴωθεν, ἀλλά τισιν, ἆρα γνωστοὶ καθεστήκασιν,
οὓς μέλλει ταῦτα καταλήψεσθαι τὰ δεινά; ἢ
ἀδιορίστως καὶ ἀπροόπτως ὑφίσταται; λέγουσιν 33
ἐκεῖνοι· Καὶ τίς τῶν ἀνθρώπων τὰ μέλλοντα
συνιδεῖν δύναται καὶ ἀκριβῶς ἐπιγνῶναι; κρεῖττον
γὰρ ἀνθρωπίνης φύσεως τοῦτο, καὶ μόνοις ἀποκλη-
ρωθὲν τοῖς ἀθανάτοις θεοῖς. καὶ ἐπαύσατο μὲν ὁ
τοῦ βασιλέως υἱὸς ἐπερωτῶν, ὠδυνήθη δὲ τὴν
Cp. Dan. iii. 19 καρδίαν ἐπὶ τῷ ὁραθέντι, καὶ ἠλλοιώθη ἡ μορφὴ
τοῦ προσώπου αὐτοῦ τῷ ἀσυνήθει τοῦ πράγματος.

Μετ' οὐ πολλὰς δὲ ἡμέρας αὖθις διερχόμενος ἐντυγχάνει γέροντι πεπαλαιωμένῳ ἐν ἡμέραις πολλαῖς, ἐρρικνωμένῳ μὲν τὸ πρόσωπον, παρειμένῳ δὲ τὰς κνήμας, συγκεκυφότι, καὶ ὅλως πεπολιωμένῳ, ἐστερημένῳ τοὺς ὀδόντας, καὶ ἐγκεκομμένα λαλοῦντι. ἔκπληξις οὖν αὐτὸν λαμβάνει· καὶ δὴ πλησίον τοῦτον ἀγαγὼν ἐπηρώτα μαθεῖν τὸ τῆς θέας παράδοξον. οἱ δὲ συμπαρόντες εἶπον· Οὗτος χρόνων ἤδη πλείστων ὑπάρχει, καὶ κατὰ μικρὸν μειουμένης αὐτῷ τῆς ἰσχύος, ἐξασθενούντων δὲ τῶν μελῶν, εἰς ἣν ὁρᾷς ἔφθασε ταλαιπωρίαν. Καὶ τί, φησί, τούτου τὸ τέλος; οἱ δὲ εἶπον αὐτῷ·

this distressing spectacle?' They, unable to conceal what he had with his own eyes seen, answered, 'These be human sufferings, which spring from corrupt matter, and from a body full of evil humours.' The young prince asked, 'Are these the fortune of all men?' They answered, 'Not of all, but of those in whom the principle of health is turned away by the badness of the humours.' Again the youth asked, 'If then this is wont to happen not to all, but only to some, can they be known on whom this terrible calamity shall fall? or is it undefined and unforeseeable?' 'What man,' said they, 'can discern the future, and accurately ascertain it? This is beyond human nature, and is reserved for the immortal gods alone.' The young prince ceased from his questioning, but his heart was grieved at the sight that he had witnessed, and the form of his visage was changed by the strangeness of the matter.

and again another, old and feeble,

Not many days after, as he was again taking his walks abroad, he happened with an old man, well stricken in years, shrivelled in countenance, feeble-kneed, bent double, grey-haired, toothless, and with broken utterance. The prince was seized with astonishment, and, calling the old man near, desired to know the meaning of this strange sight. His companions answered, 'This man is now well advanced in years, and his gradual decrease of strength, with increase of weakness, hath brought him to the misery that thou seest.' 'And,' said he, 'what will be his end?' They answered, 'Naught

and questioned his servants about them

Οὐδὲν ἄλλο ἢ θάνατος αὐτὸν διαδέξεται. Ἀλλὰ
καὶ πᾶσιν, ἔφη, τοῖς ἀνθρώποις τοῦτο πρόκειται ; ἢ καὶ τοῦτο ἐνίοις αὐτῶν συμβαίνει;
ἀπεκρίθησαν ἐκεῖνοι· Εἰ μὴ προλαβὼν ὁ θάνατος
μεταστήσει τινὰ τῶν ἐντεῦθεν, ἀδύνατον, τῶν
χρόνων προβαινόντων, μὴ εἰς ταύτης ἐλθεῖν τὴν
πεῖραν τῆς τάξεως. καί φησιν ὁ παῖς· ἐν πόσοις
οὖν ἔτεσι τοῦτο ἐπέρχεταί τινι; καὶ εἰ πάντως
πρόκειται ὁ θάνατος, καὶ οὐκ ἔστι μέθοδος τοῦτον
παραδραμεῖν, καὶ μηδὲ εἰς ταύτην ἐλθεῖν τὴν
ταλαιπωρίαν; λέγουσιν αὐτῷ· Ἐν ὀγδοήκοντα μὲν
ἢ καὶ ἑκατὸν ἔτεσιν εἰς τοῦτο τὸ γῆρας καταντῶ- 34
σιν οἱ ἄνθρωποι, εἶτα ἀποθνήσκουσι, μὴ ἄλλως
ἐνδεχομένου. χρέος γὰρ φυσικὸν ὁ θάνατός ἐστιν,
ἐξ ἀρχῆς ἐπιτεθὲν τοῖς ἀνθρώποις, καὶ ἀπαραίτητος ἡ τούτου ἐπέλευσις.

Ταῦτα πάντα ὡς εἶδέ τε καὶ ἤκουσεν ὁ συνετὸς
ἐκεῖνος καὶ φρόνιμος νεανίας, στενάξας ἐκ βάθους
καρδίας, ἔφη· Πικρὸς ὁ βίος οὗτος καὶ πάσης ὀδύνης καὶ ἀηδίας ἀνάπλεως, εἰ ταῦτα οὕτως ἔχει.
καὶ πῶς ἀμεριμνήσει τις τῇ προσδοκίᾳ τοῦ ἀδήλου
θανάτου, οὗ ἡ ἔλευσις οὐ μόνον ἀπαραίτητος, ἀλλὰ
καὶ ἄδηλος, καθὼς εἴπατε, ὑπάρχει; καὶ ἀπῆλθε
ταῦτα στρέφων ἐν ἑαυτῷ, καὶ ἀπαύστως διαλογι-
ζόμενος, καὶ πυκνὰς ποιούμενος περὶ τοῦ θανάτου
τὰς ὑπομνήσεις, πόνοις τε καὶ ἀθυμίαις ἐκ τούτου
συζῶν καὶ ἄπαυστον ἔχων τὴν λύπην. ἔλεγε γὰρ
ἐν ἑαυτῷ· Ἆρά ποτέ με ὁ θάνατος καταλήψεται;
καὶ τίς ἔσται ὁ μνήμην μου ποιούμενος μετὰ θάνατον, τοῦ χρόνου πάντα τῇ λήθῃ παραδιδόντος; καὶ
εἰ ἀποθανὼν εἰς τὸ μὴ ὂν διαλυθήσομαι; ἢ ἔστι
τις ἄλλη βιοτὴ καὶ ἕτερος κόσμος; ταῦτα καὶ τὰ

but death will relieve him.' 'But,' said he, 'is this the appointed doom of all mankind? Or doth it happen only to some?' They answered, 'Unless death come before hand to remove him, no dweller on earth, but, as life advanceth, must make trial of this lot.' Then the young prince asked in how many years this overtook a man, and whether the doom of death was without reprieve, and whether there was no way to escape it, and avoid coming to such misery. They answered him, 'In eighty or an hundred years men arrive at this old age, and then they die, since there is none other way; for death is a debt due to nature, laid on man from the beginning, and its approach is inexorable.'

How Ioasaph was sore distrest at that which he had seen and heard

When our wise and sagacious young prince saw and heard all this, he sighed from the bottom of his heart. 'Bitter is this life,' cried he, and fulfilled of all pain and anguish, if this be so. And how can a body be careless in the expectation of an unknown death, whose approach (ye say) is as uncertain as it is inexorable?' So he went away, restlessly turning over all these things in his mind, pondering without end, and ever calling up remembrances of death. Wherefore trouble and despondency were his companions, and his grief knew no ease; for he said to himself, 'And is it true that death shall one day overtake me? And who is he that shall make mention of me after death, when time delivereth all things to forgetfulness? When dead, shall I dissolve into nothingness? Or is there life beyond, and another world?' Ever fretting over these and the

τούτοις ὅμοια ἀπαύστως διενθυμούμενος ὠχριῶν κατετήκετο, κατ' ὄψιν δὲ τοῦ πατρός, ὅτε συνέβη τοῦτον ἀφικέσθαι, προσεποιεῖτο τὸ ἱλαρὸν καὶ ἄλυπον, μὴ βουλόμενος εἰς γνῶσιν τῷ πατρὶ τὰ αὐτῷ μελετώμενα ἐλθεῖν. ἐπόθει δὲ ἀκατασχέτῳ τινὶ πόθῳ καὶ ἐγλίχετο ἐντυχεῖν τινι τῷ δυναμένῳ τὴν αὐτοῦ πληροφορῆσαι καρδίαν, καὶ λόγον ἀγαθὸν ταῖς αὐτοῦ ἀκοαῖς ἐνηχῆσαι.

Τὸν προμνημονευθέντα δὲ παιδαγωγὸν αὖθις ἐπηρώτα, εἴ πού τινα γινώσκει τὸν δυνάμενον αὐτῷ συμβαλέσθαι πρὸς τὸ ποθούμενον, και τὸν νοῦν αὐτοῦ βεβαιῶσαι, δεινῶς ἰλιγγιῶντα ἐν τοῖς λογισμοῖς, καὶ μὴ δυνάμενον ἀποβαλέσθαι τὴν περὶ τούτων φροντίδα. ὁ δέ, τῶν προειρημένων πάλιν ἐπιμνησθείς, ἔλεγεν· Εἶπόν σοι καὶ πρότερον ὅπως ὁ πατήρ σου τοὺς σοφοὺς ἐκείνους καὶ ἀσκητὰς ἀεὶ περὶ τῶν τοιούτων φιλοσοφοῦντας, οὓς μὲν ἀνεῖλεν, οὓς δὲ μετ' ὀργῆς ἐδίωξε, καὶ οὐ γινώσκω νυνί τινα τοιοῦτον ἐν τῇ περιχώρῳ ταύτῃ. πολλοῦ δὲ ἐπὶ τούτοις ἄχθους ἐκεῖνος πληρωθείς, καὶ τὴν ψυχὴν δεινῶς κατατρωθείς, ἐῴκει ἀνδρὶ θησαυρὸν ἀπολέσαντι μέγαν καὶ εἰς τὴν αὐτοῦ ζήτησιν ὅλον αὐτοῦ τὸν νοῦν ἀσχολουμένῳ. ἐντεῦθεν ἀγῶνι διηνεκεῖ καὶ μερίμνῃ συνέζη, καὶ πάντα τὰ ἡδέα καὶ τερπνὰ τοῦ κόσμου ἦν ἐν ὀφθαλμοῖς αὐτοῦ ὡς ἄγος τι καὶ βδέλυγμα. οὕτως οὖν ἔχοντι τῷ νέῳ καὶ ποτνιωμένῳ κατὰ ψυχὴν τὸ ἀγαθὸν εὑρεῖν,
εἶδεν αὐτὸν ὁ πάντα βλέπων ὀφθαλμός, καὶ οὐ
1 Tim. ii. 4 παρεῖδεν ὁ θέλων πάντας σωθῆναι καὶ εἰς ἐπίγνωσιν ἀληθείας ἐλθεῖν, ἀλλά, τὴν συνήθη αὐτῷ
Ps. cxliii. 8 φιλανθρωπίαν καὶ ἐπὶ τούτῳ δείξας, ἐγνώρισεν
ὁδὸν ἣν ἔδει πορεύεσθαι τρόπῳ τοιῷδε·

like considerations, he waxed pale and wasted away, but in the presence of his father, whenever he chanced to come to him, he made as though he were cheerful and without trouble, unwilling that his cares should come to his father's knowledge. But he longed with an unrestrainable yearning, to meet with the man that might accomplish his heart's desire, and fill his ears with the sound of good tidings.

Again he enquired of the tutor of whom we have spoken, whether he knew of anybody able to help him towards his desire, and to establish a mind, dazed and shuddering at its cogitations, and unable to throw off its burden. He, recollecting their former communications, said, 'I have told thee already how thy father hath dealt with the wise men and anchorets who spend their lives in such philosophies. Some hath he slain, and others he hath wrathfully persecuted, and I wot not whether any of this sort be in this country side.' Thereat the prince was overwhelmed with woe, and grievously wounded in spirit. He was like unto a man that hath lost a great treasure, whose whole heart is occupied in seeking after it. Thenceforth he lived in perpetual conflict and distress of mind, and all the pleasures and delights of this world were in his eyes an abomination and a curse. While the youth was in this way, and his soul was crying out to discover that which is good, the eye that beholdeth all things looked upon him, and he that willeth that 'all men should be saved, and come to the knowledge of the truth,' passed him not by, but showed this man also the tender love that he hath toward mankind, and made known upon him the path whereon he needs must go. Befel it thus.

and again sought counsel of his tutor

VI

Ἐγένετο γὰρ κατ' ἐκεῖνον τὸν καιρὸν μοναχός
τις, σοφὸς τὰ θεῖα, βίῳ τε καὶ λόγῳ κοσμούμενος, 36
καὶ εἰς ἄκρον πᾶσαν μοναχικὴν μετελθὼν πολι-
τείαν· ὅθεν μὲν ὁρμώμενος καὶ ἐκ ποίου γένους οὐκ
Gen. x. 10; xi. 2; xiv. 1; Is. xi. 11; Dan. i. 2 ἔχω λέγειν, ἐν πανερήμῳ δέ τινι τῆς Σενααρίτιδος
γῆς τὰς οἰκήσεις ποιούμενος, καὶ τῆς ἱερωσύνης
τετελειωμένος τῇ χάριτι. Βαρλαὰμ ἦν ὄνομα
τούτῳ τῷ γέροντι. οὗτος οὖν ἀποκαλύψει τινὶ
θεόθεν αὐτῷ γενομένῃ γνοὺς τὰ κατὰ τὸν υἱὸν τοῦ
βασιλέως, ἐξελθὼν τῆς ἐρήμου, πρὸς τὴν οἰκουμένην κατῆλθε. καί, ἀμείψας τὸ ἑαυτοῦ σχῆμα,
ἱμάτιά τε κοσμικὰ ἀμφιασάμενος, καὶ νηὸς ἐπιβάς,
ἀφίκετο εἰς τὰ τῶν Ἰνδῶν βασίλεια, καὶ ἐμπόρου
ὑποδὺς προσωπεῖον, τὴν πόλιν καταλαμβάνει,
ἔνθα δὴ ὁ τοῦ βασιλέως υἱὸς τὸ παλάτιον εἶχε.
καί, ἡμέρας διατρίψας ἐκεῖσε πολλάς, ἠκριβο-
λογήσατο τὰ κατ' αὐτὸν καὶ τίνες οἱ τούτῳ
πλησιάζοντες. μαθὼν οὖν τὸν ἀνωτέρω ῥηθέντα
παιδαγωγὸν πάντων αὐτῷ μᾶλλον οἰκειότατον
εἶναι, προσελθὼν αὐτῷ κατ' ἰδίαν, ἔφη·

Cp. Mat. xiii. 45 Γινώσκειν σε βούλομαι, κύριέ μου, ὅτι ἔμπορος
ἐγὼ ἐκ μακρᾶς ἐλήλυθα χώρας, καὶ ὑπάρχει μοι
λίθος τίμιος, ᾧ παρόμοιος πώποτε οὐχ εὑρέθη.
καὶ οὐδενὶ μέχρι τοῦ νῦν τοῦτον ἐφανέρωσα· σοὶ
δὲ κατάδηλον ἤδη ποιῶ, συνετόν τε καὶ νουνεχῆ
βλέπων σε ἄνδρα, ὡς ἂν εἰσαγάγῃς με πρὸς τὸν 37
υἱὸν τοῦ βασιλέως, καὶ ἐπιδώσω τοῦτον αὐτῷ.
πάντων γὰρ τῶν καλῶν ἀσυγκρίτως ὑπερέχει·
δύναται καὶ τυφλοῖς τῇ καρδίᾳ φῶς δωρεῖσθαι

VI

THERE was at that time a certain monk, learned in heavenly things, graced in word and deed, a model follower of every monastic rule. Whence he sprang, and what his race, I cannot say, but he dwelt in a waste howling wilderness in the land of Senaar, and had been perfected through the grace of the priesthood. Barlaam was this elder's name. He, learning by divine revelation the state of the king's son, left the desert and returned to the world. Changing his habit, he put on lay attire, and, embarking on ship board, arrived at the seat of the empire of the Indians. Disguised as a merchant man, he entered the city, where was the palace of the king's son. There he tarried many days, and enquired diligently concerning the prince's affairs, and those that had access to him. Learning that the tutor, of whom we have spoken, was the prince's most familiar friend, he privily approached him, saying, *Of Barlaam, the monk, and his journey to the place where Ioasaph was*

'I would have thee understand, my lord, that I am a merchant man, come from a far country; and I possess a precious gem, the like of which was never yet found, and hitherto I have shewed it to no man. But now I reveal the secret to thee, seeing thee to be wise and prudent, that thou mayest bring me before the king's son, and I will present it to him. Beyond compare, it surpasseth all beautiful things; for on the blind in heart it hath virtue to *Barlaam telleth the tutor of a precious gem that he would fain show the prince,*

σοφίας, κωφῶν δὲ ὦτα ἀνοίγειν, ἀλάλοις τε φωνὴν διδόναι, καὶ ῥῶσιν τοῖς νοσοῦσι παρέχειν· τοὺς ἄφρονας σοφίζει, δαίμονας διώκει, καὶ πᾶν ὅ τι καλὸν καὶ ἐράσμιον ἀφθόνως χορηγεῖ τῷ κεκτημένῳ αὐτόν. λέγει πρὸς αὐτὸν ὁ παιδαγωγός· Ὁρῶ σε ἄνθρωπον σταθεροῦ καὶ βεβηκότος φρονήματος· τὰ δὲ ῥήματά σου ἄμετρά σε καυχᾶσθαι ἐμφαίνουσι. λίθους γὰρ καὶ μαργαρίτας πολυτελεῖς καὶ πολυτίμους πῶς ἂν σοι διηγησαίμην ὅσους ἑώρακα; ἔχοντας δὲ τοιαύτας ἃς εἴρηκας δυνάμεις οὔτε εἶδον, οὔτε ἤκουσα. ὅμως ὑπόδειξόν μοι αὐτόν, καί, εἴ ἐστι κατὰ τὸ ῥῆμά σου, θᾶττον εἰσάγω τοῦτον πρὸς τὸν τοῦ βασιλέως υἱόν, καὶ τιμὰς ὅτι μεγίστας καὶ δωρεὰς λήψῃ παρ' αὐτοῦ. πρινὴ δὲ βεβαιωθῆναί με τῇ ἀψευδεῖ τῶν ὀφθαλμῶν ὁράσει, ἀδύνατόν μοι τῷ ἐμῷ δεσπότῃ καὶ βασιλεῖ περὶ πράγματος ἀφανοῦς ταῦτα δὴ τὰ ὑπέρογκα ἀπαγγεῖλαι. ὁ δὲ Βαρλαὰμ ἔφη· Καλῶς εἶπας μήτε ἑωρακέναι πώποτε μήτε ἀκηκοέναι τοιαύτας δυνάμεις καὶ ἐνεργείας· ὁ γὰρ πρὸς σέ μου λόγος οὐ περί του τυχόντος ἐστὶ πράγματος, ἀλλὰ θαυμαστοῦ τινὸς καὶ μεγάλου. ὅτι δὲ ἐζήτησας τοῦτον θεάσασθαι, ἄκουσον τῶν ἐμῶν ῥημάτων.

Ὁ λίθος οὗτος ὁ πολύτιμος μετὰ τῶν προειρημένων ἐνεργειῶν καὶ δυνάμεων, ἔτι καὶ ταύτην κέκτηται τὴν ἰσχύν· οὐ δύναται θεάσασθαι αὐτὸν ἐκ τοῦ προχείρου ὁ μὴ ἔχων ἐρρωμένην μὲν τὴν
ὅρασιν καὶ ὑγιαίνουσαν, ἁγνὸν δὲ τὸ σῶμα καὶ 38
πάντη ἀμόλυντον. εἰ γάρ τις, μὴ τὰ δύο ταῦτα καλὰ ἔχων, προπετῶς ἐμβλέψειε τῷ τιμίῳ λίθῳ τούτῳ, καὶ αὐτὴν δήπου ἣν ἔχει ὀπτικὴν δύναμιν

bestow the light of wisdom, to open the ears of the deaf, to give speech to the dumb and strength to the ailing. It maketh the foolish wise and driveth away devils, and without stint furnisheth its possessor with everything that is lovely and desirable.' The tutor said, 'Though, to all seeming, thou art a man of staid and steadfast judgment, yet thy words prove thee to be boastful beyond measure. Time would fail me to tell thee the full tale of the costly and precious gems and pearls that I have seen. But gems, with such power as thou tellest of, I never saw nor heard of yet. Nevertheless shew me the stone; and if it be as thou affirmest, I immediately bear it to the king's son, from whom thou shalt receive most high honours and rewards. But, before I be assured by the certain witness of mine own eyes, I may not carry to my lord and master so swollen a tale about so doubtful a thing.' Quoth Barlaam, 'Well hast thou said that thou hast never seen or heard of such powers and virtues; for my speech to thee is on no ordinary matter, but on a wondrous and a great. But, as thou desiredst to behold it, listen to my words.

and of its strange and magick virtues

'This exceeding precious gem, amongst these its powers and virtues, possesseth this property besides. It cannot be seen out of hand, save by one whose eyesight is strong and sound, and his body pure and thoroughly undefiled. If any man, lacking in these two good qualities, do rashly gaze upon this precious stone, he shall, I suppose lose even the eyesight

καὶ τὰς φρένας προσαπολέσειεν. ἐγὼ δέ, οὐκ ἀμύητος τῆς ἰατρικῆς ἐπιστήμης ὑπάρχων, καθορῶ σου τοὺς ὀφθαλμοὺς μὴ ὑγιῶς ἔχοντας, καὶ δέδοικα μὴ καὶ ἧς ἔχεις ὁράσεως στέρησιν προξενήσω. ἀλλὰ τὸν υἱὸν τοῦ βασιλέως ἀκήκοα βίον μὲν ἔχειν σώφρονα, τοὺς ὀφθαλμοὺς δὲ ὡραίους καὶ ὑγιῶς ὁρῶντας· τούτου χάριν ἐκείνῳ ὑποδεῖξαι τὸν θησαυρὸν τοῦτον τεθάρρηκα. σὺ οὖν μὴ ἀμελῶς περὶ τούτου διατεθῇς, μηδὲ πράγματος τοιούτου τὸν κύριόν σου ἀποστερήσῃς. ὁ δὲ πρὸς αὐτόν, Καὶ εἰ ταῦτα, φησίν, οὕτως ἔχει, μή μοι τὸν λίθον ὑποδείξῃς· ἐν ἁμαρτίαις γὰρ πολλαῖς ὁ βίος μου ἐρρύπωται· οὐχ ὑγιῶς δὲ καὶ τὴν ὅρασιν, καθὼς εἶπας, κέκτημαι. ἀλλ' ἐγώ, τοῖς σοῖς πεισθεὶς ῥήμασι, γνωρίσαι ταῦτα τῷ κυρίῳ μου καὶ βασιλεῖ οὐκ ὀκνήσω. εἶπε ταῦτα, καὶ εἰσελθὼν κατὰ μέρος πάντα τῷ υἱῷ τοῦ βασιλέως ἀπήγγειλεν. ἐκεῖνος δέ, ὡς ἤκουσε τὰ τοῦ παιδαγωγοῦ ῥήματα, χαρᾶς τινὸς καὶ θυμηδίας πνευματικῆς ᾔσθετο, τῇ αὐτοῦ ἐμπνευσάσης καρδίᾳ, καί, ἔνθους ὥσπερ γενόμενος τὴν ψυχήν, ἐκέλευσε θᾶττον εἰσαγαγεῖν τὸν ἄνδρα.

Ὡς οὖν εἰσῆλθεν ὁ Βαρλαάμ, καὶ δέδωκεν αὐτῷ
Luke x. 5 τὴν πρέπουσαν εἰρήνην, ἐπέτρεψεν αὐτὸν καθεσθῆναι, καί, τοῦ παιδαγωγοῦ ὑποχωρήσαντος, λέγει ὁ Ἰωάσαφ τῷ γέροντι· Ὑπόδειξόν μοι τὸν πολύτιμον λίθον, περὶ οὗ μεγάλα τινὰ καὶ θαυμαστὰ λέγειν σε ὁ ἐμὸς παιδαγωγὸς διηγήσατο. ὁ δὲ Βαρλαὰμ οὕτως ἀπήρξατο τῆς πρὸς αὐτὸν διαλέξεως· Οὐ δίκαιόν ἐστιν, ὦ βασιλεῦ, ψευδῶς τι καὶ ἀπερισκέπτως πρὸς τὸ ὑπερέχον τῆς σῆς δόξης λέγειν με· πάντα γὰρ τὰ δηλωθέντα σοι

that he hath, and his wits as well. Now I, that am initiated in the physician's art, observe that thine eyes are not healthy, and I fear lest I may cause thee to lose even the eyesight that thou hast. But of the king's son, I have heard that he leadeth a sober life, and that his eyes are young and fair, and healthy. Wherefore to him I make bold to display this treasure. Be not thou then negligent herein, nor rob thy master of so wondrous a boon.' The other answered, 'If this be so, in no wise show me the gem; for my life hath been polluted by many sins, and also, as thou sayest, I am not possest of good eyesight. But I am won by thy words, and will not hesitate to make known these things unto my lord the prince.' So saying, he went in, and, word by word, reported everything to the king's son. He, hearing his tutor's words, felt a strange joy and spiritual gladness breathing into his heart, and, like one inspired, bade bring in the man forthwith.

How Barlaam was brought before Ioasaph, and discoursed with him

So when Barlaam was come in, and had in due order wished him Peace!, the prince bade him be seated. Then his tutor withdrew, and Ioasaph said unto the elder, 'Shew me the precious gem, concerning which, as my tutor hath narrated, thou tellest such great and marvellous tales.' Then began Barlaam to discourse with him thus: 'It is not fitting, O prince, that I should say anything falsely or unadvisedly to thine excellent majesty. All that hath been signified to thee from me is

παρ' ἐμοῦ ἀληθῆ εἰσι καὶ ἀναμφίλεκτα. ἀλλ', εἰ μὴ πρότερον δοκιμὴν τῆς σῆς λάβω φρονήσεως, οὐ θέμις τὸ μυστήριον φανερῶσαί σοι. φησὶ
Mat. xiii.; Mk. iv.; Luke viii. γὰρ ὁ ἐμὸς Δεσπότης· Ἐξῆλθεν ὁ σπείρων τοῦ σπεῖραι τὸν σπόρον αὐτοῦ· καὶ ἐν τῷ σπείρειν αὐτόν, ἃ μὲν ἔπεσε παρὰ τὴν ὁδόν, καὶ ἦλθε τὰ πετεινὰ καὶ κατέφαγεν αὐτά· ἄλλα δὲ ἔπεσε παρὰ τὰ πετρώδη, ὅπου οὐκ εἶχε γῆν πολλήν, καὶ εὐθέως ἐβλάστησε, διὰ τὸ μὴ ἔχειν βάθος γῆς· ἡλίου δὲ ἀνατείλαντος ἐκαυματίσθη, καί, διὰ τὸ μὴ ἔχειν ῥίζαν, ἐξηράνθη· ἄλλα δὲ ἔπεσεν ἐπὶ τὰς ἀκάνθας, καὶ ἀνέβησαν αἱ ἄκανθαι καὶ ἀπέπνιξαν αὐτά· ἄλλα δὲ ἔπεσεν ἐπὶ τὴν γῆν τὴν καλήν, καὶ ἐδίδου καρπὸν ἑκατοστεύοντα. εἰ μὲν οὖν γῆν εὕρω ἐν τῇ καρδίᾳ σου καρποφόρον καὶ ἀγαθήν, οὐκ ὀκνήσω τὸν θεῖον σπόρον ἐμφυτεῦσαί σοι καὶ φανερῶσαι τὸ μέγα μυστήριον· εἰ δὲ πετρώδης αὕτη καὶ ἀκανθώδης ἐστί, καὶ ὁδὸς πατουμένη τῷ βουλομένῳ παντί, κρεῖττον μηδόλως τοῦτον δὴ τὸν σωτήριον καταβαλεῖν σπόρον καὶ εἰς διαρπαγὴν αὐτὸν θεῖναι τοῖς πετεινοῖς καὶ θηρίοις, ὧν ἔμπροσθεν ὅλως μὴ
Mat. vii. 6 βαλεῖν τοὺς μαργαρίτας ἐντέταλμαι. ἀλλὰ πέ-
Heb. vi. 9 πεισμαι περὶ σοῦ τὰ κρείττονα καὶ ἐχόμενα σωτηρίας, ὅτι καὶ τὸν λίθον ὄψει τὸν ἀτίμητον, καὶ τῇ αἴγλῃ τοῦ φωτὸς αὐτοῦ φῶς καὶ αὐτὸς ἀξιωθήσῃ γενέσθαι, καὶ καρπὸν ἐνέγκῃς ἑκατοστεύοντα. διὰ σὲ γὰρ ἔργον ἐθέμην καὶ μακρὰν διήνυσα ὁδόν, τοῦ ὑποδεῖξαί σοι ἃ οὐχ ἑώρακας πώποτε καὶ διδάξαι ἃ οὐκ ἀκήκοας.

Εἶπε δὲ πρὸς αὐτὸν ὁ Ἰωάσαφ· Ἐγὼ μέν, πρεσβῦτα τίμιε, πόθῳ τινὶ καὶ ἔρωτι ἀκατα-

true and may not be gainsaid. But, except I first make trial of thy mind, it is not lawful to declare to thee this mystery; for my master saith, "There went out a sower to sow his seed: and, as he sowed, some seeds fell by the wayside, and the fowls of the air came and devoured them up: some fell upon stony places, where they had not much earth: and forthwith they sprang up, because they had no deepness of earth: and when the sun was up, they were scorched: and because they had no root, they withered away. And some fell among thorns; and the thorns sprung up and choked them: but others fell upon good ground, and brought forth fruit an hundredfold." Now, if I find in thine heart fruit-bearing ground, and good, I shall not be slow to plant therein the heavenly seed, and manifest to thee the mighty mystery. But and if the ground be stony and thorny, and the wayside trodden down by all who will, it were better never to let fall this seed of salvation, nor to cast it for a prey to fowls and beasts, before which I have been charged not to cast pearls. But I am "persuaded better things of thee, and things that accompany salvation,"—how that thou shalt see the priceless stone, and it shall be given thee in the light of that stone to become light, and bring forth fruit an hundredfold. Aye, for thy sake I gave diligence and accomplished a long journey, to shew thee things which thou hast never seen, and teach thee things which thou hast never heard.'

Ioasaph said unto him, 'For myself, reverend elder, I have a longing, an irresistible passion to

Ioasaph prayeth

σχέτῳ ζητῶ λόγον ἀκοῦσαι καινόν τινα καὶ ἀγαθόν, καὶ πῦρ ἔνδοθεν ἐν τῇ καρδίᾳ μου ἐκκέκαυται δεινῶς φλέγον με καὶ παρορμῶν μαθεῖν ἀναγκαίας τινὰς συζητήσεις· οὐκ ἔτυχον δὲ μέχρι τοῦ νῦν ἀνθρώπου δυναμένου πληροφορῆσαί με περὶ τούτων. εἰ δὲ τύχω σοφοῦ τινος καὶ ἐπιστήμονος, καὶ ἀκούσω λόγον σωτηρίας, οὔτε πετεινοῖς, ὡς οἶμαι, τοῦτον ἐκδώσω, οὔτε θηρίοις, οὔτε μὴν πετρώδης φανήσομαι, ὡς ἔφης, οὔτε ἀκανθώδης, ἀλλὰ καὶ εὐγνωμόνως δέξομαι καὶ εἰδημόνως τηρήσω. σὺ δέ, εἴ τι τοιοῦτον ἐπίστασαι, μὴ διακρύψῃς ἀπ' ἐμοῦ, ἀλλ' ἀνάγγειλόν μοι. ὡς γὰρ ἤκουσα ἐκ μακρᾶς ἀφικέσθαι σε γῆς, ἥσθη μου ἡ ψυχή, καὶ εὔελπις ἐγενόμην διὰ σοῦ τοῦ ποθουμένου ἐπιτυχεῖν. διὰ τοῦτο καὶ θᾶττον εἰσήγαγόν σε πρός με καὶ προσηνῶς ἐδεξάμην, ὥσπερ τινὰ τῶν συνήθων μοι καὶ ἡλικιωτῶν, εἴπερ οὐ ψευσθήσομαι τῆς ἐλπίδος. καὶ ὁ Βαρλαὰμ ἔφη· Καλῶς ἐποίησας τοῦτο καὶ
ἀξίως τῆς σῆς βασιλικῆς μεγαλοπρεπείας, ὅτι 41
μὴ τῇ φαινομένῃ προσέσχες εὐτελείᾳ, ἀλλὰ τῆς κεκρυμμένης ἐγένου ἐλπίδος.

Ἦν γάρ τις βασιλεὺς μέγας καὶ ἔνδοξος, καὶ ἐγένετο, διερχομένου αὐτοῦ ἐφ' ἅρματος χρυσοκολλήτου καὶ τῆς βασιλεῖ πρεπούσης δορυφορίας, ὑπαντῆσαι δύο ἄνδρας, διερρωγότα μὲν ἠμφιεσμένους καὶ ῥερυπωμένα, ἐκτετηκότας δὲ τὰ πρόσωπα καὶ λίαν κατωχριωμένους· ἦν δὲ γινώσκων τούτους ὁ βασιλεὺς τῷ ὑπωπιασμῷ τοῦ σώματος καὶ τοῖς τῆς ἀσκήσεως ἱδρῶσι τὸ σαρκίον ἐκδεδαπανηκότας. ὡς οὖν εἶδεν αὐτούς, καταπηδήσας εὐθὺς τοῦ ἅρματος καὶ ἐπὶ τὴν γῆν πεσών, προσ-

hear some new and goodly word, and in mine heart there is kindled fire, cruelly burning and urging me to learn the answer to some questions that will not rest. But until now I never happened on one that could satisfy me as touching them. But if I meet with some wise and understanding man, and hear the word of salvation, I shall not deliver it to the fowls of the air, I trow, nor yet to the beasts of the field; nor shall I be found either stony or thorny-hearted, as thou saidest, but I shall receive the word kindly, and guard it wisely. So if thou knowest any such like thing, conceal it not from me, but declare it. When I heard that thou wert come from a far country, my spirit rejoiced, and I had good hope of obtaining through thee that which I desire. Wherefore I called thee straightway into my presence, and received thee in friendly wise as one of my companions and peers, if so be that I may not be disappointed of my hope.' Barlaam answered, 'Fair are thy deeds, and worthy of thy royal majesty; seeing that thou hast paid no heed to my mean show, but hast devoted thyself to the hope that lieth within.

Barlaam to impart to him his treasure

'There was once a great and famous king: and it came to pass, when he was riding on a day in his golden chariot, with his royal guard, that there met him two men, clad in filthy rags, with fallen-in faces, and pale as death. Now the king knew that it was by buffetings of the body and by the sweats of the monastic life that they had thus wasted their miserable flesh. So, seeing them, he leapt anon from his chariot, fell on the ground,

APOLOGUE I. THE KING'S BROTHER AND THE TRUMPET OF DEATH

Barlaam telleth a tale much to the point

εκύνησε, καὶ ἀναστὰς περιεπλάκη αὐτοῖς προσ-
φιλέστατα κατασπαζόμενος. οἱ δὲ μεγιστᾶνες
αὐτοῦ καὶ ἄρχοντες ἐδυσχέραναν ἐπὶ τούτῳ,
ἀνάξια τῆς βασιλικῆς δόξης πεποιηκέναι αὐτὸν
νομίζοντες· μὴ τολμῶντες δὲ κατὰ πρόσωπον
ἐλέγχειν, τὸν γνήσιον αὐτοῦ ἀδελφὸν ἔλεγον
λαλῆσαι τῷ βασιλεῖ, μὴ τὸ ὕψος τοῦ διαδήματος
οὑτωσὶ καθυβρίζειν. τοῦ δὲ εἰπόντος ταῦτα τῷ
ἀδελφῷ καὶ καταμεμψαμένου τὴν ἄκαιρον αὐτοῦ
σμικρολογίαν, δέδωκεν αὐτῷ ἀπόκρισιν ὁ βασιλεύς, ἣν οὐ συνῆκεν ὁ ἀδελφὸς αὐτοῦ.

Ἔθος γὰρ ἦν ἐκείνῳ τῷ βασιλεῖ, ὅταν ἀπόφασιν θανάτου κατά τινος ἐδίδου, κήρυκα εἰς
τὴν αὐτοῦ θύραν ἀποστέλλειν μετὰ σάλπιγγος
τεταγμένης εἰς τοῦτο· καὶ τῇ φωνῇ τῆς σάλπιγγος ἐκείνης ᾔσθοντο πάντες θανάτου ἔνοχον
ἐκεῖνον ὑπάρχειν. ἑσπέρας οὖν καταλαβούσης, 42
ἀπέστειλεν ὁ βασιλεὺς τὴν σάλπιγγα τοῦ θανάτου σαλπίζειν ἐπὶ τῇ θύρᾳ τοῦ οἴκου τοῦ ἀδελφοῦ
αὐτοῦ. ὡς οὖν ἤκουσεν ἐκεῖνος τὴν σάλπιγγα
τοῦ θανάτου, ἀπέγνω τῆς ἑαυτοῦ σωτηρίας καὶ
διέθετο τὰ κατ᾽ αὐτὸν ὅλην τὴν νύκτα· ἅμα δὲ
πρωΐ, ἀμφιασάμενος μέλανα καὶ πενθήρη, μετὰ
γυναικὸς καὶ τέκνων ἀπέρχεται εἰς τὴν θύραν
τοῦ παλατίου κλαίων καὶ ὀδυρόμενος. εἰσαγα-
γὼν δὲ αὐτὸν ὁ βασιλεύς, καὶ οὕτως ἰδὼν
ὀλοφυρόμενον, ἔφη· Ὦ ἀσύνετε καὶ ἄφρον, εἰ
σὺ οὕτως ἐδειλίασας τὸν κήρυκα τοῦ ὁμοτίμου
σου ἀδελφοῦ, πρὸς ὃν οὐδὲν ὅλως ἑαυτὸν ἡμαρτηκέναι γινώσκεις, πῶς ἐμοὶ μέμψιν ἐπήγαγες ἐν
ταπεινώσει ἀσπασαμένῳ τοὺς κήρυκας τοῦ Θεοῦ
μου, τοὺς εὐηχέστερον σάλπιγγος μηνύοντάς μοι

and did obeisance. Then rising, he embraced and greeted them tenderly. But his noblemen and counsellors took offence thereat, deeming that their sovran had disgraced his kingly honour. But not daring to reprove him to the face, they bade the king's own brother tell the king not thus to insult the majesty of his crown. When he had told the king thereof, and had upbraided him for his untimely humility, the king gave his brother an answer which he failed to understand.

'It was the custom of that king, whenever he sentenced anyone to death, to send a herald to his door, with a trumpet reserved for that purpose, and at the sound of this trumpet all understood that that man was liable to the penalty of death. So when evening was come, the king sent the death-trumpet to sound at his brother's door; who, when he heard its blast, despaired of his life, and all night long set his house in order. At day-break, robed in black and garments of mourning, with wife and children, he went to the palace gate, weeping and lamenting. The king fetched him in, and seeing him in tears, said, "O fool, and slow of understanding, how didst thou, who hast had such dread of the herald of thy peer and brother (against whom thy conscience doth not accuse thee of having committed any trespass) blame me for my humility in greeting the heralds of my God, when they warned me, in gentler tones than those of the trumpet, of my death and fearful

τὸν θάνατον καὶ τὴν φοβερὰν τοῦ Δεσπότου ὑπάντησιν, ᾧ πολλὰ καὶ μεγάλα ἐμαυτὸν ἡμαρτηκέναι ἐπίσταμαι; ἰδοὺ τοίνυν τὴν σὴν ἐλέγχων ἄνοιαν τούτῳ δὴ τῷ τρόπῳ ἐχρησάμην, ὥσπερ οὖν καὶ τοὺς ὑποθεμένους σου τὴν κατ' ἐμοῦ μέμψιν θᾶττον ἀνοηταίνειν ἐλέγξω. καὶ οὕτω θεραπεύσας τὸν ἀδελφὸν αὐτοῦ καὶ ὠφελήσας οἴκαδε ἀπέστειλεν.

Cp. *Merchant of Venice*, Act II., Scenes vii. and ix.

Ἐκέλευσε δὲ γενέσθαι ἐκ ξύλων βαλάντια τέσσαρα. καὶ τὰ μὲν δύο περικαλύψας πάντοθεν χρυσίῳ, καὶ ὀστᾶ νεκρῶν ὀδωδότα βαλὼν ἐν αὐτοῖς, χρυσαῖς περόναις κατησφαλίσατο· τὰ δὲ ἄλλα πίσσῃ καταχρίσας καὶ ἀσφαλτώσας, ἐπλήρωσε λίθων τιμίων καὶ μαργαριτῶν πολυτίμων καὶ πάσης μυρεψικῆς εὐωδίας. σχοινίοις 43
τε τριχίνοις ταῦτα περισφίγξας, ἐκάλεσε τοὺς μεμψαμένους αὐτῷ μεγιστᾶνας ἐπὶ τῇ τῶν ἀνδρῶν ἐκείνων συναντήσει, καὶ προέθετο αὐτοῖς τὰ τέσσαρα βαλάντια, τοῦ ἀποτιμήσασθαι πόσου μὲν ταῦτα, πόσου δὲ ἐκεῖνα τιμήματός εἰσιν ἄξια. οἱ δὲ τὰ μὲν δύο τὰ κεχρυσωμένα τιμῆς ὅτι πλείστης εἶναι διωρίζοντο. ἔξεστι γάρ, φησίν, ἐν αὐτοῖς βασιλικὰ διαδήματα καὶ ζώνας ἀποκεῖσθαι· τὰ δὲ τῇ πίσσῃ κατακεχρισμένα καὶ τῇ ἀσφάλτῳ εὐτελοῦς τινὸς καὶ οἰκτροῦ τιμήματος ὑπάρχει. ὁ δὲ βασιλεὺς ἔφη πρὸς αὐτούς· Οἶδα κἀγὼ τοιαῦτα λέγειν ὑμᾶς· τοῖς αἰσθητοῖς γὰρ ὀφθαλμοῖς τὴν αἰσθητὴν ὄψιν κατανοεῖτε· καὶ μὴν οὐχ οὕτως δεῖ ποιεῖν. ἀλλὰ τοῖς ἔνδον ὄμμασι τὴν ἐντὸς ἀποκειμένην χρὴ βλέπειν εἴτε τιμὴν εἴτε ἀτιμίαν. καὶ ἐκέλευσεν ἀνοιγῆναι τὰ κεχρυσωμένα βαλάντια. διανοιχθέντων δέ,

meeting with that Master against whom I know that I have often grievously offended? Lo! then, it was in reproof of thy folly that I played thee this turn, even as I will shortly convict of vanity those that prompted thy reproof." Thus he comforted his brother and sent him home with a gift.

APOLOGUE II., OF THE FOUR CASKETS

Barlaam giveth another apt illustration,

'Then he ordered four wooden caskets to be made. Two of these he covered over all with gold, and, placing dead men's mouldering bones therein, secured them with golden clasps. The other two he smeared over with pitch and tar, but filled them with costly stones and precious pearls, and all manner of aromatic sweet perfume. He bound them fast with cords of hair, and called for the noblemen who had blamed him for his manner of accosting the men by the wayside. Before them he set the four caskets, that they might appraise the value of these and those. They decided that the golden ones were of greatest value, for, peradventure, they contained kingly diadems and girdles. But those, that were be-smeared with pitch and tar, were cheap and of paltry worth, said they. Then said the king to them, "I know that such is your answer, for with the eyes of sense ye judge the objects of sense, but so ought ye not to do, but ye should rather see with the inner eye the hidden worthlessness or value." Whereupon he ordered the golden chests to be opened. And when they

δεινή τις ἔπνευσε δυσωδία καὶ ἀηδεστάτη ὠράθη θέα.

Φησὶν οὖν ὁ βασιλεύς· Οὗτος ὁ τύπος τῶν τὰ λαμπρὰ μὲν καὶ ἔνδοξα ἠμφιεσμένων, πολλῇ δόξῃ καὶ δυναστείᾳ σοβαρευομένων, καὶ ἔσωθεν
Cp. Mat. xxiii. 27 ἀποζόντων νεκρῶν καὶ πονηρῶν ἔργων. εἶτα καὶ τὰ πεπισσωμένα καὶ κατησφαλτωμένα κελεύσας ἀνακαλυφθῆναι, πάντας εὔφρανε τοὺς παρόντας τῇ τῶν ἐν αὐτοῖς ἀποκειμένων φαιδρότητι καὶ εὐωδίᾳ. ἔφη δὲ πρὸς αὐτούς· Οἴδατε τίνι ὅμοια ταῦτα; τοῖς ταπεινοῖς ἐκείνοις καὶ εὐτελῆ περικειμένοις ἐνδύματα, ὧν ὑμεῖς τὸ ἐκτὸς ὁρῶντες σχῆμα, ὕβριν ἡγήσασθε τὴν ἐμὴν κατὰ πρόσω- 44
πον αὐτῶν ἐπὶ γῆς προσκύνησιν· ἐγὼ δέ, τοῖς νοεροῖς ὄμμασι τὸ τίμιον αὐτῶν καὶ περικαλλὲς κατανοήσας τῶν ψυχῶν, ἐνεδοξάσθην μὲν τῇ τούτων προσψαύσει, παντὸς δὲ στεφάνου καὶ πάσης βασιλικῆς ἀλουργίδος τιμιωτέρους αὐτοὺς ἡγησάμην. οὕτως οὖν αὐτοὺς ᾔσχυνε, καὶ ἐδίδαξε μὴ τοῖς φαινομένοις πλανᾶσθαι, ἀλλὰ τοῖς νοουμένοις προσέχειν. κατ' ἐκεῖνον τοίνυν τὸν εὐσεβῆ καὶ σοφὸν βασιλέα καὶ σὺ πεποίηκας, τῇ ἀγαθῇ ἐλπίδι προσδεξάμενός με, ἧς οὐ ψευσθήσῃ, ὡς ἔγωγε οἶμαι. εἶπε δὲ πρὸς αὐτὸν ὁ Ἰωασάφ. Ταῦτα μὲν δὴ πάντα καλῶς εἶπας καὶ εὐαρμόστως· ἀλλ' ἐκεῖνο θέλω μαθεῖν, τίς ἐστιν ὁ σὸς Δεσπότης, ὃν κατ' ἀρχὰς τοῦ λόγου περὶ τοῦ σπορέως ἐκείνου εἰρηκέναι ἔλεγες.

were thrown open, they gave out a loathsome smell and presented a hideous sight.

'Said the king, "Here is a figure of those who are clothed in glory and honour, and make great display of power and glory, but within is the stink of dead men's bones and works of iniquity." Next, he commanded the pitched and tarred caskets also to be opened, and delighted the company with the beauty and sweet savour of their stores. And he said unto them, "Know ye to whom these are like? They are like those lowly men, clad in vile apparel, whose outward form alone ye beheld, and deemed it outrageous that I bowed down to do them obeisance. But through the eyes of my mind I perceived the value and exceeding beauty of their souls, and was glorified by their touch, and I counted them more honourable than any chaplet or royal purple." Thus he shamed his courtiers, and taught them not to be deceived by outward appearances, but to give heed to the things of the soul. After the example of that devout and wise king hast thou also done, in that thou hast received me in good hope, wherein, as I ween, thou shalt not be disappointed.' Ioasaph said unto him, 'Fair and fitting hath been all thy speech; but now I fain would learn who is thy Master, who, as thou saidest at the first, spake concerning the Sower.'

with the interpretation thereof

VII

Αὖθις οὖν ἀναλαβὼν τὸν λόγον ὁ Βαρλαάμ, εἶπεν· Εἰ τὸν ἐμὸν βούλει Δεσπότην μαθεῖν, ὁ Κύριός ἐστιν Ἰησοῦς Χριστός, ὁ μονογενὴς Υἱὸς
1 Tim. vi. 15, 16 τοῦ Θεοῦ, ὁ μακάριος καὶ μόνος δυνάστης, ὁ Βασιλεὺς τῶν βασιλευόντων καὶ Κύριος τῶν κυριευόντων, ὁ μόνος ἔχων ἀθανασίαν, φῶς οἰκῶν ἀπρόσιτον, ὁ σὺν Πατρὶ καὶ ἁγίῳ Πνεύματι δοξαζόμενος. οὐκ εἰμὶ γὰρ ἐγὼ τῶν τοὺς πολλοὺς τούτους καὶ ἀτάκτους ἀναγορευόντων θεούς, καὶ τὰ ἄψυχα ταῦτα καὶ κωφὰ σεβομένων εἴδωλα· ἀλλ' ἕνα Θεὸν γινώσκω καὶ ὁμολογῶ ἐν
Mat. xxviii. 19 ; iii. 16, 17 τρισὶν ὑποστάσεσι δοξαζόμενον, Πατρί, φημί, καὶ Υἱῷ, καὶ ἁγίῳ Πνεύματι, ἐν μιᾷ δὲ φύσει καὶ οὐσίᾳ, ἐν μιᾷ δόξῃ καὶ βασιλείᾳ μὴ μεριζομένῃ. οὗτος οὖν ὁ ἐν τρισὶν ὑποστάσεσιν εἷς Θεός, ἄναρχός τε καὶ ἀτελεύτητος, αἰώνιός τε καὶ ἀΐδιος, ἄκτιστος, ἄτρεπτός τε καὶ ἀσώματος, ἀόρατος, ἀπερίγραπτος, ἀπερινόητος,
Gen. i. ; Heb. xi. 3 ; Rom. i. 20 ἀγαθὸς καὶ δίκαιος μόνος, ὁ τὰ πάντα ἐκ μὴ ὄντων ὑποστησάμενος, τά τε ὁρατὰ καὶ τὰ ἀόρατα, πρῶτον μὲν δημιουργεῖ τὰς οὐρανίους δυνάμεις καὶ ἀοράτους, ἀναρίθμητά τινα πλήθη
Heb. i. 14 ἄϋλά τε καὶ ἀσώματα, λειτουργικὰ πνεύματα τῆς τοῦ Θεοῦ μεγαλειότητος· ἔπειτα τὸν ὁρώμενον κόσμον τοῦτον, οὐρανόν τε καὶ γῆν καὶ τὴν θάλασσαν, ὅνπερ καὶ φωτὶ φαιδρύνας κατεκόσμησεν, οὐρανὸν μὲν ἡλίῳ καὶ σελήνῃ καὶ τοῖς ἄστροις, γῆν δὲ παντοίοις βλαστήμασι καὶ διαφόροις ζῴοις, τήν τε θάλασσαν πάλιν τῷ

VII

AGAIN therefore Barlaam took up his parable and said, 'If thou wilt learn who is my Master, it is Jesus Christ the Lord, the only-begotten Son of God, "the blessed and only potentate, the King of kings, and Lords of lords; who only hath immortality, dwelling in the light which no man can approach unto"; who with the Father and the Holy Ghost is glorified. I am not one of those who proclaim from the house-top their wild rout of gods, and worship lifeless and dumb idols, but one God do I acknowledge and confess, in three persons glorified, the Father, the Son, and the Holy Ghost, but in one nature and substance, in one glory and kingdom undivided. He then is in three persons one God, without beginning, and without end, eternal and everlasting, increate, immutable and incorporeal, invisible, infinite, incomprehensible, alone good and righteous, who created all things out of nothing, whether visible or invisible. First, he made the heavenly and invisible powers, countless multitudes, immaterial and bodiless, ministering spirits of the majesty of God. Afterward he created this visible world, heaven and earth and sea, which also he made glorious with light and richly adorned it; the heavens with the sun, moon and stars, and the earth with all manner of herbs and divers living beasts, and the sea in turn with all kinds of fishes. "He

Barlaam preacheth his divine master,

παμπληθεῖ τῶν νηκτῶν γένει. ταῦτα πάντα,
Ps. cxlviii. 5 αὐτὸς εἶπε, καὶ ἐγεννήθησαν, αὐτὸς ἐνετείλατο
Gen. ii. 7; i. 26 καὶ ἐκτίσθησαν. εἶτα δημιουργεῖ τὸν ἄνθρωπον
χερσὶν ἰδίαις, χοῦν μὲν λαβὼν ἀπὸ τῆς γῆς εἰς
διάπλασιν τοῦ σώματος, τὴν δὲ ψυχὴν λογικὴν
καὶ νοερὰν διὰ τοῦ οἰκείου ἐμφυσήματος αὐτῷ
δούς, ἥτις κατ' εἰκόνα καὶ ὁμοίωσιν τοῦ Θεοῦ
δεδημιουργῆσθαι γέγραπται· κατ' εἰκόνα μέν,
διὰ τὸ νοερὸν καὶ αὐτεξούσιον, καθ' ὁμοίωσιν δὲ
διὰ τὴν τῆς ἀρετῆς κατὰ τὸ δυνατὸν ὁμοίωσιν.
τοῦτον τὸν ἄνθρωπον αὐτεξουσιότητι καὶ ἀθα- 46
νασίᾳ τιμήσας, βασιλέα τῶν ἐπὶ γῆς κατέστησεν·
Gen. ii. 18 ἐποίησε δὲ ἐξ αὐτοῦ τὸ θῆλυ, βοηθὸν αὐτῷ κατ'
αὐτόν.

Gen. ii. 8 Καὶ φυτεύσας παράδεισον ἐν Ἐδὲμ κατὰ ἀνα-
τολάς, εὐφροσύνης καὶ θυμηδίας πάσης πεπληρωμένον, ἔθετο ἐν αὐτῷ τὸν ἄνθρωπον ὃν ἔπλασε,
πάντων μὲν τῶν ἐκεῖσε θείων φυτῶν κελεύσας
ἀκωλύτως μετέχειν, ἑνὸς δὲ μόνου θέμενος ἐντολὴν ὅλως μὴ γεύσασθαι, ὅπερ ξύλον τοῦ γινώσκειν καλὸν καὶ πονηρὸν κέκληται, οὕτως εἰπών.
Gen. ii. 17 ᾗ δ' ἂν ἡμέρᾳ φάγητε ἀπ' αὐτοῦ, θανάτῳ ἀποθα-
νεῖσθε. εἷς δὲ τῶν εἰρημένων ἀγγελικῶν δυνάμεων, μιᾶς στρατιᾶς πρωτοστάτης, οὐδόλως ἐν
ἑαυτῷ παρὰ τοῦ Δημιουργοῦ κακίας φυσικῆς
ἐσχηκὼς ἴχνος ἀλλ' ἐπ' ἀγαθῷ γενόμενος, αὐτεξ-
Cp. Ezek. xxviii. 12-15 ουσίῳ προαιρέσει ἐτράπη ἐκ τοῦ καλοῦ εἰς τὸ
κακόν, καὶ ἐπήρθη τῇ ἀπονοίᾳ, ἀνταραι βουληθεὶς
τῷ Δεσπότῃ καὶ Θεῷ. διὸ ἀπεβλήθη τῆς τάξεως
αὐτοῦ καὶ τῆς ἀξίας, καί, ἀντὶ τῆς μακαρίας
δόξης ἐκείνης καὶ ἀγγελικῆς ὀνομασίας, διάβολος
ἐκλήθη καὶ Σατανᾶς προσωνόμασται. ἔρριψε

spake the word and these all were made; he commanded and they were created." Then with his own hands he created man, taking dust of the ground for the fashioning of his body, but by his own in-breathing giving him a reasonable and intelligent soul, which, as it is written, was made after the image and likeness of God: after his image, because of reason and free will; after his likeness, because of the likeness of virtue, in its degree, to God. Him he endowed with free will and immortality and appointed sovran over everything upon earth; and from man he made woman, to be an helpmeet of like nature for him.

'And he planted a garden eastward in Eden, full of delight and all heart's ease, and set therein the man whom he had formed, and commanded him freely to eat of all the heavenly trees therein, but forbade him wholly the taste of a certain one which was called the tree of the knowledge of good and evil, thus saying, "In the day that ye eat thereof ye shall surely die." But one of the aforesaid angel powers, the marshall of one host, though he bore in himself no trace of natural evil from his Maker's hand but had been created for good, yet by his own free and deliberate choice turned aside from good to evil, and was stirred up by madness to the desire to take up arms against his Lord God. Wherefore he was cast out of his rank and dignity, and in the stead of his former blissful glory and angelick name received the name of the "Devil" and "Satan" for his

and telleth of the malice of the devil,

γὰρ αὐτὸν ὁ Θεὸς ὡς ἀνάξιον τῆς ἄνωθεν δόξης·
Rev. xii. 4 συναπεσπάσθη δὲ αὐτῷ καὶ συναπεβλήθη καὶ
πλῆθος πολὺ τοῦ ὑπ' αὐτὸν τάγματος τῶν
ἀγγέλων, οἵτινες, κακοὶ γεγονότες τὴν προαίρεσιν, 47
καί, ἀντὶ τοῦ ἀγαθοῦ τῇ ἀποστασίᾳ ἐξακολουθή-
σαντες τοῦ ἄρχοντος αὐτῶν, δαίμονες ὠνομά-
Rev. xii. 7-9 σθησαν, ὡς πλάνοι καὶ ἀπατεῶνες.
Ἀρνησάμενος οὖν πάντη τὸ ἀγαθὸν ὁ διάβολος,
Wisd. ii. 24 καὶ πονηρὰν προσλαβόμενος φύσιν, φθόνον ἀνεδέ-
ξατο πρὸς τὸν ἄνθρωπον, ὁρῶν ἑαυτὸν μὲν ἐκ
τηλικαύτης ἀπορριφθέντα δόξης, ἐκεῖνον δὲ πρὸς
τοιαύτην τιμὴν ἀναγόμενον, καὶ ἐμηχανήσατο
ἐκβαλεῖν αὐτὸν τῆς μακαρίας ἐκείνης διαγωγῆς.
τὸν ὄφιν οὖν ἐργαστήριον τῆς ἰδίας πλάνης λαβόμενος, δι' αὐτοῦ ὡμίλησε τῇ γυναικί, καί, πείσας
αὐτὴν φαγεῖν ἐκ τοῦ ἀπηγορευμένου ἐκείνου
Cp. 1 Tim. ii. 14 ξύλου ἐλπίδι θεώσεως, δι' αὐτῆς ἠπάτησε καὶ
τὸν Ἀδάμ, οὕτω τοῦ πρωτοπλάστου κληθέντος.
καὶ φαγὼν ὁ πρῶτος ἄνθρωπος τοῦ φυτοῦ τῆς
Gen. iii. 23 παρακοῆς ἐξόριστος γίνεται τοῦ παραδείσου τῆς
τρυφῆς ὑπὸ τοῦ Δημιουργοῦ, καί, ἀντὶ τῆς μακαρίας ζωῆς ἐκείνης καὶ ἀνωλέθρου διαγωγῆς, εἰς
τὴν ἀθλίαν ταύτην καὶ ταλαίπωρον (φεῦ μοι)
βιοτὴν ἐμπίπτει, καὶ θάνατον τὸ τελευταῖον
καταδικάζεται. ἐντεῦθεν ἰσχὺν ὁ διάβολος λαβὼν
καὶ τῇ νίκῃ ἐγκαυχώμενος, πληθυνθέντος τοῦ
γένους τῶν ἀνθρώπων, πᾶσαν κακίας ὁδὸν αὐτοῖς 48
ὑπέθετο. ὡς, ἐντεῦθεν διακόψαι τὴν πολλὴν τῆς
ἁμαρτίας φορὰν βουλόμενος, ὁ Θεὸς κατακλυσμὸν
ἐπήγαγε τῇ γῇ, ἀπολέσας πᾶσαν ψυχὴν ζῶσαν·
ἕνα δὲ μόνον εὑρὼν δίκαιον ἐν τῇ γενεᾷ ἐκείνῃ,
τοῦτον σὺν γυναικὶ καὶ τέκνοις ἐν κιβωτῷ τινι

title. God banished him as unworthy of the glory above. And together with him there was drawn away and hurled forth a great multitude of the company of angels under him, who were evil of choice, and chose, in place of good, to follow in the rebellion of their leader. These were called Devils, as being deluders and deceivers.

'Thus then did the devil utterly renounce the good, and assume an evil nature; and he conceived spite against man, seeing himself hurled from such glory, and man raised to such honour; and he schemed to oust him from that blissful state. So he took the serpent for the workshop of his own guile. Through him he conversed with the woman, and persuaded her to eat of that forbidden tree in the hope of being as God, and through her he deceived Adam also, for that was the first man's name. So Adam ate of the tree of disobedience, and was banished by his maker from that paradise of delight, and, in lieu of those happy days and that immortal life, fell alas! into this life of misery and woe, and at the last received sentence of death. Thenceforth the devil waxed strong and boastful through his victory; and, as the race of man multiplied, he prompted them in all manner of wickedness. So, wishing to cut short the growth of sin, God brought a deluge on the earth, and destroyed every living soul. But one single righteous man did God find in that generation; and him, with wife and

and of the shameful fall of man.

περισώσας, μονώτατον εἰς τὴν γῆν κατέστησεν. ἡνίκα δὲ ἤρξατο πάλιν εἰς πλῆθος τὸ τῶν ἀνθρώπων γένος χωρεῖν, ἐπελάθοντο τοῦ Θεοῦ καὶ εἰς χεῖρον ἀσεβείας προέκοψαν, διαφόροις δουλωθέντες ἁμαρτήμασι, καὶ δεινοῖς καταφθαρέντες ἀτοπήμασι, καὶ εἰς πολυσχιδῆ πλάνην διαμερισθέντες.

Οἱ μὲν γὰρ αὐτομάτως φέρεσθαι τὸ πᾶν ἐνόμισαν, καὶ ἀπρονόητα ἐδογμάτισαν, ὡς μηδενὸς ἐφεστηκότος Δεσπότου· ἄλλοι εἱμαρμένην εἰσηγήσαντο, τῇ γενέσει τὸ πᾶν ἐπιτρέψαντες· ἄλλοι πολλοὺς θεοὺς κακοὺς καὶ πολυπαθεῖς ἐσεβάσθησαν, τοῦ ἔχειν αὐτοὺς τῶν ἰδίων παθῶν καὶ δεινῶν πράξεων συνηγόρους, ὧν καὶ μορφώματα τυπώσαντες ἀνεστήλωσαν ξόανα κωφὰ καὶ ἀναίσθητα εἴδωλα, καὶ συγκλείσαντες ἐν ναοῖς προσ-
Rom. i. 25 εκύνησαν, λατρεύοντες τῇ κτίσει παρὰ τὸν
Κτίσαντα, οἱ μὲν τῷ ἡλίῳ καὶ τῇ σελήνῃ, καὶ τοῖς ἄστροις ἃ ἔθετο ὁ Θεὸς πρὸς τὸ φαῦσιν παρέχειν τῷ περιγείῳ τούτῳ κόσμῳ, ἄψυχά τε ὄντα καὶ ἀναίσθητα, τῇ προνοίᾳ τοῦ Δημιουργοῦ φωτιζόμενα καὶ διακρατούμενα, οὐ μὴν δὲ οἴκοθέν
τι δυνάμενα· οἱ δὲ τῷ πυρὶ καὶ τοῖς ὕδασι καὶ 49
τοῖς λοιποῖς στοιχείοις τῆς γῆς, ἀψύχοις καὶ ἀναισθήτοις οὖσι· καὶ οὐκ ᾐσχύνθησαν οἱ ἔμψυχοι καὶ λογικοὶ τὰ τοιαῦτα σέβεσθαι· ἄλλοι
Rom i. 23 θηρίοις καὶ ἑρπετοῖς καὶ κτήνεσι τετραπόδοις
τὸ σέβας ἀπένειμαν, κτηνωδεστέρους τῶν σεβομένων ἑαυτοὺς ἀποδεικνύντες· οἱ δὲ ἀνθρώπων τινῶν αἰσχρῶν καὶ εὐτελῶν μορφώματα ἀνετυπώσαντο, καὶ τούτους θεοὺς ἐκάλεσαν, καὶ τοὺς μὲν αὐτῶν ἄρρενας, τινὰς δὲ θηλείας ὠνόμασαν,

children, he saved alive in an Ark, and set him utterly desolate on earth. But, when the human race again began to multiply, they forgat God, and ran into worse excess of wickedness, being in subjection to divers sins and ruined in strange delusions, and wandering apart into many branches of error.

'Some deemed that everything moved by mere chance, and taught that there was no Providence, since there was no master to govern. Others brought in fate, and committed everything to the stars at birth. Others worshipped many evil deities subject to many passions, to the end that they might have them to advocate their own passions and shameful deeds, whose forms they moulded, and whose dumb figures and senseless idols they set up, and enclosed them in temples, and did homage to them, "serving the creature more than the Creator." Some worshipped the sun, moon and stars which God fixed, for to give light to our earthly sphere; things without soul or sense, enlightened and sustained by the providence of God, but unable to accomplish anything of themselves. Others again worshipped fire and water, and the other elements, things without soul or sense; and men, possest of soul and reason, were not ashamed to worship the like of these. Others assigned worship to beasts, creeping and four-footed things, proving themselves more beastly than the things that they worshipped. Others made them images of vile and worthless men, and named them gods, some of whom they called males, and some females, and they themselves set them forth as

of the delusions of fallen man,

οὓς ἐκεῖνοι αὐτοὶ ἐξέθεντο μοιχοὺς εἶναι καὶ φονεῖς, ὀργίλους καὶ ζηλωτὰς καὶ θυμαντικούς, πατροκτόνους καὶ ἀδελφοκτόνους, κλέπτας καὶ ἅρπαγας, χωλοὺς καὶ κυλλούς, καὶ φαρμακούς, καὶ μαινομένους, καὶ τούτων τινὰς μὲν τετελευτηκότας, τινὰς δὲ κεκεραυνωμένους, καὶ κοπτομένους, καὶ θρηνουμένους καὶ δεδουλευκότας ἀνθρώποις, καὶ φυγάδας γενομένους, καὶ εἰς ζῷα μεταμορφουμένους ἐπὶ πονηραῖς καὶ αἰσχραῖς μίξεσιν· ὅθεν, λαμβάνοντες οἱ ἄνθρωποι ἀφορμὰς ἀπὸ τῶν θεῶν αὐτῶν, ἀδεῶς κατεμιαίνοντο πάσῃ ἀκαθαρσίᾳ. καὶ δεινὴ κατεῖχε σκότωσις τὸ γένος ἡμῶν ἐν ἐκείνοις τοῖς χρόνοις,
Ps. xiv. 3 καὶ οὐκ ἦν ὁ συνιών, οὐκ ἦν ὁ ἐκζητῶν τὸν Θεόν.

Gen. xi.–xxv. Ἀβραὰμ δέ τις ἐν ἐκείνῃ τῇ γενεᾷ μόνος εὑρέθη τὰς αἰσθήσεις τῆς ψυχῆς ἐρρωμένας ἔχων, ὃς τῇ θεωρίᾳ τῶν κτισμάτων ἐπέγνω τὸν Δημιουργόν. Κατανοήσας γὰρ οὐρανὸν καὶ γῆν καὶ θάλασσαν, ἥλιον καὶ σελήνην καὶ τὰ λοιπά, ἐθαύμασε τὴν ἐναρμόνιον ταύτην διακόσμησιν· ἰδὼν δὲ τὸν κόσμον καὶ τὰ ἐν αὐτῷ πάντα, οὐκ αὐτομάτως γεγενῆσθαι καὶ συντηρεῖσθαι ἐνόμισεν, οὔτε μὴν τοῖς στοιχείοις τῆς γῆς ἢ τοῖς ἀψύχοις εἰδώλοις τὴν αἰτίαν τῆς τοιαύτης διακοσμήσεως προσανέθετο· ἀλλὰ τὸν ἀληθῆ Θεὸν διὰ τούτων ἐπέγνω, καὶ αὐτὸν εἶναι Δημιουργὸν τοῦ παντὸς καὶ συνοχέα συνῆκεν. ἀποδεξάμενος δὲ τοῦτον τῆς εὐγνωμοσύνης καὶ ὀρθῆς κρίσεως, ὁ Θεὸς ἐνεφάνισεν ἑαυτὸν αὐτῷ, οὐ καθὼς ἔχει φύσεως (Θεὸν γὰρ ἰδεῖν γεννητῇ φύσει ἀδύνατον), ἀλλ' οἰκονομικαῖς τισι θεοφανείαις, ὡς οἶδεν αὐτός, καὶ τελεωτέραν γνῶσιν ἐνθεὶς αὐτοῦ τῇ ψυχῇ, ἐδό-

adulterers, murderers, victims of anger, jealousy, wrath, slayers of fathers, slayers of brothers, thieves and robbers, lame and maim, sorcerers and madmen. Others they showed dead, struck by thunderbolts, or beating their breasts, or being mourned over, or in enslavement to mankind, or exiled, or, for foul and shameful unions, taking the forms of animals. Whence men, taking occasion by the gods themselves, took heart to pollute themselves in all manner of uncleanness. So an horrible darkness overspread our race in those times, and "there was none that did understand and seek after God."

'Now in that generation one Abraham alone was found strong in his spiritual senses; and by contemplation of Creation he recognized the Creator. When he considered heaven, earth and sea, the sun, moon and the like, he marvelled at their harmonious ordering. Seeing the world, and all that therein is, he could not believe that it had been created, and was upheld, by its own power, nor did he ascribe such a fair ordering to earthly elements or lifeless idols. But therein he recognized the true God, and understood him to be the maker and sustainer of the whole. And God, approving his fair wisdom and right judgement, manifested himself unto him, not as he essentially is (for it is impossible for a created being to see God), but by certain manifestations in material forms, as he alone can, and he planted in Abraham more perfect knowledge; he magnified

of Abraham, Moses and Aaron,

ξασε, καὶ οἰκεῖον ἔθετο θεράποντα, ὅς, καὶ κατὰ
διαδοχὴν τοῖς ἐξ αὐτοῦ παραπέμψας τὴν εὐσέβειαν, τὸν ἀληθῆ γνωρίζειν ἐδίδαξε Θεόν. διὸ καὶ
εἰς πλῆθος ἄπειρον τὸ σπέρμα αὐτοῦ ἐλθεῖν ὁ
Exod. xix. 5 Δεσπότης εὐδόκησε, καὶ λαὸν περιούσιον αὐτῷ
Tit. ii. 14 ὠνόμασε, καὶ δουλωθέντας αὐτοὺς ἔθνει Αἰγυπτίῳ
καὶ Φαραῷ τινι τυράννῳ σημείοις καὶ τέρασι
φρικτοῖς καὶ ἐξαισίοις ἐξήγαγεν ἐκεῖθεν διὰ
Μωσέως καὶ Ἀαρών, ἀνδρῶν ἁγίων καὶ χάριτι
προφητείας δοξασθέντων· δι' ὧν καὶ τοὺς Αἰ-
γυπτίους ἐκόλασεν ἀξίως τῆς αὐτῶν πονηρίας, καὶ
τοὺς Ἰσραηλίτας (οὕτω γὰρ ὁ λαὸς ἐκεῖνος ὁ τοῦ
Exod. xiv. 21, 22, 29 Ἀβραὰμ ἀπόγονος ἐκέκλητο) διὰ ξηρᾶς τὴν
Ἐρυθρὰν θάλασσαν διήγαγε, διασχισθέντων τῶν
ὑδάτων καὶ τεῖχος ἐκ δεξιῶν καὶ τεῖχος ἐξ εὐωνύμων γεγενημένων· τοῦ δὲ Φαραὼ καὶ τῶν
Αἰγυπτίων κατ' ἴχνος αὐτῶν εἰσελθόντων, ἐπ-
αναστραφέντα τὰ ὕδατα ἄρδην αὐτοὺς ἀπώλεσεν.
εἶτα θαύμασι μεγίστοις καὶ θεοφανείαις ἐπὶ 51
χρόνοις τεσσαράκοντα διαγαγὼν τὸν λαὸν ἐν τῇ
Ex. xvi. 4–35 ἐρήμῳ καὶ ἄρτῳ οὐρανίῳ διατρέφων, νόμον δέδωκε
Exod. xx.; Deut. v. πλαξὶ λιθίναις θεόθεν γεγραμμένον, ὅνπερ ἐνε-
χείρισε τῷ Μωσεῖ ἐπὶ τοῦ ὄρους, τύπον ὄντα καὶ
Heb. x. 1 σκιαγραφίαν τῶν μελλόντων, τῶν μὲν εἰδώλων
καὶ πάντων τῶν πονηρῶν ἀπάγοντα πράξεων,
μόνον δὲ διδάσκοντα τὸν ὄντως ὄντα Θεὸν σέβεσθαι, καὶ τῶν ἀγαθῶν ἔργων ἀντέχεσθαι·
τοιαύταις οὖν τερατουργίαις εἰσήγαγεν αὐτοὺς
εἰς ἀγαθήν τινα γῆν, ἥνπερ πάλαι τῷ πατριάρχῃ
ἐκείνῳ Ἀβραὰμ ἐπηγγείλατο δώσειν αὐτοῦ τῷ
σπέρματι. καὶ μακρὸν ἂν εἴη διηγήσασθαι ὅσα
εἰς αὐτοὺς ἐνεδείξατο μεγάλα καὶ θαυμαστά,

him and made him his own servant. Which Abraham in turn handed down to his children his own righteousness, and taught them to know the true God. Wherefore also the Lord was pleased to multiply his seed beyond measure, and called them "a peculiar people," and brought them forth out of bondage to the Egyptian nation, and to one Pharaoh a tyrant, by strange and terrible signs and wonders wrought by the hand of Moses and Aaron, holy men, honoured with the gift of prophecy; by whom also he punished the Egyptians in fashion worthy of their wickedness, and led the Israelites (for thus the people descended from Abraham were called) through the Red Sea upon dry land, the waters dividing and making a wall on the right hand and a wall on the left. But when Pharaoh and the Egyptians pursued and went in after them, the waters returned and utterly destroyed them. Then with exceeding mighty miracles and divine manifestations by the space of forty years he led the people in the wilderness, and fed them with bread from heaven, and gave the Law divinely written on tables of stone, which he delivered unto Moses on the mount, "a type and shadow of things to come" leading men away from idols and all manner of wickedness, and teaching them to worship only the one true God, and to cleave to good works. By such wondrous deeds, he brought them into a certain goodly land, the which he had promised aforetime to Abraham the patriarch, that he would give it unto his seed. And the task were long, to tell of all the mighty and marvellous works full of glory and

ἔνδοξά τε καὶ ἐξαίσια, ὧν οὐκ ἔστιν ἀριθμός, δι'
ὧν πάντων τοῦτο ἦν τὸ σπουδαζόμενον πάσης
ἀθέσμου λατρείας καὶ πράξεως τὸ τῶν ἀνθρώπων
ἀποσπάσαι γένος, καὶ εἰς τὴν ἀρχαίαν ἐπαναγαγεῖν κατάστασιν. ἀλλὰ καὶ ἔτι τῇ αὐτονομίᾳ
τῆς πλάνης ἐδουλοῦτο ἡ φύσις ἡμῶν, καὶ ἐβασί-
Rom. v. 14, λευε τῶν ἀνθρώπων ὁ θάνατος, τῇ τυραννίδι τοῦ
17 διαβόλου, καὶ τῇ καταδίκῃ τοῦ ᾅδου πάντας
παραπέμπων.

Εἰς τοιαύτην οὖν συμφορὰν καὶ ταλαιπωρίαν
ἐλθόντας ἡμᾶς οὐ παρεῖδεν ὁ πλάσας καὶ ἐκ τοῦ
μὴ ὄντος εἰς τὸ εἶναι παραγαγών, οὐδὲ ἀφῆκεν εἰς
τέλος ἀπολέσθαι τὸ τῶν χειρῶν αὐτοῦ ἔργον,
ἀλλ' εὐδοκίᾳ τοῦ Θεοῦ καὶ Πατρὸς καὶ συνεργίᾳ 52
τοῦ ἁγίου Πνεύματος, ὁ μονογενὴς Υἱὸς καὶ
John i. 18 Λόγος τοῦ Θεοῦ, ὁ ὢν εἰς τὸν κόλπον τοῦ Πατρός,
ὁ ὁμοούσιος τῷ Πατρὶ καὶ τῷ ἁγίῳ Πνεύματι, ὁ
John i. 1 προαιώνιος, ὁ ἄναρχος, ὁ ἐν ἀρχῇ ὤν, καὶ πρὸς
τὸν Θεὸν καὶ Πατέρα ὤν, καὶ Θεὸς ὤν, συγκατα-
βαίνει τοῖς ἑαυτοῦ δούλοις συγκατάβασιν ἄ-
φραστον καὶ ἀκατάληπτον, καί, Θεὸς ὢν τέλειος,
Luke i. 35 ἄνθρωπος τέλειος γίνεται ἐκ Πνεύματος ἁγίου καὶ
Is. vii. 14
John i. 13, 14 Μαρίας τῆς ἁγίας Παρθένου καὶ Θεοτόκου, οὐκ
ἐκ σπέρματος ἀνδρός, ἢ θελήματος, ἢ συναφείας,
ἐν τῇ ἀχράντῳ μήτρᾳ τῆς Παρθένου συλληφθείς,
ἀλλ' ἐκ Πνεύματος ἁγίου, καθὼς καὶ πρὸ τῆς
Luke i. 26 συλλήψεως εἷς τῶν ἀρχαγγέλων ἀπεστάλη
μηνύων τῇ Παρθένῳ τὴν ξένην σύλληψιν ἐκείνην
Matt. i. 20 καὶ τὸν ἄφραστον τόκον. ἀσπόρως γὰρ συν-
Is. xi. 1
Jer. xxxi. 22 ελήφθη ὁ Υἱὸς τοῦ Θεοῦ ἐκ Πνεύματος ἁγίου, καὶ
συμπήξας ἑαυτῷ ἐν τῇ μήτρᾳ τῆς Παρθένου
σάρκα ἐμψυχουμένην ψυχῇ λογικῇ τε καὶ νοερᾷ,

wonder, without number, which he shewed unto them, by which it was his purpose to pluck the human race from all unlawful worship and practice, and to bring men back to their first estate. But even so our nature was in bondage by its freedom to err, and death had dominion over mankind, delivering all to the tyranny of the devil, and to the damnation of hell.

Of the Incarnation of our Lord Jesus Christ,

'So when we had sunk to this depth of misfortune and misery, we were not forgotten by him that formed and brought us out of nothing into being, nor did he suffer his own handiwork utterly to perish. By the good pleasure of our God and Father, and the co-operation of the Holy Ghost, the only-begotten Son, even the Word of God, which is in the bosom of the Father, being of one substance with the Father and with the Holy Ghost, he that was before all worlds, without beginning, who was in the beginning, and was with God even the Father, and was God, he, I say, condescended toward his servants with an unspeakable and incomprehensible condescension; and, being perfect God, was made perfect man, of the Holy Ghost, and of Mary the Holy Virgin and Mother of God, not of the seed of man, nor of the will of man, nor by carnal union, being conceived in the Virgin's undefiled womb, of the Holy Ghost; as also, before his conception, one of the Archangels was sent to announce to the Virgin that miraculous conception and ineffable birth. For without seed was the Son of God conceived of the Holy Ghost, and in the Virgin's womb he formed for himself a fleshy body, animate with a reasonable and

προῆλθεν ἐν μιᾷ τῇ ὑποστάσει, δύο δὲ ταῖς
φύσεσι, τέλειος Θεός, καὶ τέλειος ἄνθρωπος, ἄ-
Ezek. xliv. 2 φθορον τὴν παρθενίαν τῆς τεκούσης καὶ μετὰ τὸν
Heb. iv. 16 Mat. vii. 7 τόκον φυλάξας, καὶ ἐν πᾶσιν ὁμοιοπαθὴς ἡμῖν
Rom. v. 12 γενόμενος χωρὶς ἁμαρτίας, τὰς ἀσθενείας ἡμῶν
ἀνέλαβε καὶ τὰς νόσους ἐβάστασεν. ἐπεὶ γὰρ
δι' ἁμαρτίας εἰσῆλθεν ὁ θάνατος εἰς τὸν κόσμον,
ἔδει τὸν λυτροῦσθαι μέλλοντα ἀναμάρτητον εἶναι 53
καὶ μὴ τῷ θανάτῳ διὰ τῆς ἁμαρτίας ὑπεύθυνον.
Ἐπὶ τριάκοντα δὲ χρόνοις τοῖς ἀνθρώποις
Mat. iii. 13, 17 συναναστραφείς, ἐβαπτίσθη ἐν τῷ Ἰορδάνῃ
ποταμῷ ὑπὸ Ἰωάννου, ἀνδρὸς ἁγίου καὶ πάντων
Mat. xi. 11 τῶν προφητῶν ὑπερκειμένου. βαπτισθέντος δὲ
αὐτοῦ, φωνὴ ἠνέχθη οὐρανόθεν ἐκ τοῦ Θεοῦ καὶ
Πατρός, λέγουσα· Οὗτός ἐστιν ὁ Υἱός μου ὁ
ἀγαπητὸς ἐν ᾧ εὐδόκησα. καὶ τὸ Πνεῦμα τὸ
Ἅγιον ἐν εἴδει περιστερᾶς κατῆλθεν ἐπ' αὐτόν.
Mat. iv. 23 καὶ ἀποτότε ἤρξατο σημεῖα ποιεῖν μεγάλα καὶ
Acts ii. 22 θαυμαστά, νεκροὺς ἀνιστῶν, τυφλοὺς φωτίζων,
δαίμονας ἀπελαύνων, κωφοὺς καὶ κυλλοὺς θεραπεύων, λεπροὺς καθαρίζων, καὶ πανταχόθεν
ἀνακαινίζων τὴν παλαιωθεῖσαν ἡμῶν φύσιν, ἔργῳ
τε καὶ λόγῳ παιδεύων καὶ διδάσκων τὴν τῆς
ἀρετῆς ὁδόν, τῆς μὲν φθορᾶς ἀπάγων, πρὸς δὲ τὴν
ζωὴν ποδηγῶν τὴν αἰώνιον. ὅθεν καὶ μαθητὰς ἐξ-
Luke vi. 13 ελέξατο δώδεκα, οὓς καὶ ἀποστόλους ἐκάλεσε· καὶ
κηρύττειν αὐτοῖς ἐπέτρεψε τὴν οὐράνιον πολιτείαν, ἣν ἦλθεν ἐπὶ τῆς γῆς ἐνδείξασθαι, καὶ οὐρανίους τοὺς ταπεινοὺς ἡμᾶς καὶ ἐπιγείους τῇ αὐτοῦ
οἰκονομίᾳ τελέσαι.
Mat. xxvii 18 Φθόνῳ δὲ τῆς θαυμαστῆς αὐτοῦ καὶ θεοπρεποῦς
πολιτείας καὶ τῶν ἀπείρων θαυμάτων οἱ ἀρχιερεῖς

intelligent soul, and thence came forth in one substance, but in two natures, perfect God and perfect man, and preserved undefiled, even after birth, the virginity of her that bore him. He, being made of like passions with ourselves in all things, yet without sin, took our infirmities and bare our sicknesses. For, since by sin death entered into the world, need was that he, that should redeem the world, should be without sin, and not by sin subject unto death.

'When he had lived thirty years among men, he was baptized in the river Jordan by John, an holy man, and great above all the prophets. And when he was baptized there came a voice from heaven, from God, even the Father, saying, "This is my beloved Son, in whom I am well pleased," and the Holy Ghost descended upon him in likeness of a dove. From that time forth he began to do great signs and wonders, raising the dead, giving sight to the blind, casting out devils, healing the lame and maim, cleansing lepers, and everywhere renewing our out-worn nature, instructing men both by word and deed, and teaching the way of virtue, turning men from destruction and guiding their feet toward life eternal. Wherefore also he chose twelve disciples, whom he called Apostles, and commanded them to preach the kingdom of heaven which he came upon earth to declare, and to make heavenly us who are low and earthly, by virtue of his Incarnation.

of his life and ministry,

'But, through envy of his marvellous and divine conversation and endless miracles, the chief priests

καὶ ἀρχηγοὶ τῶν Ἰουδαίων, ἔνθα δὴ καὶ τὰς
διατριβὰς ἐποιεῖτο, μανέντες, οἵσπερ τὰ προειρη-
μένα θαυμαστὰ σημεῖα καὶ τέρατα πεποιήκει,
ἀμνημονήσαντες πάντων, θανάτῳ αὐτὸν κατεδίκα-
Matt xxvi. 47 σαν, ἕνα τῶν μαθητῶν αὐτοῦ εἰς προδοσίαν συν- 54
αρπάσαντες· καί, κρατήσαντες αὐτόν, τοῖς ἔθνεσιν
ἔκδοτον τὴν ζωὴν τῶν ἁπάντων ἐποιήσαντο,
ἑκουσίᾳ βουλῇ ταῦτα καταδεξαμένου αὐτοῦ. ἦλθε
γὰρ δι' ἡμᾶς πάντα παθεῖν, ἵν' ἡμᾶς τῶν παθῶν
Matt. xxvii. 26 ἐλευθερώσῃ. πολλὰ δὲ εἰς αὐτὸν ἐνδειξάμενοι,
σταυρῷ τὸ τελευταῖον κατεδίκασαν. καὶ πάντα
ὑπέμεινε τῇ φύσει τῆς σαρκός, ἧς ἐξ ἡμῶν ἀνελά-
βετο, τῆς θείας αὐτοῦ φύσεως ἀπαθοῦς μεινάσης.
δύο γὰρ φύσεων ὑπάρχων, τῆς τε θείας καὶ ἧς ἐξ
ἡμῶν προσανελάβετο, ἡ μὲν ἀνθρωπεία φύσις
ἔπαθεν, ἡ δὲ θεότης ἀπαθὴς διέμεινε καὶ ἀθάνατος.
ἐσταυρώθη οὖν τῇ σαρκὶ ὁ Κύριος ἡμῶν Ἰησοῦς
1 Pet. ii. 22 Χριστός, ὢν ἀναμάρτητος. ἁμαρτίαν γὰρ οὐκ
Is. liii. 9 ἐποίησεν οὐδὲ εὑρέθη δόλος ἐν τῷ στόματι αὐτοῦ,
1 Pet. iv. 1 καὶ οὐχ ὑπέκειτο θανάτῳ· διὰ τῆς ἁμαρτίας γάρ,
ὡς καὶ προεῖπον, ὁ θάνατος εἰσῆλθεν εἰς τὸν
κόσμον· ἀλλὰ δι' ἡμᾶς ἀπέθανε σαρκὶ ἵν' ἡμᾶς
τῆς τοῦ θανάτου λυτρώσηται τυραννίδος. κατῆλ-
1 Pet. iii. 19 θεν εἰς ᾅδου, καὶ τοῦτον συντρίψας, τὰς ἀπ'
Eph. iv. 9 αἰῶνος ἐγκεκλεισμένας ἐκεῖσε ψυχὰς ἠλευθέρωσε.
τεθεὶς ἐν τάφῳ τῇ τρίτῃ ἡμέρᾳ ἐξανέστη, νικήσας
τὸν θάνατον καὶ ἡμῖν τὴν νίκην δωρησάμενος κατ' 55
αὐτοῦ, καί, ἀφθαρτίσας τὴν σάρκα ὁ τῆς ἀφθαρ-
John xx. 19 σίας πάροχος, ὤφθη τοῖς μαθηταῖς, εἰρήνην αὐτοῖς
δωρούμενος καὶ δι' αὐτῶν παντὶ τῷ γένει τῶν
ἀνθρώπων.

Luke xxiv. 50 Μεθ' ἡμέρας δὲ τεσσαράκοντα εἰς οὐρανοὺς ἀν-

and rulers of the Jews (amongst whom also he dwelt, on whom he had wrought his aforesaid signs and miracles), in their madness forgetting all, condemned him to death, having seized one of the Twelve to betray him. And, when they had taken him, they delivered him to the Gentiles, him that was the life of the world, he of his free will consenting thereto; for he came for our sakes to suffer all things, that he might free us from sufferings. But when they had done him much despite, at the last they condemned him to the Cross. All this he endured in the nature of that flesh which he took from us, his divine nature remaining free of suffering: for, being of two natures, both the divine and that which he took from us, his human nature suffered, while his Godhead continued free from suffering and death. So our Lord Jesus Christ, being without sin, was crucified in the flesh, for he did no sin, neither was guile found in his mouth; and he was not subject unto death, for by sin, as I have said before, came death into the world; but for our sakes he suffered death in the flesh, that he might redeem us from the tyranny of death. He descended into hell, and having harrowed it, he delivered thence souls that had been imprisoned therein for ages long. He was buried, and on the third day he rose again, vanquishing death and granting us the victory over death: and he, the giver of immortality, having made flesh immortal, was seen of his disciples, and bestowed upon them peace, and, through them, peace on the whole human race.

of his death, and harrowing of hell,

of his Resurrection,

'After forty days he ascended into heaven, and

Acts i. 1-11 εφοίτησε, καὶ οὕτως ἐν δεξιᾷ τοῦ Πατρὸς καθέζε-
2 Tim. iv. 1 ται, ὃς καὶ μέλλει πάλιν ἔρχεσθαι κρῖναι ζῶντας
Mat. xvi. 27 καὶ νεκρούς, καὶ ἀποδοῦναι ἑκάστῳ κατὰ τὰ ἔργα
αὐτοῦ. μετὰ δὲ τὴν ἔνδοξον αὐτοῦ εἰς οὐρανοὺς
Acts ii. 3, 4 ἀνάληψιν, ἀπέστειλε τὸ πανάγιον Πνεῦμα ἐπὶ
τοὺς ἁγίους αὐτοῦ μαθητὰς ἐν εἴδει πυρός, καὶ
ἤρξαντο ξέναις γλώσσαις λαλεῖν, καθὼς τὸ
Πνεῦμα ἐδίδου ἀποφθέγγεσθαι. ἐντεῦθεν οὖν τῇ
Mat. xxviii. 19, 20 χάριτι αὐτοῦ διεσπάρησαν εἰς πάντα τὰ ἔθνη, καὶ
ἐκήρυξαν τὴν ὀρθόδοξον πίστιν, βαπτίζοντες
αὐτοὺς εἰς τὸ ὄνομα τοῦ Πατρός, καὶ τοῦ Υἱοῦ, καὶ
τοῦ ἁγίου Πνεύματος, διδάσκοντες τηρεῖν πάσας
τὰς ἐντολὰς τοῦ Σωτῆρος. ἐφώτισαν οὖν τὰ ἔθνη
τὰ πεπλανημένα, καὶ τὴν δεισιδαίμονα πλάνην
τῶν εἰδώλων κατήργησαν. κἂν μὴ φέρων ὁ ἐχθρὸς
τὴν ἧτταν πολέμους καὶ νῦν καθ' ἡμῶν τῶν πιστῶν ἐγείρει, πείθων τοὺς ἄφρονας καὶ ἀσυνέτους 56
ἔτι τῆς εἰδωλολατρείας ἀντέχεσθαι, ἀλλ' ἀσθενὴς
Ps. ix. 6 (Sept.) ἡ δύναμις αὐτοῦ γέγονε, καὶ αἱ ῥομφαῖαι αὐτοῦ
εἰς τέλος ἐξέλιπον τῇ τοῦ Χριστοῦ δυνάμει. ἰδού
σοι τὸν ἐμὸν Δεσπότην καὶ Θεὸν καὶ Σωτῆρα δι'
ὀλίγων ἐγνώρισα ῥημάτων· τελεώτερον δὲ γνωρί-
σεις, εἰ τὴν χάριν αὐτοῦ δέξῃ ἐν τῇ ψυχῇ σου καὶ
δοῦλος αὐτοῦ καταξιωθῇς γενέσθαι.

VIII

Acts ix. 8 Τούτων ὡς ἤκουσε τῶν ῥημάτων ὁ τοῦ βασιλέως
υἱός, φῶς αὐτοῦ περιήστραψε τὴν ψυχήν· καὶ
ἐξαναστὰς τοῦ θρόνου ἐκ περιχαρείας, καὶ περιπλακεὶς τῷ Βαρλαάμ, ἔφη· Τάχα οὗτός ἐστιν,

sitteth at the right hand of the Father. And he shall come again to judge the quick and the dead, and to reward every man according to his works. After his glorious Ascension into heaven he sent forth upon his disciples the Holy Ghost in likeness of fire, and they began to speak with other tongues as the Spirit gave them utterance. From thence by his grace they were scattered abroad among all nations, and preached the true Catholic Faith, baptizing them in the name of the Father, and of the Son, and of the Holy Ghost, and teaching them to observe all the commandments of the Saviour. So they gave light to the people that wandered in darkness, and abolished the superstitious error of idolatry. Though the enemy chafeth under his defeat, and even now stirreth up war against us, the faithful, persuading the fools and unwise to cling to the worship of idols, yet is his power grown feeble, and his swords have at last failed him by the power of Christ. Lo, in few words I have made known unto thee my Master, my God, and my Saviour; but thou shalt know him more perfectly, if thou wilt receive his grace into thy soul, and gain the blessing to become his servant."

and glorious Ascension into heaven;

of the coming of the Holy Ghost, and of the spread of the Catholick Faith

VIII

When the king's son had heard these words, there flashed a light upon his soul. Rising from his seat in the fulness of his joy, he embraced Barlaam, saying: 'Most honoured sir, methinks this might be that

How Ioasaph rejoiced to hear Barlaam's good tidings

ὡς ἐγὼ εἰκάζω, τιμιώτατε τῶν ἀνθρώπων, ὁ λίθος ἐκεῖνος ὁ ἀτίμητος, ὃν ἐν μυστηρίῳ εἰκότως κατέχεις, μὴ παντὶ τῷ βουλομένῳ τοῦτον δεικνύων, ἀλλ' οἷς ἔρρωνται τὰ τῆς ψυχῆς αἰσθητήρια. ἰδοὺ 57
γάρ, ὡς ταῦτα τὰ ῥήματα ἐδεξάμην ταῖς ἀκοαῖς, φῶς γλυκύτατον εἰσέδυ μου τῇ καρδίᾳ, καὶ τὸ βαρὺ ἐκεῖνο τῆς λύπης κάλυμμα, τὸ πολὺν ἤδη χρόνον περικείμενον τῇ καρδίᾳ μου, θᾶττον περιῃρέθη. εἰ οὖν καλῶς εἰκάζω, ἀνάγγειλόν μοι· εἰ δὲ καὶ κρεῖττόν τι τῶν εἰρημένων γινώσκεις, μὴ ἀναβάλλου ἐξ αὐτῆς φανερῶσαί μοι.

Αὖθις οὖν ὁ Βαρλαὰμ ἀπεκρίνατο· Ναὶ μήν, κύριέ μου καὶ βασιλεῦ, τοῦτό ἐστι τὸ μέγα μυσ-
Col. i. 26 τήριον τὸ ἀποκεκρυμμένον ἀπὸ τῶν αἰώνων καὶ ἀπὸ τῶν γενεῶν, ἐπ' ἐσχάτων δὲ τῶν χρόνων φανερωθὲν τῷ γένει τῶν ἀνθρώπων, οὗ τὴν φανέρωσιν πάλαι τῇ τοῦ θείου Πνεύματος χάριτι
Heb. i. 1 προήγγειλαν πολλοὶ προφῆται καὶ δίκαιοι, πολυμερῶς καὶ πολυτρόπως μυηθέντες· καὶ μεγαλοφώνως καταγγείλαντες, καὶ πάντες τὴν ἐσομένην
Luke x. 24 σωτηρίαν προορῶντες, ἐπόθουν θεάσασθαι ταύτην,
Mat. xiii. 17 καὶ οὐκ ἐθεάσαντο· ἀλλ' ἐσχάτη γενεὰ αὕτη
Mk. xvi. 16 ἠξιώθη τὸ σωτήριον δέξασθαι. ὁ πιστεύσας οὖν καὶ βαπτισθεὶς σωθήσεται, ὁ δὲ ἀπιστήσας κατακριθήσεται.

Ὁ δὲ Ἰωάσαφ ἔφη· Πάντα τὰ εἰρημένα σοι ἀνενδοιάστως πιστεύω, καὶ ὃν καταγγέλλεις δοξάζω Θεόν. μόνον ἀπλανῶς μοι ταῦτα σαφήνι- 58
σον, καὶ τί με δεῖ ποιεῖν ἀκριβῶς δίδαξον· ἀλλὰ καὶ τὸ βάπτισμα τί ἐστιν, ὃ τοὺς πιστεύοντας δέξασθαι ἔφης, κατ' ἀκολουθίαν αὐτῷ πάντα μοι γνώρισον.

priceless stone which thou dost rightly keep secret, not displaying it to all that would see it, but only to those whose spiritual sense is strong. For lo, as these words dropped upon mine ear, sweetest light entered into my heart, and the heavy veil of sorrow, that hath now this long time enveloped my heart, was in an instant removed. Tell me if my guess be true: or if thou knowest aught better than that which thou hast spoken, delay not to declare it to me.'

Again, therefore, Barlaam answered, 'Yea, my lord and prince, this is the mighty mystery which hath been hid from ages and generations, but in these last days hath been made known unto mankind; the manifestation whereof, by the grace of the Holy Ghost, was foretold by many prophets and righteous men, instructed at sundry times and in divers manners. In trumpet tones they proclaimed it, and all looked forward to the salvation that should be: this they desired to see, but saw it not. But this latest generation was counted worthy to receive salvation. Wherefore he that believeth and is baptized shall be saved; but he that believeth not shall be damned.'

Said Ioasaph, 'All that thou hast told me I believe without question, and him whom thou declarest I glorify as God. Only make all plain to me, and teach me clearly what I must do. But especially go on to tell me what is that Baptism which thou sayest that the Faithful receive.'

Ἐκεῖνος δὲ πρὸς αὐτὸν ἀπεκρίνατο· Τῆς ἁγίας
ταύτης καὶ ἀμωμήτου τῶν Χριστιανῶν πίστεως
ῥίζα ὥσπερ καὶ ἀσφαλὴς ὑποβάθρα ἡ τοῦ θείου
βαπτίσματος ὑπάρχει χάρις, πάντων τῶν ἀπὸ
γενέσεως ἁμαρτημάτων κάθαρσιν ἔχουσα, καὶ
παντελῆ ῥύψιν τῶν ἀπὸ κακίας ἐπεισελθόντων
John iii. 5 μολυσμάτων. οὕτω γὰρ ὁ Σωτὴρ ἐνετείλατο δι'
ὕδατος ἀναγεννᾶσθαι καὶ Πνεύματος, καὶ εἰς τὸ
ἀρχαῖον ἐπανάγεσθαι ἀξίωμα, δι' ἐντεύξεως δηλαδὴ
καὶ τῆς σωτηρίου ἐπικλήσεως, ἐπιφοιτῶντος τῷ
ὕδατι τοῦ ἁγίου Πνεύματος. βαπτιζόμεθα τοίνυν,
Mat. xxviii. 19 κατὰ τὸν λόγον τοῦ Κυρίου, εἰς τὸ ὄνομα τοῦ
Πατρός, καὶ τοῦ Υἱοῦ, καὶ τοῦ ἁγίου Πνεύματος·
καὶ οὕτως ἐνοικεῖ τοῦ ἁγίου Πνεύματος ἡ χάρις τῇ
τοῦ βαπτισθέντος ψυχῇ, λαμπρύνουσα αὐτὴν καὶ
Gen. i. 26; ix. 6 θεοειδῆ ἀπεργαζομένη, καὶ τὸ κατ' εἰκόνα καὶ καθ'
ὁμοίωσιν αὐτῇ ἀνακαινίζουσα· καὶ λοιπὸν πάντα
τὰ παλαιὰ τῆς κακίας ἔργα ἀπορρίψαντες, συν-
θήκην πρὸς Θεὸν δευτέρου βίου καὶ ἀρχὴν
καθαρωτέρας πολιτείας ποιούμεθα, ὡς ἂν καὶ
συγκληρονόμοι ἐσόμεθα τῶν πρὸς ἀφθαρσίαν
ἀναγεννηθέντων καὶ τῆς αἰωνίου σωτηρίας ἐπι-
λαβομένων. χωρὶς δὲ βαπτίσματος οὐκ ἔστι τῆς
ἀγαθῆς ἐλπίδος ἐκείνης ἐπιτυχεῖν, κἂν πάντων 59
τῶν εὐσεβῶν εὐσεβέστερός τις γένηται. οὕτω γὰρ
ὁ ἐπὶ σωτηρίᾳ τοῦ γένους ἡμῶν ἐνανθρωπήσας
John iii. 3 Θεὸς Λόγος εἶπεν· Ἀμὴν λέγω ὑμῖν, ἐὰν μὴ
ἀναγεννηθῆτε δι' ὕδατος καὶ Πνεύματος, οὐ μὴ
εἰσέλθητε εἰς τὴν βασιλείαν τῶν οὐρανῶν. διὸ
πρὸ πάντων ἀξιῶ σε τῇ μὲν ψυχῇ δέξασθαι τὴν
πίστιν, προσελθεῖν δὲ εὐθὺς καὶ τῷ βαπτίσματι
πόθῳ θερμοτάτῳ καὶ μηδόλως πρὸς τοῦτο ἀναβάλ-

Barlaam discourseth of Holy Baptism

The other answered him thus, 'The root and sure foundation of this holy and perfect Christian Faith is the grace of heavenly Baptism, fraught with the cleansing from all original sins, and complete purification of all defilements of evil that come after. For thus the Saviour commanded a man to be born again of water and of the spirit, and be restored to his first dignity, to wit, by supplication and by calling on the Saving Name, the Holy Spirit brooding on the water. We are baptized, then, according to the word of the Lord, in the Name of the Father, and of the Son, and of the Holy Ghost: and thus the grace of the Holy Ghost dwelleth in the soul of the baptized, illuminating and making it God-like and renewing that which was made after his own image and likeness. And for the time to come we cast away all the old works of wickedness, and we make covenant with God of a second life and begin a purer conversation, that we may also become fellow-heirs with them that are born again to incorruption and lay hold of everlasting salvation. But without Baptism it is impossible to attain to that good hope, even though a man be more pious than piety itself. For thus spake God, the Word, who was incarnate for the salvation of our race, "Verily I say unto you, except ye be born of water and of the Spirit, ye shall in no wise enter into the Kingdom of Heaven." Wherefore before all things I require thee to receive faith within thy soul, and to draw near to Baptism anon with hearty desire, and on no account to delay

λεσθαι· ἐπικίνδυνον γὰρ ἡ ἀναβολή, διὰ τὸ ἄδηλον εἶναι τοῦ θανάτου τὴν προθεσμίαν.

Ὁ δὲ Ἰωάσαφ πρὸς αὐτὸν εἶπε· Καὶ τίς ἡ ἀγαθὴ ἐλπὶς ἐκείνη, ἧς ἔφης χωρὶς βαπτίσματος μὴ ἐπιτυγχάνειν; τίς δέ ἐστιν ἥνπερ βασιλείαν τῶν οὐρανῶν ἀποκαλεῖς; πόθεν δὲ τὰ τοῦ ἐνανθρωπήσαντος Θεοῦ ῥήματα σὺ ἀκήκοας; τίς δὲ ἡ τοῦ θανάτου ἄδηλος προθεσμία, περὶ ἧς μέριμνα πολλή, τῇ καρδίᾳ μου ἐνσκήψασα, ἐν λύπαις καὶ ὀδύναις δαπανᾷ μου τὰς σάρκας, καὶ αὐτῶν δὴ τῶν ὀστέων καθάπτεται; καὶ εἰ τεθνηξόμενοι εἰς τὸ μὴ ὂν διαλυθῶμεν οἱ ἄνθρωποι, ἢ ἔστιν ἄλλη τις βιοτὴ μετὰ τὴν ἐντεῦθεν ἐκδημίαν; ταῦτα καὶ τούτοις ἑπόμενα μαθεῖν ἐπεθύμουν.

Ὁ δὲ Βαρλαὰμ τοιαύτας τούτοις ἐδίδου τὰς 60
ἀποκρίσεις· Ἡ μὲν ἀγαθὴ ἐλπίς, ἣν εἴρηκα, τῆς βασιλείας ἐστὶ τῶν οὐρανῶν· αὕτη δὲ γλώσσῃ βροτείᾳ τὸ παράπαν ὑπάρχει ἀνέκφραστος· φησὶ
Is. lxiv. 4 γὰρ ἡ Γραφή· Ἃ ὀφθαλμὸς οὐκ εἶδε, καὶ οὖς οὐκ
1 Cor. ii. 9 ἤκουσε, καὶ ἐπὶ καρδίαν ἀνθρώπου οὐκ ἀνέβη, ἃ ἡτοίμασεν ὁ Θεὸς τοῖς ἀγαπῶσιν αὐτόν. ὅταν δὲ ἀξιωθῶμεν, τὸ παχὺ τοῦτο ἀποθέμενοι σαρκίον, τῆς μακαριότητος ἐκείνης ἐπιτυχεῖν, τότε αὐτός, ὁ καταξιώσας ἡμᾶς μὴ διαμαρτεῖν τῆς ἐλπίδος, διδάξει καὶ γνωριεῖ τῶν ἀγαθῶν ἐκείνων τὴν πάντα νοῦν ὑπερέχουσαν δόξαν, τὸ ἄφραστον φῶς, τὴν μὴ διακοπτομένην ζωήν, τὴν μετὰ ἀγγέλων διαγωγήν. εἰ γὰρ ἀξιωθῶμεν Θεῷ συγγενέσθαι καθ' ὅσον ἐφικτὸν ἀνθρωπίνῃ φύσει, πάντα εἰσόμεθα παρ' αὐτοῦ ἃ νῦν οὐκ ἴσμεν. τοῦτο γὰρ ἐγώ, ἐκ τῆς τῶν θεοπνεύστων Γραφῶν μεμυημένος

herein, for delay is parlous, because of the uncertainty of the appointed day of death.'

Ioasaph said unto him, 'And what is this good hope whereto thou sayest it is impossible without baptism to attain? And what this kingdom which thou callest the kingdom of Heaven? And how cometh it that thou hast heard the words of God incarnate? And what is the uncertain day of death? For on this account much anxiety hath fallen on my heart, and consumeth my flesh in pain and grief, and fasteneth on my very bones. And shall we men, appointed to die, return to nothing, or is there some other life after our departure hence? These and kindred questions I have been longing to resolve.'

Ioasaph questioneth Barlaam yet further

Thus questioned he; and Barlaam answered thus: 'The good hope, whereof I spake, is that of the kingdom of Heaven. But that kingdom is far beyond the utterance of mortal tongue; for the Scripture saith, "Eye hath not seen, nor ear heard, neither have entered into the heart of man the things which God hath prepared for them that love him." But when we have shuffled off this gross flesh, and attained to that blessedness, then will that Master, which hath granted to us not to fail of this hope, teach and make known unto us the glory of those good things, whose glory passeth all understanding:—that light ineffable, that life that hath no ending, that converse with Angels. For if it be granted us to hold communion with God, so far as is attainable to human nature, then shall we know all things from his lips which now we know not. This doth my initiation into the teaching of the divine Scriptures teach me

Barlaam telleth of future felicity,

διδαχῆς, πάντων μάλιστα βασιλείαν οὐρανῶν
τίθεμαι, τὸ πλησίον γενέσθαι τῇ θεωρίᾳ τῆς ἁγίας
1 Tim. vi. 16 καὶ ζωαρχικῆς Τριάδος, καὶ τῷ ἀπροσίτῳ φωτὶ
αὐτῆς ἐλλαμφθῆναι, τρανότερόν τε καὶ καθαρώ- 61
τερον καὶ ἀνακεκαλυμμένῳ προσώπῳ τὴν ἄρρητον
2 Cor. iii. 18 αὐτῆς δόξαν κατοπτρίζεσθαι. εἰ δὲ μὴ δυνατὸν
τὴν δόξαν ἐκείνην καὶ τὸ φῶς καὶ τὰ ἀπόρρητα
ἀγαθὰ παραστῆσαι λόγῳ, θαυμαστὸν οὐδέν· οὐκ
ἂν γὰρ ἦσαν μεγάλα καὶ ἐξαίρετα, εἴ γε ἡμῖν, τοῖς
ἐπιγείοις καὶ φθαρτοῖς καὶ τὸ βαρὺ τοῦτο καὶ
ἐμπαθὲς σαρκίον περικειμένοις, τῷ λογισμῷ τε
κατελαμβάνοντο καὶ τῷ λόγῳ παριστῶντο. οὕτω
μὲν οὖν δὴ περὶ τούτων εἰδὼς τῇ πίστει μόνῃ,
δέχου ἀνενδοιάστως μηδὲν πεπλασμένον ἔχειν,
καὶ δι' ἔργων ἀγαθῶν ἐπείχθητι τῆς ἀθανάτου
βασιλείας ἐκείνης ἐπιλαβέσθαι, ἧσπερ ὅταν ἐπι-
τύχῃς, μαθήσῃ τὸ τέλειον.

Περὶ ὧν δὲ ἠρώτησας, πῶς ἡμεῖς τοὺς λόγους
τοῦ σαρκωθέντος Θεοῦ ἀκηκόαμεν, διὰ τῶν ἱερῶν
Εὐαγγελίων ἴσθι πάντα τὰ τῆς θεανδρικῆς οἰκονομίας ἡμᾶς μεμαθηκέναι. οὕτω γὰρ ἡ ἁγία δέλτος
ἐκείνη κέκληται, ὡς ἅτε ἀθανασίαν καὶ ἀφθαρσίαν καὶ ζωὴν αἰώνιον καὶ ἁμαρτιῶν ἄφεσιν καὶ
βασιλείαν οὐρανῶν τοῖς θνητοῖς ἡμῖν καὶ φθαρτοῖς
καὶ ἐπιγείοις εὐαγγελιζομένη ἥνπερ γεγράφασιν 62
Luke i. 2 οἱ αὐτόπται καὶ ὑπηρέται τοῦ Λόγου, οὓς ἀνωτέρω
εἴρηκα, ὅτι μαθητὰς καὶ ἀποστόλους ὁ Σωτὴρ
ἡμῶν Χριστὸς ἐξελέξατο· καὶ παρέδωκαν ἡμῖν
ἐγγράφως, μετὰ τὴν ἔνδοξον τοῦ Δεσπότου εἰς
οὐρανοὺς ἄνοδον, τῆς ἐπὶ γῆς αὐτοῦ πολιτείας τάς
τε διδασκαλίας αὐτοῦ καὶ τὰ θαύματα, κατὰ τὸ
ἐγχωροῦν γραφῇ παραδοῦναι. οὕτω γὰρ πρὸς

to be the real meaning of the kingdom of Heaven; to approach the vision of the blessed and life-giving Trinity, and to be illumined with his unapproachable light, and with clearer and purer sight, and with unveiled face, to behold as in a glass his unspeakable glory. But, if it be impossible to express in language that glory, that light, and those mysterious blessings, what marvel? For they had not been mighty and singular, if they had been comprehended by reason and expressed in words by us who are earthly, and corruptible, and clothed in this heavy garment of sinful flesh. Holding then such knowledge in simple faith, believe thou undoubtingly, that these are no fictions; but by good works be urgent to lay hold on that immortal kingdom, to which when thou hast attained, thou shalt have perfect knowledge.

'As touching thy question, How it is that we have heard the words of the Incarnate God, know thou that we have been taught all that appertaineth to the divine Incarnation by the Holy Gospels, for thus that holy book is called, because it telleth us, who are corruptible and earthly, the "good spell" of immortality and incorruption, of life eternal, of the remission of sins, and of the kingdom of heaven. This book was written by the eye-witnesses and ministers of the Word, and of these I have already said that our Lord Jesus Christ chose them for disciples and apostles; and they delivered it unto us in writing, after the glorious Ascension of our Master into Heaven, a record of his life on earth, his teachings and miracles, so far as it was possible to commit them to writing. For thus, toward the end of his volume, saith he

of the Holy Gospels,

τῷ τέλει τοῦ λόγου ὁ ἐξαίρετος τῶν θείων ἐκείνων
John xxi. 25 εὐαγγελιστῶν εἴρηκεν· Ἔστι, φησί, καὶ ἄλλα
πολλὰ ὅσα ἐποίησεν ὁ Ἰησοῦς, ἅτινα ἐὰν γράφη-
ται καθ' ἓν οὐδὲ αὐτὸν οἶμαι τὸν κόσμον χωρῆσαι
τὰ γραφόμενα βιβλία.

Ἐν τούτῳ οὖν τῷ θειοτάτῳ Εὐαγγελίῳ ἐμφέρε-
ται τῆς τε σαρκώσεως, τῆς τε ἀναδείξεως, τῶν τε
θαυμάτων, τῶν τε πραγμάτων αὐτοῦ ἡ ἱστορία
Πνεύματι Θεοῦ γεγραμμένη, ἔπειτα καὶ περὶ τοῦ
ἀχράντου πάθους οὗπερ ὑπέμεινε δι' ἡμᾶς ὁ
Κύριος, τῆς τε ἁγίας καὶ τριημέρου ἐγέρσεως, καὶ
τῆς εἰς οὐρανοὺς ἀνόδου, πρὸς δὲ καὶ τῆς ἐνδόξου
καὶ φοβερᾶς αὐτοῦ δευτέρας παρουσίας. μέλλει
Mat. xxv. 31 γὰρ πάλιν ὁ Υἱὸς τοῦ Θεοῦ ἐλθεῖν ἐπὶ τῆς γῆς,
1 Thes. iv. 16 μετὰ δόξης ἀρρήτου καὶ πλήθους τῆς οὐρανίου
Rev. xx. 13 στρατιᾶς, κρῖναι τὸ γένος ἡμῶν καὶ ἀποδοῦναι
ἑκάστῳ κατὰ τὰ ἔργα αὐτοῦ. τὸν γὰρ ἄνθρωπον
Gen. ii. 7 ἐξ ἀρχῆς ὁ Θεὸς ἐκ γῆς διαπλάσας, καθὰ δὴ καὶ
προλαβὼν εἶπόν σοι, ἐνεφύσησεν εἰς αὐτὸν πνοήν,
ἥτις ψυχὴ λογική τε καὶ νοερὰ προσαγορεύεται· 63
ἐπεὶ δὲ θάνατον κατεκρίθημεν, ἀποθνήσκομεν
πάντες, καὶ οὐκ ἔστι τὸ ποτήριον τοῦτό τινα τῶν
ἀνθρώπων παραδραμεῖν· ἔστι δὲ ὁ θάνατος
χωρισμὸς ψυχῆς ἀπὸ τοῦ σώματος. ἐκεῖνο
μὲν οὖν τὸ ἐκ γῆς διαπλασθὲν σῶμα, χωρισθὲν
τῆς ψυχῆς, εἰς γῆν ὑποστρέφει, ἐξ ἧσπερ καὶ
ἐλήφθη, καὶ φθειρόμενον διαλύεται· ἡ δὲ ψυχή,
ἀθάνατος οὖσα, πορεύεται ἔνθα κελεύει ὁ Δημιουργός, μᾶλλον δὲ καθὼς αὐτὴ προητοίμασεν
ἑαυτῇ κατάλυμα ἔτι τῷ σαρκίῳ συνοῦσα. καθὼς
γάρ τις πολιτεύσηται ἐνταῦθα, μέλλει ἀπολαμ-
βάνειν ἐκεῖθεν.

that is the flower of the holy Evangelists, "And there are also many other things which Jesus did, the which, if they should be written every one, I suppose that even the world itself could not contain the books that should be written."

'So in this heavenly Gospel, written by the Spirit of God, is recorded the history of his Incarnation, his manifestation, his miracles and acts. Afterward, it telleth of the innocent suffering which the Lord endured for our sake, of his holy Resurrection on the third day, his Ascent into the heavens, and of his glorious and dreadful second coming; for the Son of God shall come again on earth, with unspeakable glory, and with a multitude of the heavenly host to judge our race, and to reward every man according to his works. For, at the beginning, God created man out of earth, as I have already told thee, and breathed into him breath, which is called a reasonable and understanding soul. But since we were sentenced to death, we die all: and it is not possible for this cup to pass any man by. Now death is the separation of the soul from the body. And that body which was formed out of earth, when severed from the soul, returneth to earth from whence also it was taken, and, decaying, perisheth; but the soul, being immortal, fareth whither her Maker calleth, or rather to the place where she, while still in the body, hath prepared for herself lodgement. For as a man hath lived here, so shall he receive reward there.

of the second coming of our Lord,

Εἶτα μετὰ πλείστους χρόνους ἐλεύσεται Χριστὸς ὁ Θεὸς ἡμῶν κρῖναι τὸν κόσμον ἐν δόξῃ
φοβερᾷ καὶ ἀνεκδιηγήτῳ, οὗ τῷ φόβῳ αἱ δυνά-
Luke xxi. 26 μεις τῶν οὐρανῶν σαλευθήσονται, καὶ πᾶσαι αἱ
στρατιαὶ τῶν ἀγγέλων τρόμῳ παρίστανται ἐνώ-
1 Thess. iv. 16 πιον αὐτοῦ. τότε ἐν φωνῇ ἀρχαγγέλου καὶ ἐν
σάλπιγγι Θεοῦ ἀναστήσονται οἱ νεκροί, καὶ παραστήσονται τῷ φοβερῷ αὐτοῦ θρόνῳ. ἔστι δὲ ἡ
ἀνάστασις συνάφεια πάλιν ψυχῆς τε καὶ σώματος.
Job. xix. 26 αὐτὸ οὖν τὸ σῶμα, τὸ φθειρόμενον καὶ διαλυό-
μενον, αὐτὸ ἀναστήσεται ἄφθαρτον. καὶ μηδαμῶς
σοι ἀπιστίας λογισμὸς περὶ τούτου ἐπέλθοι· οὐκ
ἀδυνατεῖ γὰρ τῷ ἐξ ἀρχῆς ἐκ τῆς γῆς διαπλά- 64
Ezek. xxxvii. 1–14 σαντι αὐτό, εἶτα ἀποστραφὲν εἰς γῆν ἐξ ἧς
ἐλήφθη, κατὰ τὴν τοῦ Δημιουργοῦ ἀπόφασιν,
αὖθις ἀναστῆσαι. εἰ γὰρ ἐννοήσεις πόσα ἐξ οὐκ
ὄντων ἐποίησεν ὁ Θεός, ἱκανή σοι ἔσται αὕτη
ἀπόδειξις. καὶ γὰρ γῆν λαβὼν ἐποίησεν ἄνθρωπον, γῆν οὐκ οὖσαν πρότερον· πῶς οὖν ἡ γῆ
γέγονεν ἄνθρωπος; πῶς δὲ αὕτη οὐκ οὖσα παρή-
γετο; ποίαν δὲ ὑποβάθραν ἔχει; πῶς δὲ ἐξ αὐτῆς
παρήχθησαν τὰ τῶν ἀλόγων ἄπειρα γένη, τὰ
τῶν σπερμάτων, τὰ τῶν φυτῶν; ἀλλὰ καὶ νῦν
κατανόησον ἐπὶ τῆς γεννήσεως τῆς ἡμετέρας· οὐ
σπέρμα βραχὺ ἐνίεται εἰς τὴν ὑποδεχομένην
μήτραν αὐτό; πόθεν οὖν ἡ τοσαύτη τοῦ ζώου
διάπλασις;

Τῷ οὖν ταῦτα πάντα δημιουργήσαντι ἐκ μὴ ὄντων καὶ ἔτι δημιουργοῦντι οὐκ ἀδύνατον ἐκ γῆς τὰ νενεκρωμένα καὶ διαφθαρέντα σώματα ἀναστῆσαι, ἵνα ἕκαστος ἀπολάβῃ κατὰ τὰ ἔργα αὐτοῦ· Ἐργασίας γάρ, φησίν, ὁ παρὼν καιρός, ὁ

'Then, after long seasons, Christ our God shall come to judge the world in awful glory, beyond words to tell; and for fear of him the powers of heaven shall be shaken, and all the angel hosts stand beside him in dread. Then, at the voice of the archangel, and at the trump of God, shall the dead arise and stand before his awful throne. Now the Resurrection is the re-uniting of soul and body. So that very body, which decayeth and perisheth, shall arise incorruptible. And concerning this, beware lest the reasoning of unbelief overtake thee; for it is not impossible for him, who at the beginning formed the body out of earth, when according to its Maker's doom it hath returned to earth whence it was taken, to raise the same again. If thou wilt but consider how many things God hath made out of nothing, this proof shall suffice thee. He took earth and made man, though earth was not man before. How then did earth become man? And how was earth, that did not exist, produced? And what foundation hath it? And how were countless kind of things without reason, of seeds and plants, produced out of it! Nay, now also consider the manner of our birth. Is not a little seed thrown into the womb that receiveth it? Whence then cometh such a marvellous fashioning of a living creature?

of the Resurrection of the dead,

created out of nothingness;

'So for him, who hath made everything out of nothing, and still doth make, it is not impossible to raise deadened and corrupt bodies from the earth, that every man may be rewarded according to his works; for he saith, "The present is the time for

of the day of judgement

Nazianz. Orat. ix. p. 152 δὲ μέλλων ἀνταποδόσεως. ἐπεὶ ποῦ τὸ δίκαιον τοῦ Θεοῦ, εἰ μὴ ἀνάστασις ἦν; πολλοὶ γάρ, δίκαιοι ὄντες, πολλὰ ἐν τῷ παρόντι βίῳ κακουχηθέντες καὶ τιμωρηθέντες βιαίως ἀνῃρέθησαν· ἔνιοι δέ, ἀσεβεῖς ὄντες καὶ παράνομοι, ἐν τρυφῇ καὶ εὐημερίᾳ τὴν παροῦσαν ζωὴν ἀνήλωσαν· ὁ δὲ Θεός, ἐπειδὴ ἀγαθός ἐστι καὶ δίκαιος, ὥρισεν ἡμέραν ἀναστάσεως καὶ ἐτάσεως, ἵνα, ἀπολαβοῦσα ἑκάστη ψυχὴ τὸ ἴδιον σῶμα, ὁ μὲν κακός, ἐνταῦθα τὰ ἀγαθὰ ἀπολαβών, ἐκεῖ περὶ ὧν ἥμαρτε κολασθῇ, ὁ δὲ ἀγαθός, ἐνταῦθα τιμωρηθεὶς περὶ ὧν ἥμαρτεν, ἐκεῖ τῶν ἀγαθῶν κληρονόμος γένηται· [John v. 25, 28] Ἀκούσονται γάρ, φησὶν ὁ Κύριος, οἱ ἐν τοῖς μνημείοις τῆς φωνῆς τοῦ Υἱοῦ τοῦ Θεοῦ, καὶ ἐξελεύσονται οἱ τὰ ἀγαθὰ ποιήσαντες εἰς ἀνάστασιν ζωῆς, οἱ δὲ τὰ φαῦλα πράξαντες εἰς [Dan. vii. 9] ἀνάστασιν κρίσεως, ἡνίκα καὶ θρόνοι τεθήσονται, καὶ ὁ Παλαίος τῶν ἡμερῶν καὶ πάντων Δημιουργὸς προκαθίσει, καὶ βίβλοι ἀνοιγήσονται [Rev. xx. 12] πάντων ἡμῶν τὰς πράξεις, τοὺς λόγους, τὰς ἐνθυμήσεις ἐγγεγραμμένας ἔχουσαι, καὶ ποταμὸς πυρὸς ἕλκεται, καὶ πάντα τὰ κεκρυμμένα ἀνα- [Greg. Naz. Orat. xv. p. 230] καλύπτονται. οὐδεὶς ἐκεῖ συνήγορος, ἢ πιθανότης ῥημάτων, ἢ ψευδὴς ἀπολογία, ἢ πλούτου δυναστεία, ἢ ἀξιωμάτων ὄγκος, ἢ δώρων ἄφθονοι δόσεις, κλέψαι τὴν ὀρθὴν κρίσιν ἰσχύουσιν· ἀλλ' ὁ ἀδέκαστος ἐκεῖνος καὶ ἀληθινὸς δικαστὴς ζυγοῖς δικαιοσύνης πάντα διακρινεῖ, καὶ πρᾶξιν καὶ [John v. 29] λόγον καὶ διανόημα. καὶ πορεύσονται οἱ τὰ ἀγαθὰ ποιήσαντες εἰς ζωὴν αἰώνιον, εἰς τὸ φῶς [Mk. xii. 25] τὸ ἀνεκφράστου, μετὰ ἀγγέλων εὐφραινόμενοι, τῶν ἀπορρήτων ἀγαθῶν ἀπολαύοντες, καὶ τῇ

work, the future for recompense." Else, where were the justice of God, if there were no Resurrection? Many righteous men in this present life have suffered much ill-usage and torment, and have died violent deaths; and the impious and the law-breaker hath spent his days here in luxury and prosperity. But God, who is good and just, hath appointed a day of resurrection and inquisition, that each soul may receive her own body, and that the wicked, who received his good things here, may there be punished for his misdeeds, and that the good, who was here chastised for his misdeeds, may there inherit his bliss. For, saith the Lord, "They that are in the graves shall hear the voice of the Son of God, and shall come forth; they that have done good unto the resurrection of life, and they that have done evil unto the resurrection of doom." Then also shall thrones be set, and the Ancient of days and Maker of all things shall sit as Judge, and there shall be opened books with records of the deeds and words and thoughts of all of us, and a fiery stream shall issue, and all hidden things shall be revealed. There can no advocate, no persuasive words, no false excuse, no mightiness of riches, no pomp of rank, no lavishment of bribes, avail to pervert righteous judgement. For he, the uncorrupt and truthful Judge, shall weigh everything in the balance of justice, every act, word and thought. And they that have done good shall go into life everlasting, into light unspeakable, rejoicing in the fellowship of the Angels, to enjoy bliss ineffable, standing

of the joy of the righteous,

Mat. xxv. 30 ἁγίᾳ Τριάδι καθαρῶς παριστάμενοι· οἱ δὲ τὰ 66
Is. lxvi. 24 φαῦλα πράξαντες καὶ πάντες οἱ ἀσεβεῖς καὶ
Mat. xxv. 30 Mk. ix. 43 ἁμαρτωλοὶ εἰς κόλασιν αἰώνιον, ἥτις γέεννα
Mat. xiii. 42 Luke xiii. 28 λέγεται καὶ σκότος ἐξώτερον, καὶ σκώληξ ἀκοίμητος, καὶ βρυγμὸς ὀδόντων, καὶ ἄλλα μυρία
κολαστήρια, μᾶλλον δέ, τὸ πάντων χαλεπώτατον,
τὸ ἀλλοτριωθῆναι ἀπὸ Θεοῦ καὶ ἀπερρῖφθαι τοῦ
γλυκυτάτου προσώπου αὐτοῦ, καὶ τῆς δόξης
ἐκείνης στερηθῆναι τῆς ἀνεκδιηγήτου, καὶ τὸ
παραδειγματισθῆναι ἐπὶ πάσης τῆς κτίσεως, καὶ
Dan. xii. 2 τὸ αἰσχυνθῆναι αἰσχύνην πέρας οὐκ ἔχουσαν.
μετὰ γὰρ τὸ δοθῆναι τὴν φρικτὴν ἐκείνην ἀπό-
Luke xvi. 26 φασιν, πάντα ἄτρεπτα μενεῖ καὶ ἀναλλοίωτα,
Mat. xxv. 46 μήτε τῆς τῶν δικαίων φαιδρᾶς διαγωγῆς ἐχούσης
τέλος, μήτε τῆς τῶν ἁμαρτωλῶν ταλαιπωρίας καὶ
κολάσεως λαμβανούσης πέρας· οὔτε γὰρ κριτὴς
μετ᾽ ἐκεῖνον ὑψηλότερος, οὔτε ἀπολογία δι᾽ ἔργων
δευτέρων, οὐ προθεσμία μεταποιήσεως, οὐκ ἄλλη
τις μέθοδος τοῖς κολαζομένοις, συνδιαιωνιζούσης
αὐτοῖς τῆς τιμωρίας.

2 Pet. iii. 11 Τούτων οὕτως ἐχόντων, ποταποὺς δεῖ ὑπάρχειν
ἡμᾶς ἐν ἁγίαις ἀναστροφαῖς καὶ εὐσεβέσι πολι-
τείαις, ἵνα καταξιωθῶμεν ἐκφυγεῖν τὴν μέλλουσαν
Mat. xxv. 33, 34 ἀπειλὴν καὶ σταθῆναι ἐκ δεξιῶν τοῦ Υἱοῦ τοῦ
Θεοῦ; αὕτη γὰρ ἡ στάσις τῶν δικαίων· τοῖς δὲ
ἁμαρτωλοῖς ἡ ἐξ εὐωνύμων ἀποκεκλήρωται παν-
αθλία μερίς. ἐκεῖθεν δὲ τοὺς μὲν δικαίους εὐλο- 67
γημένους ἀποκαλῶν ὁ Δεσπότης εἰς τὴν ἀτελεύτητον βασιλείαν εἰσάγει, τοὺς δὲ ἁμαρτωλούς, μετ᾽
ὀργῆς καὶ ἀρᾶς ἐκβαλὼν τοῦ προσώπου αὐτοῦ τοῦ
ἡμέρου καὶ γαληνοῦ, τὸ πάντων πικρότατον ἅμα
καὶ χαλεπώτατον, εἰς κόλασιν ἐκπέμπει αἰώνιον.

in purity before the Holy Trinity. But they that have done evil, and all the ungodly and sinners, shall go into everlasting punishment, which is called Gehenna, and outer darkness, and the worm that dieth not, and the gnashing of teeth, and a thousand other names of punishment; which meaneth rather—bitterest of all,—alienation from God, the being cast away from the sweetness of his presence, the being deprived of that glory which baffleth description, the being made a spectacle unto the whole creation, and the being put to shame, and shame that hath no ending. For, after the passing of that terrible sentence, all things shall abide immutable and unchangeable. The blissful life of the righteous shall have no close, neither shall the misery and punishment of sinners find an end: because, after him, there is no higher Judge, and no defence by after-works, no time for amendment, no other way for them that are punished, their vengeance being co-eternal with them.

'Seeing that this is so, what manner of persons ought we to be in all holy conversation and godliness, that we may be counted worthy to escape the wrath to come, and to be ranged on the right hand of the Son of God? For this is the station of the righteous: but to sinners is allotted the station of misery on the left. Then shall the Lord call the righteous "Blessed," and shall lead them into his everlasting kingdom. But, as for sinners, with anger and curse he will banish them from his serene and gentle countenance—the bitterest and hardest lot of all—and will send them away into everlasting punishment.'

and of the doom of sinners

IX

Ὁ δὲ Ἰωάσαφ πρὸς αὐτὸν ἔφη. Μεγάλα τινὰ
καὶ θαυμαστὰ πράγματα λέγεις μοι, ἄνθρωπε,
Cp. Ps. lv. 5; Is. xix. 16 φόβου πολλοῦ καὶ τρόμου ἄξια, εἰ ταῦτά γε
οὕτως ἔχει, καὶ ἔστι πάλιν, μετὰ τὸ ἀποθανεῖν
καὶ εἰς τέφραν καὶ κόνιν διαλυθῆναι, ἀνάστασις
καὶ παλιγγενεσία, ἀμοιβαί τε καὶ εὔθυναι τῶν βεβιωμένων. ἀλλὰ τίς ἡ τούτων ἀπόδειξις; καὶ πῶς,
τὸ τέως μὴ θεαθὲν μαθόντες, οὕτως ἀραρότως
καὶ ἀναμφιλέκτως ἐπιστεύσατε; τὰ μὲν γὰρ ἤδη
πραχθέντα καὶ ἔργοις φανερωθέντα, κἂν αὐτοὶ
οὐκ εἴδετε, ἀλλὰ τῶν ἱστορησάντων ἠκούσατε·
πῶς δέ, καὶ περὶ τῶν μελλόντων τοιαῦτα μεγάλα
καὶ ὑπέρογκα κηρύττοντες, ἀσφαλῆ τὴν περὶ
αὐτῶν κέκτησθε πληροφορίαν;

Καί φησιν ὁ Βαρλαάμ· Ἐκ τῶν ἤδη πραχθέντων
ἐκτησάμην καὶ τῶν μελλόντων τὴν πληροφορίαν·
οἱ γὰρ ταῦτα κηρύξαντες ἐν οὐδενὶ τῆς ἀληθείας
διαμαρτόντες, ἀλλὰ σημείοις καὶ τέρασι καὶ ποικίλαις δυνάμεσι τὰ λεχθέντα ἐμπεδωσάμενοι, αὐτοὶ
καὶ περὶ τῶν μελλόντων εἰσηγήσαντο. ὥσπερ 68
οὖν ἐνταῦθα οὐδὲν σκαιὸν καὶ πεπλασμένον
ἐδίδαξαν, ἀλλὰ πάντα φαιδρότερον ἡλίου ἔλαμψαν ὅσα τε εἶπον καὶ ἐποίησαν, οὕτω κἀκεῖ
ἀληθινὰ ἐδογμάτισαν· ἅτινα καὶ αὐτὸς ὁ Κύριος
ἡμῶν καὶ δεσπότης Ἰησοῦς Χριστὸς λόγῳ τε καὶ
John v. 25, 28 ἔργῳ ἐπιστώσατο. Ἀμὴν γάρ, φησί, λέγω ὑμῖν
ὅτι ἔρχεται ὥρα, ἐν ᾗ πάντες οἱ ἐν τοῖς μνημείοις
ἀκούσονται τῆς φωνῆς τοῦ Υἱοῦ τοῦ Θεοῦ, καὶ οἱ
ἀκούσαντες ζήσονται· καὶ αὖθις· Ἔρχεται ὥρα,

IX

IOASAPH said unto him, 'Great and marvellous, sir, are the things whereof thou tellest me, fearful and terrible, if indeed these things be so, and, if there be after death and dissolution into dust and ashes, a resurrection and re-birth, and rewards and punishments for the deeds done during life. But what is the proof thereof? And how have ye come to learn that which ye have not seen, that ye have so steadfastly and undoubtingly believed it? As for things that have already been done and made manifest in deed, though ye saw them not, yet have ye heard them from the writers of history. But, when it is of the future that ye preach tidings of such vast import, how have ye made your conviction on these matters sure?'

Ioasaph desireth proof of these sayings.

Quoth Barlaam, 'From the past I gain certainty about the future; for they that preached the Gospel, without erring from the truth, but establishing their sayings by signs and wonders and divers miracles, themselves also spake of the future. So, as in the one case they taught us nothing amiss or false, but made all that they said and did to shine clearer than the sun, so also in the other matter they gave us true doctrine, even that which our Lord and Master Jesus Christ himself confirmed both by word and deed. "Verily," he spake, "I say unto you, the hour is coming in the which all that are in the graves shall hear the voice of the Son of God and they that hear shall live:" and again, "The hour

Barlaam confirmeth them with the words of the Scriptures,

ὅτε οἱ νεκροὶ ἀκούσονται τῆς φωνῆς αὐτοῦ, καὶ
ἐκπορεύσονται, οἱ τὰ ἀγαθὰ ποιήσαντες εἰς ἀνάστασιν ζωῆς, οἱ δὲ τὰ φαῦλα πράξαντες εἰς ἀνά-
Mk. xii. 26, στασιν κρίσεως· καὶ πάλιν περὶ τῆς ἀναστάσεώς
27; Luke φησι τῶν νεκρῶν· Οὐκ ἀνέγνωτε τὸ ῥηθὲν ὑμῖν
xx. 37, 38 ὑπὸ τοῦ Θεοῦ λέγοντος· ἐγώ εἰμι ὁ Θεὸς Ἀβραὰμ
καὶ ὁ Θεὸς Ἰσαὰκ καὶ ὁ Θεὸς Ἰακώβ; οὐκ ἔστιν
ὁ Θεὸς Θεὸς νεκρῶν, ἀλλὰ ζώντων· Ὥσπερ γὰρ
συλλέγεται τὰ ζιζάνια καὶ πυρὶ καίεται, οὕτως
Mat. xiii. ἔσται ἐν τῇ συντελείᾳ αἰῶνος τούτου· ἀποστελεῖ
40–43 ὁ Υἱὸς τοῦ Θεοῦ τοὺς ἀγγέλους αὐτοῦ καὶ συλλέ-
ξουσι πάντα τὰ σκάνδαλα καὶ τοὺς ποιοῦντας τὴν
ἀνομίαν, καὶ βαλοῦσιν αὐτοὺς εἰς τὴν κάμινον
τοῦ πυρός· ἐκεῖ ἔσται ὁ κλαυθμὸς καὶ ὁ βρυγμὸς
τῶν ὀδόντων· τότε οἱ δίκαιοι ἐκλάμψουσιν ὡς ὁ
ἥλιος ἐν τῇ βασιλείᾳ τοῦ Πατρὸς αὐτῶν. ταῦτα
εἰπών, προσέθετο· Ὁ ἔχων ὦτα ἀκούειν ἀκουέτω.

Τοιούτοις μὲν λόγοις καὶ ἑτέροις πλείοσι
τὴν τῶν σωμάτων ἡμῶν ἀνάστασιν ὁ Κύριος 69
ἐφανέρωσεν· ἔργῳ δὲ τοὺς λόγους ἐπιστώσατο,
πολλοὺς ἐγείρας νεκρούς, πρὸς δὲ τῷ τέλει τῆς
John xi. ἐπὶ γῆς αὐτοῦ πολιτείας, καὶ τεταρταῖον ἤδη
1–46 καταφθαρέντα καὶ ὀδωδότα Λάζαρόν τινα φίλον
ἑαυτοῦ ἐκ τοῦ μνήματος καλέσας, καὶ ζῶντα τὸν
ἄπνουν παραστησάμενος. ἐπὶ τούτοις δὲ καὶ
1 Cor. xv. 23 αὐτὸς ὁ Κύριος ἀπαρχὴ τῆς τελείας καὶ μηκέτι
θανάτῳ ὑποπιπτούσης ἀναστάσεως γέγονε, σαρκὶ
τοῦ θανάτου γευσάμενος, ἀναστὰς δὲ τριήμερος
Col. i. 18 καὶ τῶν νεκρῶν πρωτότοκος γενόμενος. ἠγέρθησαν μὲν γὰρ καὶ ἄλλοι ἐκ τῶν νεκρῶν, ἀλλ' αὖθις
ἀπέθανον καὶ οὐκ ἔφθασαν εἰκόνα τῆς μελλούσης
ἀληθινῆς ἀναστάσεως παραστῆσαι· μόνος δὲ

cometh when the dead shall hear his voice, and shall come forth, they that have done good unto the resurrection of life, and they that have done evil unto the resurrection of damnation." And again he said concerning the resurrection of the dead, "Have ye not read that which was spoken unto you by God, saying, I am the God of Abraham, and the God of Isaac, and the God of Jacob. God is not the God of the dead but of the living." "For as the tares are gathered and burned in the fire, so shall it be in the end of this age. The Son of God shall send forth his Angels, and they shall gather all things that offend, and them which do iniquity, and shall cast them into the furnace of fire; there shall be wailing and gnashing of teeth. Then shall the righteous shine forth as the sun in the kingdom of their father." Thus spake he and added this thereto, "Who hath ears to hear, let him hear."

'In such words and many more did the Lord make manifest the resurrection of our bodies, and confirm his words in deed, by raising many that were dead. And, toward the end of his life upon earth, he called from the grave one Lazarus his friend, that had already been four days dead and stank, and thus he restored the lifeless to life. Moreover, the Lord himself became the first-fruits of that resurrection which is final and no longer subject unto death, after he had in the flesh tasted of death; and on the third day he rose again, and became the first-born from the dead. For other men also were raised from the dead, but died once more, and might not yet attain to the likeness of the future true resurrection. But he alone was the

with the ensample of Lazarus,

αὐτὸς τῆς ἀναστάσεως ἐκείνης ἀρχηγὸς ἐγένετο, πρῶτος τὴν ἀθάνατον ἐγερθεὶς ἀνάστασιν. ταῦτα (Luke i. 2) καὶ οἱ ἀπ' ἀρχῆς αὐτόπται καὶ ὑπηρέται γενόμενοι τοῦ λόγου ἐκήρυξαν. φησὶ γὰρ ὁ μακάριος (Gal. i. 1) Παῦλος, οὗ ἡ κλῆσις οὐκ ἐξ ἀνθρώπων, ἀλλ' (1 Cor. xv. 1 ff.) οὐρανόθεν γέγονε· Γνωρίζω ὑμῖν, ἀδελφοί, τὸ Εὐαγγέλιον ὃ εὐηγγελισάμην ὑμῖν· παρέδωκα γὰρ ὑμῖν ἐν πρώτοις ὃ καὶ παρέλαβον, ὅτι Χριστὸς ἀπέθανεν ὑπὲρ τῶν ἁμαρτιῶν ἡμῶν, κατὰ τὰς Γραφάς· εἰ δὲ Χριστὸς κηρύσσεται, ὅτι ἐκ νεκρῶν ἐγήγερται, πῶς λέγουσί τινες ὅτι ἀνάστασις οὐκ ἔστιν; εἰ γὰρ νεκροὶ οὐκ ἐγείρονται, οὐδὲ Χριστὸς ἐγήγερται· εἰ δὲ Χριστὸς οὐκ ἐγήγερται, ματαία ἡ πίστις ἡμῶν, ἔτι ἐστὲ ἐν ταῖς ἀνομίαις ὑμῶν· εἰ ἐν τῇ ζωῇ ταύτῃ ἠλπικότες ἐσμὲν ἐν Χριστῷ μόνον, ἐλεεινότεροι πάντων ἀνθρώπων ἐσμέν. νυνὶ δὲ Χριστὸς ἐγήγερται ἐκ νεκρῶν, ἀπαρχὴ τῶν κεκοιμημένων γενόμενος· ἐπειδὴ γὰρ δι' ἀνθρώπου ὁ θάνατος, καὶ δι' ἀνθρώπου ἀνάστασις νεκρῶν· ὥσπερ γὰρ ἐν τῷ Ἀδὰμ πάντες ἀποθνήσκουσιν, οὕτω καὶ ἐν τῷ Χριστῷ πάντες ζωοποιηθήσονται. καὶ μετ' ὀλίγα· (1 Cor. xv. 53–55) Δεῖ γὰρ τὸ φθαρτὸν τοῦτο ἐνδύσασθαι ἀφθαρσίαν καὶ τὸ θνητὸν τοῦτο ἐνδύσασθαι ἀθανασίαν· ὅταν δὲ τὸ φθαρτὸν τοῦτο ἐνδύσηται ἀφθαρσίαν καὶ τὸ θνητὸν τοῦτο ἐνδύσηται ἀθανασίαν, τότε πληρωθήσεται ὁ λόγος ὁ γεγραμμένος· Κατεπόθη ὁ θάνατος εἰς νῖκος· ποῦ σου, θάνατε, τὸ κέντρον; ποῦ σου, ᾅδη, τὸ νῖκος; καταργεῖται γὰρ τέλεον ἡ τοῦ θανάτου δύναμις τότε καὶ ἀφανίζεται, μηκέτι ὅλως ἐνεργοῦσα, ἀλλ' ἀθανασία λοιπὸν καὶ ἀφθαρσία δίδοται τοῖς ἀνθρώποις αἰώνιος.

leader of that resurrection, the first to be raised to the resurrection immortal.

'This was the preaching also of them that from the beginning were eye-witnesses and ministers of the word; for thus saith blessed Paul, whose calling was not of men, but from heaven, "Brethren, I declare unto you the Gospel which I preached unto you. For I delivered unto you first of all that which I also received, how that Christ died for our sins according to the Scriptures. Now if Christ be preached that he rose from the dead, how say some among you that there is no resurrection of the dead? For if the dead rise not, then is not Christ raised. And if Christ be not raised, your faith is vain, ye are yet in your sins. If in this life only we have hope in Christ, we are of all men most miserable. But now is Christ risen from the dead and become the first-fruits of them that slept. For since by man came death, by man came also the resurrection of the dead. For as in Adam all die, even so in Christ shall all be made alive." And after a little while, "For this corruptible must put on incorruption, and this mortal must put on immortality. So when this corruptible shall have put on incorruption, and this mortal shall have put on immortality, then shall be brought to pass the saying that is written, Death is swallowed up in victory. O death where is thy sting? O grave, where is thy victory?" For then the power of death is utterly annulled and destroyed, no longer working in us, but for the future there is given unto men immortality and incorruption for evermore.

and with the teaching of Blessed Paul,

Ἔσται οὖν, ἔσται ἀναμφιλέκτως ἡ τῶν νεκρῶν
ἀνάστασις, καὶ τοῦτο ἀνενδοιάστως πιστεύομεν·
ἀλλὰ καὶ ἀμοιβὰς καὶ εὐθύνας τῶν βεβιωμένων
γινώσκομεν κατὰ τὴν φοβερὰν ἡμέραν τῆς τοῦ
2 Pet. iii. 12, 13 Χριστοῦ παρουσίας, Δι' ἧς οὐρανοὶ πυρούμενοι
λυθήσονται καὶ στοιχεῖα καυσούμενα τήκεται, ὥς
φησί τις τῶν θεηγόρων, Καινοὺς δὲ οὐρανοὺς καὶ 71
καινὴν γῆν, κατὰ τὸ ἐπάγγελμα αὐτοῦ προσδοκῶ-
μεν. ὅτι γὰρ ἀμοιβαὶ καὶ εὔθυναι εἰσὶ τῶν ἔργων
ἐκεῖ, καὶ οὐδὲν ὅλως τῶν ἀγαθῶν ἢ τῶν πονηρῶν
παροφθήσεται, ἀλλὰ καὶ ἔργων καὶ ῥημάτων καὶ
ἐνθυμήσεων ἀνταποδόσεις ἀπόκεινται, δῆλον·
Mat. x. 42 φησὶ γὰρ ὁ Κύριος· Ὃς ἐὰν ποτίσῃ ἕνα τῶν
Mk. ix. 41 μικρῶν τούτων ποτήριον ψυχροῦ μόνον εἰς ὄνομα
μαθητοῦ, οὐ μὴ ἀπολέσῃ τὸν μισθὸν αὐτοῦ. καὶ
Mat. xxv. 31–36 πάλιν λέγει· Ὅταν ἔλθῃ ὁ Υἱὸς τοῦ ἀνθρώπου ἐν
τῇ δόξῃ αὐτοῦ, καὶ πάντες οἱ ἅγιοι ἄγγελοι μετ'
αὐτοῦ, τότε συναχθήσονται ἔμπροσθεν αὐτοῦ
πάντα τὰ ἔθνη καὶ ἀφοριεῖ αὐτοὺς ἀπ' ἀλλήλων,
ὥσπερ ὁ ποιμὴν ἀφορίζει τὰ πρόβατα ἀπὸ τῶν
ἐρίφων, καὶ στήσει τὰ μὲν πρόβατα ἐκ δεξιῶν
αὐτοῦ, τὰ δὲ ἐρίφια ἐξ εὐωνύμων· τότε ἐρεῖ ὁ
βασιλεὺς τοῖς ἐκ δεξιῶν αὐτοῦ· Δεῦτε, οἱ εὐλο-
γημένοι τοῦ Πατρός μου, κληρονομήσατε τὴν
ἡτοιμασμένην ὑμῖν βασιλείαν ἀπὸ καταβολῆς
κόσμου· ἐπείνασα γὰρ καὶ ἐδώκατέ μοι φαγεῖν,
ἐδίψησα καὶ ἐποτίσατέ με, ξένος ἤμην καὶ συν-
ηγάγετέ με, γυμνὸς καὶ περιεβάλετέ με, ἠσθένησα
καὶ ἐπεσκέψασθέ με, ἐν φυλακῇ ἤμην καὶ ἤλθετε
πρός με. τί τοῦτο λέγων; τὰς γινομένας παρ'
ἡμῶν εἰς τοὺς δεομένους εὐποιΐας ἑαυτῷ οἰκειού-
Luke xii. 8 μενος. καὶ ἐν ἑτέρῳ λέγει· Πᾶς ὅστις ὁμολογήσει

'Beyond all question, therefore, there shall be a resurrection of the dead, and this we believe undoubtingly. Moreover we know that there shall be rewards and punishments for the deeds done in our life-time, on the dreadful day of Christ's coming, "wherein the heavens shall be dissolved in fire and the elements shall melt with fervent heat," as saith one of the inspired clerks of God; "nevertheless we, according to his promise, look for new heavens and a new earth." For that there shall be rewards and punishments for men's works, and that absolutely nothing, good or bad, shall be overlooked, but that there is reserved a requital for words, deeds and thoughts, is plain. The Lord saith, "Whosoever shall give to drink unto one of these little ones a cup of cold water only, in the name of a disciple, he shall in no wise lose his reward." And again he saith, "When the Son of man shall come in his glory, and all the holy Angels with him, then before him shall be gathered all nations, and he shall separate them one from another, as a shepherd divideth his sheep from the goats. And he shall set the sheep on his right hand, but the goats on the left. Then shall the King say unto them on his right hand, 'Come ye blessed of my Father, inherit the kingdom prepared for you from the foundation of the world. For I was an hungred, and ye gave me meat: I was thirsty, and ye gave me drink: I was a stranger, and ye took me in: naked, and ye clothed me: I was sick, and ye visited me: I was in prison, and ye came unto me.'" Wherefore saith he this, except he count the kind acts we do unto the needy as done unto himself? And in another place he saith, "Whoso-

and of rewards and punishments after death

ἐν ἐμοὶ ἔμπροσθεν τῶν ἀνθρώπων, ὁμολογήσω
κἀγὼ ἐν αὐτῷ ἔμπροσθεν τοῦ Πατρός μου τοῦ ἐν
οὐρανοῖς.

Ἰδοὺ διὰ πάντων τούτων καὶ ἄλλων πλειόνων
ἐδήλωσε βεβαίας εἶναι καὶ ἀσφαλεῖς τὰς ἀμοιβὰς 72
τῶν ἀγαθῶν ἔργων· ἀλλὰ καὶ τῶν ἐναντίων εὐθύνας ἀποκεῖσθαι προκατήγγειλε διὰ παραβολῶν
Ecclus. i. 5 θαυμασίων καὶ ἐξαισίων, ἃς ἡ πηγὴ τῆς σοφίας
Luke xvi. 19 ff. πανσόφως διηγήσατο· ποτὲ μὲν πλούσιόν τινα
παρεισάγων πορφύραν καὶ βύσσον ἐνδεδυμένον,
καὶ καθ᾿ ἡμέραν λαμπρῶς εὐφραινόμενον, ἀμετά-
δοτον δὲ καὶ ἀνηλεῆ πρὸς τοὺς δεομένους ὑπάρχοντα, ὡς καὶ πτωχόν τινα Λάζαρον ὀνόματι
πρὸς τὸν πυλῶνα αὐτοῦ βεβλημένον παρα-
βλέπειν, καὶ οὐδὲ αὐτῶν τῶν τῆς τραπέζης αὐτοῦ
ψιχίων ἐπιδιδόναι αὐτῷ· ἀποθανόντων οὖν ἀμφοτέρων, ὁ μὲν πένης ἐκεῖνος καὶ ἡλκωμένος
ἀπηνέχθη, φησίν, εἰς τὸν κόλπον Ἀβραάμ, τὴν
τῶν δικαίων συναυλίαν οὕτω δηλώσας· ὁ δὲ πλούσιος παρεδόθη φλογὶ πικρᾶς βασάνου ἐν τῷ ᾅδῃ·
πρὸς ὃν Ἀβραὰμ ἔλεγεν· Ἀπέλαβες σὺ τὰ ἀγαθά
σου ἐν τῇ ζωῇ σου, καὶ Λάζαρος ὁμοίως τὰ κακά·
νῦν δὲ οὗτος μὲν παρακαλεῖται, σὺ δὲ ὀδυνᾶσαι.

Ἑτέρωθι δὲ παρεικάζων τὴν τῶν οὐρανῶν βασι-
Mat. xxii. 2 λείαν, λέγει· Ὁμοία ἐστὶν ἡ βασιλεία τῶν οὐρανῶν ἀνθρώπῳ βασιλεῖ, ὅστις ἐποίησε γάμους
τῷ υἱῷ αὐτοῦ, τὴν μέλλουσαν εὐφροσύνην καὶ
λαμπρότητα οὕτω δηλῶν. πρὸς ἀνθρώπους γὰρ
ταπεινοὺς καὶ τὰ ἐπίγεια φρονοῦντας τὸν λόγον
ποιούμενος ἐκ τῶν συνήθων αὐτοῖς καὶ γνωρίμων
ἐδίδου τὰς παραβολάς. οὐ μέντοι δὲ γάμους καὶ
τραπέζας ἐν ἐκείνῳ παρεδήλου τῷ αἰῶνι εἶναι·

ever shall confess me before men, him will I also confess before my Father which is in heaven."

'Lo, by all these examples and many more he proveth that the rewards of good works are certain and sure. Further, that punishments are in store for the bad, he foretold by parables strange and wonderful, which he, the Well of Wisdom most wisely put forth. At one time he brought into his tale a certain rich man which was clothed in purple and fine linen, and fared sumptuously every day, but who was so niggardly and pitiless toward the destitute as to overlook a certain beggar named Lazarus laid at his gate, and not even to give him of the crumbs from his table. So when one and other were dead, the poor man, full of sores, was carried away, he saith, into Abraham's bosom—for thus he describeth the habitation of the righteous—but the rich man was delivered to the fire of bitter torment in hell. To him said Abraham, "Thou in thy lifetime receivedst thy good things, and likewise Lazarus his evil things, but now he is comforted, and thou art tormented."

Barlaam reciteth the parable of Dives and Lazarus

'And otherwhere he likeneth the kingdom of heaven to a certain king which made a marriage-feast for his son and thereby he declared future happiness and splendour. For as he was wont to speak to humble and earthly minded men, he would draw his parables from homely and familiar things. Not that he meant that marriages and feasts exist in that world; but in condescension

The parable of the wedding feast,

ἀλλὰ τῇ αὐτῶν συγκαταβαίνων παχύτητι, τοιούτοις ὀνόμασι κέχρηται, γνωρίσαι αὐτοῖς τὰ
μέλλοντα βουλόμενος. πάντας μὲν οὖν, φησί, 73
Prov. ix. 3 συνεκάλεσεν ὁ βασιλεὺς ὑψηλῷ κηρύγματι συνελθεῖν εἰς τοὺς γάμους καὶ ἐμφορηθῆναι τῶν
ἀπορρήτων ἀγαθῶν ἐκείνων· πολλοὶ δὲ τῶν κε-
κλημένων ἀμελήσαντες οὐκ ἀπῆλθον, ἀλλ', ἀπα-
σχολήσαντες ἑαυτούς, οἱ μὲν εἰς ἀγρούς, οἱ δὲ εἰς
ἐμπορίας, οἱ δὲ εἰς νεονύμφους γυναῖκας, ἀπεστέρησαν ἑαυτοὺς τῆς λαμπρότητος τοῦ νυμφῶνος.
ἐκείνων δὲ ἐθελοντὶ ἀλλοτριωθέντων τῆς τερπνῆς
εὐφροσύνης, ἄλλοι προσεκλήθησαν· καὶ ἐπλήσθη
ὁ γάμος ἀνακειμένων. εἰσελθὼν δὲ ὁ βασιλεὺς
θεάσασθαι τοὺς ἀνακειμένους εἶδεν ἐκεῖ ἄνθρωπον οὐκ ἐνδεδυμένον ἔνδυμα γάμου, καὶ λέγει
αὐτῷ· Ἑταῖρε, πῶς εἰσῆλθες ὧδε μὴ ἔχων ἔνδυμα
γάμου; ὁ δὲ ἐφιμώθη. τότε εἶπεν ὁ βασιλεὺς
τοῖς διακόνοις· Δήσαντες αὐτοῦ χεῖρας καὶ πόδας,
ἄρατε αὐτόν, καὶ ἐμβάλετε εἰς τὸ σκότος τὸ
ἐξώτερον· ἐκεῖ ἔσται ὁ κλαυθμὸς καὶ ὁ βρυγμὸς
τῶν ὀδόντων. οἱ μὲν οὖν παραιτησάμενοι καὶ
μηδόλως τῆς κλήσεως ὑπακούσαντες εἰσὶν οἱ μὴ
προσδραμόντες τῇ τοῦ Χριστοῦ πίστει, ἀλλ' εἴτε
τῇ εἰδωλολατρείᾳ, εἴτε αἱρέσει τινὶ ἐμμείναντες·
ὁ δὲ μὴ ἔχων τὸ τοῦ γάμου ἔνδυμα ἐστὶν ὁ
πιστεύσας μέν, πράξεσι δὲ ῥυπαραῖς τὸ νοητὸν
ἔνδυμα κηλιδώσας, ὃς καὶ δικαίως ἐξεβλήθη τῆς
χαρᾶς τοῦ νυμφῶνος.

Mat. xxv. 1–12 Καὶ ἄλλην δὲ παραβολὴν ταύτῃ συνᾴδουσαν
παρέθηκε, δέκα τινὰς παρθένους τυπώσας, Ὧν αἱ
μὲν πέντε ἦσαν φρόνιμοι, αἱ δὲ πέντε μωραί.
αἵτινες μωραί, λαβοῦσαι τὰς λαμπάδας αὐτῶν, 74

to men's grossness, he employed these names when he would make known to them the future. So, as he telleth, the king with high proclamation called all to come to the marriage to take their fill of his wondrous store of good things. But many of them that were bidden made light of it and came not, and busied themselves: some went to their farms, some to their merchandize, and others to their newly wedded wives, and thus deprived themselves of the splendour of the bride chamber. Now when these had, of their own choice, absented themselves from this joyous merriment, others were bidden thereto, and the wedding was furnished with guests. And when the king came in to see the guests, he saw there a man which had not on a wedding garment, and he said unto him, "Friend, how camest thou in hither, not having a wedding garment?" And he was speechless. Then said the king to the servants, "Bind him hand and foot, and take him away, and cast him into outer darkness; there shall be weeping and gnashing of teeth." Now they who made excuses and paid no heed to the call are they that hasten not to the faith of Christ, but continue in idolatry or heresy. But he that had no wedding garment is he that believeth, but hath soiled his spiritual garment with unclean acts, and was rightly cast forth from the joy of the bride chamber.

'And he put forth yet another parable, in harmony with this, in his picture of the Ten Virgins, "five of whom were wise, and five were foolish. They that were foolish took their lamps and took no

and the parable of the wise and foolish virgins

οὐκ ἔλαβον μεθ' ἑαυτῶν ἔλαιον· αἱ δὲ φρόνιμοι ἔλαβον ἔλαιον· διὰ τοῦ ἐλαίου τὴν τῶν ἀγαθῶν ἔργων κτῆσιν σημαίνων. Μέσης δὲ τῆς νυκτός, φησί, κραυγὴ γέγονεν· Ἰδοὺ ὁ νυμφίος ἔρχεται· ἐξέρχεσθε εἰς ἀπάντησιν αὐτοῦ· διὰ τοῦ μεσονυκτίου τὸ ἄδηλον τῆς ἡμέρας ἐκείνης παραστήσας. τότε ἠγέρθησαν πᾶσαι αἱ παρθένοι ἐκεῖναι· Αἱ μὲν οὖν ἕτοιμοι ἐξῆλθον εἰς ἀπάντησιν τοῦ νυμφίου, καὶ εἰσῆλθον μετ' αὐτοῦ εἰς τοὺς γάμους, καὶ ἐκλείσθη ἡ θύρα· αἱ δὲ ἀνέτοιμοι, ἃς εἰκότως μωρὰς ἐκάλεσε, σβεννυμένας τὰς λαμπάδας ἑαυτῶν ὁρῶσαι, ἀπῆλθον ἀγοράσαι ἔλαιον. παραγενόμεναι δὲ κλεισθείσης ἤδη τῆς θύρας, ἔκραζον λέγουσαι· Κύριε, κύριε, ἄνοιξον ἡμῖν· ὁ δέ, φησίν, ἀποκριθεὶς εἶπεν· Ἀμήν, λέγω ὑμῖν, οὐκ οἶδα ὑμᾶς· διὰ τούτων οὖν ἁπάντων δῆλόν ἐστιν ἀνταπόδοσιν εἶναι οὐ μόνον τῶν ἐναντίων πράξεων, ἀλλὰ καὶ ῥημάτων καὶ αὐτῶν τῶν ἐνθυμήσεων.
Mat. xii. 36 εἶπεν γὰρ ὁ Σωτήρ· Λέγω ὑμῖν ὅτι πᾶν ῥῆμα ἀργὸν ὃ ἐὰν λαλήσωσιν οἱ ἄνθρωποι, ἀποδώσουσι περὶ αὐτοῦ λόγον ἐν ἡμέρᾳ κρίσεως. καὶ αὖθις·
Mat. x. 30 Ὑμῶν δέ, φησί, καὶ αἱ τρίχες τῆς κεφαλῆς ἠριθμημέναι εἰσί· διὰ τῶν τριχῶν τὰ λεπτότατα τῶν διαλογισμῶν καὶ ἐνθυμήσεων παραδηλώσας. 75
συνῳδὰ δὲ τούτοις καὶ ὁ μακάριος διδάσκει
Heb. iv. 12, 13 Παῦλος· Ζῶν γάρ, φησίν, ὁ λόγος τοῦ Θεοῦ καὶ ἐνεργής, καὶ τομώτερος ὑπὲρ πᾶσαν μάχαιραν δίστομον, καὶ διϊκνούμενος ἄχρι μερισμοῦ ψυχῆς τε καὶ πνεύματος, ἁρμῶν τε καὶ μυελῶν, καὶ κριτικὸς ἐνθυμήσεων καὶ ἐννοιῶν καρδίας· καὶ οὐκ ἔστι κτίσις ἀφανὴς ἐνώπιον αὐτοῦ, πάντα δὲ

oil with them, but the wise took oil." By the oil he signifieth the acquiring of good works. "And at midnight," he saith, "there was a cry made, 'Behold the bridegroom cometh, go ye out to meet him.'" By midnight he denoteth the uncertainty of that time. Then all those virgins arose. "They that were ready went forth to meet the bridegroom and went in with him to the marriage, and the door was shut." But they that were un-ready (whom rightly he calleth foolish), seeing that their lamps were going out, went forth to buy oil. Afterward they drew nigh, the door being now shut, and cried, saying, "Lord, Lord, open to us." But he answered and said, "Verily I say unto you, I know you not." Wherefore from all this it is manifest that there is a requital not only for overt acts, but also for words and even secret thoughts; for the Saviour said, "I say unto you, that for every idle word that men shall speak they shall give account thereof in the day of judgement." And again he saith, "But the very hairs of your head are numbered," by the hairs meaning the smallest and slightest phantasy or thought. And in harmony herewith is the teaching of blessed Paul, "For the word of God," saith he, "is quick and powerful, and sharper than any two-edged sword, and piercing even to the dividing asunder of soul and spirit, and of the joints and marrow, and is a discerner of the thoughts and intents of the heart. Neither is there any creature that is not manifest in his sight: but all things are

γυμνὰ καὶ τετραχηλισμένα τοῖς ὀφθαλμοῖς αὐτοῦ,
πρὸς ὃν ἡμῖν ὁ λόγος.

Ταῦτα καὶ οἱ προφῆται πρὸ χρόνων πολλῶν
τῇ τοῦ Πνεύματος λαμπόμενοι χάριτι ἀριδη-
Is. lxvi. 18 ff. λότατα κατήγγειλαν. φησὶ γὰρ ὁ Ἠσαΐας· Ἐγὼ
τὰ ἔργα αὐτῶν καὶ τοὺς λογισμοὺς ἐπίσταμαι καὶ
ἀνταποδώσω αὐτοῖς· ἰδοὺ συναγαγεῖν ἔρχομαι
πάντα τὰ ἔθνη καὶ τὰς γλώσσας, καὶ ἥξουσι, καὶ
ὄψονται τὴν δόξαν μου. καὶ ἔσται ὁ οὐρανὸς
καινὸς καὶ ἡ γῆ καινή, ἃ ἐγὼ ποιῶ μὲν ἐνώπιόν
μου· καὶ ἥξει πᾶσα σὰρξ τοῦ προσκυνῆσαι
ἐνώπιόν μου, λέγει Κύριος, καὶ ἐξελεύσονται, καὶ
ὄψονται τὰ κῶλα τῶν ἀνθρώπων, τῶν παρα-
βεβηκότων ἐν ἐμοί· ὁ γὰρ σκώληξ αὐτῶν οὐ
τελευτήσει, καὶ τὸ πῦρ αὐτῶν οὐ σβεσθήσεται,
καὶ ἔσονται εἰς ὅρασιν πάσῃ σαρκί. καὶ αὖθις
περὶ τῆς ἡμέρας ἐκείνης λέγει· Καὶ εἰληθήσεται ὁ
οὐρανὸς ὡς βιβλίον, καὶ πάντα τὰ ἄστρα πεσοῦν-
Is. xxxiv, 4 ται ὡς φύλλα ἐξ ἀμπέλου· ἰδοὺ γὰρ ἡμέρα Κυρίου
ἔρχεται, ἀνίατος θυμοῦ καὶ ὀργῆς, θεῖναι τὴν
οἰκουμένην ὅλην ἔρημον καὶ τοὺς ἁμαρτωλοὺς
ἀπολέσαι ἐξ αὐτῆς· οἱ γὰρ ἀστέρες τοῦ οὐρανοῦ
καὶ ὁ Ὠρίων καὶ πᾶς ὁ κόσμος τοῦ οὐρανοῦ τὸ 76
φῶς αὐτῶν οὐ δώσουσι, καὶ σκοτισθήσεται τοῦ
ἡλίου ἀνατέλλοντος, καὶ ἡ σελήνη οὐ δώσει τὸ
φῶς αὐτῆς· καὶ ἀπολῶ ὕβριν ἀνόμων καὶ ὕβριν
Is. v. 18 ὑπερηφάνων ταπεινώσω. καὶ πάλιν λέγει· Οὐαὶ
οἱ ἐπισπώμενοι τὰς ἁμαρτίας αὐτῶν ὡς σχοινίῳ
μακρῷ καὶ ὡς ζυγοῦ ἱμάντι δαμάλεως τὰς ἀνομίας·
οὐαὶ οἱ λέγοντες τὸ πονηρὸν καλὸν καὶ τὸ καλὸν
πονηρόν, οἱ τιθέντες τὸ σκότος φῶς καὶ τὸ φῶς
σκότος, οἱ τιθέντες τὸ πικρὸν γλυκὺ καὶ τὸ γλυκὺ

naked and laid bare unto the eyes of him with whom we have to do."

'These things also were proclaimed with wondrous clearness by the prophets of old time, illumined by the grace of the Spirit. For Esay saith, "I know their works and their thoughts," and will repay them. "Behold, I come to gather all nations and all tongues; and they shall come and see my glory. And the heaven shall be new, and the earth, which I make before me. And all flesh shall come to worship before me, saith the Lord. And they shall go forth, and look upon the carcasses of the men that have transgressed against me: for their worm shall not die, neither shall their fire be quenched; and they shall be a spectacle unto all flesh." And again he saith concerning that day, "And the heavens shall be rolled together as a scroll, and all the stars shall fall down as leaves from the vine. For behold, the day of the Lord cometh, cruel with wrath and fierce anger, to lay the whole world desolate and to destroy the sinners out of it. For the stars of heaven and Orion and all the constellations of heaven shall not give their light, and there shall be darkness at the sun's rising, and the moon shall not give her light. And I will cause the arrogancy of the sinners to cease, and will lay low the haughtiness of the proud." And again he saith, "Wo unto them that draw their iniquities as with a long cord, and their sins as with an heifer's cart-rope! Wo unto them that call evil good, and good evil; that put darkness for light, and light for darkness; that put bitter for sweet, and sweet for

Barlaam maketh appeal to the words of Esay,

πικρόν. οὐαὶ οἱ ἰσχύοντες ὑμῶν οἱ δυνάσται, οἱ
κιρνῶντες τὸ σίκερα, οἱ δικαιοῦντες τὸν ἀσεβῆ
ἕνεκεν δώρων καὶ τὸ δίκαιον τοῦ δικαίου αἴροντες,
Is. x. 2 οἱ ἐκκλίνοντες κρίσιν πτωχῶν καὶ ἁρπάζοντες
κρῖμα πενήτων, ὥστε εἶναι αὐτοῖς χήραν εἰς
ἁρπαγὴν καὶ ὀρφανὸν εἰς προνομήν. καὶ τί
ποιήσουσι τῇ ἡμέρᾳ τῆς ἐπισκοπῆς; καὶ πρὸς
τίνα καταφεύξονται τοῦ βοηθηθῆναι; καὶ ποῦ
καταλείψουσι τὴν δόξαν αὐτῶν τοῦ μὴ ἐμπεσεῖν
εἰς ἀπαγωγήν; ὃν τρόπον καυθήσεται καλάμη ὑπὸ
Is. v. 24 ἄνθρακος πυρὸς καὶ συγκαυθήσεται ὑπὸ φλογὸς
ἀνημμένης, ἡ ῥίζα αὐτῶν ὡς χνοῦς ἔσται, καὶ τὸ
ἄνθος αὐτῶν ὡς κονιορτὸς ἀναβήσεται· οὐ γὰρ
ἠθέλησαν τὸν νόμον Κυρίου Σαβαώθ, ἀλλὰ τὸ
λόγιον τοῦ ἁγίου Ἰσραὴλ παρώξυναν.

Zeph. i. 14–18 Τούτῳ συνᾴδων καὶ ἕτερος προφήτης φησίν·
Ἐγγὺς ἡ ἡμέρα Κυρίου ἡ μεγάλη, ἐγγὺς καὶ ταχινὴ 77
σφόδρα· φωνὴ ἡ ἡμέρας Κυρίου πικρὰ καὶ σκληρὰ
τέτακται· δυνατὴ ἡμέρα ὀργῆς ἡ ἡμέρα ἐκείνη,
ἡμέρα θλίψεως καὶ ἀνάγκης, ἡμέρα ταλαιπωρίας
καὶ ἀφανισμοῦ, ἡμέρα σκότους καὶ γνόφου, ἡμέρα
νεφέλης καὶ ὁμίχλης, ἡμέρα σάλπιγγος καὶ
κραυγῆς· καὶ ἐκθλίψω τοὺς πονηρούς, καὶ πορεύσονται ὡς τυφλοί, ὅτι τῷ Κυρίῳ ἐξήμαρτον· καὶ
τὸ ἀργύριον αὐτῶν καὶ τὸ χρυσίον οὐ μὴ δύνηται
ἐξελέσθαι αὐτοὺς ἐν ἡμέρᾳ ὀργῆς Κυρίου· ἐν πυρὶ
γὰρ ζήλου αὐτοῦ καταναλωθήσεται πᾶσα ἡ γῆ,
διότι συντέλειαν ποιήσει ἐπὶ πάντας τοὺς κατοι-
κοῦντας τὴν γῆν. πρὸς τούτοις καὶ Δαυῒδ ὁ βασι-
Ps. l. 3, 4 λεὺς καὶ προφήτης βοᾷ· Ὁ Θεὸς ἐμφανῶς ἥξει, ὁ
Θεὸς ἡμῶν, καὶ οὐ παρασιωπήσεται. πῦρ ἐνώπιον
αὐτοῦ καυθήσεται, καὶ κύκλῳ αὐτοῦ καταιγὶς

bitter! Wo unto those of you that are mighty, that are princes, that mingle strong drink, which justify the wicked for reward, and take justice from the just, and turn aside the judgement from the needy, and take away the right from the poor, that the widow may be their spoil and the fatherless their prey! And what will they do in the day of visitation, and to whom will they flee for help? And where will they leave their glory, that they fall not into arrest? Like as stubble shall be burnt by live coal of fire, and consumed by kindled flame, so their root shall be as foam, and their blossom shall go up as dust, for they would not the law of the Lord of hosts, and provoked the oracle of the Holy One of Israel."

'In tune therewith saith also another prophet, "The great day of the Lord is near, and hasteth greatly. The bitter and austere voice of the day of the Lord hath been appointed. A mighty day of wrath is that day, a day of trouble and distress, a day of wasteness and desolation, a day of blackness and gloominess, a day of clouds and thick darkness, a day of the trumpet and alarm. And I will bring distress upon the wicked, and they shall walk like blind men, because they have sinned against the Lord. Neither their silver nor their gold shall be able to deliver them in the day of the Lord's wrath; for the whole land shall be devoured by the fire of his jealousy, for he shall make a riddance of all them that dwell in the land." Moreover David, the king and prophet, crieth thus, "God shall come visibly, even our God, and shall not keep silence: a fire shall be kindled before him, and a mighty

and of other prophets

σφοδρά· προσκαλέσεται τὸν οὐρανὸν ἄνω καὶ τὴν
γῆν, τοῦ διακρῖναι τὸν λαὸν αὐτοῦ. καὶ αὖθις·
Ps. lxxxii. 8 Ἀνάστα, φησίν, Θεός, κρῖνον τὴν γῆν, ὅτι ἐνθύμιον
Ps. lxxvi. 11 ἀνθρώπου ἐξομολογήσεταί σοι· καὶ σὺ ἀποδώσεις
Ps. lxxii. 12 ἑκάστῳ κατὰ τὰ ἔργα αὐτοῦ. πολλὰ δὲ καὶ ἕτερα
τοιαῦτα ὅ τε ψαλμῳδὸς καὶ πάντες οἱ προφῆται
τῷ θείῳ πνεύματι μυηθέντες περὶ τῆς μελλούσης
κρίσεως καὶ ἀνταποδόσεως ἐκήρυξαν· ὧν τοὺς
λόγους καὶ ὁ Σωτὴρ ἀσφαλέστατα βεβαιώσας, 78
ἐδίδαξεν ἡμᾶς πιστεύειν ἀνάστασιν νεκρῶν καὶ
ἀνταπόδοσιν τῶν βεβιωμένων ζωήν τε ἀτελεύτητον τοῦ μέλλοντος αἰῶνος.

X

Ὁ δὲ Ἰωάσαφ, κατανύξεως πολλῆς ἐπὶ τούτοις πληρωθείς, σύνδακρυς ὅλος ἦν. καὶ φησὶ πρὸς τὸν γέροντα· Πάντα μοι σαφῶς ἐγνώρισας, καὶ ἀσφαλῶς διεξῆλθες τὴν φρικτὴν ταύτην καὶ θαυμαστὴν διήγησιν. τούτων οὖν προκειμένων ἡμῖν, τί χρὴ ποιεῖν, τοῦ ἐκφυγεῖν τὰς ἡτοιμασμένας τοῖς ἁμαρτωλοῖς κολάσεις, καὶ ἀξιωθῆναι τῆς χαρᾶς τῶν δικαίων;

Acts ii. 37–39 Καὶ ὁ Βαρλαὰμ ἀπεκρινατο· Γέγραπται ὅτι διδάσκοντός ποτε τοῦ Πέτρου τὸν λαόν, ὃς καὶ κορυφαῖος ἐκλήθη τῶν ἀποστόλων, κατενύγησαν τῇ καρδίᾳ, καθάπερ καὶ σὺ σήμερον, καί, εἰπόντων αὐτῶν· Τί ποιήσομεν; ὁ Πέτρος ἔφη πρὸς αὐτούς· Μετανοήσατε, καὶ βαπτισθήτω ἕκαστος ὑμῶν εἰς ἄφεσιν ἁμαρτιῶν, καὶ λήψεσθε τὴν δωρεὰν τοῦ

tempest round about him. He shall call the heaven from above, and the earth, that he may judge his people." And again he saith, "Arise, O God, judge thou the earth, because 'the fierceness of man shall turn to thy praise.' And thou shalt 'reward every man according to his works.'" And many other such things have been spoken by the Psalmist, and all the Prophets inspired by the Holy Ghost, concerning the judgement and the recompense to come. Their words also have been most surely confirmed by the Saviour who hath taught us to believe the resurrection of the dead, and the recompense of the deeds done in the flesh, and the unending life of the world to come.'

X

Ioasaph asketh how he may be saved

But Ioasaph was filled hereby with deep compunction, and was melted into tears; and he said to the elder, 'Thou hast told me everything plainly, and hast completed unerringly thy terrible and marvellous tale. With such truths set before us, what must we do to escape the punishments in store for sinners, and to gain the joy of the righteous?'

Barlaam declareth the way of salvation,

Barlaam answered: 'It is written of Peter, who was also called chief of the Apostles, that once when he was preaching the people were pricked in their heart, like thyself to-day: and when they asked, "What shall we do?", Peter said unto them, "Repent, and be baptized every one of you for the remission of sins, and ye shall receive the gift of the

Ἁγίου Πνεύματος. ὑμῖν γάρ ἐστιν ἡ ἐπαγγελία
καὶ τοῖς τέκνοις ὑμῶν καὶ πᾶσι τοῖς εἰς μακρὰν
ὅσους ἂν προσκαλέσηται Κύριος ὁ Θεὸς ἡμῶν.
ἰδοὺ οὖν καὶ ἐπὶ σὲ ἐξέχεε τὸ πλούσιον ἔλεος
αὐτοῦ, καὶ προσεκαλέσατό σε, τὸν μακρὰν αὐτοῦ
τῇ γνώμῃ ὑπάρχοντα καὶ ἀλλοτρίοις λατρεύοντα
Hab. ii. 18 οὐ θεοῖς, ἀλλὰ δαίμοσιν ὀλεθρίοις καὶ ξοάνοις
κωφοῖς καὶ ἀναισθήτοις. διὸ καὶ πρὸ πάντων
πρόσελθε τῷ κεκληκότι, παρ᾽ οὗ λήψῃ τῶν ὁρωμένων καὶ τῶν ἀοράτων ἀψευδῆ τὴν γνῶσιν. εἰ
δὲ μετὰ τὸ κληθῆναι οὐ θέλεις ἢ βραδύνεις, δικαίᾳ
Θεοῦ κρίσει ἀπόκληρος ἔσῃ, τῷ μὴ θελῆσαι μὴ 79
Acts viii. 22, 23 (?) θεληθείς· οὕτω γὰρ καὶ ὁ αὐτὸς ἀπόστολος
Πέτρος πρός τινα τῶν μαθητῶν λελάληκεν. ἐγὼ
δὲ πιστεύω ὅτι καὶ ὑπήκουσας τῆς κλήσεως, καὶ
Mat. x. 38 ἔτι τρανότερον ὑπακούσας ἀρεῖς τὸν σταυρὸν καὶ
Mk. viii. 34 ἀκολουθήσεις τῷ καλοῦντί σε Θεῷ καὶ Δεσπότῃ,
ὃς προσκαλεῖταί σε ἀπὸ θανάτου εἰς ζωὴν καὶ
1 Pet. ii. 9 ἀπὸ σκότους εἰς φῶς. τῷ ὄντι γὰρ ἡ τοῦ Θεοῦ
ἄγνοια σκότος ἐστὶ καὶ θάνατος ψυχῆς, καὶ τὸ
δουλεύειν εἰδώλοις ἐπ᾽ ὀλέθρῳ τῆς φύσεως πάσης
μοι δοκεῖ εἶναι ἀναισθησίας καὶ ἀφροσύνης
ἐπέκεινα.

Οὓς τίνι ὁμοιώσω, καὶ ποταπήν σοι εἰκόνα τῆς τούτων ἀβελτηρίας παραστήσω; ἀλλά σοι παραθήσω ὑπόδειγμα παρά τινος ἀνδρὸς σοφωτάτου λεχθὲν πρός με.

Ἔλεγε γὰρ ὅτι Ὅμοιοί εἰσιν οἱ τῶν εἰδώλων προσκυνηταὶ ἀνθρώπῳ ἰξευτῇ, ὃς κατέσχεν ἓν τῶν σμικροτάτων στρουθίων· ἀηδόνα τοῦτο καλοῦσι. λαβὼν δὲ μάχαιραν τοῦ σφάξαι αὐτὸ καὶ φαγεῖν, ἐδόθη τῇ ἀηδόνι φωνὴ ἔναρθρος. καί

Holy Ghost. For to you is the promise, and to your children, and to all that are afar off even as many as the Lord our God shall call." Behold therefore upon thee also hath he poured forth the riches of his mercy, and hath called thee that wert afar off from him in heart, and didst serve others, not Gods, but pernicious devils and dumb and senseless wooden images. Wherefore before all things approach thou him who hath called thee, and from him shalt thou receive the true knowledge of things visible and invisible. But if, after thy calling, thou be loth or slack, thou shalt be disherited by the just judgement of God, and by thy rejection of him thou shalt be rejected. For thus too spake the same Apostle Peter to a certain disciple.[1] But I believe that thou hast heard the call, and that, when thou hast heard it more plainly, thou wilt take up thy Cross, and follow that God and Master that calleth thee, calleth thee to himself from death unto life, and from darkness unto light. For, soothly, ignorance of God is darkness and death of the soul; and to serve idols, to the destruction of all nature, is to my thinking the extreme of all senselessness.

and showeth the folly of idolatry by the tale of the Fowler and the Nightingale

'But idolaters—to whom shall I compare them, and to what likeness shall I liken their silliness? Well, I will set before thee an example which I heard from the lips of one most wise.

APOLOGUE III.

'"Idol worshippers," said he, "are like a fowler who caught a tiny bird, called nightingale. He took a knife, for to kill and eat her; but the nightingale, being given the power of articulate speech,

[1] Simon Magus(?).

φησι πρὸς τὸν ἰξευτήν· Τί σοι ὄφελος, ἄνθρωπε, 80
τῆς ἐμῆς σφαγῆς; οὐ δυνήσῃ γὰρ δι' ἐμοῦ τὴν
σὴν ἐμπλῆσαι γαστέρα. ἀλλ' εἴ με τῶν δεσμῶν
ἐλευθερώσεις, δώσω σοι ἐντολὰς τρεῖς, ἃς φυλάττων μεγάλα παρ' ὅλην σου τὴν ζωὴν ὠφεληθήσῃ.
ὁ δέ, θαμβηθεὶς τῇ ταύτης λαλιᾷ, ἐπηγγείλατο, εἰ
καινόν τι παρ' αὐτῆς ἀκούσειε, θᾶττον ἐλευθερῶσαι τῆς κατοχῆς. ἐπιστραφεῖσα δὲ ἡ ἀηδὼν
λέγει τῷ ἀνθρώπῳ· Μηδέποτέ τινος τῶν ἀνεφίκτων ἐπιχειρήσῃς ἐφικέσθαι, καὶ μὴ μεταμελοῦ
ἐπὶ πράγματι παρελθόντι, καὶ ἄπιστον ῥῆμα
πώποτε μὴ πιστεύσῃς. ταύτας δὴ τὰς τρεῖς
ἐντολὰς φύλαττε, καὶ εὖ σοι γένηται. ἀγάμενος
δὲ ὁ ἀνὴρ τὸ εὐσύνοπτον καὶ συνετὸν τῶν ῥημάτων, λύσας αὐτὴν τῶν δεσμῶν κατὰ τοῦ ἀέρος
ἐξαπέστειλεν. ἡ οὖν ἀηδὼν θέλουσα μαθεῖν εἰ
ἐπέγνω ὁ ἀνὴρ τῶν λεχθέντων αὐτῷ ῥημάτων
τὴν δύναμιν καὶ εἰ ἐκαρπώσατό τινα ὠφέλειαν,
λέγει πρὸς αὐτὸν ἱπταμένη ἐν τῷ ἀέρι· Φεῦ
σου τῆς ἀβουλίας, ἄνθρωπε, ὁποῖον θησαυρὸν σήμερον ἀπώλεσας· ὑπάρχει γὰρ ἐν τοῖς
ἐγκάτοις μου μαργαρίτης, ὑπερέχων τῷ μεγέθει
στρουθοκαμήλου ᾠόν. ὡς οὖν ἤκουσε ταῦτα
ὁ ἰξευτής, συνεχύθη τῇ λύπῃ μεταμελόμενος ὅτι
ἐξέφυγεν ἡ ἀηδὼν ἐκείνη τὰς χεῖρας αὐτοῦ· καί,
πειρώμενος αὖθις κατασχεῖν αὐτήν, εἶπε· Δεῦρο
ἐν τῷ οἴκῳ μου, καί, φιλοφρονησάμενός σε καλῶς,
ἐντίμως ἐξαποστελῶ. ἡ δὲ ἀηδὼν ἔφη αὐτῷ· 81
Νῦν ἔγνων ἰσχυρῶς ἀνοηταίνειν σε· δεξάμενος
γὰρ τὰ λεχθέντα σοι προθύμως καὶ ἡδέως ἀκούσας, οὐδεμίαν ἐξ αὐτῶν ὠφέλειαν ἐπεκτήσω.
εἶπόν σοι μὴ μεταμελεῖσθαι ἐπὶ πράγματι παρελ-

said to the fowler, 'Man, what advantageth it thee to slay me? for thou shalt not be able by my means to fill thy belly. Now free me of my fetters, and I will give thee three precepts, by the keeping of which thou shalt be greatly benefited all thy life long.' He, astonied at her speech, promised that, if he heard anything new from her, he would quickly free her from her captivity. The nightingale turned towards our friend and said, 'Never try to attain to the unattainable : never regret the thing past and gone : and never believe the word that passeth belief. Keep these three precepts, and may it be well with thee.' The man, admiring the lucidity and sense of her words, freed the bird from her captivity, and sent her forth aloft. She, therefore, desirous to know whether the man had understood the force of her words, and whether he had gleaned any profit therefrom, said, as she flew aloft, 'Shame, sir, on thy fecklessness! What a treasure that hast lost to-day! For I have inside me a pearl larger than an ostrich-egg.' When the fowler heard thereof, he was distraught with grief, regretting that the bird had escaped out of his hands. And he would fain have taken her again. 'Come hither,' said he, 'into my house: I will make thee right welcome, and send thee forth with honour.' But the nightingale said unto him, 'Now I know thee to be a mighty fool. Though thou didst receive my words readily and gladly, thou hast gained no profit thereby. I bade thee never regret the thing past and gone; and

θόντι· καὶ ἰδοὺ συνεχύθης τῇ λύπῃ ὅτι σου τὰς χεῖρας ἐξέφυγον, μεταμελόμενος ἐπὶ πράγματι παρελθόντι. ἐνετειλάμην σοι μὴ ἐπιχειρεῖν τῶν ἀνεφίκτων ἐφικέσθαι, καὶ πειρᾷ κατασχεῖν με, μὴ δυνάμενος τῆς ἐμῆς ἐφικέσθαι πορείας. πρὸς τούτοις δὲ καὶ ἄπιστον ῥῆμα μὴ πιστεύειν σοι διεστειλάμην· ἀλλ' ἰδοὺ ἐπίστευσας ὑπάρχειν ἐν τοῖς ἐγκάτοις μου μαργαρίτην ὑπερβαίνοντα τὸ μέτρον τῆς ἡλικίας μου, καὶ οὐκ ἐφρόνησας συνιέναι ὅτι ὅλη ἐγὼ οὐκ ἐφικνοῦμαι τῷ μεγέθει τῶν τοῦ στρουθοκαμήλου ὠῶν, καὶ πῶς μαργαρίτην τοιοῦτον ἐχώρησα ἐν ἐμοί;

Οὕτως οὖν ἀνοηταίνουσι καὶ οἱ πεποιθότες ἐπὶ τοῖς εἰδώλοις· εἰργάσαντο γὰρ ταῦτα ταῖς χερσὶν
Is. xvii. 8 αὐτῶν, καὶ προσκυνοῦσιν ἃ ἐποίησαν οἱ δάκτυλοι αὐτῶν, λέγοντες· Οὗτοι οἱ πλαστουργοὶ ἡμῶν. πῶς οὖν πλαστουργοὺς τοὺς ὑπ' αὐτῶν δημιουργηθέντας καὶ διαπλασθέντας νομίζουσιν; ἀλλὰ καὶ τηροῦντες αὐτὰ ἐν ἀσφαλείᾳ, τοῦ μὴ ὑπὸ κλεπτῶν συληθῆναι, φύλακας ἀποκαλοῦνται τῆς σφῶν σωτηρίας· καὶ τοί γε πόσης ταῦτα ἀφροσύνης, καὶ τὸ μὴ γινώσκειν ὅτι, οὐκ ἐξαρκοῦντες ἑαυτοὺς φυλάσσειν καὶ βοηθεῖν, πῶς ἄλλοις γέ- 82
Is. viii. 19 νοιντο φύλακες καὶ σωτῆρες; τί γάρ, φησίν, ἐκζητοῦσι περὶ τῶν ζώντων τοὺς νεκρούς; κατακενοῦσι χρήματα, στήλας τοῖς δαίμοσι καὶ ἀγάλματα ἐγεῖραι, καὶ φληναφοῦσιν ἀγαθῶν παρόχους αὐτοὺς ὑπάρχειν, αἰτοῦντες παρ' αὐτῶν λαβεῖν ἅπερ οὔτε πώποτε ἐκτήσαντο, οὔτε μὴν ἔτι κτή-
Pss. cxv. 8; cxxxv. 18 σονται. διὸ γέγραπται· Ὅμοιοι αὐτοῖς γένοιντο οἱ ποιοῦντες αὐτὰ καὶ πάντες οἱ πεποιθότες ἐπ'
Is. xlvi. 6, 7 αὐτοῖς· οἵτινες, φησί, μισθωσάμενοι χρυσοχόον,

behold thou art distraught with grief because I have escaped out of thy hands—there thou regrettest a thing past and gone. I charged thee not to try to attain to the unattainable, and thou triest to catch me, though thou canst not attain to my path. Besides which, I bade thee never believe a word past belief, and behold thou hast believed that I had inside me a pearl exceeding the measure of my size, and hadst not the sense to see that my whole body doth not attain to the bulk of ostrich eggs. How then could I contain such a pearl?'"

'Thus senseless, then, are also they that trust in idols: for these be their handiwork, and they worship that which their fingers made, saying, "These be our creators." How then deem they their creators those which have been formed and fashioned by themselves? Nay more, they safeguard their gods, lest they be stolen by thieves, and yet they call them guardians of their safety. And yet what folly not to know that they, which be unable to guard and aid themselves, can in no wise guard and save others! "For" saith he, "why, on behalf of the living, should they seek unto the dead?" They expend wealth, for to raise statues and images to devils, and vainly boast that these give them good gifts, and crave to receive of their hands things which those idols never possessed, nor ever shall possess. Wherefore it is written, "May they that make them be like unto them, and so be all such as put their trust in them, who," he saith, "hire a goldsmith, and make them

ἐποίησαν χειροποίητα, καὶ κύψαντες προσεκύνη-
σαν αὐτοῖς. αἴρουσιν αὐτὰ ἐπὶ τῶν ὤμων καὶ
πορεύονται· ἐὰν δὲ θῶσιν αὐτὰ ἐπὶ τοῦ τόπου,
μενεῖ ἐν αὐτῷ, οὐ μὴ κινηθῇ. καὶ ὃς ἂν βοήσῃ
πρὸς αὐτά, οὐ μὴ εἰσακούσῃ αὐτοῦ, ἀπὸ κακῶν
Is. xlii. 17 οὐ μὴ σώσῃ αὐτόν. Διὸ αἰσχύνθητε αἰσχύνην
αἰώνιον, οἱ πεποιθότες ἐπὶ τοῖς γλυπτοῖς, οἱ
λέγοντες τοῖς χωνευτοῖς· Ὑμεῖς ἐστὲ θεοὶ ἡμῶν.
Deut. xxxii. 17, 20 Ἔθυσαν γάρ, φησί, δαιμονίοις καὶ οὐ Θεῷ, θεοῖς
οἷς οὐκ ᾔδεισαν οἱ πατέρες αὐτῶν· καινοὶ καὶ
πρόσφατοι ἥκασιν, ὅτι γενεὰ ἐξεστραμμένη ἐστὶ
καὶ οὐκ ἔστι πίστις ἐν αὐτοῖς.
Ἐκ ταύτης οὖν τῆς πονηρᾶς γενεᾶς καὶ ἀπίστου
Is. lii. 11 προσκαλεῖταί σε Κύριος, λέγων σοι· Ἔξελθε ἐκ
2 Cor. vi. 17 μέσου αὐτῶν καὶ ἀφορίσθητι, καὶ ἀκαθάρτου μὴ
Acts ii. 40 ἅψῃ, ἀλλὰ σώθητι ἐκ τῆς γενεᾶς τῆς σκολιᾶς
Mic. ii. 10 ταύτης· ἀνάστηθι καὶ πορεύου, ὅτι οὐκ ἔστι σοι
αὕτη ἀνάπαυσις· ἡ γὰρ πολυαρχία τῶν παρ'
ὑμῖν θεῶν καὶ ἄτακτον καὶ στασιῶδες καὶ παν- 83
τελῶς ἀνύπαρκτον. ἡμῖν δὲ οὐχ οὕτως ἐστίν, οὐδὲ
1 Cor. viii. 6 πολλοὶ θεοὶ καὶ κύριοι· ἀλλ' εἷς Θεὸς ὁ Πατήρ,
ἐξ οὗ τὰ πάντα καὶ ἡμεῖς εἰς αὐτόν· καὶ εἷς Κύριος
Ἰησοῦς Χριστός, δι' οὗ τὰ πάντα καὶ ἡμεῖς δι'
Col. i. 15, 16 αὐτοῦ, ὅς ἐστιν εἰκὼν τοῦ Θεοῦ τοῦ ἀοράτου,
πρωτότοκος ἁπάσης τῆς κτίσεως καὶ πάντων τῶν
αἰώνων, ὅτι ἐν αὐτῷ ἐκτίσθη τὰ πάντα, τὰ ἐν τοῖς
οὐρανοῖς καὶ τὰ ἐπὶ τῆς γῆς, τὰ ὁρατὰ καὶ τὰ
ἀόρατα, εἴτε Θρόνοι, εἴτε Κυριότητες, εἴτε Ἀρχαί,
John i. 3 εἴτε Ἐξουσίαι· Τὰ πάντα δι' αὐτοῦ ἐγένετο, καὶ
χωρὶς αὐτοῦ ἐγένετο οὐδὲ ἓν ὃ γέγονε· καὶ ἓν
Πνεῦμα Ἅγιον, ἐν ᾧ τὰ πάντα, τὸν Κύριον καὶ
John vi. 63 ζωοποιόν, Θεὸν καὶ θεοποιοῦν, Πνεῦμα ἀγαθόν,

gods, and they fall down, yea, they worship them. They bear them upon the shoulders, and go forward. And if they set them in their place, they stand therein: they shall not remove. Yea, one shall cry unto them, yet can they not answer him, nor save him out of his trouble." "Wherefore be ye ashamed with everlasting shame, ye that trust in graven images, that say to the molten images, Ye are our gods." "For they sacrificed," he saith, "unto devils, and not to God; to gods whom their fathers knew not. There came new and fresh gods; because it is a froward generation, and there is no faith in them."

'Wherefore out of this wicked and faithless generation the Lord calleth thee to him, saying, "Come out from among them, and be thou separate, and touch no unclean thing," but "save thyself from this untoward generation." "Arise thou, and depart, for this is not thy rest;" for that divided lordship, which your gods hold, is a thing of confusion and strife and hath no real being whatsoever. But with us it is not so, neither have we many gods and lords, but one God, the Father, of whom are all things, and we unto him: and one Lord Jesus Christ, by whom are all things and we by him, "who is the image of the invisible God, the first born of every creature" and of all ages, "for in him were all things created that are in the heavens and that are upon the earth, visible and invisible, whether they be thrones, or dominions, or principalities, or powers." "All things were made by him, and without him was not anything made that was made:" and one Holy Ghost, in whom are all things, "the Lord and Giver of life," God and making God, the good Spirit, the right Spirit, "the

Barlaam confesseth his faith in the Holy Trinity,

John xvi. 7 Πνεῦμα εὐθές, Πνεῦμα παράκλητον, Πνεῦμα
Rom. viii. 15 υἱοθεσίας. τούτων Θεὸς μὲν ἕκαστον καθ' ἑαυτὸ
θεωρούμενον· ὡς ὁ Πατὴρ καὶ ὁ Υἱός, ὡς ὁ Υἱὸς
καὶ τὸ Πνεῦμα τὸ Ἅγιον, εἷς δὲ Θεὸς ἐν τρισί, μία
φύσις, μία βασιλεία, μία δύναμις, μία δόξα, μία
οὐσία, διαιρετὴ ταῖς ὑποστάσεσι καὶ μόνον. εἷς
γὰρ ὁ Πατήρ, ᾧ καὶ ἴδιον ἡ ἀγεννησία· εἷς δὲ ὁ
μονογενὴς Υἱός, καὶ ἴδιον αὐτῷ ἡ γέννησις· ἓν
John xv. 26 δὲ τὸ Ἅγιον Πνεῦμα, καὶ ἴδιον αὐτῷ ἡ ἐκπόρευσις.
οὕτω γὰρ ἡμεῖς, ἐκ φωτὸς τοῦ Πατρὸς φῶς περι- 84
λαμφθέντες τὸν Υἱὸν ἐν φωτὶ τῷ Ἁγίῳ Πνεύματι,
μίαν δοξάζομεν θεότητα ἐν τρισὶν ὑποστάσεσι·
καὶ αὐτός ἐστιν ἀληθινὸς καὶ μόνος Θεός, ὁ ἐν
Rom. xi. 36 Τριάδι γινωσκόμενος, ὅτι ἐξ αὐτοῦ καὶ δι' αὐτοῦ
καὶ εἰς αὐτὸν τὰ πάντα.

Τούτου τῇ χάριτι τὰ κατὰ σὲ γνοὺς κἀγὼ ἀπεστάλην διδάξαι σε ἃ μεμάθηκα καὶ τετήρηκα ἐξ
Mk. xvi. 16 ἀρχῆς εἰς τήνδε τὴν πολιάν. εἰ οὖν πιστεύσεις
καὶ βαπτισθῇς, σωθήσῃ· εἰ δὲ ἀπιστήσεις, κατα-
κριθήσῃ. ταῦτα γὰρ ἃ σήμερον ὁρᾷς καὶ οἷς σε-
μνύνῃ, ἥ τε δόξα καὶ τρυφὴ καὶ ὁ πλοῦτος καὶ
πᾶσα ἡ τοῦ βίου ἀπάτη, ὅσον οὔπω παρέρχεται,
ἐκβαλοῦσι δέ σε καὶ μὴ βουλόμενον ἐντεῦθεν.
καὶ τὸ μὲν σῶμα κατακλεισθήσεται σμικροτάτῳ
μνήματι μονώτατον καταλειφθέν, πάσης τε ἀπο-
στερηθὲν φίλων καὶ συγγενῶν ἑταιρείας· οἰχή-
σεται δὲ τὰ τερπνὰ τοῦ κόσμου, καὶ πολλὴ ἀηδία
καὶ δυσώδης φθορά, ἀντὶ τῆς νυνὶ καλλονῆς καὶ
εὐοσμίας, περιχυθήσεται· τὴν δὲ ψυχήν σου
βαλοῦσιν ἐν τοῖς καταχθονίοις τῆς γῆς, ἐν τῇ καταδίκῃ τοῦ ᾅδου, ἕως τῆς τελευταίας ἀναστάσεως,
ἡνίκα πάλιν ἀπολαβοῦσα ἡ ψυχὴ τὸ ἑαυτῆς 85

Spirit the Comforter," "the Spirit of adoption." Of these each person, severally, is God. As the Father is, so also is the Son, and as the Son, so also the Holy Ghost. And there is one God in three, one nature, one kingdom, one power, one glory, one substance, distinct in persons, and so only distinct. One is the Father, whose property it is not to have been begotten; one is the only-begotten Son, and his property it is to have been begotten; and one is the Holy Ghost, and his property it is that he proceedeth. Thus illuminated *by* that light, which is the Father, *with* that light, which is the Son, *in* that light, which is the Holy Ghost, we glorify one Godhead in three persons. And he is one very and only God, known in the Trinity: for of him and through him, and unto him are all things.

and telleth Ioasaph of the doom of sinners,

'By his grace also, I came to know thy case, and was sent to teach thee the lessons that I have learned and observed from my youth even to these grey hairs. If then thou shalt believe and be baptized, thou shalt be saved; but if thou believe not, thou shalt be damned. All the things that thou seest to-day, wherein thou gloriest,—pomp, luxury, riches, and all the deceitfulness of life,—quickly pass away; and they shall cast thee hence whether thou wilt or no. And thy body will be imprisoned in a tiny grave, left in utter loneliness, and bereft of all company of kith and kin. And all the pleasant things of the world shall perish; and instead of the beauty and fragrance of to-day, thou shalt be encompassed with horror and the stink of corruption. But thy soul shall they hurl into the nether-regions of the earth, into the condemnation of Hades, until the final resurrection, when re-united to her body, she shall be cast forth from

σῶμα ἐκριφθήσεται ἐκ προσώπου Κυρίου, καὶ
παραδοθήσεται πυρὶ γεέννης ἀτελεύτητα φλογι-
ζούσης. ταῦτά σοι συμβήσεται καὶ πολλῷ τούτων χείρονα, εἰ ἐμμείνῃς τῇ ἀπιστίᾳ.

Εἰ δὲ προθύμως ὑπακούσεις τῷ καλοῦντί σε
εἰς σωτηρίαν, καί, προσδραμὼν αὐτῷ πόθῳ καὶ
χαρᾷ, τῷ φωτὶ αὐτοῦ σημειωθήσῃ, καὶ ἀμεταστρεπτὶ αὐτῷ ἀκολουθήσεις, πάντα μὲν ἀπαρνησάμενος, αὐτῷ μόνῳ κεκολλημένος, ὁποίας τεύξῃ
Prov. iii. 24, 25 ἀσφαλείας καὶ εὐφροσύνης ἄκουσον· Ἐὰν κάθῃ,
ἄφοβος ἔσῃ· ἐὰν δὲ καθεύδῃς, ἡδέως ὑπνώσεις,
καὶ οὐ φοβηθήσῃ πτόησιν ἐπελθοῦσαν, οὐδὲ ὁρμὰς
τῶν ἀσεβῶν δαιμόνων ἐπερχομένας· ἀλλὰ πορεύσῃ
Prov. xxviii. 1 πεποιθὼς ὡς λέων, καὶ ζήσῃ μετ' εὐφροσύνης καὶ
Is. li. 11 ἀγαλλιάματος αἰωνίου· ἐπὶ γὰρ τῆς κεφαλῆς σου
ἀγαλλίασις καὶ αἴνεσις, καὶ εὐφροσύνη καταλή-
ψεταί σε· ἔνθα ἀπέδρα ὀδύνη, λύπη καὶ στεναγ-
Is. lviii. 8, 9 μός· τότε ῥαγήσεται πρώϊμον τὸ φῶς σου, καὶ τὰ 86
ἰάματά σου ταχὺ ἀνατελεῖ, καὶ προπορεύσεται
ἔμπροσθέν σου ἡ δικαιοσύνη σου, καὶ ἡ δόξα τοῦ
Θεοῦ περιστελεῖ σε· τότε βοήσῃ, καὶ ὁ Θεὸς
εἰσακούσεταί σου· ἔτι λαλοῦντός σου ἐρεῖ· Ἰδοὺ
Is. xliii. 25, 26 πάρειμι· ἐγὼ γάρ εἰμι ὁ ἐξαλείφων τὰς ἀνομίας
σου καὶ οὐ μνησθῶ· σὺ δὲ μνήσθητι καὶ κριθῶ-
μεν· λέγε σὺ τὰς ἀνομίας σου, ἵνα δικαιωθῇς.
καὶ ἐὰν ὦσιν αἱ ἁμαρτίαι σου ὡς φοινικοῦν, ὡς
Is. i. 18, 20 χιόνα λευκανῶ· ἐὰν δὲ ὦσιν ὡς κόκκινον, ὡς ἔριον
λευκανῶ. τὸ γὰρ στόμα Κυρίου ἐλάλησε ταῦτα.

the presence of the Lord and be delivered to hell fire, which burneth everlastingly. These, and far worse haps than these, shall be thy destiny, if thou continue in unbelief.

'But and if thou readily obey him that calleth thee to salvation, and if thou run unto him with desire and joy, and be signed with his light, and follow him without turn, renouncing every thing, and cleaving only unto him, hear what manner of security and happiness shall be thine. "When thou sittest down, thou shalt not be afraid of sudden fear. When thou liest down, sweet shall be thy sleep." And thou shalt not be afraid of terror coming or the assaults of evil spirits, but shalt go thy way bold as any lion, and shalt live in bliss and everlasting joyaunce. For "joy and praise shall crown thy head, and gladness shall befall thee there, where pain and sorrow and wailing shall flee away." "Then shall thy light break forth as the morning, and thine health shall rise speedily: and thy righteousness shall go before thee, and the glory of the Lord shall be thy reward." Then shalt thou call, and the Lord shall answer; while thou art yet speaking, he shall say, "Here am I." "I, even I, am he that blotteth out thy transgressions, and will not remember them. Put me in remembrance: let us plead together: declare thou thy sins that thou mayst be justified." "Though thy sins be as scarlet, I will make them white as snow: though they be red as crimson I will make them white as wool, for the mouth of the Lord hath spoken it."'

and the blessings of the righteous

XI

Λέγει πρὸς αὐτὸν ὁ Ἰωάσαφ· Πάντα σου τὰ
ῥήματα καλὰ καὶ θαυμαστά εἰσι, κἀγὼ ἐπίστευσα
καὶ πιστεύω, πᾶσαν μὲν εἰδωλολατρείαν ἀπὸ
καρδίας μισήσας· καί, πρὸ τοῦ εἰσελθεῖν γάρ σε
πρός με, πλαγίως πως καὶ διστάζων πρὸς ταύτην
διέκειτό μου ἡ ψυχή· νυνὶ δὲ τέλειον μῖσος
Cp. Ps. cxxxix. 22 ἐμίσησα, μαθὼν παρὰ σοῦ τὴν ματαιότητα τούτων
καὶ τὴν ἀφροσύνην τῶν αὐτοῖς λατρευόντων.
Ποθῶ δὲ τοῦ ἀληθινοῦ Θεοῦ δοῦλος γενέσθαι,
εἴπερ οὐκ ἀπώσεταί με τὸν ἀνάξιον διὰ τὰς ἐμὰς
ἀνομίας, ἀλλὰ συγχωρήσει μοι πάντα, φιλάνθρωπος ὢν καὶ εὔσπλαγχνος, καθὰ διδάσκεις, καὶ
ἀξιώσει με δοῦλον αὐτοῦ γενέσθαι. ἤδη οὖν
ἑτοίμως ἔχω καὶ τὸ βάπτισμα δέξασθαι, καὶ
πάντα ὅσα εἴπῃς μοι φυλάξαι. τί δὲ χρή με
ποιεῖν μετὰ τὸ βάπτισμα; καὶ εἰ ἀρκεῖ τοῦτο
μόνον πρὸς σωτηρίαν, τὸ πιστεῦσαι καὶ βαπτι- 87
σθῆναι, ἢ καὶ ἄλλα τινὰ δεῖ προστιθέναι;

Καί φησι πρὸς αὐτὸν ὁ Βαρλαάμ· Ἄκουσον
τί δεῖ ποιεῖν μετὰ τὸ βάπτισμα· πάσης μὲν
ἁμαρτίας καὶ παντὸς πάθους ἀπέχεσθαι, ἐποικο-
δομεῖν δὲ ἐπὶ τῷ θεμελίῳ τῆς ὀρθοδόξου πίστεως
Jas. ii. 26 τὴν τῶν ἀρετῶν ἐργασίαν, ἐπειδὴ πίστις χωρὶς
τῶν ἔργων νεκρά ἐστιν, ὥσπερ καὶ ἔργα πίστεως
Cp. Gal. v. 16 ff. δίχα. φησὶ γὰρ ὁ Ἀπόστολος· Ἐν πνεύματι
περιπατεῖτε, καὶ ἐπιθυμίαν σαρκὸς οὐ μὴ τελέ-
σητε· φανερὰ δέ ἐστι τὰ ἔργα τῆς σαρκὸς ἅτινά
ἐστι, μοιχεῖαι, πορνεῖαι, ἀκαθαρσίαι, ἀσέλγειαι,
εἰδωλολατρεῖαι, φαρμακεῖαι, ἔχθραι, ἔρις, ζῆλοι,

XI

IOASAPH said unto him, 'All thy words are fair and wonderful, and, while thou spakest, I believed them and still believe them; and I hate all idolatry with all my heart. And indeed, even before thy coming hither, my soul was, in uncertain fashion, doubtful of it. But now I hate it with a perfect hatred, since I have learned from thy lips the vanity thereof, and the folly of those who worship idols; and I yearn to become the servant of the true God, if haply he will not refuse me, that am unworthy by reason of my sins, and I trust that he will forgive me everything, because he is a lover of men, and compassionate, as thou tellest me, and will count me worthy to become his servant. So I am ready anon to receive baptism, and to observe all thy sayings. But what must I do after baptism? And is this alone sufficient for salvation, to believe and be baptized, or must one add other services thereto?'

Ioasaph declareth his faith, and his desire to be baptized

Barlaam answered him, 'Hear what thou must do after baptism. Thou must abstain from all sin, and every evil affection, and build upon the foundation of the Catholick Faith the practice of the virtues; for faith without works is dead, as also are works without faith. For, saith the Apostle, Walk in the Spirit, and ye shall not fulfil the lust of the flesh. Now the works of the flesh are manifest, which are these: Adultery, fornication, uncleanness, lasciviousness, idolatry, witchcraft,

Barlaam describeth the conversation of true Christian men,

θυμοί, ἐρίθειαι, διχοστασίαι, αἱρέσεις, φθόνοι,
φόνοι, φιλαργυρίαι, λοιδορίαι, φιληδονίαι, μέθαι,
κῶμοι, ὑπερηφανίαι, καὶ τὰ ὅμοια τούτοις· ἃ
προλέγω ὑμῖν, καθὼς καὶ προεῖπον, ὅτι οἱ τὰ
τοιαῦτα πράσσοντες βασιλείαν Θεοῦ οὐ κληρο-
νομήσουσιν· ὁ δὲ καρπὸς τοῦ πνεύματός ἐστιν
ἀγάπη, χαρά, εἰρήνη, μακροθυμία, χρηστότης,
ἀγαθωσύνη, πίστις, πραότης, ἐγκράτεια, ἁγια-
σμὸς ψυχῆς καὶ σώματος, ταπείνωσις καρδίας
καὶ συντριβή, ἐλεημοσύνη, ἀμνησικακία, φιλανθρωπία, ἀγρυπνία, μετάνοια ἀκριβὴς πάντων
τῶν προγεγονότων σφαλμάτων, δάκρυον κατανύξεως, πένθος ὑπέρ τε τῶν ἰδίων ἁμαρτιῶν καὶ
τῶν τοῦ πλησίον, καὶ τὰ τούτοις ὅμοια, ἅτινα,
ὥσπερ τινὲς βαθμίδες καὶ κλίμακες ἀλλήλων
ἐχόμεναι καὶ ὑπ' ἀλλήλων συγκροτούμεναι, εἰς 88
οὐρανὸν τὴν ψυχὴν ἀναφέρουσιν. ἰδοὺ τούτων
ἐντετάλμεθα, μετὰ τὸ βάπτισμα, ἀντέχεσθαι,
τῶν δ' ἐναντίων ἀπέχεσθαι.

Prov. xxvi. 11; 2 Pet. ii. 22 Εἰ δὲ μετὰ τὸ λαβεῖν τὴν ἐπίγνωσιν τῆς
ἀληθείας, τῶν προτέρων αὖθις ἐπιληψόμεθα
νεκρῶν ἔργων, καὶ ὡς κύων ἐπὶ τὸν ἴδιον ἔμετον
ἐπιστρέψομεν, συμβήσεται ἡμῖν τὸ ὑπὸ τοῦ
Cp. Luke xi. 24–26 Κυρίου εἰρημένον. Ὅταν γάρ, φησί, τὸ ἀκάθαρτον
Πνεῦμα ἐξέλθῃ ἀπὸ τοῦ ἀνθρώπου (τῇ χάριτι
δηλαδὴ τοῦ βαπτίσματος), διέρχεται δι' ἀνύδρων
τόπων, ζητοῦν ἀνάπαυσιν, καὶ οὐχ εὑρίσκει·
μὴ φέρον δὲ ἐπὶ πολὺ ἄοικον καὶ ἀνέστιον
περιπλανᾶσθαι, λέγει· Ἐπιστρέψω εἰς τὸν οἶκόν
μου, ὅθεν ἐξῆλθον. καί, ἐλθόν, εὑρίσκει σεσαρω-
μένον καὶ κεκοσμημένον, κενὸν δὲ καὶ σχολάζοντα,
μὴ ὑποδεξάμενον τὴν ἐργασίαν τῆς χάριτος, μηδὲ

hatred, variance, emulations, wrath, strife, seditions, heresies, envyings, murders, love of money, railing, love of pleasure, drunkenness, revelling, arrogance, and such like, of the which I tell you before, as I have also told you in time past, that they which do such things shall not inherit the Kingdom of God. But the fruit of the Spirit is love, joy, peace, long-suffering, gentleness, goodness, faith, meekness, temperance, sanctification of soul and body, lowliness of heart and contrition, almsgiving, forgiveness of injuries, loving-kindness, watchings, perfect repentance of all past offences, tears of compunction, sorrow for our own sins and those of our neighbours, and the like. These, even as steps and ladders that support one another and are clinched together, conduct the soul to heaven. Lo, to these we are commanded to cleave after baptism, and to abstain from their contraries.

warneth Ioasaph against sins after baptism,

'But if, after receiving the knowledge of the truth, we again lay hold on dead works, and, like a dog, return to our vomit, it shall happen unto us according to the word of the Lord; "for," saith he, "when the unclean spirit is gone out of a man" (to wit, by the grace of baptism) "he walketh through dry places, seeking rest, and finding none." But enduring not for long to wander homeless and hearthless, he saith, "I will return to my house whence I came out." And, when he cometh, he findeth it swept and garnished, but empty and unoccupied, not having received the operation of grace, nor having filled itself with the riches of the

πληρώσαντα ἑαυτὸν τῷ πλούτῳ τῶν ἀρετῶν.
τότε πορεύεται καὶ λαμβάνει μεθ' ἑαυτοῦ ἕτερα
ἑπτὰ Πνεύματα πονηρότερα ἑαυτοῦ· καὶ εἰσ-
ελθόντα κατοικεῖ ἐκεῖ· καὶ γίνεται τὰ ἔσχατα
τοῦ ἀνθρώπου ἐκείνου χείρονα τῶν πρώτων. τὸ
Col. ii. 14 γὰρ βάπτισμα τῶν μὲν προημαρτημένων πάντων
τὰ χειρόγραφα, τῷ ὕδατι ἐνθάπτον, παντελεῖ
ἀφανισμῷ παραδίδωσι, καὶ εἰς τὸ ἑξῆς τεῖχος 89
ἡμῖν ἐστιν ἀσφαλὲς καὶ προπύργιον καὶ ὅπλον
κραταιὸν εἰς τὴν τοῦ ἐχθροῦ παράταξιν· οὐ μὴν
δὲ ἀναιρεῖ τὸ αὐτεξούσιον, οὔτε τῶν μετὰ τὸ
βάπτισμα ἁμαρτανομένων ἔχει συγχώρησιν, οὔτε
Eph. iv. 5 δευτέρας κολυμβήθρας κατάδυσιν. ἓν γὰρ ὁμο-
λογοῦμεν βάπτισμα· καὶ χρὴ πάσῃ φυλακῇ
τηρεῖν ἑαυτούς, μὴ δευτέροις ἐμπεσεῖν μολυσμοῖς,
ἀλλὰ τῶν ἐντολῶν ἐπιλαβέσθαι τοῦ Κυρίου.
Mat. xxviii. 19, 20 εἰπὼν γὰρ πρὸς τοὺς Ἀποστόλους, Πορευθέντες
μαθητεύσατε πάντα τὰ ἔθνη, βαπτίζοντες αὐτοὺς
εἰς τὸ ὄνομα τοῦ Πατρὸς καὶ τοῦ Υἱοῦ καὶ τοῦ
Ἁγίου Πνεύματος, οὐ μέχρι τούτου ἔστη· ἀλλὰ
προσέθετο, Διδάσκοντες αὐτοὺς τηρεῖν πάντα ὅσα
ἐνετειλάμην ὑμῖν.

Mat. v. 3 ff. Ἐνετείλατο δὲ πτωχοὺς μὲν εἶναι τῷ πνεύματι, οὓς μακαρίζει καὶ τῆς βασιλείας τῶν
οὐρανῶν ἀξίους ἀποκαλεῖ. εἶτα πενθεῖν ἐν τῷ
παρόντι ὑποτίθεται βίῳ, ἵνα τῆς μελλούσης
παρακλήσεως ἀξιωθῶμεν, πραεῖς τε εἶναι καὶ
ἀεὶ πεινῶντας καὶ διψῶντας τὴν δικαιοσύνην,
ἐλεήμονάς τε καὶ εὐμεταδότους, οἰκτίρμονας καὶ
συμπαθεῖς, καθαροὺς τῇ καρδίᾳ, ἀπεχομένους 90
ἀπὸ παντὸς μολυσμοῦ σαρκὸς καὶ πνεύματος,
εἰρηνοποιοὺς πρός τε τοὺς πλησίον καὶ πρὸς τὴν

virtues. Then goeth he, and taketh to him seven other spirits more wicked than himself; and they enter in and dwell there: and the last state of that man becometh worse than the first." For baptism burieth in the water and completely blotteth out the hand-writing of all former sins, and is to us for the future a sure fortress and tower of defence, and a strong weapon against the marshalled host of the enemy; but it taketh not away free will, nor alloweth the forgiving of sins after baptism, or immersion in the font a second time. For it is one baptism that we confess, and need is that we keep ourselves with all watchfulness that so we fall not into defilement a second time, but hold fast to the commandments of the Lord. For when he said to the Apostles, "Go make disciples of all nations, baptizing them in the name of the Father, and of the Son, and of the Holy Ghost," he did not stop there, but added, "teaching them to observe all things whatsoever I have commanded you."

'Now he commanded men to be poor in spirit, and such he calleth blessed and worthy of the kingdom of heaven. Again he chargeth us to mourn in the present life, that we may obtain comfort hereafter, and to be meek, and to be ever hungering and thirsting after righteousness: to be merciful, and ready to distribute, pitiful and compassionate, pure in heart, abstaining from all defilement of flesh and spirit, peacemakers with our neighbours and with our own souls,

and speaketh of the commands of Christ,

ἑαυτῶν ψυχήν, ὑποτάξαντας δηλονότι τὸ χεῖρον
τῷ κρείττονι καὶ τὸν μεταξὺ αὐτῶν διηνεκῆ
πόλεμον ὀρθῇ κρίσει εἰρηνοποιήσαντας, ὑπομένειν τε πάντα διωγμὸν καὶ πᾶσαν θλῖψιν καὶ
ὀνειδισμόν, ἕνεκεν δικαιοσύνης ὑπὲρ τοῦ ὀνόματος
αὐτοῦ ἡμῖν ἐπαγόμενον, ἵνα τῆς αἰωνίου χαρᾶς
ἐν τῇ λαμπρᾷ τῶν δώρων διανομῇ ἀξιωθῶμεν.
ἀλλὰ καὶ ἐν τῷ κόσμῳ οὕτως παρακελεύεται
λάμπειν τὸ φῶς ἡμῶν ἔμπροσθεν τῶν ἀνθρώπων,
ὅπως ἴδωσι, φησί, τὰ καλὰ ἔργα ὑμῶν, καὶ
δοξάσωσι τὸν Πατέρα ὑμῶν τὸν ἐν τοῖς οὐρανοῖς.
Exod. xx. Ὁ μὲν γὰρ τοῦ Μωσέως νόμος, ὁ πάλαι δοθεὶς
13; Deut. v. τοῖς Ἰσραηλίταις, Οὐ φονεύσεις, λέγει, οὐ μοι-
χεύσεις, οὐ κλέψεις, οὐ ψευδομαρτυρήσεις· ὁ δὲ
Mat. v. 21 ff. Χριστός φησιν, ὅτι Πᾶς ὁ ὀργιζόμενος τῷ ἀδελφῷ
αὐτοῦ εἰκῇ, ἔνοχος ἔσται τῇ κρίσει. ὃς δ' ἂν εἴπῃ,
Μωρέ, ἔνοχος ἔσται εἰς τὴν γέενναν τοῦ πυρός·
καὶ ὅτι, Ἐὰν προσφέρῃς τὸ δῶρόν σου ἐπὶ τὸ
θυσιαστήριον, κἀκεῖ μνησθῇς ὅτι ὁ ἀδελφός σου
ἔχει τι κατὰ σοῦ, ἄφες ἐκεῖ τὸ δῶρόν σου ἐπὶ τὸ
θυσιαστήριον, καὶ ἀπελθὼν πρῶτον διαλλάγηθι
τῷ ἀδελφῷ σου· καὶ ὅτι Πᾶς ὁ ἐμβλέπων γυναῖκα
πρὸς τὸ ἐπιθυμῆσαι, ἤδη ἐμοίχευσεν αὐτὴν ἐν τῇ 91
καρδίᾳ αὐτοῦ· τὸν μολυσμὸν τῆς ψυχῆς καὶ τὴν
τοῦ πάθους συγκατάθεσιν μοιχείαν καλέσας.
ἀλλὰ καὶ τοῦ νόμου τὴν ἐπιορκίαν κωλύοντος, ὁ
Χριστὸς οὐδὲ ὅλως ὀμνύειν, πλὴν τοῦ Ναὶ καὶ τοῦ
Exod. xxi. 28; Deut. xix. 21 Οὔ, ἐνετείλατο. ὀφθαλμὸν ἀντὶ ὀφθαλμοῦ καὶ
ὀδόντα ἀντὶ ὀδόντος ἐκεῖ· ἐνταῦθα δέ· Ὅστις σε
Mat. v. 39 ff. ῥαπίσει εἰς τὴν δεξιὰν σιαγόνα, στρέψον αὐτῷ,
φησί, καὶ τὴν ἄλλην· καὶ τῷ θέλοντί σοι κριθῆναι
καὶ τὸν χιτῶνά σου λαβεῖν, ἄφες αὐτῷ καὶ τὸ

by bringing the worse into subjection to the better, and thus by a just decision making peace in that continual warfare betwixt the twain; also to endure all persecution and tribulation and reviling, inflicted upon us for righteousness' sake in defence of his name, that we may obtain everlasting felicity in the glorious distribution of his rewards. Ay, and in this world he exhorteth us to let our "light so shine before men, that they may see," he saith, "your good works, and glorify your Father which is in heaven."

'For the law of Moses, formerly given to the Israelites, saith, "Thou shalt not kill; thou shalt not commit adultery; thou shalt not steal; thou shalt not bear false witness:" but Christ saith "Whosoever is angry with his brother without a cause shall be in danger of the judgement; and whosoever shall say, Thou fool, shall be in danger of hell fire:" and, "if thou bring thy gift to the altar, and there rememberest that thy brother hath aught against thee, leave there thy gift before the altar, and go thy way and first be reconciled to thy brother." And he also saith, "Whosoever looketh on a woman to lust after her, hath committed adultery with her in his heart." And hereby he calleth the defilement and consent of the affection adultery. Furthermore, where the law forbade a man to forswear himself, Christ commanded him to swear not at all beyond Yea and Nay. There we read, "Eye for eye and tooth for tooth": here, "Whosoever shall smite thee on thy right cheek, turn to him the other also. And if any man will sue thee at the law, and take

showing how much more excellent is the Gospel than the law of Moses

ἱμάτιον· καὶ ὅστις σε ἀγγαρεύσει μίλιον ἕν,
ὕπαγε μετ᾽ αὐτοῦ δύο· τῷ αἰτοῦντί σε δίδου, καὶ
τὸν θέλοντα ἀπὸ σοῦ δανείσασθαι μὴ ἀποστραφῇς·
ἀγαπᾶτε τοὺς ἐχθροὺς ὑμῶν, εὐλογεῖτε τοὺς κατα-
ρωμένους ὑμᾶς, καλῶς ποιεῖτε τοῖς μισοῦσιν ὑμᾶς,
καὶ προσεύχεσθε ὑπὲρ τῶν ἐπηρεαζόντων ὑμᾶς
καὶ διωκόντων, ὅπως γένησθε υἱοὶ τοῦ Πατρὸς ὑμῶν
τοῦ ἐν τοῖς οὐρανοῖς, ὅτι τὸν ἥλιον αὐτοῦ ἀνα-
τέλλει ἐπὶ πονηροὺς καὶ ἀγαθούς, καὶ βρέχει ἐπὶ
Mat. vii. 1; Luke vi. 37 δικαίους καὶ ἀδίκους. μὴ κρίνετε, ἵνα μὴ κριθῆτε·
Mat. vi. 14, 19 ἄφετε, καὶ ἀφεθήσεται ὑμῖν. μὴ θησαυρίζετε
ὑμῖν θησαυροὺς ἐπὶ τῆς γῆς, ὅπου σὴς καὶ βρῶσις
Ibid. vi. 19 ἀφανίζει καὶ ὅπου κλέπται διορύσσουσι καὶ
κλέπτουσι· θησαυρίζετε δὲ ὑμῖν θησαυροὺς ἐν
οὐρανῷ, ὅπου οὔτε σὴς οὔτε βρῶσις ἀφανίζει καὶ
ὅπου κλέπται οὐ διορύσσουσιν, οὐδὲ κλέπτουσιν· 92
ὅπου γάρ ἐστιν ὁ θησαυρὸς ὑμῶν, ἐκεῖ ἔσται καὶ
ἡ καρδία ὑμῶν. μὴ μεριμνᾶτε τῇ ψυχῇ ὑμῶν τί
φάγητε καὶ τί πίητε, μηδὲ τῷ σώματι ὑμῶν τί ἐν-
δύσησθε· οἶδε γὰρ ὁ Πατὴρ ὑμῶν ὁ οὐράνιος ὅτι
χρῄζετε τούτων ἁπάντων· ὃς οὖν τὴν ψυχὴν δοὺς
καὶ τὸ σῶμα, δώσει πάντως καὶ τροφὴν καὶ
Ibid. vi. 26 ἔνδυμα, ὁ τὰ πετεινὰ τοῦ οὐρανοῦ τρέφων καὶ τὰ
κρίνα τοῦ ἀγροῦ τοιαύτῃ κοσμῶν ὡραιότητι.
ζητεῖτε δέ, φησί, πρῶτον τὴν βασιλείαν τοῦ Θεοῦ
καὶ τὴν δικαιοσύνην αὐτοῦ, καὶ ταῦτα πάντα
προστεθήσεται ὑμῖν. μὴ μεριμνήσητε εἰς τὴν
αὔριον· ἡ γὰρ αὔριον τὰ ἑαυτῆς μεριμνήσει.
Ibid. vii. 12 πάντα ὅσα ἂν θέλητε ἵνα ποιῶσιν ὑμῖν οἱ ἄνθρω-
Ibid. vii. 13, 14 ποι, οὕτω καὶ ὑμεῖς ποιεῖτε αὐτοῖς. εἰσέλθετε
διὰ τῆς στενῆς πύλης, ὅτι πλατεῖα ἡ πύλη καὶ
εὐρύχωρος ἡ ὁδὸς ἡ ἀπάγουσα εἰς τὴν ἀπώλειαν,

away thy coat, let him have thy cloke also. And whosoever shall compel thee to go a mile, go with him twain. Give to him that asketh thee, and from him that would borrow of thee turn not thou away. Love your enemies, bless them that curse you, do good to them that hate you, and pray for them which despitefully use you and persecute you; that ye may be the children of your Father which is in heaven: for he maketh his sun to rise on the evil and on the good, and sendeth rain on the just and on the unjust. Judge not, that ye be not judged. Forgive, and ye shall be forgiven. Lay not up for yourselves treasures upon earth, where moth and rust doth corrupt, and where thieves break through and steal: but lay up for yourselves treasures in heaven, where neither moth nor rust doth corrupt, and where thieves do not break through nor steal: for where your treasure is, there will your heart be also. Take no thought for your life, what ye shall eat, or what ye shall drink; nor yet for your body, what ye shall put on: for your heavenly Father knoweth that ye have need of all these things." He therefore that gave life and body will assuredly give food and raiment: he that feedeth the fowls of the air and arrayeth with such beauty the lilies of the field. "But, seek ye first," saith Christ, "the kingdom of God, and his righteousness; and all these things shall be added unto you. Take therefore no thought for the morrow: for the morrow shall take thought for the things of itself. Therefore all things whatsoever ye would that men should do to you, do ye even so to them. Enter ye in at the strait gate: for wide is the gate, and broad is the way that leadeth to destruction, and many

καὶ πολλοί εἰσιν οἱ εἰσερχόμενοι δι᾽ αὐτῆς· στενὴ
καὶ τεθλιμμένη ἡ ὁδὸς ἡ ἀπάγουσα εἰς τὴν ζωήν,
Mat. vii. 21 καὶ ὀλίγοι εἰσὶν οἱ εὑρίσκοντες αὐτήν. οὐ πᾶς ὁ
λέγων μοι, Κύριε, Κύριε, εἰσελεύσεται εἰς τὴν
βασιλείαν τῶν οὐρανῶν, ἀλλ᾽ ὁ ποιῶν τὸ θέλημα
Mat. x. 37. 38 τοῦ Πατρός μου τοῦ ἐν οὐρανοῖς. ὁ φιλῶν πατέρα
ἢ μητέρα ὑπὲρ ἐμὲ οὐκ ἔστι μου ἄξιος, καὶ ὁ φιλῶν
υἱὸν ἢ θυγατέρα ὑπὲρ ἐμὲ οὐκ ἔστι μου ἄξιος· καὶ
ὃς οὐ λαμβάνει τὸν σταυρὸν αὐτοῦ καὶ ἀκολουθεῖ
ὀπίσω μου, οὐκ ἔστι μου ἄξιος. ἰδοὺ ταῦτα καὶ
τὰ τούτοις ὅμοια ἐνετείλατο ὁ Σωτὴρ τοῖς ἀπο- 93
στόλοις διδάσκειν τοὺς πιστούς· καὶ ταῦτα
πάντα ὀφείλομεν φυλάττειν, εἴπερ ποθοῦμεν τῆς
2 Tim. iv. 8 τελειότητος ἐπιτυχεῖν καὶ τῶν ἀφθάρτων στεφάνων ἀξιωθῆναι τῆς δικαιοσύνης, οὓς ἀποδώσει
Κύριος ἐν ἐκείνῃ τῇ ἡμέρᾳ ὁ δίκαιος κριτὴς πᾶσι
τοῖς ἠγαπηκόσι τὴν ἐπιφάνειαν αὐτοῦ.

Λέγει ὁ Ἰωάσαφ πρὸς τὸν γέροντα· Ταύτης οὖν τῆς ἀκριβείας τῶν δογμάτων χρηζούσης καὶ τὴν ἀκραιφνῆ ταύτην πολιτείαν, ἐὰν μετὰ τὸ βάπτισμα συμβῇ με ἑνὸς ἢ δύο τῶν ἐντολῶν τούτων διαμαρτεῖν, ἆρα διαμαρτάνων ἔσομαι ὅλου τοῦ σκοποῦ, καὶ ματαία ἔσται πᾶσα ἡ ἐλπίς;

Ὁ δὲ Βαρλαὰμ ἔφη· Μὴ οὕτως ὑπολάμβανε ταῦτα. ὁ γὰρ ἐπὶ σωτηρίᾳ τοῦ γένους ἡμῶν ἐνανθρωπήσας Θεὸς Λόγος, εἰδὼς τὴν πολλὴν ἀσθένειαν καὶ ταλαιπωρίαν τῆς φύσεως ἡμῶν, οὐδὲ ἐν τούτῳ τῷ μέρει ἀφῆκεν ἡμᾶς ἀνιάτρευτα νοσεῖν· ἀλλ᾽ ὡς πάνσοφος ἰατρὸς τῇ ὀλισθηρᾷ ἡμῶν καὶ φιλαμαρτήμονι γνώμῃ συνέμιξε τὸ φάρμακον τῆς μετανοίας, κηρύξας ταύτην εἰς ἄφεσιν ἁμαρτιῶν. μετὰ γὰρ τὸ λαβεῖν ἡμᾶς τὴν

there be which go in thereat. Strait and narrow is the way which leadeth unto life and few there be that find it. Not every one that saith unto me, Lord, Lord, shall enter into the kingdom of heaven; but he that doeth the will of my Father which is in heaven. He that loveth father or mother more than me is not worthy of me; and he that loveth son and daughter more than me is not worthy of me. And he that taketh not up his cross and followeth after me, is not worthy of me." Lo these and the like of these be the things which the Saviour commanded his Apostles to teach the Faithful: and all these things we are bound to observe, if we desire to attain to perfection and receive the incorruptible crowns of righteousness, which the Lord, the righteous judge, shall give at that day unto all them that have loved his appearing.'

Ioasaph's question concerning sins after baptism

Ioasaph said unto the elder, 'Well then, as the strictness of these doctrines demandeth such chaste conversation, if, after baptism, I chance to fail in one or two of these commandments, shall I therefore utterly miss the goal, and shall all my hope be vain?'

Barlaam telleth of the baptism of tears and repentance

Barlaam answered, 'Deem not so. God, the Word, made man for the salvation of our race, aware of the exceeding frailty and misery of our nature, hath not even here suffered our sickness to be without remedy. But, like a skilful leech, he hath mixed for our unsteady and sin-loving heart the potion of repentance, prescribing this for the remission of sins. For

ἐπίγνωσιν τῆς ἀληθείας, καὶ ἁγιασθῆναι δι' ὕδατος
καὶ πνεύματος, πάσης τε ἁμαρτίας καὶ παντὸς 94
ῥύπου ἀμογητὶ καθαρθῆναι, ἐὰν συμβῇ ἔν τισι
παραπτώμασιν ἡμᾶς ἁμαρτημάτων ἐμπεσεῖν, οὐκ
ἔστι μὲν διὰ βαπτίσματος δευτέρα ἀναγέννησις ἐν
ὕδατι τῆς κολυμβήθρας διὰ τοῦ πνεύματος ἐγ-
γινομένη καὶ τελείως ἡμᾶς ἀναχωνεύουσα. τοῦτο
γὰρ τὸ δώρημα ἅπαξ δέδοται· ἀλλὰ διὰ μετανοίας
ἐμπόνου καὶ θερμῶν δακρύων, κόπων τε καὶ ἱδρώ-
των, γίνεται καθαρισμὸς καὶ συγχώρησις τῶν
Luke i. 78 πταισμάτων διὰ σπλάγχνα ἐλέους Θεοῦ ἡμῶν.
βάπτισμα γὰρ ἐκλήθη καὶ ἡ τῶν δακρύων πηγή,
κατὰ χάριν τοῦ Δεσπότου, ἀλλὰ πόνου καὶ χρόνου
δεόμενον· καὶ πολλοὺς τῶν πολλῶν διεσώσατο
πταισμάτων· καθότι οὐκ ἔστιν ἁμαρτία νικῶσα
τὴν τοῦ Θεοῦ φιλανθρωπίαν, εἴπερ φθάσομεν
μετανοῆσαι καὶ δάκρυσι πταισμάτων αἶσχος
ἀπονίψασθαι, καὶ μὴ προλαβὼν ὁ θάνατος ῥερυπω-
μένους ἡμᾶς ἐκβαλεῖ τῶν ἐντεῦθεν· οὐκ ἔστι γὰρ
Ps. vi. 5 ἐν τῷ ᾅδῃ ἐξομολόγησις, οὐδὲ μετάνοια· ἕως δὲ
ἐν τοῖς ζῶσιν ὦμεν, τοῦ θεμελίου τῆς ὀρθοδόξου
Cp. Eccles. x. 18 πίστεως ἀρραγοῦς διαμένοντος, κἂν τι τῆς δοκώ-
σεως ἢ τῆς ἐνδομήσεως παραλυθῇ, ἔξεστι τὸ
Cp. Rev. xxi. 18 σαθρωθὲν τοῖς πταίσμασι τῇ μετανοίᾳ αὖθις
ἀνακαινίσαι. πλῆθος γὰρ οἰκτιρμῶν Θεοῦ ἀριθ-
μῆσαι καὶ μέγεθος ἐλέους αὐτοῦ μετρῆσαι
ἀδύνατον· ἁμαρτήματα δὲ οἷά περ ἂν ὦσι καὶ
πταίσματα μέτρῳ ὑπόκεινται καὶ ἀριθμητὰ εἶναι
συμβαίνει. τὰ οὖν μέτρῳ καὶ ἀριθμῷ ὑποκείμενα
πταίσματα ἡμῶν τὸ ἀμέτρητον ἔλεος καὶ τοὺς 95
ἀναριθμήτους οἰκτιρμοὺς τοῦ Θεοῦ νικῆσαι οὐ
δύναται.

after that we have received the knowledge of the truth, and have been sanctified by water and the Spirit, and cleansed without effort from all sin and all defilement, if we should fortune to fall into any transgression, there is, it is true, no second regeneration made within us by the spirit through baptism in the water of the font, and wholly re-creating us (that gift is given once for all): but, by means of painful repentance, hot tears, toils and sweats, there is a purifying and pardoning of our offences through the tender mercy of our God. For the fount of tears is also called baptism, according to the grace of the Master, but it needeth labour and time; and many hath it saved after many a fall; because there is no sin too great for the clemency of God, if we be quick to repent, and purge the shame of our offences, and death overtake us not, and depart us not from this life still defiled; for in the grave there is no confession nor repentance. But as long as we are among the living, while the foundation of our true faith continueth unshattered, even if somewhat of the outer roof-work or inner building be disabled, it is allowed to renew by repentance the part rotted by sins. It is impossible to count the multitude of the mercies of God, or measure the greatness of his compassion: whereas sins and offences, of whatever kind, are subject to measure and may be numbered. So our offences, being subject to measure and number, cannot overcome the immeasurable compassion, and innumerable mercies of God.

Διὸ οὐ προσετάχθημεν ἐπὶ τοῖς ἡμαρτημένοις
ἀπογινώσκειν, ἀλλ᾽ ἐπιγινώσκειν τὴν ἀγαθότητα
τοῦ Θεοῦ, καὶ καταγινώσκειν τῶν ἁμαρτημάτων
ὧν ἡ ἄφεσις πρόκειται διὰ φιλανθρωπίαν τοῦ
Χριστοῦ, ὃς ὑπὲρ τῶν ἁμαρτιῶν ἡμῶν τὸ ἴδιον
ἐξέχεεν αἷμα. πολλαχόθεν δὲ τῆς γραφῆς διδα-
σκόμεθα τὴν δύναμιν τῆς μετανοίας, καὶ μάλιστα
ἐκ τῶν προσταγμάτων καὶ παραβολῶν τοῦ Κυ-
Mat. iv. 17 ρίου ἡμῶν Ἰησοῦ Χριστοῦ. Ἀπὸ τότε γάρ, φησίν,
ἤρξατο ὁ Ἰησοῦς διδάσκειν καὶ λέγειν· Μετα-
νοεῖτε· ἤγγικε γὰρ ἡ βασιλεία τῶν οὐρανῶν.
Luke xv. 11 ff. ἀλλὰ καὶ ἐν παραβολῇ υἱόν τινα εἰσηγεῖται,
λαβόντα τὴν τοῦ πατρὸς οὐσίαν καὶ εἰς χώραν
ἀποδημήσαντα μακράν, κἀκεῖ ἐν ἀσωτίᾳ πάντα
καταναλώσαντα, εἶτα, λιμοῦ κατὰ τὴν χώραν
ἐκείνην γενομένου, ἀπελθόντα καὶ κολληθέντα
ἑνὶ τῶν πονηρῶν πολιτῶν τῆς πολυαμαρτήτου
χώρας ἐκείνης· ὃς καὶ ἔπεμψεν αὐτόν, φησίν,
εἰς τοὺς ἀγροὺς αὐτοῦ βόσκειν χοίρους· τὴν
τραχυτάτην καὶ βδελυρὰν ἁμαρτίαν οὕτω καλέσας. πολλὰ οὖν μογήσας, καὶ εἰς ἐσχάτην
ἐληλακὼς ταλαιπωρίαν, ὡς μηδὲ τῆς βρομώδους
τῶν χοίρων τροφῆς τὴν ἰδίαν ἰσχύειν ἐμπλῆσαι
γαστέρα, εἰς συναίσθησιν ὀψέ ποτε ἐλθὼν τῆς
τοιαύτης αἰσχύνης, θρηνῶν ἑαυτὸν ἔλεγε· Πόσοι 96
μίσθιοι τοῦ πατρός μου περισσεύονται ἄρτων,
ἐγὼ δὲ λιμῷ ἀπόλλυμαι. ἀναστὰς πορεύσομαι
πρὸς τὸν πατέρα μου, καὶ ἐρῶ αὐτῷ· Πάτερ,
ἥμαρτον εἰς τὸν οὐρανὸν καὶ ἐνώπιόν σου, καὶ
οὐκ εἰμὶ ἄξιος κληθῆναι υἱός σου· ποίησόν με ὡς
ἕνα τῶν μισθίων σου. καὶ ἀναστὰς ἦλθε πρὸς
τὸν πατέρα αὐτοῦ. ὁ δέ, πόρρωθεν ἰδὼν αὐτόν,

'Wherefore we are commanded not to despair for our trespasses, but to acknowledge the goodness of God, and condemn the sins whereof forgiveness is offered us by reason of the loving-kindness of Christ, who for our sins shed his precious blood. In many places of Scripture we are taught the power of repentance, and especially by the precepts and parables of our Lord Jesus Christ. For it saith, "From that time began Jesus to preach and to say, 'Repent ye, for the kingdom of heaven is at hand.'" Moreover he setteth before us, in a parable, a certain son that had received his father's substance, and taken his journey into a far country, and there spent all in riotous living. Then, when there arose a famine in that land, he went and joined himself to one of the citizens of that land of iniquity, who sent him into his fields to feed swine,—thus doth he designate the most coarse and loathsome sin. When, after much labour, he had come to the utmost misery, and might not even fill his belly with the husks that the swine did eat, at last he came to perceive his shameful plight, and, bemoaning himself, said, "How many hired servants of my father's have bread enough and to spare, and I perish with hunger! I will arise and go to my father, and will say unto him, 'Father, I have sinned against heaven and before thee, and am no more worthy to be called thy son: make me as one of thy hired servants.'" And he arose, and came to his father. But, when he was yet a great

Barlaam telleth of the parables of the Prodigal Son,

ἐσπλαγχνίσθη, καὶ προσδραμὼν ἐνηγκαλίσατο
καὶ συμπαθῶς κατεφίλησε· καὶ τῆς προτέρας
ἀξιώσας τιμῆς ἑορτὴν χαρμόσυνον ἐπὶ τῇ αὐτοῦ
ἀνευρέσει ἐποιήσατο, θύσας τὸν μόσχον τὸν
σιτευτόν. ἰδοὺ ταύτην τὴν παραβολὴν περὶ τῶν
ἐξ ἁμαρτιῶν ὑποστρεφόντων καὶ ἐν μετανοίᾳ
Luke xv. 4 ff. προσπιπτόντων ἡμῖν ἐξηγήσατο. ἀλλὰ καὶ ποι-
μένα τινὰ ἀγαθὸν αὖθις δηλοῖ ἑκατὸν ἐσχηκότα
πρόβατα καί, τοῦ ἑνὸς ἀπολωλότος, καταλιπόντα
τὰ ἐνενηκονταεννέα, εἰς ἐπιζήτησιν τοῦ ἀλωμένου
ἐξελθεῖν, ἕως εὑρὼν αὐτό, καὶ τοῖς ὤμοις ἀναλαβών, τοῖς ἀπλανέσι συγκατέμιξε, συγκαλέσας
τοὺς φίλους καὶ τοὺς γείτονας εἰς εὐωχίαν ἐν τῇ
τούτου εὑρέσει. Οὕτω, φησὶν ὁ Σωτήρ, χαρὰ ἔσται
ἐν οὐρανῷ ἐπὶ ἑνὶ ἁμαρτωλῷ μετανοοῦντι, ἢ ἐπὶ
ἐνενηκονταεννέα δικαίοις, οἵτινες οὐ χρείαν ἔχουσι
μετανοίας.

Ἀμέλει καὶ ὁ κορυφαῖος τῶν μαθητῶν Πέτρος,
ἡ τῆς πίστεως πέτρα, κατ᾿ αὐτὸν τὸν καιρὸν τοῦ
σωτηρίου πάθους, πρὸς μικρὸν ἐγκαταλειφθεὶς
οἰκονομικῇ τινι ἐγκαταλείψει, ὡς ἂν γνῷ τῆς
ἀνθρωπίνης ἀσθενείας τὸ εὐτελὲς καὶ ταλαί-
Luke xxii. 62 πωρον, ἀρνήσεως περιπέπτωκεν ἐγκλήματι· εἶτ᾿
εὐθὺς μνησθεὶς τῶν τοῦ Κυρίου ῥημάτων, ἐξελθὼν 97
ἔξω ἔκλαυσε πικρῶς· καὶ τοῖς θερμοῖς ἐκείνοις
δάκρυσι τὴν ἧτταν ἀνακαλεσάμενος ἑτεραλκέα
τὴν νίκην εἰργάσατο. ἐμπειροπόλεμος γὰρ ὤν,
εἰ καὶ πέπτωκεν, οὐκ ἐξελύθη, οὐδ᾿ ἀπέγνω
ἑαυτόν· ἀλλ᾿ ἀναπηδήσας προσήγαγε πικρότατα
δάκρυα ἀπὸ καρδίας θλιβομένης· καὶ παραυτίκα
ὁ πολέμιος θεασάμενος αὐτά, ὥσπερ ὑπὸ φλογὸς
σφοδροτάτης τὰς ὄψεις φλεγόμενος, ἀπεπήδησε

way off, his father saw him, and had compassion, and ran, and embraced him, and kissed him tenderly, and, restoring him to his former rank, made a feast of joyaunce because his son was found again, and killed the fatted calf. Lo, this parable, Jesus spake to us, concerneth such as turn again from sin, and fall at his feet in repentance. Again, he repre- senteth a certain good shepherd that had an hundred sheep, and, when one was lost, left the ninety and nine, and went forth to seek that which was gone astray, until he found it: and he laid it on his shoulders, and folded it with those that had not gone astray, and called together his friends and neighbours to a banquet, because that it was found. "Likewise," saith the Saviour, "joy shall be in heaven over one sinner that repenteth, more than over ninety and nine just persons which need no repentance."

and of the Good Shepherd,

'And, in sooth, even the chief of the disciples, Peter, the Rock of the Faith, in the very season of the Saviour's Passion, failing for a little while in his stewardship, that he might understand the worthlessness and misery of human frailty, fell under the guilt of denial. Then he straightway remembered the Lord's words, and went out and wept bitterly, and with those hot tears made good his defeat, and transferred the victory to his own side. Like a skilful man of war, though fallen, he was not undone, nor did he despair, but, springing to his feet, he brought up, as a reserve, bitter tears from the agony of his soul; and straight- way, when the enemy saw that sight, like a man whose eyes are scorched with a fierce flame, he leaped

and of the fall and rising again of St. Peter,

φεύγων μακρὰν καὶ δεινῶς ὀλολύζων. ὁ δὲ κορυφαῖος κορυφαῖος ἦν αὖθις, ὥσπερ διδάσκαλος τῆς
οἰκουμένης χειροτονηθείς, οὕτω δὴ καὶ μετανοίας
ὑπογραμμὸς γενόμενος. μετὰ δὲ τὴν θείαν ἀνέ-
John xxi. 16, 17 γερσιν τρίτον προσειπὼν ὁ Χριστός, Πέτρε, φιλεῖς
με; τὸ τρισσὸν τῆς ἀρνήσεως διωρθώσατο, τοῦ
ἀποστόλου ἀποκρινομένου· Ναί, Κύριε, σὺ οἶδας
ὅτι φιλῶ σε.

Ἐκ πάντων οὖν τουτων καὶ ἄλλων πολλῶν καὶ
ἀριθμοῦ ὑπερκειμένων παραδειγμάτων μανθάνομεν
τὴν δύναμιν τῶν δακρύων καὶ τῆς μετανοίας·
μόνον ὁ τρόπος ταύτης ἀξιόλογος, γενέσθω ἐκ
διαθέσεως βδελυσσομένης τὴν ἁμαρτίαν, μισούσης
τε ταύτην καὶ καταγινωσκούσης, δάκρυσι δὲ
κεχρημένης, καθώς φησιν ὁ προφήτης Δαυίδ·
Ps. vi. 6 Ἐκοπίασα ἐν τῷ στεναγμῷ μου· λούσω καθ' 98
ἑκάστην νύκτα τὴν κλίνην μου· ἐν δάκρυσί μου
τὴν στρωμνήν μου βρέξω. καὶ λοιπὸν ὁ καθαρισμὸς τῶν ἁμαρτημάτων γενήσεται διὰ τοῦ
αἵματος τοῦ Χριστοῦ, ἐν τῷ μεγέθει τοῦ ἐλέους
αὐτοῦ, καὶ τῷ πλήθει τῶν οἰκτιρμῶν τοῦ Θεοῦ
Is. i. 18 τοῦ εἰπόντος ὅτι, Ἐὰν ὦσιν αἱ ἁμαρτίαι ὑμῶν ὡς
φοινικοῦν, ὡς χιόνα λευκανῶ, καὶ τὰ ἑξῆς.

Ταῦτα μὲν οὖν οὕτως ἔχει καὶ οὕτως πιστεύο-
Cp. 1 Tim. ii. 4; iv. 3 μεν· χρὴ δέ, μετὰ τὸ λαβεῖν τὴν ἐπίγνωσιν τῆς
ἀληθείας καὶ τῆς ἀναγεννήσεως καὶ υἱοθεσίας
ἀξιωθῆναι καὶ μυστηρίων γεύσασθαι θείων,
πάσῃ δυνάμει ἀσφαλίζεσθαι τοῦ μὴ πίπτειν.
τὸ γὰρ πίπτειν οὐ πρέπει τῷ ἀθλητῇ, ἐπειδὴ
πολλοὶ πεσόντες ἀναστῆναι οὐκ ἠδυνήθησαν· οἱ
μέν, τοῖς πάθεσι θύραν ἀνοίξαντες, καὶ δυσαποσπάστως αὐτοῖς προσμείναντες, οὐκ ἔτι ἴσχυσαν

off and fled afar, howling horribly. So the chief became chief again, as he had before been chosen teacher of the whole world, being now become its pattern of penitence. And after his holy resurrection Christ made good this three-fold denial with the three-fold question, "Peter, lovest thou me?", the Apostle answering, "Yea, Lord, thou knowest that I love thee."

proving thereby the power of repentance,

'So from all these and many other examples beyond count we learn the virtue of tears and repentance. Only the manner thereof must be noted—it must arise from a heart that abominateth sin and weepeth, as saith the prophet David, "I am weary of my groaning: every night will I wash my bed and water my couch with my tears." Again the cleansing of sins will be wrought by the blood of Christ, in the greatness of his compassion and the multitude of the mercies of that God who saith, "Though your sins be as scarlet, I will make them white as snow," and so forth.

but bidding Ioasaph to take heed lest he fall

'Thus therefore it is, and thus we believe. But after receiving the knowledge of the truth and winning regeneration and adoption as sons, and tasting of the divine mysteries, we must strive hard to keep our feet lest we fall. For to fall becometh not the athlete, since many have fallen and been unable to rise. Some, opening a door to sinful lusts, and clinging obstinately to them, have no more had

πρὸς μετάνοιαν παλινδρομῆσαι· οἱ δέ, προαν-
αρπασθέντες ὑπὸ τοῦ θανάτου, καὶ μὴ φθάσαντες
διὰ μεταγνώσεως ἑαυτοὺς τοῦ ῥύπου τῆς ἁμαρτίας
ἐκπλῦναι, κατεδικάσθησαν. καὶ διὰ τοῦτο ἐπικίνδυνον τὸ πίπτειν ἐν οἱῳδήποτε πάθει· ἐὰν δὲ
συμβῇ πεσεῖν, εὐθὺς ἀναπηδῆσαι χρή, καὶ στῆναι
πάλιν εἰς τὸν καλὸν ἀγῶνα· καὶ ὁσάκις ἂν τοῦτο 99
συμβῇ, κἀκεῖνο αὐτίκα ἔστω τὸ τῆς ἐγέρσεως καὶ
Zech. i. 3 στάσεως ἕως τῆς τελευτῆς. Ἐπιστράφητε γὰρ
πρός με, καὶ ἐπιστραφήσομαι πρὸς ὑμᾶς, λέγει
Κύριος ὁ Θεός.

XII

Πρὸς ταῦτα ὁ Ἰωάσαφ εἶπε· Πῶς οὖν τις φυλάξει ἑαυτὸν μετὰ τὸ βάπτισμα καθαρὸν ἀπὸ πάσης ἁμαρτίας; κἂν γάρ ἐστιν, ὡς λέγεις, τοῖς πταίουσι μετάνοια, ἀλλ' ἐν κόπῳ καὶ πόνῳ, κλαυθμῷ τε καὶ πένθει, ἅπερ οὐκ εὐκατόρθωτα τοῖς πολλοῖς εἶναί μοι δοκῶ· ἀλλὰ μᾶλλον ἤθελον εὑρεῖν ὁδὸν τοῦ φυλάττειν ἀκριβῶς τὰ προστάγματα τοῦ Θεοῦ καὶ μὴ ἐκκλίνειν ἀπ' αὐτῶν, μηδέ, μετὰ τὴν συγχώρησιν τῶν προτέρων κακῶν, παροργίζειν αὖθις τὸν γλυκύτατον Δεσπότην καὶ Θεόν.

Ὁ δὲ Βαρλαὰμ ἔφη· Καλῶς εἶπας ταῦτα, κύριέ μου βασιλεῦ· τοῦτο καὶ ἐμοὶ καταθύμιον ὑπάρχει· ἀλλ' ἐργῶδές ἐστι καὶ κομιδῇ ἀδύνατον τὸ πυρὶ συναναστρεφόμενόν τινα μὴ καπνίζεσθαι. δυσκατόρθωτον οὖν καὶ λίαν ἄναντες δεδεμένον τοῖς τοῦ βίου πράγμασι καὶ ταῖς αὐτοῦ ἀσχολούμενον

strength to hasten back to repentance; and others, being untimely snatched by death, and having not made speed enough to wash them from the pollution of their sin, have been damned. And for this cause it is parlous to fall into any kind of sinful affection whatsoever. But if any man fall, he must at once leap up, and stand again to fight the good fight: and, as often as there cometh a fall, so often must there at once ensue this rising and standing, unto the end. For, "Turn ye unto me, and I will turn unto you," saith the Lord God.'

XII

To this said Ioasaph, 'But how, after baptism, shall a man keep himself clear from all sin? For even if there be, as thou sayest, repentance for them that stumble, yet it is attended with toil and trouble, with weeping and mourning; things which, methinks, are not easy for the many to accomplish. But I desired rather to find a way to keep strictly the commandments of God, and not swerve from them, and, after his pardoning of my past misdeeds, never again to provoke that most sweet God and Master.'

Ioasaph enquireth how he may keep himself from falling

Barlaam answered, 'Well said, my lord and king. That also is my desire; but it is hard, nay quite impossible, for a man living with fire not to be blackened with smoke: for it is an uphill task, and one not easy of accomplishment, for a man that is tied to the matters of this life and busied with its cares

Barlaam warneth him of the temptations of life in this world,

μερίμναις καὶ ταραχαῖς, πλούτῳ τε καὶ τρυφῇ συζῶντα, ἀκλινῶς βαδίζειν τὴν ὁδὸν τῶν ἐντολῶν τοῦ
Κυρίου, καὶ καθαρὸν ἑαυτὸν ἐκ τούτων περισώσα-
Mat. vi. 24 σθαι. φησὶ γὰρ ὁ Κύριος· Οὐδεὶς δύναται δυσὶ
κυρίοις δουλεύειν· ἢ γὰρ τὸν ἕνα μισήσει καὶ 100
τὸν ἕτερον ἀγαπήσει, ἢ τοῦ ἑνὸς ἀνθέξεται καὶ τοῦ
ἑτέρου καταφρονήσει· οὐ δύνασθε Θεῷ δουλεύειν
καὶ μαμωνᾷ. γράφει δὲ καὶ ὁ ἠγαπημένος αὐτοῦ
μαθητής, Ἰωάννης ὁ εὐαγγελιστὴς καὶ θεολόγος,
1 John ii. 15–17 ἐν τῇ κατ' αὐτὸν ἐπιστολῇ οὕτως· Μὴ ἀγαπᾶτε
τὸν κόσμον, μηδὲ τὰ ἐν τῷ κόσμῳ· ἐάν τις ἀγαπᾷ
τὸν κόσμον, οὐκ ἔστιν ἡ ἀγάπη τοῦ Πατρὸς ἐν
αὐτῷ, ὅτι πᾶν τὸ ἐν τῷ κόσμῳ, ἡ ἐπιθυμία τῆς
σαρκὸς καὶ ἡ ἐπιθυμία τῶν ὀφθαλμῶν καὶ ἡ ἀλαζονεία τοῦ βίου, οὐκ ἔστιν ἐκ τοῦ Πατρός, ἀλλ' ἐκ
τοῦ κόσμου ἐστί. καὶ ὁ κόσμος παράγεται καὶ ἡ
ἐπιθυμία αὐτοῦ· ὁ δὲ ποιῶν τὸ θέλημα τοῦ Θεοῦ
μένει εἰς τὸν αἰῶνα.

Ταῦτα οὖν οἱ θεῖοι καὶ θεοφόροι Πατέρες ἡμῶν
κατανοήσαντες, καὶ τοῦ Ἀποστόλου ἀκούσαντες,
Acts xiv. 22 ὅτι διὰ πολλῶν θλίψεων δεῖ ἡμᾶς εἰσελθεῖν εἰς
τὴν βασιλείαν τῶν οὐρανῶν, ἔσπευσαν μετὰ τὸ
ἅγιον βάπτισμα ἄμωμον καὶ ἀκηλίδωτον τὸ τῆς
ἀφθαρσίας διατηρῆσαι ἔνδυμα· ὅθεν οἱ μὲν αὐτῶν
καὶ ἕτερον προσέθεντο βάπτισμα προσλαβέσθαι,
τὸ δι' αἵματός φημι καὶ διὰ μαρτυρίου· βάπτισμα
γὰρ καὶ τοῦτο ὠνόμασται, καὶ πάνυ γε τιμιώτατον καὶ αἰδεσιμώτατον· δευτέροις γὰρ οὐ μολύνε-
Mk. x. 38, 39 ται ἁμαρτίας μολυσμοῖς· ὅπερ καὶ ὁ Κύριος ἡμῶν
ὑπὲρ ἡμῶν καταδεξάμενος βάπτισμα εἰκότως
ἐκάλεσεν. ἐντεῦθεν αὐτοῦ μιμηταὶ καὶ ζηλωταὶ
γενόμενοι, πρότερον μὲν οἱ αὐτόπται αὐτοῦ 101

and troubles, and liveth in riches and luxury, to walk unswervingly in the way of the commandments of the Lord, and to preserve his life pure of these evils. "For," saith the Lord, "no man can serve two masters; for either he will hate the one and love the other; or else he will hold to the one and despise the other. Ye cannot serve God and Mammon." So also writeth the beloved Evangelist and Divine in his Epistle, thus saying, "Love not the world, neither the things that are in the world. If any man love the world, the love of the Father is not in him. For all that is in the world, the lust of the flesh, and the lust of the eyes, and the pride of life, is not of the Father, but is of the world. And the world passeth away, and the lust thereof; but he that doeth the will of God abideth for ever."

and praiseth that other baptism—the baptism of martyrdom—

'These things were well understood by our holy and inspired fathers; and mindful of the Apostle's word that we must through much tribulation enter into the Kingdom of Heaven, they strove, after holy baptism, to keep their garment of immortality spotless and undefiled. Whence some of them also thought fit to receive yet another baptism; I mean that which is by blood and martyrdom. For this too is called baptism, the most honourable, and reverend of all, inasmuch as its waters are not polluted by fresh sin; which also our Lord underwent for our sakes, and rightly called it baptism. So as imitators and followers of him, first his eyewitness, disciples,

καὶ μαθηταὶ καὶ ἀπόστολοι, ἔπειτα δὲ καὶ πᾶς ὁ
τῶν ἁγίων μαρτύρων χορός, τοῖς θεραπευταῖς τῶν
εἰδώλων βασιλεῦσι καὶ τυράννοις ἑαυτοὺς ὑπὲρ
τοῦ ὀνόματος τοῦ Χριστοῦ ἐκδόντες, πᾶν εἶδος
κολαστηρίων ὑπέμειναν, θηρίοις προσομιλήσαντες
1 Tim. iv. 7 καὶ πυρὶ καὶ ξίφεσι, καί, τὴν καλὴν ὁμολογίαν
ὁμολογήσαντες, τὸν δρόμον τετελεκότες καὶ τὴν
πίστιν τετηρηκότες, τῶν τῆς δικαιοσύνης ἐπέτυχον
βραβείων, τῶν Ἀγγέλων ὁμοδίαιτοι καὶ τοῦ
Χριστοῦ συγκληρονόμοι γενόμενοι· ὧν ἡ ἀρετὴ
Ps. xix. 4 τοσοῦτον ἔλαμψεν, ὡς εἰς πᾶσαν τὴν γῆν τὸν
φθόγγον αὐτῶν ἐξελθεῖν, καὶ εἰς τὰ πέρατα τῆς
οἰκουμένης τῶν κατορθωμάτων αὐτῶν ἀστράψαι
Cp. 2 Kings xiii. 21; Ecclus. xlviii. 14; Acts v. 15; xix. 12 τὴν λαμπηδόνα. τούτων, οὐ τὰ ῥήματα μόνον καὶ
τὰ ἔργα, ἀλλὰ καὶ αὐτὰ τὰ αἵματα καὶ τὰ ὀστᾶ
πάσης ἁγιότητος πλήρη ὑπάρχουσι, δαίμονας μὲν
κατὰ κράτος ἐλαύνοντα, ἀνιάτων δὲ νοσημάτων
ἰάσεις τοῖς πίστει προσψαύουσι παρέχοντα· καὶ
2 Kings ii. 8. 14 τὰ ἱμάτια δὲ καὶ εἴ τι ἄλλο τοῖς τιμίοις αὐτῶν
προσήγγισε σώμασι, τῇ κτίσει πάσῃ πάντοτέ
ἐστιν αἰδέσιμα. περὶ ὧν πολύς ἐστιν ὁ λόγος
κατὰ μέρος τὰς αὐτῶν ἀριστείας διηγήσασθαι.

Ἐπεὶ δὲ οἱ μὲν ἀπηνεῖς ἐκεῖνοι καὶ θηριώδεις τύ-
Cp. Mat. xxi. 41 ραννοι κακοὶ κακῶς ἀπώλοντο, καὶ ὁ διωγμὸς
ἔπαυσε, βασιλεῖς δὲ πιστοὶ ἀνὰ πᾶσαν τὴν οἰκουμένην ἐβασίλευσαν, διαδεξάμενοι ἕτεροι καὶ μιμη- 102
σάμενοι τὸν ζῆλον ἐκείνων καὶ τὸν θεῖον πόθον,
λέγω δὲ τῶν μαρτύρων, καὶ τῷ αὐτῷ ἔρωτι τὰς
ψυχὰς τρωθέντες, ἄριστα διεσκόπουν ἀρρύπαντον
Cp. Rom. xii. 1 τὴν ψυχὴν καὶ τὸ σῶμα τῷ Κυρίῳ παραστῆσαι,
πάσας τὰς τῶν παθῶν περικόψαντες ἐνεργείας,
καὶ παντὸς μολυσμοῦ σαρκὸς καὶ πνεύματος

and Apostles, and then the whole band of holy martyrs yielded themselves, for the name of Christ, to kings and tyrants that worshipped idols, and endured every form of torment, being exposed to wild beasts, fire and sword, confessing the good confession, running the course and keeping the faith. Thus they gained the prizes of righteousness, and became the companions of Angels, and fellow-heirs with Christ. Their virtue shone so bright that their sound went out into all lands, and the splendour of their good deeds flashed like lightning into the ends of the earth. Of these men, not only the words and works, but even the very blood and bones are full of all sanctity, mightily casting out devils, and giving to such as touch them in faith the healing of incurable diseases: yea, and even their garments, and anything else that hath been brought near their honoured bodies, are always worthy of the reverence of all creation. And it were a long tale to tell one by one their deeds of prowess.

and recounteth the glories of the Martyrs

'But when those cruel and brutal tyrants brought their miserable lives to a miserable end, and persecution ceased, and Christian kings ruled throughout the world, then others too in succession emulated the Martyrs' zeal and divine desire, and, wounded at heart with the same love, considered well how they might present soul and body without blemish unto God, by cutting off all the workings of sinful lusts and purifying themselves of every

Barlaam telleth of the hermits,

ἑαυτοὺς ἐκκαθάραντες. ἐπεὶ δὲ οὐκ ἄλλως τοῦτο,
ἀλλὰ διὰ τῆς φυλακῆς τῶν ἐντολῶν τοῦ Χριστοῦ
κατορθοῦσθαι ἔγνωσαν, τὴν δὲ φυλακὴν τῶν
ἐντολῶν καὶ τὴν ἐργασίαν τῶν ἀρετῶν δυσχερῶς
ἐν μέσῳ τῶν τοῦ κόσμου θορύβων προσγίνεσθαι
κατενόησαν, ἄλλον τινὰ βίον ξένον καὶ ἐνηλλαγ-
μένον ἑαυτοῖς ἐπετηδεύσαντο, καί, κατὰ τὴν θείαν
Mat. xix. 29 φωνήν, πάντα καταλιπόντες, γονεῖς, τέκνα, φίλους,
συγγενεῖς, πλοῦτον καὶ τρυφήν. καὶ πάντα τὰ ἐν τῷ
κόσμῳ μισήσαντες, πρὸς τὰς ἐρήμους, ὥσπερ τινὲς
Cp. Heb. xi. 37, 38 φυγάδες, ᾤχοντο, ὑστερούμενοι, θλιβόμενοι, κακου-
χούμενοι, ἐν ἐρημίαις πλανώμενοι καὶ ὄρεσι καὶ
σπηλαίοις καὶ ταῖς ὀπαῖς τῆς γῆς, πάντων τῶν
ἐπὶ γῆς τερπνῶν τε καὶ ἀπολαυστικῶν ἑαυτοὺς
μακρύναντες, καὶ αὐτοῦ δὲ τοῦ ἄρτου καὶ σκεπά-
σματος λίαν ἐνδεῶς ἔχοντες· δύο ταῦτα πραγ- 103
ματευσάμενοι, ἵνα, μὴ ὁρῶντες τὰς ὕλας τῶν
παθῶν, προρρίζους αὐτῶν τὰς ἐπιθυμίας ἐκ τῆς
ψυχῆς ἀνασπάσωσι, καί, τὰς αὐτῶν ἐξαλείψαντες
μνήμας, ἔρωτα καὶ πόθον τῶν θείων καὶ οὐρανίων
ἐν ἑαυτοῖς ἐμφυτεύσωσι· πρὸς τούτοις, ἵνα, διὰ
τῆς κακοπαθείας τὸ σαρκίον ἐκδαπανήσαντες καὶ
μάρτυρες τῇ προαιρέσει γενόμενοι, μὴ ἀποτύχωσι
τῆς εὐκλείας τῶν δι' αἵματος τελειωθέντων, ἀλλὰ
μιμηταὶ καὶ αὐτοὶ τῶν τοῦ Χριστοῦ παθημάτων,
ὅσον τὸ ἐπ' αὐτοῖς, γενόμενοι, καὶ τῆς ἀτελευτήτου
βασιλείας συμμέτοχοι ἔσονται. οὕτως οὖν ἄριστα
διασκεψάμενοι, τὸν μονάδα καὶ ἡσύχιον μετῆλθον
βίον, τινὲς μὲν αἴθριοι διακαρτερήσαντες, τῷ φλογ-
μῷ τοῦ καύσωνος καὶ κρυμοῖς ἀγρίοις καὶ ὄμβροις
καὶ ταραχαῖς ἀνέμων ταλαιπωρούμενοι· οἱ δέ, καλύ-
βας πηξάμενοι, ἢ σπηλαίοις καὶ ἄντροις ὑποκρυ-

defilement of flesh and spirit. But, as they perceived that this could only be accomplished by the keeping of the commandments of Christ, and that the keeping of his commandments and the practice of the virtues was difficult to attain in the midst of the turmoils of the world, they adopted for themselves a strange and changed manner of life, and, obedient to the voice divine, forsook all, parents, children, friends, kinsfolk, riches and luxury, and, hating everything in the world, withdrew, as exiles, into the deserts, being destitute, afflicted, evil entreated, wandering in wildernesses and mountains, and in dens and caves of the earth, self-banished from all the pleasures and delights upon earth, and standing in sore need even of bread and shelter. This they did for two causes: firstly, that never seeing the objects of sinful lust, they might pluck such desires by the root out of their soul, and blot out the memory thereof, and plant within themselves the love and desire of divine and heavenly things: and secondly, that, by exhausting the flesh by austerities, and becoming Martyrs in will, they might not miss the glory of them that were made perfect by blood, but might be themselves, in their degree, imitators of the sufferings of Christ, and become partakers of the kingdom that hath no end. Having then come to this wise resolve, they adopted the quiet of monastic life, some facing the rigours of the open air, and braving the blaze of the scorching heat and fierce frosts and rain-storms and tempestuous winds, others spending their lives in the hovels which they had builded them, or in the hiding of holes and caverns.

of their poverty and self-denial,

of their aim and hope,

βέντες, διέζησαν. οὕτω δὲ τὴν ἀρετὴν μετερχόμενοι, πᾶσαν σαρκικὴν παράκλησιν καὶ ἀνάπαυσιν εἰς τέλος ἀπηρνήσαντο, λαχάνων ὠμῶν καὶ βοτανῶν, ἢ ἀκροδρύων, ἢ ἄρτου ξηροῦ καὶ πάνυ σκληροῦ στοιχήσαντες διαίτῃ, μὴ τῇ ποιότητι μόνον ἀποταξάμενοι τῶν ἡδέων, ἀλλά, τῷ περιόντι τῆς ἐγκρατείας, καὶ πρὸς τὴν ποσότητα τὸ φιλότιμον ἑαυτῶν παρατείναντες. τοσοῦτον γὰρ καὶ αὐτῶν τῶν εὐτελῶν καὶ ἀναγκαιοτάτων μετελάμβανον βρωμάτων, ὅσον ἀποζῆν μόνον. οἱ μὲν γὰρ αὐτῶν, ὅλας τὰς τῆς ἑβδομάδος ἡμέρας ἄσιτοι διατελοῦντες, τῇ κυριακῇ τροφῆς μετελάμβανον· οἱ δὲ δὶς τῆς ἑβδομάδος ταύτης μεμνη- 104
μένοι· ἄλλοι δὲ παρὰ μίαν, ἢ καὶ καθ' ἑσπέραν, ἐσιτοῦντο ὅσον μόνον τροφῆς ἀπογεύεσθαι. εὐχαῖς τε καὶ ἀγρυπνίαις μικροῦ πρὸς τὸν τῶν ἀγγέλων παρημιλλήθησαν βίον, χαίρειν εἰπόντες χρυσίου καὶ ἀργυρίου τῇ κτήσει παντάπασι, πράσεις τε καὶ ἀγορασίας ἐπιλαθόμενοι εἶναι ὅλως ἐν ἀνθρώποις.

Φθόνος δὲ καὶ ἔπαρσις, οἱ μάλιστα τοῖς ἀγαθοῖς ἔργοις ἀκολουθεῖν εἰωθότες, οὐκ ἔσχον χώραν ἐν αὐτοῖς. οὐδὲ γὰρ ὁ ἐλάττων ἐν τοῖς τῆς ἀσκήσεως ἱδρῶσι κατὰ τοῦ μᾶλλον διαλάμποντος βασκανίας λογισμὸν ὅλως ἐν ἑαυτῷ ὑπεδέχετο· οὐδ' αὖ πάλιν τὸν μεγάλα κατορθοῦντα κατὰ τῶν ἀσθενεστέρων πρὸς οἴησιν ἐπῆρεν ἡ ἀλαζονεία ἢ ἐξουθενεῖν τὸν πλησίον, ἢ ἐγκαυχᾶσθαι τῇ ἀσκήσει, καὶ μεγαλοφρονεῖν ἐπὶ τοῖς κατορθώμασιν, ἀπατήσασα. ὁ γὰρ τὸ πλέον ἔχων εἰς ἀρετήν, οὐ πόνοις ἰδίοις, ἀλλὰ Θεοῦ δυνάμει, τὸ πᾶν ἐπιγράφων, ταπεινόφρονι γνώμῃ ἔπειθεν ἑαυτὸν μηδὲν ὅλως ἐργά-

Thus, in pursuit of virtue, they utterly denied themselves all fleshly comfort and repose, submitting to a diet of uncooked herbs and worts, or acorns, or hard dry bread, not merely saying good-bye to delights in their quality, but, in very excess of temperance, extending their zeal to limit even the quantity of enjoyment. For even of those common and necessary meats they took only so much as was sufficient to sustain life. Some of them continued fasting the whole week, and partook of victuals only of a Sunday: others thought of food twice only in the week: others ate every other day, or daily at eventide—that is, took but a taste of food. In prayers and watchings they almost rivalled the life of Angels, bidding a long farewell to the possession of gold and silver, and quite forgetting that buyings and sellings are concerns of men.

'But envy and pride, the evils most prone to follow good works, had no place amongst them. He that was weaker in ascetic exercises entertained no thought of malice against him of brighter example. Nor again was he, that had accomplished great feats, deceived and puffed up by arrogance to despise his weaker brethren, or set at nought his neighbour, or boast of his rigours, or glory in his achievements. He that excelled in virtue ascribed nothing to his own labours, but all to the power of God, in humility of mind persuading himself that his labours were

and commendeth the rigours and purity of their life,

ζεσθαι, ἀλλὰ καὶ πλειόνων ὀφειλέτην εἶναι, καθά
φησιν ὁ Κύριος· Ὅταν ποιήσητε πάντα τὰ δια-
Luke xvii. 10 ταχθέντα ὑμῖν, λέγετε, ὅτι Ἀχρεῖοι δοῦλοί ἐσμεν,
ὅτι ὃ ὠφείλομεν ποιῆσαι πεποιήκαμεν. οἱ δὲ
πάλιν οὐδὲ ποιῆσαί ποτε τὰ διατεταγμένα ἔπει-
θον ἑαυτούς, ἀλλὰ πλείονα εἶναι τῶν ἤδη κατ-
ωρθωμένων τὰ ἐλλείποντα. καὶ ὁ ἐλαττούμενος
πάλιν ἐν τῇ ἀσκήσει, διὰ σωματικὴν ἴσως ἀσθέ- 105
νειαν, ἐξευτέλιζε ταλανίζων ἑαυτόν, ῥαθυμίᾳ
γνώμης, οὐχὶ φύσεως ἀσθενείᾳ, τὸ ὑστέρημα
λογιζόμενος. οὕτως οὖν ἄλλος ἄλλου καὶ πάντες
ἁπάντων ἦσαν μετριώτεροι· κενοδοξίας δὲ πάθος
ἢ ἀνθρωπαρεσκείας ποῦ ἐν ἐκείνοις; οἵτινες, τὴν
οἰκουμένην φυγόντες, διὰ τοῦτο οἰκοῦσι τὴν
ἔρημον, οὐκ ἀνθρώποις, ἀλλὰ Θεῷ τὰ κατορθώματα δεικνύναι βουλόμενοι, παρ' οὗ καὶ τῶν
κατορθωμάτων τὰς ἀμοιβὰς ἐλπίζουσι, καλῶς
ἐπιστάμενοι ὅτι αἱ διὰ κενοδοξίαν ἐπιτελούμεναι
ἀσκήσεις ἄμισθοι, δι' ἔπαινον γὰρ ἀνθρώπων,
καὶ οὐ διὰ τὸν Θεὸν γίνονται· ὅθεν καὶ διπλῶς
οἱ τοιοῦτοι ἀδικοῦνται, τὸ σῶμα κατατήκοντες
καὶ μισθὸν μὴ λαμβάνοντες. οἱ δὲ τῆς ἄνω δόξης
ὀρεγόμενοι καὶ πρὸς ταύτην ἐπειγόμενοι πάσης
τῆς ἐπιγείου καὶ ἀνθρωπίνης κατεφρόνησαν.

Ἔχουσι δὲ τὰς οἰκήσεις οἱ μὲν ἐν παντελεῖ ἀναχωρήσει καὶ μονίᾳ τὸν ἀγῶνα διανύοντες, μακρύναντες ἑαυτοὺς τῆς τῶν ἀνθρώπων συναυλίας παρ' ὅλον αὐτῶν τὸν τῆς ζωῆς χρόνον καὶ Θεῷ πλησιάσαντες· οἱ δέ, πόρρωθεν ἀλλήλων τὰς οἰκήσεις πηξάμενοι, ταῖς Κυριακαῖς εἰς ἐκκλησίαν μίαν φοιτῶσι, καὶ τῶν θείων μυστηρίων κοινωνοῦσι, τῆς ἀναιμάκτου φημὶ θυσίας, τοῦ

nought and that he was debtor even for more, as saith the Lord, "When ye shall have done all those things which are commanded you, say, 'We are unprofitable servants: we have done that which was our duty to do.'" Others again persuaded themselves that they had not done even the things which they were commanded to do, but that the things left undone outnumbered the things already well done. Again, he that was far behind in austerity, perchance through bodily weakness, would disparage and blame himself, attributing his failure to slothfulness of mind rather than to natural frailty. So each excelled each, and all excelled all in this sweet reasonableness. But the spirit of vain glory and pleasing of men—what place had it among them? For they had fled from the world, and were dwelling in the desert, to the end that they might show their virtues not to men, but to God, from whom also they hope to receive the rewards of their good deeds, well aware that religious exercises performed for vain glory go without recompense; for these are done for the praise of men and not for God. Whence all that do thus are doubly defrauded: they waste their body, and receive no reward. But they who yearn for glory above, and strive thereafter, despise all earthly and human glory.

and their love toward God and man

'As to their dwellings, some monks finish the contest in utter retirement and solitude, having removed themselves far from the haunts of men throughout the whole of their earthly life-time, and having drawn nigh to God. Others build their homes at a distance one from another, but meet on the Lord's Day at one Church, and communicate of

He describeth their dwellings and assemblies

ἀχράντου σώματος καὶ τοῦ τιμίου αἵματος τοῦ Χριστοῦ, ἃ τοῖς πιστοῖς εἰς ἄφεσιν ἁμαρτιῶν, φωτισμόν τε καὶ ἁγιασμὸν ψυχῆς καὶ σώματος ὁ Κύριος ἐδωρήσατο· καί, ἑστιῶντες ἀλλήλους γυμνασίᾳ τῶν θείων λόγων καὶ ταῖς ἠθικαῖς παραινέσεσι, τούς τε κρυπτοὺς τῶν ἀντιπάλων δημοσιεύοντες πολέμους, ὥστε μὴ ἁλῶναι τούτοις τινὰ τῆς πάλης ἀγνοοῦντα τὴν μέθοδον, οἴκαδε 106
πάλιν ἕκαστος ἐπανέρχονται, τὸ τῆς ἀρετῆς μέλι τοῖς σίμβλοις τῶν καρδιῶν φιλοτίμως ἐναποτιθέντες, καὶ γεωργοῦντες καρπὸν γλυκύτατον καὶ τῆς ἐπουρανίου τραπέζης ἐπάξιον.

Ἄλλοι δὲ κοινοβιακὸν μετέρχονται βίον· οἵτινες, πλήθη πολυάνθρωπα ἐπὶ τὸ αὐτὸ ἀθροισθέντες, ὑφ' ἑνὶ ταξιάρχῃ καὶ προεστῶτι, τῷ πάντων διαφορωτάτῳ, ἑαυτοὺς ἔταξαν, πᾶν θέλημα ἑαυτῶν μαχαίρᾳ τῆς ὑπακοῆς ἀποσφάξαντες· καὶ δούλους ὠνητοὺς ἑαυτοὺς ἑκουσίως λογισάμενοι, οὐκ ἔτι ἑαυτοῖς ζῶσιν, ἀλλ' ᾧ διὰ τὸν τοῦ Χριστοῦ πόθον ἑαυτοὺς καθυπέταξαν· οἰκειότερον δὲ μᾶλλον
Gal. ii. 20 εἰπεῖν, ζῶσιν οὐκ ἔτι ἑαυτοῖς, ζῇ δὲ ἐν αὐτοῖς ὁ Χριστός, ᾧ ἠκολούθησαν πάντα ἀπαρνησάμενοι. τοῦτο γάρ ἐστιν ἀναχώρησις, κόσμου ἑκούσιον μῖσος, καὶ ἄρνησις φύσεως πόθῳ τῶν ὑπὲρ φύσιν. οὗτοι τοίνυν ὡς ἄγγελοι ἐπὶ τῆς γῆς πολιτεύονται, ψαλμοὺς καὶ ὕμνους ὁμοθυμαδὸν τῷ Κυρίῳ ᾄδοντες, καὶ ὁμολογηταὶ τοῖς ἄθλοις τῆς ὑπακοῆς χρηματίζοντες· ἐφ' οἷς καὶ τὸ δεσποτικὸν πλη-
Mat. xviii. 20 ροῦται λόγιον. φησὶ γάρ· Ὅπου εἰσὶ δύο ἢ τρεῖς συνηγμένοι εἰς τὸ ἐμὸν ὄνομα, ἐκεῖ εἰμὶ ἐν μέσῳ αὐτῶν, οὐκ εἰς τοῦτο τὸ μέτρον τὴν ἐπὶ τῷ ὀνόματι αὐτοῦ συναγωγὴν περικλείσας, ἀλλὰ

the Holy Mysteries, I mean the unbloody Sacrifice of the undefiled Body and precious Blood of Christ, which the Lord gave to the Faithful for the remission of sins, for the enlightenment and sanctification of soul and body. They entertain one another with the exercises of the divine Oracles and moral exhortations, and make public the secret wiles of their adversaries, that none, through ignorance of the manner of wrestling, may be caught thus. Then turn they again, each to his own home, eagerly storing the honey of virtue in the cells of their hearts, and husbanding sweet fruits worthy of the heavenly board.

He telleth of monastic orders and of their rule,

'Others again spend their life in monasteries. These gather in multitudes in one spot, and range themselves under one superior and president, the best of their number, slaying all self-will with the sword of obedience. Of their own free choice they consider themselves as slaves bought at a price, and no longer live for themselves, but for him, to whom, for Christ his sake, they have become obedient; or rather, to speak more properly, they live no more for themselves, but Christ liveth in them, whom to follow, they renounce all. This is retirement, a voluntary hatred of the world, and denial of nature by desire of things above nature. These men therefore live the lives of Angels on earth, chanting psalms and hymns with one consent unto the Lord, and purchasing for themselves the title of Confessors by labours of obedience. And in them is fulfilled the word of the Lord, when he saith, "Where two or three are gathered together in my name, there am I in the midst of them." By this number he limiteth not the gathering together in his name, but by "two

διὰ τῶν δύο ἢ τριῶν ἀδιόριστον τὸν ἀριθμὸν δηλώσας. εἴτε γὰρ ὀλίγοι, εἴτε πολλοὶ διὰ τὸ ἅγιον αὐτοῦ συναχθῶσιν ὄνομα, αὐτῷ διαπύρῳ λατρεύοντες πόθῳ, ἐκεῖ παρεῖναι τοῦτον πιστεύομεν ἐν μέσῳ τῶν αὐτοῦ δούλων.

Τούτοις τοῖς τύποις καὶ ταῖς τοιαύταις ἀγωγαῖς
οἱ γήϊνοι καὶ χοϊκοὶ τὸν βίον ἐζήλωσαν τῶν 107
οὐρανίων, ἐν νηστείαις καὶ εὐχαῖς καὶ ἀγρυπνίαις, ἐν δάκρυσι θερμοῖς καὶ ἀμετεωρίστῳ πένθει, ἐν ξενιτείᾳ καὶ μνήμῃ θανάτου, ἐν πραότητι καὶ ἀοργησίᾳ, ἐν σιωπῇ χειλέων, ἐν ἀκτημοσύνῃ καὶ πτωχείᾳ, ἐν ἁγνείᾳ καὶ σωφροσύνῃ, ἐν ταπεινόφρονι γνώμῃ καὶ ἡσυχίᾳ, ἐν ἀγάπῃ τελείᾳ πρὸς τὸν Θεὸν καὶ τὸν πλησίον, τὸν παρόντα ἐκτελέσαντες βίον καὶ ἄγγελοι τοῖς τρόποις γενόμενοι. ὅθεν Θεὸς θαύμασι καὶ σημείοις καὶ ποικίλαις δυνάμεσιν
Ps. xix. 4 αὐτοὺς κατεκόσμησε, καὶ τὸν φθόγγον τῆς θαυμαστῆς αὐτῶν πολιτείας εἰς τὰ πέρατα διηχεῖσθαι τῆς οἰκουμένης πεποίηκε. καὶ εἴπερ σοι τὸν βίον ἑνὸς αὐτῶν ἐπὶ στόματος φέρων κατὰ μέρος διηγήσομαι, ὃς καὶ ἀρχηγὸς γεγενῆσθαι τῆς κατὰ μοναχοὺς πολιτείας λέγεται (Ἀντώνιος δὲ ὄνομα αὐτῷ), γνώσῃ πάντως ἐκ τοῦ ἑνὸς δένδρου τῶν ὁμογενῶν καὶ ὁμοειδῶν καρπῶν τὴν γλυκύτητα, καὶ οἵαν ἐκεῖνος ἔθετο τῆς ἀσκήσεως ὑποβάθραν, οἵαν δὲ τὴν ὀροφὴν ἐπήξατο, καὶ ὁποίων ἠξιώθη παρὰ τοῦ Σωτῆρος τυχεῖν χαρισμάτων. πολλοὶ δὲ καὶ ἄλλοι μετ᾿ ἐκεῖνον τὸν ἴσον ἀγωνισάμενοι ἀγῶνα τῶν ὁμοίων ἔτυχον στεφάνων τε καὶ γερῶν.

Μακάριοι οὗτοι καὶ τρισμακάριοι οἱ τὸν Θεὸν ἀγαπήσαντες, καὶ διὰ τὴν ἀγάπην αὐτοῦ καταφρονήσαντες πάντων. ἐδάκρυσαν γὰρ πενθοῦντες ἡμέρας καὶ νυκτός, ἵνα τῆς ἀλήκτου τύχωσι

or three" signifieth that the number is indefinite. For, whether there be many, or few, gathered together because of his holy name, serving him with fervent zeal, there we believe him to be present in the midst of his servants.

'By these ensamples and such like assemblies men of earth and clay imitate the life of heavenly beings, in fastings and prayers and watchings, in hot tears and sober sorrow, as soldiers in the field with death before their eyes, in meekness and gentleness, in silence of the lips, in poverty and want, in chastity and temperance, in humbleness and quietude of mind, in perfect charity toward God and their neighbour, carrying their present life down to the grave, and becoming Angels in their ways. Wherefore God hath graced them with miracles, signs and various virtues and made the voice of their marvellous life to be sounded forth to the ends of the world. If I open my mouth to declare in every point the life of one of them who is said to have been the founder of the monastic life, Antony by name, by this one tree thou shalt assuredly know the sweet fruits of other trees of the like kind and form, and shalt know what a foundation of religious life that great man laid, and what a roof he built, and what gifts he merited to receive from the Saviour. After him many fought the like fight and won like crowns and guerdons.

of their angelick life, and of one Antony their founder,

Blessed, yea, thrice blessed, are they that have loved God, and, for his love's sake, have counted every thing as nothing worth. For they wept and mourned, day and night, that they might gain everlasting comfort: they humbled themselves

and calleth them blessed for their sufferings here and their glory hereafter

Mat. xxiii. 12 παρακλήσεως· ἐταπείνωσαν ἑαυτοὺς ἑκουσίως, ἵν'
ἐκεῖ ὑψωθῶσι· κατέτηξαν τὰς ἑαυτῶν σάρκας
πείνῃ τε καὶ δίψῃ καὶ ἀγρυπνίᾳ ἵν' ἐκεῖ διαδέξη-
ται αὐτοὺς ἡ τρυφὴ καὶ ἀγαλλίασις τοῦ παραδεί- 108
σου· σκήνωμα γεγόνασι τοῦ ἁγίου Πνεύματος τῇ
2 Cor. vi. 16 καθαρότητι τῆς καρδίας, καθὼς γέγραπται· Ἐνοι-
Gal. vi. 14 κήσω ἐν αὐτοῖς καὶ ἐμπεριπατήσω· ἐσταύρωσαν
Mat. xxv. 31 ἑαυτοὺς τῷ κόσμῳ, ἵν' ἐκ δεξιῶν τοῦ σταυρωθέντος
Eph. vi. 14 σταθῶσι· περιεζώσαντο τὰς ὀσφύας αὐτῶν ἐν
Mat. xxv. 1–13 ἀληθείᾳ, καὶ ἑτοίμους ἔσχον ἀεὶ τὰς λαμπάδας,
προσδοκῶντες τὴν ἔλευσιν τοῦ ἀθανάτου νυμφίου.
νοεροὺς γὰρ κτησάμενοι ὀφθαλμούς, προεώρων
διηνεκῶς τὴν φρικτὴν ὥραν ἐκείνην, τήν τε
θεωρίαν τῶν μελλόντων ἀγαθῶν καὶ τῆς αἰωνίου
κολάσεως ἀχώριστον τῆς ἑαυτῶν ἔσχον καρδίας·
καὶ ἐσπούδασαν καμεῖν, ἵνα τῆς ἀϊδίου δόξης μὴ
ἀποτύχωσι. γεγόνασιν ἀπαθεῖς ὥσπερ ἄγγελοι·
καὶ νῦν μετ' ἐκείνων χορεύουσιν, ὧν καὶ τὸν βίον
ἐμιμήσαντο. μακάριοι οὗτοι καὶ τρισμακάριοι,
ὅτι ἀπλανέσι τοῖς τοῦ νοὸς ὀφθαλμοῖς κατενόησαν
τὴν τῶν παρόντων ματαιότητα, καὶ τῆς ἀνθρωπίνης εὐπραγίας τὸ ἄστατον καὶ ἀνώμαλον, καί,
ταύτην ἀπαρνησάμενοι, τὰ αἰώνια ἑαυτοῖς ἐθησαύ-
Mat. vi. 20 ρισαν ἀγαθά, καὶ τῆς μηδέποτε διαπιπτούσης
μήτε θανάτῳ διακοπτομένης ἐπελάβοντο ζωῆς.

Τούτους οὖν τοὺς θαυμασίους καὶ ὁσίους ἄνδρας
καὶ ἡμεῖς οἱ εὐτελεῖς καὶ ἀνάξιοι μιμεῖσθαι σπου-
δάζομεν, οὐκ ἐφικνούμεθα δὲ τῷ ὕψει τῆς οὐρανο- 109
πολίτου αὐτῶν διαγωγῆς· ἀλλά, κατὰ τὸ ἐνὸν
τῆς ἀσθενοῦς ἡμῶν καὶ ταλαιπώρου δυνάμεως,
τὸν βίον αὐτῶν χαρακτηρίζομεν καὶ τὸ σχῆμα
περιβεβλήμεθα, κἂν τῶν ἔργων διαμαρτάνωμεν.

willingly, that there they might be exalted: they afflicted the flesh with hunger and thirst and vigil, that there they might come to the pleasures and joys of Paradise. By their purity of heart they became a tabernacle of the Holy Ghost, as it is written, "I will dwell in them and walk in them." They crucified themselves unto the world, that they might stand at the right hand of the Crucified: they girt their loins with truth, and alway had their lamps ready, looking for the coming of the immortal bridegroom. The eye of their mind being enlightened, they continually looked forward to that awful hour, and kept the contemplation of future happiness and everlasting punishment immovable from their hearts, and pained themselves to labour, that they might not lose eternal glory. They became passionless as the Angels, and now they weave the dance in their fellowship, whose lives also they imitated. Blessed, yea, thrice blessed are they, because with sure spiritual vision they discerned the vanity of this present world and the uncertainty and inconstancy of mortal fortune, and cast it aside, and laid up for themselves everlasting blessings, and laid hold of that life which never faileth, nor is broken by death.

With their blessedness he contrasteth the falseness and misery of this present world,

These then are the marvellous holy men whose examples we, that are poor and vile, strive to imitate, but cannot attain to the high level of the life of these heavenly citizens. Nevertheless, so far as is possible for our weakness and feeble power, we take the stamp of their lives, and wear their habit, even though we fail to equal their works; for we are

πρόξενον γὰρ ἀναμαρτησίας τὸ θεῖον ἐπάγγελμα
τοῦτο καὶ συνεργὸν τῆς ἐκ τοῦ θείου βαπτίσματος δοθείσης ἡμῖν ἀφθαρσίας ἐπιστάμεθα. καί,
τοῖς λόγοις ἑπόμενοι τῶν μακαρίων ἐκείνων, πάνυ
καταγινώσκομεν τῶν φθαρτῶν τούτων καὶ ἐπικήρων τοῦ βίου πραγμάτων, ἐν οἷς οὐδὲν ἔστιν
εὑρεῖν βέβαιον, οὐδὲ ὁμαλόν, οὐδὲ ἐπὶ τῶν αὐτῶν
Eccles. 1, 14 ἱστάμενον· ἀλλὰ ματαιότης ἐστὶ τὰ πάντα καὶ
προαίρεσις πνεύματος, πολλὰς ἐν ἀτόμῳ φέροντα
τὰς μεταβολάς· ὀνείρων γὰρ καὶ σκιᾶς, καὶ αὔρας
κατὰ τὸν ἀέρα πνεούσης, εἰσὶν ἀσθενέστερα·
μικρὰ καὶ πρὸς ὀλίγον ἡ χάρις, καὶ οὐδὲ χάρις·
ἀλλὰ πλάνη τις καὶ ἀπάτη τῆς τοῦ κόσμου κακίας, ὅνπερ μὴ ἀγαπᾶν ὅλως, μισεῖν δὲ μᾶλλον ἐκ
καρδίας δεδιδάγμεθα. καὶ ἔστι γε κατὰ ἀλήθειαν
μισητὸς οὗτος καὶ ἀπευκταῖος· ὅσα γὰρ δωρεῖται
τοῖς φίλοις αὐτοῦ, μετ' ὀργῆς αὖθις αὐτὰ ἀφαρ-
πάζει, γυμνοὺς δὲ παντὸς ἀγαθοῦ καὶ αἰσχύνην
ἠμφιεσμένους, φορτία τε περικειμένους βαρέα, τῇ
αἰωνίᾳ παραπέμψει θλίψει· οὓς δ' αὖ πάλιν ὑψοῖ, 110
τῇ ἐσχάτῃ θᾶττον ταπεινοῖ ταλαιπωρίᾳ, ὑπο-
ποδίους αὐτοὺς τιθεὶς καὶ ἐπίχαρμα πάντων τῶν
ἐχθρῶν αὐτῶν. τοιαῦται οὖν αἱ χάριτες αὐτοῦ·
τοιαῦτα τὰ δωρήματα αὐτοῦ. ἐχθρὸς γάρ ἐστι
τῶν φίλων αὐτοῦ, καὶ ἐπίβουλος πάντων τῶν
ποιούντων αὐτοῦ τὰ θελήματα, καὶ καταράσσων
δεινῶς τοὺς ἐπερειδομένους ἐπ' αὐτόν, καὶ ἐκνευρί-
ζων τοὺς ἐπ' αὐτῷ πεποιθότας. συνθήκας τίθησι
μετὰ τῶν ἀφρόνων καὶ ἐπαγγελείας ψευδεῖς,
ἵνα μόνον αὐτοὺς ἐπισπάσηται· ἐκείνων δὲ
ἀγνωμονησάντων, ἀγνώμων αὐτὸς καὶ ψευδὴς
διαδείκνυται, μηδὲν ὧν συνέθετο ἀποπληρῶν.

assured that this holy profession is a means to perfection and an aid to the incorruption given us by holy baptism. So, following the teachings of these blessed Saints, we utterly renounce these corruptible and perishable things of life, wherein may be found nothing stable or constant, or that continueth in one stay; but all things are vanity and vexation of spirit, and many are the changes that they bring in a moment; for they are slighter than dreams and a shadow, or the breeze that bloweth the air. Small and short-lived is their charm, that is after all no charm, but illusion and deception of the wickedness of the world; which world we have been taught to love not at all, but rather to hate with all our heart. Yea, and verily it is worthy of hatred and abhorrence; for whatsoever gifts it giveth to its friends, these in turn in passion it taketh away, and shall hand over its victims, stripped of all good things, clad in the garment of shame, and bound under heavy burdens, to eternal tribulation. And those again whom it exalteth, it quickly abaseth to the utmost wretchedness, making them a foot-stool and a laughing stock for their enemies. Such are its charms, such its bounties. For it is an enemy of its friends, and traitor to such as carry out its wishes: dasheth to dire destruction all them that lean upon it, and enervateth those that put their trust therein. It maketh covenants with fools and fair false promises, only that it may allure them to itself. But, as they have dealt treacherously, it proveth itself treacherous and false in fulfilling

which is vain and treacherous,

σήμερον γὰρ βρώμασιν ἡδέσι τὸν φάρυγγα αὐτῶν καταλεάνας, κατάβρωμα τοῖς ἐχθροῖς ὅλους αὐτοὺς αὔριον τίθησι. σήμερον βασιλέα τινὰ δείκνυσι, καὶ αὔριον δουλείᾳ τινὶ πονηρᾷ παραδίδωσι· σήμερον μυρίοις εὐθηνούμενον ἀγα-
Demosth. 170, 16 θοῖς, αὔριον προσαίτην καὶ οἰκοτρίβων οἰκότριβα. 111
σήμερον στέφανον δόξης αὐτοῦ τῇ κορυφῇ ἐπιτίθησιν· αὔριον τὸ πρόσωπον τῇ γῇ καταράσσει. σήμερον κοσμεῖ τὸν τράχηλον αὐτοῦ λαμπραῖς ἀξιωμάτων τιμαῖς· αὔριον ταπεινοῖ σιδηροῖς κλοιοῖς δεσμούμενον. ποθητὸν πρὸς μικρὸν τοῖς πᾶσι τοῦτον ἐργάζεται, μισητὸν δὲ μετ᾽ ὀλίγον ἰσχυρῶς καὶ ἐβδελυγμένον. σήμερον εὐφραίνει, καὶ αὔριον θρήνοις αὐτὸν καὶ κοπετοῖς κατατήκει. ὁποῖον δὲ τούτων καὶ τὸ τέλος ἐπιτίθησιν ἄκουσον· οἰκήτορας γεέννης τοὺς ἠγαπηκότας αὐτὸν ἐλεεινῶς ἀπεργάζεται. τοιαύτην ἔχει γνώμην ἀεί, τοιαύτην πρόθεσιν ἀτεχνῶς. οὔτε τοὺς παρελθόντας θρηνεῖ, οὔτε τοὺς καταλειφθέντας οἰκτείρει. ἐκείνους γὰρ δεινῶς ἀπατήσας καὶ τοῖς ἄρκυσιν αὐτοῦ κατακλείσας, πρὸς τούτους αὖθις τὰ τῆς ἐπιστήμης μετενεγκεῖν πειρᾶται, μὴ θέλων τινὰ τῶν χαλεπῶν αὐτοῦ ἐκφυγεῖν παγίδων.

Τοὺς μὲν οὖν τοιούτῳ δουλεύοντας ἀπηνεῖ καὶ πονηρῷ δεσπότῃ τοῦ ἀγαθοῦ καὶ φιλανθρώπου φρενοβλαβῶς ἑαυτοὺς μακρύναντας, εἰς τὰ παρόντα δὲ κεχηνότας πράγματα καὶ τούτοις προστετηκότας, μηδόλως τῶν μελλόντων λαμβάνοντας ἔννοιαν, καὶ εἰς μὲν τὰς σωματικὰς ἀπολαύσεις 112
ἀδιαλείπτως ἐπειγομένους, τὰς δὲ ψυχὰς ἐῶντας λιμῷ κατατήκεσθαι καὶ μυρίοις ταλαιπωρεῖσθαι κακοῖς, ὁμοίους εἶναι δοκῶ ἀνδρὶ φεύγοντι ἀπὸ

none of its pledges. To-day it tickleth their gullet with pleasant dainties; to-morrow it maketh them nought but a gobbet for their enemies. To-day it maketh a man a king: to-morrow it delivereth him into bitter servitude. To-day its thrall is fattening on a thousand good things; to-morrow he is a beggar, and drudge of drudges. To-day it placeth on his head a crown of glory; to-morrow it dasheth his face upon the ground. To-day it adorneth his neck with brilliant badges of dignity; to-morrow it humbleth him with a collar of iron. For a little while it causeth him to be the desire of all men; but after a time it maketh him their hate and abomination. To-day it gladdeneth him: but to-morrow it weareth him to a shadow with lamentations and wailings. What is the end thereof, thou shalt hear. Ruthlessly it bringeth its former lovers to dwell in hell. Such is ever its mind, such its purposes. It lamenteth not its departed, nor pitieth the survivor. For after that it hath cruelly duped and entangled in its meshes the one party, it immediately transferreth the resources of its ingenuity against the other, not willing that any should escape its cruel snares.

and maketh this plain by the tale of THE MAN AND THE UNICORN

APOLOGUE IV

'These men that have foolishly alienated themselves from a good and kind master, to seek the service of so harsh and savage a lord, that are all agog for present joys and are glued thereto, that take never a thought for the future, that always grasp after bodily enjoyments, but suffer their souls to waste with hunger, and to be worn with myriad ills, these I consider to be like a man flying before the

προσώπου μαινομένου μονοκέρωτος, ὅς, μὴ φέρων
τὸν ἦχον τῆς αὐτοῦ βοῆς καὶ τὸν φοβερὸν αὐτοῦ
μυκηθμόν, ἀλλ' ἰσχυρῶς ἀποδιδράσκων τοῦ μὴ
γενέσθαι τούτου κατάβρωμα, ἐν τῷ τρέχειν αὐτὸν
ὀξέως μεγάλῳ τινὶ περιπέπτωκε βόθρῳ· ἐν δὲ
τῷ ἐμπίπτειν αὐτῷ, τὰς χεῖρας ἐκτείνας, καὶ
φυτοῦ τινος δραξάμενος, κραταιῶς τοῦτο κατέσχε,
καὶ ἐπὶ βάσεώς τινος τοὺς πόδας στηρίξας, ἔδοξεν
ἐν εἰρήνῃ λοιπὸν εἶναι καὶ ἀσφαλείᾳ. βλέψας
δὲ ὁρᾷ δύο μῦας, λευκὸν μὲν τὸν ἕνα, μέλανα
δὲ τὸν ἕτερον, διεσθίοντας ἀπαύστως τὴν ῥίζαν
τοῦ φυτοῦ, οὗ ἦν ἐξηρτημένος, καὶ ὅσον οὔπω
ἐγγίζοντας ταύτην ἐκτεμεῖν. κατανοήσας δὲ τὸν
πυθμένα τοῦ βόθρου, δράκοντα εἶδε φοβερὸν τῇ
θέᾳ, πῦρ πνέοντα καὶ δριμύτατα βλοσυροῦντα,
τὸ στόμα τε δεινῶς περιχάσκοντα καὶ καταπιεῖν
αὐτὸν ἐπειγόμενον. ἀτενίσας δὲ αὖθις τῇ βάσει
ἐκείνῃ, ἐφ' ᾗ τοὺς πόδας εἶχεν ἐρηρεισμένους,
τέσσαρας εἶδε κεφαλὰς ἀσπίδων τοῦ τοίχου
προβεβληκυίας, ἐφ' οὗ ἐπεστήρικτο. ἀναβλέψας
δὲ τοὺς ὀφθαλμούς, ὁρᾷ ἐκ τῶν κλάδων τοῦ φυτοῦ
ἐκείνου μικρὸν ἀποστάζον μέλι. ἐάσας οὖν διασκέψασθαι περὶ τῶν περιεχουσῶν αὐτῷ συμφο-
ρῶν, ὅπως ἔξωθεν μὲν ὁ μονόκερως δεινῶς ἐκμανεὶς 113
ζητεῖ τοῦτον καταφαγεῖν, κάτωθεν δὲ ὁ πικρὸς
δράκων κέχηνε καταπιεῖν, τὸ δὲ φυτὸν ὃ περιεδέδρακτο ὅσον οὔπω ἐκκόπτεσθαι ἔμελλε, τούς
τε πόδας ἐπ' ὀλισθηρᾷ καὶ ἀπίστῳ βάσει ἐπεστή-
ρικτο· τῶν τοσούτων οὖν καὶ τοιούτων φρικτῶν
θεαμάτων ἀλογίστως ἐπιλαθόμενος, ὅλῳ νοῒ μέλιτος ἐκείνου τοῦ μικροῦ γέγονε τῆς ἡδύτητος
ἐκκρεμής.

face of a rampant unicorn, who, unable to endure the sound of the beast's cry, and its terrible bellowing, to avoid being devoured, ran away at full speed. But while he ran hastily, he fell into a great pit; and as he fell, he stretched forth his hands, and laid hold on a tree, to which he held tightly. There he established some sort of foot-hold and thought himself from that moment in peace and safety. But he looked and descried two mice, the one white, the other black, that never ceased to gnaw the root of the tree whereon he hung, and were all but on the point of severing it. Then he looked down to the bottom of the pit and espied below a dragon, breathing fire, fearful for eye to see, exceeding fierce and grim, with terrible wide jaws, all agape to swallow him. Again looking closely at the ledge whereon his feet rested, he discerned four heads of asps projecting from the wall whereon he was perched. Then he lift up his eyes and saw that from the branches of the tree there dropped a little honey. And thereat he ceased to think of the troubles whereby he was surrounded; how, outside, the unicorn was madly raging to devour him: how, below, the fierce dragon was yawning to swallow him: how the tree, which he had clutched, was all but severed; and how his feet rested on slippery, treacherous ground. Yea, he forgat, without care, all those sights of awe and terror, and his whole mind hung on the sweetness of that tiny drop of honey.

The pit, the dragon, and the dripping honey

Αὕτη ἡ ὁμοίωσις τῶν τῇ ἀπάτῃ τοῦ παρόντος προστετηκότων βίου, ἧσπερ τὴν σαφήνειαν αὐτίκα λέξω σοι. ὁ μὲν μονόκερως τύπος ἂν εἴη τοῦ θανάτου, τοῦ διώκοντος ἀεὶ καὶ καταλαβεῖν ἐπειγομένου τὸ Ἀδαμιαῖον γένος· ὁ δὲ βόθρος ὁ κόσμος ἐστὶ πλήρης ὑπάρχων παντοίων κακῶν καὶ θανατηφόρων παγίδων· τὸ φυτὸν δὲ τὸ ὑπὸ τῶν δύο μυῶν ἀπαύστως συγκοπτόμενον, ὃ περιεδέδρακτο, ὁ δίαυλος ὑπάρχει τῆς ἑκάστου ζωῆς, ὁ δαπανώμενος καὶ ἀναλισκόμενος διὰ τῶν ὡρῶν τοῦ ἡμερονυκτίου καὶ τῇ ἐκτομῇ κατὰ μικρὸν προσεγγίζων· αἱ δὲ τέσσαρες ἀσπίδες τὴν ἐπὶ τεσσάρων σφαλερῶν καὶ ἀστάτων στοιχείων σύστασιν τοῦ ἀνθρωπείου σώματος αἰνίττονται, ὧν ἀτακτούντων καὶ ταραττομένων ἡ τοῦ σώματος καταλύεται σύστασις· πρὸς τούτοις καὶ ὁ πυρώδης ἐκεῖνος καὶ ἀπηνὴς δράκων τὴν φοβερὰν εἰκονίζει τοῦ ᾅδου γαστέρα, τὴν μαιμάσσουσαν ὑποδέξασθαι τοὺς τὰ παρόντα τερπνὰ τῶν μελλόντων ἀγαθῶν προκρίνοντας. ὁ δὲ τοῦ μέλιτος σταλαγμὸς τὴν γλυκύτητα ἐμφαίνει τῶν τοῦ κόσμου ἡδέων, δι' ἧς ἐκεῖνος ἀπατῶν τοὺς ἑαυτοῦ φίλους οὐκ ἐᾷ τῆς σφῶν προνοήσασθαι σωτηρίας.

XIII

Ταύτην ὁ Ἰωάσαφ λίαν ἀποδεξάμενος τὴν 114
παραβολήν, ἔφη· Ὡς ἀληθὴς ὁ λόγος οὗτος καὶ πάνυ ἁρμοδιώτατος. μὴ οὖν ὀκνήσῃς τοιούτους ἀεί μοι τύπους ὑποδεικνύειν, ἵνα γνῶ ἀκριβῶς ὁποῖος ὑπάρχει ὁ καθ' ἡμᾶς [1] βίος, καὶ τίνων τοῖς ἑαυτοῦ φίλοις πρόξενος γίνεται.

[1] ἡμᾶς, Bois. ὑμᾶς (?).

'This is the likeness of those who cleave to the deceitfulness of this present life,—the interpretation whereof I will declare to thee anon. The unicorn is the type of death, ever in eager pursuit to overtake the race of Adam. The pit is the world, full of all manner of ills and deadly snares. The tree, which was being continually fretted by the two mice, to which the man clung, is the course of every man's life, that spendeth and consuming itself hour by hour, day and night, and gradually draweth nigh its severance. The fourfold asps signify the structure of man's body upon four treacherous and unstable elements which, being disordered and disturbed, bring that body to destruction. Furthermore, the fiery cruel dragon betokeneth the maw of hell that is hungry to receive those who choose present pleasures rather than future blessings. The dropping of honey denoteth the sweetness of the delights of the world, whereby it deceiveth its own friends, nor suffereth them to take timely thought for their salvation.' The interpretation of the tale

XIII

IOASAPH received this parable with great joy and said, 'How true this story is, and most apt! Grudge not, then, to shew me other such like figures, that I may know for certain what the manner of our life is, and what it hath in store for its friends.' Ioasaph heareth the tale with joy

Ὁ δὲ γέρων εἶπεν· Ὅμοιοι αὖθίς εἰσιν οἱ ἐρασθέντες τῶν τοῦ βίου τερπνῶν καὶ τῇ τούτου
γλυκανθέντες ἡδύτητι, τῶν μελλόντων τε καὶ μὴ
σαλευομένων τὰ ῥευστὰ καὶ ἀσθενῆ προτιμήσαντες, ἀνθρώπῳ τινὶ τρεῖς ἐσχηκότι φίλους, ὧν
τοὺς μὲν δύο περιπαθῶς ἐτίμα, καὶ σφοδρῶς τῆς
αὐτῶν ἀγάπης ἀντείχετο, μέχρι θανάτου ὑπὲρ
αὐτῶν ἀγωνιζόμενος καὶ προκινδυνεύειν αἱρού-
μενος· πρὸς δὲ τὸν τρίτον πολλῇ ἐφέρετο κατα-
φρονήσει, μήτε τιμῆς, μήτε τῆς προσηκούσης
αὐτὸν πώποτε ἀξιώσας ἀγάπης, ἀλλ' ἢ μικράν
τινα καὶ οὐδαμινὴν εἰς αὐτὸν προσποιούμενος
φιλίαν. καταλαμβάνουσιν οὖν ἐν μιᾷ φοβεροί
τινες καὶ ἐξαίσιοι στρατιῶται, σπεύδοντες ταχύ-
τητι πολλῇ πρὸς τὸν βασιλέα τοῦτον ἀγαγεῖν,
λόγον ἀποδώσοντα ὑπὲρ ὀφειλῆς μυρίων ταλάντων. στενοχωρούμενος δὲ ἐκεῖνος ἐζήτει βοηθόν,
τὸν συναντιλαβέσθαι αὐτῷ ἐν τῷ φρικτῷ τοῦ
βασιλέως λογοθεσίῳ δυνάμενον. δραμὼν οὖν
πρὸς τὸν πρῶτον αὐτοῦ καὶ πάντων γνησιώτατον
Cp. John xiii. 37 φίλον, λέγει. Οἶδας, ὦ φίλε, ὡς ἀεὶ ἐθέμην τὴν
ψυχήν μου ὑπὲρ σοῦ· νυνὶ δὲ χρῄζω βοηθείας ἐν
τῇ ἡμέρᾳ ταύτῃ τῆς κατεχούσης με ἀνάγκης.
πόσων οὖν ἐπαγγέλλῃ συναντιλαβέσθαι μοι νῦν; 115
καὶ τίς ἡ παρὰ σοῦ προσγινομένη μοι ἐλπίς,
προσφιλέστατε; ἀποκριθεὶς οὖν ἐκεῖνος ἔφη·
Οὐκ εἰμί σου φίλος, ἄνθρωπε· οὐκ ἐπίσταμαι τίς
εἶ. ἄλλους γὰρ ἔχω προσφιλεῖς, μεθ' ὧν δεῖ με
σήμερον εὐφραίνεσθαι, καὶ φίλους αὐτοὺς εἰς τὸ
ἑξῆς κτήσασθαι. παρέχω δέ σοι ἰδοὺ ῥάκια δύο,
τοῦ ἔχειν σε ταῦτα ἐν τῇ ὁδῷ ᾗ πορεύῃ, ἅτινα
οὐδέν σε τὸ παράπαν ὠφελήσουσι. καὶ μηδεμίαν

Barlaam telleth the tale of the Man and his Three Friends, APOLOGUE V

The elder answered, 'Again, those who are enamoured of the pleasures of life, and glamoured by the sweetness thereof, who prefer fleeting and paltry objects to those which are future and stable, are like a certain man who had three friends. On the first two of these he was extravagantly lavish of his honours, and clave passionately to their love, fighting to the death and deliberately hazarding his life for their sakes. But to the third he bore himself right arrogantly, never once granting him the honour nor the love that was his due, but only making show of some slight and inconsiderable regard for him. Now one day he was apprehended by certain dread and strange soldiers, that made speed to hale him to the king, there to render account for a debt of ten thousand talents. Being in a great strait, this debtor sought for a helper, able to take his part in this terrible reckoning with the king. So he ran to his first and truest friend of all, and said, "Thou wottest, friend, that I ever jeopardied my life for thy sake. Now to-day I require help in a necessity that presseth me sore. In how many talents wilt thou undertake to assist me now? What is the hope that I may count upon at thy hands, O my dearest friend?" The other answered and said unto him, "Man, I am not thy friend: I know not who thou art. Other friends I have, with whom I must needs make merry to-day, and so win their friendship for the time to come. But, see, I present thee with two ragged garments, that thou mayest have them on the way whereon thou goest, though they will do thee no manner of good.

ἄλλην παρ' ἐμοῦ προσδοκήσῃς ἐλπίδα. τούτων ἀκούσας ἐκεῖνος καὶ ἀπογνοὺς ἣν ἐξ αὐτοῦ βοήθειαν ἤλπιζε, πρὸς τὸν ἕτερον πορεύεται φίλον, καί φησι· Μέμνησαι, ὦ ἑταῖρε, ὅσης ἀπήλαυσας παρ' ἐμοῦ τιμῆς καὶ εὐγνωμοσύνης· σήμερον δέ, θλίψει περιπεσὼν καὶ συμφορᾷ μεγίστῃ, χρῄζω συνεργοῦ. πόσον οὖν ἰσχύεις μοι συγκοπιάσαι; ἐξ αὐτῆς γνώρισόν μοι. ὁ δέ φησιν· Οὐ σχολάζω σήμερον συναγωνίσασθαί σοι· μερίμναις γὰρ κἀγὼ καὶ περιστάσεσι περιπεσὼν ἐν θλίψει εἰμί. μικρὸν δ' ὅμως συνοδεύσω σοι, κἂν μηδὲν ὠφελήσω σε· καί, θᾶττον ὑποστρέψας οἴκαδε, ταῖς ἰδίαις ἔσομαι ἀσχολούμενος μερίμναις. κεναῖς οὖν κἀκεῖθεν ὑποστρέψας χερσὶν ὁ ἄνθρωπος καὶ πάντοθεν ἀπορούμενος, ἐταλάνιζεν ἑαυτὸν τῆς ματαίας ἐλπίδος τῶν ἀγνωμόνων αὐτοῦ φίλων, καὶ τῶν ἀνοήτων ταλαιπωριῶν ὧν ὑπὲρ τῆς ἐκείνων ἀγάπης ὑπέστη. ἀπέρχεται λοιπὸν πρὸς τὸν τρίτον φίλον αὐτοῦ, ὃν οὐδέποτε 116
ἐθεράπευσεν, οὐδὲ κοινωνὸν τῆς ἑαυτοῦ εὐφροσύνης προσεκαλέσατο· καί φησι πρὸς αὐτὸν κατῃσχυμμένῳ τε καὶ κατηφιῶντι τῷ προσώπῳ· Οὐκ ἔχω στόμα διᾶραι πρὸς σέ, γινώσκων ἀκριβῶς ὅτι οὐ μέμνησαί μου πώποτε εὐεργετήσαντός σε, ἢ προσφιλῶς διατεθέντος σοι. ἀλλ' ἐπεὶ συμφορά με κατέλαβε χαλεπωτάτη, οὐδαμόθεν δὲ τῶν λοιπῶν μου φίλων εὗρον σωτηρίας ἐλπίδα, παρεγενόμην πρὸς σέ, δυσωπῶν, εἰ ἔστι σοι ἰσχύς, μικράν τινα βοήθειαν παρασχεῖν μοι. μὴ οὖν ἀπαγορεύσῃς, μηνίσας μου τῆς ἀγνωμοσύνης. ὁ δέ φησιν ἱλαρῷ καὶ χαρίεντι προσώπῳ· Ναὶ δὴ φίλον ἐμὸν γνησιώτατον ὁμο-

Further help from me thou mayest expect none." The other, hearing this, despaired of the succour whereon he had reckoned, and went to his second friend, saying, "Friend, thou rememberest how much honour and kindness thou hast enjoyed at my hands. To-day I have fallen into tribulation and sorrow, and need a helping hand. To what extent then canst thou share my labour? Tell me at once." Said he, "I have on leisure today to share thy troubles. I too have fallen among cares and perils, and am myself in tribulation. Howbeit, I will go a little way with thee, even if I shall fail to be of service to thee. Then will I turn quickly homeward, and busy myself with mine own anxieties." So the man returned from him too empty-handed and baulked at every turn; and he cried misery on himself for his vain hope in those ungrateful friends, and the unavailing hardships that he had endured through love of them. At the last he went away to the third friend, whom he had never courted, nor invited to share his happiness. With countenance ashamed and downcast, he said unto him, "I can scarce open my lips to speak with thee, knowing full well that I have never done thee service, or shown thee any kindness that thou mightest now remember. But seeing that a heavy misfortune hath overtaken me, and that I have found nowhere among my friends any hope of deliverance, I address myself to thee, praying thee, if it lie in thy power, to afford me some little aid. Bear no grudge for my past unkindness, and refuse me not." The other with a smiling and gracious countenance answered, "Assuredly I own thee my very true friend. I have

how they proved themselves in his distress,

λογῶ σε ὑπάρχειν· καὶ, τῆς μικρᾶς ἐκείνης μεμνημένος σου εὐποιίας, σὺν τόκῳ σήμερον ἀποδώσω σοι. μὴ φοβοῦ τοίνυν, μηδὲ δέδιθι· ἐγώ σου γὰρ προπορεύσομαι, ἐγὼ δυσωπήσω ὑπὲρ σοῦ τὸν βασιλέα, καὶ οὐ μὴ παραδῶ σε εἰς χεῖρας ἐχθρῶν σου. θάρσει οὖν, προσφιλέστατε, καὶ μὴ λυποῦ. τότε κατανυγεὶς ἐκεῖνος ἔλεγε μετὰ δακρύων· Οἴμοι τί πρῶτον θρηνήσω, καὶ τί κλαύσομαι πρῶτον; τῆς ματαίας μου καταγνώσομαι προσπαθείας εἰς τοὺς ἀμνήμονας καὶ ἀχαρίστους καὶ ψευδεῖς φίλους ἐκείνους; ἢ τὴν φρενοβλαβῆ ταλανίσω ἀγνωμοσύνην, ἥνπερ τῷ ἀληθεῖ τούτῳ 117
καὶ γνησίῳ ἐνεδειξάμην φίλῳ;

Ὁ δὲ Ἰωάσαφ, καὶ τοῦτον μετὰ θαύματος δεξάμενος τὸν λόγον, τὴν σαφήνειαν ἐζήτει. καί φησιν ὁ Βαρλαάμ· Ὁ πρῶτος φίλος ἂν εἴη ἡ τοῦ πλούτου περιουσία καὶ ὁ τῆς φιλοχρηματίας ἔρως, ἐφ' ᾧ μυρίοις ὁ ἄνθρωπος περιπίπτει κινδύνοις, καὶ πολλὰς ὑπομένει ταλαιπωρίας· ἐλθούσης δὲ τῆς τελευταίας τοῦ θανάτου προθεσμίας οὐδὲν ἐκ πάντων ἐκείνων, εἰ μὴ τὰ πρὸς κηδείαν ἀνόνητα ῥάκια, λαμβάνει. δεύτερος δὲ φίλος κέκληται γυνή τε καὶ τέκνα καὶ οἱ λοιποὶ συγγενεῖς τε καὶ οἰκεῖοι, ὧν τῇ προσπαθείᾳ κεκολλημένοι δυσαποσπάστως ἔχομεν, αὐτῆς τῆς ψυχῆς καὶ τοῦ σώματος ἕνεκεν τῆς αὐτῶν ὑπερορῶντες ἀγάπης· οὐδεμιᾶς δέ τις ἐξ αὐτῶν ἀπώνατο ὠφελείας τῇ ὥρᾳ τοῦ θανάτου· ἀλλ' ἢ μόνον μέχρι τοῦ μνήματος συνοδεύουσιν αὐτῷ παρεπόμενοι, εἶτ', εὐθὺς ἐπαναστραφέντες, τῶν ἰδίων ἔχονται μεριμνῶν καὶ περιστάσεων, οὐκ ἔλαττον λήθῃ τὴν μνήμην, ἢ τὸ σῶμα τοῦ ποτε προσφιλοῦς

not forgotten those slight services of thine: and I will repay them to-day with interest. Fear not therefore, neither be afraid. I will go before thee and entreat the king for thee, and will by no means deliver thee into the hands of thine enemies. Wherefore be of good courage, dear friend, and fret not thyself." Then, pricked at heart, the other said with tears, "Wo is me! Which shall I first lament, or which first deplore? Condemn my vain preference for my forgetful, thankless and false friends, or blame the mad ingratitude that I have shown to thee, the sincere and true?"'

Ioasaph heard this tale also with amazement and asked the interpretation thereof. Then said Barlaam, 'The first friend is the abundance of riches, and love of money, by reason of which a man falleth into the midst of ten thousand perils, and endureth many miseries: but when at last the appointed day of death is come, of all these things he carrieth away nothing but the useless burial cloths. By the second friend is signified our wife and children and the remnant of kinsfolk and acquaintance, to whom we are passionately attached, and from whom with difficulty we tear ourselves away, neglecting our very soul and body for the love of them. But no help did man ever derive from these in the hour of death, save only that they will accompany and follow him to the sepulchre, and then straightway turning them homeward again they are occupied with their own cares and matters, and bury his memory in oblivion as they have buried his body in the grave. But the

and the interpretation thereof

καλύψαντες τάφῳ. ὁ δ' αὖ τρίτος φίλος ὁ παρεωραμένος καὶ φορτικός, ὁ μὴ προσιτός, ἀλλὰ φευκτὸς καὶ οἷον ἀποτρόπαιος, ὁ τῶν ἀρίστων ἔργων χορὸς καθέστηκεν, οἷον πίστις, ἐλπίς, ἀγάπη, ἐλεημοσύνη, φιλανθρωπία, καὶ ὁ λοιπὸς τῶν ἀρετῶν ὅμιλος, ὁ δυνάμενος προπορεύεσθαι ἡμῶν ἐξερχομένων τοῦ σώματος, ὑπὲρ ἡμῶν τε δυσωπῆσαι τὸν
Cp. Luke xvi. 9 Κύριον, καὶ τῶν ἐχθρῶν ἡμᾶς λυτρούμενος καὶ δεινῶν φορολόγων, τῶν λογοθέσιον ἡμῖν πικρὸν ἐν τῷ ἀέρι κινούντων, καὶ χειρώσασθαι πικρῶς ζητούντων. οὗτός ἐστιν ὁ εὐγνώμων φίλος καὶ
ἀγαθός, ὁ καὶ τὴν μικρὰν ἡμῶν εὐπραγίαν ἐπὶ 118
μνήμης φέρων καὶ σὺν τόκῳ ἡμῖν πᾶσαν ἀποδιδούς.

XIV

Αὖθις οὖν ὁ Ἰωάσαφ, Εὖ σοι γένοιτο παρὰ Κυρίου τοῦ Θεοῦ, ὦ σοφώτατε τῶν ἀνθρώπων. εὔφρανας γάρ μου τὴν ψυχὴν τοῖς καταλλήλοις σου καὶ ἀρίστοις ῥήμασι. τοιγαροῦν ἀνατύπωσόν μοι καὶ ἔτι εἰκόνα τῆς ματαιότητος τοῦ κόσμου, καὶ πῶς ἄν τις ἐν εἰρήνῃ καὶ ἀσφαλείᾳ τοῦτον διέλθοι.

Ἀναλαβὼν δὲ τὸν λόγον ὁ Βαρλαὰμ ἔφη, Ἄκουσον καὶ τούτου δὴ τοῦ προβλήματος ὁμοίωσιν. πόλιν τινὰ μεμάθηκα μεγάλην, ἧς οἱ πολῖται τοιαύτην ἐσχήκεσαν ἔκπαλαι συνήθειαν, τὸ ἐπιλαμβάνεσθαι ξένου τινὸς καὶ ἀγνώστου ἀνδρός, μηδὲν τῶν νόμων τῆς πόλεως καὶ παραδόσεων ὅλως ἐπισταμένου, καὶ τοῦτον βασιλέα καθιστᾶν ἑαυτοῖς, πάσης ἀπολαύοντα ἐξουσίας καὶ τῶν

third friend, that was altogether neglected and held cheap, whom the man never approached, but rather shunned and fled in horror, is the company of good deeds,—faith, hope, charity, alms, kindliness, and the whole band of virtues, that can go before us, when we quit the body, and may plead with the Lord on our behalf, and deliver us from our enemies and dread creditors, who urge that strict rendering of account in the air, and try bitterly to get the mastery of us. This is the grateful and true friend, who beareth in mind those small kindnesses that we have shown him and repayeth the whole with interest.'

XIV

Ioasaph desireth yet another parable

AGAIN said Ioasaph, 'The Lord God prosper thee, O thou wisest of men! For thou hast gladdened my soul with thine apt and excellent sayings. Wherefore sketch me yet another picture of the vanity of the world, and how a man may pass through it in peace and safety.'

Barlaam telleth of the city that had strangers for its kings, APOLOGUE VI

Barlaam took up his parable and said, 'Hear then a similitude of this matter too. I once heard tell of a great city whose citizens had, from old time, the custom of taking some foreigner and stranger, who knew nothing of their laws and traditions, and of making him their king, to enjoy absolute power,

αὐτοῦ θελημάτων ἀκωλύτως ἐχόμενον, ἄχρι συμπληρώσεως ἐνιαυσιαίου χρόνου. εἶτ', ἐξαίφνης ἐν πάσῃ αὐτοῦ τυγχάνοντος ἀμεριμνίᾳ, τρυφῶντός τε καὶ σπαταλῶντος ἀδεῶς, καὶ συνδιαιωνίζειν αὐτῷ τὴν βασιλείαν εἰσαεὶ δοκοῦντος, ἐπεγειρόμενοι κατ' αὐτοῦ, καὶ τὴν βασιλικὴν ἀφελόμενοι στολήν, γυμνόν τε ἀνὰ πᾶσαν θριαμβεύσαντες τὴν πόλιν, ἐξόριστον ἔπεμπον εἰς μακρὰν ἀπῳκισμένην καὶ μεγάλην τινὰ νῆσον, ἐν ᾗ, μήτε διατροφῆς εὐπορῶν μήτε ἐνδυμάτων, ἐν λιμῷ καὶ γυμνότητι δεινῶς κατετρύχετο, τῆς παρ' ἐλπίδα δοθείσης αὐτῷ τρυφῆς καὶ θυμηδίας εἰς λύπην αὖθις καὶ παρ' ἐλπίδα πᾶσαν καὶ προσδοκίαν μεταμειφθείσης. κατὰ τὸ παρακολουθῆσαν τοίνυν ἔθος τῶν πολιτῶν ἐκείνων, προεχειρίσθη τις ἀνὴρ
εἰς τὴν βασιλείαν συνέσει πολλῇ τὸν λογισμὸν 119
κατάκομον ἔχων, ὃς αὐτίκα μὴ συναρπασθεὶς τῇ ἐξαίφνης αὐτῷ προσπεσούσῃ εὐθηνίᾳ, μηδὲ τῶν προβεβασιλευκότων καὶ ἀθλίως ἐκβληθέντων τὴν ἀμεριμνίαν ζηλώσας, ἐμμέριμνον εἶχε καὶ ἐναγώνιον τὴν ψυχὴν πῶς ἂν τὰ κατ' αὐτὸν εὖ διάθοιτο. τῇ συχνῇ δὲ μελέτῃ ἀκριβωσάμενος, ἔγνω διά τινος σοφωτάτου συμβούλου τὴν συνήθειαν τῶν πολιτῶν, καὶ τὸν τόπον τῆς διηνεκοῦς ἐξορίας· ὅπως τε χρὴ ἑαυτὸν ἀσφαλίσασθαι ἀπλανῶς ἐδιδάχθη. ταῦτ' οὖν ὡς ἔγνω, καὶ ὅτι δεῖ αὐτὸν ὅσον οὔπω ἐκείνην καταλαμβάνειν τὴν νῆσον, τὴν δ' ἐπίκτητον ταύτην καὶ ἀλλοτρίαν βασιλείαν ἀλλοτρίοις αὖθις καταλιμπάνειν, ἀνοίξας τοὺς θησαυροὺς αὐτοῦ ὧνπερ τέως ἀνειμένην εἶχε καὶ ἀκώλυτον τὴν χρῆσιν, καὶ λαβὼν χρημάτων πλῆθος, χρυσοῦ τε καὶ

and follow his own will and pleasure without hindrance, until the completion of a year. Then suddenly, while he was living with never a care in rioting and wantonness, without fear, and alway supposing that his reign would only terminate with his life, they would rise up against him, strip him bare of his royal robes, lead him in triumph up and down the city, and thence dispatch him beyond their borders into a distant great island; there, for lack of food and raiment, in hunger and nakedness he would waste miserably away, the luxury and pleasure so unexpectedly showered upon him changed as unexpectedly into woe. In accordance therefore with the unbroken custom of these citizens, a certain man was ordained to the kingship. But his mind was fertile of understanding, and he was not carried away by this sudden access of prosperity, nor did he emulate the heedlessness of the kings that had gone before him, and had been miserably expelled, but his soul was plunged in care and trouble how he might order his affairs well. After long and careful search, he learned from a wise counsellor the custom of the citizens, and the place of perpetual banishment, and was taught of him without guile how to ensure himself against this fate. So with this knowledge that within a very little while he must reach that island and leave to strangers this chance kingdom among strangers, he opened the treasures whereof he had awhile absolute and unforbidden use, and took a great store of money and huge masses of gold and silver and

and of the stranger king that looked well to his future welfare

ἀργύρου καὶ λίθων τιμίων ἁδρότατον ὄγκον,
πιστοτάτοις παραδοὺς οἰκέταις, εἰς ἐκείνην προέ-
πεμψεν, εἰς ἣν ἔμελλεν ἀπάγεσθαι, νῆσον. συν-
τελεσθέντος δὲ τοῦ ἐμπροθέσμου ἐνιαυτοῦ, στα-
σιάσαντες οἱ πολῖται γυμνὸν αὐτόν, ὡς καὶ τοὺς
πρὸ αὐτοῦ, τῇ ἐξορίᾳ παρέπεμψαν. οἱ μὲν οὖν
λοιποὶ ἀνόητοι καὶ πρόσκαιροι βασιλεῖς δεινῶς
ἐλίμωττον· ὁ δέ, τὸν πλοῦτον προαποθέμενος 120
ἐκεῖνον, εὐθηνίᾳ διηνεκεῖ συζῶν καὶ τρυφὴν
ἀδάπανον ἔχων, φόβον τε παντάπασιν ἀποσεισάμενος τῶν ἀτάκτων καὶ πονηρῶν πολιτῶν,
τῆς σοφωτάτης ἑαυτὸν ἐμακάριζεν εὐβουλίας.

Πόλιν οὖν νόει μοι τὸν μάταιον τοῦτον καὶ
ἀπατεῶνα κόσμον, πολίτας δὲ τὰς ἀρχὰς καὶ
Eph. vi. 12 τὰς ἐξουσίας τῶν δαιμόνων, τοὺς κοσμοκράτορας
τοῦ σκότους τοῦ αἰῶνος τούτου, τοὺς δελεάζοντας
ἡμᾶς τῷ λείῳ τῆς ἡδονῆς, καὶ ὡς περὶ ἀφθάρτων
ὑποτιθεμένους διανοεῖσθαι τῶν φθαρτῶν καὶ
ἐπικήρων, ὡς ἅτε συνδιαιωνιζούσης ἡμῖν καὶ
ἀθάνατα τῆς τούτων συνυπαρχούσης ἀπολαύσεως. οὕτως οὖν ἀπατηθέντων ἡμῶν καὶ μηδεμίαν περὶ τῶν μονίμων ἐκείνων καὶ αἰωνίων
βουλευσαμένων, μήτε τι ταμιευσαμένων ἑαυτοῖς
εἰς τὸν ἐκεῖθεν βίον, αἰφνίδιος ἡμῖν ἐφίσταται
ὄλεθρος ὁ τοῦ θανάτου. τότε δὴ τότε γυμνοὺς
ἡμᾶς τῶν ἐντεῦθεν οἱ πονηροὶ καὶ πικροὶ δεξά-
μενοι πολῖται τοῦ σκότους, ὡς ἐκείνοις τὸν
ἅπαντα προσαναλώσαντας χρόνον, ἀπάγουσιν
Job. x. 21 εἰς γῆν σκοτεινὴν καὶ γνοφεράν, εἰς γῆν σκότους
αἰωνίου, οὗ οὐκ ἔστι φέγγος, οὐδὲ ὁρᾶν ζωὴν
βροτῶν. σύμβουλον δὲ ἀγαθόν, τὸν τἀληθῆ
πάντα γνωρίσαντα καὶ τὰ σωτήρια διδάξαντα

precious stones and delivered the same to trusty servants and sent them before him to the island whither he was bound. When the appointed year came to an end, the citizens rose against him, and sent him naked into banishment like those that went before him. But while the rest of these foolish kings, kings only for a season, were sore anhungred, he, that had timely deposited his wealth, passed his time in continual plenty mid dainties free of expense, and, rid of all fear of those mutinous and evil citizens, could count himself happy on his wise forethought.

The interpretation of the parable,

'Understand thou, therefore, that the city is this vain and deceitful world; that the citizens are the principalities and powers of the devils, the rulers of the darkness of this world, who entice us by the soft bait of pleasure, and counsel us to consider corruptible and perishable things as incorruptible, as though the enjoyment that cometh from them were co-existent with us, and immortal as we. Thus then are we deceived; we have taken no thought concerning the things which are abiding and eternal, and have laid up in store for ourselves no treasure for that life beyond, when of a sudden there standeth over us the doom of death. Then, then at last do those evil and cruel citizens of darkness, that received us, dispatch us stript of all worldly goods,—for all our time has been wasted on their service—and carry us off "to a dark land and a gloomy, to a land of eternal darkness, where there is no light, nor can one behold the life of men." As for that good counsellor, who made known all the truth and taught

ἐπιτηδεύματα τῷ συνετῷ καὶ σοφωτάτῳ βασιλεῖ,
τὴν ἐμὴν ὑπολάμβανε εὐτελῆ χθαμαλότητα, ὃς
τὴν ἀγαθὴν ὁδὸν καὶ ἀπλανῆ ὑποδεῖξαί σοι ἥκω,
τοῖς αἰωνίοις μὲν καὶ ἀτελευτήτοις ἐνάγων κἀκεῖσε
πάντα συμβουλεύων ἀποθέσθαι, ἀπάγων δὲ τοῦ
πλάνου κόσμου τούτου, ὅνπερ κἀγὼ δυστυχῶς 121
ἐφίλουν, καὶ τῶν αὐτοῦ ἀντειχόμην τερπνῶν τε
καὶ ἀπολαυστικῶν. κατανοήσας δὲ τοῖς ἀπλανέσι τοῦ νοὸς ὀφθαλμοῖς πῶς ἐν τούτοις πᾶς ὁ
τῶν ἀνθρώπων κατατρίβεται βίος, τῶν μὲν
παραγινομένων, τῶν δὲ ἀπαιρόντων, καὶ μηδενὸς
ἔχοντος τὸ στάσιμόν τε καὶ βέβαιον, μήτε τῶν
πλουτούντων ἐν τῷ πλούτῳ, μήτε τῶν δυνατῶν
ἐν τῇ ἰσχύϊ, μήτε τῶν σοφῶν ἐν τῇ σοφίᾳ, μηδ'
αὖ τῶν εὐημερούντων ἐν τῇ εὐημερίᾳ, μήτε
τῶν τρυφώντων ἐν τῇ σπατάλῃ, μήτε τῶν
ἀσφαλῶς δοκούντων βιοῦν ἐν τῇ ματαίᾳ αὐτῶν
καὶ ἀδρανεστάτῃ ἀσφαλείᾳ, μήτε ἐν ἄλλῳ τινὶ
τῶν ἐνταῦθα ἐπαινουμένων, ἀλλ' ἔοικε τὸ πρᾶγμα
Greg. Naz. Orat. xvi. p. 251 χειμάρρων παρόδῳ ἀμετρήτῳ θαλάσσης ἐμπι-
πτόντων βυθῷ (ῥευστὰ γὰρ οὕτως εἰσὶ τὰ
παρόντα πάντα καὶ πρόσκαιρα), συνῆκα ὡς τὰ
τοιαῦτα μάταια σύμπαντα καὶ ὄνησις αὐτῶν
οὐδεμία, ἀλλ', ὥσπερ τὰ πρότερον πάντα λήθῃ
κέκρυπται, εἴτε δόξαν εἴποις, εἴτε βασιλείαν,
εἴτε ἀξιωμάτων λαμπρότητας, εἴτε δυναστείας
ὄγκον, εἴτε τυράννων θρασύτητα, εἴτε τι τῶν
τοιούτων, οὕτως καὶ τὰ ἐνεστῶτα εἰς τοὺς ἑξῆς
καὶ μετέπειτα χρόνους ἀμαυρωθήσεται. ὧνπερ
κἀγὼ εἷς ὑπάρχων τῇ συνήθει πάντως ἀλλοιώσει
ὑποπεσοῦμαι, καὶ καθὼς οἱ πρὸ ἐμοῦ δι' αἰῶνος
τέρπεσθαι τοῖς παροῦσιν οὐ συνεχωρήθησαν,

that sagacious and wise king the way of salvation, understand thou that I, thy poor and humble servant, am he, who am come hither for to shew thee the good and infallible way to lead thee to things eternal and unending, and to counsel thee to lay up all thy treasure there; and I am come to lead thee away from the error of this world, which, to my woe, I also loved, and clave to its pleasures and delights. But, when I perceived, with the unerring eyes of my mind how all human life is wasted in these things that come and go; when I saw that no man hath aught that is stable and stedfast, neither the rich in his wealth, nor the mighty in his strength, nor the wise in his wisdom, nor the prosperous in his prosperity, nor the luxurious in his wantonness, nor he that dreameth of security of life in that vain and feeble security of his dreams, nor any man in any of those things that men on earth commend ('tis like the boundless rush of torrents that discharge themselves into the deep sea, thus fleeting and temporary are all present things); then, I say, I understood that all such things are vanity, and that their enjoyment is naught; and, that even as the past is all buried in oblivion, be it past glory, or past kingship, or the splendour of rank, or amplitude of power, or arrogance of tyranny, or aught else like them, so also present things will vanish in the darkness of the days to come. And, as I am myself of the present, I also shall doubtless be subject to its accustomed change; and, even as my fathers before me were not allowed to take delight for ever in the present world, so also shall it be with me.

which Barlaam applieth to his own case and that of the prince

οὕτως ἔσται καὶ ἐπ' ἐμοί. κατεῖδον γὰρ οἷα τοὺς ἀνθρώπους ὁ τύραννος οὗτος καὶ ταραχώδης κατεργάζεται κόσμος, μετατιθεὶς αὐτοὺς ἐντεῦθεν κἀκεῖθεν, οὓς μὲν ἐκ πλούτου πρὸς πενίαν, οὓς δὲ 122
ἐκ πενίας εἰς δόξαν, τούτους μὲν ὑπεξάγων τοῦ βίου, ἄλλους δὲ αὖθις ἀντεισάγων, τινὰς μὲν σοφοὺς καὶ συνετοὺς ἀποδοκιμάζων, ἀτίμους τε καὶ εὐτελεῖς τοὺς τιμίους καὶ περιφανεῖς ἐργαζόμενος, ἄλλους δὲ ἀσόφους τε καὶ ἀσυνέτους ἐπὶ θρόνου καθίζων δόξης, τιμίους τε τοὺς ἀτίμους καὶ ἀφανεῖς πᾶσι δεικνύων.

Καὶ ἔστιν ἰδεῖν τὸ τῶν ἀνθρώπων γένος μηδόλως κατὰ πρόσωπον τῆς αὐτοῦ ἀπηνοῦς τυραννίδος ἔχον στάσιν· ἀλλ', ὡς ὅταν περιστερά, φεύγουσα ἀετὸν εἴτε ἱέρακα, τόπους ἐκ τόπων ἀμείβῃ, νῦν μὲν τούτῳ τῷ δένδρῳ, αὖθις ἐκείνῳ τῷ θάμνῳ, εἶτ' εὐθὺς τρώγλαις τῶν πετρῶν καὶ παντοίαις ἀκάνθαις ἑαυτὴν προσαράσσουσα, καὶ οὐδαμοῦ εὑρίσκουσα προσφύγιον ἀσφαλές, ἐν σάλῳ καὶ ταλαντώσει ταλαιπωρεῖται διηνεκεῖ, οὕτως εἰσὶν οἱ τοῖς παροῦσιν ἐπτοημένοι, ὑφ' ὁρμῆς μὲν ἀλογίστου ἀθλίως πονοῦντες, μηδόλως δέ τι ἔχοντες βέβαιον ἢ ἀσφαλές, μήτ' ἐπιστάμενοι εἰς ὁποῖον καταντῶσι τέλος, καὶ ποῦ τούτους ὁ μάταιος ἄγει βίος, ᾧ καθυπέταξαν ἑαυτοὺς λίαν δυστυχῶς καὶ ἀθλίως, πονηρὰ μὲν ἑλόμενοι ἀντὶ ἀγαθῶν, μετελθόντες δὲ κακίαν ἀντὶ χρηστότητος, ἢ τίς ὁ τὰς ψυχρὰς τῶν πολλῶν καὶ μοχθηρῶν αὐτῶν καμάτων διαδεξάμενος ἐπικαρπίας, εἴτε οἰκεῖος, εἴτε ἀλλότριος· καὶ πολλάκις οὐδὲ φίλος ὅλως ἢ γνωστός, ἀλλ' ἐχθρὸς καὶ πολέμιος.

For I have observed how this tyrannical and troublesome world treateth mankind, shifting men hither and thither, from wealth to poverty, and from poverty to honour, carrying some out of life and bringing others in, rejecting some that are wise and understanding, making the honourable and illustrious dishonoured and despised, but seating others who are unwise and of no understanding upon a throne of honour, and making the dishonoured and obscure to be honoured of all.

Barlaam bewaileth the vain restlessness of human life, and telleth of the way of peace

'One may see how the race of mankind may never abide before the face of the cruel tyranny of the world. But, as when a dove fleeing from an eagle or a hawk flitteth from place to place, now beating against this tree, now against that bush, and then anon against the clefts of the rocks and all manner of bramble-thorns, and, nowhere finding any safe place of refuge, is wearied with continual tossing and crossing to and fro, so are they which are flustered by the present world. They labour painfully under unreasoning impulse, on no sure or firm bases: they know not to what goal they are driving, nor whither this vain life leadeth them—this vain life, whereto they have in miserable folly subjected themselves, choosing evil instead of good, and pursuing vice instead of goodness; and they know not who shall inherit the cold fruits of their many heavy labours, whether it be a kinsman or a stranger, and, as oft times it haps, not even a friend or acquaintance at all, but an enemy and foeman.

Ταῦτα πάντα καὶ τὰ τούτοις ἑπόμενα διακρίνας
ἐν τῷ τῆς ψυχῆς κριτηρίῳ, ἐμίσησα τὸν σύμ-
παντά μου βίον τὸν ἐν τοῖς ματαίοις ἀναλωθέντα,
ὃν διήγαγον τοῖς περὶ γῆς πόνοις προστετηκώς.
ἀποβαλλομένῳ δέ μοι τῆς ψυχῆς τὴν τούτων 123
προσπάθειαν καὶ ἀπορρίψαντι κατέφανη τὰ τῷ
ὄντι ἀγαθά, τὸ φοβεῖσθαι τὸν Θεὸν καὶ ποιεῖν
αὐτοῦ τὸ θέλημα. τοῦτο γὰρ ἔγνων πάντων τῶν
Ps. cxi. 10 ἀγαθῶν κεφάλαιον ὑπάρχειν· τοῦτο καὶ ἀρχὴ
σοφίας λέγεται καὶ σοφία τετελειωμένη· ζωὴ γάρ
ἐστιν ἄλυπος καὶ ἀνεπηρέαστος τοῖς ἀντεχομένοις
αὐτῆς, καὶ τοῖς ἐπερειδομένοις ἐπ᾽ αὐτὴν ὡς ἐπὶ
Κύριον ἀσφαλής. ἐπιστήσας οὖν μου τὸν λογι-
Ps. cxix. 32 σμὸν τῇ ἀπλανεστάτῃ ὁδῷ τῶν ἐντολῶν τοῦ
Prov. viii. 8 Κυρίου, καὶ γνοὺς ἀκριβῶς μηδὲν ἐν αὐτῇ σκολιὸν ἢ στραγγαλιῶδες ὑπάρχειν, μήτε φαράγγων
καὶ σκοπέλων ἀκανθῶν τε καὶ τριβόλων πεπληρωμένην, ἀλλ᾽ ὅλην λείαν καθεστηκέναι καὶ
ὁμαλήν, τέρπουσαν μὲν τοὺς ὀφθαλμοὺς τῶν
αὐτὴν ὁδευόντων ταῖς φανοτάταις θεωρίαις ὡραΐ-
Is. lii. 7 ζουσαν δὲ τοὺς πόδας, καὶ ὑποδύουσαν τὴν ἑτοι-
Rom. x. 15 μασίαν τοῦ εὐαγγελίου τῆς εἰρήνης, τοῦ ἀσφαλῶς
Eph. vi. 15 τε καὶ συντόμως βαδίζειν· ἥνπερ πάντων δικαίως
προέκρινα, καὶ οἰκοδομεῖν ἠρξάμην τὴν πεσοῦσάν
μου τῆς ψυχῆς καὶ φθαρεῖσαν οἰκίαν.

Οὕτως μου τὰ κατ᾽ ἐμαυτὸν διατιθεμένου καὶ
τὸ σφαλερὸν τοῦ νοὸς ἐπανορθοῦντος, ῥημάτων
ἀκήκοα σοφοῦ τινος διδασκάλου τοιαῦτά μοι
ἐμβοῶντος· Ἐξέλθετε, ἔφη, πάντες οἱ ποθοῦντες
σωθῆναι· ἀποχωρίσθητε τῆς ματαιότητος τοῦ 124
1 Cor. vii. 31 κόσμου· παράγει γὰρ τὸ σχῆμα αὐτοῦ μικρὸν
ὅσον, καὶ ἰδοὺ οὐκ ἔσται. ἐξέλθετε ἀμεταστρεπτί,

'On all these things, and others akin to them, I held judgement in the tribunal of my soul, and I came to hate my whole life that had been wasted in these vanities, while I still lived engrossed in earthly things. But when I had put off from my soul the lust thereof, and cast it from me, then was there revealed unto me the true good, to fear God and do his will; for this I saw to be the sum of all good. This also is called the beginning of wisdom, and perfect wisdom. For life is without pain and reproach to those that hold by her, and safe to those who lean upon her as upon the Lord. So, when I had set my reason on the unerring way of the commandments of the Lord, and had surely learned that there is nothing froward or perverse therein, and that it is not full of chasms and rocks, nor of thorns and thistles, but lieth altogether smooth and even, rejoicing the eyes of the traveller with the brightest sights, making beautiful his feet, and shoeing them with "the preparation of the Gospel of peace," that he may walk safely and without delay, this way, then, I rightly chose above all others, and began to rebuild my soul's habitation, which had fallen into ruin and decay.

Of the voice that called Barlaam to come out from the world

'In such wise was I devising mine estate, and establishing mine unstable mind, when I heard the words of a wise teacher calling loudly to me thus, "Come ye out," said he, "all ye that will to be saved. Be ye separate from the vanity of the world, for the fashion thereof quickly passeth away, and behold it shall not be. Come ye out, without

μὴ προῖκα δὲ καὶ ἀμισθί, ἀλλ' ἐφόδια φερόμενοι
ζωῆς αἰωνίου· μακρὰν γὰρ μέλλετε βαδίζειν ὁδόν,
πολλῶν ἔχουσαν χρείαν τῶν ἐντεῦθεν ἐφοδίων.
καὶ καταλαμβάνετε τὸν αἰώνιον τόπον χώρας
ἔχοντα δύο, πολλὰς ἐν ἑαυταῖς μονὰς ἐχούσας, ὧν
τὴν μὲν μίαν ἡτοίμασεν ὁ Θεὸς τοῖς ἀγαπῶσιν
αὐτὸν καὶ τὰς αὐτοῦ φυλάττουσιν ἐντολάς, παντοίων οὖσαν ἀγαθῶν πεπληρωμένην, ἧσπερ οἱ
ἀξιωθέντες ἐν ἀφθαρσίᾳ ζήσονται διηνεκεῖ, τῆς
Is. xxxv. 10 ἀνωλέθρου ἀπολαύοντες ἀθανασίας, ἔνθα ἀπέδρα
ὀδύνη, λύπη καὶ στεναγμός· ἡ δὲ δευτέρα, σκότους οὖσα μεστὴ καὶ θλίψεως καὶ ὀδύνης, τῷ
Mat. xxv. 41 διαβόλῳ ἡτοίμασται καὶ τοῖς ἀγγέλοις αὐτοῦ, ἐν
ᾗ βληθήσονται καὶ οἱ δι' ἔργων πονηρῶν ἑαυτοῖς
ταύτην προξενήσαντες, οἱ τῶν ἀφθάρτων καὶ
αἰωνίων τὰ παρόντα ἀνταλλαξάμενοι καὶ ὅλους
ἑαυτοὺς κατάβρωμα τοῦ αἰωνίου πυρὸς ποιησάμενοι.

Ταύτης ἐγὼ τῆς φωνῆς ἀκούσας καὶ τὸ ἀψευδὲς
αὐτῆς ἐπιγνούς, ἐκεῖνο καταλαβεῖν τὸ κατάλυμα
ἔργον ἐθέμην, τὸ πάσης μὲν ἀπηλλαγμένον
ὀδύνης τε καὶ λύπης, τοσαύτης δὲ ἀσφαλείας καὶ
τοιούτων ἀγαθῶν πλῆρες ὑπάρχον, ὧν ἡ γνῶσις
νυνὶ μὲν ἐκ μέρους ἐστὶν ἐν ἐμοί, νηπίῳ τε ὄντι
1 Cor. xiii. 9–12 τὴν πνευματικὴν ἡλικίαν καὶ ὡς δι' ἐσόπτρων καὶ
αἰνιγμάτων τὰ ἐκεῖθεν βλέποντι· ὅτε δὲ ἔλθῃ τὸ
τέλειον, καὶ ἐπιγνώσομαι πρόσωπον πρὸς πρόσ-
Rom. vii. 25 ωπον, τότε τὸ ἐκ μέρους καταργηθήσεται. εὐχαριστῶ τοίνυν τῷ Θεῷ διὰ Ἰησοῦ Χριστοῦ τοῦ
Rom. viii. 2, 6 Κυρίου ἡμῶν· ὁ γὰρ νόμος τοῦ πνεύματος τῆς
ζωῆς ἐν Χριστῷ Ἰησοῦ ἠλευθέρωσέ με ἀπὸ τοῦ
νόμου τῆς ἁμαρτίας καὶ τοῦ θανάτου, καὶ διή-

turning back, not for nothing and without reward, but winning supplies for travelling to life eternal, for ye are like to journey a long road, needing much supplies from hence, and ye shall arrive at the place eternal that hath two regions, wherein are many mansions; one of which places God hath prepared for them that love him and keep his commandments, full of all manner of good things; and they that attain thereto shall live for ever in incorruption, enjoying immortality without death, where pain and sorrow and sighing are fled away. But the other place is full of darkness and tribulation and pain, prepared for the devil and his angels, wherein also shall be cast they who by evil deeds have deserved it, who have bartered the incorruptible and eternal for the present world, and have made themselves fuel for eternal fire."

Barlaam counselleth Ioasaph to lay up for himself treasure in heaven

'When I heard this voice, and recognized the truth, I did my diligence to attain to that abode, that is free from all pain and sorrow, and full of security and all good things, whereof I have knowledge now only in part, being but a babe in my spiritual life, and seeing the sights yonder as through mirrors and riddles; but when that which is perfect is come, and I shall see face to face, then that which is in part shall be done away. Wherefore I thank God through Jesus Christ our Lord; for the law of the Spirit of life in Christ Jesus hath made me free from the law of sin and of death, and hath opened mine

νοιξέ μου τοὺς ὀφθαλμοὺς ἁπλανῶς κατιδεῖν ὅτι τὸ φρόνημα τῆς σαρκὸς θάνατος, τὸ δὲ φρόνημα τοῦ πνεύματος ζωὴ καὶ εἰρήνη. καὶ καθάπερ οὖν ἐγώ, τῶν παρόντων ἐπιγνοὺς τὴν ματαιότητα, τέλειον αὐτὰ ἐμίσησα μῖσος, οὕτω δὴ καὶ σὲ γινώσκειν περὶ τούτων συμβουλεύω, ἵνα ὡς ἀλλοτρίοις διατεθῇς αὐτοῖς καὶ θᾶττον παρερχομένοις, ἀφελόμενος δ' ἐντεῦθεν πάντα, θησαυρίσῃς σεαυτῷ ἐν τῷ ἀφθάρτῳ αἰῶνι θησαυρὸν ἀσύλητον, πλοῦτον ἀδαπάνητον, ἔνθα σε δεῖ ἀνυπερθέτως πορευθῆναι, ἵνα, ὅταν ἀπέλθῃς, οὐχ ὑστερούμενος ἔσῃ, ἀλλὰ πλούτῳ βρίθων, καθάπερ σοι τὴν τούτων ἀνεθέμην ἀνωτέρω καταλληλοτάτην εἰκόνα.

XV

Λέγει δὲ ὁ Ἰωάσαφ τῷ γέροντι· Πῶς οὖν δυνήσομαι θησαυροὺς χρήματων καὶ πλούτου ἐκεῖσε 126
προπέμπειν, ὡς ἂν ἄσυλον αὐτῶν καὶ ἀνώλεθρον
τὴν ἀπόλαυσιν ἀπελθὼν εὕρω; πῶς δὲ δείξω τὸ
πρὸς τὰ παρόντα μου μῖσος, καὶ τῶν αἰωνίων
ἀνθέξομαι; μάλα σαφήνισόν μοι. καί φησιν ὁ
Βαρλαάμ· Ἡ μὲν τοῦ πλούτου τούτου πρὸς τὸν
αἰώνιον τόπον προπομπὴ ταῖς χερσὶ γίνεται τῶν
πενήτων. φησὶ γάρ τις τῶν προφητῶν, Δανιὴλ ὁ
Dan. iv. 24 σοφώτατος, τῷ βασιλεῖ Βαβυλῶνος· Διὰ τοῦτο,
βασιλεῦ, ἡ βουλή μου ἀρεσάτω σοι· καὶ τὰς
ἁμαρτίας σου ἐν ἐλεημοσύναις λύτρωσαι καὶ
τὰς ἀδικίας σου ἐν οἰκτιρμοῖς πενήτων. λέγει δὲ
Luke xvi. 9 καὶ ὁ Σωτήρ· Ποιήσατε ἑαυτοῖς φίλους ἐκ τοῦ

eyes to see clearly that the will of the flesh is death, but the will of the Spirit is life and peace. And even as I did discern the vanity of present things and hate them with a perfect hatred, so likewise I counsel thee to decide thereon, that thou mayest treat them as something alien and quickly passing away, and mayest remove all thy store from earth and lay up for thyself in the incorruptible world a treasure that can not be stolen, wealth inexhaustible, in that place whither thou must shortly fare, that when thou comest thither thou mayest not be destitute, but be laden with riches, after the manner of that aptest of parables that I lately showed thee.'

XV

Barlaam declareth the virtue of almsgiving

SAID Ioasaph unto the elder, 'How then shall I be able to send before me thither treasures of money and riches, that, when I depart hence, I may find these unharmed and unwasted for my enjoyment? How must I show my hatred for things present and lay hold on things eternal? This make thou right plain unto me.' Quoth Barlaam, 'The sending before thee of money to that eternal home is wrought by the hands of the poor. For thus saith one of the prophets, Daniel the wise, unto the king of Babylon, "Wherefore, O Prince, let my counsel be acceptable unto thee, and redeem thy sins by almsgiving, and thine iniquities by showing mercy to the poor." The Saviour also saith, "Make to

μαμωνᾶ τῆς ἀδικίας, ἵν', ὅταν ἐκλίπητε, δέξωνται
Cp. Luke xi. 41; xii. 33; xix. 8; Mat. xix. 21 ὑμᾶς εἰς τὰς αἰωνίους σκηνάς. καὶ πολὺν ἄνω τε
καὶ κάτω λόγον ὁ Δεσπότης τῆς ἐλεημοσύνης καὶ
μεταδόσεως τῶν πενήτων ποιεῖται, καθὼς ἐν τῷ
Εὐαγγελίῳ μανθάνομεν. οὕτως μὲν οὖν ἀσφαλέστατα λίαν ἐκεῖσε προπέμψεις πάντα ταῖς τῶν
Mat. xxv. 40 δεομένων χερσίν· ὅσα γὰρ εἰς τούτους ποιήσεις,
ἑαυτῷ ὁ Δεσπότης οἰκειούμενος πολυπλασίως σε
ἀνταμείψεται· νικᾷ γὰρ ἀεὶ ταῖς τῶν δωρεῶν 127
ἀντιδόσεσι τοὺς ἀγαπῶντας αὐτόν. τούτῳ μὲν οὖν τῷ τρόπῳ τέως τοὺς θησαυροὺς τοῦ σκότους τοῦ αἰῶνος τούτου συλήσας, ᾧ τεταλαιπώρηκας πολὺν ἤδη χρόνον ἐκδουλεύων, καλῶς ἐκ τούτων πρὸς τὸ μέλλον ἐφοδιασθήσῃ, καὶ τοῦ ἀλλοτρίου ἀφελόμενος σεαυτῷ πάντα προαποθήσῃ, διὰ τῶν ῥευστῶν τούτων καὶ προσκαίρων τὰ ἑστῶτα καὶ μένοντα ἐξωνησάμενος· ἔπειτα, τοῦ Θεοῦ συνεργοῦντός σοι, καταινοήσεις τὸ ἄστατον τοῦ κόσμου καὶ ἀνώμαλον, καί, χαίρειν πᾶσιν εἰπών, πρὸς τὸ μέλλον μεθορμισθήσῃ, παραδραμὼν μὲν τὰ παρατρέχοντα, τοῖς ἐλπιζομένοις δὲ καὶ ἱσταμένοις προστεθήσῃ, καὶ τὸ σκότος μὲν ἀπολιπὼν σὺν τῇ σκιᾷ τοῦ θανάτου, μισήσας δὲ τὸν κόσμον
Eph. vi. 12 καὶ κοσμοκράτορα, καὶ τὴν φθειρομένην σάρκα
1 Tim. vi. 16 ἐχθρὰν ἑαυτῷ λογισάμενος, τῷ φωτὶ προσδράμῃς
Mk. viii. 34 τῷ ἀπροσίτῳ, καί, τὸν σταυρὸν ἐπ' ὤμων ἄρας,
ἀκολουθήσεις αὐτῷ ἀμεταστρεπτί, ἵνα καὶ σὺν αὐτῷ δοξασθῇς καὶ τῆς οὐκ ἔτι μεταπιπτούσης ζωῆς οὐδὲ ἀπατηλῆς ἀναδειχθῇς κληρονόμος.

Ὁ δὲ Ἰωάσαφ· Τὸ πάντων οὖν, φησίν, ὑπεριδεῖν καὶ ἐπίπονον οὕτως ἀναλαβέσθαι βίον, κα-

yourselves friends of the mammon of unrighteousness; that, when ye fail, they may receive you into everlasting habitations." And, in divers places, the Master maketh much mention of almsgiving and liberality to the poor, as we learn in the Gospel. Thus shalt thou most surely send all thy treasure before thee by the hands of the needy, for whatsoever thou shalt do unto these the Master counteth done unto himself, and will reward thee manifold; for, in the recompense of benefits, he ever surpasseth them that love him. So in this manner by seizing for awhile the treasures of the darkness of this world, in whose slavery for a long time past thou hast been miserable, thou shalt by these means make good provision for thy journey, and by plundering another's goods thou shalt store all up for thyself, with things fleeting and transient purchasing for thyself things that are stable and enduring. Afterwards, God working with thee, thou shalt perceive the uncertainty and inconstancy of the world, and saying farewell to all, shalt remove thy barque to anchor in the future, and, passing by the things that pass away, thou shalt hold to the things that we look for, the things that abide. Thou shalt depart from darkness and the shadow of death, and hate the world and the ruler of the world; and, counting thy perishable flesh thine enemy, thou shalt run toward the light that is unapproachable, and taking the Cross on thy shoulders, shalt follow Christ without looking back, that thou mayest also be glorified with him, and be made inheritor of the life that never changeth nor deceiveth.'

which Christ himself hath commended

Ioasaph said, 'When thou spakest a minute past of despising all things, and taking up such a life of

Ioasaph would fain know

θάπερ εἴρηκας ἀνωτέρω, παράδοσίς ἐστιν ἀρχαία
ἐκ τῆς τῶν ἀποστόλων κατιοῦσα διδαχῆς; ἢ
ἔναγχος ὑμῖν ἐπινενόηται τῇ τοῦ νοὸς ὑμῶν
ἐπιστήμῃ, ὡς κρεῖττον ἐκλεξαμένοις τοῦτο;

Πρὸς ὃν ὁ γέρων ἔφη· Οὐ νόμον προσφάτως 128
εἰσενεχθέντα διδάσκω σε (μὴ γένοιτο), ἀλλ' ἔκπα-
Luke xviii. 18 λαι δοθέντα ἡμῖν. εἶπεν γὰρ ὁ Κύριος πλουσίῳ
Mat. xix. 16 τινὶ ἐπερωτήσαντι αὐτόν, Τί ποιήσας ζωὴν
Mk. x. 21 αἰώνιον κληρονομήσω; καὶ καυχωμένῳ πάντα
φυλάξαι τὰ γεγραμμένα ἐν τῷ νόμῳ, Ἕν σοι, φησίν,
ὑστερεῖ· ὕπαγε, ὅσα ἔχεις πώλησον καὶ δὸς
πτωχοῖς, καὶ ἕξεις θησαυρὸν ἐν οὐρανοῖς· καὶ
δεῦρο ἀκολούθει μοι, ἄρας τὸν σταυρόν. ὁ δὲ
ταῦτα ἀκούσας περίλυπος ἐγένετο· ἦν γὰρ πλούσιος σφόδρα. ἰδὼν δὲ αὐτὸν ὁ Ἰησοῦς περίλυπον
Luke xviii. 24 γενόμενον, εἶπε· Πῶς δυσκόλως οἱ τὰ χρήματα
ἔχοντες εἰσελεύσονται εἰς τὴν βασιλείαν τοῦ Θεοῦ.
εὐκοπώτερον γάρ ἐστι κάμηλον διὰ τρυμαλιᾶς
ῥαφίδος διελθεῖν, ἢ πλούσιον εἰς τὴν βασιλείαν
τοῦ Θεοῦ εἰσελθεῖν. ταύτης οὖν τῆς ἐντολῆς
πάντες ἀκούσαντες οἱ ἅγιοι ἀποχωρισθῆναι
πάντῃ τῆς τοιαύτης τοῦ πλούτου δυσκολίας
ἐφρόντισαν· καὶ πάντα σκορπίσαντες, καὶ διὰ
τῆς τῶν πενήτων διαδόσεως πλοῦτον ἑαυτοῖς
αἰώνιον προαποθέμενοι, ἦραν τὸν σταυρὸν καὶ τῷ
Χριστῷ ἠκολούθησαν, οἱ μὲν μαρτυρικῶς, καθὰ
δὴ καὶ εἶπόν σοι, τελειωθέντες, οἱ δὲ ἀσκητικῶς
ἀγωνισάμενοι, καὶ μηδὲν ἐκείνων ἀπολιπόντες τῇ
ἀγωγῇ τῆς ἀληθινῆς ταύτης φιλοσοφίας. ἐντολὴν οὖν ταύτην εἶναι γίνωσκε Χριστοῦ τοῦ 129
βασιλέως ἡμῶν καὶ Θεοῦ, ἀπάγουσαν ἡμᾶς τῶν
φθαρτῶν, καὶ τῶν ἀϊδίων μετόχους ἐργαζομένην.

toil, was that an old tradition handed down from the teaching of the Apostles, or is this a late invention of your wits, which ye have chosen for yourselves as a more excellent way?'

by what authority Barlaam speaketh

The elder answered and said, 'I teach thee no law introduced but yesterday, God forbid! but one given unto us of old. For when a certain rich young man asked the Lord, "What shall I do to inherit eternal life?" and boasted that he had observed all that was written in the Law, Jesus said unto him, "One thing thou lackest yet. Go sell all that thou hast and distribute unto the poor, and thou shalt have treasure in heaven, and come, take up thy cross and follow me." But when the young man heard this he was very sorrowful: for he was very rich. And when Jesus saw that he was very sorrowful, he said, "How hardly shall they which have riches enter into the kingdom of God! For it is easier for a camel to go through the eye of a needle, than for a rich man to enter into the kingdom of God!" So, when all the Saints heard this command, they thought fit by all means to withdraw from this hardness of riches. They parted with all their goods, and by this distribution of their riches to the poor laid up for themselves eternal riches; and they took up their Cross and followed Christ, some being made perfect by martyrdom, even as I have already told thee; and some by the practice of self-denial falling not a whit short of those others in the life of the true philosophy. Know thou, then, that this is a command of Christ our King and God, which leadeth us from things corruptible and maketh us partakers of things everlasting.'

Barlaam telleth of the command of Christ to sell all and follow him,

Παλαιᾶς οὖν, φησὶν ὁ Ἰωάσαφ, καὶ οὕτως ἀναγκαίας οὔσης τῆς τοιαύτης φιλοσοφίας, πῶς οὐ πολλοὶ ζηλοῦσι σήμερον τουτονὶ τὸν βίον;

Ὁ δὲ γέρων ἔφη· Πολλοὶ μὲν ἐζήλωσαν καὶ ζηλοῦσιν, οἱ πλεῖστοι δὲ ὀκνοῦσι καὶ ἀναδύονται·
Mat. vii. 13 Ὀλίγοι γάρ, καθά φησιν ὁ Κύριος, οἱ τῆς στενῆς
Luke xiii. 23 ὁδοῦ καὶ τεθλιμμένης ὁδοιπόροι, τῆς ἀνειμένης δὲ καὶ πλατείας οἱ πλείους. οἱ γὰρ καθάπαξ ὑπὸ φιλοχρηματίας καὶ τῶν τῆς φιληδονίας κακῶν ἁλόντες, τῇ κενῇ δὲ καὶ ματαίᾳ προστετηκότες δόξῃ, δυσαποσπάστως αὐτῶν ἔχουσιν, ὡς ἅτε δούλους ἑαυτοὺς ἑκουσίως ἀπεμπολήσαντες ἀλλοτρίῳ δεσπότῃ, καὶ ἀπ᾽ ἐναντίας ἱστάμενοι τῷ ταῦτα ἐπιτάττοντι Θεῷ, καὶ δέσμιοι αὐτῷ κατεχόμενοι. ψυχὴ γὰρ καθάπαξ ἀπογνοῦσα τῆς οἰκείας σωτηρίας, τὰς ἡνίας αὐτῆς ἐνδοῦσα ταῖς ἀλόγοις ἐπιθυμίαις, πανταχοῦ περιφέρεται. διὰ τοῦτο ὀλοφυρόμενος ὁ Προφήτης τὴν περικεχυμένην ἄνοιαν ταῖς τοιαύταις ψυχαῖς, καὶ τῆς ἐπικειμένης
Ps. iv. 2 αὐταῖς ἀχλύος τὴν παχύτητα θρηνῶν, ἔλεγεν Υἱοὶ ἀνθρώπων, ἕως πότε βαρυκάρδιοι; ἱνατί ἀγαπᾶτε ματαιότητα καὶ ζητεῖτε ψεῦδος; ὅτῳ τις καὶ τῶν
Greg. Naz. Orat. ix. p. 151 ἡμετέρων σοφῶν διδασκάλων, θεολογικώτατος ἀνήρ, συνᾴδων, καί τινα παρ᾽ ἑαυτοῦ προστιθείς,
ἐκβοᾷ πᾶσιν ὡς ἐξ ἀπόπτου τινὸς καὶ ὑψηλοτάτης 130
περιωπῆς· Υἱοὶ ἀνθρώπων, ἕως πότε βαρυκάρδιοι; ἱνατί ἀγαπᾶτε ματαιότητα καὶ ζητεῖτε ψεῦδος; μέγα τι τὸν ἐνταῦθα βίον καὶ τὴν τρυφὴν καὶ τὸ μικρὸν δοξάριον καὶ τὴν ταπεινὴν δυναστείαν καὶ τὴν ψευδομένην εὐημερίαν ὑπολαμβάνοντες, ἃ μὴ τῶν ἐχόντων μᾶλλον ἐστὶν ἢ τῶν ἐλπισάντων,

Said Ioasaph, 'If, then, this kind of philosophy be so ancient and so salutary, how cometh it that so few folk now-a-days follow it?'

The elder answered, 'Many have followed, and do follow it; but the greatest part hesitate and draw back. For few, saith the Lord, are the travellers along the strait and narrow way, but along the wide and broad way many. For they that have once been taken prisoners by the love of money, and the evils that come from the love of pleasure, and are given up to idle and vain glory, are hardly to be torn therefrom, seeing that they have of their own free will sold themselves as slaves to a strange master, and setting themselves on the opposite side to God, who gave these commands, are held in bondage to that other. For the soul that hath once rejected her own salvation, and given the reins to unreasonable lusts, is carried about hither and thither. Therefore saith the prophet, mourning the folly that encompasseth such souls, and lamenting the thick darkness that lieth on them, "O ye sons of men, how long will ye be of heavy heart? Why love ye vanity, and seek after leasing?" And in the same tone as he, but adding thereto some thing of his own, one of our wise teachers, a most excellent divine, crieth aloud to all, as from some exceeding high place of vantage, "O ye sons of men, how long will ye be of heavy heart? Why love ye vanity and seek after leasing? Trow ye that this present life, and luxury, and these shreds of glory, and petty lordship and false prosperity are any great thing?"—things which no more belong to those that possess them than to them that hope for them, nor to these latter any more than to those who never thought of them:

and of the vanity of men who will not obey that call.

οὐδὲ τούτων μᾶλλον ἢ τῶν οὐδὲ προσδοκησάντων, ὥσπερ χοῦς ὑπὸ λαίλαπος ἄλλοτε εἰς ἄλλους ῥιπιζόμενα καὶ μεταρριπτούμενα, ἢ ὥσπερ καπνὸς διαρρέοντα, καὶ ὡς ὄναρ παίζοντα, καὶ ὡς σκιὰ μὴ κρατούμενα, οὔτε ἀπόντα δυσέλπιστα τοῖς οὐ κεκτημένοις, οὔτε παρόντα πιστὰ τοῖς ἔχουσιν.

Οὕτως οὖν τοῦ Σωτῆρος ἐντελλομένου, τῶν Προφητῶν τε καὶ Ἀποστόλων κηρυττόντων, καὶ τῶν ἁγίων πάντων ἔργῳ τε καὶ λόγῳ εἰς τὴν τῆς ἀρετῆς συνωθούντων ἡμᾶς ἀπλανεστάτην ὁδόν, κἂν ὀλίγοι οἱ ταύτην ὁδεύοντες, πλείους δὲ οἱ τὴν εὐρύχωρον καὶ πρὸς ἀπώλειαν ἄγουσαν προκρίνοντες, οὐκ ἐκ τούτου ἡ πολιτεία τῆς ἐνθέου ταύτης κατασμικρυνθήσεται φιλοσοφίας, ἀλλά, καθάπερ ὁ ἥλιος, εἰς φαῦσιν πᾶσιν ἀνατέλλων, ἀφθόνως αὐτοῦ τὰς ἀκτῖνας προπέμπει πάντας φωτίζεσθαι προτρεπόμενος, οὕτω καὶ ἡ ἀληθὴς φιλοσοφία τοὺς αὐτῆς ἐραστὰς ἡλίου δίκην φωταγωγεῖ καὶ περιθάλπει καὶ λαμπροὺς ἀποδείκνυσιν. εἰ δέ τινες, μύσαντες τοὺς ὀφθαλμούς, κατιδεῖν αὐτοῦ τὸ φέγγος οὐ θελήσουσιν, οὔτε μεμπτέος παρὰ τοῦτο ὁ ἥλιος οὔτε τοῖς λοιποῖς παροπτέος, οὔτε μὴν ἡ δόξα τῆς αὐτοῦ λαμπρότητος διὰ τῆς ἐκείνων ἀτιμασθήσεται ἀβελτηρίας· ἀλλ᾽ ἐκεῖνοι μὲν 131
τοῦ φωτὸς ἑαυτοὺς ἀποστερήσαντες ὡς τυφλοὶ ψηλαφήσουσι τοῖχον, πολλοῖς δὲ ἐμπεσοῦνται βόθροις, καὶ πολλαῖς ἐκκεντηθήσονται τὰς ὄψεις ἀκάνθαις, ὁ δὲ ἥλιος ἐπὶ τῆς ἰδίας ἱστάμενος λαμπρότητος φωτιεῖ τοὺς ἀνακεκαλυμμένῳ προσώπῳ τὸ φέγγος αὐτοῦ κατοπτριζομένους. τὸν αὐτὸν δὴ τρόπον καὶ τὸ τοῦ Χριστοῦ φῶς φαίνει μὲν πᾶσι πλουσίως, μεταδιδὸν ἡμῖν τῆς αὐτοῦ λαμπηδόνος·

things like the dust carried and whirled about to and fro by the tempest, or vanishing as the smoke, or delusive as a dream, or intangible as a shadow; which, when absent, need not be despaired of by them that have them not, and, when present, cannot be trusted by their owners.

'This then was the commandment of the Saviour; this the preaching of the Prophets and Apostles; in such wise do all the Saints, by word and deed, constrain us to enter the unerring road of virtue. And though few walk therein and more choose the broad way that leadeth to destruction, yet not for this shall the life of this divine philosophy be minished in fame. But as the sun, rising to shine on all, doth bounteously send forth his beams, inviting all to enjoy his light, even so doth our true philosophy, like the sun, lead with her light those that are her lovers, and warmeth and brighteneth them. But if any shut their eyes, and will not behold the light thereof, not for that must the sun be blamed, or scorned by others: still less shall the glory of his brightness be dishonoured through their silliness. But while they, self-deprived of light, grope like blind men along a wall, and fall into many a ditch, and scratch out their eyes on many a bramble bush, the sun, firmly established on his own glory, shall illuminate them that gaze upon his beams with unveiled face. Even so shineth the light of Christ on all men abundantly, imparting to us of his

who are like those that shut their eyes against the blessed light of the sun

μετέχει δὲ ἕκαστος καθ' ὅσον ἐφέσεως ἔχει καὶ προθυμίας· οὔτε γὰρ ἀποστερεῖ τινα τῶν βουλο-
Mal. iv. 2 μένων αὐτῷ ἐνατενίζειν ὁ ἥλιος τῆς δικαιοσύνης, οὔτε μὴν βιάζεται τοὺς ἑκουσίως τὸ σκότος ἐκλεγομένους· ἀλλὰ τῇ ἰδίᾳ ἕκαστος ἐφεῖται αὐτεξουσίῳ προαιρέσει, ἕως ἐν τῷ παρόντι βίῳ ἐστί.

Cp. S. John Dam. De fide orth. Bk. II. ch. xxii.-xxvii.

Τοῦ δὲ Ἰωάσαφ πυθομένου Τί τὸ αὐτεξούσιον καὶ τί προαίρεσις, φησὶν ὁ γέρων· Αὐτεξουσιότης μέν ἐστι ψυχῆς λογικῆς θέλησις, ἀκωλύτως κινουμένη πρὸς ὅπερ ἂν βούλοιτο, εἴτε ἀρετὴν εἴτε κακίαν, οὕτως ὑπὸ τοῦ Δημιουργοῦ γενομένης. αὐτεξουσιότης αὖθίς ἐστι νοερᾶς ψυχῆς κίνησις αὐτοκρατής. προαίρεσις δέ ἐστιν ὄρεξις βουλευτικὴ τῶν ἐφ' ἡμῖν, ἢ βούλευσις ὀρεκτικὴ τῶν ἐφ' ἡμῖν· τοῦ γὰρ προκριθέντος ἐκ τῆς βουλῆς ἐφιέμεθα προαιρούμενοι. βουλὴ δέ ἐστιν ὄρεξις ζητητικὴ περὶ τῶν ἐφ' ἡμῖν πρακτικῶν γινομένη· βουλεύεται γάρ τις, εἰ ὤφειλε μετελθεῖν τὸ πρᾶγμα ἢ οὔ. εἶτα κρίνει τὸ κρεῖττον, καὶ γίνεται κρίσις. εἶτα διατίθεται καὶ ἀγαπᾷ τὸ ἐκ τῆς βουλῆς κριθέν, καὶ λέγεται γνώμη· ἐὰν γὰρ κρίνῃ,
καὶ μὴ διατεθῇ πρὸς τὸ κριθέν, ἤγουν ἀγαπήσῃ 132
αὐτό, οὐ λέγεται γνώμη. εἶτα μετὰ τὴν διάθεσιν γίνεται προαίρεσις, ἤγουν ἐπιλογή· προαίρεσις γάρ ἐστι δύο προκειμένων τὸ ἓν αἱρεῖσθαι καὶ ἐκλέγεσθαι τοῦτο πρὸ τοῦ ἑτέρου. καὶ τοῦτο φανερόν, ὅτι βουλή ἐστι μετ' ἐπικρίσεως ἡ προαίρεσις, καὶ ἐξ αὐτῆς τῆς ἐτυμολογίας· προαιρετὸν γάρ ἐστι τὸ ἕτερον πρὸ τοῦ ἑτέρου αἱρετόν· οὐδεὶς δὲ προκρίνει τι μὴ βουλευσάμενος, οὐδὲ προαιρεῖ-

lustre. But every man shareth thereof in proportion to his desire and zeal. For the Sun of righteousness disappointeth none of them that would fix their gaze on him, yet doth he not compel those who willingly choose darkness; but every man, so long as he is in this present life, is committed to his own free will and choice.'

Ioasaph asked, 'What is free will and what is choice?' The elder answered, 'Free will is the willing of a reasonable soul, moving without hindrance toward whatever it wisheth, whether to virtue or to vice, the soul being thus constituted by the Creator. Free will again is the sovran motion of an intelligent soul. Choice is desire accompanied by deliberation, or deliberation accompanied by desire for things that lie in our power; for in choosing we desire that which we have deliberately preferred. Deliberation is a motion towards enquiry about actions possible to us; a man deliberateth whether he ought to pursue an object or no. Then he judgeth which is the better, and so ariseth judgement. Then he is inclined towards it, and loveth that which was so judged by the deliberative faculty, and this is called resolve; for, if he judge a thing, and yet be not inclined toward the thing that he hath judged, and love it not, it is not called resolve. Then, after inclination toward it, there ariseth choice or rather selection. For choice is to choose one or other of two things in view, and to select this rather than that. And it is manifest that choice is deliberation *plus* discrimination, and this from the very etymology. For that which is the "object of choice" is the thing chosen before the other thing. And no man preferreth a thing without deliberation, nor maketh a choice

Barlaam defineth free will and choice.

ται μὴ προκρίνας. ἐπειδὴ γὰρ οὐ πάντα τὰ δόξαντα ἡμῖν εὖ ἔχειν εἰς ἔργον ἀγαγεῖν προθυμούμεθα, τότε προαίρεσις καὶ προαιρετὸν γίνεται τὸ προκριθὲν ἐκ τῆς βουλῆς, ὅταν προσλάβῃ τὴν ὄρεξιν. καὶ οὕτω συνάγεται προαίρεσιν εἶναι ὄρεξιν βουλευτικὴν τῶν ἐφ' ἡμῖν· τοῦ γὰρ προκριθέντος ἐκ τῆς βουλῆς ἐφιέμεθα προαιρούμενοι. πᾶσα γὰρ βουλὴ πράξεως ἕνεκα καὶ διὰ πρᾶξιν· καὶ οὕτω πάσης μὲν προαιρέσεως βουλὴ ἡγεῖται, πάσης δὲ πράξεως προαίρεσις. διὰ τοῦτο οὐ μόνον αἱ πράξεις, ἀλλὰ καὶ τὰ κατὰ διάνοιαν, ἅτινα τὰς προαιρέσεις παριστῶσι, καὶ στεφάνους καὶ κολάσεις προξενοῦσιν. ἀρχὴ γὰρ ἁμαρτίας καὶ δικαιοπραγίας προαίρεσίς ἐστιν ἐν τοῖς ἐφ' ἡμῖν καταγομένη· ὧν γὰρ αἱ ἐνέργειαι ἐφ' ἡμῖν, τούτων καὶ αἱ πράξεις αἱ κατὰ τὴν ἐνέργειαν ἐφ' ἡμῖν· ἐφ' ἡμῖν δὲ αἱ κατὰ τὴν ἀρετὴν ἐνέργειαι, ἐφ' ἡμῖν ἄρα καὶ αἱ ἀρεταί· κυρίως γὰρ ἐφ' ἡμῖν ἐστι τὰ ψυχικὰ πάντα καὶ περὶ ὧν βουλευόμεθα. οὕτως
αὐτεξουσίως βουλευομένων τῶν ἀνθρώπων καὶ 133
αὐτεξουσίως προαιρουμένων, καθ' ὅσον ἂν τις προαιρῆται, κατὰ τοσοῦτον καὶ μετέχει τοῦ θείου φωτὸς καὶ προκόπτει ἐν τοῖς τῆς φιλοσοφίας ἐπιτηδεύμασι· διαφοραὶ γὰρ προαιρέσεως εἰσί. καὶ καθάπερ τινὲς πηγαὶ ὑδάτων ἐκ τῶν τῆς γῆς λαγόνων ἀναπεμπόμεναι, αἱ μὲν ἐπιπολαίως τῆς γῆς ἐκβλύζουσιν, αἱ δὲ μικρόν τι βαθύτερον, αἱ δὲ λίαν βαθέως, τούτων δὲ τῶν ὑδάτων τὰ μὲν προσεχῶς ἐκβλύζοντα καὶ τῇ γεύσει γλυκέα, τὰ δὲ βαθέως ἐξερχόμενα καὶ ἁλμυρίζοντα ἢ θεαφίζοντα, καὶ τὰ μὲν ἀφθόνως ἐκδιδόμενα, τὰ δὲ κατὰ μικρὸν

without having conceived a preference. For, since we are not zealous to carry into action all that seemeth good to us, choice only ariseth and the deliberately preferred only becometh the chosen, when desire is added thereto. Thus we conclude that choice is desire accompanied by deliberation for things that lie in our power; in choosing we desire that which we have deliberately preferred. All deliberation aimeth at action and dependeth on action; and thus deliberation goeth before all choice, and choice before all action. For this reason not only our actions, but also our thoughts, inasmuch as they give occasion for choice, bring in their train crowns or punishments. For the beginning of sin and righteous dealing is choice, exercised in action possible to us. Where the power of activity is ours, there too are the actions that follow that activity in our power. Virtuous activities are in our power, therefore in our power are virtues also; for we are absolute masters over all our souls' affairs and all our deliberations. Since then it is of free will that men deliberate, and of free will that men choose, a man partaketh of the light divine, and advanceth in the practice of this philosophy in exact measure of his choice, for there are differences of choice. And even as water-springs, issuing from the hollows of the earth, sometimes gush forth from the surface soil, and sometimes from a lower source, and at other times from a great depth, and even as some of these waters bubble forth continuously, and their taste is sweet, while others that come from deep wells are brackish or sulphurous, even as some pour forth in abundance while others flow drop by drop, thus, understand

and showeth that virtue lieth within our power

στάζοντα· οὕτως καὶ ἐπὶ τῶν προαιρέσεων νόει, τὰς μὲν ταχείας εἶναι καὶ λίαν θερμοτάτας, τὰς δὲ νωθρὰς καὶ ψυχράς, καὶ τὰς μὲν ὅλως ἐπὶ τὰ καλὰ τὴν ῥοπὴν κεκτημένας, τὰς δὲ πρὸς τὸ ἐναντίον πάσῃ δυνάμει ἀποκλινούσας. κατὰ γοῦν τὰς αὐτῶν διαθέσεις καὶ αἱ πρὸς τὰς πράξεις ἀκολουθοῦσιν ὁρμαί.

XVI

Λέγει δὲ ὁ Ἰωάσαφ πρὸς τὸν γέροντα· Εἰσὶν οὖν καὶ ἕτεροί τινες νῦν οἱ κατὰ ταῦτα κηρύττοντες ὥσπερ σύ; ἢ μόνος εἶ σήμερον ὁ ταῦτα διδάσκων καὶ οὕτως μισητὸν τὸν παρόντα βίον διηγούμενος;

Ὁ δὲ ἀποκριθεὶς εἶπεν· Ἐν τῇ καθ' ὑμᾶς 134
δυστυχεστάτῃ χώρᾳ ταύτῃ οὐδένα γινώσκω. ἡ γὰρ τοῦ σοῦ πατρὸς τυραννὶς μυρίοις τούτους θανάτοις περιέβαλε, καὶ ἔργον ἔθετο μὴ τὸ σύνολον ἀκούεσθαι ἐν ὑμῖν τὸ τῆς θεογνωσίας κήρυγμα. ἐν πάσαις δὲ ταῖς λοιπαῖς γλώσσαις ᾄδεται ταῦτα καὶ δοξάζεται, οἷς μὲν ὀρθοτάτῳ λόγῳ, ἄλλοις δὲ διεστραμμένως, τοῦ πολεμίου τῶν ἡμετέρων ψυχῶν ἐκκλίνειν αὐτοὺς τῆς εὐθείας ποιησαμένου καὶ ἀλλοτρίαις καταμερισαμένου
Cp. 2 Pet. iii. 16 δόξαις, καὶ ῥήσεις τινὰς τῶν Γραφῶν ἄλλως καὶ οὐ κατὰ τὸν ἐγκείμενον νοῦν μεθερμηνεύειν διδάξαντος. μία δέ ἐστιν ἡ ἀλήθεια, ἡ κηρυχθεῖσα διὰ τῶν ἐνδόξων ἀποστόλων καὶ τῶν θεοφόρων πατέρων, καὶ ἐν τῇ καθολικῇ Ἐκκλησίᾳ τῇ ἀπὸ περάτων ἕως περάτων τῆς οἰκουμένης ἡλίου φαιδρότερον διαλάμπουσα, ἧσπερ ἐγὼ κῆρυξ καὶ διδάσκαλος ἀπεστάλην σοι.

thou, is it also with our choices. Some choices are swift and exceeding fervent, others languid and cold: some have a bias entirely toward virtue, while others incline with all their force to its opposite. And like in nature to these choices are the ensuing impulses to action.'

XVI

Ioasaph learneth his father's evil practices,

Ioasaph said unto the elder, 'Are there now others, too, who preach the same doctrines as thou? Or art thou to-day the only one that teacheth this hatred of the present world?'

The other answered and said, 'In this your most unhappy country I know of none: the tyranny of thy father hath netted all such in a thousand forms of death; and he hath made it his aim that the preaching of the knowledge of God be not once heard in your midst. But in all other tongues these doctrines are sung and glorified, by some in perfect truth, but by others perversely; for the enemy of our souls hath made them decline from the straight road, and divided them by strange teachings, and taught them to interpret certain sayings of the Scriptures falsely, and not after the sense contained therein. But the truth is one, even that which was preached by the glorious Apostles and inspired Fathers, and shineth in the Catholick Church above the brightness of the sun from the one end of the world unto the other; and as an herald and teacher of that truth have I been sent to thee.'

Εἶπε δὲ ὁ Ἰωάσαφ πρὸς αὐτόν· Οὐδὲν οὖν τούτων ὁ ἐμὸς μεμάθηκε πατήρ;

Καί φησιν ὁ γέρων· Τρανῶς μὲν καὶ προσηκόντως οὐδὲν μεμάθηκε· βύων γὰρ τὰς αἰσθήσεις, τὸ ἀγαθὸν ἑκὼν οὐ προσδέχεται, πρὸς τὸ κακὸν αὐτοπροαιρέτως τὴν ῥοπὴν κεκτημένος.

Ἀλλ' ἤθελον, φησὶν ὁ Ἰωάσαφ, κἀκεῖνον ταῦτα
Mat. xix. 26 μυηθῆναι. Ὁ δὲ γέρων· Τὰ παρὰ ἀνθρώποις,
Mk. x. 27 εἶπεν, ἀδύνατα, παρὰ τῷ Θεῷ πάντα δυνατά ἐστι.
Cp. 1 Cor. vii. 16 τί γὰρ οἶδας εἰ σὺ σώσεις τὸν πατέρα σου, καὶ
τρόπῳ θαυμασίῳ γεννήτωρ τοῦ σοῦ χρηματίσεις
γεννήτορος; Ἀκήκοα γὰρ βασιλέα τινὰ γεγονέναι 135
πάνυ καλῶς τὴν ἑαυτοῦ οἰκονομοῦντα βασιλείαν.
πράως τε καὶ ἠπίως τῷ ὑπ' αὐτὸν κεχρημένον
λαῷ, ἐν τούτῳ δὲ μόνῳ σφαλλόμενον, τῷ μὴ
πλουτεῖν τὸν τῆς θεογνωσίας φωτισμόν, ἀλλὰ τῇ
πλάνῃ τῶν εἰδώλων κατέχεσθαι. εἶχε δέ τινα
σύμβουλον ἀγαθὸν καὶ παντοίως κεκοσμημένον
τῇ τε πρὸς τὸν Θεὸν εὐσεβείᾳ καὶ τῇ λοιπῇ πάσῃ
ἐναρέτῳ σοφίᾳ· ὅς, ἀχθόμενος καὶ δυσχεραίνων
ἐπὶ τῇ πλάνῃ τοῦ βασιλέως καὶ βουλόμενος
αὐτὸν περὶ τούτου ἐλέγξαι, ἀνεχαιτίζετο τῆς
ὁρμῆς, δεδοικὼς μὴ κακῶν πρόξενος ἑαυτῷ τε καὶ
τοῖς αὐτοῦ ἑταίροις γένοιτο καὶ τὴν γινομένην δι'
αὐτοῦ πολλῶν ὠφέλειαν περικόψειεν. ἐζήτει δὲ
ὅμως καιρὸν εὔθετον τοῦ ἑλκύσαι αὐτὸν πρὸς τὸ
ἀγαθόν. φησὶν οὖν ἐν μιᾷ νυκτὶ πρὸς αὐτὸν ὁ
βασιλεύς· Δεῦρο δή, ἐξέλθωμεν καὶ ἐμπεριπατήσωμεν τὴν πόλιν, εἴ πού τι τῶν ὠφελούντων
ὀψόμεθα. ἐμπεριπατούντων δὲ αὐτῶν τὴν πόλιν,
εἶδον φωτὸς αὐγὴν ἀπό τινος τρυμαλιᾶς λάμπουσαν· καί, ταύτῃ τοὺς ὀφθαλμοὺς ἐπιβαλόντες,

Ioasaph said unto him, 'Hath my father then, learned naught of these things?'

The elder answered, 'Clearly and duly he hath learned naught; for he stoppeth up his senses, and will not admit that which is good, being of his own free choice inclined to evil.'

'Would God,' said Ioasaph, 'that he too were instructed in these mysteries!' The elder answered, 'The things that are impossible with men are possible with God. For how knowest thou whether thou shalt save thy sire, and in wondrous fashion be styled the spiritual father of thy father?

and desireth to turn him therefrom

'I have heard that, once upon a time, there was a king who governed his kingdom right well, and dealt kindly and gently with his subjects, only failing in this point, that he was not rich in the light of the knowledge of God, but held fast to the errors of idolatry. Now he had a counsellor, which was a good man and endued with righteousness toward God and with all other virtuous wisdom. Grieved and vexed though he was at the error of the king, and willing to convince him thereof, he nevertheless drew back from the attempt, for fear that he might earn trouble for himself and his friends, and cut short those services which he rendered to others. Yet sought he a convenient season to draw his sovereign toward that which was good. One night the king said unto him, "Come now, let us go forth and walk about the city, if haply we may see something to edify us." Now while they were walking about the city, they saw a ray of light shining through an aperture. Fixing their eyes there-

Barlaam telleth of the king and his counsellor that went abroad in the city for to see sights,

APOLOGUE VII

βλέπουσιν ὑπόγειόν τι ἀντρῶδες οἴκημα, ἐν ᾧ προὐκαθέζετο ἀνὴρ ἐσχάτῃ συζῶν πενίᾳ καὶ εὐτελῆ τινα περικείμενος ῥάκια. παρίστατο δὲ ἡ γυνὴ αὐτοῦ οἶνον κιρνῶσα. τοῦ δὲ ἀνδρὸς τὴν κύλικα ἐπὶ χεῖρας λαβόντος, λιγυρὸν ᾄδουσα μέλος ἐκείνη τέρψιν αὐτῷ ἐνεποίει ὀρχουμένη καὶ τὸν ἄνδρα ἐγκωμίοις καταθέλγουσα. οἱ περὶ τὸν βασιλέα τοίνυν, ἐπὶ ὥραν ἱκανὴν ταῦτα κατανοοῦντες, ἐθαύμαζον ὅτι, τοιαύτῃ πιεζόμενοι πενίᾳ ὡς μήτε οἴκου εὐπορεῖν μήτ' ἐσθῆτος, οὕτως εὐθύμως τὸν βίον διῆγον· καί φησιν ὁ βασιλεὺς 136
τῷ πρωτοσυμβούλῳ αὐτοῦ· Ὢ τοῦ θαύματος, φίλε, ὅτι ἐμοί τε καὶ σοὶ οὐδὲ οὕτως ὁ καθ' ἡμᾶς ποτε ἤρεσε βίος, τοσαύτῃ δόξῃ καὶ τρυφῇ περ διαλάμπων, ὡς ἡ εὐτελὴς αὕτη καὶ ταλαίπωρος ζωὴ τούτους δὴ τοὺς ἀνοήτους τέρπει, καὶ ἡδύνει λεῖος αὐτοῖς καὶ προσηνὴς ὁ τραχὺς οὗτος καὶ ἀπευκταῖος βίος καταφαινόμενος. εὐκαίρου δὲ δραξάμενος ὁ πρωτοσύμβουλος ὥρας, ἔφη· Ἀλλὰ σοί γε, βασιλεῦ, πῶς ἡ τούτων φαίνεται βιοτή; Πάντων, φησὶν ὁ βασιλεύς, ὧν πώποτε ἑώρακα ἀηδεστάτη καὶ δυστυχεστάτη, βδελυκτή τε καὶ ἀποτρόπαιος. τότε λέγει πρὸς αὐτὸν ὁ πρωτοσύμβουλος, Οὕτω, οὖν, εὖ ἴσθι, βασιλεῦ, καὶ πολλῷ χαλεπώτερος ὁ καθ' ἡμᾶς λελόγισται βίος τοῖς ἐπόπταις καὶ μύσταις τῆς ἀϊδίου δόξης ἐκείνης καὶ τῶν πάντα νοῦν ὑπερβαινόντων ἀγαθῶν· αἵ τε χρυσῷ καταστίλβουσαι οἰκίαι καὶ τὰ λαμπρὰ ταῦτα ἐνδύματα, καὶ ἡ λοιπὴ τοῦ βίου τούτου τρυφή, σκυβάλων τε καὶ ἀμαυρῶν εἰσιν ἀηδέστερα τοῖς ὀφθαλμοῖς τῶν **εἰδότων** τὰ
Heb. ix. 11 ἀνεκδιήγητα κάλλη τῶν ἐν οὐρανοῖς ἀχειροτεύ-

on, they descried an underground cavernous chamber, in the forefront of which there sat a man, plunged in poverty, and clad in rags and tatters. Beside him stood his wife, mixing wine. When the man took the cup in his hands, she sung a clear sweet melody, and delighted him by dancing and cozening him with flatteries. The king's companions observed this for a time, and marvelled that people, pinched by such poverty as not to afford house and raiment, yet passed their lives in such good cheer. The king said to his chief counsellor, "Friend, how marvellous a thing it is, that our life, though bright with such honour and luxury, hath never pleased us so well as this poor and miserable life doth delight and rejoice these fools: and that this life, which appeareth to us so cruel and abominable, is to them sweet and alluring!" The chief counsellor seized the happy moment and said, "But to thee, O king, how seemeth their life?" "Of all that I have ever seen," quoth the king, "the most hateful and wretched, the most loathsome and abhorrent." Then spake the chief counsellor unto him, "Such, know thou well, O king, and even more unendurable is our life reckoned by those who are initiated into the sight of the mysteries of yonder everlasting glory, and the blessings that pass all understanding. Your palaces glittering with gold, and these splendid garments, and all the delights of this life are more loathsome than dung and filth in the eyes of those that know the unspeakable beauties of the tabernacles

and of the man and his wife whom they saw making merry in extreme poverty,

and how the counsellor taught the king the meaning of that sight;

κτων σκηνωματῶν, τῆς θεοϋφάντου τε στολῆς καὶ
Cp. Jas. i. 12 τῶν ἀφθάρτων διαδημάτων, ἃ ἡτοίμασεν ὁ Θεὸς
τοῖς ἀγαπῶσιν αὐτόν, ὁ πάντων Δημιουργὸς καὶ
Κύριος. ὃν τρόπον γὰρ ἀνοηταίνειν ἡμῖν οὗτοι 137
ἐλογίσθησαν, πολλῷ πλέον ἡμεῖς, οἱ τῷ κόσμῳ
περιπλανώμενοι καὶ αὐταρεσκοῦντες ἐν τῇ ψευδο-
μένῃ ταύτῃ δόξῃ καὶ ἀνοήτῳ τρυφῇ, θρήνων ἐσμὲν
ἄξιοι καὶ δακρύων ἐν ὀφθαλμοῖς τῶν γευσαμένων
τῆς γλυκύτητος τῶν ἀγαθῶν ἐκείνων.

Ὁ δὲ βασιλεὺς τούτων ἀκούσας, καὶ ἐννεὸς
ὥσπερ γενόμενος, ἔφη· Τίνες οὖν ἐκεῖνοί εἰσιν οἱ
κρείττονα τῆς καθ᾽ ἡμᾶς κεκτημένοι ζωήν; Πάντες, φησὶν ὁ πρωτοσύμβουλος, οἱ τὰ αἰώνια
προτιμήσαντες τῶν προσκαίρων. αὖθις οὖν τοῦ
βασιλέως μαθεῖν ζητοῦντος τίνα τὰ αἰώνια,
φησὶν ὁ ἀνήρ· Βασιλεία ἀδιάδοχος, καὶ ζωὴ μὴ
ὑποκειμένη θανάτῳ, καὶ πλοῦτος μηδέποτε ὑφορώμενος πενίαν, χαρά τε καὶ εὐφροσύνη πάσης
ἀμέτοχος λύπης καὶ ἀχθηδόνος, καὶ εἰρήνη
διηνεκὴς ἐλευθέρα πάσης ἔχθρας καὶ φιλονεικίας.
τούτων οἱ καταξιωθέντες ἀπολαύειν μακάριοι,
καὶ τοῦτο πολλάκις· ἄλυπον γὰρ καὶ ἄμοχθον
ζήσουσιν εἰς αἰῶνας ζωήν, πάντων τῶν ἡδέων
καὶ τερπνῶν τῆς τοῦ Θεοῦ βασιλείας ἀμογητὶ
ἀπολαύοντες, καὶ τῷ Χριστῷ ἀτελεύτητα συμβα-
σιλεύοντες. καί, Τίς ἄξιος τούτων ἐπιτυχεῖν;
εἰπόντος τοῦ βασιλέως, ἐκεῖνος ἀπεκρίνατο·
Πάντες οἱ τῆς ἐκεῖσε ἀπαγούσης ὁδοῦ δραξάμενοι·
ἀκώλυτος γὰρ ἡ εἴσοδος τοῖς θελήσασι μόνον.
ὁ δὲ βασιλεύς· Καὶ τίς, φησίν, ἡ ἐκεῖσε φέρουσα
τρίβος; πρὸς ὃν ἔφη ὁ λαμπρὸς τὴν ψυχὴν 138
John xvii. 3 ἐκεῖνος· Τὸ γινώσκειν τὸν μόνον ἀληθινὸν Θεόν,

in heaven made without hands, and the apparel woven by God, and the incorruptible diadems which God, the Creator and Lord of all, hath prepared for them that love him. For like as this couple were accounted fools by us, so much the more are we, who go astray in this world and please ourselves in this false glory and senseless pleasure, worthy of lamentation and tears in the eyes of those who have tasted of the sweets of the bliss beyond."

'When the king heard this, he became as one dumb. He said, "Who then are these men that live a life better than ours?" "All," said the chief-counsellor "who prefer the eternal to the temporal." Again, when the king desired to know what the eternal might be the other replied, "A kingdom that knoweth no succession, a life that is not subject unto death, riches that dread no poverty: joy and gladness that have no share of grief and vexation; perpetual peace free from all hatred and love of strife. Blessed, thrice blessed are they that are found worthy of these enjoyments! Free from pain and free from toil is the life that they shall live for ever, enjoying without labour all the sweets and pleasaunce of the kingdom of God, and reigning with Christ world without end."

how the king desired to know of the matter,

'"And who is worthy to obtain this?" asked the king. The other answered, "All they that hold on the road that leadeth thither; for none forbiddeth entrance, if a man but will."

'Said the king, "And what is the way that beareth thither?" That bright spirit answered, "To know the only true God, and Jesus Christ, his

καὶ Ἰησοῦν Χριστὸν τὸν μονογενῆ αὐτοῦ Υἱὸν καὶ τὸ Ἅγιον καὶ ζωοποιὸν Πνεῦμα.

Ὁ τοίνυν βασιλεύς, τῆς ἀλουργίδος σύνεσιν ἔχων ἀξίαν, ἔφη πρὸς αὐτόν· Καὶ τί τὸ κωλῦσάν σε μέχρι τοῦ νῦν μὴ γνωρίσαι μοι περὶ τούτων; οὐκ ἀναβολῆς γὰρ καὶ ὑπερθέσεως ἄξιά μοι δοκεῖ ὑπάρχειν ταῦτα, εἴ γε ἀληθῆ τυγχάνει· εἰ δὲ ἀμφίβολά ἐστιν, ἐμπόνως δεῖ ζητῆσαι μέχρις ὅτου τὸ ἀναμφίλεκτον εὕροιμι. Οὐκ ἀμελείᾳ, φησὶν ὁ ἀνήρ, ἢ ῥᾳθυμίᾳ συνεχόμενος, περὶ τούτων ὤκνησά σοι γνωρίσαι, ἀληθῆ περ ὄντα καὶ πάντη ἀναμφίλεκτα, ἀλλὰ τὸ ὑπερέχον αἰδούμενος τῆς σῆς δόξης, μή ποτε ὀχληρότερός σοι φανείην· εἰ οὖν προστάσσεις τῷ σῷ οἰκέτῃ ὑπομιμνήσκειν σοι εἰς τὸ ἑξῆς περὶ τούτων τῷ σῷ ἔσομαι καθυπηρετῶν προστάγματι. Ναί, φησὶν ὁ βασιλεύς, μὴ καθ' ἡμέραν μόνον, ἀλλὰ καὶ ἐφ' ἑκάστης ὥρας τὴν τούτων μνήμην διηνεκῶς ἀνακαίνιζε· οὐκ ἀμελῶς γὰρ χρὴ τούτοις προσέχειν, ἀλλὰ καὶ λίαν θερμῶς καὶ σπουδαίως.

Ἀκηκόαμεν οὖν, φησὶν ὁ Βαρλαάμ, εὐσεβῶς τὸν βασιλέα τοῦτον ζῆσαι τὸ ἑξῆς, καὶ ἀκυμάντως τὸν παρόντα διανύσαντα βίον, τῆς μελλούσης μὴ ἀποτυχεῖν μακαριότητος. εἰ τοίνυν καὶ τῷ σῷ πατρὶ τοιαῦτά τις ἐν ἐπιτηδείῳ προσυπομνήσει καιρῷ, τάχα συνήσει καὶ γνώσεται ὅσοις 139
συνεσχέθη κακοῖς, καὶ τούτων ἐκκλίνας ἐκλέξεται
2 Pet. 1. 9 τὸ ἀγαθόν· ἐπεὶ τό γε νῦν ἔχον τυφλός ἐστι, μυωπάζων, τοῦ ἀληθινοῦ φωτὸς ἑαυτὸν ἀποστερήσας, αὐτομολῶν δὲ πρὸς τὸ τῆς ἀσεβείας σκότος.

only-begotten Son, and the Holy and quickening Spirit."

'The king, endowed with understanding worthy of the purple, said unto him, "What hath hindered thee until now from doing me to wit of these things? For they appear to me too good to be put off or passed over, if they indeed be true; and, if they be doubtful, I must search diligently, until I find the truth without shadow of doubt."

and was led to prefer the eternal to things temporal,

'The chief counsellor said, "It was not from negligence or indifference that I delayed to make this known unto thee, for it is true and beyond question, but 'twas because I reverenced the excellency of thy majesty, lest thou mightest think me a meddler. If therefore thou bid thy servant put thee in mind of these things for the future, I shall obey thy behest." "Yea," said the king, "not every day only, but every hour, renew in me the remembrance thereof: for it behoveth us not to turn our mind inattentively to these things, but with very fervent zeal."

and lived thereafter in holiness and joy

'We have heard,' said Barlaam, 'that this king lived, for the time to come, a godly life, and, having brought his days without tempest to an end, failed not to gain the felicity of the world to come. If then at a convenient season one shall call these things to thy father's mind also, peradventure he shall understand and know the dire evil in which he is held, and turn therefrom and choose the good; since, for the present at least, "he is blind and cannot see afar off," having deprived himself of the true light and being a deserter of his own accord to the darkness of ungodliness.'

Εἶπε δὲ ὁ Ἰωάσαφ πρὸς αὐτόν· Τὰ μὲν τοῦ ἐμοῦ πατρὸς ἄγοιτο Κύριος καθὼς κελεύει· αὐτῷ γάρ, καθὰ δὴ καὶ εἶπας, πάντα δυνατὰ καθέστηκε τὰ παρὰ ἀνθρώποις ἀδύνατα· ἐγὼ δέ, διὰ τῶν σῶν ἀνυπερβλήτων ῥημάτων, τῆς τῶν παρόντων καταγνοὺς ματαιότητος, ἀποστῆναι μὲν τούτων πάντη διανενόημαι, καὶ μετὰ σοῦ τὸ λοιπὸν τῆς ζωῆς μου διανύσαι, ἵνα μὴ διὰ τῶν προσκαίρων τούτων καὶ ῥευστῶν τῆς τῶν αἰωνίων καὶ ἀφθάρτων ἐκπέσω ἀπολαύσεως.

Πρὸς ὃν ὁ γέρων ἀπεκρίνατο· Εἰ τοῦτο ποιήσεις, ὅμοιος ἔσῃ νεανίσκῳ τινὶ φρονιμωτάτῳ, περὶ οὗ ἀκήκοα πλουσίων γεγονέναι καὶ ἐνδόξων γονέων· ᾧτινι ὁ πατὴρ μνηστευσάμενος τὴν θυγατέρα τινὸς τῶν εὐγενείᾳ καὶ πλούτῳ διαφερόντων λίαν ὡραιοτάτην, κοινολογησάμενος δὲ πρὸς τὸν παῖδα περὶ τοῦ γάμου, καὶ ὅπως ἦν αὐτῷ μελετώμενα ἀπαγγείλας, ἀκούσας ἐκεῖνος, καὶ ὡς ἀπηχές τι καὶ ἄτοπον ἀποσεισάμενος τὸ πρᾶγμα, φυγὰς ᾤχετο καταλιπὼν τὸν πατέρα. πορευόμενος δὲ ξενίζεται ἐν οἰκίᾳ γηραιοῦ τινος πένητος, τοῦ καύσωνος τῆς ἡμέρας ἑαυτὸν διαναπαύων.

Ἡ δὲ θυγάτηρ τοῦ πένητος, μονογενὴς οὖσα 140
καὶ παρθένος, καθεζομένη πρὸ τῶν θυρῶν, εἰργάζετο μὲν ταῖς χερσί, τῷ δὲ στόματι ἀσιγήτως τὸν Θεὸν εὐλόγει εὐχαριστοῦσα αὐτῷ ἐκ βαθέων ψυχῆς· τῶν ταύτης δὲ ὕμνων ἀκούσας ὁ νέος ἔφη· Τί σου, γύναι, τὸ ἐπιτήδευμα; χάριν δὲ τίνος, οὕτω περ οὖσα εὐτελὴς καὶ πτωχή, ὡς ἐπί τισι μεγάλοις δωρήμασιν εὐχαριστεῖς, τὸν δοτῆρα ὑμνοῦσα; Ἡ δὲ πρὸς αὐτὸν ἀπεκρίνατο· Οὐκ

Ioasaph said unto him, 'The Lord undertake my father's matters, as he ordereth! For, even as thou sayest, the things that are impossible with men, are possible with him. But for myself, thanks to thine unsurpassable speech, I renounce the vanity of things present, and am resolved to withdraw from them altogether, and to spend the rest of my life with thee, lest, by means of these transitory and fleeting things, I lose the enjoyment of the eternal and incorruptible.'

Ioasaph desireth to flee from the world

The elder answered him, 'This do, and thou shalt be like unto a youth of great understanding of whom I have heard tell, that was born of rich and distinguished parents. For him his father sought in marriage the exceeding fair young daughter of a man of high rank and wealth. But when he communed with his son concerning the espousals, and informed him of his plans, the son thought it strange and ill-sounding, and cast it off, and left his father and went into exile. On his journey he found entertainment in the house of a poor old man, where he rested awhile during the heat of the day.

Barlaam likeneth Ioasaph to a young man that fled from a rich and noble bride

APOLOGUE VIII

Now this poor man's daughter, his only child, a virgin, was sitting before the door, and, while she wrought with her hands, with her lips she loudly sang the praises of God with thanksgiving from the ground of her heart. The young man heard her hymn of praise and said, "Damsel, what is thine employment? and wherefore, poor and needy as thou art, givest thou thanks as though for great blessings, singing praise to the Giver?" She answered, "Knowest thou not that, as a little

and, meeting a poor man's daughter, desired the rather to marry her, for her piety and wit,

οἶσθα ὅτι, καθάπερ φάρμακον μικρὸν ἐκ μεγάλων νοσημάτων πολλάκις ῥύεται τὸν ἄνθρωπον, οὕτω δὴ καὶ τὸ ἐπὶ τοῖς μικροῖς εὐχαριστεῖν τῷ Θεῷ μεγάλων πρόξενον γίνεται; ἐγὼ τοίνυν, θυγάτηρ οὖσα γέροντος πτωχοῦ, εὐχαριστῶ ἐπὶ τοῖς μικροῖς τούτοις καὶ εὐλογῶ τὸν Θεόν, εἰδυῖα ὡς ὁ ταῦτα δοὺς καὶ μείζονα δύναται δοῦναι. καὶ ταῦτα μὲν περὶ τῶν ἔξωθεν καὶ οὐχ ἡμετέρων,
ἐξ ὧν οὔτε τοῖς πολλὰ κεκτημένοις τι προσγί- 141
νεται κέρδος (ἵνα μὴ εἴπω ὅτι καὶ ζημία πολλάκις), οὔτε τοῖς ἐλάττονα λαβοῦσιν ἐπέρχεται βλάβη, τὴν αὐτὴν ἀμφοτέρων ὁδευόντων ὁδὸν καὶ πρὸς τὸ αὐτὸ ἐπειγομένων τέλος· ἐν δὲ τοῖς ἀναγκαιοτάτοις καὶ καιριωτάτοις πολλῶν ἀπήλαυσα καὶ μεγίστων τοῦ Δεσπότου μου δωρημάτων, οὐμενοῦν ἐχόντων ἀριθμὸν ἢ εἰκασμῷ ὑποπιπτόντων. κατ' εἰκόνα γὰρ Θεοῦ γεγένημαι καὶ τῆς αὐτοῦ γνώσεως ἠξίωμαι, καὶ λόγῳ παρὰ πάντα τὰ ζῷα κεκόσμημαι, καὶ ἐκ θανάτου πρὸς
Luke i. 78 τὴν ζωὴν ἀνακέκλημαι διὰ σπλάγχνα ἐλέους Θεοῦ ἡμῶν, καὶ τῶν αὐτοῦ μετέχειν μυστηρίων ἐξουσίαν ἔλαβον, καὶ ἡ τοῦ παραδείσου θύρα ἀνέῳκται, ἀκώλυτον, εἴπερ θελήσω, παρέχουσά μοι τὴν εἴσοδον. τῶν τοσούτων οὖν καὶ τοιούτων δωρημάτων, ὧν ἐπίσης μετέχουσι πλούσιοί τε καὶ πένητες, ἀξίως εὐχαριστῆσαι πάντῃ μοι
ἀδύνατον, εἰ δὲ καὶ τὴν μικρὰν ταύτην ὑμνο- 142
λογίαν οὐ προσάξω τῷ δωρησαμένῳ, ποίαν ἕξω ἀπολογίαν;

Ὁ δὲ νεώτερος τὴν πολλὴν αὐτῆς ὑπερθαυμάσας σύνεσιν, τὸν αὐτῆς προσκαλεσάμενος πατέρα. Δός μοι, φησί, τὴν θυγατέρα σου·

medicine often times delivereth a man from great ailments, even so the giving of thanks to God for small mercies winneth great ones? Therefore I, the daughter of a poor old man, thank and bless God for these small mercies, knowing that the Giver thereof is able to give even greater gifts. And this applieth but to those external things that are not our own from whence there accrueth no gain to those who possess much (not to mention the loss that often ariseth), nor cometh there harm to those who have less; for both sorts journey along the same road, and hasten to the same end. But, in things most necessary and vital, many and great the blessings I have enjoyed of my Lord, though indeed they are without number and beyond compare. I have been made in the image of God, and have gained the knowledge of him, and have been endowed with reason beyond all the beasts, and have been called again from death unto life, through the tender mercy of our God, and have received power to share in his mysteries; and the gate of Paradise hath been opened to me, allowing me to enter without hindrance, if I will. Wherefore for gifts so many and so fine, shared alike by rich and poor, I can indeed in no wise praise him as I ought, yet if I fail to render to the Giver this little hymn of praise, what excuse shall I have?"

shown in her thanksgivings to God,

'The youth, astonished at her wit, called to her father, and said unto him, "Give me thy daughter:

ἠγάπησα γὰρ τὴν σύνεσιν αὐτῆς καὶ εὐσέβειαν.
ὁ δὲ γέρων ἔφη· Οὐκ ἔξεστί σοι ταύτην λαβεῖν
τὴν πένητος θυγατέρα, πλουσίων ὄντι γονέων.
αὖθις δὲ ὁ νέος, Ναί, φησί, ταύτην λήψομαι,
εἴπερ οὐκ ἀπαγορεύεις· θυγάτηρ γάρ μοι μεμνή-
στευται εὐγενῶν καὶ πλουσίων, καὶ ταύτην ἀποσεισάμενος φυγῇ ἐχρησάμην· τῆς δὲ σῆς θυγατρὸς
διὰ τὴν εἰς Θεὸν εὐσέβειαν καὶ τὴν νουνεχῆ
σύνεσιν ἐρασθείς, συναφθῆναι αὐτῇ προτεθύμη-
μαι. ὁ δὲ γέρων πρὸς αὐτὸν ἔφησεν· Οὐ δύναμαί
σοι ταύτην δοῦναι τοῦ ἀπαγαγεῖν ἐν τῷ οἴκῳ
τοῦ πατρός σου καὶ τῶν ἐμῶν χωρίσαι ἀγκαλῶν·
μονογενὴς γάρ μοί ἐστιν. Ἀλλ' ἐγώ, φησὶν ὁ
νεανίσκος, παρ' ὑμῖν μενῶ, καὶ τὴν ὑμῶν ἀναδέ-
ξομαι πολιτείαν. εἶτα καὶ τὴν λαμπρὰν ἀποθέμενος ἐσθῆτα, τὰ τοῦ γέροντος αἰτησάμενος
περιεβάλλετο. πολλὰ δὲ ἐκεῖνος ἐκπειράσας
αὐτὸν καὶ ποικίλως τὸν αὐτοῦ δοκιμάσας λογισμόν, ὡς ἔγνω σταθερᾶς ὑπάρχειν αὐτὸν διανοίας
καὶ ὡς οὐκ ἔρωτι ἀφροσύνης κατεχόμενος αἰτεῖται
τὴν αὐτοῦ θυγατέρα, ἀλλ' ἔρωτι εὐσεβείας εἵλετο
πενιχρῶς ζῆν, ταύτην προκρίνας τῆς αὐτοῦ δόξης
καὶ εὐγενείας, κρατήσας αὐτὸν τῆς χειρός, εἰσήγαγεν εἰς τὸ ἑαυτοῦ ταμιεῖον, καὶ ὑπέδειξε πλοῦτον πολὺν ἀποκείμενον αὐτῷ καὶ χρημάτων
ἀναρίθμητον ὄγκον, ὅσον οὐ τεθέατο πώποτε ὁ
νεανίσκος. καί φησι πρὸς αὐτόν· Τέκνον, ταῦτα 143
πάντα σοι δίδωμι, ἀνθ' ὧν ᾑρετίσω τῆς ἐμῆς
θυγατρὸς ἀνὴρ γενέσθαι, γενέσθαι δὲ καὶ κληρονόμος τῆς ἐμῆς οὐσίας. ἥνπερ κληρονομίαν κατα-
σχὼν ἐκεῖνος πάντας ὑπερῆρε τοὺς ἐνδόξους τῆς
γῆς καὶ πλουσίους.

for I love her wisdom and piety." But the elder said, "It is not possible for thee, the son of wealthy parents, to take this a beggar's daughter." Again the young man said, "Yea, but I will take her, unless thou forbid: for a daughter of noble and wealthy family hath been betrothed unto me in marriage, and her I have cast off and taken to flight. But I have fallen in love with thy daughter because of her righteousness to God-ward, and her discreet wisdom, and I heartily desire to wed her." But the old man said unto him, "I cannot give her unto thee, to carry away to thy father's house, and depart her from mine arms, for she is mine only child." "But," said the youth, "I will abide here with your folk and adopt your manner of life." Thereupon he stripped him of his own goodly raiment, and asked for the old man's clothes and put them on. When the father had much tried his purpose, and proved him in manifold ways, and knew that his intent was fixed, and that it was no light passion that led him to ask for his daughter, but love of godliness that constrained him to embrace a life of poverty, preferring it to his own glory and noble birth, he took him by the hand, and brought him into his treasure-house, where he showed him much riches laid up, and a vast heap of money, such as the young man had never beheld. And he said unto him, "Son, all these things give I unto thee, forasmuch as thou hast chosen to become the husband to my daughter, and also thereby the heir of all my substance." So the young man acquired the inheritance, and surpassed all the famous and wealthy men of the land.'

and, being constant in his desire, came to great prosperity thereby

XVII

Εἶπε δὲ ὁ Ἰωάσαφ πρὸς τὸν Βαρλαάμ· Προσηκόντως καὶ αὕτη τὰ κατ' ἐμὲ παρίστησιν ἡ διήγησις· ὅθεν σοι καὶ περὶ ἐμοῦ ταῦτα λελέχθαι δοκῶ. ἀλλὰ τίς ἡ πεῖρα δι' ἧς γνῶναι ζητεῖς τὸ σταθερὸν τῆς ἐμῆς διανοίας;

Καὶ ὁ γέρων ἔφη· Ἐγὼ μὲν καὶ πεπείρακα ἤδη
καὶ ἔγνωκα ὁποίας ὑπάρχεις ἐχέφρονος καὶ
σταθερᾶς διανοίας καὶ ψυχῆς τῷ ὄντι εὐθυτάτης.
ἀλλὰ τὸ τέλος τῆς κατὰ σὲ πράξεως βεβαιώσει
Eph. iii. 14 ταῦτα. τούτου χάριν κάμπτω τὰ γόνατά μου
πρὸς τὸν ἐν Τριάδι δοξαζόμενον Θεὸν ἡμῶν, τὸν
πάντων δημιουργὸν ὁρατῶν τε καὶ ἀοράτων, τὸν
ὄντως ὄντα καὶ ἀεὶ ὄντα, μήτε ἀρχὴν ἐσχηκότα
πώποτε τῆς ἐνδόξου ὑπάρξεως αὐτοῦ, μήτ' ἔχοντα
τέλος, τὸν φοβερὸν καὶ παντοδύναμον, ἀγαθόν
Eph. i. 17–19 τε καὶ εὔσπλαγχνον, ἵνα φωτίσῃ τοὺς ὀφθαλμοὺς
τῆς καρδίας σου, καὶ δώῃ σοι πνεῦμα σοφίας
καὶ ἀποκαλύψεως ἐν ἐπιγνώσει αὐτοῦ, εἰς τὸ 144
εἰδέναι σε τίς ἐστιν ἡ ἐλπὶς τῆς κλήσεως αὐτοῦ,
καὶ τίς ὁ πλοῦτος τῆς δόξης τῆς κληρονομίας
αὐτοῦ ἐν τοῖς ἁγίοις, καὶ τί τὸ ὑπερβάλλον
μέγεθος τῆς δυνάμεως αὐτοῦ εἰς ἡμᾶς τοὺς
Eph. ii. 19–22 πιστεύοντας, ἵνα μηκέτι ξένος ἔσῃ καὶ πάροικος,
ἀλλὰ συμπολίτης τῶν ἁγίων καὶ οἰκεῖος Θεοῦ,
ἐπῳκοδομημένος ἐπὶ τῷ θεμελίῳ τῶν ἀποστόλων
καὶ προφητῶν, ὄντος ἀκρογωνιαίου αὐτοῦ τοῦ
Κυρίου ἡμῶν Ἰησοῦ Χριστοῦ, ἐν ᾧ πᾶσα οἰκοδομὴ συναρμολογουμένη αὔξει εἰς ναὸν ἅγιον ἐν
Κυρίῳ.

XVII

SAID Ioasaph unto Barlaam, 'This story also fitly setteth forth mine own estate. Whence also me thinketh that thou hadst me in mind when thou spakest it. But what is the proof whereby thou seekest to know the steadfastness of my purpose?'

Ioasaph applieth the tale to his own case

Said the elder, 'I have already proved thee, and know how wise and steadfast is thy purpose, and how truly upright is thine heart. But the end of thy fortune shall confirm it. For this cause I bow my knees unto our God glorified in Three Persons, the Maker of all things visible and invisible, who verily is, and is for ever, that never had beginning of his glorious being, nor hath end, the terrible and almighty, the good and pitiful, that he may enlighten the eyes of thine heart, and give thee the spirit of wisdom and revelation in the knowledge of him, that thou mayest know what is the hope of his calling, and what the riches of the glory of his inheritance in the Saints, and what is the exceeding greatness of his power to us-ward who believe; that thou mayest be no more a stranger and sojourner, but a fellow-citizen with the Saints, and of the household of God, being built upon the foundation of the Apostles and Prophets, Jesus Christ our Lord himself being the chief corner-stone, in whom all the building fitly framed together groweth unto an holy temple in the Lord.'

Barlaam prayeth that Ioasaph's eyes may be opened to see the glory of God,

Ὁ δὲ Ἰωάσαφ, σφόδρα κατανυγεὶς τὴν καρδίαν, ἔφη· Ταῦτα δὴ πάντα κἀγὼ ποθῶν γνῶναι δέομαί σου· γνώρισόν μοι τόν τε πλοῦτον τῆς δόξης τοῦ Θεοῦ καὶ τὸ ὑπερβάλλον τῆς αὐτοῦ δυνάμεως.

Εἶπε δὲ πρὸς αὐτὸν ὁ Βαρλαάμ· Τῷ Θεῷ εὔχομαι διδάξαι σε ταῦτα, καὶ τὴν γνῶσιν τῶν τοιούτων ἐνθεῖναί σου τῇ ψυχῇ· ἐπεὶ παρὰ ἀνθρώποις τὴν αὐτοῦ λεχθῆναι δόξαν καὶ δύναμιν τὸ παράπαν ἀδύνατον, κἂν πᾶσαι αἱ τῶν νυνὶ καὶ τῶν πώποτε γενομένων ἀνθρώπων γλῶσσαι ἓν
John i. 18 γένωνται. Θεὸν γάρ, φησὶν ὁ εὐαγγελιστὴς καὶ θεολόγος, οὐδεὶς ἑώρακε πώποτε· ὁ μονογενὴς Υἱός, ὁ ὢν εἰς τὸν κόλπον τοῦ Πατρός, ἐκεῖνος ἐξηγήσατο. τοῦ δὲ ἀοράτου καὶ ὑπεραπείρου τὴν δόξαν καὶ τὴν μεγαλωσύνην τίς ἰσχύσει γηγενῶν καταλαβέσθαι, εἰ μὴ ᾧ ἂν αὐτὸς ἀπο- 145
καλύψῃ καθ' ὅσον βούλεται, ὥσπερ τοῖς προφήταις αὐτοῦ καὶ ἀποστόλοις ἀπεκάλυψεν; ἡμεῖς δὲ ἐκ τοῦ κηρύγματος αὐτῶν καὶ ἐξ αὐτῆς τῆς τῶν πραγμάτων φύσεως, κατὰ τὸ ἐγχωροῦν
Ps. xix. 1 ἡμῖν μανθάνομεν. λέγει γὰρ ἡ Γραφή· Οἱ οὐρανοὶ διηγοῦνται δόξαν Θεοῦ, ποίησιν δὲ χειρῶν
Rom. i. 20 αὐτοῦ ἀναγγέλλει τὸ στερέωμα· καί, Τὰ ἀόρατα αὐτοῦ ἀπὸ κτίσεως κόσμου τοῖς ποιήμασι νοούμενα καθορᾶται, ἥ τε ἀΐδιος αὐτοῦ δύναμις καὶ θεότης.

Καθάπερ γάρ τις, οἰκίαν ἰδὼν λαμπρῶς καὶ ἐντέχνως κατεσκευασμένην ἢ σκεῦος εὐφυῶς συνηρμοσμένον, τὸν οἰκοδόμον ἢ τέκτονα εὐθὺς ἂν ἐννοήσας θαυμάσειεν, οὕτω κἀγώ, ἐκ μὴ ὄντων διαπλασθεὶς καὶ εἰς τὸ ὂν παραχθείς, εἰ καὶ τὸν

Ioasaph, keenly pricked at the heart, said, 'All this I too long to learn: and I beseech thee make known to me the riches of the glory of God, and the exceeding greatness of his power.'

Barlaam said unto him, 'I pray God to teach thee this, and to plant in thy soul the knowledge of the same; since with men it is impossible that his glory and power be told, yea, even if the tongues of all men that now are and have ever been were combined in one. For, as saith the Evangelist and Divine, "No man hath seen God at any time; the only begotten Son, which is in the bosom of the Father, he hath declared him." But the glory and majesty of the invisible and infinite God, what son of earth shall skill to comprehend it, save he to whom he himself shall reveal it, in so far as he will, as he hath revealed it, to his Prophets and Apostles? But we learn it, so far as in us lieth, by their teaching, and from the very nature of the world. For the Scripture saith, "The heavens declare the glory of God, and the firmament sheweth his handiwork"; and, "The invisible things of him from the creation of the world are clearly understood by the things that are made, even his eternal power and Godhead."

which passeth human power to tell

'Even as a man, beholding an house splendidly and skilfully builded, or a vessel fairly framed, taketh note of the builder or workman and marvelleth thereat, even so I that was fashioned out of nothing and brought into being, though I cannot see the

He showeth that glory made manifest in man,

πλάστην καὶ παροχέα θεάσασθαι οὐ δεδύνημαι,
ἀλλ' ἐκ τῆς εὐαρμόστου καὶ θαυμασιωτάτης μου
κατασκευῆς εἰς γνῶσιν ἦλθον τῆς αὐτοῦ σοφίας,
οὐ καθ' ὅ τί ἐστιν, ἀλλὰ καθὰ δεδύνημαι νοεῖν,
ὅτι οὐκ αὐτομάτως παρήχθην, οὐδὲ ἀφ' ἑαυτοῦ
γεγένημαι, ἀλλ' αὐτὸς ἔπλασέ με καθὼς ἠβου-
λήθη, πάντων μὲν προκατάρχειν τάξας τῶν
κτισμάτων, τινῶν δὲ καὶ ἐλαττώσας, καὶ συντρι-
βέντα πάλιν κρείττονι ἀνακαινίσει ἀναπλάσας,
εἶτα καὶ ὑπεξάγων τῶν ἐντεῦθεν τῷ θείῳ αὐτοῦ
προστάγματι καὶ πρὸς ἑτέραν μετατιθεὶς βιοτὴν
ἀτελεύτητον καὶ αἰώνιον, ἐν οὐδενὶ τούτων δυναμένου μου ἀνθίστασθαι τῇ ἰσχύϊ τῆς αὐτοῦ προ-
Mat. vi. 27 νοίας, μήτε τι προστιθέναι ἐμαυτῷ μήτε ὑφαιρεῖν, 146
εἴτε καθ' ἡλικίαν εἴτε κατὰ τὸ τῆς μορφῆς εἶδος,
μήτε τὰ πεπαλαιωμένα μοι ἀνακαινίζειν ἐξι-
σχῦσαι, μήτε τὰ διεφθαρμένα ἐπανορθοῦν. οὐδεὶς
γὰρ τῶν ἀνθρώπων τούτων τι ἴσχυσέ ποτε κατερ-
γάσασθαι, οὔτε βασιλεύς, οὔτε σοφός, οὔτε πλούσιος, οὔτε δυνάστης, οὔτε τις ἄλλος ἀνθρώπινα
Wisd. vii. 5, 6 μετερχόμενος ἐπιτηδεύματα· Οὐδεὶς γάρ, φησί,
βασιλέων ἢ τῶν ἐν ὑπεροχαῖς ὄντων ἑτέραν ἔσχε
γενέσεως ἀρχήν, μία δὲ πάντων εἴσοδος εἰς τὸν
βίον, ἔξοδός τε ἴση.

Ἐκ τούτων οὖν τῶν περὶ ἐμὲ εἰς γνῶσιν τῆς
τοῦ Δημιουργοῦ μεγαλουργίας χειραγωγοῦμαι·
σὺν τούτοις δὲ καὶ τὴν εὐάρμοστον κατασκευὴν
καὶ συντήρησιν τῆς κτίσεως ἁπάσης ἐννοῶν, ὅτι
αὐτὰ μὲν καθ' ἑαυτὰ τροπῇ ὑπόκεινται πάντα καὶ
ἀλλοιώσει, τὰ μὲν νοητὰ κατὰ προαίρεσιν, τήν τε
ἐν τῷ καλῷ προκοπὴν καὶ τὴν ἐκ τοῦ καλοῦ ἀπο-
φοίτησιν, τὰ δὲ αἰσθητὰ κατὰ γένεσιν καὶ φθοράν,

maker and provider, yet from his harmonious and marvellous fashioning of me have come to the knowledge of his wisdom, not to the full measure of that wisdom, but to the full compass of my powers; yea I have seen that I was not brought forth by chance, nor made of myself, but that he fashioned me, as it pleased him, and set me to have dominion over his creatures, howbeit making me lower than some; that, when I was broken, he re-created me with a better renewal; and that he shall draw me by his divine will from this world and place me in that other life that is endless and eternal; and that in nothing I could withstand the might of his providence, nor add anything to myself nor take anything away, whether in stature or bodily form, and that I am not able to renew for myself that which is waxen old, nor raise that which hath been destroyed. For never was man able to accomplish aught of these things, neither king, nor wise man, nor rich man, nor ruler, nor any other that pursueth the tasks of men. For he saith, "There is no king, or mighty man, that had any other beginning of birth. For all men have one entrance into life, and the like going out."

and in the whole creation,

So from mine own nature, I am led by the hand to the knowledge of the mighty working of the Creator; and at the same time I think upon the well-ordered structure and preservation of the whole creation, how that in itself it is subject everywhere to variableness and change, in the world of thought by choice, whether by advance in the good, or departure from it, in the world of sense by birth and decay, increase and decrease, and change in quality and motion in space. And thus all things

αὔξησίν τε καὶ μείωσιν, καὶ τὴν κατὰ ποιότητα
μεταβολὴν καὶ τοπικὴν κίνησιν, καὶ ἐκ τούτων
κηρύττουσι φωναῖς ἀλαλήτοις ὑπὸ τοῦ ἀκτίστου
καὶ ἀτρέπτου καὶ ἀναλλοιώτου γεγενῆσθαι Θεοῦ, 147
συνέχεσθαί τε, καὶ συντηρεῖσθαι, καὶ ἀεὶ προνο-
εῖσθαι. πῶς γὰρ ἂν αἱ ἐναντίαι φύσεις εἰς ἑνὸς
κόσμου συμπλήρωσιν ἀλλήλαις συνεληλύθεισαν
καὶ ἀδιάλυτοι μεμενήκεισαν, εἰ μή τις παντο-
δύναμος δύναμις ταῦτα συνεβίβασε καὶ ἀεὶ συνε-
Wisd. xi. 25 τήρει ἀδιάλυτα; Πῶς γὰρ ἔμεινεν ἄν τι, εἰ μὴ
αὐτὸς ἠθέλησεν; ἢ τὸ μὴ κληθὲν ὑπ' αὐτοῦ πῶς
ἂν διετηρήθη; φησὶν ἡ Γραφή.

Εἰ γὰρ πλοῖον ἀκυβέρνητον οὐ συνίσταται, ἀλλ' εὐκόλως καταποντίζεται, καὶ οἰκία μικρὰ οὐκ ἂν στῇ χωρὶς τοῦ προνοοῦντος, πῶς ἂν ὁ κόσμος ἐπὶ τοσούτων χρόνων συνέστη, δημιούργημα οὕτω μὲν μέγα, οὕτω δὲ καλὸν καὶ θαυμαστόν, ἄνευ ἐνδόξου τινὸς καὶ μεγάλης καὶ θαυμαστῆς διακυβερνήσεως καὶ πανσόφου προνοίας; ἰδοὺ γὰρ ὁ οὐρανὸς πόσον ἔχει χρόνον, καὶ οὐκ ἠμαυρώθη· τῆς γῆς ἡ δύναμις οὐκ ἠτόνησε, τοσοῦτον τίκτουσα χρόνον· αἱ πηγαὶ οὐκ ἐπέλιπον ἀναβλύζειν ἐξ οὗ γεγόνασιν· ἡ θάλασσα, τοσούτους δεχομένη ποταμούς, οὐχ ὑπερέβη τὸ μέτρον· οἱ δρόμοι τοῦ ἡλίου καὶ τῆς σελήνης οὐκ ἠλλοίωνται· αἱ τάξεις τῆς ἡμέρας καὶ τῆς νυκτὸς οὐ μετετράπησαν. ἐκ τούτων πάντων ἡ ἄφατος τοῦ Θεοῦ δύναμις καὶ
μεγαλοπρέπεια ἡμῖν ἐμφανίζεται, μαρτυρουμένη 148
ὑπὸ προφητῶν καὶ ἀποστόλων· ἀλλ' οὐδεὶς κατ' ἀξίαν νοῆσαι ἢ εὐφημῆσαι τὴν δόξαν αὐτοῦ δυνήσεται. πάντα γὰρ τά τε νοητὰ καὶ ὅσα ὑπὸ τὴν

proclaim, by voices that cannot be heard, that they were created, and are held together, and preserved, and ever watched over by the providence of the uncreate, unturning and unchanging God. Else how could diverse elements have met, for the consummation of a single world, one with another, and remained inseparable, unless some almighty power had knit them together, and still were keeping them from dissolution? "For how could anything have endured, if it had not been his will? or been preserved, if not called by him?" as saith the Scripture.

'A ship holdeth not together without a steersman, but easily foundereth; and a small house shall not stand without a protector. How then could the world have subsisted for long ages,—a work so great, and so fair and wondrous,—without some glorious mighty and marvellous steersmanship and all-wise providence? Behold the heavens, how long they have stood, and have not been darkened: and the earth hath not been exhausted, though she hath been bearing offspring so long. The water-springs have not failed to gush out since they were made. The sea, that receiveth so many rivers, hath not exceeded her measure. The courses of Sun and Moon have not varied: the order of day and night hath not changed. From all these objects is declared unto us the unspeakable power and magnificence of God, witnessed by Prophets and Apostles. But no man can fitly conceive or sound forth his glory. For the

and proveth that the world subsisteth by divine Providence,

αἴσθησιν ὁ θεῖος Ἀπόστολος, ὁ τὸν Χριστὸν ἔχων
1 Cor. xiii. 9, 10 ἐν ἑαυτῷ λαλοῦντα, κατανοήσας εἶπεν· Ἐκ
μέρους γινώσκομεν καὶ ἐκ μέρους προφητεύομεν·
ὅταν δὲ ἔλθῃ τὸ τέλειον, τότε τὸ ἐκ μέρους
καταργηθήσεται. διὸ καί, ἐκπληττόμενος τὸν
ὑπεράπειρον πλοῦτον τῆς σοφίας αὐτοῦ καὶ
Rom. xi. 33 γνώσεως, διαρρήδην ἔφησεν· Ὦ βάθους πλούτου,
καὶ σοφίας, καὶ γνώσεως Θεοῦ· ὡς ἀνεξερεύνητα
τὰ κρίματα αὐτοῦ, καὶ ἀνεξιχνίαστοι αἱ ὁδοὶ
αὐτοῦ.

2 Cor. xii. 2, 4 Εἰ δὲ ἐκεῖνος, ὁ μέχρι τρίτου φθάσας οὐρανοῦ
καὶ ἀρρήτων ἀκούσας ῥημάτων, τοιαύτας ἀφῆκε
φωνάς, τίς τῶν κατ᾽ ἐμὲ ὅλως ἀντοφθαλμῆσαι
ταῖς ἀβύσσοις τῶν τοσούτων ἰσχύσειε μυστηρίων,
καὶ εἰπεῖν τι κατὰ γνώμην, ἢ ἐνθυμηθῆναι ἀξίως
τῶν λεγομένων δυνήσεται, εἰ μή τι αὐτὸς ὁ τῆς
σοφίας χορηγός, ὁ τῶν ἀσόφων διορθωτὴς παρά-
σχοι. ἐν γὰρ τῇ χειρὶ αὐτοῦ καὶ ἡμεῖς καὶ
οἱ λόγοι ἡμῶν, πᾶσά τε φρόνησις καὶ σύνεσις
παρ᾽ αὐτῷ καὶ συνέσεως ἐπιστήμη· καὶ αὐτὸς ἡμῖν
δέδωκε τὴν τῶν ὄντων γνῶσιν ἀψευδῆ, εἰδέναι
σύστασιν κόσμου καὶ ἐνέργειαν στοιχείων, ἀρχὴν
τε καὶ τέλος καὶ μεσότητα χρόνων, τροπῶν διαλ-
Cp. Wisd. xi. 21 ff. λαγὰς καὶ μεταβολὰς καιρῶν, καὶ ὅτι πάντα
μέτρῳ καὶ σταθμῷ διέταξε. τὸ γὰρ μεγάλως 149
ἰσχύειν αὐτῷ πάρεστι πάντοτε, καὶ κράτει βρα-
χίονος αὐτοῦ τίς ἀντιστήσεται; ὅτι ὡς ῥοπὴ ἐκ
πλαστίγγων ὅλος ὁ κόσμος ἐναντίον αὐτοῦ, καὶ
ὡς ῥανὶς δρόσου ὀρθρινῆς κατελθοῦσα ἐπὶ γῆς·
ἐλεεῖ δὲ πάντας, ὅτι πάντα δύναται, καὶ παρορᾷ
ἁμαρτήματα ἀνθρώπων εἰς μετάνοιαν· οὐδὲν γὰρ
βδελύσσεται, οὐδὲ ἀποστρέφεται τῶν προστρε-

holy Apostle, that had Christ speaking within him, after perceiving all objects of thought and sense, still said, "We know in part, and we prophesy in part. But when that which is perfect is come, then that which is in part shall be done away." Wherefore also, astonied at the infinite riches of his wisdom and knowledge, he cried for all to understand, "O the depth of the riches both of the wisdom and knowledge of God! how unsearchable are his judgments, and his ways past finding out!"

which passeth man's understanding

'Now, if he, that attained unto the third heaven and heard such unspeakable words, uttered such sentences, what man of my sort shall have strength to look eye to eye upon the abysses of such mysteries, or speak rightly thereof, or think meetly of the things whereof we speak, unless the very giver of wisdom, and the amender of the unwise, vouchsafe that power? For in his hand are we and our words, and all prudence and knowledge of wisdom is with him. And he himself hath given us the true understanding of the things that are; to know the structure of the world, the working of the elements, the beginning, end and middle of times, the changes of the solstices, the succession of seasons, and how he hath ordered all things by measure and weight. For he can shew his great strength at all times, and who may withstand the power of his arm? For the whole world before him is as a little grain of the balance, yea, as a drop of the morning dew that falleth down upon the earth. But he hath mercy upon all; for he can do all things, and winketh at the sins of men, because they should amend. For he abhorreth

χόντων αὐτῷ, ὁ μόνος ἀγαθὸς καὶ φιλόψυχος δεσπότης· εὐλογημένον εἴη τὸ ὄνομα τῆς δόξης Cp. Dan. iii. 52 (Sept.) αὐτοῦ τὸ ἅγιον καὶ ὑπερύμνητον καὶ ὑπερυψούμενον εἰς τοὺς αἰῶνας. Ἀμήν.

XVIII

Εἶπε δὲ πρὸς αὐτὸν ὁ Ἰωάσαφ· Εἰ πάνυ πολὺν χρόνον ἐσκόπησας, σοφώτατε, πῶς ἂν ἄριστα τὴν λύσιν τῶν προβληθέντων ζητημάτων ἡμῖν σαφηνίσαις, οὐκ ἂν ἄμεινον τοῦτό μοι ποιῆσαι ἐδόκεις, ἢ τοιαῦτά μοι λέγων ὁποῖά μοι νῦν ἐξεῖπας, δημιουργὸν μὲν πάντων καὶ συνοχέα τὸν Θεὸν διδάξας, ἀκατάληπτον δὲ λογισμοῖς ἀνθρωπίνοις τὴν δόξαν τῆς μεγαλωσύνης αὐτοῦ λόγοις ἀναντιρρήτοις ἀποδείξας, καὶ ὅτι οὐκ ἄλλος τις ἰσχύει ταύτης ἐφικέσθαι, ἀλλ' οἷς ἂν αὐτός, καθ' ὅσον κελεύει, ἀποκαλύψειε. διό σου τὴν λογιωτάτην ὑπερτεθαύμακα σοφίαν.

Ἀλλά μοι φράσον, μακαριώτατε, πόσων μὲν χρόνων αὐτὸς ὑπάρχεις, ἐν ποίοις δὲ τόποις τὰς διατριβὰς κέκτησαι, τίνας δὲ τοὺς συμφιλοσοφοῦντάς σοι ἔχεις. κραταιῶς γάρ μου ἡ ψυχὴ τῆς σῆς ἐξήρτηται, καὶ οὐδαμῶς σου τὸν πάντα μου χρόνον τῆς ζωῆς χωρισθῆναι θέλω.

Ὁ δὲ γέρων ἔφη· Χρόνων μὲν εἰμί, ὡς εἰκάζω, τεσσαρακονταπέντε· ἐν ἐρήμοις δὲ τῆς γῆς Σεναὰρ διάγων συναγωνιστὰς κέκτημαι τοὺς πρὸς τὸν δρόμον τῆς ἄνω πορείας συμπονοῦντας καὶ συναμιλλωμένους.

nothing, nor turneth away from them that run unto him, he, the only good Lord and lover of souls. Blessed be the holy name of his glory, praised and exalted above all for ever! Amen.'

XVIII

IOASAPH said unto him, 'If thou hadst for a long time considered, most wise Sir, how thou mightest best declare to me the explanation of the questions that I propounded, methinks thou couldest not have done it better than by uttering such words as thou hast now spoken unto me. Thou hast taught me that God is the Maker and preserver of all things; and in unanswerable language thou hast shown me that the glory of his majesty is incomprehensible to human reasonings, and that no man is able to attain thereto, except those to whom, by his behest, he revealeth it. Wherefore am I lost in amaze at thine eloquent wisdom.

Ioasaph rendereth thanks to Barlaam

'But tell me, good Sir, of what age thou art, and in what manner of place is thy dwelling, and who are thy fellow philosophers; for my soul hangeth fast on thine, and fain would I never be parted from thee all the days of my life.'

and asketh his age, and his abode

The elder said, 'Mine age is, as I reckon, forty and five years, and in the deserts of the land of Senaar do I dwell. For my fellow combatants I have those who labour and contend together with me on the course of the heavenly journey.'

Πῶς, φησὶν ὁ Ἰωάσαφ, ταῦτά μοι λέγεις; ἐπέκεινα γάρ μοι φαίνῃ τῶν ἑβδομήκοντά που ἐνιαυτῶν. τίς οὖν ὁ λόγος σοι τῶν τεσσαρακονταπέντε βούλεται χρόνων; οὐ δοκεῖς γάρ μοι ἐν τούτῳ ἀληθεύειν.

Εἶπε δὲ Βαρλαὰμ πρὸς αὐτόν· Εἰ μὲν τοὺς
ἀπὸ γενέσεως χρόνους μου μαθεῖν ζητεῖς, καλῶς
τούτους ἀπείκασας ἐπέκεινα τῶν ἑβδομήκοντά
που ὑπάρχειν· ἀλλ' ἔμοιγε οὐδόλως εἰς μέτρον
ζωῆς ἐλογίσθησαν ὅσοι τῇ ματαιότητι τοῦ κόσμου
δεδαπάνηντο. ὅτε γὰρ ἔζων τῷ σαρκίῳ δεδου-
λωμένος ταῖς ἁμαρτίαις, νεκρὸς ἤμην τὸν ἔσω 151
ἄνθρωπον. τοὺς οὖν τῆς νεκρώσεως χρόνους οὐκ
Gal. vi. 14 ἄν ποτε ζωῆς ὀνομάσαιμι. ἐξ ὅτου δὲ ὁ κόσμος
Eph. iv. 22 ἐμοὶ ἐσταύρωται, κἀγὼ τῷ κόσμῳ, καί, ἀποθέμενος τὸν παλαιὸν ἄνθρωπον, τὸν φθειρόμενον
κατὰ τὰς ἐπιθυμίας τῆς ἀπάτης, οὐκ ἔτι ζῶ τῇ
Gal. ii. 20 σαρκί, ἀλλὰ ζῇ ἐν ἐμοὶ ὁ Χριστός, ὃ δὲ ζῶ τῇ
πίστει ζῶ τῇ τοῦ Υἱοῦ τοῦ Θεοῦ, τοῦ ἀγαπή-
σαντός με καὶ παραδόντος ἑαυτὸν ὑπὲρ ἐμοῦ,
τούτους εἰκότως καὶ ζωῆς χρόνους καὶ ἡμέρας σωτηρίας καλέσαιμι, οὓς περὶ τὰ τεσσαρακονταπέντε συναριθμῶν ἔτη, κατὰ λόγον σοι καὶ οὐκ ἀπὸ σκοποῦ τὴν τούτων ἐξεῖπον ἀρίθμησιν. καὶ σὺ τοίνυν τοῦ τοιούτου ἔχου λογισμοῦ ἑκάστοτε, μηδόλως ζῆν ὑπολαμβάνων τοὺς νενεκρωμένους μὲν πρὸς πᾶσαν ἀγαθοεργίαν, ζῶντας δὲ ταῖς ἁμαρτίαις καὶ τῷ κοσμοκράτορι καθυπουργοῦντας τῶν κάτω συρομένων, ἐν ἡδοναῖς τε καὶ ἐπιθυμίαις πονηραῖς τὸν βίον δαπανῶντας· ἀλλὰ τεθανατωμένους τούτους εὖ ἴσθι τυγχάνειν καὶ νενεκρωμένους τῇ τῆς ζωῆς ἐνεργείᾳ. τὴν γὰρ

'What sayest thou?' quoth Ioasaph. 'Thou seemest to me upwards of seventy years old. How speakest thou of forty and five? Herein methinks thou tellest not the truth.'

Ioasaph is perplexed by Barlaam's answer,

Barlaam said unto him, 'If it be the number of years from my birth that thou askest, thou hast well reckoned them at upwards of seventy. But, for myself, I count not amongst the number of my days the years that I wasted in the vanity of the world. When I lived to the flesh in the bondage of sin, I was dead in the inner man; and those years of deadness I can never call years of life. But now the world hath been crucified to me, and I to the world, and I have put off the old man, which is corrupt according to the deceitful lusts, and live no longer to the flesh, but Christ liveth in me; and the life that I live, I live by the faith of the Son of God, who loved me and gave himself for me. And the years, that have passed since then, I may rightly call years of life, and days of salvation. And in numbering these at about forty and five, I reckoned by the true tale, and not off the mark. So do thou also alway hold by this reckoning; and be sure that there is no true life for them that are dead to all good works, and live in sin, and serve the world-ruler of them that are dragged downward, and waste their time in pleasures and lusts: but rather be well assured that these are dead and defunct in the activity of life. For a wise

but learneth from him how truly to number the years of life

Basil, Hom. de trist. ἁμαρτίαν θάνατον τῆς ἀθανάτου ψυχῆς σοφός
τις ἐκάλεσεν εἰκότως· φησὶ δὲ καὶ ὁ Ἀπόστολος·
Rom. vi. 10 Ὅτε δοῦλοι ἦτε τῆς ἁμαρτίας, ἐλεύθεροι ἦτε 152
τῇ δικαιοσύνῃ· τίνα οὖν καρπὸν εἴχετε τότε, ἐφ'
οἷς νῦν ἐπαισχύνεσθε; τὸ γὰρ τέλος ἐκείνων
θάνατος. νυνὶ δὲ ἐλευθερωθέντες ἀπὸ τῆς ἁμαρτίας, δουλωθέντες δὲ τῷ Θεῷ, ἔχετε τὸν καρπὸν
ὑμῶν εἰς ἁγιασμόν, τὸ δὲ τέλος ζωὴν αἰώνιον. τὰ
γὰρ ὀψώνια τῆς ἁμαρτίας θάνατος, τὸ δὲ χά-
ρισμα τοῦ Θεοῦ ζωὴ αἰώνιος.

Εἶπε δὲ ὁ Ἰωάσαφ πρὸς αὐτόν· Ἐπείπερ ἡ ἐν
σαρκὶ ζωὴ οὐκ ἐν μέτρῳ ζωῆς σοι λελόγισται,
οὐδὲ τὸν θάνατον τοῦτον, ὃν ὑφίστανται πάντες,
θάνατόν σοι λογίζεσθαι χρή.

Ὁ δὲ γέρων ἀπεκρίνατο· Ἀναμφιλέκτως καὶ
περὶ τούτων οὕτως ἔχω, μηδόλως τὸν πρόσκαιρον
τουτονὶ θάνατον τρέμων, μήτε θάνατον αὐτὸν
τοπαράπαν ἀποκαλῶν, εἴ γε τὴν ὁδὸν τῶν
ἐντολῶν τοῦ Θεοῦ βαδίζοντά με καταλάβῃ, διαβατήριον δὲ μᾶλλον ἐκ θανάτου πρὸς ζωὴν τὴν
Col. iii. 3 κρείττονα καὶ τελειοτέραν καὶ ἐν Χριστῷ κρυπτομένην, ἧσπερ ποθοῦντες τυχεῖν οἱ ἅγιοι
πάνυ τῇ παρούσῃ ἐδυσχέραινον. διό φησιν ὁ
2 Cor. v. 1-4 Ἀπόστολος· Οἴδαμεν ὅτι, ἐὰν ἡ ἐπίγειος ἡμῶν
οἰκία τοῦ σκήνους καταλυθῇ, οἰκοδομὴν ἐκ Θεοῦ
ἔχομεν οἰκίαν ἀχειροποίητον, αἰώνιον, ἐν τοῖς
οὐρανοῖς· καὶ γὰρ ἐν τούτῳ στενάζομεν, τὸ
οἰκητήριον ἡμῶν τὸ ἐξ οὐρανοῦ ἐπενδύσασθαι
ἐπιποθοῦντες, εἴ γε καὶ ἐνδυσάμενοι οὐ γυμνοὶ
εὑρεθησόμεθα· καὶ γὰρ οἱ ὄντες ἐν τῷ σκήνει 153
στενάζομεν βαρούμενοι, ἐφ' ᾧ οὐ θέλομεν ἐκδύσασθαι, ἀλλ' ἐπενδύσασθαι, ἵνα καταποθῇ τὸ

man hath fitly called sin the death of the immortal soul. And the Apostle also saith, "When ye were the servants of sin, ye were free from righteousness. What fruit had ye then in those things whereof ye are now ashamed? for the end of those things is death. But now being made free from sin, and become servants to God, ye have your fruit unto holiness, and the end everlasting life. For the wages of sin is death, but the gift of God is eternal life."'

Ioasaph said unto him, 'Since thou reckonest not the life in the flesh in the measure of life, neither canst thou reckon that death, which all men undergo, as death.'

The elder answered, 'Without doubt thus think I of these matters also, and fear this temporal death never a whit, nor do I call it death at all, if only it overtake me walking in the way of the commandments of God, but rather a passage from death to the better and more perfect life, which is hid in Christ, in desire to obtain which the Saints were impatient of the present. Wherefore saith the Apostle, "We know that if our earthly house of this tabernacle be dissolved, we have a building of God, a house not made with hands, eternal in the heavens. For in this we groan, earnestly desiring to be clothed upon with our house which is from heaven: if so be that being clothed we shall not be found naked. For we that are in this tabernacle do groan, being burdened: not for that we would be unclothed, but clothed upon, that mortality might be swallowed up of life." And

Barlaam layeth bare the true nature of death

Rom. vii. 24 θνητὸν ὑπὸ τῆς ζωῆς. καὶ πάλιν· Ταλαίπωρος
ἐγὼ ἄνθρωπος, τίς με ῥύσεται ἐκ τοῦ σώματος
Phil. i. 23 τοῦ θανάτου τούτου; καὶ αὖθις· Ἐπιθυμῶ ἀνα-
Ps. xlii. 2 λῦσαι καὶ σὺν Χριστῷ εἶναι. ὁ δὲ Προφήτης,
Πότε ἥξω, φησί, καὶ ὀφθήσομαι τῷ προσώπῳ
τοῦ Θεοῦ; ὅτι δὲ καὶ ἐμοὶ τῷ πάντων ἐλαχιστο-
τέρῳ οὐδόλως τὸν αἰσθητὸν θάνατον δεδοικέναι
δοκεῖ, ἔξεστί σοι γνῶναι τῷ παρ' οὐδὲν θέμενόν
με τὴν τοῦ σοῦ πατρὸς ἀπειλὴν ἀδεῶς παραγενέσθαι πρὸς σὲ καὶ τὸν σωτήριόν σοι καταγγεῖλαι λόγον, ἀκριβῶς περ εἰδότα ὡς, εἰ ἔλθοι
αὐτῷ εἰς γνῶσιν ταῦτα, μυρίοις με, εἰ δυνατόν,
καθυποβαλεῖ θανάτοις. ἀλλ' ἔγωγε, τὸν τοῦ
Θεοῦ λόγον πάντων προκρίνων καὶ αὐτοῦ ποθῶν
ἐπιτυχεῖν, οὔτε πτοοῦμαι τὸν πρόσκαιρον θάνατον, οὔτε τῆς τοιαύτης αὐτὸν προσηγορίας ἄξιον
ὅλως ἀποκαλῶ, τῇ Δεσποτικῇ πειθόμενος ἐντολῇ,
Mat. x. 28 τῇ λεγούσῃ· Μὴ φοβεῖσθε ἀπὸ τῶν ἀποκτεινόν-
των τὸ σῶμα, τὴν δὲ ψυχὴν μὴ δυναμένων ἀπο-
κτεῖναι· φοβήθητε δὲ μᾶλλον τὸν δυνάμενον καὶ
ψυχὴν καὶ σῶμα ἀπολέσαι ἐν γεέννῃ.

Ταῦτα μὲν οὖν, φησὶν ὁ Ἰωάσαφ, τῆς ἀληθινῆς
ὑμῶν φιλοσοφίας τὰ κατορθώματα, ὑπεραναβε-
βηκότα λίαν τὴν τῶν γηΐνων φύσιν τῶν δυσαποσπάστως τῆς παρούσης ἐχόντων ζωῆς· καὶ
μακάριοι ὑμεῖς τοιαύτης ἐχόμενοι ἀνδρειοτάτης 154
γνώμης. τίς δέ σου καὶ τῶν σὺν σοὶ ἐν τῇ τοιαύτῃ
ἐρήμῳ ἡ διατροφή, πόθεν δὲ τὰ ἐνδύματα καὶ
ποταπά, γνώρισόν μοι φιλαλήθως.

Ὁ δὲ Βαρλαὰμ φησίν. Ἡ μὲν διατροφὴ ἐκ τῶν
εὑρισκομένων ἐστὶν ἀκροδρύων καὶ βοτανῶν ὧν ἡ
ἔρημος τρέφει, δρόσῳ ποτιζομένη οὐρανίῳ καὶ τῇ

again, "O wretched man that I am! who shall deliver me from the body of this death?" And once more, "I desire to depart and be with Christ." And the prophet saith, "When shall I come and appear before the presence of God?" Now that I the least of all men, choose not to fear bodily death, thou mayest learn by this, that I have set at nought thy father's threat, and come boldly unto thee, and have preached to thee the tidings of salvation, though I knew for sure that, if this came to his knowledge, he would, were that possible, put me to a thousand deaths. But I, honouring the word of God afore all things, and longing to win it, dread not temporal death, nor reckon it at all worthy of such an appellation, in obedience to my Lord's command, which saith, "Fear not them which kill the body, but are not able to kill the soul: but rather fear him which is able to destroy both soul and body in hell."'

'These then,' said Ioasaph, 'are the good deeds of that true philosophy, that far surpass the nature of these earthly men who cleave fast to the present life. Blessed are ye that hold to so noble a purpose! But tell me truly what is thy manner of life and that of thy companions in the desert, and from whence cometh your raiment and of what sort may it be? Tell me as thou lovest truth.'

Ioasaph enquireth after his life in the desert

Said Barlaam, 'Our sustenance consisteth of acorns and herbs that we find in the desert, watered by the dew of heaven, and in obedience to the Crea-

Gen. i. 29, 30 προστάξει τοῦ Δημιουργοῦ εἴκουσα, ἐφ' οἷς οὐδείς
Cp. Xen. Symp. iii. 9 ἐστιν ὁ μαχόμενος ἡμῖν καὶ φιλονεικῶν καὶ τὸ
πλέον ζητῶν ἁρπάζειν τῷ τῆς πλεονεξίας ὅρῳ
τε καὶ λόγῳ· ἀλλ' ἀφθόνως πᾶσι πρόκειται
ἀνήροτος τροφὴ καὶ αὐτοσχέδιος τράπεζα. εἰ δέ
ποτε καὶ τῶν πλησιαζόντων τις πιστῶν ἀδελφῶν
ἄρτου ἐνέγκοι εὐλογίαν, ὡς παρὰ τῆς προνοίας
πεμφθέντα δεχόμεθα τοῦτον ἐπ' εὐλογίᾳ τῶν
πιστῶς προσενεγκόντων. τὰ δὲ ἐνδύματα ἀπὸ
ῥακίων εἰσὶ τριχίνων καὶ μηλωταρίων ἢ σεβεν-
νίνων, πεπαλαιωμένα πάντα καὶ πολύρραφα,
πάνυ κατατρύχοντα τὸ ἀσθενὲς τοῦτο σαρκίον.
Cp. Joh. Chrys. Ecl. p. 431 τὸ αὐτὸ γὰρ ἡμῖν ἐστι περιβόλαιον θέρους τε καὶ
χειμῶνος, ὅπερ οὐδόλως, ἐξ ὅτου ἐνδυσόμεθα, 155
ἐκδύσασθαι θέμις, μέχρις ἂν παλαιωθὲν τέλεον
διαφθαρῇ. οὕτω γὰρ ταῖς τοῦ κρύους καὶ φλογώσεως ἀνάγκαις ταλαιπωρούμενοι τὴν τῶν μελλόν-
2 Esd. ii. 45 των τῆς ἀφθαρσίας ἐνδυμάτων ποριζόμεθα ἑαυτοῖς
ἀμφίασιν.

Τοῦ δὲ Ἰωάσαφ εἰπόντος· Πόθεν δέ σου τοῦτο τὸ ἱμάτιον ὃ περιβέβλησαι; ὁ γέρων ἔφη· Ἐν χρήσει τοῦτο παρά τινος τῶν πιστῶν ἀδελφῶν εἴληφα, τὴν πρός σε μέλλων πορείαν ποιήσασθαι· οὐ γὰρ ἔδει με τῷ συνήθει ἐνδύματι παραγενέσθαι. καθάπερ τις ἔχων προσφιλέστατον συγγενῆ αἰχμάλωτον ἐν ἀλλοδαπεῖ ἀπαχθέντα ἔθνει, καὶ τοῦτον βουλόμενος ἐκεῖθεν ἐξαγαγεῖν, ἀποθέμενος αὐτοῦ τὴν ἐσθῆτα καὶ τὸ τῶν ὑπεναντίων ὑποδὺς προσωπεῖον τὴν ἐκείνων καταλάβοι χώραν, καὶ πολυτρόπως τὸν οἰκεῖον τῆς πικρᾶς ἐλευθερώσειε τυραννίδος· τὸν αὐτὸν δὴ τρόπον κἀγὼ τὰ κατά σε μυηθείς, τοῦτο περιθέμενος

tor's command; and for this there is none to fight and quarrel with us, seeking by the rule and law of covetousness to snatch more than his share, but in abundance for all is food provided from unploughed lands, and a ready table spread. But, should any of the faithful brethren in the neighbourhood bring a blessed dole of bread, we receive it as sent by providence, and bless the faith that brought it. Our raiment is of hair, sheepskins or shirts of palm fibre, all thread-bare and much patched, to mortify the frailty of the flesh. We wear the same clothing winter and summer, which, once put on, we may on no account put off until it be old and quite outworn. For by thus afflicting our bodies with the constraints of cold and heat we purvey for ourselves the vesture of our future robes of immortality.'

Barlaam telleth how he cometh to be clad in other attire,

Ioasaph said, 'But whence cometh this garment that thou wearest?' The elder answered, 'I received it as a loan from one of our faithful brethren, when about to make my journey unto thee; for it behoved me not to arrive in mine ordinary dress. If one had a beloved kinsman carried captive into a foreign land, and wished to recover him thence, one would lay aside one's own clothing, and put on the guise of the enemy, and pass into their country and by divers crafts deliver one's friend from that cruel tyranny. Even so I also, having been made aware of thine estate, clad myself in

τὸ σχῆμα, ἦλθον τὸν σπόρον τοῦ θείου κηρύγματος τῇ σῇ καταβαλεῖν καρδίᾳ, καὶ τῆς
δουλείας λυτρώσασθαι τοῦ δεινοῦ κοσμοκρά- 156
τορος. καὶ νῦν ἰδοὺ τῇ τοῦ Θεοῦ δυνάμει, ὅσον τὸ ἐπ' ἐμοί, τὴν διακονίαν μου πεποίηκα, τὴν αὐτοῦ καταγγείλας σοι γνῶσιν καὶ τὸ τῶν προφητῶν καὶ ἀποστόλων γνωρίσας κήρυγμα, διδάξας τε ἀπλανῶς καὶ φιλαλήθως τὴν τῶν παρόντων ματαιότητα καὶ οἵων κακῶν ὁ κόσμος γέμει, χαλεπῶς ἀπατῶν τοὺς αὐτῷ πειθομένους καὶ πολυτρόπως αὐτοὺς παγιδεύων. λοιπὸν πορευθῆναί με δεῖ ὅθεν ἐλήλυθα. καὶ τηνικαῦτα, τὸ ἀλλότριον ἀποθέμενος σχῆμα, τὸ ἴδιον ἔσομαι ἐνδεδυμένος.

Δυσωπεῖ τοίνυν τὸν γέροντα ὁ Ἰωάσαφ ὀφθῆναι αὐτῷ τῷ συνήθει αὐτοῦ ἐνδύματι. τότε ὁ Βαρλαὰμ ἀπεκδυσάμενος ὃ ἦν περιβεβλημένος ἱμάτιον, θέαμα ὤφθη φοβερὸν τῷ Ἰωάσαφ. ἦν γὰρ ἡ πᾶσα μὲν τῆς σαρκὸς ποιότης δεδαπανημένη, μεμελανωμένον δὲ τὸ δέρμα ἐκ τῆς ἡλιακῆς φλογώσεως καὶ περιτεταμένον τοῖς ὀστέοις, ὡς εἴ τις δοράν τινα περιτείνει ἐν λεπτοῖς καλάμοις· τρίχινον δέ τι ῥάκος ἐρρικνωμένον καὶ λίαν τραχὺ περιεζώννυτο ἐξ ὀσφύος μέχρι γονάτων· ὅμοιον δὲ τούτου παλλίον περιεβέβλητο κατὰ τῶν ὤμων.

Ὑπερθαυμάσας δὲ ὁ Ἰωάσαφ τῆς σκληρᾶς ταύτης διαγωγῆς τὸ ἐπίπονον, καὶ τὸ τῆς καρτερίας ὑπερβάλλον ἐκπλαγείς, σφοδρῶς ἐδάκρυε, καί φησι πρὸς τὸν γέροντα· Ἐπεί με

this dress, and came to sow the seed of the divine message in thine heart, and ransom thee from the slavery of the dread ruler of this world. And now behold by the power of God, as far as in me lay, I have accomplished my ministry, announcing to thee the knowledge of him, and making known unto thee the preaching of the Prophets and Apostles, and teaching thee unerringly and soothly the vanity of the present life, and the evils with which this world teems, which cruelly deceiveth them that trust therein, and taketh them in many a gin. Now must I return thither whence I came, and thereupon doff this robe belonging to another, and don mine own again.'

Ioasaph therefore begged the elder to shew himself in his wonted apparel. Then did Barlaam strip off the mantle that he wore, and lo, a terrible sight met Ioasaph's eyes: for all the fashion of his flesh was wasted away, and his skin blackened by the scorching sun, and drawn tight over his bones like an hide stretched over thin canes. And he wore an hair shirt, stiff and rough, from his loins to his knees, and over his shoulders there hung a coat of like sort.[1]

and showeth Ioasaph his own raiment beneath the borrowed cloak

But Ioasaph, being sore amazed at the hardship of his austere life, and astonished at his excess of endurance, burst into tears, and said to the elder, 'Since thou

Ioasaph would fain go with Barlaam

[1] The Latin *pallium*. παλλίον, or πάλλιον, is used by Epiphanius and others. See E. A. Sophocles' *Greek Lexicon*.

τῆς πικρᾶς τοῦ διαβόλου δουλείας ἐλευθερῶσαι
Ps. cxli. 9 ἥκεις, τέλος σου τῇ εὐεργεσίᾳ ἐπιθεὶς Ἐξάγαγε
ἐκ φυλακῆς τὴν ψυχήν μου, καί, παραλαβών 157
με μετὰ σοῦ, ἄγωμεν ἐντεῦθεν, ἵνα τέλεον λελυ-
τρωμένος τῆς τοῦ κόσμου ἀπάτης τὴν σφραγῖδα
τηνικαῦτα δέξωμαι τοῦ σωτηρίου βαπτίσματος,
καὶ κοινωνός σοι τῆς θαυμαστῆς ταύτης φιλοσοφίας καὶ ὑπερφυοῦς ἀσκήσεως γένωμαι.

Εἶπε δὲ Βαρλαὰμ πρὸς αὐτόν· Νεβρὸν δορκάδος ἔτρεφέ τις τῶν πλουσίων. αὐξηθεῖσα δὲ αὕτη τὰς ἐρήμους ἐπόθει, τῇ φυσικῇ ἑλκομένη ἕξει. ἐξελθοῦσα τοίνυν ἐν μιᾷ, εὑρίσκει ἀγέλην δορκάδων βοσκομένων καὶ ἐχομένη τούτων περιῆγεν ἐν τοῖς πεδίοις τοῦ δρυμοῦ, ὑποστρέφουσα μὲν τὸ πρὸς ἑσπέραν, ἅμα δὲ πρωΐ, τῇ τῶν ὑπουργούντων ἀμελείᾳ, ἐξερχομένη καὶ τοῖς ἀγρίοις συναγελάζουσα. ἐκείνων δὲ πορρωτέρω μεταθεμένων νέμεσθαι, συνηκολούθησε καὶ αὐτή. οἱ δὲ τοῦ πλουσίου ὑπηρέται, τοῦτο αἰσθόμενοι, ἐφ᾿ ἵππων ἀναβάντες, κατεδίωξαν ὀπίσω αὐτῶν, καὶ τὴν μὲν ἰδίαν δορκάδα ζωγρήσαντες, καὶ ἐπαναστρέψαντες οἴκαδε, ἀπρόϊτον τοῦ λοιποῦ ἔθεντο· τῆς δὲ λοιπῆς ἀγέλης τὰς μὲν ἀπέκτειναν, τὰς δὲ κακῶς διέθεντο. τὸν αὐτὸν δὴ τρόπον δέδοικα γενέσθαι καὶ ἐφ᾿ ἡμᾶς, εἰ συνακολουθήσεις μοι· μήποτε καὶ τῆς σῆς ἀποστερηθῶ συνοικήσεως, καὶ κακῶν πολλῶν τοῖς ἑταίροις μου γένωμαι πρόξενος κρίματός τε αἰωνίου τῷ σῷ γεννήτορι. ἀλλὰ τοῦτό σε βούλεται ὁ Κύριος, νῦν μὲν σημειωθῆναι τῇ σφραγῖδι τοῦ θείου βαπτίσματος, καὶ μένειν ἐπὶ χώρας, πάσης ἀντεχόμενον εὐσεβείας καὶ τῆς τῶν ἐντολῶν

art come to deliver me from the slavery of the devil, crown thy good service to me, and "bring my soul out of prison," and take me with thee, and let us go hence, that I may be fully ransomed from this deceitful world and then receive the seal of saving Baptism, and share with thee this thy marvellous philosophy, and this more than human discipline.'

But Barlaam said unto him, 'A certain rich man once reared the fawn of a gazelle; which, when grown up, was impelled by natural desire to long for the desert. So on a day she went out and found an herd of gazelles browsing; and, joining them, she would roam through the glades of the forest, returning at evenfall, but issuing forth at dawn, through the heedlessness of her keepers, to herd with her wild companions. When these removed, to graze further afield, she followed them. But the rich man's servants, when they learned thereof, mounted on horseback, and gave chase, and caught the pet fawn, and brought her home again, and set her in captivity for the time to come. But of the residue of the herd, some they killed, and roughly handled others. Even so I fear that it may happen unto us also if thou follow me; that I may be deprived of thy fellowship, and bring many ills to my comrades, and everlasting damnation to thy father. But this is the will of the Lord concerning thee; thou now indeed must be signed with the seal of holy Baptism, and abide in this country, cleaving to all righteousness, and the fulfilling of the commandments of

Barlaam telleth of the tame gazelle that herded with the wild, APOLOGUE IX

and applieth it to Ioasaph's case

τοῦ Χριστοῦ ἐργασίας. ἐπὰν δὲ δῴη καιρὸν ὁ 158
πάντων δοτὴρ τῶν καλῶν, τηνικαῦτα καὶ ἐλεύσῃ πρὸς ἡμᾶς, καὶ τὸ ὑπόλοιπον τῆς παρούσης ζωῆς ἀλλήλοις συνοικήσαιμεν. πέποιθα δὲ τῷ Κυρίῳ καὶ ἐν τῇ μελλούσῃ διαγωγῇ ἀδιαστάτους ἡμᾶς εἶναι.

Αὖθις δὲ ὁ Ἰωάσαφ δακρύων φησὶ πρὸς αὐτόν· Εἰ τῷ Κυρίῳ ταῦτα δοκεῖ, τὸ θέλημα αὐτοῦ γενέσθω. τελειώσας οὖν με λοιπὸν τῷ θείῳ βαπτίσματι, καὶ λαβὼν παρ' ἐμοῦ χρήματα καὶ ἱμάτια εἰς διατροφὴν καὶ ἀμφίασιν σοῦ τε καὶ τῶν ἑταίρων σου, ἄπελθε εἰς τὸν τόπον τῆς ἀσκήσεώς σου, τῇ τοῦ Θεοῦ εἰρήνῃ φρουρούμενος. κἀμοῦ μὴ διαλίπῃς ὑπερευχόμενος, ἵνα μὴ ἐκπέσοιμι τῆς ἐλπίδος μου, ἀλλὰ θᾶττον ἰσχύσω καταλαβεῖν σε καὶ ἐν ἡσυχίᾳ βαθείᾳ τῆς παρὰ σοῦ ἀπολαύειν ὠφελείας.

Ὁ δὲ Βαρλαὰμ ἔφη· Τὴν μὲν τοῦ Χριστοῦ σε λαβεῖν σφραγῖδα τὸ κωλῦον οὐδέν. εὐτρέπισον λοιπὸν σεαυτόν· καί, τοῦ Κυρίου συνεργοῦντος, τελειωθήσῃ. περὶ ὧν δὲ εἶπας χρημάτων τοῖς ἑταίροις μου παρασχεῖν, πῶς ἔσται τοῦτο, σὲ τὸν πένητα τοῖς πλουσίοις ἐλεημοσύνην διδόναι; οἱ πλούσιοι γὰρ ἀεὶ τοὺς πένητας εὐεργετοῦσιν, οὐ μὴν δὲ οἱ ἄποροι τοὺς εὐπόρους. ὁ γὰρ ἔσχατος πάντων τῶν ἑταίρων μου πλουσιώτερός σου ἀσυγκρίτως καθέστηκεν. ἀλλὰ πέποιθα εἰς τοὺς οἰκτιρμοὺς τοῦ Θεοῦ καί σε ὅσον οὔπω ὑπερπλουτῆσαι· καὶ οὐκ εὐμετάδοτος τηνικαῦτα ἔσῃ.

Εἶπε δὲ ὁ Ἰωάσαφ πρὸς αὐτόν· Σαφήνισόν μοι τὸν λόγον, πῶς ὁ πάντων ἔσχατος τῶν σῶν

Christ; but when the Giver of all good things shall give thee opportunity, then shalt thou come to us, and for the remainder of this present life we shall dwell together; and I trust in the Lord also that in the world to come we shall not be parted asunder.'

Again Ioasaph, in tears, said unto him, 'If this be the Lord's pleasure, his will be done! For the rest, perfect me in holy Baptism. Then receive at my hands money and garments for the support and clothing both of thyself and thy companions, and depart to the place of thy monastic life, and the peace of God be thy guard! But cease not to make supplications on my behalf, that I may not fall away from my hope, but may soon be able to reach thee, and in peace profound may enjoy thy ministration.' **Ioasaph would give alms to Barlaam and his companions,**

Barlaam answered, 'Nought forbiddeth thee to receive the seal of Christ. Make thee ready now; and, the Lord working with thee, thou shalt be perfected. But as concerning the money that thou didst promise to bestow on my companions, how shall this be, that thou, a poor man, shouldest give alms to the rich? The rich always help the poor, not the needy the wealthy. And the least of all my comrades is incomparably richer than thou. But I trust in the mercies of God that thou too shalt soon be passing rich as never afore: and then thou wilt not be ready to distribute.' **but Barlaam forbiddeth this,**

Ioasaph said unto him, 'Make plain to me this saying; how the least of all thy companions

ἑταίρων ὑπέρκειταί μου τῷ πλούτῳ, οὗσπερ πολλῇ συζῆν ἀκτημοσύνῃ καὶ ἐσχάτῃ ταλαιπω- 159
ρεῖσθαι πτωχείᾳ πρὸ μικροῦ ἔλεγες, πῶς δὲ νῦν μὲν πένητά με ἀποκαλεῖς, ὅταν δὲ ὑπερπλουτήσω οὐκ ἂν μετάδοτον γενέσθαι λέγεις τὸν εὐμετάδοτον νῦν καθεστηκότα;

Ὁ δὲ Βαρλαὰμ ἀπεκρίνατο· Οὐ πτωχείᾳ τούτους ἔφην ταλαιπωρεῖσθαι, ἀλλὰ πλούτῳ κομᾶν ἀκενώτῳ. τὸ γὰρ ἀεὶ τοῖς χρήμασι προστιθέναι χρήματα, καὶ μὴ τῆς ὁρμῆς χαλινοῦσθαι, ἀλλὰ καὶ πλειοτέρων ἀκορέστως ὀρέγεσθαι, τοῦτο πενίας ἐσχάτης ἐστί. τοὺς δὲ τῶν παρόντων μὲν ὑπεριδόντας πόθῳ τῶν αἰωνίων,
Phil. iii. 8 καὶ σκύβαλα ταῦτα ἡγησαμένους, ἵνα Χριστὸν μόνον κερδήσωσι, πᾶσαν δὲ βρωμάτων καὶ ἐνδυμάτων ἀποθεμένους μέριμναν καὶ τῷ Κυρίῳ ταύτην ἐπιρρίψαντας, εὐφραινομένους δὲ τῇ ἀκτησίᾳ, ὡς οὐκ ἄν τις τῶν φιλοκόσμων εὐφρανθείη πλούτῳ καὶ χρήμασι βρίθων, καὶ τὸν πλοῦτον τῆς ἀρετῆς ἀφθόνως ἑαυτοῖς συναγηοχότας, ταῖς ἐλπίσι τε τῶν ἀτελευτήτων τρεφομένους ἀγαθῶν, εἰκότως πλουσιωτέρους σου καὶ πάσης τῆς ἐπιγείου βασιλείας καλέσαιμι. τοῦ δὲ Θεοῦ συνεργοῦντός σοι, ἐπιλήψῃ καὶ αὐτὸς τῆς τοιαύτης πνευματικῆς περιουσίας, ἥνπερ ἐν ἀσφαλείᾳ τηρῶν καὶ τοῦ πλείονος ἀεὶ δικαίως ἐφιέμενος, οὐκ ἂν θελήσειάς τι ταύτης κατακενοῦν ὅλως. αὕτη γάρ ἐστιν ἀληθὴς περιουσία· ὁ δὲ τοῦ αἰσθητοῦ πλούτου ὄγκος βλάψειε μᾶλλον τοὺς αὐτοῦ φίλους ἢ ὠφελήσειεν. εἰκότως οὖν πενίαν ἐσχάτην τοῦτον ἀπεκάλεσα, ὅνπερ οἱ ἐρασταὶ τῶν οὐρανίων ἀγαθῶν πάντῃ ἀπαρνησά-

surpasseth me in riches—thou saidest but now that they lived in utter penury, and were pinched by extreme poverty—and why thou callest me a poor man, but sayest that, when I shall be passing rich, I, who am ready to distribute, shall be ready to distribute no more.'

showing that it is his companions that possess the true wealth

Barlaam answered, 'I said not that these men were pinched by poverty, but that they plume themselves on their inexhaustible wealth. For to be ever adding money to money, and never to curb the passion for it, but insatiably to covet more and more, betokeneth the extreme of poverty. But those who despise the present for love of the eternal and count it but dung, if only they win Christ, who have laid aside all care for meat and raiment and cast that care on the Lord, and rejoice in penury as no lover of the world could rejoice, were he rolling in riches, who have laid up for themselves plenteously the riches of virtue, and are fed by the hope of good things without end, may more fitly be termed rich than thou, or any other earthly kingdom. But, God working with thee, thou shalt lay hold on such spiritual abundance that, if thou keep it in safety and ever rightfully desire more, thou shalt never wish to dispend any part of it. This is true abundance: but the mass of material riches will damage rather than benefit its friends. Meetly therefore called I it the extreme of poverty, which the lovers of heavenly blessings utterly renounce and eschew, and flee from it, as a man

μενοι ἔφυγον ἀπ' αὐτοῦ, ὡς φεύγει τις ἀπὸ ὄφεως. 160
εἰ δέ, ὃν ἀπέκτειναν ἐχθρὸν καὶ τοῖς ποσὶ συνεπά-
τησαν οἱ συνασκηταί μου καὶ συστρατιῶται, τοῦτον αὖθις ζῶντα παρὰ σοῦ λαβὼν αὐτοῖς
ἀπενέγκω, καὶ πρόξενος πολέμων καὶ παθῶν
γένωμαι, ἔσομαι αὐτοῖς πάντως ἄγγελος πονηρός·
ὅπερ μὴ γένοιτό μοι ποιῆσαι.

Τὰ αὐτὰ δέ μοι νόει καὶ περὶ ἐνδυμάτων. τοῖς
γὰρ ἀπεκδυσαμένοις τὴν τῆς παλαιότητος κατα-
φθορὰν καὶ τὸ τῆς παρακοῆς ἔνδυμα, ὅσον τὸ ἐπ'
Gal. iii. 27 αὐτοῖς, ἀποθεμένοις, τὸν Χριστὸν δὲ ὡς ἱμάτιον
σωτηρίου καὶ χιτῶνα εὐφροσύνης ἐνδεδυμένοις,
πῶς αὐτοὺς πάλιν τοὺς δερματίνους ἀμφιάσαιμι
χιτῶνας καὶ τὸ τῆς αἰσχύνης περιθήσομαι περιβόλαιον; ἀλλὰ τοὺς μὲν ἐμοὺς ἑταίρους μηδενὸς
τῶν τοιούτων ἐπιδεομένους γινώσκων, τῇ τῆς ἐρήμου δὲ ἀρκουμένους ἀσκήσει καὶ τρυφὴν ταύτην
λογιζομένους ἀληθεστάτην, τὰ χρήματα καὶ
ἱμάτια, ἅπερ τούτοις ἔλεγες παρασχεῖν, τοῖς πένησι
διανείμας, θησαυρὸν ἑαυτῷ εἰς τὸ μέλλον ἄσυλον
θησαύρισον, τὸν Θεὸν ἑαυτῷ ταῖς ἐκείνων εὐχαῖς
ἐπίκουρον θέμενος· οὕτω γὰρ μᾶλλον συνεργῷ τῷ
πλούτῳ πρὸς τὰ καλὰ χρήσαιο. εἶτα καὶ τὴν
Eph. vi. 13–17 πανοπλίαν τοῦ πνεύματος περιβαλλόμενος, καὶ
τὴν μὲν ὀσφὺν ἐν ἀληθείᾳ περιζωσάμενος, ἐνδυσά-
μενος δὲ καὶ τὸν τῆς δικαιοσύνης θώρακα, περιθέ-
μενός τε καὶ τὴν περικεφαλαίαν τοῦ σωτηρίου,
καὶ τοὺς πόδας ἐν ἑτοιμασίᾳ τοῦ Εὐαγγελίου τῆς
εἰρήνης ὑποδησάμενος, μετὰ χεῖράς τε τὸν τῆς πίστεως ἀναλαβὼν θυρεόν, καὶ τὴν τοῦ πνεύματος
μάχαιραν, ἥ ἐστι ῥῆμα Θεοῦ, καὶ πάντοθεν ἄριστα 161
καθοπλισθεὶς καὶ περιφραξάμενος, οὕτω πεποι-

fleeth from an adder. But if I take from thee and so bring back to life that foe, whom my comrades in discipline and battle have slain and trampled under foot, and carry him back to them, and so be the occasion of wars and lusts, then shall I verily be unto them an evil angel, which heaven forfend!

'Let the same, I pray thee, be thy thoughts about raiment. As for them that have put off the corruption of the old man, and, as far as possible, cast away the robe of disobedience, and put on Christ as a coat of salvation and garment of gladness, how shall I again clothe these in their coats of hide, and gird them about with the covering of shame? But be assured that my companions have no need of such things, but are content with their hard life in the desert, and reckon it the truest luxury; and bestow thou on the poor the money and garments which thou promisedst to give unto our monks, and lay up for thyself, for the time to come, treasure that cannot be stolen, and by the orisons of these poor folk make God thine ally; for thus shalt thou employ thy riches as an help toward noble things. Then also put on the whole armour of the Spirit, having thy loins girt about with truth, and having on the breast-plate of righteousness, and wearing the helmet of salvation, and having thy feet shod with the preparation of the gospel of peace, and taking in thine hands the shield of faith, and the sword of the spirit, which is the word of God. And, being thus excellently armed and guarded on

He biddeth Ioasaph give alms to the poor and win thereby the blessing of the Lord

θὼς πρὸς τὸν κατὰ τῆς ἀσεβείας ἔξελθε πόλεμον, ὡς ἄν, ταύτην τροπωσάμενος καὶ τὸν αὐτῆς ἀρχηγὸν διάβολον εἰς γῆν καταρράξας, τοῖς τῆς νίκης στεφάνοις κοσμηθήσῃ ἐκ τῆς ζωαρχικῆς δεξιᾶς τοῦ Δεσπότου.

XIX

Τοῖς τοιούτοις οὖν δόγμασι καὶ λόγοις σωτηρίοις κατηχήσας ὁ Βαρλαὰμ τὸν τοῦ βασιλέως υἱὸν καὶ πρὸς τὸ θεῖον βάπτισμα εὐτρεπίσας, νηστεύειν τε καὶ εὔχεσθαι ἐντειλάμενος, κατὰ τὸ ἔθος, ἐφ' ἱκανὰς ἡμέρας, οὐ διέλιπε συχνάζων πρὸς αὐτόν, καὶ πᾶσαν δογματικὴν φωνὴν τῆς ὀρθοδόξου πίστεως ἐκδιδάσκων καὶ τὸ θεῖον Εὐαγγέλιον ὑπαγορεύων αὐτῷ, πρὸς δὲ καὶ τὰς ἀποστολικὰς παραινέσεις καὶ τὰς προφητικὰς ῥήσεις ἑρμηνεύων· θεοδίδακτος γὰρ ὢν ὁ ἀνὴρ πᾶσαν ἐπὶ στόματος Παλαιάν τε καὶ Καινὴν Γραφὴν ἔφερε, καί, τῷ θείῳ κινούμενος Πνεύματι, ἐφώτισεν αὐτὸν πρὸς τὴν ἀληθῆ θεογνωσίαν. ἐν αὐτῇ δὲ τῇ ἡμέρᾳ ὅτε βαπτισθῆναι ἔμελλε, διδάσκων αὐτόν, ἔλεγεν· Ἰδοὺ τὴν τοῦ Χριστοῦ
Ps. iv. 6 ἐπείγῃ λαβεῖν σφραγῖδα, καὶ τῷ φωτὶ σημειωθῆναι τοῦ προσώπου Κυρίου. καὶ υἱὸς μὲν γίνῃ Θεοῦ, ναὸς δὲ τοῦ ἁγίου καὶ ζωοποιοῦ Πνεύματος. πίστευε τοίνυν εἰς Πατέρα, καὶ Υἱόν, καὶ Ἅγιον Πνεῦμα, τὴν ἁγίαν καὶ ζωαρχικὴν Τριάδα ἐν τρισὶν ὑποστάσεσι καὶ μιᾷ θεότητι δοξαζομένην, 162
διαιρετὴν μὲν ταῖς ὑποστάσεσι καὶ ταῖς ὑποστατικαῖς ἰδιότησιν, ἡνωμένην δὲ τῇ οὐσίᾳ· ἕνα μὲν

every side, in this confidence go forth to the warfare against ungodliness, until, this put to flight, and its prince, the devil, dashed headlong to the earth, thou be adorned with the crowns of victory from the right hand of thy master, the Lord of life.'

XIX

With such like doctrines and saving words did Barlaam instruct the king's son, and fit him for holy Baptism, charging him to fast and pray, according to custom, several days; and he ceased not to resort unto him, teaching him every article of the Catholick Faith and expounding him the holy Gospel. Moreover he interpreted the Apostolick exhortations and the sayings of the Prophets: for, taught of God, Barlaam had alway ready on his lips the Old and New Scripture; and, being stirred by the Spirit, he enlightened his young disciple to see the true knowledge of God. But on the day, whereon the prince should be baptized, he taught him, saying, 'Behold thou art moved to receive the seal of Christ, and be signed with the light of the countenance of the Lord: and thou becomest a son of God, and temple of the Holy Ghost, the giver of life. Believe thou therefore in the Father, and in the Son, and in the Holy Ghost, the holy and life-giving Trinity, glorified in three persons and one Godhead, different indeed in persons and personal properties, but united

Barlaam prepareth Ioasaph for baptism

instructing him in the doctrine of the Holy Trinity,

γινώσκων Θεὸν ἀγέννητον, τὸν Πατέρα, ἕνα δὲ
γεννητὸν Κύριον, τὸν Υἱόν, φῶς ἐκ φωτός, Θεὸν
ἀληθινὸν ἐκ Θεοῦ ἀληθινοῦ, γεννηθέντα πρὸ πάντων τῶν αἰώνων· ἀγαθοῦ γὰρ Πατρὸς ἀγαθὸς
ἐγεννήθη Υἱός, φωτὸς δὲ τοῦ ἀγεννήτου φῶς
ἐξέλαμψε τὸ ἀΐδιον, καὶ ἐκ τῆς ὄντως ζωῆς ἡ
ζωοποιὸς προῆλθε πηγή, καὶ ἐκ τῆς αὐτοδυνάμεως
Wisd. vii. 26; Heb. i. 3 ἡ τοῦ Υἱοῦ δύναμις ἐξεφάνη, ὅς ἐστιν ἀπαύγασμα
John i. 2, 3 τῆς δόξης καὶ Λόγος ἐνυπόστατος, ἐν ἀρχῇ ὢν
πρὸς τὸν Θεὸν καὶ Θεὸς ἄναρχός τε καὶ ἀΐδιος· δι'
οὗ τὰ πάντα ἐγένετο τὰ ὁρατὰ καὶ τὰ ἀόρατα·
John xv. 26 καὶ ἓν εἰδὼς Πνεῦμα Ἅγιον, τὸ ἐκ τοῦ Πατρὸς
ἐκπορευόμενον, Θεὸν τέλειον, καὶ ζωοποιόν, καὶ
ἁγιασμοῦ παρεκτικόν, ταυτοθελές, ταυτοδύναμον,
συναΐδιον, ἐνυπόστατον. οὕτως οὖν προσκύνει
τὸν Πατέρα καὶ τὸν Υἱὸν καὶ τὸ Ἅγιον Πνεῦμα ἐν
τρισὶν ὑποστάσεσιν, εἴτ' οὖν ἰδιότησι, καὶ θεότητι
μιᾷ· κοινὸν μὲν γὰρ τῶν τριῶν ἡ θεότης, καὶ μία
αὐτῶν ἡ φύσις, μία οὐσία, μία δόξα, μία βασι-
Greg. Naz. Orat. xxv. 16 λεία, μία δύναμις, μία ἐξουσία· κοινὸν δὲ Υἱῷ
καὶ Ἁγίῳ Πνεύματι τὸ ἐκ τοῦ Πατρός, ἴδιον δὲ τοῦ 163
Πατρὸς μὲν ἡ ἀγεννησία, Υἱοῦ δὲ ἡ γέννησις,
Πνεύματος δὲ ἡ ἐκπόρευσις.

Οὕτω μὲν οὖν ταῦτα πίστευε· καταλαβεῖν δὲ
τὸν τρόπον τῆς γεννήσεως ἢ τῆς ἐκπορεύσεως μὴ
Ps. cxix. 7 ἐπιζήτει (ἀκατάληπτος γάρ)· ἐν εὐθύτητι καρδίας
ἀπεριέργως προσδέχου ὅτι ὁ Πατὴρ καὶ ὁ Υἱὸς
καὶ τὸ Ἅγιον Πνεῦμα κατὰ πάντα ἕν εἰσι, πλὴν
τῆς ἀγεννησίας καὶ τῆς γεννήσεως καὶ τῆς ἐκπορεύσεως, καὶ ὅτι ὁ μονογενὴς Υἱὸς καὶ Λόγος
τοῦ Θεοῦ καὶ Θεὸς διὰ τὴν ἡμετέραν σωτηρίαν
Eph. i. 5 κατῆλθεν ἐπὶ τῆς γῆς εὐδοκίᾳ τοῦ Πατρὸς καὶ

in substance; acknowledging one God unbegotten, the Father; and one begotten Lord, the Son, light of light, very God of very God, begotten before all worlds; for of the good Father is begotten the good Son, and of the unbegotten light shone forth the everlasting light; and from very life came forth the life-giving spring, and from original might shone forth the might of the Son, who is the brightness of his glory and the Word in personality, who was in the beginning with God, and God without beginning and without end, by whom all things, visible and invisible, were made: knowing also one Holy Ghost, which proceedeth from the Father, perfect, life-giving and sanctifying God, with the same will, the same power, coëternal and impersonate. Thus therefore worship thou the Father, and the Son, and the Holy Ghost, in three persons or properties and one Godhead. For the Godhead is common of the three, and one is their nature, one their substance, one their glory, one their kingdom, one their might, one their authority; but it is common of the Son and of the Holy Ghost that they are of the Father; and it is proper of the Father that he is unbegotten, and of the Son that he is begotten, and of the Holy Ghost that he proceedeth.

'This therefore be thy belief; but seek not to understand the manner of the generation or procession, for it is incomprehensible. In uprightness of heart and without question accept the truth that the Father, and the Son, and the Holy Ghost, are in all points one except in the being unbegotten, and begotten, and proceeding; and that the only-begotten Son, the Word of God, and God, for our salvation came down upon earth, by the good

and charging him to accept it in unquestioning faith

συνεργίᾳ τοῦ ἁγίου Πνεύματος, ἀσπόρως συλλη-
Mat. i. 20, 23 φθεὶς ἐν τῇ μήτρᾳ τῆς ἁγίας Παρθένου καὶ Θεο-
Luke i. 35; τόκου Μαρίας διὰ Πνεύματος Ἁγίου, καὶ ἀφθόρως
Is. vii. 11 ἐξ αὐτῆς γεννηθείς, καὶ ἄνθρωπος τέλειος γενόμενος, καὶ ὅτι αὐτὸς Θεὸς τέλειός ἐστι καὶ ἄνθρωπος τέλειος, γενόμενος ἐκ δύο φύσεων, θεότητός
τε καὶ ἀνθρωπότητος, καὶ ἐν δύο φύσεσι νοεραῖς,
θελητικαῖς τε καὶ ἐνεργητικαῖς καὶ αὐτεξουσίοις,
καὶ κατὰ πάντα τελείως ἐχούσαις κατὰ τὸν
ἑκάστῃ πρέποντα ὅρον τε καὶ λόγον, θεότητι,
φημί, καὶ ἀνθρωπότητι, μιᾷ δὲ συνθέτῳ ὑποστάσει. καὶ ταῦτα ἀπεριέργως δέχου, μηδόλως τὸν
Phil. ii. 7 τρόπον μαθεῖν ἐκζητῶν, πῶς ἑαυτὸν ἐκένωσεν ὁ
Υἱὸς τοῦ Θεοῦ καὶ ἄνθρωπος γέγονεν ἐκ παρθενι- 164
κῶν αἱμάτων ἀσπόρως τε καὶ ἀφθάρτως, ἢ τίς ἡ
τῶν δύο φύσεων ἐν μιᾷ ὑποστάσει συνέλευσις;
πίστει γὰρ ταῦτα ἐδιδάχθημεν κατέχειν τὰ
θειώδως ἡμῖν ἐκ τῆς θείας Γραφῆς εἰρημένα· τὸν
δὲ τρόπον καὶ ἀγνοοῦμεν καὶ λέγειν οὐ δυνάμεθα.

Luke i. 78 Πίστευε τὸν Υἱὸν τοῦ Θεοῦ, τὸν διὰ σπλάγχνα
ἐλέους γενόμενον ἄνθρωπον, πάντα τε ἀναδέξασθαι τὰ τῆς ἀνθρωπότητος φυσικὰ καὶ ἀδιάβλητα
πάθη (ἐπείνησε γάρ, καὶ ἐδίψησε, καὶ ὕπνωσε,
καὶ ἐκοπίασε, καὶ ἠγωνίασε φύσει τῆς ἀνθρωπότητος, καὶ ὑπὲρ τῶν ἀνομιῶν ἡμῶν ἤχθη εἰς
θάνατον, ἐσταυρώθη, καὶ ἐτάφη, θανάτου γευσάμενος, τῆς θεότητος ἀπαθοῦς καὶ ἀτρέπτου δια-
μεινάσης· οὐδὲν γὰρ ὅλως τῶν παθῶν τῇ ἀπαθεῖ
προσάπτομεν φύσει· ἀλλὰ τῷ προσλήμματι γινώσκομεν αὐτὸν παθόντα καὶ ταφέντα, καὶ τῇ θείᾳ
δόξῃ ἐκ νεκρῶν ἀναστάντα, ἐν ἀφθαρσίᾳ τε εἰς
2 Tim. iv. 1 οὐρανοὺς ἀνεληλυθότα), καὶ ἥξειν πάλιν μετὰ

pleasure of the Father, and, by the operation of the Holy Ghost, was conceived without seed in the womb of Mary the holy Virgin and Mother of God, by the Holy Ghost, and was born of her without defilement and was made perfect man and that he is perfect God and perfect man, being of two natures, the Godhead and the manhood, and in two natures, endowed with reason, will, activity, and free will, and in all points perfect according to the proper rule and law in either case, that is in the Godhead and the manhood, and in one united person. And do thou receive these things without question, never seeking to know the manner, how the Son of God emptied himself, and was made man of the blood of the Virgin, without seed and without defilement; or what is this meeting in one person of two natures. For by faith we are taught to hold fast those things that have been divinely taught us out of Holy Scripture; but of the manner we are ignorant, and cannot declare it.

He telleth of the Life and Passion of the Lord Jesus Christ,

'Believe thou that the Son of God, who, of his tender mercy was made man, took upon him all the affections that are natural to man, and are blameless (he hungered and thirsted and slept and was weary and endured agony in his human nature, and for our transgressions was led to death, was crucified and was buried, and tasted of death, his Godhead continuing without suffering and without change; for we attach no sufferings whatsoever to that nature which is free from suffering, but we recognize him as suffering and buried in that nature which he assumed, and in his heavenly glory rising again from the dead, and in immortality ascending into heaven); and believe that he shall come again, with

δόξης κρῖναι ζῶντας καὶ νεκροὺς οἷς αὐτὸς οἶδε
λόγοις θεοειδεστέρου σώματος, καὶ ἀποδώσειν
John v. 28 ἑκάστῳ τοῖς δικαίοις αὐτοῦ σταθμοῖς. ἀναστήσονται γὰρ οἱ νεκροὶ καὶ ἐγερθήσονται οἱ ἐν τοῖς
Cp. Dan. xii. 2 μνημείοις· καὶ οἱ μὲν τὰς τοῦ Χριστοῦ φυλά-
ξαντες ἐντολὰς καὶ τῇ ὀρθῇ συναπελθόντες πίστει
John viii. 24 κληρονομήσουσι ζωὴν αἰώνιον, οἱ δ' ἐν ἁμαρτίαις
καταφθαρέντες καὶ τῆς ὀρθῆς ἐκκλίναντες πίστεως
Mat. xxv. 46 εἰς κόλασιν αἰώνιον ἀπελεύσονται. πίστευε μὴ
οὐσίαν τινὰ εἶναι τοῦ κακοῦ ἢ βασιλείαν, μηδὲ
ἄναρχον αὐτὴν ὑπολάμβανε ἢ παρ' ἑαυτῆς ὑπο-
στᾶσαν, ἢ παρὰ τοῦ Θεοῦ γενομένην· ἄπαγε
τῆς ἀτοπίας· ἀλλ' ἡμέτερον ἔργον τοῦτο καὶ τοῦ
διαβόλου, ἐκ τῆς ἡμετέρας ἀπροσεξίας ἐπεισελθὸν
ἡμῖν διὰ τὸ αὐτεξουσίους ἡμᾶς γεγενῆσθαι, καὶ
αὐτοπροαιρέτῳ βουλήσει τοῦτο ἐκλέγεσθαι, εἴτε
Eph. iv. 5 ἀγαθόν, εἴτε καὶ φαῦλον. πρὸς τούτοις ὁμολόγει
ἓν βάπτισμα ἐξ ὕδατος καὶ Πνεύματος εἰς
ἄφεσιν ἁμαρτιῶν.

Δέχου καὶ τὴν μετάληψιν τῶν ἀχράντων τοῦ
Χριστοῦ μυστηρίων, πιστεύων ἐν ἀληθείᾳ σῶμα
καὶ αἷμα ὑπάρχειν Χριστοῦ τοῦ Θεοῦ ἡμῶν, ἃ
δέδωκε τοῖς πιστοῖς εἰς ἄφεσιν ἁμαρτιῶν. ἐν τῇ
1 Cor. xi. 23–25 νυκτὶ γὰρ ᾗ παρεδίδοτο, διαθήκην καινὴν διέθετο
Mat. xxvi. 26–28 τοῖς ἁγίοις αὐτοῦ μαθηταῖς καὶ ἀποστόλοις,
καὶ δι' αὐτῶν πᾶσι τοῖς εἰς αὐτὸν πιστεύουσιν,
Mark xiv. 22–24 εἰπών· Λάβετε, φάγετε· τοῦτό ἐστι τὸ σῶμά μου
Luke xxii. 19, 20 ὑπὲρ ὑμῶν κλώμενον εἰς ἄφεσιν ἁμαρτιῶν.
ὁμοίως δὲ καὶ τὸ ποτήριον λαβὼν δέδωκεν
αὐτοῖς, λέγων· Πίετε ἐξ αὐτοῦ πάντες· τοῦτό

glory, to judge quick and dead, and by the words, which himself knoweth, of that diviner body,[1] and to reward every man by his own just standards. For the dead shall rise again, and they that are in their graves shall awake: and they that have kept the commandments of Christ, and have departed this life in the true faith shall inherit eternal life, and they, that have died in their sins, and have turned aside from the right faith, shall go away into eternal punishment. Believe not that there is any true being or kingdom of evil, nor suppose that it is without beginning, or self-originate, or born of God: out on such an absurdity! but believe rather that it is the work of us and the devil, come upon us through our heedlessness, because we were endowed with free-will, and we make our choice, of deliberate purpose, whether it be good or evil. Beside this, acknowledge one Baptism, by water and the Spirit, for the remission of sins.

and of the Holy Eucharist

'Receive also the Communion of the spotless Mysteries of Christ, believing in truth that they are the Body and Blood of Christ our God, which he hath given unto the faithful for the remission of sins. For in the same night in which he was betrayed he ordained a new testament with his holy disciples and Apostles, and through them for all that should believe on him, saying, "Take, eat: this is my Body, which is broken for you, for the remission of sins." After the same manner also he took the cup, and gave unto them saying, "Drink ye all of this: this is my Blood, of the new testament, which

[1] Greg. Naz. Orat xl. 45. *οὐκ ἔτι μὲν σάρκα, οὐκ ἀσώματον δέ, οἷς αὐτὸς οἶδε λόγοις, θεοειδεστέρου σώματος, κ.τ.λ.*

ἐστι τὸ αἷμά μου, τὸ τῆς καινῆς διαθήκης, τὸ
ὑπὲρ ὑμῶν ἐκχυνόμενον εἰς ἄφεσιν ἁμαρτιῶν·
τοῦτο ποιεῖτε εἰς τὴν ἐμὴν ἀνάμνησιν. αὐτὸς οὖν 166
Heb. iv. 12 ὁ Λόγος τοῦ Θεοῦ ὁ ζῶν, καὶ ἐνεργής, καὶ πάντα
ποιῶν τῇ δυνάμει αὐτοῦ, ποιεῖ καὶ μετασκευάζει
διὰ τῆς θείας ἐνεργείας τὸν ἄρτον καὶ τὸν οἶνον
Cyril. Cat. xxiii. 19 τῆς προσφορᾶς σῶμα αὐτοῦ καὶ αἷμα, τῇ ἐπιφοι-
τήσει τοῦ Ἁγίου Πνεύματος, εἰς ἁγιασμὸν καὶ
φωτισμὸν τῶν πόθῳ μεταλαμβανόντων.

John Damascene, De fid. orth. iv. 16 Προσκύνει πιστῶς τιμῶν καὶ ἀσπαζόμενος τὸ
σεβάσμιον ἐκτύπωμα τοῦ Δεσποτικοῦ χαρακτῆ-
ρος τοῦ δι' ἡμᾶς ἐνανθρωπήσαντος Θεοῦ Λόγου,
αὐτὸν δοκῶν τὸν Κτίστην ὁρᾶν ἐν τῇ εἰκόνι. Ἡ
Basil, De Spiritu Sancto, ch. 18 τιμὴ γὰρ τῆς εἰκόνος, φησί τις τῶν ἁγίων, ἐπὶ
τὸ πρωτότυπον διαβαίνει· πρωτότυπον δέ ἐστι
τὸ εἰκονιζόμενον, ἐξ οὗ τὸ παράγωγον γίνεται.
τὴν γὰρ ἐν εἰκόνι βλέποντες γραφήν, τοῖς τοῦ
νοὸς ὀφθαλμοῖς πρὸς τὴν ἀληθινὴν διαβαίνομεν
ἰδέαν οὗ ἐστιν ἡ εἰκών, εὐσεβῶς προσκυνοῦντες
τὴν τοῦ δι' ἡμᾶς σαρκωθέντος μορφήν, οὐ θεοποιούμενοι, ἀλλ' ὡς εἰκόνα τοῦ σαρκωθέντος Θεοῦ
Phil. ii. 7 κατασπαζόμενοι, πόθῳ καὶ ἀγάπῃ τοῦ κενώ-
σαντος ἑαυτὸν δι' ἡμᾶς μέχρι καὶ δούλου μορφῆς·
John Damascene, De fid. orth. iv. 16 ὁμοίως καὶ τῆς ἀχράντου Μητρὸς αὐτοῦ καὶ
πάντων τῶν ἁγίων τὰ ἐκτυπώματα τούτῳ τῷ
λόγῳ περιπτυσσόμενοι. ὡσαύτως δὲ καὶ τὸν
ibid. 11 τύπον τοῦ ζωοποιοῦ καὶ σεβασμίου σταυροῦ
πίστει προσκυνῶν κατασπάζου διὰ τὸν κρεμα-
σθέντα ἐν αὐτῷ σαρκὶ ἐπὶ σωτηρίᾳ τοῦ γένους 167
ἡμῶν Χριστὸν τὸν Θεὸν καὶ Σωτῆρα τοῦ κόσμου,
Cp. Wisd. xvi. 6 καὶ δόντα ἡμῖν τοῦτον σύμβολον τῆς κατὰ τοῦ δια-
Cyril. Cat. xiii. 36 βόλου νίκης· φρίττει γὰρ καὶ τρέμει, μὴ φέρων

is shed for you for the remission of sins: this do in remembrance of me." He then, the Word of God, being quick and powerful, and, working all things by his might, maketh and transformeth, through his divine operation, the bread and wine of the oblation into his own Body and Blood, by the visitation of the Holy Ghost, for the sanctification and enlightenment of them that with desire partake thereof.

Barlaam instructeth Ioasaph in the worship of Images

'Faithfully worship, with honour and reverence, the venerable likeness of the features of the Lord, the Word of God, who for our sake was made man, thinking to behold in the Image thy Creator himself. "For the honour of the Image, saith one of the Saints, passeth over to the original." The original is the thing imaged, and from it cometh the derivation. For when we see the drawing in the Image, in our mind's eye we pass over to the true form of which it is an Image, and devoutly worship the form of him who for our sake was made flesh, not making a god of it, but saluting it as an image of God made flesh, with desire and love of him who for us men emptied himself, and even took the form of a servant. Likewise also for this reason we salute the pictures of his undefiled Mother, and of all the Saints. In the same spirit also faithfully worship and salute the emblem of the life-giving and venerable Cross, for the sake of him that hung thereon in the flesh, for the salvation of our race, Christ the God and Saviour of the world, who gave it to us as the sign of victory over the devil; for the devil trembleth and quaketh

καθορᾶν αὐτοῦ τὴν δύναμιν. ἐν τοῖς τοιούτοις
δόγμασι καὶ μετὰ τοιαύτης πίστεως βαπτι-
σθήσῃ, ἄτρεπτον ταύτην καὶ ἀμιγῆ πάσης αἱρέσεως φυλάττων μέχρις ἐσχάτης ἀναπνοῆς. πᾶσαν
δὲ διδασκαλίαν καὶ πᾶσαν δογματικὴν φωνήν,
ταύτῃ τῇ ἀμωμήτῳ ἀνθισταμένην πίστει, βδε-
λύσσου, καὶ ἀλλοτρίωσιν λογίζου εἶναι Θεοῦ.
Gal. i. 8 φησὶ γὰρ ὁ Ἀπόστολος, ὅτι Κἂν ἡμεῖς ἢ ἄγγελος
ἐξ οὐρανοῦ εὐαγγελίζηται ὑμῖν παρ' ὃ εὐηγγελι-
σάμεθα ὑμῖν, ἀνάθεμα ἔστω. οὐκ ἔστι γὰρ ἄλλο
Εὐαγγέλιον καὶ ἄλλη πίστις, πλὴν ἡ διὰ τῶν
ἀποστόλων κηρυχθεῖσα, καὶ διὰ τῶν θεοφόρων
Πατέρων ἐν διαφόροις συνόδοις βεβαιωθεῖσα, καὶ
τῇ καθολικῇ Ἐκκλησίᾳ βεβαιωθεῖσα.[1]

Ταῦτα εἰπὼν ὁ Βαρλαάμ, καὶ τὸ τῆς πίστεως
A.D. 325 σύμβολον τὸ ἐκτεθὲν ἐν τῇ κατὰ Νίκαιαν συνόδῳ
Mat. xxviii. 19 διδάξας τὸν τοῦ βασιλέως υἱόν, ἐβάπτισεν αὐτὸν
εἰς τὸ ὄνομα τοῦ Πατρός, καὶ τοῦ Υἱοῦ, καὶ τοῦ
Ἁγίου Πνεύματος εἰς τὴν κολυμβήθραν τοῦ ὕδατος
τὴν οὖσαν ἐν τῷ παραδείσῳ αὐτοῦ. καὶ ἦλθεν ἐπ'
αὐτὸν ἡ χάρις τοῦ Ἁγίου Πνεύματος. ἐπανελθὼν
δὲ εἰς τὸν αὐτοῦ κοιτῶνα, καὶ τὴν ἱερὰν ἐπιτε-
λέσας μυσταγωγίαν τῆς ἀναιμάκτου θυσίας,
μετέδωκεν αὐτῷ τῶν ἀχράντων τοῦ Χριστοῦ
Luke x. 21 μυστηρίων, καὶ ἠγαλλιάσατο τῷ Πνεύματι, δόξαν 16
ἀναπέμπων Χριστῷ τῷ Θεῷ.

1 Pet. i. 3, 4 Εἶπε δὲ πρὸς αὐτὸν ὁ Βαρλαάμ· Εὐλογητὸς ὁ
Θεὸς καὶ Πατὴρ τοῦ Κυρίου ἡμῶν Ἰησοῦ Χρι-
στοῦ, ὁ κατὰ τὸ πολὺ ἔλεος αὐτοῦ ἀναγεννήσας
σε εἰς ἐλπίδα ζῶσαν, εἰς κληρονομίαν ἄφθαρτον
καὶ ἀμίαντον, καὶ ἀμάραντον, τετηρημένην ἐν

[1] A misprint for παραδοθεῖσα.

at the virtue thereof, and endureth not to behold it. In such doctrines and in such faith shalt thou be baptized, keeping thy faith unwavering and pure of all heresy until thy latest breath. But all teaching and every speech of doctrine contrary to this blameless faith abhor, and consider it an alienation from God. For, as saith the Apostle, "Though we, or an angel from heaven, preach any other gospel unto you than that which we have preached unto you, let him be accursed." For there is none other Gospel or none other Faith than that which hath been preached by the Apostles, and established by the inspired Fathers at divers Councils, and delivered to the Catholick Church.'

Ioasaph is baptized

When Barlaam had thus spoken, and taught the king's son the Creed which was set forth at the Council of Nicæa, he baptized him in the name of the Father, and of the Son, and of the Holy Ghost, in the pool of water which was in his garden. And there came upon him the grace of the Holy Spirit. Then did Barlaam come back to his chamber, and offer the holy Mysteries of the unbloody Sacrifice, and communicate him with the undefiled Mysteries of Christ: and Ioasaph rejoiced in spirit, giving thanks to Christ his God.

Barlaam giveth thanks to God, and biddeth Ioasaph walk

Then said Barlaam unto him, 'Blessed be the God and Father of our Lord Jesus Christ, which according to his abundant mercy hath begotten thee again unto a lively hope, to an inheritance incorruptible and undefiled, that fadeth not away,

οὐρανοῖς, ἐν Χριστῷ Ἰησοῦ τῷ Κυρίῳ ἡμῶν διὰ
Rom. vi. 22 Πνεύματος ἁγίου. σήμερον γὰρ ἐλευθερωθεὶς ἀπὸ
τῆς ἁμαρτίας ἐδουλώθης τῷ Θεῷ, τὸν ἀρραβῶνα
Rom. xiii. 12 δεξάμενος τῆς αἰωνίου ζωῆς, καί, τὸ σκότος ἀπο-
Rom. viii. 21 λιπών, φῶς ἐνεδύσω, καταταγεὶς εἰς τὴν ἐλευθε-
John i. 12 ρίαν τῆς δόξης τῶν τέκνων τοῦ Θεοῦ· Ὅσοι γάρ,
φησίν, ἔλαβον αὐτόν, ἔδωκεν αὐτοῖς ἐξουσίαν
τέκνα Θεοῦ γενέσθαι, τοῖς πιστεύουσιν εἰς τὸ
Gal. iv. 7 ὄνομα αὐτοῦ· ὥστε οὐκέτι εἶ δοῦλος, ἀλλ' υἱὸς
καὶ κληρονόμος Θεοῦ διὰ Ἰησοῦ Χριστοῦ ἐν
2 Pet. iii. 14 Πνεύματι Ἁγίῳ. διό, ἀγαπητέ, σπούδασον ἄσπι-
λος καὶ ἀμώμητος αὐτῷ εὑρεθῆναι, ἐργαζόμενος
Jas. ii. 26 τὸ ἀγαθὸν ἐπὶ τῷ θεμελίῳ τῆς πίστεως· πίστις
Greg. Naz. Orat. xl. γὰρ χωρὶς ἔργων νεκρά ἐστιν, ὥσπερ καὶ ἔργα
p.146, *supra* δίχα πίστεως, καθὼς καὶ πρότερον μέμνημαι
1 Pet. ii. 1, 2 λαλήσας σοι. ἀποθέμενος οὖν λοιπὸν πᾶσαν 169
κακίαν, καὶ πάντα τὰ ἔργα τοῦ παλαιοῦ ἀν-
θρώπου μισήσας τὰ φθειρόμενα κατὰ τὰς ἐπιθυμίας τῆς ἀπάτης, ὡς ἀρτιγέννητον βρέφος τὸ
λογικὸν καὶ ἄδολον γάλα τῶν ἀρετῶν ἐπιπόθησον
πιεῖν, ἵνα ἐν αὐτῷ αὐξηθῇς, καὶ φθάσῃς εἰς τὴν
ἐπίγνωσιν τῶν ἐντολῶν τοῦ Υἱοῦ τοῦ Θεοῦ, εἰς
Eph. iv. 13, 14 ἄνδρα τέλειον, εἰς μέτρον ἡλικίας τοῦ πληρώματος τοῦ Χριστοῦ, μηκέτι νήπιος ὢν ταῖς φρεσί,
κλυδωνιζόμενος καὶ περιφερόμενος τῇ ζάλῃ καὶ
1 Cor. xiv. 20 τρικυμίᾳ τῶν παθῶν, ἀλλὰ τῇ μὲν κακίᾳ
νηπιάζων, πρὸς δὲ τὸ ἀγαθὸν στερέμνιον καὶ
Eph. iv. 1 πεπαγιωμένον ἔχων τὸν νοῦν, καὶ ἀξίως περι-
πατῶν τῆς κλήσεως ἧς ἐκλήθης ἐν φυλακῇ
τῶν ἐντολῶν τοῦ Κυρίου, ἀποσεισάμενος ἑαυτοῦ
καὶ ἀλλοτριώσας τὴν ματαιότητα τῆς προ-
Eph. iv. 17, 18 τέρας ἀναστροφῆς, καθὼς τὰ ἔθνη περιπατεῖ

reserved in heaven in Christ Jesus our Lord by the Holy Ghost; for to-day thou hast been made free from sin, and hast become the servant of God, and hast received the earnest of everlasting life: thou hast left darkness and put on light, being enrolled in the glorious liberty of the children of God. For he saith, "As many as received him, to them gave he power to become the sons of God, even to them that believe on his name." Wherefore thou art no more a servant, but a son and an heir of God through Jesus Christ in the Holy Ghost. Wherefore, beloved, give diligence that thou mayest be found of him without spot and blameless, working that which is good upon the foundation of faith: for faith without works is dead, as also are works without faith; even as I remember to have told thee afore. Put off therefore now all malice, and hate all the works of the old man, which are corrupt according to the deceitful lusts; and, as new-born babe, desire to drink the reasonable and sincere milk of the virtues, that thou mayest grow thereby, and attain unto the knowledge of the commandments of the Son of God, unto a perfect man, unto the measure of the stature of the fulness of Christ: that thou mayest henceforth be no more a child in mind, tossed to and fro, and carried about on the wild and raging waves of thy passions: or rather in malice be a child, but have thy mind settled and made steadfast toward that which is good, and walk worthy of the vocation wherewith thou wast called, in the keeping of the commandments of the Lord, casting off and putting far from thee the vanity of thy former conversation, henceforth walking not as the Gentiles

worthy of his calling,

ἐν τῇ ματαιότητι τοῦ νοὸς αὐτῶν, ἐσκοτισμένοι
τῇ διανοίᾳ καὶ ἀπηλλοτριωμένοι τῆς δόξης τοῦ
Θεοῦ, ὑποτεταγμένοι ταῖς ἐπιθυμίαις αὐτῶν καὶ
ἀλόγοις ὁρμαῖς. σὺ δέ, ὥσπερ προσῆλθες Θεῷ
Eph. v. 9 ζῶντι καὶ ἀληθινῷ, οὕτω δὴ καὶ ὡς υἱὸς φωτὸς 170
Gal. v. 22 περιπάτησον. ὁ γὰρ καρπὸς τοῦ Πνεύματος ἐν
πάσῃ ἀγαθοσύνῃ, καὶ δικαιοσύνῃ, καὶ ἀληθείᾳ,
καὶ τὸν ἐνδυθέντα σοι σήμερον νέον ἄνθρωπον
μηκέτι τῇ προτέρᾳ καταφθείρῃς παλαιότητι·
ἀλλ' ἀνακαινίζου καθ' ἑκάστην ἐν δικαιοσύνῃ,
καὶ ὁσιότητι, καὶ ἀληθείᾳ· δυνατὸν γὰρ τοῦτο
p. 284 παντὶ τῷ βουλομένῳ, καθάπερ ἀκούεις ὅτι ἐξουσίαν δέδωκε τέκνα Θεοῦ γενέσθαι τοῖς πιστεύουσιν
εἰς τὸ ὄνομα αὐτοῦ, ὥστε οὐκέτι δυνάμεθα λέγειν
ὅτι ἀδύνατος ἡμῖν ἡ κτῆσις τῶν ἀρετῶν· εὔκολος
Mat. vii. 14 γὰρ ἡ ὁδὸς καὶ ῥᾳδία. εἰ γὰρ καὶ στενή πως καὶ
Cp. 1 Cor. ix. 27 τεθλιμμένη κέκληται διὰ τὸν ὑπωπιασμὸν τοῦ
σώματος, ἀλλ' ὅμως ποθεινή ἐστι καὶ θεία διὰ
Eph. v. 15 τὴν ἐλπίδα τῶν μελλόντων ἀγαθῶν τοῖς μὴ ἀσό-
Eph. v. 17 φως περιπατοῦσιν, ἀλλ' ἀκριβῶς συνιοῦσι τί τὸ
Eph. vi. 11 θέλημα τοῦ Θεοῦ, καὶ τὴν πανοπλίαν αὐτοῦ ἀμπ-
εχομένοις εἰς παράταξιν τῶν μεθοδειῶν τοῦ ἀντικειμένου, καὶ ἐν προσευχῇ καὶ δεήσει εἰς αὐτὸ
Eph. vi. 18 τοῦτο ἀγρυπνοῦσιν ἐν πάσῃ ὑπομονῇ καὶ ἐλπίδι.
σὺ οὖν, καθὼς ἤκουσας παρ' ἐμοῦ καὶ ἐδιδάχθης,
καὶ βεβαίαν κατεβάλου κρηπῖδα, ἐν αὐτῇ περισ-
σεύου, αὐξανόμενος καὶ προκόπτων, καὶ τὴν
1 Tim. i. 18, 19 καλὴν στρατευόμενος στρατείαν, ἔχων πίστιν καὶ
ἀγαθὴν συνείδησιν δι' ἔργων ἀγαθῶν μαρτυρου- 171
1 Tim. vi. 11 μένην, καὶ διώκων δικαιοσύνην, εὐσέβειαν, πίστιν,
ἀγάπην, ὑπομονήν, πραότητα, ἐπιλαβόμενος τῆς
αἰωνίου ζωῆς εἰς ἣν ἐκλήθης. πᾶσαν δὲ ἡδονὴν

walk in the vanity of their mind, having their understanding darkened, alienated from the glory of God, in subjection to their lusts and unreasonable affections. But as for thee, even as thou hast approached the living and true God, so walk thou as a child of light; for the fruit of the Spirit is in all goodness and righteousness and truth; and no longer destroy by the works of the old man the new man, which thou hast to-day put on. But day by day renew thyself in righteousness and holiness and truth: for this is possible with every man that willeth, as thou hearest that unto them that believe on his name he hath given power to become the sons of God; so that we can no longer say that the acquiring of virtues is impossible for us, for the road is plain and easy. For, though with respect to the buffeting of the body, it hath been called a strait and narrow way, yet through the hope of future blessings is it desirable and divine for such as walk, not as fools but circumspectly, understanding what the will of God is, clad in the whole armour of God to stand in battle against the wiles of the adversary, and with all prayer and supplication watching thereunto, in all patience and hope. Therefore, even as thou hast heard from me, and been instructed, and hast laid a sure foundation, do thou abound therein, increasing and advancing, and warring the good warfare, holding faith and a good conscience, witnessed by good works, following after righteousness, godliness, faith, charity, patience, meekness, laying hold on eternal life whereunto thou wast called. But remove far

and to present his soul spotless before God;

καὶ ἐπιθυμίαν τῶν παθῶν μὴ μόνον τῇ κατὰ πρᾶξιν ἐνεργείᾳ μακρύνῃς ἀπὸ σοῦ, ἀλλὰ καὶ ταῖς κατ' ἔννοιαν ἐνθυμήσεσιν, ὡς ἂν ἀμόλυντόν σου τὴν ψυχὴν τῷ Θεῷ ὑποδείξῃς. οὐ μόνον γὰρ αἱ πράξεις, ἀλλὰ καὶ αἱ ἐνθυμήσεις ἡμῶν, ἀνάγραπτοι οὖσαι, στεφάνων ἢ τιμωριῶν πρόξενοι γίνονται· ταῖς καθαραῖς δὲ καρδίαις ἐνοικεῖν τὸν Χριστὸν ἅμα Πατρὶ καὶ Ἁγίῳ Πνεύματι ἐπιστάμεθα. ὡς δ' αὖ πάλιν καπνὸς μελίσσας, οὕτω τοὺς πονηροὺς λογισμοὺς ἐκδιώκειν ἡμῶν τὴν τοῦ θείου Πνεύματος χάριν μεμαθήκαμεν. διὸ ἐπιμελῶς πρὸς τοῦτο ἔχων πάντα διαλογισμὸν ἐμπαθείας ἀπαλείψας τῆς ψυχῆς, τὰς ἀρίστας ἐμφύτευσον ἐννοίας, ναὸν σεαυτὸν ποιῶν τοῦ Ἁγίου Πνεύματος. ἐκ τῶν διαλογισμῶν γὰρ καὶ πρὸς τὰς κατ' ἐνέργειαν πράξεις ἐρχόμεθα· καὶ πᾶν ἔργον, ἀπὸ ἐννοίας καὶ ἐνθυμήσεως προκόπτον, μικρᾶς ἐπιλαμβάνεται ἀρχῆς, εἶτα ταῖς κατὰ μικρὸν αὐξήσεσιν εἰς μεγάλα καταλήγει.

Διὰ τοῦτο μηδὲ ὅλως σου κυριεῦσαι συνήθειαν ἐάσῃς κακήν, ἀλλὰ νεαρᾶς ἔτι οὔσης, ἔξελέ σου τῆς καρδίας τὴν πονηρὰν ῥίζαν, ἵνα μή, ἐμφυεῖσα καὶ ἐν τῷ βάθει τὰς ῥίζας ἐμπήξασα, χρόνου καὶ κόπου δεηθῇ τοῦ ἐκριζωθῆναι. διὰ τοῦτο γὰρ ἀεὶ τὰ μείζονα τῶν ἁμαρτημάτων ἐπεισέρχεται ἡμῖν καὶ καταδυναστεύει τῶν ἡμετέρων ψυχῶν, ὅτι τὰ ἐλάττονα δοκοῦντα εἶναι, οἷον ἐνθυμήσεις πονηραί, 172
Menander; (1 Cor. xv. 33) λόγοι ἀπρεπεῖς, ὁμιλίαι κακαί, τῆς προσηκούσης οὐ τυγχάνει διορθώσεως. ὥσπερ γὰρ ἐν τοῖς σώμασιν οἱ μικρῶν καταφρονήσαντες τραυμάτων σηπεδόνας πολλάκις καὶ θάνατον ἑαυτοῖς προεξέ-

from thee all pleasure and lust of the affections, not only in act and operation, but even in the thoughts of thine heart, that thou mayest present thy soul without blemish to God. For not our actions only, but our thoughts also are recorded, and procure us crowns or punishments: and we know that Christ, with the Father and the Holy Ghost, dwelleth in pure hearts. But, just as smoke driveth away bees, so, we learn, do evil imaginations drive out of us the Holy Spirit's grace. Wherefore take good heed hereto, that thou blot out every imagination of sinful passion from thy soul, and plant good thoughts therein, making thyself a temple of the Holy Ghost. For from imaginations we come also to actual deeds, and every work, advancing from thought and reflection, catcheth at small beginnings, and then, by small increases, arriveth at great endings.

'Wherefore on no account suffer any evil habit to master thee; but, while it is yet young, pluck the evil root out of thine heart, lest it fasten on and strike root so deep that time and labour be required to uproot it. And the reason that greater sins assault us and get the mastery of our souls is that those which appear to be less, such as wicked thoughts, unseemly words and evil communications, fail to receive proper correction. For as in the case of the body, they that neglect small wounds often bring mortification and death upon themselves, so too with the

and he warneth him to beware the beginnings of evil,

νησαν, οὕτω καὶ τῶν ψυχῶν, οἱ τῶν μικρῶν
ὑπερορῶντες παθῶν καὶ ἁμαρτημάτων, τὰ μείζονα
ἐπεισάγουσι· καθ' ὅσον δὲ τὰ μείζονα ἐπεισέρχεται αὐτοῖς, ἐν ἕξει γινομένη ἡ ψυχὴ κατα-
Prov. xviii. φρονεῖ. Ἀσεβὴς γάρ, φησίν, ἐλθὼν εἰς βάθος
3 Prov. xxvi. κακῶν καταφρονεῖ, καὶ λοιπὸν ὥσπερ ὗς ἐγκυλιν-
11 δούμενος βορβόρῳ ἥδεται, οὕτω καὶ ἡ ψυχὴ
2 Pet. ii. 22 ἐκείνη, ταῖς κακαῖς συνηθείαις καταχωσθεῖσα,
οὐδὲ αἴσθησιν λαμβάνει τῆς τῶν ἁμαρτημάτων
δυσωδίας, ἀλλὰ τέρπεται μᾶλλον αὐταῖς καὶ
ἐνηδύνεται, ὡς ἀγαθοῦ τινος τῆς κακίας ἀντεχο-
μένη· κἂν ὀψὲ δή ποτε ἀνανεύουσα εἰς αἴσθησιν
ἔλθῃ, κόπῳ πολλῷ καὶ ἱδρῶτι ἐλευθεροῦται, οἷς
ἐθελοντὶ κατεδούλευσεν ἑαυτὴν τῇ πονηρᾷ συν-
ηθείᾳ.

Διὰ τοῦτο πάσῃ δυνάμει μάκρυνον ἑαυτὸν ἀπὸ πάσης ἐννοίας καὶ ἐνθυμήσεως πονηρᾶς καὶ πάσης ἐμπαθοῦς συνηθείας· μᾶλλον δὲ ταῖς ἀρεταῖς ἔθιζε ἑαυτὸν καὶ ἐν ἕξει τῆς τούτων γενοῦ ἐργασίας. εἰ γὰρ μικρὸν κοπιάσεις ἐν αὐτοῖς καὶ ἐν ἕξει γενέσθαι ἰσχύσεις, ἀκόπως λοιπὸν τῇ τοῦ Θεοῦ συνεργείᾳ προκόψεις. ἡ γὰρ ἕξις τῆς ἀρετῆς τῇ ψυχῇ ποιωθεῖσα, ὡς ἅτε φυσικὴν συγγένειαν πρὸς αὐτὴν ἔχουσα καὶ τὸν Θεὸν
συνεργὸν κεκτημένη, δυσμετάβλητος γίνεται καὶ 173
λίαν ἀσφαλεστάτη, καθὼς ὁρᾷς ὅτι ἡ ἀνδρεία καὶ φρόνησις, σωφροσύνη τε καὶ δικαιοσύνη δυσμετάβληταί εἰσιν, ἕξεις οὖσαι τῆς ψυχῆς καὶ ποιότητες καὶ ἐνέργειαι διὰ βάθους κεχωρηκυῖαι. εἰ γὰρ τὰ πάθη τῆς κακίας, οὐ φυσικὰ ἡμῖν ὄντα, ἀλλ' ἔξωθεν ἐπεισελθόντα, ἡνίκα ἐν ἕξει γένωνται, δυσμετάβλητά εἰσι, πόσῳ μᾶλλον ἡ ἀρετή, καὶ

soul: thus they that overlook little passions and sins bring on greater ones. And the more those greater sins grow on them, the more doth the soul become accustomed thereto and think light of them. For he saith, "When the wicked cometh to the depth of evil things, he thinketh light of them": and finally, like the hog, that delighteth to wallow in mire, the soul, that hath been buried in evil habits, doth not even perceive the stink of her sin, but rather delighteth and rejoiceth therein, cleaving to wickedness as it were good. And even if at last she issue from the mire and come to herself again, she is delivered only by much labour and sweat from the bondage of those sins, to which she hath by evil custom enslaved herself.

and to form the habit of virtue

'Wherefore with all thy might remove thyself far from every evil thought and fancy, and every sinful custom; and school thyself the rather in virtuous deeds, and form the habit of practising them. For if thou labour but a little therein, and have strength to form the habit, at the last, God helping thee, thou shalt advance without labour. For the habit of virtue, taking its quality from the soul, seeing that it hath some natural kinship therewith and claimeth God for an help-mate, becometh hard to alter and exceeding strong; as thou seest, courage and prudence, temperance and righteousness are hard to alter, being deeply seated habits, qualities and activities of the soul. For if the evil affections, not being natural to us, but attacking us from without, be hard to alter when they become habits, how much harder shall it be to shift virtue, which hath been by

φυσικῶς ἡμῖν ἐμφυτευθεῖσα ὑπὸ τοῦ Δημιουργοῦ καὶ αὐτὸν ἐπίκουρον ἔχουσα, εἰ, μικρὸν ἀγωνισαμένων ἡμῶν, ἐν ἕξει ῥιζωθῇ τῇ ψυχῇ, δυσμετάβλητος ἔσται;

XX

Ὅθεν μοι ταύτης ἐργάτης διηγήσατό τις, ὅτι
Μετὰ τὸ προσλαβέσθαι με τὴν θείαν θεωρίαν ἐν
ἕξει βεβαιοτάτῃ καὶ τῇ ταύτης μελέτῃ ποιωθῆναι
τὴν ψυχήν, βουληθείς ποτε ἀπόπειραν αὐτῆς ποιήσασθαι,
κατέσχον τὸν νοῦν μου, μὴ συγχωρήσας
τῇ κατ᾽ ἔθος ἐπιβαλεῖν μελέτῃ· καὶ ἔγνων αὐτὸν
ἀνιώμενον καὶ δυσφοροῦντα καὶ πρὸς αὐτὴν ἀσχέτῳ
ἐπειγόμενον πόθῳ, μηδόλως δὲ πρὸς ἐναντίαν
τινὰ ἐνθύμησιν ἀποκλῖναι ἰσχύοντα· ἡνίκα δὲ
μικρὸν ἐνέδωκα τὰς ἡνίας, ὀξυδρόμως εὐθὺς ἀνέδραμε
πρὸς τὴν ἑαυτοῦ ἐργασίαν, καθά φησιν ὁ
Ps. xlii. 1 Προφήτης· Ὃν τρόπον ἐπιποθεῖ ἡ ἔλαφος ἐπὶ τὰς
πηγὰς τῶν ὑδάτων, οὕτως ἐπιποθεῖ ἡ ψυχή μου
πρὸς τὸν Θεόν, τὸν ἰσχυρόν, τὸν ζῶντα. ἀποδέδεικται
οὖν ἐκ πάντων τούτων, ὡς ἐφ᾽ ἡμῖν
ἐστιν ἡ κτῆσις τῆς ἀρετῆς, καὶ ἡμεῖς ταύτης
κύριοι καθεστήκαμεν εἴτε θελήσομεν αὐτῆς
ἀνθέξεσθαι, εἴτε τὴν ἁμαρτίαν προκρῖναι. οἱ
μὲν οὖν δουλωθέντες τῇ κακίᾳ δυσαποσπάστως 174
αὐτῆς ἔχουσι, καθὰ δὴ προλαβὼν εἶπον.

Luke i. 78 Σὺ δὲ λοιπὸν ἐλευθερωθεὶς ταύτης διὰ σπλάγχνα ἐλέους Θεοῦ ἡμῶν, καὶ τὸν Χριστὸν ἐνδεδυμένος τῇ τοῦ θείου Πνεύματος χάριτι, ὅλον σεαυτὸν μετάθες ἐπὶ τὸν Κύριον, καὶ μηδόλως

nature planted in us by our Maker, and hath him for an help-mate, if so be, through our brief endeavour, it shall have been rooted in habit in the soul?'

XX

Barlaam telleth of the case of one that had made a practice of virtue

'WHEREFORE a practician of virtue once spake to me on this wise: "After I had made divine meditation my constant habit, and through the practice of it my soul had received her right quality, I once resolved to make trial of her, and put a check upon her, not allowing her to devote herself to her wonted exercises. I felt that she was chafing and fretting, and yearning for meditation with an ungovernable desire, and was utterly unable to incline to any contrary thought. No sooner had I given her the reins than immediately she ran in hot haste to her own task, as saith the Prophet, 'Like as the hart desireth the water brooks, so longeth my soul after the strong, the living God.'" Wherefore from all these proofs it is evident that the acquirement of virtue is within our reach, and that we are lords over it, whether we will embrace or else the rather choose sin. They then, that are in the thraldom of wickedness, can hardly be torn away therefrom, as I have already said.

He biddeth Ioasaph hold converse with his God in prayer,

'But thou, who hast been delivered therefrom, through the tender mercy of our God, and hast put on Christ by the grace of the Holy Ghost, now transfer thyself wholly to the Lord's side, and never open a

Cp. Acts xiv. 27

ἔτι τοῖς πάθεσι θύραν ἀνοίξῃς· ἀλλὰ τῇ εὐωδίᾳ καὶ λαμπρότητι τῶν ἀρετῶν κοσμήσας σου τὴν ψυχήν, ναὸν αὐτὴν ποίησον τῆς ἁγίας Τριάδος, τῇ ταύτης θεωρίᾳ πάσας σου τὰς τοῦ νοὸς δυνάμεις ἀπασχολήσας. εἰ γὰρ βασιλεῖ τις ἐπιγείῳ συνδιάγων καὶ διαλεγόμενος μακαριστὸς πᾶσι δείκνυται, ὁ Θεῷ διαλέγεσθαι καὶ συνεῖναι τῷ νοῒ καταξιωθεὶς πόσης ἀπολαύσεται μακαριότητος; αὐτὸν οὖν ἐνοπτρίζου πάντοτε, καὶ αὐτῷ προσομίλει. πῶς δὲ προσομιλήσεις Θεῷ; τῇ διὰ προσευχῆς καὶ δεήσεως πρὸς αὐτὸν ἐγγύτητι. ὁ γὰρ πόθῳ θερμοτάτῳ καὶ καρδίᾳ κεκαθαρμένῃ προσευχόμενος, πάντων μὲν τῶν ὑλικῶν καὶ χαμαιζήλων μακρύνας τὸν νοῦν, ὡς ἐνώπιος δὲ ἐνωπίῳ παριστάμενος τῷ Θεῷ, φόβῳ τε καὶ τρόμῳ τὰς δεήσεις αὐτῷ προσάγων, ὁ τοιοῦτος ὁμιλεῖ αὐτῷ καὶ πρόσωπον πρὸς πρόσωπον αὐτῷ διαλέγεται.

Πάρεστι γὰρ πανταχοῦ ὁ ἀγαθὸς ἡμῶν Δεσπότης ἐπακούων τῶν εἰλικρινῶς καὶ καθαρῶς προσερχομένων αὐτῷ, καθάπερ φησὶν ὁ Προφήτης·

Ps. xxxiv. 5

Ὀφθαλμοὶ Κυρίου ἐπὶ δικαίους, καὶ ὦτα αὐτοῦ εἰς δέησιν αὐτῶν. καὶ διὰ τοῦτο οἱ Πατέρες τὴν προσευχὴν ἕνωσιν ἀνθρώπου πρὸς Θεὸν ὁρίζονται, καὶ ἔργον ἀγγέλων ταύτην καλοῦσι, καὶ τῆς μελλούσης εὐφροσύνης προοίμιον.

John Clim. Scala, gradus 28; John Chrys. Orat. 1 & 2, de Orat.

ἐπεὶ γὰρ βασιλείαν οὐρανῶν τὴν ἐγγύτητα καὶ θεωρίαν τῆς Ἁγίας Τριάδος πλέον πάντων τίθενται, πρὸς τοῦτο δὲ καὶ ἡ τῆς εὐχῆς προσεδρεία τὸν νοῦν χειραγωγεῖ, εἰκότως προοίμιον καὶ οἱονεὶ προεικόνισμα ἐκείνης τῆς μακαριότητος κέκληται αὕτη. οὐ πᾶσα δὲ εὐχὴ οὑτωσὶ καθέστηκεν, ἀλλ' ἡ

door to thy passions, but adorn thy soul with the sweet savour and splendour of virtue, and make her a temple of the Holy Trinity, and to his contemplation see thou devote all the powers of thy mind. He that liveth and converseth with an earthly king is pointed out by all as a right happy man: what happiness then must be his who is privileged to converse and be in spirit with God! Behold thou then his likeness alway, and converse with him. How shalt thou converse with God? By drawing near him in prayer and supplication. He that prayeth with exceeding fervent desire and pure heart, his mind estranged from all that is earthly and grovelling, and standeth before God, eye to eye, and presenteth his prayers to him in fear and trembling, such an one hath converse and speaketh with him face to face.

'Our good Master is present everywhere, hearkening to them that approach him in purity and truth, as saith the Prophet, "The eyes of the Lord are over the righteous, and his ears are open unto their cry." For this reason the Fathers define Prayer as "the union of man with God," and call it "Angels' work," and "the prelude of gladness to come." For since they lay down before all things that "the kingdom of heaven" consisteth in nearness to and contemplation of the Holy Trinity, and since all the importunity of prayer leadeth the mind thither, prayer is rightly called "the prelude" and, as it were, the "fore-glimpse" of that blessedness. But not all prayer is of this nature, but only such prayer as

and expoundeth to him the power of prayer

τῆς προσηγορίας ταύτης ὄντως ἀξία, ἡ Θεὸν
ἔχουσα διδάσκαλον, τὸν διδόντα εὐχὴν τῷ εὐχο-
μένῳ, ἡ πάντων τῶν ἐπὶ γῆς ὑπεραρθεῖσα καὶ τῷ
Δεσπότῃ Θεῷ ἀμέσως ἐντυγχάνουσα.

Ταύτην σεαυτῷ περιποιοῦ, καὶ εἰς ταύτην
ἀγωνίζου τὴν προκοπήν· ἱκανὴ γὰρ ὑπάρχει ἐκ
γῆς εἰς οὐρανοὺς ἀνυψῶσαί σε. οὐκ ἀπαρασκεύως
δὲ καὶ ὡς ἔτυχε προκόψεις ἐν ταύτῃ· ἀλλά, πάντων τῶν παθῶν τὴν ψυχὴν προκαθάρας, καὶ
πάσης πονηρᾶς ἐνθυμήσεως ταύτην ἀποσμήξας
ὡς καθαρὸν καὶ νεόσμηκτον ἔσοπτρον, πάσης τε 176
μνησικακίας καὶ μήνιδος σεαυτὸν μακρύνας, ἥτις
πλέον πάντων τὰς ἡμετέρας εὐχὰς πρὸς Θεὸν
ἀνάγεσθαι κωλύει, πᾶσί τε τοῖς ἡμαρτηκόσι σοι
ἀπὸ καρδίας ἀφεὶς τὰ πλημμελήματα, καὶ ἐν
Schol. on Scala by John Clim. p. 443 ἐλεημοσύναις καὶ οἰκτιρμοῖς πενήτων τὴν εὐχὴν
πτερώσας, προσάγαγε τῷ Θεῷ μετὰ θερμῶν
δακρύων. οὕτως εὐχόμενος δυνήσῃ εἰπεῖν ὡς ὁ
μακάριος Δαυΐδ· οὗτος γὰρ βασιλεὺς ὢν καὶ
μυρίαις ἑλκόμενος φροντίσι, πάντων δὲ τῶν
παθῶν τὴν ψυχὴν αὐτοῦ καθαρίσας, ἔλεγε πρὸς
Ps. cxix. 163 τὸν Θεόν· Ἀδικίαν ἐμίσησα καὶ ἐβδελυξάμην,
τὸν δὲ νόμον σου ἠγάπησα· ἑπτάκις τῆς ἡμέρας
ᾔνεσά σε ἐπὶ τὰ κρίματα τῆς δικαιοσύνης· ἐφύλαξεν ἡ ψυχή μου τὰ μαρτύριά σου καὶ ἠγά-
πησεν αὐτὰ σφόδρα· ἐγγισάτω ἡ δέησίς μου
ἐνώπιόν σου, Κύριε· κατὰ τὸ λόγιόν σου συνέ-
τισόν με.

Is. lviii. 8, 9 Οὕτως βοῶντός σου ὁ Θεὸς ἐπακούσεται· ἔτι
λαλοῦντός σου, ἐρεῖ· Ἰδοὺ πάρειμι. εἰ τοιαύτην
οὖν κτήσῃ εὐχήν, μακάριος ἔσῃ· ἀμήχανον γὰρ
ἄνθρωπον, μετὰ τοιαύτης προθυμίας εὐχόμενον 177

is worthy of the name, which hath God for its teacher, who giveth prayer to him that prayeth; prayer which soareth above all things on earth and entreateth directly with God.

'This acquire thou for thyself, and strive to advance thereto, for it is able to exalt thee from earth to heaven. But without preparation and at hap-hazard thou shalt not advance therein. But first purify thy soul from all passion, and cleanse it like a bright and newly cleansed mirrour from every evil thought, and banish far all remembrance of injury and anger, which most of all hindereth our prayers from ascending to God-ward: and from the heart forgive all those that have trespassed against thee, and with alms and charities to the poor lend wings to thy prayer, and so bring it before God with fervent tears. Thus praying thou shalt be able to say with blessed David, who, for all that he was king, and distraught with ten thousand cares, yet cleansed his soul from all passions, and could say unto God, "As for iniquity, I hate and abhor it, but thy law do I love. Seven times a day do I praise thee, because of thy righteous judgements. My soul hath kept thy testimonies, and loved them exceedingly. Let my complaint come before thee, O Lord: give me understanding according to thy word."

as shown in the psalm of blessed David,

'While thou art calling thus, the Lord shall hear thee: while thou art yet speaking, he shall say, "Behold I am here." If then thou attain to such prayer, blessed shalt thou be; for it is impossible for a man praying and calling upon

prayer, which raiseth men to heaven

καὶ παρακαλοῦντα τὸν Θεόν, μὴ καθ' ἑκάστην προκόπτειν ἐν τῷ ἀγαθῷ καὶ πασῶν ὑπερίπτασθαι τῶν τοῦ ἐχθροῦ παγίδων. ὁ γὰρ διαθερμάνας
which of them? αὐτοῦ τὴν διάνοιαν, καθάπερ τις τῶν ἁγίων ἔφησε,
Καὶ τὴν ψυχὴν ἀναστήσας, καὶ πρὸς τὸν οὐρανὸν ἑαυτὸν μετοικίσας, καὶ οὕτω τὸν Δεσπότην τὸν ἑαυτοῦ καλέσας, καὶ τῶν ἰδίων ἁμαρτημάτων ἀναμνησθείς, καὶ περὶ τῆς συγχωρήσεως τούτων διαλεχθείς, καὶ δάκρυσι θερμοτάτοις δεηθεὶς ἵλεω γενέσθαι αὐτῷ τὸν φιλάνθρωπον, ἀπὸ τῆς ἐν τοῖς λόγοις καὶ διαλογισμοῖς τούτοις διατριβῆς πᾶσαν ἀποτίθεται βιωτικὴν φροντίδα καὶ τῶν ἀνθρωπίνων παθῶν ὑψηλότερος γίνεται, καὶ Θεῷ συνόμιλος ἀξιοῦται κληθῆναι· οὗπερ τί γένοιτ' ἂν μακαριώτερον ἢ ὑψηλότερον; ἀξιώσαι σε οὖν Κύριος τῆς τοιαύτης ἐπιτυχεῖν μακαριότητος.

Ἰδοὺ γάρ σοι τὴν ὁδὸν ὑπέδειξα τῶν ἐντολῶν
Acts xx. 27 τοῦ Κυρίου, καὶ οὐδὲν ὑπεστειλάμην τοῦ μὴ ἀναγγεῖλαί σοι πᾶσαν τὴν βουλὴν τοῦ Θεοῦ. καὶ ἐγὼ μὲν ἤδη τὴν πρός σέ μου διακονίαν τετέλεκα· λοιπὸν αὐτὸς ἀναζωσάμενος τὴν ὀσφὺν τῆς διανοίας σου, κατὰ τὸν καλέσαντά σε ἅγιον,
1 Pet. i. 13 ff. καὶ αὐτὸς ἅγιος ἐν πάσῃ ἀναστροφῇ γενοῦ· Ἅγιοι γὰρ γίνεσθε, διότι ἐγὼ ἅγιός εἰμι, λέγει Κύριος. γράφει δὲ καὶ ὁ κορυφαιότατος τῶν ἀποστόλων· Εἰ Πατέρα, φησίν, ἐπικαλεῖσθε τὸν ἀπροσωπο-
λήπτως κρίνοντα κατὰ τὸ ἑκάστου ἔργον, ἐν φόβῳ 178
τὸν τῆς παροικίας ὑμῶν χρόνον ἀναστράφητε, εἰδότες ὅτι οὐ φθαρτοῖς, ἀργυρίῳ ἢ χρυσίῳ, ἐλυτρώθητε ἐκ τῆς ματαίας ὑμῶν ἀναστροφῆς πατροπαραδότου, ἀλλὰ τιμίῳ αἵματι, ὡς ἀμνοῦ ἀμώμου καὶ ἀσπίλου, Χριστοῦ.

God with such purpose not to advance daily in that which is good, and soar over all the snares of the enemy. For, as saith one of the Saints, "He that hath made fervent his understanding, and hath lift up his soul and migrated to heaven, and hath thus called upon his Master, and remembered his own sins, and spoken concerning the forgiveness of the same, and with hot tears hath besought the Lover of mankind to be merciful to him: such an one, I say, by his continuance in such words and considerations, layeth aside every care of this life, and waxeth superior to human passions, and meriteth to be called an associate of God." Than which state what can be more blessed and higher? May the Lord vouchsafe thee to attain to this blessedness!

Barlaam putteth Ioasaph once more in mind of his redemption,

'Lo I have shown thee the way of the commandments of the Lord, and have not shunned to declare unto thee all the counsel of God. And now I have fulfilled my ministry unto thee. It remaineth that thou gird up the loins of thy mind, obedient to the Holy One that hath called thee, and be thou thyself holy in all manner of conversation: for, "Be ye holy: for I am holy," saith the Lord. And the chief prince of the Apostles also writeth, saying, "If ye call on the Father, who without respect of persons judgeth according to every man's work, pass the time of your sojourning here in fear; knowing that ye were not redeemed with corruptible things, as silver and gold, from your vain conversation received by tradition from your fathers, but with the precious blood of Christ, as of a lamb without blemish and without spot."

Ταῦτα οὖν πάντα ἐν καρδίᾳ τιθέμενος, μέμνησο ἀδιαλείπτως, πρὸ ὀφθαλμῶν ἔχων ἀεὶ τὸν φόβον τοῦ Θεοῦ καὶ τὸ φρικῶδες αὐτοῦ κριτήριον, τὴν φαιδρότητά τε τῶν δικαίων ἣν μέλλουσιν ἐν ἐκείνῳ ἀπολαβεῖν τῷ αἰῶνι, καὶ τὴν κατήφειαν τῶν ἁμαρτωλῶν ἐν τῷ σκότει τῷ βαθυτάτῳ, τὴν ἀσθένειάν τε καὶ ματαιότητα τῶν παρόντων καὶ
Is. xi. 6 τὸ τῶν μελλόντων ἀτελεύτητον, ὅτι Πᾶσα σὰρξ χόρτος καὶ πᾶσα δόξα ἀνθρώπου ὡς ἄνθος χόρτου· ἐξηράνθη ὁ χόρτος καὶ τὸ ἄνθος αὐτοῦ ἐξέπεσε, τὸ δὲ ῥῆμα Κυρίου μένει εἰς τὸν αἰῶνα. ταῦτα μελέτα διὰ παντός· καὶ ἡ εἰρήνη τοῦ Θεοῦ εἴη μετὰ σοῦ, φωτίζουσά σε καὶ συνετίζουσα καὶ εἰς τὴν ὁδὸν ἄγουσα τῆς σωτηρίας, καὶ πᾶν θέλημα πονηρὸν πόρρω διώκουσα τοῦ νοός σου, σφραγίζουσα δὲ τὴν ψυχήν σου τῷ τοῦ σταυροῦ σημείῳ, ἵνα μηδέν σοι πλησιάσῃ τῶν τοῦ πονηροῦ σκανδάλων, ἀλλ' ἀξιωθῇς ἐν πάσῃ τελειότητι τῶν ἀρετῶν τῆς μελλούσης ἐπιτυχεῖν ἀτελευτήτου καὶ ἀδιαδόχου βασιλείας, καὶ τῷ φωτὶ περιλαμφθῆναι τῆς μακαρίας καὶ ζωαρχικῆς Τριάδος, τῆς ἐν Πατρὶ καὶ Υἱῷ καὶ ἁγίῳ Πνεύματι δοξαζομένης.

XXI

Τοιούτοις οὖν ἠθικοῖς ῥήμασι νουθετήσας ὁ τιμιώτατος γέρων τὸν τοῦ βασιλέως υἱόν, εἰς τὴν 179
ἰδίαν ἀπῄει ξενίαν. οἱ δὲ ὑπηρέται τοῦ νέου καὶ παιδαγωγοὶ τὴν συχνὴν αὐτοῦ εἰσέλευσιν ἐν τῷ παλατίῳ ὁρῶντες ἐθαύμαζον. εἷς δὲ τῶν προεχόντων ἐν αὐτοῖς, ὃν ὡς πιστότατον καὶ εὐγνώ-

'All these things therefore store thou up in thine heart, and remember them unceasingly, ever keeping before thine eyes the fear of God, and his terrible judgement seat, and the splendour of the righteous which they shall receive in the world to come, and the shame of sinners in the depths of darkness, and the frailty and vanity of things present, and the eternity of things hereafter; for, "All flesh is grass, and all the glory of man as the flower of grass. The grass withereth, and the flower thereof falleth away: but the word of the Lord endureth for ever." Meditate upon these things alway and the peace of God be with thee, enlightening and informing thee, and leading thee into the way of salvation, chasing afar out of thy mind every evil wish, and sealing thy soul with the sign of the Cross, that no stumbling block of the evil one come nigh thee, but that thou mayest merit, in all fulness of virtue, to obtain the kingdom that is to come, without end or successor, and be illumined with the light of the blessed life-giving Trinity, which, in the Father, and in the Son, and in the Holy Ghost, is glorified.'

of the vanity of life, and of judgement to come

XXI

With such moral words did the reverend elder exhort the king's son, and then withdrew to his own hospice. But the young prince's servants and tutors marvelled to see the frequency of Barlaam's visits to the palace; and one of the chiefest among them,

Zardan, a tutor of Ioasaph, is troubled about Barlaam's visits

μονα κατέστησεν ὁ βασιλεὺς ἐπὶ τοῦ παλατιου τοῦ υἱοῦ αὐτοῦ, Ζαρδὰν καλούμενος, φησὶ πρὸς τὸν τοῦ βασιλέως υἱόν· Οἶδας πάντως, ὦ δέσποτα, ὅσος ἐπ' ἐμοὶ ὁ τοῦ σοῦ πατρὸς φόβος καὶ ὅση μου ἡ πρὸς αὐτὸν πίστις· διό με ὡς οἰκέτην πιστότατον καθυπηρετεῖν σοι παρεκελεύσατο. νυνὶ δὲ τὸν ἄνδρα τοῦτον τὸν ξένον συχνῶς ὁρῶν ὁμιλοῦντά σοι, δέδοικα μή ποτε τῆς τῶν Χριστιανῶν εἴη θρησκείας, πρὸς ἣν λίαν ἀπεχθῶς ὁ σὸς πατὴρ διάκειται· καὶ τῆς θανατηφόρου εὑρεθήσομαι ὑπεύθυνος ψήφου. εἴτε οὖν τῷ βασιλεῖ τὰ περὶ αὐτοῦ γνώρισον, εἴτε τοῦ λοιποῦ παῦσαι τούτῳ προσομιλεῖν· εἰ δὲ μή, ἔκβαλόν με τοῦ σοῦ προσώπου, ὡς ἂν μὴ μεμπτέος ὦ, καὶ ἄλλον αἴτησαι τὸν πατέρα σου ἀγαγεῖν ἐνταῦθα.

Ὁ δὲ τοῦ βασιλέως υἱὸς ἔφη πρὸς αὐτόν· Τοῦτο πρὸ πάντων, ὦ Ζαρδάν, ποίησον. καθέσθητι σὺ ἔνδοθεν τοῦ παραπετάσματος, καὶ ἄκουσον τῆς αὐτοῦ πρός με ὁμιλίας· καὶ εἶθ' οὕτως λαλήσω σοι τί δεῖ ποιῆσαι.

Μέλλοντος δὲ τοῦ Βαρλαὰμ εἰσελθεῖν πρὸς αὐτόν, εἰσήγαγε τὸν Ζαρδὰν ἐντὸς τοῦ παραπετάσματος, καὶ λέγει τῷ γέροντι· Ἀνακεφαλαίωσαί μοι τὰ τῆς ἐνθέου σου διδασκαλίας, ὡς ἂν κραταιότερον ἐμφυτευθῇ μου τῇ καρδίᾳ. ὑπολαβὼν δὲ ὁ Βαρλαὰμ πολλὰ περὶ Θεοῦ καὶ τῆς εἰς αὐτὸν εὐσεβείας ἐφθέγγετο, καὶ ὡς αὐτὸν μόνον δεῖ ἀγαπᾶν ἐξ ὅλης καρδίας, καὶ ἐξ ὅλης ψυχῆς, καὶ ἐξ ὅλης τῆς διανοίας, καὶ τὰς αὐτοῦ φυλάττειν ἐντολὰς φόβῳ τε καὶ πόθῳ. καὶ ὅτι αὐτός ἐστιν ὁ ποιητὴς ὁρατῶν τε πάντων καὶ ἀοράτων. ἐφ' οἷς καὶ τὴν τοῦ πρώτου ἀνθρώπου

whom, for his fidelity and prudence, the king had set over his son's palace, named Zardan, said to the prince, 'Thou knowest well, sir, how much I dread thy father, and how great is my faith toward him: wherefore he ordered me, for my faithfulness, to wait upon thee. Now, when I see this stranger constantly conversing with thee, I fear he may be of the Christian religion, toward which thy father hath a deadly hate; and I shall be found subject to the penalty of death. Either then make known to thy father this man's business, or in future cease to converse with him. Else cast me forth from thy presence, that I be not blameable, and ask thy father to appoint another in my room.'

The king's son said unto him, 'This do, Zardan, first of all. Sit thou down behind the curtain, and hear his communication with me: and then thus will I tell thee what thou oughtest to do.'

Ioasaph admitteth Zardan to overhear Barlaam's discourse

So when Barlaam was about to enter into his presence, Ioasaph hid Zardan within the curtain, and said to the elder, 'Sum me up the matter of thy divine teaching, that it may the more firmly be implanted in my heart.' Barlaam took up his parable and uttered many sayings touching God, and righteousness toward him, and how we must love him alone with all our heart, and with all our soul, and with all our mind, and keep his commandments with fear and love: and how he is the Maker of all things visible and invisible. Thereon he called to remembrance the creation

διάπλασιν ὑπεμίμνησκε, τήν τε δοθεῖσαν αὐτῷ ἐντολὴν καὶ τὴν ταύτης παράβασιν, καὶ τὴν ἐπὶ τῇ παραβάσει τοῦ πλάσαντος καταδίκην. εἶτα καθεξῆς τὰ ἀγαθὰ ἀπηριθμεῖτο, ὧν ἀθετήσαντες τὴν ἐντολὴν ἑαυτοὺς ἀπεκλείσαμεν· καὶ αὖθις ἐμέμνη- 181
το τῶν λυπηρῶν, ὅσα μετὰ τὴν ἐκείνων ἀποτυχίαν κατέλαβεν ἀθλίως ἡμᾶς. ἐπὶ τούτοις τὰ τῆς φιλανθρωπίας ἐπῆγεν, ὅπως τῆς ἡμετέρας φροντίζων ὁ Δημιουργὸς σωτηρίας διδασκάλους ἀπέστειλε καὶ προφήτας τὴν τοῦ Μονογενοῦς κηρύττοντας σάρκωσιν· ἔπειτα καὶ τὴν ἐκείνου κάθοδον, τὴν ἐνανθρώπησιν, τὰς εὐεργεσίας, τὰ θαύματα, καὶ τὰ ὑπὲρ ἡμῶν τῶν ἀχαρίστων παθήματα, τὸν σταυρόν, τὴν λόγχην, τὸν ἑκούσιον θάνατον· τέλος, τὴν ἐπανόρθωσιν ἡμῶν, τὴν ἀνάκλησιν, τὴν εἰς τὸ πρῶτον ἀγαθὸν ἐπάνοδον· μετὰ ταῦτα, τὴν ἐκδεχομένην τοὺς ἀξίους τῶν οὐρανῶν βασιλείαν, τὴν ἀποκειμένην τοῖς φαύλοις βάσανον, τὸ μὴ σβεννύμενον πῦρ, τὸ μὴ λῆγον σκότος, τὸν ἀθάνατον σκώληκα, καὶ ὅσην ἄλλην οἱ τῆς ἁμαρτίας δοῦλοι κόλασιν ἑαυτοῖς ἐθησαύρισαν. ταῦτα διεξελθὼν καὶ εἰς ἠθικὴν διδασκαλίαν τὸν λόγον τελέσας, πολλά τε περὶ καθαρότητος βίου διαλεχθείς, καὶ τῆς τῶν παρόντων ματαιότητος καταγνούς, τὴν ἀθλιότητά τε τῶν τούτοις προστετηκότων διελέγξας, εἰς εὐχὴν κατέληξε. καὶ ἀπερίτρεπτον αὐτῷ ἐπευξάμενος καὶ ἀκλινῆ τὴν ὁμολογίαν τῆς ὀρθοδόξου πίστεως, ἀνεπίληπτόν τε τὸν βίον καὶ καθαρωτάτην τὴν πολιτείαν, ὁ μέν, τέλος ἐπιθεὶς τῇ εὐχῇ, πρὸς τὴν ξενίαν αὖθις ἀπῄει.

of the first man, the command given unto him, and his transgression thereof, and the sentence pronounced by the Creator for this transgression. Then he reckoned up in order the good things wherefrom we excluded ourselves by the disannulling of his commandment. Again he made mention of the many grievous misfortunes that unhappily overtook man, after the loss of the blessings. Besides this he brought forward God's love toward mankind; how our Maker, heedful of our salvation, sent forth teachers and prophets proclaiming the Incarnation of the Only-begotten. Then he spake of the Son, his dwelling among men, his deeds of kindness, his miracles, his sufferings for us thankless creatures, his Cross, his spear, his voluntary death; finally, of our recovery and recall, our return to our first good estate; after this, of the kingdom of heaven awaiting such as are worthy thereof; of the torment in store for the wicked; the fire that is not quenched, the never ending darkness, the undying worm, and all the other tortures which the slaves of sin have laid up in store for themselves. When he had fully related these matters, he ended his speech with moral instruction, and dwelt much upon purity of life, and utterly condemned the vanity of things present, and proved the utter misery of such as cleave thereto, and finally made an end with prayer. And therewith he prayed for the prince, that he might hold fast the profession of the Catholick Faith without turning and without wavering, and keep his life blameless and his conversation pure, and so ending with prayer again withdrew to his hospice.

Barlaam summeth up for the prince the teaching of the Church

Ὁ δὲ τοῦ βασιλέως υἱός, τὸν Ζαρδὰν προσκαλεσάμενος καὶ τὴν αὐτοῦ γυμνάζων διάθεσιν, ἔφη· Ἤκουσας ὁποῖά μοι ὁ σπερμολόγος οὗτος διαλέγεται, ἀπατῆσαί με ταῖς κεναῖς αὐτοῦ πιθανολογίαις πειρώμενος καὶ ἀποστερῆσαι τῆς τερπνῆς ταύτης εὐφροσύνης καὶ ἀπολαύσεως, καὶ ξένῳ λατρεῦσαι
Θεῷ; ὁ δὲ Ζαρδάν· Τί σοι ἔδοξεν, ἔφη, ὦ βασιλεῦ, 182
πειράζειν με τὸν σὸν οἰκέτην; οἶδα κατὰ βάθος εἰσδῦναί σου τῇ καρδίᾳ τοὺς λόγους τοῦ ἀνδρός· εἰ μὴ γὰρ τοῦτο ἦν, οὐκ ἂν αὐτῷ ἡδέως τε καὶ ἀδιαλείπτως ὡμίλεις. καί γε ἡμεῖς οὐκ ἀγνοοῦμεν τουτὶ τὸ κήρυγμα· ἀλλ' ἐξ ὅτου ὁ σὸς πατὴρ διωγμὸν ἄσπονδον κατὰ τῶν Χριστιανῶν ἐξήγειρεν, ἀπηλάθησαν αὐτοὶ τῶν ἐντεῦθεν, καὶ ἐσίγησε τὸ κήρυγμα αὐτῶν. εἰ δὲ νῦν ἀρεστόν σοι τὸ δόγμα κατεφάνη καὶ τὸ σκληρὸν αὐτοῦ καὶ ἐπίπονον ἀναδέξασθαι ἰσχύεις, κατευθυνθείη σου τὰ θελήματα εἰς τὸ ἀγαθόν. ἐγὼ δὲ τί ποιήσω, πρὸς μὲν τὴν τοιαύτην σκληρότητα μηδ' ἀντοφθαλμῆσαι δυνάμενος, τῷ δὲ φόβῳ τοῦ βασιλέως τὴν ψυχὴν ἐν ὀδύναις καὶ ἀλγηδόσι μεριζόμενος; τί ἀπολογήσομαι αὐτῷ, ἀμελῶς τοῖς αὐτοῦ διατεθεὶς προστάγμασι, καὶ τῷ ἀνδρὶ τούτῳ τῆς πρὸς σὲ παραχωρήσας εἰσόδου;

Ἔφη δὲ πρὸς αὐτὸν ὁ τοῦ βασιλέως υἱός· Ἐγὼ μέν, τῆς πολλῆς σου πρός με εὐγνωμοσύνης μηδεμίαν ἄλλην ἀξίαν ἀμοιβὴν γινώσκων, ταύτην καὶ ὑπεραξίαν εὑρηκὼς ἐπ' εὐεργεσίᾳ τῇ σῇ, κατάδηλον ποιῆσαί σοι τὸ ὑπὲρ φύσιν ἀγαθὸν ἔργον πεποίηκα, τοῦ γνωρίσαι σε εἰς ὃ γεγένησαι καὶ τὸν Δημιουργὸν ἐπιγνῶναι ἀπολιπόντα τε τὸ
σκότος τῷ φωτὶ προσδραμεῖν· καὶ ἤλπιζον ἅμα 183

But the king's son called Zardan forth, and, to try his disposition, said unto him, 'Thou hast heard what sort of discourses this babbler maketh me, endeavouring to be-jape me with his specious follies, and rob me of this pleasing happiness and enjoyment, to worship a strange God.' Zardan answered, 'Why hath it pleased thee, O prince, to prove me that am thy servant? I wot that the words of that man have sunk deep into thine heart; for, otherwise, thou hadst not listened gladly and unceasingly to his words. Yea, and we also are not ignorant of this preaching. But from the time when thy father stirred up truceless warfare against the Christians, the men have been banished hence, and their teaching is silenced. But if now their doctrine commend itself unto thee, and if thou have the strength to accept its austerity, may thy wishes be guided straight toward the good! But for myself, what shall I do, that am unable to bear the very sight of such austerity, and through fear of the King am divided in soul with pain and anguish? What excuse shall I make, for neglecting his orders, and giving this fellow access unto thee?'

Ioasaph trieth Zardan, but may not beguile him,

The King's son said unto him, 'I knew full well that in none other wise could I requite thee worthily for thy much kindness: and therefore have I tasked myself to make known unto thee this more than human good, which doth even exceed the worth of thy good service, that thou mightest know to what end thou wast born, and acknowledge thy Creator, and, leaving darkness, run to the light. And I hoped that when thou heardest

and pleadeth with him to say nought to the king

τῷ ἀκοῦσαί σε πόθῳ ἀσχέτῳ τούτῳ ἀκολουθῆσαι. ἀλλ' ἐψεύσθην, καθὼς ὁρῶ, τῆς ἐλπίδος,
χλιαρῶς σε βλέπων πρὸς τὰ λαληθέντα διακείμενον. τῷ δὲ βασιλεῖ καὶ πατρί μου εἰ
ταῦτα δηλώσεις, οὐδὲν ἕτερον ποιήσεις ἢ μερίμναις
αὐτοῦ καὶ λύπαις τὴν ψυχὴν ἀηδίσεις. ἀλλ',
εἴπερ αὐτῷ εὐγνωμονεῖς, μηδόλως ἄχρι καιροῦ τοῦ
προσήκοντος ἀναγγείλῃς τι περὶ τούτων. ταῦτα
Cp. Theogn. 106, 107 μὲν πρὸς αὐτὸν λαλήσας, ἐφ' ὑδάτων ἐδόκει σπεί-
ρειν· εἰς ψυχὴν γὰρ ἀσύνετον οὐκ εἰσελεύσεται
σοφία.

Τῇ ἐπαύριον δὲ ὁ Βαρλαὰμ ἐλθὼν τὰ τῆς ἀπο-
δημίας ὡμίλει· ὁ δέ, τὸν τούτου μὴ φέρων
χωρισμόν, τὴν ψυχὴν ἠνιᾶτο καὶ δακρύων τοὺς
ὀφθαλμοὺς ἐπεπλήρωτο. πολλὰ δὲ ὁ γέρων
αὐτῷ διαλεχθείς, καὶ ἀκλόνητον διαμένειν ἐν τῷ
ἀγαθῷ μαρτυράμενος, λόγοις τε παρακλητικοῖς
στηρίξας αὐτοῦ τὴν καρδίαν, ἱλαρῶς αὐτὸν ἐξ-
αποστεῖλαι ἠξίου· ἅμα δὲ καὶ προέλεγεν οὐκ εἰς
μακρὸν αὐτοὺς ἑνοῦσθαι ἑνώσει ἀδιαιρέτῳ. ὁ δὲ
τοῦ βασιλέως υἱός, μὴ δυνάμενος ἐπὶ πλεῖον
κόπους τῷ γέροντι παρέχειν καὶ τῆς ποθουμένης
αὐτὸν κωλύειν ὁδοῦ, ἅμα δὲ καὶ ὑφορώμενος μὴ 184
δῆλα τὰ περὶ αὐτὸν ὁ Ζαρδὰν ἐκεῖνος τῷ βασιλεῖ
ποιήσηται καὶ τιμωρίαις αὐτὸν ὑποβάλῃ, λέγει
πρὸς αὐτόν· Ἐπείπερ σοι τοῦτο ἔδοξε, πάτερ
πνευματικὲ καὶ διδασκάλων ἄριστε καὶ καλοῦ
παντὸς ἐμοὶ πρόξενε, τοῦ καταλιπεῖν με τῇ τοῦ
κόσμου ματαιότητι συναναστρέφεσθαι καὶ σὲ
πορευθῆναι εἰς τὸν τῆς πνευματικῆς ἀναπαύσεως
τόπον, οὐκ ἔτι σε κατέχειν καὶ παρεμποδίζειν
τολμῶ. ἄπιθι οὖν τῇ τοῦ Θεοῦ εἰρήνῃ φρουρού-

thereof thou wouldst follow it with irresistible desire. But, as I perceive, I am disappointed of my hope, seeing that thou art listless to that which hath been spoken. But if thou reveal these secrets to the king my father, thou shalt but distress his mind with sorrows and griefs. If thou be well disposed to him, on no account reveal this matter to him until a convenient season.' Speaking thus, he seemed to be only casting seed upon the water; for wisdom shall not enter into a soul void of understanding.

Barlaam taketh his leave of Ioasaph,

Upon the morrow came Barlaam and spake of his departure: but Ioasaph, unable to bear the separation, was distressed at heart, and his eyes filled with tears. The elder made a long discourse, and adjured him to continue unshaken in good works, and with words of exhortation established his heart, and begged him to send him cheerfully on his way; and at the same time he foretold that they should shortly be at one, never to be parted more. But Ioasaph, unable to impose fresh labours on the elder, and to restrain his desire to be on his way, and suspecting moreover that the man Zardan might make known his case to the King and subject him to punishment, said unto Barlaam, 'Since it seemeth thee good, my spiritual father, best of teachers and minister of all good to me, to leave me to live in the vanity of the world, while thou journeyest to thy place of spiritual rest, I dare no longer let and hinder thee. Depart therefore, with the peace of God for thy guardian, and ever in thy worthy

μενος, καὶ τῆς ἐμῆς ἀθλιότητος ἐν ταῖς τιμίαις σου εὐχαῖς διὰ παντὸς μέμνησο διὰ τὸν Κύριον, ἵνα δυνηθῶ καταλαβεῖν σε καὶ τὸ σὸν βλέπειν τίμιον πρόσωπον πάντοτε. ποίησον δέ μου μίαν αἴτησιν· καί, ἐπείπερ οὐκ ἠθέλησάς τι λαβεῖν ὑπὲρ τῶν συνασκητῶν σου, δέξαι κἂν ὑπὲρ σεαυτοῦ μικρόν τι χρῆμα εἰς διατροφὴν καὶ ἱμάτιον εἰς ἀμφίασιν. ὁ δὲ πρὸς αὐτὸν ἀπεκρίνατο· Εἰ ὑπὲρ τῶν ἀδελφῶν μου οὐκ ἐδεξάμην τι παρὰ σοῦ (οὐδὲ γὰρ ἐκεῖνοι χρῄζουσιν ἐπιλαβέσθαι τῶν ὑλῶν τοῦ κόσμου ὧν ἑκόντες ἐμάκρυναν), πῶς ἐμαυτῷ περιποιήσομαι ὅπερ ἐκείνοις ἀπηγόρευσα; εἰ μὲν γὰρ καλὸν ἦν ἡ τῶν χρημάτων κτῆσις, ἐκείνοις ἂν πρὸ ἐμοῦ τούτων μετέδωκα· ἐπεὶ δὲ ὀλεθρίαν τὴν αὐτῶν ἐπίσταμαι κτῆσιν, οὔτε ἐκείνους, οὔτε μὴν ἐμαυτὸν τοῖς τοιούτοις ὑποβαλῶ βρόχοις.

Ὡς δὲ καὶ ἐν τούτῳ πείθειν οὐκ εἶχε, δευτέρας ἱκετηρίας ἀρχή, καὶ δευτέραν πάλιν αἴτησιν ποιεῖται, μὴ πάντη αὐτοῦ παριδεῖν τὰς δεήσεις, μηδὲ 185
πᾶσαν αὐτῷ καταχέαι τὴν ἀθυμίαν, ἀλλὰ καταλιπεῖν αὐτῷ τὸ ἐρρικνωμένον ἱμάτιον ἐκεῖνο καὶ τραχὺ παλλίον, ἅμα μὲν εἰς μνήμην τῆς τοῦ διδασκάλου ἀσκήσεως, ἅμα δὲ εἰς φυλακτήριον αὐτῷ ἀπὸ πάσης σατανικῆς ἐνεργείας, λαβεῖν δὲ παρ' αὐτοῦ ἕτερον ἀντ' ἐκείνου· Ὡς ἄν, τὸ παρ' ἐμοῦ, φησί, δοθὲν ὁρῶν, τὴν ἐμὴν ἐπὶ μνήμης φέρῃς ταπεινότητα.

Ὁ δὲ γέρων ἔφη· Τὸ μὲν παλαιὸν καὶ διερρωγὸς δοῦναί σοι καὶ λαβεῖν καινὸν ἔνδυμα, οὐ θέμις, ἵνα μὴ τοῦ μικροῦ κόπου μου τὴν ἀμοιβὴν ἐνθάδε ἀπολαβεῖν κατακριθῶ· ἵνα δέ σου τὴν

prayers, for the Lord's sake, think upon my misery, that I may be enabled to overtake thee, and behold thine honoured face for ever. But fulfil this my one request; since thou couldest not receive aught for thy fellow monks, yet for thyself accept a little money for sustenance, and a cloak to cover thee.' But Barlaam answered and said unto him, 'Seeing that I would not receive aught for my brethren (for they need not grasp at the world's chattels which they have chosen to forsake), how shall I acquire for myself that which I have denied them? If the possession of money were a good thing, I should have let them share it before me. But, as I understand that the possession thereof is deadly, I will hazard neither them nor myself in such snares.'

and refuseth to take a gift at parting

But when Ioasaph had failed once again to persuade Barlaam, 'twas but a sign for a second petition, and he made yet another request, that Barlaam should not altogether overlook his prayer, nor plunge him in utter despair, but should leave him that stiff shirt and rough mantle, both to remind him of his teacher's austerities and to safe-guard him from all the workings of Satan, and should take from him another cloak instead, in order that 'When thou seest my gift,' said he, 'thou mayest bear my lowliness in remembrance.'

Ioasaph would lief keep Barlaam's hair shirt and mantle

But the elder said, 'It is not lawful for me to give thee my old and worn out vestment, and take one that is new, lest I be condemned to receive here the recompense of my slight labour. But, not to

Barlaam granteth him his desire,

προθυμίαν μὴ ἐγκόψω, παλαιὰ καὶ μηδὲν τῶν
ἐμῶν διαφέροντα ἔστωσαν τὰ διδόμενά μοι παρὰ
σοῦ. ζητήσας δὲ ὁ τοῦ βασιλέως υἱὸς τρίχινα
ῥάκη παλαιά, καὶ ταῦτα δοὺς τῷ γέροντι, τὰ
ἐκείνου λαβὼν ἔχαιρε, πάσης πορφύρας καὶ
βασιλικῆς ἁλουργίδος τιμιώτερα ταῦτα ἀσυγκρίτως ἡγούμενος.

Ὁ δὲ θειότατος Βαρλαάμ, ἀπιέναι ὅσον οὔπω
βουλόμενος, τὰ τῆς ἐκδημίας ὡμίλει, καὶ τελευταίαν αὐτῷ διδασκαλίαν προσῆγεν· Ἀδελφέ,
λέγων, ἠγαπημένε καὶ τέκνον γλυκύτατον, ὃ διὰ
1 Cor. iv. 15 τοῦ Εὐαγγελίου ἐγέννησα, οἶδας τίνι ἐστρατεύθης
βασιλεῖ καὶ πρὸς τίνα τὰς ὁμολογίας σου διέθου.
δεῖ οὖν βεβαίας ταύτας φυλάξαι, καὶ τὰ τῆς
στρατείας προθύμως τελέσαι, ὅσα ὑπέσχου ἐν
τῇ τῆς ὁμολογίας χάρτῃ τῷ πάντων Δεσπότῃ, 186
πάσης παρούσης τῆς ἐπουρανίου στρατιᾶς καὶ
συμμαρτυρούσης, ἅμα δὲ καὶ ἀπογραφομένης τὰ
ὁμολογηθέντα, ἅτινα φυλάττων μακάριος ἔσῃ.
μηδὲν οὖν τῶν παρόντων Θεοῦ καὶ τῶν αὐτοῦ
προκρίνῃς ἀγαθῶν. τί γὰρ ἂν οὕτω φοβερὸν εἴη
τῶν παρόντων, ὡς γέεννα πυρὸς αἰωνίου, μήτε τοῦ
καίοντος ὅλως φῶς ἔχοντος, μήτε τοῦ κολάζοντός
ποτε λήγοντος; τί δὲ πάλιν τῶν τοῦ κόσμου
καλῶν τηλικοῦτον εὐφράνοι, ὡς Θεὸς αὐτὸς ἐκεῖνος
τοῖς ἀγαπήσασι χαριζόμενος; οὗπερ τὸ κάλλος μὲν
ἄφατον, δυναστεία δὲ ἄμαχος καὶ ἡ δόξα ἀΐδιος·
οὗπερ τὰ ἀγαθά, τὰ τοῖς αὐτοῦ φίλοις ἀποκείμενα, πάντων τῶν ὁρωμένων ἀσυγκρίτως ὑπερέ-
1 Cor. ii. 9 χει, ἃ ὀφθαλμὸς οὐκ εἶδε, καὶ οὖς οὐκ ἤκουσε, καὶ
ἐπὶ καρδίαν ἀνθρώπου οὐκ ἀνέβη· ὧν κληρονόμος

thwart thy willing mind, let the garments given me by thee be old ones, nothing different from mine own.' So the king's son sought for old shirts of hair, which he gave the aged man, rejoicing to receive his in exchange, deeming them beyond compare more precious than any regal purple.

Now saintly Barlaam, all but ready for to start, spake concerning his journey, and delivered Ioasaph his last lesson, saying, 'Brother beloved, and dearest son, whom I have begotten through the Gospel, thou knowest of what King thou art the soldier, and with whom thou hast made thy covenant. This thou must keep steadfastly, and readily perform the duties of thy service, even as thou didst promise the Lord of all in the script of thy covenant, with the whole heavenly host present to attest it, and record the terms; which if thou keep, thou shalt be blessed. Esteem therefore nought in the present world above God and his blessings. For what terror of this life can be so terrible as the Gehenna of eternal fire, that burneth and yet hath no light, that punisheth and never ceaseth? And which of the goodly things of this world can give such gladness as that which the great God giveth to those that love him? Whose beauty is unspeakable, and power invincible, and glory everlasting; whose good things, prepared for his friends, exceed beyond comparison all that is seen; which eye hath not seen, nor ear heard, neither have entered into the heart of man:

and biddeth him farewell

ἀναδειχθείης, τῇ τοῦ Θεοῦ φρουρούμενος κραταιοτάτῃ χειρί.

Ὁ δὲ τοῦ βασιλέως υἱός, δάκρυσι συγκεχυ- 187
μένος, ἠνιᾶτο καὶ ἤσχαλλε, φιλοστόργου πατρὸς
καὶ διδασκάλου ἀρίστου ἀπολειφθῆναι μὴ ἀνεχό-
μενος· Καὶ τίς μοι, φησίν, ὦ πάτερ, τὴν σὴν
πληρώσει τάξιν; ὑπὸ τίνι δὲ ἐγὼ τοιούτῳ ποιμένι
καὶ ὁδηγῷ ψυχικῆς σωτηρίας γενήσομαι; τί τοῦ
σοῦ παραμύθιον ποιήσομαι πόθου; ἰδοὺ γὰρ ἐμὲ
τὸν πονηρὸν δοῦλον καὶ ἀποστάτην τῷ Θεῷ
προσήγαγες, καὶ εἰς υἱοῦ καὶ κληρονόμου κατέ-
Mat. xviii. 12 στησας τάξιν, καὶ τὸν ἀπολωλότα καὶ ὀρειάλωτον,
τὸν παντὶ θηρίῳ ἕτοιμον εἰς βοράν, ἐζήτησας,
καὶ τοῖς ἀπλανέσι κατέμιξας Θεοῦ προβάτοις·
καὶ ἔδειξάς μοι τὴν ἐπίτομον τῆς ἀληθείας ὁδόν,
Cp. Luke i. 79; Ps. lxxxviii. 5 ἐξαγαγών με τοῦ σκότους καὶ τῆς σκιᾶς τοῦ
θανάτου, καί, τοὺς πόδας μου μεταγαγὼν ἐκ
τῆς ὀλισθηρᾶς καὶ θανατηφόρου καὶ σκολιωτάτης
καὶ καμπύλης ἀτραποῦ, μεγάλων καὶ θαυμασίων
μοι γέγονας πρόξενος ἀγαθῶν, καὶ ὧν οὐδεὶς
ἐξαρκέσειε λόγος τὸ ὑπερέχον διηγήσασθαι.
μεγάλων καὶ αὐτὸς ὑπὲρ ἐμοῦ τοῦ μικροῦ
μετάσχοις τοῦ Θεοῦ δωρεῶν· καὶ τῆς ἐμῆς
εὐχαριστίας ὑστέρημα πληρῶσαι Κύριος, ὁ μόνος
νικῶν ταῖς τῶν δωρεῶν ἀντιδόσεσι τοὺς αὐτὸν
ἀγαπῶντας.

Ὁ δὲ Βαρλαάμ, τῆς θρηνῳδίας αὐτὸν ἐκ-
κόπτων, ἀναστὰς εἰς εὐχὴν ἵστατο, καὶ τὼ
χεῖρε εἰς οὐρανοὺς διάρας· Ὁ Θεός, ἔλεγε, καὶ
Πατὴρ τοῦ Κυρίου ἡμῶν Ἰησοῦ Χριστοῦ, ὁ
φωτίσας τὰ πρὶν ἐσκοτισμένα, καὶ τὴν ὁρατὴν 188
ταύτην καὶ ἀόρατον κτίσιν ἐκ τοῦ μὴ ὄντος

whereof mayest thou be shown an inheritor, preserved by the mighty hand of God!'

Here the king's son burst into tears of pain and vexation, unable to bear the parting from a loving father and excellent teacher. 'And who,' quoth he, 'shall fill thy place, O my father? And whom like unto thee shall I find to be shepherd and guide of my soul's salvation? What consolation may I find in my loss of thee? Behold thou hast brought me, the wicked and rebellious servant, back to God, and set me in the place of son and heir! Thou hast sought me that was lost and astray on the mountain, a prey for every evil beast, and folded me amongst the sheep that had never wandered. Thou hast shown me the direct road to truth, bringing me out of darkness and the shadow of death, and, changing the course of my feet from the slippery, deadly, crooked and winding pathway, hast ministered to me great and marvellous blessings, whereof speech would fail to recount the exceeding excellence. Great be the gifts that thou receivest at God's hand, on account of me who am small! And may the Lord, who in the rewards of his gifts alone overpasseth them that love him, supply that which is lacking to my gratitude!'

Ioasaph is sore distrest at his loss

Here Barlaam cut short his lamentation, and rose and stood up to pray, lifting up his either hand, and saying, 'O God and Father of our Lord Jesu Christ, which didst illuminate the things that once were darkened, and bring this visible and invisible

Barlaam's parting prayer

παραγαγών, ὁ τὸ σὸν ἐπιστρέψας πλάσμα καὶ μὴ ἐάσας ἡμᾶς ὀπίσω τῆς ἀφροσύνης ἡμῶν πορεύεσθαι, εὐχαριστοῦμέν σοι, καὶ τῇ σῇ σοφίᾳ καὶ δυνάμει τῷ Κυρίῳ ἡμῶν Ἰησοῦ Χριστῷ, δι' οὗ καὶ τοὺς αἰῶνας ἐποίησας, πεσόντας τε ἡμᾶς ἀνέστησας, καὶ πεπλημμεληκόσι τὰς ἁμαρτίας ἀφῆκας, πλανηθέντας ἐπανήγαγες, αἰχμαλωτισθέντας ἐλυτρώσω, τεθνηκότας ἐζωποίησας τῷ τιμίῳ τοῦ Υἱοῦ σου καὶ δεσποτικῷ αἵματι. σὲ οὖν ἐπικαλοῦμαι, καὶ τὸν μονογενῆ σου Υἱόν, καὶ τὸ πανάγιόν σου Πνεῦμα· ἔπιδε ἐπὶ τὸ λογικόν σου πρόβατον τοῦτο, τὸ προσελθὸν δι' ἐμοῦ τοῦ ἀναξίου εἰς θυσίαν σοι, καὶ ἁγίασον αὐτοῦ τὴν ψυχὴν τῇ σῇ δυνάμει καὶ χάριτι·
Cp. Ps. lxxx. 14 ἐπίσκεψαι τὴν ἄμπελον ταύτην τὴν φυτευθεῖσαν διὰ τοῦ Ἁγίου σου Πνεύματος, καὶ δὸς αὐτὴν καρποφορῆσαι καρπὸν δικαιοσύνης· ἐνίσχυσον αὐτόν, βεβαιῶν ἐν αὐτῷ τὴν διαθήκην σου, καὶ ἐξελοῦ τῆς ἀπάτης τοῦ διαβόλου. τῇ σοφίᾳ
Ps. cxliii. 10 τοῦ ἀγαθοῦ σου Πνεύματος δίδαξον αὐτὸν ποιεῖν τὸ θέλημά σου, καὶ τὴν βοήθειάν σου μὴ ἀφέλῃς ἀπ' αὐτοῦ, ἀξιῶν σὺν ἐμοὶ τῷ ἀχρείῳ σου οἰκέτῃ τῶν ἀτελευτήτων σου ἀγαθῶν κληρονόμον γενέσθαι, ὅτι εὐλογητὸς εἶ καὶ δεδοξασμένος εἰς τοὺς αἰῶνας. ἀμήν.

Τελέσας δὲ τὴν εὐχὴν καὶ ἐπιστραφείς, κατησπάσατο τὸ τέκνον ἤδη τοῦ ἐπουρανίου Πατρός. 189
εἰρήνην τε αὐτῷ ἐπευξάμενος καὶ σωτηρίαν αἰώνιον, ἐξῆλθε τοῦ παλατίου, καὶ ἀπῄει χαίρων καὶ εὐχαριστῶν τῷ Θεῷ, τῷ εὐοδώσαντι τὴν ὁδὸν αὐτοῦ εἰς ἀγαθόν.

creation out of nothing, and didst turn again this thine handiwork, and sufferedst us not to walk after our foolishness, we give thanks to thee and to thy Wisdom and Might, our Lord Jesu Christ, by whom thou didst make the worlds, didst raise us from our fall, didst forgive us our trespasses, didst restore us from wandering, didst ransom us from captivity, didst quicken us from death by the precious blood of thy Son our Lord. Upon thee I call, and upon thine only begotten Son, and upon the Holy Ghost. Look upon this thy spiritual sheep that hath come to be a sacrifice unto thee through me thine unworthy servant, and do thou sanctify his soul with thy might and grace. Visit this vine, which was planted by thy Holy Spirit, and grant it to bear fruit, the fruit of righteousness. Strengthen him, and confirm in him thy covenant, and rescue him from the deceit of the devil. With the wisdom of thy good Spirit teach him to do thy will, and take not thy succour from him, but grant unto him, with me thine unprofitable servant, to become an inheritor of thine everlasting bliss, because thou art blessed and glorified for ever, Amen.'

When that he had ended his prayer, he turned him round and embraced Ioasaph, now a son of his heavenly father, wishing him eternal peace and salvation, and he departed out of the palace, and went his way, rejoicing and giving thanks to God, who had well ordered his steps for good.

Barlaam quitteth the palace

XXII

Ὁ Ἰωάσαφ δέ, μετὰ τὸ ἐξελθεῖν τὸν Βαρλαάμ,
εὐχῇ ἑαυτὸν ἐδίδου καὶ δάκρυσι θερμοτάτοις,
Ps. lxx. 1 καὶ ἔλεγεν· Ὦ Θεός, εἰς τὴν βοήθειάν μου πρό-
σχες. Κύριε, εἰς τὸ βοηθῆσαί μοι σπεῦσον, ὅτι
Ps. ix. 35 σοὶ ἐγκαταλέλειπται ὁ πτωχός, ὀρφανῷ σὺ ἦσθα
Ps. lxxxvi. 16 βοηθός· ἐπίβλεψον ἐπ' ἐμὲ καὶ ἐλέησόν με, ὁ
1 Tim. ii. 4 πάντας θέλων σωθῆναι καὶ εἰς ἐπίγνωσιν ἀληθείας ἐλθεῖν, σῶσόν με καὶ ἐνίσχυσόν με τὸν
ἀνάξιον τοῦ πορευθῆναι τὴν ὁδὸν τῶν ἁγίων
σου ἐντολῶν, ὅτι ἐγὼ μὲν ἀσθενὴς καὶ ταλαίπωρος καὶ ποιῆσαι τὸ ἀγαθὸν οὐχ ἱκανός· σὺ
δὲ σώζειν με δυνατός, ὁ πάντα τὰ ὁρατὰ καὶ
τὰ ἀόρατα συγκρατῶν καὶ συνέχων. μὴ ἐάσῃς
με ὀπίσω τῶν θελημάτων τῆς σαρκὸς τῶν πο-
Ps. cxliii. 10 νηρῶν πορεύεσθαι· ἀλλὰ τὸ σὸν δίδαξον ποιεῖν
θέλημα, καὶ συντήρησόν με εἰς τὴν αἰώνιόν σου
καὶ μακαρίαν ζωήν. ὦ Πάτερ, καὶ Υἱέ, καὶ θεῖον
Πνεῦμα, ἡ ὁμοούσιος καὶ ἀδιαίρετος Θεότης, σὲ
ἐπικαλοῦμαι καὶ σὲ δοξάζω· σὲ γὰρ ὑμνεῖ πᾶσα
κτίσις, καὶ σὲ δοξολογοῦσιν αἱ νοεραὶ τῶν
ἀσωμάτων δυνάμεις εἰς τοὺς αἰῶνας. ἀμήν.

Ἔκτοτε οὖν πάσῃ φυλακῇ ἐτήρει ἑαυτόν,
καθαρότητα ψυχῆς τε καὶ σώματος ἑαυτῷ περι-
ποιούμενος, ἐγκρατείᾳ τε συζῶν καὶ προσευχαῖς
ὁλονύκτοις καὶ δεήσεσιν. ἡμέρας μὲν γὰρ πολ- 190
λάκις περικοπτόμενος τῇ τε τῶν συνόντων αὐτῷ
συναυλίᾳ, ἔσθ' ὅτε καὶ τῇ τοῦ βασιλέως πρὸς
αὐτὸν ἐπιδημίᾳ ἢ τῇ αὐτοῦ εἰς ἐκεῖνον μετα-
κλήσει, ἡ νὺξ αὐτῷ τὰ τῆς ἡμέρας ἀνεπλήρου

XXII

After Barlaam was gone forth, Ioasaph gave himself unto prayer and bitter tears, and said, 'O God, haste thee to help me: O Lord, make speed to help me, because the poor hath committed himself unto thee; thou art the helper of the orphan. Look upon me, and have mercy upon me; thou who willest have all men to be saved and to come unto the knowledge of the truth, save me, and strengthen me, unworthy though I be, to walk the way of thy holy commandments, for I am weak and miserable, and not able to do the thing that is good. But thou art mighty to save me, who sustainest and holdest together all things visible and invisible. Suffer me not to walk after the evil will of the flesh, but teach me to do thy will, and preserve me unto thine eternal and blissful life. O Father, Son, and Holy Ghost, the consubstantial and undivided Godhead, I call upon thee and glorify thee. Thou art praised by all creation; thou art glorified by the intelligent powers of the Angels for ever and ever. Amen.'

Ioasaph calleth on God for help,

From that time forth he kept himself with all vigilance, seeking to attain purity of soul and body, and living in continency and prayers and intercessions all night long. In the day-time he was often interrupted by the company of his fellows, and at times by a visit from the king, or a call to the king's presence, but the night would then make good the

and continueth in vigil and prayer

ὑστερήματα, ἐν εὐχαῖς καὶ δάκρυσι μέχρι διαφαύματος ἱσταμένου αὐτοῦ καὶ τὸν Θεὸν ἐπικαλουμένου· ὅθεν τὸ προφητικὸν ἐκεῖνο ῥῆμα ἐπ' αὐτὸν
Ps. cxxxiii.2 (Sept.) ἐπληροῦτο· Ἐν ταῖς νυξὶν ἐπάρατε τὰς χεῖρας ὑμῶν εἰς τὰ ἅγια, καὶ εὐλογεῖτε τὸν Κύριον.

Ὁ δὲ Ζαρδὰν ἐκεῖνος, τὴν τοιαύτην αὐτοῦ αἰσθόμενος διαγωγὴν καὶ λύπης πληρούμενος, μερίμναις τε δειναῖς τὴν ψυχὴν βαλλόμενος, οὐκ εἶχεν ὅ τι καὶ δράσειε· τέλος, τῇ ἀνίᾳ καταπονηθείς, εἰς τὸν ἑαυτοῦ ἀπεδήμησεν οἶκον, ἀρρωστεῖν προσποιούμενος. ὡς δὲ εἰς γνῶσιν τῷ βασιλεῖ τοῦτο ἐληλύθει, ἄλλον μὲν ἀντ' αὐτοῦ τῶν πιστοτάτων καθυπηρετεῖν τῷ υἱῷ ἐξαπέστειλεν· αὐτὸς δέ, τῆς τοῦ Ζαρδὰν ἐπιμελούμενος ὑγείας, ἰατρὸν αὐτῷ πέμπει δοκιμώτατον καὶ φροντίδος ὅτι πολλῆς ἀξιοῖ θεραπευθῆναι.

Ὁ δὲ ἰατρός, ἐπεὶ τῷ βασιλεῖ οὗτος κεχαρισμένος ἦν, ἐπιμελῶς ἐπεσκέψατο, καί, ἄριστα διαγνοὺς τὰ κατ' αὐτόν, τῷ βασιλεῖ θᾶττον ἀναγγέλλει, ὡς Ἐγώ, φησί, οὐδενὸς νοσήματος αἴτιον ἐν τῷ ἀνθρώπῳ εὑρεῖν δεδύνημαι· ἔνθεν τοι καὶ ὑπολαμβάνω, ἀθυμίᾳ τινὶ τὴν ψυχὴν βληθέντα, τοῦτον μαλακισθῆναι. ὁ δὲ βασιλεύς, τούτων ἀκούσας τῶν ῥημάτων, ὑπέλαβε βαρέως αὐτῷ τὸν υἱὸν διατεθῆναι, καὶ τούτου χάριν λυπηθέντα αὐτὸν ὑποχωρῆσαι. μαθεῖν δὲ τὸ πρᾶγμα ἀκολούθως βουλόμενος, δεδήλωκε τῷ
Ζαρδάν, ὡς Αὔριον ἐλεύσομαι, φησί, θεωρῆσαί 191
σε, καὶ τὰ τῆς ἐπισυμβάσης σοι διαγνῶναι ἀρρωστίας.

Ὁ Ζαρδὰν δέ, ταύτης ἀκούσας τῆς ἀγγελιας, ἅμα πρωῒ περιβαλλόμενος αὐτοῦ τὸ ἱμάτιον,

shortcomings of the day, whilst he stood, in prayer and weeping until daybreak, calling upon God. Whence in him was fulfilled the saying of the prophet, 'In nights raise your hands unto holy things; and bless ye the Lord.'

But Zardan observed Ioasaph's way of life, and was full of sorrow, and his soul was pierced with grievous anxieties; and he knew not what to do. At the last, worn down with pain, he withdrew to his own home, feigning sickness. When this had come to the knowledge of the king he appointed in his place another of his trusty men to minister unto his son, while he himself, being concerned for Zardan's health, sent a physician of reputation, and took great pains that he should be healed.

Zardan is troubled thereat and feigneth sickness

The physician, seeing that Zardan was in favour with the king, attended him diligently, and, having right well judged his case, soon made this report to the king; 'I have been unable to discover any root of disease in the man: wherefore I suppose that this weakness is to be ascribed to distress of spirit.' But, on hearing his words, the king suspected that his son had been wroth with Zardan, and that this slight had caused his retirement. So, wishing to search the matter, he sent Zardan word, saying 'To-morrow I shall come to see thee, and judge of the malady that hath befallen thee.'

The physician cannot detect his disease

But Zardan, on hearing this message, at daybreak wrapt his cloak around him and went to the king,

Zardan visiteth the king

πορεύεται πρὸς τὸν βασιλέα. καὶ εἰσελθὼν προσεκύνησεν αὐτῷ ἐπὶ τῆς γῆς. ὁ δὲ βασιλεύς, Τί, φησί, παρεβιάσω ἑαυτὸν παραγενέσθαι; αὐτὸς γὰρ ἤθελον ἐπισκέψασθαί σε, καὶ πᾶσι γνωρίσαι τὴν πρὸς σέ μου φιλίαν. ὁ δὲ ἀντέφησεν· Ἡ ἐμή, βασιλεῦ, ἀσθένεια οὐκ ἔστι τῶν συνήθων ἀνθρώποις ἀρρωστιῶν· ἀλλ' ἐκ λυπηρᾶς καὶ ἐμμερίμνου ψυχῆς τῆς καρδίας ὀδυνωμένης συνωδυνήθη τὸ σῶμα. ἀφροσύνη δέ μοι ἦν οὕτως ἔχοντά με μὴ δουλικῶς πρὸς τὸ σὸν παραγενέσθαι κράτος, ἀλλὰ τὴν σὴν βασιλείαν προσμένειν ἕως ἐμοῦ τοῦ οἰκέτου σκυλῆναι. τοῦ βασιλέως οὖν πυνθανομένου τίς ἡ τῆς ἀθυμίας αὐτοῦ αἰτία, ὑπολαβὼν ὁ Ζαρδάν, Μέγας ἐμοὶ κίνδυνος, ἔφη· καὶ μεγάλων ἐγὼ τιμωριῶν ἄξιος, πολλῶν δὲ θανάτων ἔνοχος καθέστηκα, ὅτι σοῦ τοῖς προστάγμασιν ἀμελῶς διατεθεὶς ἀνίας σοι πολλῆς ὅσον οὐδέπω πρόξενος γέγονα.

Αὖθις δὲ ὁ βασιλεύς, Καὶ τίνα σὺ ἀμέλειαν ἠμέληκας; ἤρετο· τί δὲ τὸ περιέχον σε δέος; Ἐν τῇ περὶ τὸν κύριόν μου τὸν υἱόν σου ἀκριβείᾳ ἠμέληκα, ἔφη. πονηρὸς γὰρ ἄνθρωπος καὶ γόης ἐλθὼν ὡμίλησεν αὐτῷ τὰ τῆς θρησκείας τῶν Χριστιανῶν. εἶτα διηγεῖται κατὰ μέρος τῷ βασιλεῖ τὰ λαληθέντα παρὰ τοῦ γέροντος πρὸς τὸν υἱὸν αὐτοῦ, καὶ μεθ' ὅσης ἡδονῆς ἐκεῖνος τὸν λόγον ἐδέξατο, καὶ ὡς ὅλος τοῦ Χριστοῦ ἐγεγόνει. πρὸς δὲ καὶ 192
τὴν κλῆσιν ἐδήλου τοῦ γέροντος, Βαρλαὰμ τοῦτον καλεῖσθαι εἰπών. ἀκηκόει γὰρ καὶ πρότερον ὁ βασιλεὺς τὰ περὶ τοῦ Βαρλαὰμ καὶ τῆς ἀκροτάτης ἀσκήσεως αὐτοῦ. ὡς δ' εἰς ἀκοὰς ταῦτα ἦλθε τῷ βασιλεῖ, κλόνῳ εὐθὺς ἐκ τῆς περιπε-

and entered and fell in obeisance on the ground. The king spake unto him, 'Why hast thou forced thyself to appear? I was minded to visit thee myself, and so make known to all my friendship for thee.' He answered, 'My sickness, O king, is no malady common to man; but pain of heart, arising from an anxious and careful mind, hath caused my body to suffer in sympathy. It had been folly in me, being as I am, not to attend as a slave before thy might, but to wait for thy Majesty to be troubled to come to me thy servant.' Then the king enquired after the cause of his despondency; Zardan answered and said, 'Mighty is my peril, and mighty are the penalties that I deserve, and many deaths do I merit, for that I have been guilty of neglect of thy behests, and have brought on thee such sorrow as ne'er before.'

Zardan discovoreth to the king the visit of Barlaam

Again said the king, 'And of what neglect hast thou been guilty? And what is the dread that encompasseth thee?' 'I have been guilty,' said he, 'of negligence in my close care of my lord thy son. There came an evil man and a sorcerer, and communicated to him the precepts of the Christian religion.' Then he related to the king, point by point, the words which the old man spake with his son, and how gladly Ioasaph received his word, and how he had altogether become Christ's. Moreover he gave the old man's name, saying that it was Barlaam. Even before then the king had heard tell of Barlaam's ways and his extreme severity of life; but, when this came to the ears of the king, he was

σούσης αὐτῷ ἀθυμίας βάλλεται, καὶ θυμοῦ πληροῦται, μικροῦ καὶ ἀποπήγνυται τῷ ἀκούσματι. καὶ αὐτίκα προσκαλεῖται Ἀραχήν τινα οὕτω λεγόμενον, ὃς καὶ τῶν δευτερείων μετὰ τὸν βασιλέα ἠξιοῦτο, καὶ πρῶτος αὐτῷ ἐν πάσαις ταῖς ἀποκρύφοις συμβουλίαις ἐτύγχανεν· ἅμα δὲ καὶ τῆς ἀστρολογίας ἐπιστήμων ἦν ὁ ἀνήρ. πρὸς ὃν παραγενόμενον τὸ συμβὰν ὁ βασιλεὺς σὺν ἀθυμίᾳ πολλῇ καὶ ἀδημονίᾳ διηγεῖται. ὁ δέ, τὸν τάραχον αὐτοῦ καὶ τὴν σύγχυσιν τῆς ψυχῆς θεασάμενος, Ἀτάραχά σοι, φησί, ἔστω καὶ ἄλυπα, Ὦ βασιλεῦ· οὐκ ἀνέλπιστον γὰρ ἡμῖν ἔτι τὸ μεταπεσεῖν αὐτόν· ἀλλὰ καὶ λίαν βεβαιότατα γινώσκω θᾶττον αὐτὸν καὶ ἐξαρνήσασθαι τὴν τοῦ πλάνου ἐκείνου διδασκαλίαν, καὶ τῷ σῷ συνθέσθαι θελήματι.

Τούτοις οὖν τοῖς ῥήμασι τὸν βασιλέα εἰς τὸ εὐθυμότερον ὁ Ἀραχὴς μεταβαλών, τῇ περὶ τὸ πρᾶγμα διασκέψει μελέτην ἐποιοῦντο. Καὶ τοῦτο, φησίν, ὦ βασιλεῦ, πρὸ πάντων ποιήσωμεν· καταλαβεῖν σπεύσωμεν τὸν δεινὸν Βαρλαάμ. καὶ εἰ τούτου ἐπιτύχωμεν, οὐκ ἀστοχήσομεν, εὖ οἶδα, 193
τοῦ σκοποῦ, οὐδὲ ψευσθησόμεθα τῆς ἐλπίδος. ἀλλ' ἐκεῖνος αὐτός, ἢ ῥήμασι πιθανοῖς ἢ βασάνων ὀργάνοις πολυειδέσι πεισθείς, ἄκων ἂν ὁμολογήσειε ψευδῆ καὶ πεπλανημένα φάσκειν, καὶ τὸν κύριόν μου καὶ υἱόν σου τοῦ πατρῴου ἔχεσθαι μεταπείσειε δόγματος. εἰ δὲ ἐκεῖνον μὲν καταλαβεῖν οὐ δυνηθείημεν, ἕτερον ἐγὼ ἐπίσταμαι πρεσβύτην μονερημίτην, Ναχὼρ καλούμενον, ὅμοιον τῷ Βαρλαὰμ κατὰ πάντα, ὃν οὐκ ἔστι διαγνῶναι μὴ ἐκεῖνον ὑπάρχειν, τῆς ἡμετέρας

straightway astonied by the dismay that fell on him, and was filled with anger, and his blood well-nigh curdled at the tidings. Immediately he bade call one Araches, who held the second rank after the king, and was the chief in all his private councils: besides which the man was learned in star-lore. When he was come, with much despondency and dejection the king told him of that which had happened. He, seeing the king's trouble and confusion of mind, said, 'O king, trouble and distress thyself no more. We are not without hope that the prince will yet change for the better: nay, I know for very certain that he will speedily renounce the teaching of this deceiver, and conform to thy will.'

The king calleth for his counsellor Araches

By these words then did Araches set the king in happier frame of mind; and they turned their thoughts to the thorough sifting of the matter. 'This, O king,' said Araches, 'do we first of all. Make we haste to apprehend that infamous Barlaam. If we take him, I am assured that we shall not miss the mark, nor be cheated of our hope. Barlaam himself shall be persuaded, either by persuasion or by divers engines of torture, against his will to confess that he hath been talking falsely and at random, and shall persuade my lord, thy son, to cleave to his father's creed. But if we fail to take Barlaam, I know of an eremite, Nachor by name, in every way like unto him: it is impossible to distinguish the one from the other. He

Araches plotteth how to recover Ioasaph to idolatry

δόξης ὄντα, καὶ διδάσκαλον ἐμὸν ἐν τοῖς μαθήμασι γενόμενον. τούτῳ ὑπαγορεύσας ἐγώ, νύκτωρ ἀπελθών, πάντα κατὰ μέρος ἀφηγήσομαι. εἶτα, κρατηθῆναι τὸν Βαρλαὰμ διαφημήσαντες, τοῦτον παραστησόμεθα· ὃς καὶ Βαρλαὰμ ἑαυτὸν ὀνομάσας, τὰ τῶν Χριστιανῶν πρεσβεύειν προσποιήσεται, καὶ τούτους διεκδικῶν φανήσεται. εἶτα, μετὰ πολλὴν διάλεξιν ἡττώμενος, κατὰ κράτος ἐκνικηθήσεται. καὶ ταῦτα ὁ τοῦ βασιλέως υἱὸς θεώμενος, ὡς ὁ Βαρλαὰμ μὲν ἡττήθη, τὰ δὲ ἡμέτερα ὑπερνικᾷ, τοῖς νικῶσι πάντως συνθήσεται· μέγα πρὸς τούτοις καὶ τὸ τὴν σὴν αἰδεῖσθαι βασιλείαν καὶ τὰ σοὶ κεχαρισμένα ποιεῖν τιθέμενος. ἐπιστραφήσεται γὰρ καὶ ὁ τὸ προσωπεῖον τοῦ Βαρλαὰμ ὑποδύς, καὶ πεπλανῆσθαι αὐτὸν διαβεβαιώσειε.

Ἥσθη ὁ βασιλεὺς ἐπὶ τοῖς λαληθεῖσι, καὶ ἄριστα βουλεύσασθαι ἔδοξε, κεναῖς ἐπερειδόμενος ἐλπίσιν. ἔνθεν τοι καὶ τὸν Βαρλαὰμ ἔναγχος 194
μαθὼν ὑποχωρῆσαι, χειρώσασθαι ἔσπευδε. λόχοις οὖν καὶ λοχαγοῖς τῶν διεξόδων τὰς πλείους διειληφώς, μίαν δὲ τῶν ὁδῶν, ἣν πασῶν μᾶλλον ὑφωρᾶτο, αὐτός, ἵπποις ἐπιβάς, ἀνὰ κράτος ἐδίωκε, προκαταλαβεῖν αὐτὸν ἐκ παντὸς τρόπου διανοούμενος. ἐν ὅλαις δὲ ἓξ ἡμέραις κοπιάσας, μάτην τεταλαιπωρήκει. εἶτα, αὐτὸς μὲν ἔν τινι τῶν βασιλικῶν παλατίων ἐν τοῖς ἀγροῖς διακειμένῳ προσμείνας, τὸν Ἀραχὴν μετὰ ἱππέων οὐκ ὀλίγων ἕως αὐτῆς τῆς Σενααρίτιδος ἐρήμου ἐπὶ ζήτησιν ἀπέστειλε τοῦ Βαρλαάμ. καταλαβὼν δὲ ἐκεῖνος τὸν τόπον, πάντας τοὺς περιοίκους διετάραξε· καὶ τῶνδε μὴ ἑωρακέναι ποτὲ τὸν ἄνδρα

is of our opinion, and was my teacher in studies. I will give him the hint, and go by night, and tell him the full tale. Then will we blazon it abroad that Barlaam hath been caught; but we shall exhibit Nachor, who, calling himself Barlaam, shall feign that he is pleading the cause of the Christians and standing forth as their champion. Then, after much disputation, he shall be worsted and utterly discomfited. The prince, seeing Barlaam worsted, and our side victorious, will doubtless join the victors; the more so that he counteth it a great duty to reverence thy majesty, and do thy pleasure. Also the man who hath played the part of Barlaam shall be converted, and stoutly proclaim that he hath been in error.'

The king sendeth Araches in pursuit of Barlaam

The king was delighted with his words, and rocked himself on idle hopes, and thought it excellent counsel. Thereupon, learning that Barlaam was but lately departed, he was zealous to take him prisoner. He therefore occupied most of the passes with troops and captains, and, himself, mounting his chariot, gave furious chase along the one road of which he was especially suspicious, being minded to surprise Barlaam at all costs. But though he toiled by the space of six full days, his labour was but spent in vain. Then he himself remained behind in one of his palaces situate in the country, but sent forward Araches, with horsemen not a few, as far as the wilderness of Senaar, in quest of Barlaam. When Araches arrived in that place, he threw all the neighbour folk into commotion: and when they constantly affirmed that they had

βεβαιωσαμένων, ἐπὶ τὰς ἐρήμους ὁ ἄρχων τοὺς
εὐσεβεῖς θηρεύσων ἐξῄει. πολύ τε τῆς ἐρήμου
διοδεύσας διάστημα, ὄρη τε περικυκλώσας καὶ
ἀτριβεῖς φάραγγας πεζεύσας καὶ δυσβάτους, μετὰ
τῶν σὺν αὐτῷ ὄχλων ἀκρώρειάν τινα καταλαβών,
καὶ στὰς ἐπ᾽ αὐτῆς, ὁρᾷ κατὰ τὴν ὑπώρειαν φά- 195
λαγγα ἐρημιτῶν περιπατοῦσαν. καὶ εὐθὺς τῷ
τοῦ ἄρχοντος προστάγματι πάντες ἐπ᾽ αὐτοὺς
θέουσιν ἀπνευστί, ἄλλος ἄλλον τοῖς δρόμοις
φθάσαι φιλονεικοῦντες· καὶ φθάσαντες, περιεχύθησαν αὐτοῖς κύνες ὡσεὶ πολλοὶ ἢ θηρία
πονηρά τινα καὶ μισάνθρωπα· καὶ κρατοῦσι τοὺς
ἄνδρας τῷ τε εἴδει καὶ τῇ καταστάσει σεμνοτά-
τους, καὶ τὰ σήμαντρα τῆς ἐρημικῆς καταστάσεως
ἐπὶ τῶν προσώπων φέροντας· καὶ τούτους σύρον-
τες τῷ ἄρχοντι παρέστησαν, οὐ θορυβηθέντας
ὅλως, οὐκ ἀγεννές τι καὶ σκυθρωπὸν ἐνδειξα-
μένους ἢ φθεγξαμένους. ὁ δὲ προάγων αὐτῶν καὶ
οἱονεὶ καθηγούμενος πήραν ἐβάσταζε τριχίνην,
μεστὴν λειψάνων προεκδημησάντων τινῶν ἁγίων
Πατέρων.

Κατανοήσας δὲ αὐτοὺς ὁ Ἀραχής, ὡς οὐκ εἶδε τὸν Βαρλαὰμ (ἐγίνωσκε γὰρ αὐτόν), συνεχύθη τῇ λύπῃ. λέγει δὲ πρὸς αὐτούς· Ποῦ ἔστιν ὁ ἀπατεὼν ἐκεῖνος, ὁ τὸν υἱὸν πλανήσας τοῦ βασιλέως; ὁ δὲ τὴν πήραν βαστάζων ἀπεκρίνατο· Οὐκ ἔστιν ἐκεῖνος ἐν ἡμῖν· μηδὲ γένοιτο· φεύγει γὰρ ἡμᾶς τῇ τοῦ Χριστοῦ διωκόμενος χάριτι. ἐν ὑμῖν δὲ τὰς οἰκήσεις ἔχει· ὁ ἄρχων ἔφη· Γινώσκεις οὖν αὐτόν; Ναί, φησὶν ὁ ἐρημίτης· οἶδα τὸν ἀπατεῶνα λεγόμενον, ὅς ἐστιν ὁ διάβολος, ὁ μέσον ὑμῶν κατοικῶν καὶ παρ᾽ ὑμῶν λατρευόμενός τε

never seen the man, he went forth into the desert places, for to hunt out the Faithful. When he had gone through a great tract of desert, and made the circuit of the fells around, and journeyed a-foot over untrodden and pathless ravines, he and his hosts arrived at a plateau. Standing thereon, he descried at the foot of the mountain a company of hermits a-walking. Straightway at their governor's word of command all his men ran upon them in breathless haste, vying one with another, who should arrive first. When they arrived, they came about the monks like so many dogs, or evil beasts that plague mankind. And they seized these men of reverend mien and mind, that bore on their faces the hall-mark of their hermit life, and haled them before the governor; but the monks showed no sign of alarm, no sign of meanness or sullenness, and spake never a word. Their leader and captain bore a wallet of hair, charged with the relics of some holy Fathers departed this life.

Araches captureth a band of monks,

When Araches beheld them, but saw no Barlaam—for he knew him by sight—he was overwhelmed with grief, and said unto them, 'Where is that deceiver who hath led the king's son astray?' The bearer of the wallet answered, 'He is not amongst us, God forbid! For, driven forth by the grace of Christ, he avoideth us; but amongst you he hath his dwelling.' The governor said, 'Thou knowest him then?' 'Yea,' said the hermit, 'I know him that is called the deceiver, which is the devil, who dwelleth in your midst and is worshipped

and questioneth them concerning Barlaam

καὶ θεραπευόμενος. ὁ ἄρχων λέγει· Περὶ τοῦ Βαρλαὰμ ἐγὼ τὴν ζήτησιν ἔχω, καὶ τοῦτον ἠρόμην σε μαθεῖν ποῦ ἔστιν· ὁ δὲ μοναχός· Καὶ ἵνα τί, 196
φησίν, ἀλληνάλλως ἐλάλησας, περὶ τοῦ ἀπατήσαντος τὸν υἱὸν τοῦ βασιλέως τὴν πεῦσιν προσαγαγών; εἰ γὰρ τὸν Βαρλαὰμ ἐζήτεις, ἔδει σε πάντως εἰπεῖν· Ποῦ ἔστιν ὁ ἐκ τῆς πλάνης ἐπιστρέψας καὶ σώσας τὸν τοῦ βασιλέως υἱόν; ἐκεῖνος γὰρ ἀδελφὸς ἡμῶν ὑπάρχει καὶ συνασκητής· ἐκ πολλῶν δὲ ἤδη ἡμερῶν οὐ τεθεάμεθα αὐτόν. ὁ δὲ Ἀραχής· Τὸ οἴκημα αὐτοῦ, φησίν, ὑπόδειξον. ὁ ἀσκητὴς ἀπεκρίνατο· Εἰ θεάσασθαι ὑμᾶς ἤθελεν, ἐκεῖνος ἂν εἰς συνάντησιν ὑμῶν ἐξῆλθεν. ἡμῖν δ' οὖν οὐκ ἔξεστι τὸ δωμάτιον αὐτοῦ ὑμῖν γνωρίσαι.

Θυμοῦ ἐπὶ τούτῳ ἐμπίμπλαται ὁ ἄρχων, καί φησι πρὸς αὐτόν, ὀργίλον ἅμα καὶ θηριῶδες ἐμβλέψας· Ξένῳ νυνὶ θανάτῳ ὑμᾶς θανατώσω, εἰ ἐξ αὐτῆς τὸν Βαρλαὰμ οὐ παραστήσετέ μοι· Καὶ τί, φησὶν ὁ ἀσκητής, ὁρᾷς ἐν ἡμῖν, οὗπερ ἀντεχόμενοι δυσαποσπάστως τῆς παρούσης διακεισόμεθα ζωῆς, καὶ τὸν παρὰ σοῦ ἐπαχθησόμενον φοβηθῶμεν θάνατον; χάριν γάρ σοι μᾶλλον ὁμολογήσομεν, ὅτι τῆς ἀρετῆς ἐχομένους τοῦ βίου ἐξήγαγες. δεδοίκαμεν γὰρ οὐ μικρῶς τὸ τοῦ τέλους ἄδηλον, μὴ εἰδότες πῶς ἔχοντας ἡμᾶς καταλήψεται, μή που γνώμης ὄλισθος ἢ ἐπήρειά 197
τις δαιμονικὴ τῆς προαιρέσεως τὴν ἔνστασιν μεταστρέψῃ, καὶ ἕτερα φρονεῖν ἢ ποιεῖν παρὰ τὰ τῷ Θεῷ ὡμολογημένα μεταπείσειεν. ὅθεν τυχεῖν ὧν ἐλπίζετε ὅλως ἀπειπόντες, μὴ ὀκνήσητε ποιεῖν ὅπερ βούλεσθε. οὔτε γὰρ τὸ τοῦ θεοφιλοῦς ἡμῶν

and served by you.' The governor said, 'It is for Barlaam that I make search, and I asked thee of him, to learn where he is.' The monk answered, 'And wherefore then spakest thou in this ambiguous manner, asking about him that had deceived the king's son? If thou wast seeking Barlaam, thou shouldest certainly have said, "Where is he that hath turned from error and saved the king's son?" Barlaam is our brother and fellow-monk. But now for many days past we have not seen his face.' Said Araches, 'Show me his abode.' The monk answered, 'Had he wished to see you, he would have come forth to meet you. As for us, it is not lawful to make known to you his hermitage.'

Thereupon the governor waxed full of indignation, and, casting a haughty and savage glance upon him, said, 'Ye shall die no ordinary death, except ye immediately bring Barlaam before me.' 'What,' said the monk, 'seest thou in our case that should by its attractions cause us to cling to life, and be afraid of death at thy hands? Whereas we should the rather feel grateful to thee for removing us from life in the close adherence to virtue. For we dread, not a little, the uncertainty of the end, knowing not in what state death shall overtake us, lest perchance a slip of the inclination, or some despiteful dealing of the devil, may alter the constancy of our choice, and mis-persuade us to think or do contrary to our covenants with God. Wherefore abandon all hope of gaining the knowledge that ye desire, and shrink not to work your will. We shall neither reveal the dwelling-

The monks defy Araches

ἀδελφοῦ οἰκητήριον, καίτοι γε εἰδότες, ὑποδείξομεν, οὔτε ἄλλα τινὰ ὑμῖν λανθάνοντα μοναστήρια προδώσομεν, ταύτῃ τὸν θάνατον ἐκφυγεῖν κακῶς ἀνεχόμενοι· ἀλλὰ καλῶς μᾶλλον θανούμεθα, ἱδρῶτας ἀρετῆς πρότερον, καὶ νῦν ἀνδραγαθίας αἷμα, τῷ Θεῷ προσενέγκαντες.

Οὕτω παρρησιασαμένους οὐκ ἐνεγκὼν ὁ ἀλιτήριος, ἀλλὰ πρὸς τὸ γενναῖον τοῦ φρονήματος ὀξύτατα κινηθείς, πολλαῖς αὐτοὺς περιέβαλε πληγαῖς καὶ βασάνοις· ὧν τὸ μεγαλόψυχον καὶ γενναῖον καὶ τῷ τυράννῳ ἄξιον θαύματος ἐνομίσθη. ὡς δὲ μετὰ πολλὰς τιμωρίας πείθειν οὐκ εἶχεν, οὔτε ὑποδεῖξαί τις αὐτῷ τὸν Βαρλαὰμ ἠνείχετο, λαβὼν τούτους, ἐπὶ τὸν βασιλέα κελεύει τυπτομένους καὶ προπηλακιζομένους ἄγεσθαι, βαστάζοντας καὶ τὴν πήραν τῶν λειψάνων.

XXIII

Δι᾽ ἡμερῶν δὲ οὐκ ὀλίγων προσάγει τούτους τῷ βασιλεῖ, καὶ τὰ κατ᾽ αὐτοὺς δῆλα τίθησιν. εἶτα παριστᾷ κατὰ πρόσωπον αὐτοῦ δεινὰ θυμομαχοῦντος. καὶ ὃς ἰδὼν αὐτούς, τῷ θυμῷ ὑπερζέσας, μαινομένῳ ἐῴκει. τύπτεσθαί τε αὐτοὺς ἀνηλεῶς
κελεύσας, ὡς εἶδε ταῖς πληγαῖς χαλεπῶς κατα- 198
κοπέντας, μόλις τῆς πολλῆς ἀνενεγκὼν μανίας, παύσασθαι τοὺς τύπτοντας κελεύει. καί φησι πρὸς αὐτούς· Τί τὰ ὀστᾶ ταῦτα τῶν τεθνεώτων περιφέρετε; εἰ, ὧν τὰ ὀστᾶ εἰσι ποθοῦντες, ταῦτα βαστάζετε, ταύτῃ τῇ ὥρᾳ θήσομαι καὶ ὑμᾶς μετ᾽ αὐτῶν, ἵνα, τῶν ποθουμένων τυχόντες, χάριν μοι

place of our brother, whom God loveth, although we know it, nor shall we betray any other monasteries unbeknown to ye. We will not endure to escape death by such cowardice. Nay, liefer would we die honourably, and offer unto God, after the sweats of virtue, the life-blood of courage.'

Araches tormenteth the monks and at the last sendeth them to the king

That man of sin could not brook this boldness of speech, and was moved to the keenest passion against this high and noble spirit, and afflicted the monks with many stripes and tortures. Their courage and nobility won admiration even from that tyrant. But, when after many punishments he failed to persuade them, and none of them consented to discover Barlaam, he took and ordered them to be led to the king, bearing with them the wallet with the relics, and to be beaten and shamefully entreated as they went.

XXIII

The king receiveth them cruelly and asketh why they carry relics in a wallet

After many days Araches brought them to the king, and declared their case. Then he set them before the bitterly incensed king: and he, when he saw them, boiled over with fury and was like to one mad. He ordered them to be beaten without mercy, and, when he saw them cruelly mangled with scourges, could scarcely restrain his madness, and order the tormentors to cease. Then said he unto them, 'Why bear ye about these dead men's bones? If ye carry these bones through affection for those men to whom they belong, this very hour I will set you in their company, that ye may meet your

ὁμολογήσητε. ὁ δὲ τῆς θείας ἐκείνης φάλαγγος
ἔξαρχος καὶ καθηγητὴς παρ᾽ οὐδὲν τὰς τοῦ
βασιλέως τιθέμενος ἀπειλάς, ὡς μηδενὸς αὐτῷ
συμβεβηκότος ἀνιαροῦ, ἐλευθέρᾳ φωνῇ καὶ λαμ-
προτάτῳ προσώπῳ καὶ τὴν ἐνοικοῦσαν τῇ ψυχῇ
Cp. John σημαίνοντι χάριν ἔφη· Τὰ ὀστᾶ ταῦτα τὰ καθαρὰ
Dam. adv. καὶ ἅγια περιφέρομεν, ὦ βασιλεῦ, τὸν πόθον τε
Constant. ἀφοσιούμενοι ὧν εἰσι θαυμασίων ἀνδρῶν, καὶ τῆς
labal. 2; Chrys. Ad ἀσκήσεως αὐτῶν καὶ θεοφιλοῦς πολιτείας εἰς
Romanos Hom. 32 μνήμην ἑαυτοὺς ἄγοντες καὶ πρὸς τὸν ὅμοιον διε-
γείροντες ζῆλον, τὴν ἀνάπαυσίν τε ἐνοπτριζόμενοι
καὶ τρυφὴν ἐν ᾗ νῦν διάγουσι· καὶ τούτους μὲν
μακαρίζοντες, ἀλλήλους δὲ παραθήγοντες τοῖς
2 Kings xiii. αὐτῶν ἐξακολουθεῖν ἴχνεσι σπεύδομεν. πρὸς δέ,
21; Ecclus. καὶ τὴν τοῦ θανάτου ἑαυτοῖς περιποιούμεθα μνή-
xlviii. 13; Acts v. μην, πάνυ ὠφέλιμον οὖσαν καὶ πρὸς τοὺς τῆς
14–16; xix. 11, 12 ἀσκήσεως ἀγῶνας προθύμως ἀναπτεροῦσαν, καὶ 199
ἁγιασμὸν δὲ τῇ τούτων ἀρυόμεθα προσψαύσει.

Αὖθις δὲ ὁ βασιλεύς, Εἰ ὠφέλιμος, φησίν, ἡ τοῦ θανάτου μνήμη, καθὼς φατε, τί μὴ τοῖς ἐν τοῖς σώμασιν ὑμῶν ὀστέοις τὴν τούτου ὑποδέχεσθε μνήμην, τοῖς οἰκείοις ὑμῖν καὶ ὅσον οὔπω φθαρησομένοις, ἤπερ τοῖς ἀλλοτρίοις τούτοις καὶ διεφθαρμένοις;

Καὶ ὁ μοναχός, Πέντε μέν, φησίν, ἐμοῦ εἰρηκότος αἰτίας τῆς τῶν λειψάνων περιφορᾶς, πρὸς μίαν αὐτὸς ἀνταποκρινόμενος, χλευάζειν ἡμᾶς δοκεῖς· ἀλλ᾽ ἐναργέστερον, εὖ ἴσθι, τὰ τῶν προτετελευτηκότων ὀστᾶ τὴν τοῦ θανάτου παριστῶσι μνήμην, ἤγε τῶν ζώντων. ἀλλ᾽, ἐπείπερ ταῦθ᾽ οὕτως εἶναι γινώσκεις καὶ τὰ ἐν τῇ σαρκί σου ὀστᾶ τὸν θάνατόν σοι ὑποτυποῦσι, τί μὴ καὶ

lost friends and be duly grateful to me.' The captain and leader of that godly band, setting at naught the king's threats, showing no sign of the torment that he had undergone, with free voice and radiant countenance that signified the grace that dwelt in his soul, cried out, 'We carry about these clean and holy bones, O king, because we attest in due form our love of those marvellous men to whom they belong: and because we would bring ourselves to remember their wrestlings and lovely conversation, to rouse up ourselves to the like zeal; and because we would catch some vision of the rest and felicity wherein they now live, and thus, as we call them blessed, and provoke one another to emulate them, strive to follow in their footsteps: because moreover, we find thereby that the thought of death, which is right profitable, lendeth wings of zeal to our religious exercises; and lastly, because we derive sanctification from their touch.'

Their leader telleth of the virtue of relics,

Again said the king, 'If the thought of death be profitable, as ye say, why should ye not reach that thought of death by the bones of the bodies that are now your own, and are soon to perish, rather than by the bones of other men which have already perished?'

The monk said, 'Five reasons I gave thee, why we carry about these relics; and thou, making answer to one only, art like to be mocking us. But know thou well that the bones of them, that have already departed this life, bring the thought of death more vividly before us than do the bones of the living. But since thou judgest otherwise, and since the bones of thine own body are to thee a type of death, why dost thou not recollect thy latter

and rebuketh the king

αὐτός, τῆς ὅσον οὔπω ἐλευσομένης μνημονεύων τελευτῆς, εὖ τὰ σεαυτοῦ διατίθης, ἀλλὰ πάσαις μὲν τὴν ψυχήν σου ἐκδέδωκας παρανομίαις, βιαίως δὲ καὶ ἀνηλεῶς ἀναιρεῖς τοὺς λατρευτὰς τοῦ Θεοῦ καὶ τῆς εὐσεβείας ἐραστάς, τοὺς μηδέν σοι ἠδικηκότας, μηδέ σοι τῶν παρόντων τι συμμεριζομένους ἢ ἀφελέσθαι φιλονεικοῦντας;

Ὁ δὲ βασιλεὺς ἔφη· Τοὺς δεινοὺς ὑμᾶς καὶ λαοπλάνους εἰκότως κολάζω, ὅτι πάντας ἀπατᾶτε, ἀπέχεσθαι τῶν τερπνῶν τοῦ βίου ὑποτιθέμενοι, καί, ἀντὶ τῆς γλυκείας ζωῆς καὶ τῆς ποθεινοτάτης ἐπιθυμίας καὶ ἡδονῆς, τὴν σκληρὰν καὶ ῥυπώδη ταύτην καὶ πιναρὰν ἐκλέγεσθαι ἀγωγὴν ἐκβιά- 200
ζεσθε, καὶ τὴν τῶν θεῶν τιμὴν τῷ Ἰησοῦ ἀπονέμειν κηρύττετε. ἵνα οὖν μή, τῇ ὑμετέρᾳ ἀπάτῃ ἐξακολουθοῦντες, οἱ λαοὶ ἔρημον τὴν γῆν καταλίπωσι, καί, τῶν πατρίων ἀποστάντες θεῶν, ἀλλοτρίῳ λατρεύσωσι, τιμωρίαις ὑμᾶς καὶ θανάτοις ὑποβαλεῖν δίκαιον ἔκρινα.

Ὁ δὲ μοναχὸς φησίν· Εἰ πάντας μετέχειν τῶν ἀγαθῶν τοῦ βίου ὀρέγῃ, τί μὴ πᾶσιν ἐπ' ἴσης μεταδίδως τῆς τρυφῆς καὶ τοῦ πλούτου, ἀλλ' οἱ μὲν πλείους πενίᾳ ταλαιπωροῦνται, σὺ δὲ τὰ αὐτῶν προσαφαρπάζων τοῖς ἑαυτοῦ προστίθης; οὐκ ἄρα τῆς τῶν πολλῶν φροντίζεις σωτηρίας, ἀλλὰ τὴν ἰδίαν πιαίνεις σάρκα, ὕλην ἑτοιμάζων τῇ τῶν σκωλήκων καταβρώσει. διὰ τοῦτο, καὶ τὸν τῶν πάντων ἀπαρνησάμενος Θεόν, τοὺς μὴ ὄντας προσηγόρευσας θεούς, τοὺς πάσης παρανομίας ἐφευρετάς, ἵνα σοι, κατὰ μίμησιν αὐτῶν ἀσελγαίνοντι καὶ παρανομοῦντι, τὸ μιμητὴς ἀναγορεύεσθαι τῶν θεῶν σου προσγένηται. οἷα γὰρ οἱ θεοὶ ὑμῶν

end so shortly to come, and set thine house in order, instead of giving up thy soul to all kinds of iniquities, and violently and unmercifully murdering the servants of God and lovers of righteousness, who have done thee no wrong, and seek not to share with thee in present goods, nor are ambitious to rob thee of them?'

The king answereth them with revilings

Said the king, 'I do well to punish you, ye clever misleaders of the folk, because ye deceive all men, counselling them to abstain from the enjoyments of life; and because, instead of the sweets of life and the allures of appetite and pleasure, ye constrain them to choose the rough, filthy and squalid way, and preach that they should render to Jesus the honour due unto the gods. Accordingly, in order that the people may not follow your deceits and leave the land desolate, and, forsaking the gods of their fathers, serve another, I think it just to subject you to punishment and death.'

Their leader chideth the king for his sin and folly,

The monk answered, 'If thou art eager that all should partake of the good things of life, why dost thou not distribute dainties and riches equally amongst all? And why is it that the common herd are pinched with poverty, while thou addest ever to thy store by seizing for thyself the goods of others? Nay, thou carest not for the weal of the many, but fattenest thine own flesh, to be meat for the worms to feed on. Wherefore also thou hast denied the God of all, and called them gods that are not, the inventors of all wickedness, in order that, by wantonness and wickedness after their example, thou mayest gain the title of imitator of the gods.

ἔπραξαν, πῶς οὐχὶ καὶ οἱ προσέχοντες αὐτοῖς ἄνθρωποι πράξουσι; πλάνην οὖν μεγάλην πεπλάνησαι, ὦ βασιλεῦ. δέδοικας δὲ μή τινας τοῦ λαοῦ πείσαιμεν, τοῖς ἡμετέροις συνθεμένους, ἀποστῆναί σου τῆς χειρὸς καὶ τῇ τὰ πάντα συνεχούσῃ προσοικειωθῆναι χειρί· θέλεις γὰρ πολλοὺς εἶναι τοὺς ὑπουργοὺς τῆς σῆς πλεονεξίας, ἵν' αὐτοὶ μὲν ταλαιπωρῶσι, σοὶ δὲ τὰ παρ' αὐτῶν προσγένοιτο κέρδη. ὃν τρόπον κύνας τις τρέφων ἢ ὄρνεα εἰς θήραν τιθασσευόμενα, πρὸ μὲν τῆς θήρας κολακεύων ταῦτα φαίνοιτο, ἡνίκα δὲ κατά- 201
σχωσί τι τῶν θηρευομένων, βιαίως αὐτῶν τοῦ στόματος τὸ θηρευθὲν ἀφαρπάζει· οὕτω δὴ καὶ σύ, πολλοὺς θέλων ἔχειν τοὺς φόρους σοι καὶ τέλη ἐκ γῆς καὶ θαλάσσης κομίζοντας, λέγεις μὲν τῆς αὐτῶν φροντίζειν σωτηρίας, ἀπώλειαν δὲ αὐτοῖς προξενῶν αἰώνιον, πρὸ δὲ πάντων σεαυτῷ, ἵνα μόνον σοι ὁ σκυβάλων καὶ σαπριῶν ἀχρηστότερος βρίθοιτο πλοῦτος, λέληθας σκότος ἀντὶ φωτὸς κατέχων. ἀλλ' ἀνάνηψον τοῦ καταχθονίου ὕπνου τούτου, διάνοιξόν σου τοὺς μεμυκότας ὀφθαλμούς, καὶ ἴδε τὴν περιλάμπουσαν πᾶσι τοῦ Θεοῦ ἡμῶν δόξαν· καὶ σύ ποτε
Ps. xciv. 8 σεαυτοῦ γενοῦ· Σύνετε γάρ, ἄφρονες ἐν τῷ λαῷ, καὶ μωροί ποτε φρονήσατε, φησὶν ὁ προφήτης· σύνες ὅτι οὐκ ἔστι θεός, πλὴν τοῦ Θεοῦ ἡμῶν, καὶ οὐκ ἔστι σωτηρία, εἰ μὴ ἐν αὐτῷ.

Ὁ δὲ βασιλεύς· Τῆς μωρᾶς σου ταύτης φλυαρίας παυσάμενος, τὸν Βαρλαὰμ αὐτίκα μοι ὑπόδειξον, ἢ πειρασθήσῃ κολαστηρίων ὀργάνων, ὧν οὐδέποτε πεῖραν εἴληφας. ὁ μεγαλόφρων οὖν καὶ γενναιότατος ἀσκητὴς καὶ τῆς οὐρανίου φιλο-

For, as your gods have done, why should not also the men that follow them do? Great then is the error that thou hast erred, O king. Thou fearest that we should persuade certain of the people to join with us, and revolt from thy hand, and place themselves in that hand that holdeth all things, for thou willest the ministers of thy covetousness to be many, that they may be miserable while thou reapest profit from their toil; just as a man, who keepeth hounds or falcons tamed for hunting, before the hunt may be seen to pet them, but, when they have once seized the quarry, taketh the game with violence out of their mouths. So also thou, willing that there should be many to pay thee tribute and toll from land and water, pretendest to care for their welfare, but in truth bringest on them and above all on thyself eternal ruin; and simply to pile up gold, more worthless than dung or rottenness, thou hast been deluded into taking darkness for light. But recover thy wits from this earthly sleep: open thy sealed eyes, and behold the glory of God that shineth round about us all; and come at length to thyself. For saith the prophet, "Take heed, ye unwise among the people, and, O ye fools, understand at last." Understand thou that there is no God except our God, and no salvation except in him.'

showing the falseness of his heart

But the king said, 'Cease this foolish babbling, and anon discover to me Barlaam: else shalt thou taste instruments of torture such as thou hast never tasted before.' That noble-minded, great-hearted monk, that lover of the heavenly philosophy, was not

σοφίας ἐραστὴς κατ' οὐδένα τρόπον ταῖς τοῦ βασιλέως ἀπειλαῖς μετετρέπετο· ἀλλ' ἀτρέμας ἑστὼς ἔλεγεν· Οὐ τὰ παρὰ σοῦ θεσπιζόμενα ποιεῖν, ὦ βασιλεῦ, προστετάγμεθα, ἀλλὰ τὰ παρὰ τοῦ Δεσπότου ἡμῶν καὶ Θεοῦ κεκελευσμένα, ὃς σωφροσύνην ἡμᾶς ἐκδιδάσκει τοῦ πασῶν τῶν ἡδονῶν καὶ ἐπιθυμιῶν κρατεῖν, καὶ ἀνδρείαν 202
ἐξασκεῖν, ὥστε πάντα πόνον καὶ πᾶσαν κάκωσιν ὑπὲρ τῆς δικαιοσύνης ὑπομένειν. ὅσα γοῦν ἐπάξεις ἡμῖν ὑπὲρ τῆς εὐσεβείας δεινὰ μᾶλλον εὐεργετήσεις. ποίει οὖν ὃ βούλει· ἡμεῖς γὰρ ἔξω τοῦ καθήκοντος πρᾶξαί τι οὐκ ἀνεξόμεθα, οὐδὲ ἁμαρτίᾳ ἑαυτοὺς ἐκδώσομεν. μὴ μικρὰν γὰρ ταύτην νομίσῃς ἁμαρτίαν, εἰ τὸν συναγωνιστὴν ἡμῶν καὶ συστρατιώτην εἰς τὰς σὰς προδώσομεν χεῖρας. ἀλλ' οὐ γὰρ γελάσεις καθ' ἡμῶν τὸν γέλωτα τοῦτον, κἂν μυρίοις ἡμᾶς περιβάλῃς θανάτοις· οὐχ οὕτως γὰρ ἡμεῖς ἄνανδροι, ὡς φόβῳ τῶν σῶν βασάνων τὴν ἡμετέραν προδοῦναι φιλοσοφίαν, καὶ ἀνάξιόν τι δρᾶσαι τῆς θείας νομοθεσίας. πρὸς ταῦτα πᾶν, εἴ τι γινώσκεις, ἀμυν-
Phil. i. 21 τήριον εὐτρέπιζε ὄργανον· ἡμῖν γὰρ τὸ ζῆν Χριστός ἐστι, καὶ τὸ θανεῖν ὑπὲρ αὐτοῦ κέρδος ἄριστον.

Ἐπὶ τούτοις θυμῷ ἐξαφθείς, ὁ κρατῶν ἐκέλευσε τὰς μὲν θεολόγους αὐτῶν ἐκκοπῆναι γλώσσας ἐξορυχθῆναι δὲ τοὺς ὀφθαλμούς, χεῖράς τε ὁμοῦ ἀποτμηθῆναι καὶ πόδας. τῆς δ' ἀποφάσεως δοθείσης, οἱ μὲν ὑπασπισταὶ περιστάντες αὐτοῖς καὶ δορυφόροι μισανθρώπως καὶ ἀνηλεῶς ἠκρωτηρίαζον· καὶ τὰς μὲν γλώσσας ὀγκινίσκοις τῶν 203
στομάτων ἐξελκύσαντες, θηριωδῶς ἀπέτεμνον, τοὺς

moved by the king's threats, but stood unflinching, and said, 'We are not commanded to fulfil thy hest, O king, but the orders of our Lord and God who teacheth us temperance, that we should be lords over all pleasures and passions, and practise fortitude, so as to endure all toil and all ill-treatment for righteousness' sake. The more perils that thou subjectest us to for the sake of our religion, the more shalt thou be our benefactor. Do therefore as thou wilt: for we shall not consent to do aught outside our duty, nor shall we surrender ourselves to sin. Deem not that it is a slight sin to betray a fellow-combatant and fellow-soldier into thy hands. Nay, but thou shalt not have that scoff to make at us; no, not if thou put us to ten thousand deaths. We be not such cowards as to betray our religion through dread of thy torments, or to disgrace the law divine. So then, if such be thy purpose, make ready every weapon to defend thy claim; for to us to live is Christ, and to die for him is the best gain.'

and defieth his threats of torture

Incensed with anger thereat, the monarch ordered the tongues of these Confessors to be rooted out, and their eyes digged out, and likewise their hands and feet lopped off. Sentence passed, the henchmen and guards surrounded and mutilated them, without pity and without ruth. And they plucked out their tongues from their mouths with prongs, and severed them with brutal severity, and they digged out their

The martyrdom of the monks

ὀφθαλμοὺς δὲ σιδηροῖς ἐξώρυττον ὄνυξιν, ἀρθρεμβόλοις δὲ ὀργάνοις τὰς χεῖρας αὐτῶν καὶ τοὺς πόδας ἐξαρθροῦντες ἀπέτεμνον. οἱ δὲ μακάριοι ἐκεῖνοι καὶ αἰδήμονες καὶ γενναῖοι τὸν λογισμόν, ὡς πρὸς εὐωχίαν καλούμενοι, ἀνδρείως προσήρχοντο ταῖς βασάνοις, ἀλλήλους παραθήγοντες καὶ πρὸς τὸν διὰ Χριστὸν θάνατον ἀφόβως χωροῦντες.

Ἐν τοιαύταις οὖν πολυειδέσι τιμωρίαις τὰς καρτερικὰς αὐτῶν ψυχὰς τῷ Κυρίῳ παρέθεντο οἱ ἱεροὶ ἀσκηταί, ἑπτακαίδεκα τὸν ἀριθμὸν τελοῦντες. ὁμολογουμένως οὖν αὐτοκράτωρ ἐστὶ τῶν
Josephus παθῶν ὁ εὐσεβὴς λογισμός, καθάπερ τις τῶν οὐχ
Eleazar ἡμετέρων ἔφησεν, ἄθλους διηγούμενος πρεσβύτου
2 Macc. vi., vii. ἱερέως καὶ παίδων ἑπτὰ σὺν ὁμόφρονι μητρί, τοῦ πατρῴου ὑπεραθλησάντων νόμου, ὧν τῆς καρτερίας καὶ μεγαλοψυχίας οὐδὲν καθυστέρησαν οἱ θαυμάσιοι οὗτοι πατέρες καὶ τῆς ἄνω Ἱερουσαλὴμ πολῖται καὶ κληρονόμοι.

XXIV

Τούτων οὖν εὐσεβῶς τελειωθέντων, ὁ βασιλεὺς τῷ πρωτοσυμβούλῳ ἔλεγεν Ἀραχῇ πρὸς τὴν δευτέραν ἀποβλέψαι βουλήν, τοῦ πρώτου διαμαρτόντος, καὶ τὸν Ναχὼρ ἐκεῖνον προσκαλέσασθαι. ὁ γοῦν Ἀραχὴς νυκτὶ βαθείᾳ τὸ ἐκείνου καταλαβὼν σπήλαιον (τὰς ἐρήμους γὰρ ᾤκει, μαντικαῖς σχολάζων τέχναις), καὶ πάντα αὐτῷ τὰ βεβουλευμένα σαφηνίσας, πρὸς τὸν βασιλέα ἅμα πρωῒ ἐπανέρχεται. καὶ δὴ ἱππεῖς αὐτῷ αὖθις

eyes with iron claws, and stretched their arms and legs on the rack, and lopped them off. But those blessed, shamefast, noble-hearted men went bravely to torture like guests to a banquet, exhorting one another to meet death for Christ his sake undaunted.

The triumph of holy courage over pain

In such divers tortures did these holy monks lay down their lives for the Lord. They were in all seventeen. By common consent, the pious mind is superior to sufferings, as hath been said by one, but not of us, when narrating the martydom of the aged priest, and of the seven sons with their equally brave mother when contending for the law of their fathers: whose bravery and lofty spirit, however, was equalled by these marvellous fathers and citizens and heirs of Hierusalem that is above.

XXIV

Of the plot of Araches and the king, and of the taking of Nachor the sorcerer, who feigneth himself to be Barlaam

After the monks had made this godly end, the king bade Araches, his chief councillor, now that they had failed of their first plan, to look to the second and summon the man Nachor. At dead of night Araches repaired to his cave (he dwelt in the desert practising the arts of divination), and told him of their plans, and returned to the king at day-break. Again he demanded horsemen, and

ζητήσας ἐπὶ ἔρευναν τοῦ Βαρλαὰμ ἐξέρχεσθαι 204
προσεποιεῖτο. ἐξελθόντι δὲ καὶ τὰς ἐρήμους ἐμπεριπατοῦντι ὁρᾶται αὐτῷ ἀνήρ τις ἐκ φάραγγός τινος ἐξερχόμενος. τοῦ δὲ καταδιώκειν αὐτὸν κελεύσαντος, φθάνουσι τὸ τάχος, καὶ συλλαβόντες πρὸς αὐτὸν ἄγουσι. τοῦ δὲ πυνθανομένου τίς τε εἴη καὶ ποίας θρησκείας ἢ τί καλούμενος, Χριστιανὸν μὲν ἐκεῖνος ἑαυτὸν ἀπεκάλεσε, Βαρλαὰμ δὲ ὠνόμασε, καθάπερ δεδίδακτο. χαρᾶς δὲ πλησθεὶς ὁ Ἀραχής, ὡς ἐδείκνυε, τάχιστα τοῦτον λαβών, πρὸς τὸν βασιλέα ἐπανέρχεται· καὶ δὴ μηνύσας παρίστησιν αὐτόν. καί φησιν ὁ βασιλεὺς εἰς ἐπήκοον πάντων τῶν παρισταμένων· Σὺ εἶ ὁ τοῦ δαίμονος ἐργάτης Βαρλαάμ; ὁ δὲ ἀντέφησεν· Τοῦ Θεοῦ ἐργάτης εἰμί, καὶ οὐ τῶν δαιμόνων. μὴ οὖν με λοιδόρει. πολλὰς γάρ μοι ὁμολογεῖν χάριτας ὀφειλέτης εἶ, ὅτι τὸν υἱόν σου θεοσεβεῖν ἐδίδαξα, πάσης ἀπαλλάξας ἀπάτης
καὶ τῷ ἀληθινῷ καταλλάξας Θεῷ, καὶ πᾶσαν παι- 205
δεύσας ἀρετῆς ἰδέαν. αὖθις δὲ ὁ βασιλεύς, ὀργιζόμενος ὥσπερ, ἔφη· Ἔδει μέν σε μηδὲ λόγου τὸ παράπαν ἀξιώσαντα, ἢ τόπον ἀπολογίας δόντα, ἀλλ' ἀνερωτήτως θανατῶσαι. ἀλλ' ἀνέχομαί σου τοῦ θράσους, τῆς προσηκούσης μοι ἕνεκεν φιλανθρωπίας, ἕως τακτῇ ἡμέρᾳ ἐξετάσω τὰ περὶ σοῦ. καὶ εἰ μὲν πεισθείης μοι συγγνώμης ἀξιωθήσῃ· εἰ δὲ μή, κακῶς ἀπολῇ. οὕτως εἰπὼν τῷ Ἀραχῇ τοῦτον παραδίδωσι, φυλάττειν ἀκριβέστατα ἐντειλάμενος.

Τῇ δὲ ἐπαύριον ἀναζεύξας ἐκεῖθεν, πρὸς τὸ ἴδιον ἐπάνεισι παλάτιον. καὶ ἐξηχοῦετο κρατηθῆναι τὸν Βαρλαάμ, ὥστε καὶ τὸν βασιλέως

made as though he went in quest of Barlaam. When he was gone forth, and was walking the desert, a man was seen to issue from a ravine. Araches gave command to his men to pursue him. They took and brought him before their master. When asked who he was, what his religion and what his name, the man declared himself a Christian and gave his name as Barlaam, even as he had been instructed. Araches made great show of joy, apprehended him and returned quickly to the king, and told his tale and produced his man. Then said the king in the hearing of all present, 'Art thou the devil's workman, Barlaam?' But he denied it, saying, 'I am God's workman, not the devil's. Revile me not; for I am thy debtor to render me much thanks, because I have taught thy son to serve God, and have turned him from error to the true God, and have schooled him in all manner of virtue.' Feigning anger, again spake the king, 'Though I ought to allow thee never a word, and give thee no room for defence, but rather do thee to death without question, yet such is my humanity that I will bear with thine effrontery until on a set day I try thy cause. If thou be persuaded by me, thou shalt receive pardon: if not, thou shalt die the death.' With these words he delivered him to Araches, commanding that he should be most strictly guarded.

Nachor is brought before the king

On the morrow the king removed thence, and came back to his own palace, and it was blazoned abroad that Barlaam was captured, so that the

Ioasaph heareth of the taking of the mock Barlaam,

ἀκούσαντα υἱὸν δεινῶς τὴν ψυχὴν ἀλγῆσαι, καὶ
μηδόλως τῶν δακρύων ἐγκρατὴς δύνασθαι εἶναι.
στεναγμοῖς δὲ καὶ θρήνοις τὸν Θεὸν ἐδυσώπει, καὶ
εἰς βοήθειαν αὐτὸν ἐπεκαλεῖτο τοῦ γέροντος. οὐ
Ps. cxlv. 9 παρεῖδεν οὖν αὐτὸν ὀδυρόμενον ὁ ἀγαθός· χρηστὸς
Ps. xx. 1 γάρ ἐστι τοῖς ὑπομένουσιν αὐτὸν ἐν ἡμέρᾳ θλίψεως, καὶ γινώσκων τοὺς εὐλαβουμένους αὐτόν·
ὃς καὶ τῷ νέῳ δι' ὁράματος νυκτερινοῦ πάντα
γνωρίζει, καὶ ἰσχὺν αὐτῷ ἐντίθησι, καὶ εἰς τὸν
τῆς εὐσεβείας παραθαρρύνει ἀγῶνα. ἔξυπνος
δὲ γενόμενος, χαρᾶς τε πλήρη καὶ θάρσους καὶ
φωτὸς γλυκυτάτου, τὴν πρὸ μικροῦ λυπουμένην
αὐτοῦ καὶ ἀλγοῦσαν εὑρίσκει καρδίαν. ὁ δὲ
βασιλεύς, οὕτω ταῦτα δράσας καὶ οὕτω διανοη-
θείς, ἔχαιρε, καλῶς διασκέπτεσθαι οἰόμενος, καὶ
τῷ Ἀραχῇ μεγίστην ἀπονέμων τὴν χάριν. ἀλλ' 206
Ps. xxvi. 12 ἐψεύσατο ἡ ἀδικία ἑαυτῇ, τὸ τοῦ θείου φάναι
Δαυΐδ, καὶ ἡ δικαιοσύνη νικᾷ τὴν ἀνομίαν, τέλεον
αὐτὴν καταβαλοῦσα καὶ τὸ μνημόσυνον αὐτῆς
Ps. ix. 6 ἀπολέσασα μετ' ἤχου, ὡς ἐν τοῖς ἑξῆς δηλώσειεν
ὁ λόγος.

Μετὰ γοῦν δύο ἡμέρας ὁ βασιλεὺς παραγίνεται πρὸς τὸ τοῦ υἱοῦ παλάτιον. καὶ τούτου εἰς ὑπάντησιν ἐξελθόντος, οὐκ ἠσπάσατο συνήθως ὁ πατήρ· ἀλλ', ἀχθομένῳ ὥσπερ καὶ ὀργιζομένῳ ἐοικώς, εἰσελθὼν ἐν τῷ βασιλικῷ κοιτῶνι, σκυθρωπάζων ἐκαθέσθη. εἶτα, τὸν υἱὸν προσκαλεσάμενος, ἔφη· Τίς ἡ διηχοῦσά μου τὰς ἀκοὰς φήμη, τέκνον, καὶ ἀθυμίαις μου τὴν ψυχὴν κατατήκουσα; οὐδένα γὰρ τῶν ἀνθρώπων τοσαύτης ἐμπιπλᾶσθαι χαρᾶς ποτε οἶμαι ἐπὶ τέκνου γεννήσει, ὅσης ἐγὼ ἐπὶ σοὶ μετέσχον θυμηδίας·

king's son heard thereof and was exceeding sad at heart, and could in no wise refrain from weeping. With groans and lamentations he importuned God, and called upon him to succour the aged man. Nor did the good God despise his complaint, for he is loving with them that abide him in the day of trouble, and knoweth them that fear him. Wherefore in a night-vision he made known the whole plot to the young prince, and strengthened and cheered him for the trial of his righteousness. So, when the prince awoke from sleep, he found that his heart, erstwhile so sore and heavy, was now full of joyaunce, courage and pleasant light. But the king rejoiced at that which he had done and planned, imagining that he was well advised, and showering thanks on Araches. But wickedness lied to itself, to use the words of holy David, and righteousness overcame iniquity, completely overthrowing it, and causing the memorial thereof to perish with sound, as our tale in its sequel shall show.

but learneth the truth in a vision

After two days the king visited his son's palace. When his son came forth for to meet him, instead of kissing him, as was his wont, the father put on a show of distress and anger, and entered the royal chamber, and there sat down frowning. Then calling to his son, he said, 'Child, what is this report that soundeth in mine ears, and weareth away my soul with despondency? Never, I ween, was man more filled with gladness of heart at the birth of a son than was I at thine; and, I trow,

The king visiteth Ioasaph and pleadeth with him to renounce the new faith,

οὐδ᾽ αὖ πάλιν λυπηθῆναί τινα καὶ κακῶς παρὰ
παιδὸς διατεθῆναι δοκῶ, ὡς σύ με νῦν διέθηκας
καὶ τὴν ἐμὴν ἠτίμασας πολιάν, τὸ φῶς τε 207
περιῆρας τῶν ὀφθαλμῶν μου καὶ τὴν τῶν ἐμῶν
Cp. Job. iii. 25 νεύρων ἐξέκοψας ἰσχύν· φόβος γὰρ ὃν ἐφοβούμην
περὶ σοῦ ἦλθέ μοι, καὶ ὃν ἐδεδοίκειν συνήντησέ
Cp. Ecclus. xviii. 31 μοι. καὶ γέγονας τῶν ἐχθρῶν μου ἐπίχαρμα καὶ
τῶν ὑπεναντίων μου κατάγελως. ἀπαιδεύτῳ
φρενὶ καὶ νηπιώδει γνώμῃ τοῖς τῶν ἀπατεώνων
ῥήμασιν ἐξακολουθήσας, καὶ τὴν βουλὴν τῶν
κακοφρόνων τῆς ἐμῆς προκρίνας βουλῆς, καὶ τῶν
ἡμετέρων θεῶν τὸ σέβας καταλιπών, ἀλλοτρίῳ
ἐλάτρευσας Θεῷ. ἵνα τί, τέκνον, ταῦτα πεποίηκας; καὶ ὃν ἤλπιζον ἐν πάσῃ ἐκτρέφειν ἀσφαλείᾳ
καὶ τοῦ γήρως ἔχειν βακτηρίαν καὶ ἰσχύν, διά-
δοχόν τε ἄριστον καταλιμπάνειν τῆς βασιλείας,
τὰ τῶν ἐχθρῶν οὐκ ᾐδέσθης καὶ πολεμίων ἐνδείξασθαι εἰς ἐμέ; οὐκ ἔδει σε ἐμοὶ μᾶλλον πείθεσθαι καὶ τοῖς ἐμοῖς ἕπεσθαι δόγμασιν, ἢ τοῦ
δολίου καὶ σαπροῦ γέροντος εἴκειν ταῖς φληνά-
φοις μωρολογίαις, τοῦ πικράν σοι ἀντὶ τῆς
γλυκείας ὑποθεμένου ζωήν, καὶ ἀντὶ τῆς ποθεινοτάτης τρυφῆς τὴν σκληρὰν καὶ τραχεῖαν
ὁδεύειν ὁδόν, ἣν ὁ τῆς Μαρίας Υἱὸς ἰέναι προτρέ- 208
πεται, οὐ δέδοικας δὲ τῶν μεγίστων θεῶν τὴν
ὀργήν, μὴ κεραυνῷ σε βαλοῦσιν, ἢ σκηπτῷ
θανατώσουσιν, ἢ χάσματι γῆς καταποντίσουσιν,
ἀνθ᾽ ὧν τοὺς τοσαῦτα ἡμᾶς εὐηργετηκότας καὶ
διαδήματι βασιλείας κατακοσμήσαντας, καὶ ἔθνη
πολυάνθρωπα ὑποτάξαντας, καὶ σὲ παρ᾽ ἐλπίδα
δι᾽ εὐχῆς ἐμῆς καὶ δεήσεως γεννηθῆναι καὶ τοῦ
γλυκυτάτου μετέχειν φωτὸς τούτου παρασκευά-

never was man so distressed and cruelly treated by child as I have now been by thee. Thou hast dishonoured my grey hairs, and taken away the light of mine eyes, and loosed the strength of my sinews; "for the thing which I greatly feared concerning thee is come upon me, and that which I was afraid of hath come unto me." Thou art become a joy to mine enemies, and a laughing-stock to mine adversaries. With untutored mind and childish judgement thou hast followed the teaching of the deceivers and esteemed the counsel of the malicious above mine; thou hast forsaken the worship of our gods and become the servant of a strange God. Child, wherefore hast thou done this? I hoped to bring thee up in all safety, and have thee for the staff and support of mine old age, and leave thee, as is most meet, to succeed me in my kingdom, but thou wast not ashamed to play against me the part of a relentless foe. And shouldst thou not rather have listened to me, and followed my injunctions, than have obeyed the idle and foolish pratings of that crafty old knave, who taught thee to choose a sour life instead of a sweet, and abandon the charms of dalliance, to tread the hard and rough road, which the Son of Mary ordereth men to go? Dost thou not fear the displeasure of the most puissant gods, lest they strike thee with lightning, or quell thee with thunderbolt, or overwhelm thee in the yawning earth, because thou hast rejected and scorned those deities that have so richly blessed us, and adorned our brow with the kingly diadem, and made populous nations to be our servants, that, beyond my hope, in answer to my prayer and supplication,

into which a deceiver hath betrayed him,

and to return to the worship of his gods

σαντας, παρωσάμενος καὶ ἐξουθενήσας, τῷ ἐσταυρωμένῳ προσεκολλήθης, ταῖς ματαίαις ἐλπίσι τῶν αὐτοῦ θεραπόντων φενακισθείς, καινούς τινας μυθολογούντων αἰῶνας καὶ νεκρῶν σωμάτων ἀνάστασιν ληρούντων, καὶ ἄλλα μυρία πρὸς ἀπάτην τῶν ἀνοήτων παρεισαγόντων; ἀλλά γε νῦν, φίλτατε υἱέ, εἴ τι μοι πείθῃ τῷ πατρί, μακρὰν τοῖς μακροῖς τούτοις λήροις χαίρειν εἰπών, θῦσον προσελθὼν τοῖς εὐμενέσι θεοῖς, 209
ἑκατόμβαις τε αὐτοὺς καὶ σπονδαῖς ἐκμειλιξώμεθα, ἵνα συγγνώμην σοι τοῦ πταίσματος παράσχοιντο· δυνατοὶ γάρ εἰσι καὶ ἰσχύοντες εὐεργετεῖν τε καὶ τιμωρεῖσθαι, καί σοι παράδειγμα τῶν λεγομένων, ἡμεῖς οἱ δι' αὐτῶν εἰς ταύτην τὴν ἀρχὴν προελθόντες, καὶ χάριτας αὐτοῖς τῆς εὐεργεσίας, τάς τε πρὸς τοὺς σεβομένους τιμὰς καὶ τὰς πρὸς τοὺς μὴ πειθομένους αὐτοῖς θύειν κολάσεις παρέχοντες.

Πολλὰς οὖν τοιαύτας βαττολογίας τοῦ βασιλέως διεξελθόντος, τὰ μὲν ἡμέτερα διακωμῳδοῦντος καὶ διαβάλλοντος, τὰ τῶν εἰδώλων δὲ ἐγκωμιάζοντος καὶ ἐπαινοῦντος, ἰδὼν ὁ θειότατος νεανίας ὡς οὐκ ἔτι δεῖται τὸ πρᾶγμα γωνίας καὶ ἐπικρύψεως, ἀλλὰ λυχνίας καὶ περιωπῆς, μᾶλλον ὥστε φανερὸν ἅπασι καταστῆναι, παρρησίας καὶ θάρσους ὑποπλησθείς, ἔφη.

Ὅ μοι πέπρακται, δέσποτα, οὐκ ἂν ἀρνηθείην. τὸ σκότος ἐξέφυγον, τῷ φωτὶ προσδραμών· καὶ τὴν πλάνην ἀπέλιπον, τῇ ἀληθείᾳ οἰκειωθείς· καὶ τοῖς δαίμοσιν ἀποταξάμενος, Χριστῷ συνε- 210
ταξάμην, τῷ τοῦ Θεοῦ καὶ Πατρὸς Υἱῷ καὶ Λόγῳ, οὗ τῷ ῥήματι παρήχθη τὸ πᾶν ἐκ μὴ

allowed thee to be born, and see the sweet life of day, and hast joined thyself unto the Crucified, duped by the hopes of his servants who tell thee fables of worlds to come, and drivel about the resurrection of dead bodies, and bring in a thousand more absurdities to catch fools? But now, dearest son, if thou hast any regard for me thy father, bid a long farewell to these long-winded follies, and come sacrifice to the gracious gods, and let us propitiate them with hecatombs and drink-offerings, that they may grant thee pardon for thy fall; for they be able and strong to bless and to punish. And wouldst thou have an example of that which I say? Behold us, who by them have been advanced to this honour, repaying them for their kindness by honouring their worshippers and chastising the runagates.'

Now when the king had ended all this idle parleying, gainsaying and slandering of our religion, and belauding and praising of his idolatry, the saintly young prince saw that the matter needed no further to be hid in a corner, but to be lighted and made plain to the eyes of all; and, full of boldness and courage, he said.

'That which I have done, sir, I will not deny. I have fled from darkness and run to the light: I have left error and joined the household of truth: I have deserted the service of devils, and joined the service of Christ, the Son and Word of God the Father, at whose decree the world was

Ioasaph answereth his father boldly,

ὄντων, ὃς καί, τὸν ἄνθρωπον ἐκ χοὸς διαπλάσας,
ζωτικὴν ἐνεφύσησε πνοήν, ἐν παραδείσῳ τε
τῆς τρυφῆς ἔθετο διαιτᾶσθαι, παραβάντα δὲ
τὴν ἐντολὴν αὐτοῦ καὶ τῷ θανάτῳ ὑπόδικον
γενόμενον, τῇ ἐξουσίᾳ τε τοῦ δεινοῦ κοσμοκράτορος ὑπαχθέντα, οὐκ ἀπέστη πάντα ποιῶν
πρὸς τὴν ἀρχαίαν βουλόμενος ἐπαναγαγεῖν τιμήν.
διὸ αὐτὸς ὁ πάσης τῆς κτίσεως ποιητὴς καὶ τοῦ
ἡμετέρου γένους δημιουργὸς ἄνθρωπος ἐγένετο δι'
Mat. i. 23 ἡμᾶς καὶ ἐπὶ γῆς ἐλθὼν ἐκ Παρθένου ἁγίας τοῖς
Baruch. iii. 37 ἀνθρώποις συνανεστρέφετο, καὶ ὑπὲρ ἡμῶν τῶν
ἀγνωμόνων οἰκετῶν ὁ Δεσπότης θάνατον κατεδέ-
Phil. ii. 8 ξατο καὶ θάνατον τὸν διὰ σταυροῦ, ὅπως λυθῇ
τῆς ἁμαρτίας ἡ τυραννίς, ὅπως ἡ προτέρα κατα-
δίκη ἀναιρεθῇ, ὅπως ἀνοιγῶσι πάλιν ἡμῖν αἱ
οὐρανοῦ πύλαι. ἐκεῖ γὰρ τὴν φύσιν ἡμῶν ἀνή-
γαγε καὶ ἐπὶ θρόνου δόξης κεκάθικε, βασιλείαν
τε τὴν ἀτελεύτητον ἐδωρήσατο τοῖς αὐτὸν ἀγα- 211
πῶσι καὶ ἀγαθὰ τὰ κρείττονα καὶ λόγου καὶ
ἀκοῆς. αὐτὸς γάρ ἐστιν ὁ κραταιὸς καὶ μόνος
1 Tim. vi. 15 δυνάστης, ὁ Βασιλεὺς τῶν βασιλευόντων καὶ
Rev. xix. 16 Κύριος τῶν κυριευόντων, οὗ τὸ κράτος ἄμαχον
καὶ ἡ δυναστεία ἀνείκαστος, ὁ μόνος ἅγιος καὶ
ἐν ἁγίοις ἀναπαυόμενος, ὁ σὺν Πατρὶ καὶ Ἁγίῳ
Πνεύματι δοξαζόμενος, εἰς ἃ βεβάπτισμαι. καὶ
ὁμολογῶ, δοξάζω τε καὶ προσκυνῶ ἕνα Θεὸν
ἐν τρισὶν ὑποστάσεσιν ὁμοούσιόν τε καὶ ἀσύγ-
χυτον, ἄκτιστόν τε καὶ ἀθάνατον, αἰώνιον,
ἄπειρον, ἀπεριόριστον, ἀσώματον, ἀπαθῆ, ἄτρεπτον, ἀναλλοίωτον, ἀόριστον, πηγὴν ἀγαθότητος
καὶ δικαιοσύνης καὶ φωτὸς ἀϊδίου, πάντων κτισμάτων ὁρατῶν τε καὶ ἀοράτων ποιητήν, συνέ-

brought out of nothing; who, after forming man out of clay, breathed into him the breath of life, and set him to live in a paradise of delight, and, when he had broken his commandment and was become subject unto death, and had fallen into the power of the dread ruler of this world, did not fail him, but wrought diligently to bring him back to his former honour. Wherefore he, the framer of all Creation and maker of our race, became man for our sake, and, coming from a holy Virgin's womb, on earth conversed with men: for us ungrateful servants did the master endure death, even the death of the Cross, that the tyranny of sin might be destroyed, that the former condemnation might be abolished, that the gates of heaven might be open to us again. Thither he hath exalted our nature, and set it on the throne of glory, and granted to them that love him an everlasting kingdom and joys beyond all that tongue can tell, or ear can hear. He is the mighty and only potentate, King of kings and Lord of lords, whose might is invincible, and whose lordship is beyond compare, who only is holy and dwelleth in holiness, who with the Father and with the Holy Ghost is glorified; into this faith I have been baptized. And I acknowledge and glorify and worship One God in Three persons, of one substance, and not to be confounded, increate and immortal, eternal, infinite, boundless, without body, without passions, immutable, unchangeable, undefinable, the fountain of goodness, righteousness and everlasting light, maker of all things visible and invisible,

confessing his Christian faith,

χοντά τε πάντα καὶ συντηροῦντα, πάντων προνοούμενον, κρατοῦντά τε πάντων καὶ βασιλεύ-
John i. 3 οντα. οὔτε γὰρ ἐγένετό τι τῶν ὄντων χωρὶς αὐτοῦ, οὔτε τῆς αὐτοῦ προνοίας ἄνευ συνίστασθαί τι δύναται· αὐτὸς γάρ ἐστι πάντων ἡ ζωή, πάντων ἡ σύστασις, πάντων ὁ φωτισμός, ὅλος γλυκασμὸς καὶ ἐπιθυμία ἀκόρεστος, καὶ πάντων τῶν ἐφετῶν τὸ ἀκρότατον. τὸ καταλιπεῖν οὖν τὸν οὕτως ἀγαθόν, οὕτω σοφόν, οὕτω δυνατὸν Θεόν, καὶ δαίμοσιν ἀκαθάρτοις, δημιουργοῖς πάντων τῶν παθῶν, λατρεῦσαι, ξοάνοις τε κωφοῖς καὶ ἀλάλοις σέβας ἀπονεῖμαι, τοῖς μήτε οὖσί τι μήτε ἐσομένοις, πόσης οὐκ ἂν εἴη πέρα ἀνοίας
Ps. cxiv. 5; cxxxv. 16 καὶ παραφροσύνης; πότε γὰρ ἠκούσθη τις λαλιὰ 212
ἢ λόγος παρ' αὐτῶν; πότε κἂν σμικρὰν ἀπόκρισιν τοῖς εὐχομένοις αὐτοῖς δεδώκασι; πότε περιεπάτησαν ἢ αἴσθησίν τινα ἐδέξαντο; οὔτε γὰρ οἱ ἱστάμενοί ποτε καθέδρας ἐμνήσθησαν, οὔτε οἱ καθήμενοι ἀναστάντες ὤφθησαν. τούτων τὸ εἰδεχθὲς καὶ δυσῶδες καὶ ἀναίσθητον, ἔτι δὲ καὶ
Basil, on Is. x. 11 τῶν ἐνεργούντων ἐν αὐτοῖς καὶ δι' αὐτῶν ὑμᾶς ἀπατώντων δαιμόνων τὸ σαθρὸν καὶ ἀσθενὲς παρὰ ἀνδρὸς ἁγίου μαθών, καὶ τῆς αὐτῶν κακίας
Ps. cxxxix. 22 καταπτύσας, καὶ τέλειον μῖσος μισήσας αὐτούς, τῷ ζῶντι καὶ ἀληθινῷ συνεταξάμην Θεῷ· καὶ αὐτῷ δουλεύσω μέχρι τελευταίας ἀναπνοῆς, ἵνα καὶ εἰς τὰς αὐτοῦ χεῖρας ἔλθοι μου τὸ πνεῦμα. τῶν τοιούτων οὖν συναντησάντων μοι ἀνεκδιηγήτων ἀγαθῶν, ἔχαιρον μὲν τῆς δουλείας ἀπαλλαγεὶς τῶν πονηρῶν δαιμόνων καὶ τῆς δεινῆς ἀνακληθεὶς αἰχμαλωσίας, καὶ τῷ φωτὶ περιλαμφθεὶς τοῦ προσώπου Κυρίου· ἠνιώμην δὲ

containing and sustaining all things, provident for all, ruler and King of all. Without him was there nothing made, nor without his providence can aught subsist. He is the life of all, the support of all, the light of all, being wholly sweetness and insatiable desire, the summit of aspiration. To leave God, then, who is so good, so wise, so mighty, and to serve impure devils, makers of all sinful lusts, and to assign worship to deaf and dumb images, that are not, and never shall be, were not that the extreme of folly and madness? When was there ever heard utterance or language from their lips? When have they given even the smallest answer to their bedesmen? When have they walked, or received any impression of sense? Those of them that stand have never thought of sitting down; and those that sit have never been seen to rise. From an holy man have I learned the ugliness, ill savour and insensibility of these idols, and, moreover, the rottenness and weakness of the devils that operate in them and by them deceive you; and I loathe their wickednesses and, hating them with a perfect hatred, have joined myself to the living and true God, and him will I serve until my latest breath, that my spirit also may return into his hands. When these unspeakable blessings came in my path, I rejoiced to be freed from the bondage of evil devils, and to be reclaimed from dire captivity and to be illumined with the light of the countenance of the Lord. But my soul was distressed and divided

abjuring all idolatry,

καὶ τὴν ψυχὴν ἐμεριζόμην, ὅτι μὴ καὶ αὐτὸς ὁ δεσπότης μου καὶ πατὴρ τῶν τοιούτων μετεῖχες εὐεργεσιῶν. ἀλλὰ δεδοικώς σου τῆς γνώμης τὸ δυσπειθές, κατεῖχον ἐν ἐμαυτῷ τὴν λύπην, μὴ παροργίσαι σε βουλόμενος, τὸν Θεὸν δὲ ἀπαύστως ἱκέτευον ἑλκῦσαί σε πρὸς ἑαυτὸν καὶ τῆς
μακρᾶς ἀνακαλέσασθαι ἐξορίας ἧς αὐτὸς προε- 213
ξένησας σεαυτῷ, δραπέτης οἴμοι τῆς εὐσεβείας γενόμενος καὶ κακίας ὑπηρέτης πάσης καὶ ἀσεβείας. ἐπεὶ δὲ αὐτός, ὦ πάτερ, εἰς ἐμφανὲς τὰ κατ᾽ ἐμὲ ἤγαγες, τὸ πᾶν τῆς ἐμῆς ἄκουε γνώμης· οὐ ψεύσομαι τὰς πρὸς Χριστόν μου συνθήκας, οὐ, μὰ τὸν ἐξαγοράσαντά με τῆς δουλείας τῷ
1 Pet. i. 19 τιμίῳ αὐτοῦ αἵματι, κἂν μυριάκις με δεῖ ἀποθανεῖν ὑπὲρ αὐτοῦ, θανοῦμαι. τὰ περὶ ἐμοῦ
Mk. xiv. 6 τοίνυν οὕτως εἰδώς, μηκέτι κόπους σεαυτῷ πάρεχε, μεταπείθειν με ἐπιχειρῶν τῆς καλῆς ὁμολογίας. ὡς γάρ σοι τοῦ οὐρανοῦ ἐπιλαβέσθαι δόξαντι τῇ χειρί, ἢ τὰ θαλάττια ξηρᾶναι πελάγη, ἄπρακτον ἂν τὸ ἐγχείρημα ἦν καὶ ἀνήνυτον, οὕτω δὴ καὶ τοῦτο γίνωσκε εἶναι. ἢ τοίνυν αὐτός, τῆς ἐμῆς ἀκούσας βουλῆς, τῷ Χριστῷ οἰκειώθητι, καὶ τῶν ὑπὲρ ἔννοιαν λήψῃ ἀγαθῶν, κοινωνοί τε ἀλλήλοις ἐσόμεθα, ὥσπερ τῆς φύσεως, οὕτω δὴ καὶ τῆς πίστεως· ἢ τῆς σῆς ἀποστήσομαι, εὖ ἴσθι, υἱότητος, καὶ τῷ Θεῷ μου λατρεύ- 214
σω καθαρῷ συνειδότι.

Ταῦτα οὖν πάντα ὡς ἤκουσεν ὁ βασιλεύς, ὀξύτατα κινηθεὶς καὶ θυμῷ ἀσχέτῳ καταληφθείς, ὀργίλως αὐτῷ ἐλάλει, καὶ πικρῶς τοὺς ὀδόντας ἔβρυχε, μαινομένῳ ἐοικώς· Καὶ τίς, φησίν, ὁ τοιούτων μοι αἴτιος τῶν κακῶν, ἢ αὐτὸς ἐγὼ

asunder, that thou, my lord and father, didst not share in my blessings. Yet I feared the stubbornness of thy mind, and kept my grief to myself, not wishing to anger thee; but, without ceasing, I prayed God to draw thee to himself, and call thee back from the long exile that thou hast imposed upon thyself, a runagate alas! from righteousness, and a servant of all sin and wickedness. But sith thou thyself, O my father, hast brought mine affairs to light, hear the sum of my resolve: I will not be false to my covenant with Christ; no, I swear it by him that bought me out of slavery with his own precious blood; even if I must needs die a thousand deaths for his sake, die I will. Knowing then how matters now stand with me, prithee, no longer trouble thyself in endeavouring to persuade me to change my good confession. For as it were a thankless and never ending task for thee to try to grasp the heavens with thy hand, or to dry up the waters of the sea, so hard were it for thee to change me. Either then now listen to my counsel, and join the household of Christ, and so thou shalt gain blessings past man's understanding, and we shall be fellows with one another by faith, even as by nature; or else, be well assured, I shall depart thy sonship, and serve my God with a clear conscience.'

and imploring his father to do likewise

Now when the king heard all these words, he was furiously enraged: and, seized with ungovernable anger, he cried out wrathfully against him, and gnashed his teeth fiercely, like any madman. 'And who,' said he, 'is blameable for all my misfortunes

The king in hot anger casteth reproaches on his son

οὕτως σοι διατεθεὶς καὶ τοιαῦτα ἐπὶ σοὶ ἐργασά-
μενος ἃ οὐδεὶς πώποτε τῶν πατέρων πεποίηκε;
διό σου τῆς γνώμης τὸ σκολιὸν καὶ φιλόνεικον,
δύναμιν τῇ ἐξουσίᾳ προσλαβόμενον, κατὰ τῆς
ἐμῆς κεφαλῆς μανῆναί σε πεποίηκε. δικαίως οὖν
ἐν τῇ σῇ γεννήσει οἱ ἀστρολόγοι δεινὸν εἶπον 215
ἀποβήσεσθαί σε καὶ παμπόνηρον ἄνδρα, ἀλαζόνα
τε καὶ γονεῦσιν ἀπειθῆ. ἀλλὰ νῦν, εἰ τὴν ἐμὴν
ἀκυρώσεις βουλὴν καὶ τῆς ἐμῆς ἀποστήσῃ υἱότητος, ὡς ἐχθρός σοι διατεθείς, ἐκεῖνα ποιήσω σοι,
ἅπερ οὐδὲ πολεμίοις τις ἐνεδείξατο.

Αὖθις δὲ ἐκεῖνος, Τί, φησίν, ὦ βασιλεῦ, εἰς
ὀργὴν ἀνήφθης; ὅτι τοιούτων ἐγὼ ἠξίωμαι ἀγαθῶν, λελύπησαι; καὶ τίς ποτε πατὴρ ἐπὶ τῇ τοῦ
υἱοῦ εὐτυχίᾳ ἀχθόμενος ὡράθη; ἢ πῶς πατὴρ ὁ
τοιοῦτος, καὶ οὐκ ἐχθρός, λογισθείη; οὐκοῦν οὐδὲ
ἐγὼ τοῦ λοιποῦ πατέρα μού σε καλέσω· ἀλλ᾽
ἀποστήσομαί σου, ὥσπερ τις φεύγει ἀπὸ ὄφεως,
εἰ γνώσομαι φθονεῖν σε τὴν ἐμὴν σωτηρίαν, εἰς
ἀπώλειαν δὲ βιαίᾳ συνωθεῖν με χειρί. εἰ γὰρ
βιάζειν με καὶ τυραννεῖν θελήσειας, καθὰ δὴ καὶ
εἶπας, οὐδὲν ἄλλο κερδανεῖς, εὖ ἴσθι, ἢ τὸ ἀντὶ
πατρὸς τύραννος καὶ φονεὺς κληθῆναι μόνον· ἐπεὶ
ῥᾷόν σοι ἀετοῦ ἴχνεσιν ἐφικέσθαι καὶ κατ᾽ αὐτὸν
Cp. Prov. xxx. 19 τὸν ἀέρα διίπτασθαι, ἢ τὴν ἐμὴν μεταπείσειν[1] εἰς
Χριστὸν πίστιν, καὶ ἣν αὐτῷ ὡμολόγησα καλὴν
ὁμολογίαν. ἀλλὰ σύνες, ὦ πάτερ, καί, τὴν λήμην
καὶ ἀχλὺν ἀποτινάξας τῶν τοῦ νοὸς ὀμμάτων, ἀνά- 216
βλεψον ἰδεῖν τὸ πᾶσι περιλάμπον τοῦ Θεοῦ μου
φῶς, καὶ αὐτός ποτε περιλάμφθητι τῷ γλυκυτάτῳ
τούτου φωτί. ἵνα τί γὰρ ὅλως τοῖς πάθεσι καὶ

[1] μεταπείθειν?

but myself, who have dealt with thee so kindly, and cared for thee as no father before? Hence the perversity and contrariness of thy mind, gathering strength by the licence that I gave thee, hath made thy madness to fall upon mine own pate. Rightly prophesied the astrologers in thy nativity that thou shouldest prove a knave and villain, an impostor and rebellious son. But now, if thou wilt make void my counsel, and cease to be my son, I will become thine enemy, and entreat thee worse than ever man yet entreated his foes.'

Ioasaph seeketh to allay the king's wrath,

Again said Ioasaph, 'Why, O king, hast thou been kindled to wrath? Art thou grieved that I have gained such bliss? Why, what father was ever seen to be sorrowful in the prosperity of his son? Would not such an one be called an enemy rather than a father? Therefore will I no more call thee my father, but will withdraw from thee, as a man fleeth from a snake, if I know that thou grudgest me my salvation, and with violent hand forcest me to destruction. If thou wilt force me, and play the tyrant, as thou hast threatened, be assured that thou shalt gain nought thereby save to exchange the name of father for that of tyrant and murderer. It were easier for thee to attain to the ways of the eagle, and, like him, cleave the air, than to alter my loyalty to Christ, and that good confession that I have confessed in him. But be wise, O my father, and shake off the rheum and mist from the eyes of thy mind, lift them aloft and look upward to view the light of my God that enlighteneth all around, and be thyself, at last, enlightened with this light most sweet. Why art thou wholly given up to the

θελήμασιν ἐξεδόθης τῆς σαρκός, καὶ ἀνάνευσις[1]
Cp. Is. xl. 6, 7 οὐκ ἔστι; γνῶθι ὅτι πᾶσα σὰρξ χόρτος καὶ πᾶσα
δόξα ἀνθρώπου ὡς ἄνθος χόρτου· ἐξηράνθη ὁ
χόρτος καὶ τὸ ἄνθος αὐτοῦ ἐκπέπτωκε, τὸ δὲ ῥῆμα
τοῦ Κυρίου μου, τὸ εὐαγγελισθὲν ἐπὶ πάντας,
μενεῖ εἰς τὸν αἰῶνα. τί οὖν οὕτως ἐμμανῶς ἀντέχῃ
καὶ περιέχῃ τῆς δίκην τῶν ἐαρινῶν ἀνθέων μαραι-
νομένης καὶ ἀφανιζομένης δόξης, καὶ τῆς βδελυρᾶς
καὶ δυσώδους τρυφῆς, καὶ τῶν τῆς γαστρὸς καὶ
ὑπὸ γαστέρα μιαρωτάτων παθῶν, ἅτινα πρὸς
καιρὸν ἡδύνουσι τὰς αἰσθήσεις τῶν ἀνοήτων,
ὕστερον μέντοι πικροτέρας χολῆς ποιοῦνται τὰς 217
ἀναδόσεις, ὅταν αἱ μὲν σκιαὶ αὗται καὶ τὰ ἐνύπνια
τοῦ ματαίου τούτου παρέλθωσι βίου, ἐν ὀδύνῃ δὲ
διηνεκεῖ πυρὸς ἀσβέστου καὶ σκοτεινοῦ κατακλει-
σθῶσιν οἱ τούτων ἐρασταί, καὶ τῆς ἀνομίας ἐργά-
Is. lxvi. 24 ται, ἔνθα ὁ σκώληξ αὐτοὺς ὁ ἀκοίμητος ἀτελεύτητα
Mark ix. 44, 46, 48 κατεσθίει, καὶ τὸ πῦρ ἄληκτα καὶ ἀκατάσβεστα
εἰς αἰῶνας κατακαίει ἀπεράντους; μεθ᾽ ὧν οἴμοι
καὶ αὐτὸς κατακλεισθεὶς καὶ χαλεπῶς ὀδυνώμενος,
πολλὰ μὲν μεταγνώσῃ τῶν δεινῶν βουλευμάτων,
πολλὰ δὲ ἐπιζητήσεις τὰς νῦν ἡμέρας καὶ τῶν
ἐμῶν ἐπιμνησθήσῃ ῥημάτων· ἀλλ᾽ ὄφελος τῆς
Ps. vi. 5 μεταμελείας οὐκ ἔσται. ἐν γὰρ τῷ ᾅδῃ ἐξομολόγη-
Greg. Naz. Orat. ix. p. 152 σις καὶ μετάνοια οὐχ ὑπάρχει· ἀλλ᾽ ὁ παρὼν
ὡρίσθη καιρὸς τῆς ἐργασίας, ὁ δὲ μέλλων τῆς
ἀνταποδόσεως. εἰ μὲν γὰρ τὰ παρόντα τερπνὰ
οὐκ ἀφανισμῷ ὑπέκειτο καὶ ῥοῇ, ἀλλὰ συνδιαιωνίζειν ἔμελλε τοῖς αὐτῶν δεσπόταις, οὐδὲ οὕτως
ἔδει τῶν τοῦ Χριστοῦ δωρεῶν καὶ ὑπὲρ ἔννοιαν

[1] De baptismo usurpatum significat emersionem, ap. Joh. Chryst. Caten. in Joh. c. 3.

passions and desires of the flesh, and why is there no looking upward? Know thou that all flesh is grass and all the glory of man as the flower of grass. The grass withereth, and the flower thereof falleth away; but the word of my Lord, which by the gospel is preached unto all, shall endure for ever. Why then dost thou thus madly cling to and embrace that glory, which, like spring flowers, fadeth and perisheth, and to beastly unsavoury wantonness, and to the abominable passions of the belly and the members thereunder, which for a season please the senses of fools, but afterwards make returns more bitter than gall, when the shadows and dreams of this vain life are passed away, and the lovers thereof, and workers of iniquity are imprisoned in the perpetual pain of dark and unquenchable fire, where the worm that sleepeth not gnaweth for ever, and where the fire burneth without ceasing and without quenching through endless ages? And with these sinners alas! thou too shalt be imprisoned and grievously tormented, and shalt bitterly rue thy wicked counsels, and bitterly regret thy days that now are, and think upon my words, but there shall be no advantage in repentance; for in death there is no confession and repentance. But the present is the set time for work: the future for reward. Even if the pleasures of the present world were not evanescent and fleeting, but were to endure for ever with their owners, not even thus should any man choose them before the gifts of Christ, and the good things that pass

showing him the vanity of his present power and pleasures,

ἀγαθῶν ταῦτα προκρῖναι· καθ' ὅσον γὰρ ὁ ἥλιος
τῆς βαθείας ἐστὶ νυκτὸς λαμπρότερος καὶ διαυγέ-
στερος, τοσοῦτον καὶ πολλῷ πλέον τὰ ἐπηγγελμένα ἀγαθὰ τοῖς ἀγαπῶσι τὸν Θεὸν πάσης
ἐπιγείου βασιλείας καὶ δόξης ἐνδοξότερά τε ὑπάρχει καὶ μεγαλοπρεπέστερα, καὶ ἔδει πάντως τὰ
μείζονα τῶν εὐτελεστέρων προκρῖναι. ἐπεὶ δὲ καὶ
ῥευστὰ τὰ τῇδε πάντα καὶ φθορᾷ ὑποκείμενα ὡς
Job. xiv. 2 ὄναρ τε καὶ ὡς σκιὰ καὶ ἐνύπνιον παρέρχεται καὶ 218
Ps. cxliv. 4 ἀφανίζεται, καὶ αὔραις μᾶλλον ἔστι πιστεύειν
Wisd. v. 10 οὐχ ἱσταμέναις καὶ νηὸς ποντοπορούσης ἴχνεσιν ἢ
ἀνθρώπων εὐημερίᾳ, πόσης εὐηθείας ἤ, μᾶλλον
εἰπεῖν, ἀνοίας τε καὶ παραφροσύνης τὰ φθαρτὰ
καὶ ἐπίκηρα, ἀσθενῆ τε καὶ οὐδαμινά, τῶν ἀφθάρτων προκρῖναι καὶ αἰωνίων, ἀκηράτων τε καὶ
ἀτελευτήτων, καὶ τῇ προσκαίρῳ τούτων ἀπολαύσει τῆς ἀδιαδόχου στερηθῆναι τῶν ἀγαθῶν ἐκείνων ἀπολαύσεως; οὐ συνήσεις ταῦτα, ὦ πάτερ;
οὐ παραδραμεῖς τὰ παρατρέχοντα, καὶ προσθήσῃ
τοῖς ἐπιμένουσιν; οὐ προτιμήσεις τὴν κατοικίαν
τῆς παροικίας, τὸ φῶς τοῦ σκότους, τὸ πνεῦμα
τῆς σαρκός, τὴν αἰώνιον ζωὴν τῆς σκιᾶς τοῦ θανάτου, τὰ μὴ λυόμενα τῶν ῥεόντων; οὐκ ἐκφεύξῃ τῆς
χαλεπῆς δουλείας τοῦ δεινοῦ κοσμοκράτορος,
τοῦ πονηροῦ, φημί, διαβόλου, καὶ τῷ ἀγαθῷ καὶ
εὐσπλάγχνῳ καὶ πανοικτίρμονι οἰκειωθήσῃ Δεσπότῃ; οὐ, τῆς τῶν πολλῶν ἀποστὰς καὶ ψευ-
1 Thess. i. 9 δωνύμων θεῶν λατρείας, τῷ ἑνὶ λατρεύσεις
ἀληθινῷ καὶ ζῶντι Θεῷ; εἰ γὰρ καὶ ἥμαρτες αὐτῷ,
πολλὰ βλασφημήσας καὶ τοὺς αὐτοῦ θεράποντας
δειναῖς ἀνελὼν τιμωρίαις, ἀλλὰ δέξεταί σε, εὖ 219
οἶδα, ὁ ἀγαθὸς ἐπιστρέψαντα καὶ πάντων σου

man's understanding. Soothly, as the sun surpasseth in radiance and brightness the dead of night, even so, and much more so, doth the happiness promised to those that love God excel in glory and magnificence all earthly kinship and glory; and there is utter need for a man to choose the more excellent before the more worthless. And forasmuch as everything here is fleeting and subject to decay, and passeth and vanisheth as a dream, and as a shadow and vision of sleep; and as one may sooner trust the unstable breezes, or the tracks of a ship passing over the waves, than the prosperity of men, what simplicity, nay, what folly and madness it is to choose the corruptible and perishable, the weak things of no worth, rather than the incorruptible and everlasting, the imperishable and endless, and, by the temporal enjoyment of these things, to forfeit the eternal fruition of the happiness to come! Wilt thou not understand this, my father? Wilt thou not haste past the things which haste pass thee, and attach thyself to that which endureth? Wilt thou not prefer a home land to a foreign land, light to darkness, the spirit to the flesh, eternal life to the shadow of death, the indestructible to the fleeting? Wilt thou not escape from the grievous bondage of the cruel prince of this world, I mean the evil one, the devil, and become the servant of the good, tenderhearted, and all merciful Lord? Wilt thou not break away from serving thy many gods, falsely so called, and serve the one, true and living God? Though thou hast sinned against him often times by blaspheming him, and often times by slaying his servants with dread torments, yet, I know well, that if thou turn again, he shall in his kindness receive thee, and no

and the surety and steadfastness of things eternal

ἀμνημονεύσει τῶν πλημμελημάτων· οὐ βούλεται
Cp. Ez. xxxiii. 11 γὰρ τὸν θάνατον τοῦ ἁμαρτωλοῦ, ὡς τὸ ἐπιστρέψαι καὶ ζῆν αὐτόν, ὁ ἐκ τῶν ἀνεκδιηγήτων κατελ-
θὼν ὑψωμάτων ἐπὶ ζήτησιν τῶν πλανηθέντων
ἡμῶν, σταυρόν τε καὶ μάστιγας καὶ θάνατον ὑπομείνας δι' ἡμᾶς, καὶ τῷ τιμίῳ αὐτοῦ αἵματι ἐξ-
Cp. Rom. vii. 14 αγοράσας ἡμᾶς τοὺς πεπραμένους ὑπὸ τὴν
ἁμαρτίαν. αὐτῷ ἡ δόξα καὶ αἴνεσις εἰς τοὺς
αἰῶνας. ἀμήν.

Τοῦ δὲ βασιλέως ἐκπλήξει τε ἅμα καὶ ὀργῇ λη-
φθέντος, τὸ μὲν ἐπὶ τῇ τοῦ παιδὸς συνέσει καὶ τοῖς
ἀναντιρρήτοις αὐτοῦ ῥήμασι, τὸ δὲ ἐφ' ᾧ ἐκείνου
οὐ διέλιπεν ἐνδιαβάλλων θεοὺς καὶ ὅλον αὐτοῦ
μυκτηρίζων καὶ χλευάζων τὸν βίον, τὸ μὲν τοῦ
λόγου φαιδρὸν διὰ τὴν ἔνδον οὐκ ἐδέξατο τοῦ
σκότους παχύτητα, τιμωρήσασθαι δὲ αὐτὸν ἢ
κακῶς τι διαθέσθαι τῇ φυσικῇ μὴ δυνάμενος
στοργῇ, τὸ δὲ μεταπείσειν αὐτὸν ἀπειλαῖς πάντη
ἀπογνούς, φοβηθεὶς μή, πλείονας κινήσας πρὸς
αὐτὸν λόγους, ἐκείνου παρρησιαζομένου καὶ τὰ
τῶν θεῶν διακωμῳδοῦντος καὶ χλευάζοντος, εἰς
πλείονα θυμὸν ἐξαφθείς, τῶν ἐναντίων εἰς αὐτόν
τι διαπράξοιτο, μετ' ὀργῆς ἀναστάς, ὑπεχώρησεν,
Εἴθε μηδόλως ἐγεννήθης, εἰπών, μήτ' εἰς φῶς
προῆλθες, τοιοῦτος μέλλων ἔσεσθαι, βλάσφημος
εἰς τοὺς θεοὺς καὶ τῆς πατρικῆς ἀποστάτης φιλίας τε καὶ νουθεσίας. ἀλλ' οὐκ εἰς τέλος τῶν
ἀηττήτων καταμωκήσῃ θεῶν, οὐδ' ἐπὶ πολὺ χαρή-
σονται οἱ ὑπεναντίοι, οὐδ' αἱ τούτων ἰσχύσουσι
γοητεῖαι. εἰ μὴ γὰρ εὐήκοος γενήσῃ μοι καὶ τοῖς 220
θεοῖς εὐγνώμων, πολλαῖς πρότερον ἐκδώσας σε

more remember thine offences: because he willeth not the death of a sinner but rather that he may turn and live—he, who came down from the unspeakable heights, to seek us that had gone astray: who endured for us Cross, scourge and death; who bought with his precious blood us who had been sold in bondage under sin. Unto him be glory and praise for ever and ever! Amen.'

The king departeth from Ioasaph in anger

The king was overwhelmed with astonishment and anger; with astonishment, at his son's wisdom and unanswerable words; with anger, at the persistence with which he denounced his father's gods, and mocked and ridiculed the whole tenour of his life. He could not admit the glory of his discourse because of the grossness of the darkness within, but natural affection forbad him to punish his son, or evilly to entreat him, and he utterly despaired of moving him by threats. Fearing then that, if he argued further with him, his son's boldness and bitter satire of the gods might kindle him to hotter anger, and lead him to do him a mischief, he arose in wrath and withdrew. 'Would that thou hadst never been born,' he cried, 'nor hadst come to the light of day, destined as thou wert to be such an one, a blasphemer of the gods, and a renegade from thy father's love and admonition! But thou shalt not alway mock the invincible gods, nor shall their enemies rejoice for long, nor shall these knavish sorceries prevail. For except thou become obedient unto me, and right-minded toward the gods, I will first deliver thee to sundry

καὶ ποικίλαις τιμωρίαις, κακηγκάκως[1] θανατώσω, οὐχ ὡς υἱῷ σοι διατεθείς, ἀλλ' ὡς ἐχθρῷ τινι καὶ ἀποστάτῃ.

XXV

Ταῦτα τοῦ πατρὸς ἀπειλησαμένου καὶ μετ'
ὀργῆς ὑποχωρήσαντος, εἰς τὸν ἑαυτοῦ κοιτῶνα ὁ
υἱὸς εἰσελθών, καὶ πρὸς τὸν οἰκεῖον ἀγωνοθέτην
Cp. Ps. cxxx. 1 τοὺς ὀφθαλμοὺς ἀνατείνας, Κύριε, ὁ Θεός μου, ἐκ
βάθους ἀνέκραξε τῆς καρδίας, γλυκεῖα ἐλπὶς καὶ
ἀψευδὴς ἐπαγγελία, ἡ κραταιὰ καταφυγὴ τῶν
σοὶ προσανακειμένων, ἴδε μου τὴν συντριβὴν τῆς
Ps. xxxviii. 21 καρδίας ἱλέῳ καὶ εὐμενεῖ ὄμματι, καὶ μὴ ἐγκαταλίπῃς με, μηδὲ ἀποστῇς ἀπ' ἐμοῦ· ἀλλά, κατὰ
τὴν ἀψευδῆ σου ὑπόσχεσιν, γενοῦ μετ' ἐμοῦ τοῦ
ἀναξίου καὶ εὐτελοῦς· σὲ γὰρ γινώσκω καὶ ὁμολογῶ ποιητὴν καὶ προνοητὴν πάσης κτίσεως.
αὐτὸς οὖν με ἐνίσχυσον ἐν ταύτῃ τῇ καλῇ ὁμο-
Cp. Ps. xxv. 16 λογίᾳ μέχρι τελευταίας διαμεῖναι ἀναπνοῆς· ἐπίβλεψον ἐπ' ἐμὲ καὶ ἐλέησόν με, καὶ παράστηθι
ἐκ πάσης διατηρῶν με σατανικῆς ἐνεργείας ἀλώ- 221
βητον· ἐπίβλεψον, βασιλεῦ· διαπέφλεκται γὰρ
ἰσχυρῶς ἡ ψυχή μου τῷ σῷ πόθῳ, καὶ ἐκκέ-
Cp. Is. xliv. 8 καυται ὡς ἐν δίψῃ καύματος ἐν ἀνύδρῳ, σὲ ἐπι-
Ps. xlii. 1 ποθοῦσα τὴν πηγὴν τῆς ἀθανασίας. μὴ παρα-
Ps. lxxiv. 19 δῴης τοῖς θηρίοις ψυχὴν ἐξομολογουμένην σοι·
τῆς ψυχῆς τοῦ πτωχοῦ σου μὴ ἐπιλάθῃ εἰς τέλος·
ἀλλὰ παράσχου μοι τῷ ἁμαρτωλῷ παρ' ὅλην μου
τὴν ζωὴν ὑπὲρ τοῦ σοῦ ὀνόματος καὶ τῆς σῆς

[1] Also κακιγκάκως, p. 236 of Boissonade.

tortures, and then put thee to the cruellest death, dealing with thee not as with a son, but as with an enemy and rebel.'

XXV

Ioasaph prayeth for strength and comfort

In such wise did the father threaten and wrathfully retire. But the son entered his own bedchamber, and lifted up his eyes to the proper judge of his cause, and cried out of the depth of his heart, 'O Lord my God, my sweet hope and unerring promise, the sure refuge of them that are wholly given up to thee, with gracious and kindly eye look upon the contrition of my heart, and leave me not, neither forsake me. But, according to thine unerring pledge, be thou with me, thine unworthy and sorry servant. Thee I acknowledge and confess, the maker and provider of all creation. Therefore do thou thyself enable me to continue in this good confession, until my dying breath: look upon me, and pity me; and stand by and keep me unhurt by any working of Satan. Look upon me, O King: for my heart is enkindled with longing after thee, and is parched as with burning thirst in the desert, desiring thee, the well of immortality. Deliver not to the wild beasts my soul that confesseth thee: forget not the soul of the poor for ever; but grant me that am a sinner throughout my length of days to suffer all things for thy name's sake and in

ὁμολογίας πάντα παθεῖν, καὶ ὅλον ἐμαυτόν σοι καταθῦσαι· σοῦ γὰρ ἐνδυναμοῦντος καὶ οἱ ἀσθενεῖς ὑπερισχύσουσιν, ὅτι μόνος εἶ σύμμαχος ἀήττητος καὶ Θεὸς ἐλεήμων, ὃν εὐλογεῖ πᾶσα κτίσις τὸν δεδοξασμένον εἰς τοὺς αἰῶνας. ἀμήν.

Οὕτως εὐξάμενος θείας ᾔσθετο παρακλήσεως τῇ αὐτοῦ ἐπιφοιτησάσης καρδίᾳ, καὶ θάρσους ἐμπλησθεὶς εὐχόμενος ὅλην διετέλεσε τὴν νύκτα. ὁ δὲ βασιλεὺς Ἀραχῇ τῷ φίλῳ κοινολογησάμενος τὰ περὶ τοῦ παιδός, καὶ τὴν ἀπότομον αὐτοῦ παρρησίαν ἀμετάθετόν τε δηλώσας γνώμην, βουλὴν τίθεται φίλιον ὁ Ἀραχὴς ὅτι μάλιστα καὶ θεραπευτικὴν πρὸς αὐτὸν ποιήσασθαι τὴν ὁμιλίαν, ταῖς κολακείαις ἐλπίζων ἴσως ἐφελκύσασθαι. ἔρχεται τοιγαροῦν τῇ ἐπαύριον πρὸς τὸν υἱόν· καὶ καθίσας ἐγγύτερον τοῦτον προσεκαλέσατο. εἶτα περιπλακεὶς κατεφίλει, πράως ὑπερχόμενος καὶ ἠπίως, Ὦ τέκνον ποθεινότατον, εἰρηκώς, καὶ φιλούμενον, τίμησον τὴν τοῦ σοῦ πατρὸς πολιάν, καί, τῆς ἐμῆς ἀκούσας δεήσεως, προσελθὼν θυσίαν τοῖς θεοῖς προσάγαγε. οὕτω 222
γὰρ ἐκείνους τε εὐμενεῖς ἕξεις, καὶ μακρότητα ἡμερῶν, δόξης τε πάσης καὶ βασιλείας ἀνεπηρεάστου καὶ παντοίων ἀγαθῶν μετουσίαν παρ' αὐτῶν ἀπολήψῃ, ἐμοί τε τῷ πατρὶ ἔσῃ κεχαρισμένος διὰ βίου παντός, καὶ πᾶσιν ἀνθρώποις τίμιός τε καὶ ἐπαινετός. μέγα γὰρ εἰς ἐπαίνου λόγον τῷ πατρὶ ὑπακούειν, καὶ μάλιστα ἐπ' ἀγαθῷ καὶ τῇ εἰς θεοὺς εὐνοίᾳ. τί δέ, τέκνον, ὑπέλαβες; πότερον ὡς ἑκὼν τῆς ἀγαθῆς ἐκκλίνας ὁδοῦ τὴν ἐναντίαν ἰέναι προέκρινα, ἢ ἀγνοίᾳ καὶ ἀπειρίᾳ τοῦ ἀγαθοῦ τοῖς ὀλεθρίοις ἐμαυτὸν

the confession of thee, and to sacrifice my whole self unto thee. For, with thy might working in them, even the feeble shall wax exceeding strong; for thou only art the unconquerable ally and merciful God, whom all creation blesseth, glorified for ever and ever. Amen.'

The king again visiteth his son,

When he had thus prayed, he felt divine comfort stealing over his heart, and, fulfilled with courage, he spent the whole night in prayer. Meanwhile the king communed with Araches, his friend, as touching his son's matters, and signified to him his son's sheer audacity and unchangeable resolution. Araches gave counsel that he should, in his dealings with him, show the utmost kindness and courtesy, in the hope, perchance, of alluring him by flattering attentions. The day following, the king came to his son, and sat down, and called him to his side. He embraced and kissed him affectionately, coaxing him gently and tenderly, and said, 'O my darling and well-beloved son, honour thou thy father's grey hairs: listen to my entreaty, and come, do sacrifice to the gods; thus shalt thou win their favour, and receive at their hands length of days, and the enjoyment of all glory and of an undisputed kingdom, and happiness of every sort. Thus shalt thou be well pleasing to me thy father throughout life and be honoured and lauded of all men. It is a great count in the score of praise to be obedient to thy father, especially in a good cause, and to gain the goodwill of the gods. What thinkest thou, my son? Is it that I have willingly declined from the right, and chosen to travel on the wrong road: or that, from ignorance and inexperience of

and pleadeth tenderly with him to return to his old ways

ἐξέδωκα; ἀλλ', εἰ μὲν ἑκόντα με νομίζεις τοῦ συμφέροντος προτιμᾶν τὰ κακὰ καὶ τῆς ζωῆς προκρίνειν τὸν θάνατον, πάνυ μοι δοκεῖς, τέκνον, τῆς ὀρθῆς ἀποσφαλῆναι κρίσεως. ἢ οὐχ ὁρᾷς ὅση κακουχίᾳ καὶ ταλαιπωρίᾳ πολλάκις ἐμαυτὸν ἐκδίδωμι ἐν ταῖς κατὰ τῶν ἐχθρῶν ἐκστρατείαις, ἢ ἄλλαις τισὶ τοῦ κοινοῦ προστασίαις ἀσχολούμενος, ὡς καὶ πείνης τε καὶ δίψης, πεζοπορίας τε καὶ χαμαικοιτίας, οὕτω δεῆσαν, μὴ φείσασθαι; πλούτου δὲ καὶ χρημάτων τοσαύτη μοι πρόσεστιν ὑπεροψία τε καὶ καταφρόνησις, ὡς ἀφθόνως ἔσθ' ὅτε τὰ ταμιεῖα πάντα τοῦ ἐμοῦ παλατίου κατακενῶσαι εἰς τὸ ἀνοικοδομῆσαι τοὺς τῶν θεῶν μεγίστους ναοὺς καὶ παντοίῳ τούτους καταλαμπρῦναι κόσμῳ ἢ τοῖς στρατοπέδοις ἀφθόνως διανεῖμαι τοὺς θησαυροὺς τῶν χρημάτων. τοιαύτης οὖν μετέχων τῶν ἀπολαυστικῶν ὑπεροψίας καὶ τῆς ἐν τοῖς δεινοῖς καρτερίας, εἰ τὴν τῶν Γαλιλαίων ἐγίνωσκον θρησκείαν κρείττονα τῆς ἐν χερσὶν ὑπάρχειν, πόσης ἂν οὐκ ἔκρινα τὸ πρᾶγμα σπουδῆς ἄξιον, πάντων 223
μὲν ὑπεριδεῖν καὶ τὴν ἐμαυτοῦ περιποιήσασθαι σωτηρίαν; εἰ δὲ ἄγνοιάν μοι καὶ ἀπειρίαν τοῦ καλοῦ καταγινώσκεις, σύνες ὅσας πολλάκις νύκτας ἀΰπνους διετέλεσα, ζητήματός τινος προτεθέντος, ἔσθ' ὅτε καὶ οὐ πολὺ ἀναγκαίου, μὴ παρέχων ὅλως ἐμαυτῷ ἀνάπαυσιν, πρὶν ἢ τοῦ ζητουμένου σαφῆ καὶ εὐπρεπεστάτην εὕροιμι τὴν λύσιν.

Εἰ οὖν τῶν προσκαίρων τούτων πραγμάτων οὐδὲ τὸ σμικρότατον ἔχω εὐκαταφρόνητον, ἄχρις οὗ πάντα συμφερόντως καὶ ἐπὶ λυσιτελείᾳ τῶν

the good, I have given myself to destruction? Well, if thou thinkest that I willingly prefer the evil to the profitable, and choose death before life, thou seemest to me, son, completely to have missed the goal in jud ing. Dost thou not see to what discomfort and trouble I often expose myself in mine expeditions against my foes, or when I am engaged in divers other business for the public good, not sparing myself. even hunger and thirst, if need be, the march on foot, or the couch on the ground? As for riches and money, such is my contempt and scorn thereof, that I have at times ungrudgingly lavished all the stores of my palace, to build mighty temples for the gods, and to adorn them with all manner of splendour, or else to distribute liberal largess to my soldiers. Possessing then, as I also do, this contempt of pleasure and this courage in danger, what zeal would I not have devoted to contemning all else, and winning my salvation, had I only found that the religion of the Galileans were better than mine own? But, if thou condemnest me for ignorance and inexperience of the good, consider how many sleepless nights I have spent, with some problem before me, oft-times no very important one, giving myself no rest until I had found the clear and most apt solution.

Seeing then that I reckon that not even the least of these temporal concerns is unworthy of thought until all be fitly completed for the advantage of all and

He professeth to have learnt by testing,

ἁπάντων ἐπιτελεσθείη, καὶ οὐδενὶ ἑτέρῳ ἀκριβέστερον ἡ τῶν ἀπορρήτων διάγνωσις ἐν πάσῃ, ὡς οἶμαι, τῇ ὑφηλίῳ διερευνᾶσθαι ὡς ἐμοὶ παρὰ πάντων μεμαρτύρηται, πῶς τὰ θεῖα, καὶ ἃ σέβεσθαι καὶ θεολογεῖν θέμις, εὐκαταφρόνητα ἂν ἐλογισάμην, καὶ μὴ πάσῃ σπουδῇ, πάσῃ δυνάμει, ὅλῃ τῇ ψυχῇ καὶ ὅλῳ τῷ νοΐ, εἰς τὴν τούτων ἀπησχόλησα ἐμαυτὸν ζήτησιν, τοῦ εὑρεῖν τἀληθῆ καὶ πρεπωδέστατα; καί γε ἐζήτησα ἐμπόνως, πολλὰς μὲν νύκτας ἴσα ταῖς ἡμέραις ἐν τούτοις ἀναλώσας, πολλοὺς δὲ σοφοὺς καὶ ἐπιστήμονας εἰς τήνδε τὴν βουλὴν συγκαλέσας, πολλοῖς δὲ καὶ τῶν λεγομένων Χριστιανῶν ὁμιλήσας. καὶ τῇ ἀόκνῳ συζητήσει καὶ διαπύρῳ ἐρεύνῃ εὑρέθη μοι ἡ τῆς ἀληθείας ὁδός, παρὰ σοφῶν τῇ τε λογιότητι καὶ συνέσει τετιμημένων μαρτυρηθεῖσα ὡς οὐκ ἔστιν ἄλλη πίστις εἰ μὴ ἣν σήμερον πορευόμεθα, τοῖς μεγίστοις θεοῖς 224
λατρεύοντες καὶ τῆς γλυκείας βιοτῆς καὶ ἐνηδόνου ἀντεχόμενοι, τῆς πᾶσιν ἀνθρώποις παρ' αὐτῶν δεδωρημένης, ἥτις τερπνότητος ὅτι πλείστης καὶ θυμηδίας πεπλήρωται, ἣν οἱ τῶν Γαλιλαίων ἔξαρχοι καὶ μυσταγωγοὶ ἀφρόνως ἀπώσαντο, ὡς καὶ τὸ γλυκὺ τοῦτο φῶς καὶ τὰ τερπνὰ πάντα, ἅπερ εἰς ἀπόλαυσιν ἐχαρίσαντο ἡμῖν οἱ θεοί, ἐλπίδι τινὸς ἑτέρας ἀδήλου ζωῆς ἑτοίμως
1 Tim. i. 7 προΐεσθαι, μὴ εἰδότες τί λέγουσιν ἢ περὶ τίνων διαβεβαιοῦνται.

Σὺ δέ, φίλτατε υἱέ, τῷ σῷ πείσθητι πατρὶ δι' ἀκριβοῦς καὶ ἀληθεστάτης ἐρεύνης τὸ ὄντως καλὸν εὑρηκότι. ἰδοὺ γὰρ ἀποδέδεικται ὡς οὔτε ἑκών, οὔτε μὴν ἀγνοίας τρόπῳ, διήμαρτον τοῦ

seeing that all (I ween) bear me witness that no man under the sun can search out secrets with more diligence than I, how then could I have considered divine things, that call for worship and serious consideration, unworthy of thought, and not rather have devoted all my zeal and might, all my mind and soul to the investigation thereof, to find out the right and the true? Aye, and I have laboriously sought thereafter. Many nights and days have I spent thus: many wise and learned men have I called to my council; and with many of them that are called Christians have I conversed. By untiring enquiry and ardent search I have discovered the pathway of truth, witnessed by wise men honoured for their intelligence and wit,—that there is none other faith than ours. This is the path that we tread to-day, worshipping the most puissant gods, and holding fast to that sweet and delightsome life, given by them to all men, fulfilled with all manner of pleasure and gladness of heart, which the leaders and priests of the Galileans have in their folly rejected; so that, in hope of some other uncertain life, they have readily cast away this sweet light, and all those pleasures which the gods have bestowed on us for enjoyment, and all the while know not what they say, nor whereof they confidently affirm.

the truth of idol-worship,

'But thou, dearest son, obey thy father, who, by diligent and honest search, hath found the real good. Lo, I have shown thee that, neither willingly, no, nor by way of ignorance, have I failed of the

and biddeth Ioasaph to follow where he has trod

ἀγαθοῦ, ἀλλ' εὗρον καὶ προσελαβόμην· ἐπιποθῶ
δὲ καὶ σὲ μὴ ἀνοήτως πλανᾶσθαι, ἀλλ' ἐμοὶ
ἀκολουθῆσαι. αἰδέσθητι οὖν τὸν πατέρα σου.
ἢ οὐκ οἶδας ὁποῖόν ἐστι καλὸν τῷ πατρὶ
πείθεσθαι καὶ αὐτῷ ἐν πᾶσι χαρίζεσθαι; ὡς
ἔμπαλιν ὀλέθριον καὶ ἐπάρατον τὸ πατέρα παρα-
πικραίνειν καὶ τὰς αὐτοῦ παρ' οὐδὲν τιθέναι 225
ἐντολάς; ὅσοι γὰρ τοῦτο ἐποίησαν, κακοὶ κακῶς
ἀπώλοντο· οἷς σύ, τέκνον, μὴ συναριθμηθείης·
ἀλλά, τὰ τῷ τεκόντι κεχαρισμένα ποιῶν, πάντων
ἐπιτύχοις τῶν ἀγαθῶν, καὶ κληρονόμος γένοιο
τῆς εὐλογίας τῆς ἐμῆς καὶ βασιλείας.

Ὁ δὲ μεγαλόφρων καὶ εὐγενὴς ὡς ἀληθῶς
νεανίας τῆς τοῦ πατρὸς περιττολογίας καὶ ἀνοή-
του ἀντιβολῆς ἀκούσας, καὶ γνοὺς τὰς τοῦ
Zech. iii. 1 σκολιοῦ δράκοντος μηχανάς, ὡς ἐκ τῶν δεξιῶν
Ps. cix. 5 αὐτοῦ τοῖς ποσὶν ἡτοίμασε παγίδα, κατακάμψαι
τὴν θεοειδῆ ψυχὴν τεχναζόμενος καὶ πρὸς τὸ
προκείμενον ἐμποδίσαι βραβεῖον, τὸ δεσποτικὸν
Mat. x. 34 ff. πρὸ ὀφθαλμῶν ἔθετο πρόσταγμα, Οὐκ ἦλθον
βαλεῖν εἰρήνην, εἰπόντος, ἀλλὰ μάχην καὶ μά-
χαιραν· ἦλθον γὰρ διχάσαι υἱὸν κατὰ τοῦ πατρὸς
αὐτοῦ καὶ θυγατέρα κατὰ τῆς μητρὸς αὐτῆς, καὶ
τὰ ἑξῆς. καί, ὅτι Ὁ φιλῶν πατέρα ἢ μητέρα
ὑπὲρ ἐμέ, οὐκ ἔστι μου ἄξιος, καί, Ὅστις με
ἀρνήσεται ἔμπροσθεν τῶν ἀνθρώπων, ἀρνήσομαι
αὐτὸν κἀγὼ ἔμπροσθεν τοῦ Πατρός μου τοῦ ἐν
οὐρανοῖς. ταῦτα λογισάμενος, καὶ τῷ θείῳ φόβῳ
τὴν ψυχὴν πεδήσας, τῷ πόθῳ τε καὶ ἔρωτι 226
Eccles. iii. 8 ἐνισχύσας, τὸ Σολομόντειον ἐκεῖνο ῥῆμα πάνυ
κατὰ καιρὸν ἐξελάβετο, Καιρός, φάσκον, τοῦ
φιλῆσαι καὶ καιρὸς τοῦ μισῆσαι, καιρὸς πολέμου

good, but rather that I have found and laid hold thereon. And I earnestly desire that thou too shouldest not wander as a fool, but shouldest follow me. Have respect then unto thy father. Dost thou not know how lovely a thing it is to obey one's father, and please him in all ways? Contrariwise, how deadly and cursed a thing it is to provoke a father and despise his commands? As many as have done so, have come to a miserable end. But be not thou, my son, one of their number. Rather do that which is well pleasing to thy sire, and so mayest thou obtain all happiness and inherit my blessing and my kingdom!'

Ioasaph, seeing the snare laid for him, prayeth again for strength

The high-minded and noble youth listened to his father's windy discourse and foolish opposition, and recognized therein the devices of the crooked serpent, and how standing at his right hand he had prepared a snare for his feet, and was scheming how to overthrow his righteous soul, and hinder him of the prize laid up in store. Therefore the prince set before his eyes the commandment of the Lord, which saith, 'I came not to send peace, but strife and a sword. For I am come to set a man at variance against his father, and a daughter against her mother, and so forth; and 'He that loveth father or mother more than me is not worthy of me'; and 'Whosoever shall deny me before men, him will I also deny before my Father which is in heaven.' When he had considered these things, and fettered his soul with divine fear, and strengthened it with longing desire and love, right opportunely he remembered the saying of Solomon, 'There is a time to love, and a time to hate; a time of war, and a

καὶ καιρὸς εἰρήνης. καὶ πρῶτα μέν, κατὰ νοῦν
Ps. lvii. 1, 2 εὐξάμενος, Ἐλέησόν με, Κύριε, εἶπεν, ὁ Θεός,
ἐλέησόν με, ὅτι ἐπὶ σοὶ πέποιθεν ἡ ψυχή μου,
καὶ ἐν τῇ σκιᾷ τῶν πτερύγων σου ἐλπιῶ ἕως
οὗ παρέλθῃ ἡ ἀνομία. κεκράξομαι πρὸς τὸν
Θεὸν τὸν ὕψιστον, τὸν Θεὸν τὸν εὐεργετήσαντά
με, καὶ τὰ ἑξῆς τοῦ ψαλμοῦ.

Exod. xx. 12 Εἶτά φησι πρὸς τὸν βασιλέα· Τὸ μὲν θερα-
πεύειν πατέρα καὶ τοῖς αὐτοῦ ὑπείκειν προστάγμασιν, εὐνοίᾳ τε καὶ φιλίᾳ καθυπηρετεῖν, ὁ κοινὸς
ἡμᾶς διδάσκει Δεσπότης, φυσικὴν ἡμῖν τὴν τοιαύτην ἐγκατασπείρας στοργήν. ὅταν δὲ ἡ τῶν
γονέων σχέσις καὶ φιλία πρὸς αὐτὸν φέρῃ τὸν
κίνδυνον τὴν ψυχὴν καὶ τοῦ Δημιουργοῦ πόρρω
Mat. v. 29; ποιῇ, ἐκκόπτειν ταύτην παντάπασι προστετάγ-
xviii. 9; Mk. ix. 47 μεθα, καὶ μηδόλως εἴκειν τοῖς χωρίζουσιν ἡμᾶς
τοῦ Θεοῦ, ἀλλὰ μισεῖν τούτους καὶ ἀποστρέφε-
σθαι, κἂν πατὴρ ὁ τὰ ἀπευκταῖα ἐπιτάττων εἴη,
κἂν μήτηρ, κἂν βασιλεύς, κἂν τῆς ζωῆς αὐτῆς 227
κύριος. διὰ ταῦτα τῆς πατρικῆς μὲν σχέσεως
ἕνεκα τὸν Θεὸν ζημιωθῆναι τῶν ἀδυνάτων μοί
ἐστι. διὸ μήτε σεαυτῷ κόπους πάρεχε, μήτε ἐμοί·
1 Thess. i. 9 ἀλλ' ἢ πείσθητι καὶ τῷ ζῶντι ἄμφω καὶ ἀληθινῷ
λατρεύσωμεν Θεῷ· ἃ γὰρ νῦν σέβῃ εἴδωλα εἰσί,
Ps. cxv. 4 χειρῶν ἀνθρωπίνων ἔργα, πνοῆς ἔρημα καὶ κωφά,
μηδὲν ὅλως ἢ μόνην ἀπώλειαν καὶ τιμωρίαν αἰώνιον τοῖς αὐτὰ σεβομένοις προξενοῦντα.

Εἰ δὲ μὴ τοῦτο βούλοιο, ποίει εἰς ἐμὲ ὅπερ σοι
Cp. Rom. viii. 38, 39 δοκεῖ· δοῦλος γάρ εἰμι τοῦ Χριστοῦ, καὶ οὔτε θω-
πείαις, οὔτε κολάσεσι τῆς αὐτοῦ ἀποστήσομαι
ἀγάπης, καθὰ δὴ καὶ τῇ προτεραίᾳ εἶπόν σοι,
μέσον ἐμβαλὼν τὸ τοῦ Δεσπότου μου ὄνομα καὶ

time of peace.' First of all he prayed in silence, and said, 'Have mercy of me, Lord God, have mercy of me; for my soul trusteth in thee; and under the shadow of thy wings I shall hope till wickedness overpass. I shall cry to the highest God; to God that did well to me,' and the rest of the psalm.

He convicteth his father of grievous error,

Then said Ioasaph to the king, 'To honour one's father, and to obey his commands, and to serve him with good will and affection is taught us by the Lord of us all, who hath implanted in our hearts this natural affection. But, when loving devotion to our parents bringeth our soul into peril, and separateth her from her Maker, then we are commanded, at all costs, to cut it out, and, on no account, to yield to them that would depart us from God, but to hate and avoid them, even if it be our father that issueth the abominable command, or our mother, or our king, or the master of our very life. Wherefore it is impossible for me, out of devotion to my father, to forfeit God. So, prithee, trouble not thyself, nor me: but be persuaded, and let us both serve the true and living God, for the objects of thy present worship are idols, the works of men's hands, devoid of breath, and deaf, and give nought but destruction and eternal punishment to their worshippers.

'But if this be not thy pleasure, deal with me even as thou wilt: for I am a servant of Christ, and neither flatteries nor torments shall separate me from his love, as I told thee yesterday, swearing it by my Master's name, and confirming

ἀσφαλέστατα τὸν λόγον ἐμπεδωσάμενος. ὅτι δὲ
μήτε ἑκὼν ἔφησας κακουργεῖν, μήτε μὴν ἀγνοίᾳ
διαμαρτάνειν τοῦ ἀγαθοῦ, ἀλλὰ πολλῇ καὶ ἐμπόνῳ
συζητήσει τοῦτο ἔγνως ὄντως εἶναι καλόν, τὸ
εἰδώλοις λατρεύειν καὶ ταῖς ἡδοναῖς τῶν παθῶν
προσηλοῦσθαι, κακουργεῖν μέν σε ἐθελοντὶ οὐκ
ἔχω λέγειν. ὅτι δὲ πολλή σοι περικέχυται ἀγνω-
Ex. x. 21 σίας ἀχλὺς καὶ ὡς ἐν σκότει ψηλαφητῷ πορευόμενος οὐδόλως ὁρᾷς φωτὸς κἂν μικράν τινα
μαρμαρυγήν, ὅθεν τὴν εὐθεῖαν ἀπολέσας κρημνοῖς
καὶ φάραγξι δεινοῖς περιπεπλάνησαι, τοῦτο κἀγὼ
βεβαίως ἐπίσταμαι καὶ σέ, πάτερ, γινώσκειν 228
βούλομαι. διὸ σκότος ἀντὶ φωτὸς κατέχων καὶ
θανάτου ὥσπερ ζωῆς ἀντεχόμενος, οἴει συμφερόντως βεβουλεῦσθαι καὶ λυσιτελῶς ἐντεθυμῆσθαι·
ἀλλ' οὐκ ἔστι ταῦτα, οὐκ ἔστιν. οὔτε γὰρ ἅπερ
Basil, Comment. in Isaiam, x. 11 σέβῃ θεοί εἰσιν, ἀλλὰ στῆλαι δαιμόνων, πᾶσαν
αὐτῶν τὴν μυσαρὰν ἐνέργειαν ἔνδον ἔχουσαι· οὔτε
ἥνπερ γλυκεῖαν ἀποκαλεῖς καὶ ἐνήδονον βιοτήν,
τερπνότητός τε καὶ θυμηδίας δοκεῖς πεπληρῶ-
σθαι, τῆς τοιαύτης ἔχει φύσεως, ἀλλὰ βδελυκτή
ἐστιν αὕτη, κατά γε τὸν τῆς ἀληθείας λόγον, καὶ
Prov. xxiv. 13 ἀποτρόπαιος. πρὸς καιρὸν γὰρ γλυκαίνει καὶ
p. 186 λεαίνει τὸν φάρυγγα, ὕστερον δὲ πικροτέρας χολῆς
ποιεῖται τὰς ἀναδόσεις, ὡς ὁ ἐμὸς ἔφη διδάσκαλος,
Heb. iv. 12 καὶ ἠκονημένη μᾶλλον μαχαίρας διστόμου.

Καὶ πῶς ἄν σοι τὰ ταύτης κακὰ διηγησαίμην;
Ps. cxxxix. 18 ἐξαριθμήσομαι αὐτά, καὶ ὑπὲρ ἄμμον πληθυν-
θήσονται. ἄγκιστρον γάρ ἐστι τοῦ διαβόλου, ὡς
δέλεαρ τὴν βδελυρὰν περικειμένην ἡδονήν, δι' οὗ
Prov. xiv. 12; xvi. 25 τοὺς ἀπατωμένους, εἰς τὸν τοῦ ᾅδου καθέλκει
πυθμένα. τὰ δὲ παρὰ τοῦ ἐμοῦ Δεσπότου ἐπηγ-

the word with surest oath. But, whereas thou saidest that thou didst neither wilfully do wrong, nor didst fail of the mark through ignorance, but after much laborious enquiry hadst ascertained that it was truly a good thing to worship idols and to be riveted to the pleasures of the passions—that thou art wilfully a wrong doer, I may not say. But this I know full well, and would have thee know, O my father, that thou art surrounded with a dense mist of ignorance, and, walking in darkness that may be felt, seest not even one small glimmer of light. Wherefore thou hast lost the right pathway, and wanderest over terrible cliffs and chasms. Holding darkness for light, and clinging to death as it were life, thou deemest that thou art well advised, and hast reflected to good effect: but it is not so, not so. The objects of thy veneration are not gods but statues of devils, charged with all their filthy power; nor is the life, which thou pronouncest sweet and pleasant, and thinkest to be full of delight and gladness of heart, such in kind: but the same is abominable, according to the word of truth, and to be abhorred. For for a time it sweeteneth and tickleth the gullet, but afterwards it maketh the risings more bitter than gall (as said my teacher), and is sharper than any two-edged sword.

'How shall I describe to thee the evils of this life? I will tell them, and they shall be more in number than the sand. For such life is the fishhook of the devil, baited with beastly pleasure, whereby he deceiveth and draggeth his prey into the depth of hell. Whereas the good things, promised by my Master,

and warneth him of the approach of Doomsday,

γελμένα ἀγαθά, ἅπερ σὺ ἀδήλου ζωῆς ἐλπίδα
ὠνόμασας, ἀψευδῆ εἰσι καὶ ἀναλλοίωτα, τέλος
οὐκ οἶδε, φθορᾷ οὐχ ὑπόκειται· λόγος οὐκ ἔστιν ὁ
παραστῆσαι τὸ μέγεθος τῆς δόξης ἐκείνης καὶ
τερπνότητος ἰσχύων, τῆς χαρᾶς τῆς ἀνεκλαλήτου, 229
τῆς διηνεκοῦς εὐφροσύνης. πάντες μὲν γάρ, καθάπερ αὐτὸς ὁρᾷς, ἀποθνήσκομεν, καὶ οὐκ ἔστιν
Ps. lxxxix. 47 ἄνθρωπος ὃς ζήσεται καὶ οὐκ ὄψεται θάνατον·
μέλλομεν δὲ πάντες ἀνίστασθαι, ἡνίκα ἐλεύσεται
Κύριος Ἰησοῦς Χριστός, ὁ Υἱὸς τοῦ Θεοῦ, ἐν
Luke xxi. 25 δόξῃ ἀνεκλαλήτῳ καὶ δυνάμει φοβερᾷ, ὁ μόνος
1 Tim. vi. 15 Βασιλεὺς τῶν βασιλευόντων καὶ Κύριος τῶν κυρ-
Phil. ii. 10 ιευόντων, ᾧ πᾶν γόνυ κάμψει ἐπουρανίων καὶ ἐπιγείων καὶ καταχθονίων· καὶ τοσαύτην ἐμποιήσει
Mk. xiii. 25 τότε τὴν ἔκστασιν, ὡς καὶ αὐτὰς ἐκπλαγῆναι τὰς
Luke xxi. 26 οὐρανίους δυνάμεις· καὶ παραστήσονται αὐτῷ
Dan. vii. 10 τρόμῳ χίλιαι χιλιάδες καὶ μύριαι μυριάδες ἀγγέλων καὶ ἀρχαγγέλων, καὶ πάντα ἔσται φόβου
1 Cor. xv. 52 καὶ τρόμου μεστά. σαλπιεῖ γὰρ εἷς τῶν ἀρχαγ-
Is. xxxiv. 4 γέλων ἐν σάλπιγγι Θεοῦ, καὶ εὐθὺς ὁ οὐρανὸς μὲν
εἱλιγήσεται ὡς βιβλίον, ἡ γῆ δὲ ἀναρρηγνυμένη
ἀναπέμψει τὰ τεθνεῶτα σώματα τῶν πώποτε
1 Cor. xv. 45 γενομένων ἀνθρώπων, ἐξ οὗ γέγονεν ὁ πρῶτος
ἄνθρωπος Ἀδὰμ μέχρι τῆς ἡμέρας ἐκείνης. καὶ
1 Cor. xv. 52 τότε πάντες οἱ ἀπ᾽ αἰῶνος θανόντες ἐν ῥιπῇ ὀφθαλμοῦ ζῶντες παραστήσονται τῷ βήματι τοῦ ἀθανά- 230
του Δεσπότου, καὶ ἕκαστος λόγον δώσει ὑπὲρ ὧν
Mat. xiii. 43 ἔπραξε. τότε οἱ δίκαιοι λάμψουσιν ὡς ἥλιος, οἱ
πιστεύσαντες εἰς Πατέρα καὶ Υἱὸν καὶ Ἅγιον
Πνεῦμα, καὶ ἐν ἔργοις ἀγαθοῖς τελέσαντες τὸν
παρόντα βίον. πῶς δέ σοι διηγήσομαι τὴν μέλλουσαν αὐτοὺς τότε διαδέχεσθαι δόξαν; κἂν γὰρ

which thou callest "the hope of some other uncertain life," are true and unchangeable; they know no end, and are not subject to decay. There is no language that can declare the greatness of yonder glory and delight, of the joy unspeakable, and the everlasting gladness. As thou thyself seest, we all die; and there is no man that shall live and not see death. But one day we shall all rise again, when our Lord Jesus Christ shall come, the Son of God, in unspeakable glory and dread power, the only King of kings, and Lord of lords; to whom every knee shall bow, of things in heaven, and things in earth, and things under the earth. Such terror shall he then inspire that the very powers of heaven shall be shaken: and before him there shall stand in fear thousand thousands, and ten thousand times ten thousand of Angels and Archangels, and the whole world shall be full of fear and terror. For one of the Archangels shall sound with the trump of God, and immediately the heavens shall be rolled together as a scroll; and the earth shall be rent, and shall give up the dead bodies of all men that ever were since the first man Adam until that day. And then shall all men that have died since the beginning of the world in the twinkling of an eye stand alive before the judgement seat of the immortal Lord, and every man shall give account of his deeds. Then shall the righteous shine forth as the sun; they that believed in the Father, Son and Holy Ghost, and ended this present life in good works. And how can I describe to thee the glory that shall receive them at that day? For though I compare their brightness and beauty

when the powers of the heavens shall be shaken

τῷ ἡλιακῷ παραβάλλω φωτὶ τὴν λαμπρότητα
αὐτῶν καὶ τὸ κάλλος, κἂν ἀστραπῇ τῇ φανοτάτῃ,
Is. lxiv. 4 οὐδὲν τῆς λαμπρότητος ἐκείνης ἄξιον ἐρῶ. ὀφθαλ-
1 Cor. ii. 9 μὸς γὰρ οὐκ εἶδε καὶ οὖς οὐκ ἤκουσε καὶ ἐπὶ καρδίαν ἀνθρώπου οὐκ ἀνέβη, ἃ ἡτοίμασεν ὁ Θεὸς τοῖς
ἀγαπῶσιν αὐτὸν ἐν τῇ βασιλείᾳ τῶν οὐρανῶν, ἐν
1 Tim. vi. 16 τῷ φωτὶ τῷ ἀπροσίτῳ, ἐν τῇ δόξῃ τῇ ἀπορρήτῳ
καὶ ἀτελευτήτῳ.

Καὶ οἱ μὲν δίκαιοι τοιούτων τεύξονται τῶν
ἀγαθῶν τοιαύτης δὲ τῆς μακαριότητος· οἱ δὲ τὸν
ὄντως ὄντα Θεὸν ἀρνησάμενοι, καὶ τὸν πλάστην
καὶ δημιουργὸν ἀγνοήσαντες, δαίμοσι δὲ μιαροῖς
λατρεύσαντες, καὶ εἰδώλοις κωφοῖς τὸ σέβας
ἀπονείμαντες, τὰς ἡδονάς τε τοῦ ματαίου βίου 231
Cp. 2 Pet. ii. 22 τούτου ποθήσαντες, καὶ δίκην χοίρων τῷ βορβόρῳ τῶν παθῶν κυλισθέντες, καὶ πάσης κακίας
ὁρμητήριον τὰς ἑαυτῶν ψυχὰς ποιησάμενοι,
Heb. iv. 13 σταθήσονται γυμνοὶ καὶ τετραχηλισμένοι, κατ-
ῃσχυμένοι καὶ κατηφεῖς, ἐλεεινοὶ καὶ τῷ σχήματι
καὶ τῷ πράγματι, ὄνειδος προκείμενοι πάσῃ τῇ
κτίσει. πάντα δὲ αὐτῶν τὰ ἐν λόγῳ, τὰ ἐν
ἔργῳ, τὰ ἐν διανοίᾳ, πρὸ προσώπου αὐτῶν
ἐλεύσονται. εἶτα, μετὰ τὴν αἰσχύνην ἐκείνην
τὴν χαλεπωτάτην καὶ τὸ ὄνειδος ἐκεῖνο τὸ
Mk. ix. 43; Mat. xiii. 42; Luke xiii. 28 ἀφόρητον, καταδικασθήσονται εἰς τὸ πῦρ τῆς
γεέννης τὸ ἄσβεστον καὶ ἀφεγγές, εἰς τὸ σκότος
τὸ ἐξώτερον, τὸν βρυγμὸν τῶν ὀδόντων καὶ σκώληκα τὸν ἰοβόλον. αὕτη ἡ μερὶς αὐτῶν, οὗτος
ὁ κλῆρος, οἷς εἰς αἰῶνας συνέσονται τοὺς ἀτελευ-
τήτους τιμωρούμενοι, ἀνθ' ὧν, τὰ ἐν ἐπαγγελίαις
ἀγαθὰ παρωσάμενοι, διὰ πρόσκαιρον ἁμαρτίας
ἡδονὴν κόλασιν αἰώνιον ἐξελέξαντο. ὑπὲρ δὴ

to the light of the sun or to the brightest lightning-flash, yet should I fail to do justice to their brightness. Eye hath not seen, nor ear heard, neither have entered into the heart of man, the things which God hath prepared for them that love him, in the kingdom of heaven, in the light which no man can approach unto, in his unspeakable and unending glory.

'Such joys and such bliss shall the righteous obtain, but they that have denied the only true God and not known their Maker and Creator, but have worshipped foul devils, and rendered homage to dumb idols, and loved the pleasures of this vain world, and, like swine, wallowed in the mire of sinful lusts, and made their lives a headquarters for all wickedness, shall stand naked and laid bare, downright ashamed and downcast, pitiable in appearance and in fact, set forth for a reproach to all creation. All their life in word, deed and thought shall come before their faces. Then, after this bitter disgrace and unbearable reproach, shall they be sentenced to the unquenchable and light-less fire of Gehenna, unto the outer darkness, the gnashing of teeth and the venomous worm. This is their portion, this their lot, in the which they shall dwell together in punishment for endless ages, because they rejected the good things offered them in promise, and, for the sake of the pleasure of sin for a season, made choice of eternal punishment. For these

when the wicked shall receive their punishment and the righteous their reward

τούτων, ὥστε τῆς ἀρρήτου μὲν χαρᾶς ἐκείνης
ἐπιτυχεῖν καὶ τῆς ἀπορρήτου δόξης ἀπολαύειν,
τοῖς ἀγγέλοις δὲ ἀντιλάμπειν, καὶ τῷ ἀγαθῷ καὶ
Wisd. v. 1 γλυκυτάτῳ Δεσπότῃ μετὰ παρρησίας παρίστα-
σθαι, τὰς πικροτάτας δὲ τιμωρίας καὶ ἀτελευ-
τήτους καὶ τὴν ὀδυνηρὰν ἐκείνην ἐκφυγεῖν αἰσχύνην, πόσα οὐκ ἄξιον προέσθαι καὶ χρήματα καὶ 232
σώματα, μᾶλλον δὲ καὶ αὐτὰς τὰς ψυχάς; τίς
οὕτως ἀγεννής, τίς οὕτως ἀσύνετος, ὡς μὴ
μυρίους ὑποστῆναι προσκαίρους θανάτους, ἵνα
τοῦ αἰωνίου ἀπαλλαγῇ καὶ ἀτελευτήτου θανάτου,
τὴν ζωὴν δὲ κληρονομήσῃ τὴν μακαρίαν τε καὶ
ἀνώλεθρον, καὶ τῷ φωτὶ περιλαμφθῇ τῆς μακαρίας καὶ ζωαρχικῆς Τριάδος;

XXVI

Τούτων ἀκούσας ὁ βασιλεὺς τῶν ῥημάτων, καὶ
τὸ στερέμνιον καὶ ἀνένδοτον ἰδὼν τοῦ παιδὸς
μήτε κολακείαις εἴκοντος μήτε λόγων πειθοῖ,
μὴ τιμωριῶν ἀπειλαῖς, ἐθαύμαζε μὲν ἐπὶ τῇ
πιθανότητι τοῦ λόγου καὶ ταῖς ἀναντιρρήτοις
ἀποκρίσεσιν, ἠλέγχετο δὲ ὑπὸ τοῦ συνειδότος,
ἀληθῆ λέγειν αὐτὸν καὶ δίκαια ὑποδεικνύοντος·
ἀλλ' ἀνθείλκετο ὑπὸ τῆς πονηρᾶς συνηθείας καὶ
τῶν ἐν ἕξει βεβαιωθέντων ἐν αὐτῷ παθῶν, ὑφ'
Ps. xxxii. 6 ὧν ὡς ἐν κημῷ κατείχετο καὶ χαλινῷ, τῷ φωτὶ
μὴ συγχωρούμενος προσβλέψαι τῆς ἀληθείας.
ὅθεν πάντα λίθον, τὸ τοῦ λόγου, κινῶν, εἴχετο
τοῦ πάλαι σκοποῦ, τὴν προμελετηθεῖσαν αὐτῷ
μετὰ τοῦ Ἀραχῆ σκῆψιν εἰς ἔργον ἀγαγεῖν

reasons—to obtain that unspeakable bliss, to enjoy that ineffable glory, to equal the Angels in splendour, and to stand with boldness before the good and most sweetest Lord, to escape those bitter and unending punishments and that galling shame—time after time, were it not worth men's while to sacrifice their riches and bodies, nay, even their very lives? Who is so cowardly, who so foolish, as not to endure a thousand temporal deaths, to escape eternal and everlasting death, and to inherit life, blissful and imperishable, and to shine in the light of the blessed and life-giving Trinity?'

XXVI

The king offereth to hold debate on the truth of his religion

When the king heard these words, and saw the steadfastness, and unbuxomness of his son, who yielded neither to flattery, nor persuasion, nor threat, he marvelled indeed at the persuasiveness of his speech and his irrefutable anwers, and was convicted by his own conscience secretly assuring him that Ioasaph spake truly and aright. But he was dragged back by his evil habit and passions, which, from long use, had taken firm grip on him, and held him in as with bit and bridle, and suffered him not to behold the light of truth. So he left no stone unturned, as the saying is, and adhered to his old purpose, determining to put into action the plot which he and Araches had between them devised. Said he to his

βουλόμενος. καί φησι τῷ παιδί; Ἔδει μέν σε,
ὦ τέκνον, τοῖς ἐμοῖς ἁπλῶς εἴκειν ἐν πᾶσι
προστάγμασιν· ἀλλ' ἐπεί, σκληρὸς ὢν καὶ ἀπει-
θής, ἰσχυρῶς οὕτως ἀντέστης μοι, τὴν ἰδίαν
ἐνιστάμενος γνώμην κυριωτέραν πάντων ποιήσασθαι, δεῦρο δὴ τῇ ματαίᾳ ἐνστάσει χαίρειν
ἄμφω εἰπόντες, πειθοῖ πολιτευσώμεθα. καὶ ἐπεὶ
ὁ σὲ ἀπατήσας Βαρλαὰμ σιδηροδέσμιος παρ' 233
ἐμοὶ τυγχάνει, ἐκκλησιάσας ἐκκλησίαν μεγάλην,
καὶ πάντας ἡμετέρους τε καὶ Γαλιλαίους ἐπὶ τὸ
αὐτὸ συγκαλέσας, κήρυκάς τε διαρρήδην βοᾶν
θεσπίσας τοῦ μηδένα τῶν Χριστιανῶν δεδοικέναι,
ἀλλ' ἀφόβως πάντας συνεισελθεῖν, κοινῇ διασκε-
ψώμεθα γνώμῃ. καὶ ἤ, πείσαντες, ὑμεῖς μετὰ
τοῦ ὑμετέρου Βαρλαὰμ τεύξεσθε ὧν ἐσπουδάκατε·
ἤ, πεισθέντες, σὺν ἑκουσίᾳ τῇ γνώμῃ τοῖς προσ-
τάγμασί μου ὑπείκειν προθυμηθείητε.

Ὁ δὲ φρόνιμος τῷ ὄντι καὶ ἐχέφρων νεανίας,
διὰ τοῦ θεόθεν αὐτῷ ἐμφανισθέντος ὁράματος
τὴν τοῦ βασιλέως προδεδιδαγμένος σκαιωρίαν,
ἔφη· Τὸ θέλημα τοῦ Κυρίου γενέσθω, καὶ ἔστω
καθὼς ἐκέλευσας· αὐτὸς γὰρ ὁ ἀγαθὸς Θεὸς καὶ
Δεσπότης δῴη τῆς εὐθείας μὴ πλανηθῆναι ἡμᾶς·
Ps. lvii. 1 ἐπ' αὐτῷ γὰρ πέποιθεν ἡ ψυχή μου, καὶ αὐτὸς
ἐλεήσει με. τότε δὴ τότε κελεύει ὁ βασιλεὺς
πάντας ἀθροίζεσθαι εἰδωλολάτρας τε καὶ Χρισ-
τιανούς, γραμμάτων μὲν πανταχοῦ διαπεφοιτηκότων, κηρύκων τε ἀνὰ πάσας τὰς κωμοπόλεις
βοώντων τοῦ μηδένα τῶν Χριστιανῶν δεδοικέναι
ὥστε ἀδόκητόν τι ὑποστῆναι, ἀλλ' ἀδεῶς πάντας
καθ' ἑταιρείαν καὶ συγγένειαν ἐπὶ τὸ αὐτὸ συνελθεῖν ἐπὶ φιλαλήθει καὶ οὐ βεβιασμένῃ συζητήσει,

son, 'Although, child, thou oughtest in all points simply to give in to my commands, yet, because thou art stubborn and disobedient, and hast thus stiffly opposed me, insisting that thine own opinion should prevail over all, bid we now farewell to vain insistance, and let persuasion be now our policy. And, forasmuch as Barlaam, thy deceiver, is here, my prisoner in iron chains, I will make a great assembly, and summon all our people and your Galileans, to one place; and I will charge heralds to proclaim expressly that none of the Christians shall fear, but that all shall muster without dread; and we will hold debate together. If your side win, then shall ye and your Barlaam gain your desires; but if ye lose, then shall ye with right good will yield yourselves to my commands.'

The king summoneth Christians and idolaters to the trial

But this truly wise and prudent youth, forewarned, by the heavenly vision sent him, of his father's mischief, replied, 'The Lord's will be done! Be it according to thy command! May our good God and Lord himself vouchsafe that we wander not from the right way, for my soul trusteth in him, and he shall be merciful unto me.' There and then did the king command all, whether idolaters or Christians, to assemble. Letters were despatched in all quarters: heralds proclaimed it in every village town that no Christian need fear any secret surprise, but all might come together without fear, as friends and kindred,

μετὰ τοῦ ἐξάρχου καὶ καθηγεμόνος αὐτῶν μελλούσῃ γενέσθαι Βαρλαάμ. ὡσαύτως δὲ καὶ τοὺς
Acts xix. 35 μύστας καὶ νεωκόρους τῶν εἰδώλων καὶ σοφοὺς
τῶν Χαλδαίων καὶ Ἰνδῶν, τοὺς κατὰ πᾶσαν τὴν
ὑπ' αὐτὸν ἀρχὴν ὄντας, συνεκαλέσατο, καί τινας 234
οἰωνοσκόπους καὶ γόητας καὶ μάντεις, ὅπως ἂν
Χριστιανῶν περιγένοιντο.

Καὶ δὴ συνῆλθον πρὸς τὸν βασιλέα πλῆθος
πολὺ τῆς μυσαρᾶς αὐτοῦ θρησκείας· Χριστιανῶν
δὲ εἷς εὑρέθη μόνος εἰς βοήθειαν ἐλθὼν τοῦ νομι-
ζομένου Βαρλαάμ, ὀνόματι Βαραχίας. οἱ μὲν γὰρ
τῶν πιστῶν θανόντες ἦσαν ὑπὸ τῆς τῶν κατὰ
πόλιν ἀρχόντων μανίας κατασφαγέντες· οἱ δὲ ἐν
ὄρεσιν ἀπεκρύπτοντο καὶ σπηλαίοις τῷ φόβῳ τῶν
ἐπικειμένων δεινῶν. ἄλλοι δὲ ἐδεδοίκεισαν τὴν
ἀπειλὴν τοῦ βασιλέως, καὶ οὐκ ἐτόλμων ἑαυτοὺς
εἰς φῶς ἀγαγεῖν· ἀλλὰ νυκτερινοὶ ἦσαν θεοσεβεῖς,
ἐν τῷ λεληθότι τῷ Χριστῷ λατρεύοντες καὶ μηδαμῶς παρρησιαζόμενοι. ἐκεῖνος δὲ μόνος, γενναῖος ὢν τὴν ψυχήν, εἰς συναγωνισμὸν ἦλθε τῆς
ἀληθείας.

Προκαθίσας τοίνυν ὁ βασιλεὺς ἐπὶ βήματος
ὑψηλοῦ τε καὶ μετεώρου, συνεδριάζειν αὐτῷ τὸν
υἱὸν ἐκέλευσεν. ὁ δέ, τῇ πρὸς τὸν πατέρα εὐλα-
βείᾳ καὶ τιμῇ τοῦτο μὴ θελήσας ποιῆσαι, ἐπὶ τῆς
γῆς πλησίον αὐτοῦ ἐκάθισε. παρέστησαν τοίνυν
1 Cor. i. 20 οἱ ἐπιστήμονες τῆς μωρανθείσης παρὰ τοῦ Θεοῦ
σοφίας, ὧν ἐπλανήθη ἡ ἀσύνετος καρδία, καθώς φη-
Rom. i. 21–23 σιν ὁ Ἀπόστολος· Δοκοῦντες γὰρ εἶναι σοφοὶ ἐμω- 235
ράνθησαν, καὶ ἤλλαξαν τὴν δόξαν τοῦ ἀφθάρτου
Θεοῦ ἐν ὁμοιώματι θνητῶν ἀνθρώπων καὶ τετρα-
πόδων καὶ ἑρπετῶν. οὗτοι συνῆλθον συνᾶραι

for the honest and unrestrained enquiry that should be held with their chief and captain, Barlaam. In like manner also he summoned the initiate and the temple-keepers of his idols, and wise men of the Chaldeans and Indians that were in all his kingdom, beside certain augurs, sorcerers and seers, that they might get the better of the Christians.

Barachias appeareth as a champion of the true Faith

Then were there gathered together multitudes that held his loathly religion; but of the Christians was there found one only that came to the help of the supposed Barlaam. His name was Barachias. For of the Faithful, some were dead, having fallen victims to the fury of the governors of the cities; and some were hiding in mountains and dens, in dread of the terrors hanging over them; while others had feared the threats of the king, and durst not adventure themselves into the light of day, but were worshippers by night, serving Christ in secret, and in no wise boldly confessing him. So noble-hearted Barachias came alone to the contest, to help and champion the truth.

The king sitteth to judge the cause,

The king sat down before all on a doom-stool high and exalted, and bade his son sit beside him. He, in reverence and awe of his father, consented not thereto, but sat near him on the ground. There stood the learned in the wisdom which God hath made foolish, whose unwise hearts had gone astray, as saith the Apostle; for, 'professing themselves to be wise, they became fools, and changed the glory of the uncorruptible God into an image made like to corruptible man, and four-footed beasts, and creeping things.' These were assembled for to join argument

λόγον πρὸς τὸν τοῦ βασιλέως υἱὸν καὶ τοὺς περὶ αὐτόν, καὶ ἐπληροῦτο ἐπ' αὐτοῖς τὸ τῆς παροιμίας, ὅτι πρὸς λέοντα δορκὰς μάχης ἥπτετο.[1] ὁ μὲν γὰρ
Ps. xci. 9 τὸν Ὕψιστον ἔθετο καταφυγὴν αὐτοῦ, καὶ ἐν τῇ
Ps. lvii. 1 σκιᾷ ἤλπισε τῶν αὐτοῦ πτερύγων· οἱ δὲ τοῖς
Ps. cxlvi. 2 ἄρχουσιν ἐπεποίθεσαν τοῦ αἰῶνος τούτου τοῖς
Eph. vi. 12 καταργουμένοις, καὶ τῷ κοσμοκράτορι τοῦ σκότους, ᾧ καθυπέταξαν ἑαυτοὺς ἐλεεινῶς καὶ ἀθλίως.

Ἄγεται τοίνυν ὁ Ναχὼρ τὸν Βαρλαὰμ ὑποκρινόμενος· καὶ οἱ μὲν περὶ τὸν βασιλέα τοῦ τοιούτου εἴχοντο σκοποῦ· ἑτέρα δὲ πάλιν ἡ σοφὴ πρόνοια ἄνωθεν ᾠκονόμει. παρισταμένων γὰρ τούτων ἁπάντων φησὶν ὁ βασιλεὺς τοῖς ῥήτορσιν αὐτοῦ καὶ φιλοσόφοις, μᾶλλον δὲ τοῖς λεωπλάνοις καὶ ἀσυνέτοις τὴν καρδίαν· Ἰδοὺ δὴ ἀγὼν ὑμῖν πρόκειται καὶ ἀγώνων ὁ μέγιστος. δυοῖν γὰρ θάτερον γενήσεται ὑμῖν· ἢ τὰ ἡμέτερα κρατύναντας,
καὶ πλανᾶσθαι τὸν Βαρλαὰμ καὶ τοὺς σὺν αὐτῷ 236
ἐλέγξαντας, δόξης μεγίστης καὶ τιμῆς παρ' ἡμῶν τε καὶ πάσης τυχεῖν τῆς συγκλήτου καὶ στεφάνοις νίκης καταστεφθῆναι· ἢ ἡττηθέντας σὺν πάσῃ αἰσχύνῃ κακιγκάκως[2] θανατωθῆναι, πάντα δὲ τὰ ὑμέτερα τῷ δήμῳ δοθῆναι, ὡς ἂν παντάπασιν ἐξαρθῇ τὸ μνημόσυνον ὑμῶν ἀπὸ τῆς γῆς. τὰ μὲν γὰρ σώματα ὑμῶν θηρίοις δώσω παρανάλωμα, τὰ δὲ τέκνα ὑμῶν διηνεκεῖ καταδουλώσω δουλείᾳ.

Τούτων οὕτως εἰρημένων τῷ βασιλεῖ, ὁ υἱὸς αὐτοῦ ἔφη· Κρῖμα δίκαιον σήμερον ἔκρινας, ὦ βασιλεῦ· κρατύναι Κύριος ταύτην σου τὴν γνώμην. κἀγὼ δὲ τὰ αὐτά φημι τῷ ἐμῷ διδασκάλῳ.

[1] μὴ πὸς λέοντα δυρκὰς ἅψωμαι μάχης. Suidas, Lexicon.
[2] κακηγκάκως on p. 220 of Boissonade above.

with the king's son and his fellows, and on them was fulfilled the proverb, 'Gazelle against lion.' The one made the most High his house of defence, and his hope was under the shadow of his wings; while the others trusted in the princes of this world, who are made of none effect, and in the ruler of the darkness of this world, to whom they have subjected themselves miserably and wretchedly.

Now came on Nachor, in the disguise of Barlaam; and the king's side were like to reach their goal; but, once again, very different was the ordering of the wise providence of God. When all the company was come, thus spake the king to his orators and philosophers, or rather to the deceivers of his people, and fools at heart, 'Behold now, there lieth before you a contest, even the mightiest of contests; for one of two things shall befall you. If ye establish our cause, and prove Barlaam and his friends to be in error, ye shall have your fill of glory and honour from us and all the senate, and shall be crowned with crowns of victory. But if ye be worsted, in all ignominy ye shall pitiably perish, and all your goods shall be given to the people, that your memorial may be clean blotted out from off the earth. Your bodies will I give to be devoured by wild beasts and your children will I deliver to perpetual slavery.'

and biddeth his spokesman be mindful of the greatness of the issue

When the king had thus spoken, his son said, 'A righteous doom hast thou judged this day, O king. The Lord establish this thy mind! I too have the same bidding for my teacher.' And, turning

Ioasaph, too, admonisheth his orator Nachor, the mock Barlaam

καὶ ἐπιστραφεὶς λέγει τῷ Ναχώρ, ὃς ἐνομίζετο
Βαρλαὰμ εἶναι· Οἶδας, ὦ Βαρλαάμ, ἐν τίνι με
δόξῃ εὕρηκας καὶ τρυφῇ· καὶ λόγοις πλείστοις
ἔπεισάς με τῶν μὲν πατρῴων ἀποστῆναι νόμων
τε καὶ ἐθῶν, ἀγνώστῳ δὲ λατρεῦσαι Θεῷ, ἀρρήτων τινῶν καὶ αἰωνίων ἀγαθῶν ἐπαγγελίαις
ἑλκύσας μου τὸν νοῦν τοῖς σοῖς ἐξακολουθῆσαι
δόγμασι καὶ τὸν ἐμὸν παραπικρᾶναι πατέρα τε
καὶ δεσπότην; νῦν οὖν ὡς ἐπὶ τρυτάνης νόμιζε
σεαυτὸν ἑστάναι. εἰ μὲν γάρ, νικήσας τὴν προκει-
μένην πάλην, ἀληθῆ σου τὰ δόγματα δείξεις ἅ
μοι ἐδίδαξας, πλανωμένους δὲ ἐλέγξεις τοὺς σήμερον ἡμῖν ἀντιπίπτοντας, σὺ μὲν δοξασθήσῃ ὡς
οὐδεὶς τῶν πώποτε γεγονότων καὶ κήρυξ ἀληθείας
κληθήσῃ, ἐγὼ δὲ τῇ σῇ ἐμμενῶ διδαχῇ καὶ τῷ
Χριστῷ λατρεύσω, καθὰ δὴ καὶ ἐκήρυξας, μέχρι
τῆς τελευταίας μου ἀναπνοῆς· εἰ δέ, ἡττηθεὶς
εἴτε δόλῳ εἴτε ἀληθείᾳ, αἰσχύνης μοι σήμερον
πρόξενος γένῃ, θᾶττον ἐκδικήσω μου τὴν ὕβριν,
χερσὶν οἰκείαις τήν τε καρδίαν σου καὶ τὴν γλῶτ-
ταν ἐξορύξας, κυσί τε βορὰν ταῦτα σὺν τῷ λοιπῷ 237
σου σώματι παραδούς, ἵνα παιδευθῶσι πάντες διὰ
σοῦ μὴ πλανᾶν υἱοὺς βασιλέων.

Τούτων ἀκούσας ὁ Ναχὼρ τῶν ῥημάτων, σκυ-
Ps. vii. 16 θρωπὸς ἦν λίαν καὶ κατηφής, ὁρῶν ἑαυτὸν ἐμπί-
Ps. xxxi. 5 πτοντα τῷ βόθρῳ ᾧ εἰργάσατο καὶ τῇ παγίδι ᾗ
Ps. xxxvii. 15 ἔκρυψε συλλαμβανόμενον, καὶ τὴν ῥομφαίαν αὐτοῦ εἰς καρδίαν αὐτοῦ κατανοῶν εἰσδυομένην.
Συλλογισάμενος οὖν καθ' ἑαυτόν, τῷ τοῦ βασιλέως υἱῷ μᾶλλον ἔγνω προστεθῆναι καὶ τὰ
ἐκείνου κρατῦναι, τοῦ διαφυγεῖν τὸν ἐπηρτημένον
αὐτῷ κίνδυνον, ὡς ἐκείνου εὐλόγως δυναμένου

round to Nachor, who was supposed to be Barlaam, he said, 'Thou knowest, Barlaam, in what splendour and luxury thou foundest me. With many a speech thou persuadedst me to leave my father's laws and customs, and to serve an unknown God, drawn by the promise of some unspeakable and eternal blessings, to follow thy doctrines and to provoke to anger my father and lord. Now therefore consider that thou art weighed in the balance. If thou overcome in the wrestling, and prove that the doctrines, which thou hast taught me, be true, and show that they, that try a fall with us, be in error, thou shalt be magnified as no man heretofore, and shalt be entitled "herald of truth"; and I will abide in thy doctrine and serve Christ, even as thou didst preach, until my dying breath. But if thou be worsted, by foul play or fair, and thus bring shame on me to-day, speedily will I avenge me of mine injury; with mine own hands will I quickly tear out thy heart and thy tongue, and throw them with the residue of thy carcase to be meat for the dogs, that others may be lessoned by thee not to cozen the sons of kings.'

When Nachor heard these words, he was exceeding sorrowful and downcast, seeing himself falling into the destruction that he had made for other, and being drawn into the net that he had laid privily, and feeling the sword entering into his own soul. So he took counsel with himself, and determined rather to take the side of the king's son, and make it to prevail, that he might avoid the danger hanging over him, because the prince was

Nachor, dreading Ioasaph, resolveth to plead his cause in good faith

τιμωρήσασθαι αὐτόν, εἴπερ παραπικραίνων εὑρεθείη. τὸ δὲ πᾶν τῆς θείας ἦν προνοίας σοφῶς
διὰ τῶν ἐναντίων τὰ ἡμέτερα βεβαιούσης. ὡς
γὰρ εἰς λόγους ἦλθον ἀλλήλοις οἱ μύσται τῶν
Numb. xxii.-xxiv. εἰδώλων καὶ ὁ Ναχώρ, καθάπερ τις ἄλλος Βαλαὰμ ὃς ἐπὶ τοῦ Βαλάκ ποτε, ἐπαράσασθαι τὸν
Ἰσραὴλ προθέμενος, πολυειδέσιν αὐτὸν εὐλό-
γησεν εὐλογίαις, οὕτως καὶ ὁ Ναχὼρ ἰσχυρῶς
τοῖς ἀσόφοις καὶ ἀσυνέτοις σοφοῖς ἀντικαθίστατο.

Καθεζομένου γὰρ τοῦ βασιλέως ἐπὶ τοῦ θρόνου, 238
συνεδριάζοντος καὶ τοῦ υἱοῦ, καθάπερ ἔφημεν,
Ps. lxiv. 3 παρεστώτων δὲ τῶν ὥσπερ ῥομφαίαν τὰς γλώσσας ἀκονησάντων ἐπὶ καθαιρέσει τῆς ἀληθείας
Is. lix. 4 ἀσόφων ῥητόρων, οἵ, τὸ τοῦ Ἡσαΐου, κύουσι
πόνον καὶ τίκτουσιν ἀνομίαν, συνελθόντων δὲ
ἀπείρων λαῶν εἰς θέαν τοῦ ἀγῶνος ὥστε μαθεῖν
ὁπότερον μέρος τὴν νίκην ἀποίσεται, λέγει τῷ
Ναχὼρ εἷς τῶν ῥητόρων, ὁ τῶν σὺν αὐτῷ πάντων
διαφορώτατος· σὺ εἶ ὁ ἀναισχύντως οὕτως καὶ
ἰταμῶς εἰς τοὺς θεοὺς ἡμῶν ἐξυβρίζων Βαρλαάμ,
καὶ τὸν φίλτατον υἱὸν τοῦ βασιλέως τοιαύτῃ
περιβαλὼν τῇ πλάνῃ καὶ τῷ ἐσταυρωμένῳ διδάξας λατρεύειν; καὶ ὁ Ναχώρ· Ἐγώ εἰμι, ἀπεκρίνατο, ἐγώ εἰμι Βαρλαάμ, ὁ τοὺς θεούς σου μὲν
ἐξουθενῶν, καθὼς εἴρηκας, τὸν υἱὸν δὲ τοῦ βασιλέως οὐ πλάνῃ περιβαλών, ἀλλὰ πλάνης ἀπαλλάξας καὶ τῷ ἀληθινῷ προσοικειωσάμενος Θεῷ.
καὶ ὁ ῥήτωρ· Τῶν μεγάλων, φησί, καὶ θαυμασίων
ἀνδρῶν τῶν πᾶσαν σοφίας ἐπιστήμην ἐξευρη-
κότων θεοὺς ὑψηλοὺς καὶ ἀθανάτους ἐκείνους
ὀνομαζόντων, καὶ πάντων τῶν ἐπὶ γῆς βασιλέων
καὶ ἐνδόξων αὐτοῖς προσκυνούντων καὶ σεβο-

doubtless able to requite him, should he be found to provoke him. But this was all the work of divine providence that was wisely establishing our cause by the mouth of our adversaries. For when these idol-priests and Nachor crossed words, like another Barlaam, who, of old in the time of Balak, when purposing to curse Israel, loaded him with manifold blessings, so did Nachor mightily resist these unwise and unlearned wise men.

There sat the king upon his throne, his son beside him, as we have said. There beside him stood these unwise orators who had whetted their tongues like a sharp sword, to destroy truth, and who (as saith Esay) conceive mischief and bring forth iniquity. There were gathered innumerable multitudes, come to view the contest and see which side should carry off the victory. Then one of the orators, the most eminent of all his fellows, said unto Nachor, 'Art thou that Barlaam which hath so shamelessly and audaciously blasphemed our gods, and hath enmeshed our king's well beloved son in the net of error, and taught him to serve the Crucified?' Nachor answered, 'I am he, I am Barlaam, that, as thou sayest, doth set your gods at nought: but the king's son have I not enmeshed in error; but rather from error have I delivered him, and brought him to the true God.' The orator replied, 'When the great and marvellous men, who have discovered all knowledge of wisdom, do call them high and immortal gods, and when all the kings and honourable men upon earth do worship and adore them, how waggest thou tongue

μένων, πῶς αὐτὸς γλῶσσαν κατ' αὐτῶν κινεῖς,
καὶ ὅλως ἀποθρασύνεσθαι τὰ τοιαῦτα τολμᾷς;
Τίς δὲ ἡ ἀπόδειξις μὴ τούτους εἶναι θεούς, ἀλλὰ
τὸν ἐσταυρωμένον; ὑπολαβὼν δὲ ὁ Ναχὼρ τὸν
μὲν ῥήτορα ἐκεῖνον οὐδόλως ἀποκρίσεως ἠξίωσε·
Acts xiii. 16 κατασείσας δὲ τῇ χειρὶ τὸ πλῆθος σιγᾶν, ἀνοίξας 239
Numb. xxii. 28; 2 Pet. ii 16 τὸ στόμα αὐτοῦ, καθάπερ ὁ τοῦ Βαλαὰμ ὄνος, ἃ
οὐ προέθετο εἰπεῖν ταῦτα λελάληκε· καί φησι
πρὸς τὸν βασιλέα·

XXVII

Ἐγώ, βασιλεῦ, προνοίᾳ Θεοῦ ἦλθον εἰς τὸν
Cp. 2 Macc. vii. 28 κόσμον· καὶ θεωρήσας τὸν οὐρανὸν καὶ γῆν καὶ
θάλασσαν, ἥλιόν τε καὶ σελήνην καὶ τὰ λοιπά,
ἐθαύμασα τὴν διακόσμησιν τούτων. ἰδὼν δὲ τὸν
κόσμον καὶ τὰ ἐν αὐτῷ πάντα, ὅτι κατὰ ἀνάγκην
κινεῖται, συνῆκα τὸν κινοῦντα καὶ διακρατοῦντα
εἶναι Θεόν· πᾶν γὰρ τὸ κινοῦν ἰσχυρότερον τοῦ
κινουμένου, καὶ τὸ διακρατοῦν ἰσχυρότερον τοῦ
διακρατουμένου ἐστίν. αὐτὸν οὖν λέγω εἶναι
Θεὸν τὸν συστησάμενον τὰ πάντα καὶ διακρατοῦντα, ἄναρχον καὶ ἀΐδιον, ἀθάνατον καὶ ἀπροσ-
δεῆ, ἀνώτερον πάντων τῶν παθῶν καὶ ἐλαττω-
μάτων, ὀργῆς τε καὶ λήθης καὶ ἀγνοίας καὶ τῶν
Cp. Col. i. 17 λοιπῶν. δι' αὐτοῦ δὲ τὰ πάντα συνέστηκεν. οὐ
Acts xvii. 25 χρῄζει θυσίας καὶ σπονδῆς, οὐδὲ πάντων τῶν
φαινομένων· πάντες δὲ αὐτοῦ χρῄζουσι.

Τούτων οὕτως εἰρημένων περὶ Θεοῦ, καθὼς ἐμὲ
ἐχώρησε περὶ αὐτοῦ λέγειν, ἔλθωμεν καὶ ἐπὶ
τὸ ἀνθρώπινον γένος, ὅπως ἴδωμεν τίνες αὐτῶν
μετέχουσι τῆς ἀληθείας καὶ τίνες τῆς πλάνης. 240

against them, and, in brief, how durst thou be so mighty brazen-faced? What is the manner of thy proof that the Crucified is God, and these be none?' Then replied Nachor, disdaining even to answer the speaker. He beckoned with his hand to the multitude to keep silence, and opening his mouth, like Balaam's ass, spake that which he had not purposed to say, and thus addressed the king.

XXVII

'By the providence of God, O king, came I into the world; and when I contemplated heaven and earth and sea, the sun and moon, and the other heavenly bodies, I was led to marvel at their fair order. And, when I beheld the world and all that therein is, how it is moved by law, I understood that he who moveth and sustaineth it is God. That which moveth is ever stronger than that which is moved, and that which sustaineth is stronger than that which is sustained. Him therefore I call God, who constructed all things and sustaineth them, without beginning, without end, immortal, without want, above all passions, and failings, such as anger, forgetfulness, ignorance, and the like. By him all things consist. He hath no need of sacrifice, or drink-offering, or of any of the things that we see, but all men have need of him.

Nachor beginneth his discourse (APOLOGY OF ARISTIDES)

'Now that I have said thus much concerning God, according as he hath granted me to speak concerning himself, come we now to the human race, that we may know which of them partake of truth, and

Of idolaters, Jews and Christians

φανερὸν γάρ ἐστιν ἡμῖν, ὦ βασιλεῦ, ὅτι τρία γένη
εἰσὶν ἀνθρώπων ἐν τῷδε τῷ κόσμῳ· ὧν εἰσὶν οἱ
τῶν παρ' ὑμῶν λεγομένων θεῶν προσκυνηταί,
καὶ Ἰουδαῖοι, καὶ Χριστιανοί· αὐτοὶ δὲ πάλιν,
οἱ τοὺς πολλοὺς σεβόμενοι θεούς, εἰς τρία διαι-
ροῦνται γένη, Χαλδαίους τε καὶ Ἕλληνας καὶ
Αἰγυπτίους· οὗτοι γὰρ γεγόνασιν ἀρχηγοὶ καὶ
διδάσκαλοι τοῖς λοιποῖς ἔθνεσι τῆς τῶν πολυω-
νύμων θεῶν λατρείας καὶ προσκυνήσεως. ἴδωμεν
οὖν τίνες τούτων μετέχουσι τῆς ἀληθείας καὶ
τίνες τῆς πλάνης.

Οἱ μὲν γὰρ Χαλδαῖοι, οἱ μὴ εἰδότες Θεόν,
ἐπλανήθησαν ὀπίσω τῶν στοιχείων καὶ ἤρξαντο
Rom. i. 25 σέβεσθαι τὴν κτίσιν παρὰ τὸν κτίσαντα αὐτούς·
ὧν καὶ μορφώματά τινα ποιήσαντες ὠνόμασαν
ἐκτυπώματα τοῦ οὐρανοῦ καὶ τῆς γῆς καὶ τῆς
θαλάσσης, ἡλίου τε καὶ σελήνης, καὶ τῶν λοιπῶν
στοιχείων ἢ φωστήρων, καί, συγκλείσαντες ναοῖς,
προσκυνοῦσι θεοὺς καλοῦντες, οὓς καὶ τηροῦσιν
ἀσφαλῶς ἵνα μὴ κλαπῶσιν ὑπὸ ληστῶν. καὶ
οὐ συνῆκαν ὅτι πᾶν τὸ τηροῦν μεῖζον τοῦ τηρου-
μένου ἐστί, καὶ ὁ ποιῶν μείζων ἐστὶ τοῦ ποιου-
μένου· εἰ γὰρ ἀδυνατοῦσιν οἱ θεοὶ αὐτῶν περὶ
τῆς ἰδίας σωτηρίας, πῶς ἄλλοις σωτηρίαν χα-
ρίσονται; πλάνην οὖν μεγάλην ἐπλανήθησαν οἱ
Χαλδαῖοι, σεβόμενοι ἀγάλματα νεκρὰ καὶ ἀνωφελῆ. καὶ θαυμάζειν μοι ἐπέρχεται, ὦ βασιλεῦ,
πῶς οἱ λεγόμενοι φιλόσοφοι αὐτῶν οὐδόλως
συνῆκαν ὅτι καὶ αὐτὰ τὰ στοιχεῖα φθαρτά ἐστιν.
εἰ δὲ τὰ στοιχεῖα φθαρτά ἐστι καὶ ὑποτασσόμενα
κατὰ ἀνάγκην, πῶς εἰσι θεοί; εἰ δὲ τὰ στοιχεῖα 241

which of error. It is manifiest to us, O king, that there are three races of men in this world: those that are worshippers of them whom ye call gods, and Jews, and Christians. And again those who serve many gods are divided into three races, Chaldeans, Greeks and Egyptians, for these are to the other nations the leaders and teachers of the service and worship of the gods whose name is legion. Let us therefore see which of these hold the truth, and which error.

Of idolaters, and first of the Chaldeans

'The Chaldeans, which knew not God, went astray after the elements and began to worship the creature rather than their Creator, and they made figures of these creatures and called them likenesses of heaven, and earth and sea, of sun and moon, and of the other elements or luminaries. And they enclose them in temples, and worship them under the title of gods, and guard them in safety lest they be stolen by robbers. They have not understood how that which guardeth is ever greater than that which is guarded, and that the maker is greater than the thing that is made; for, if the gods be unable to take care of themselves, how can they take care of others? Great then is the error that the Chaldeans have erred in worshipping lifeless and useless images. And I am moved to wonder, O king, how they, who are called philosophers among them, fail to understand that even the very elements are corruptible. But if the elements are corruptible and subject to necessity, how are they gods? And if the elements

οὐκ εἰσὶ θεοί, πῶς τὰ ἀγάλματα, ἃ γέγονεν εἰς τιμὴν αὐτῶν, θεοὶ ὑπάρχουσιν;

Ἔλθωμεν οὖν, ὦ βασιλεῦ, ἐπὶ αὐτὰ τὰ στοιχεῖα, ὅπως ἀποδείξωμεν περὶ αὐτῶν ὅτι οὐκ εἰσὶ θεοί, ἀλλὰ φθαρτὰ καὶ ἀλλοιούμενα, ἐκ τοῦ μὴ ὄντος παραχθέντα προστάγματι τοῦ ὄντως[1] Θεοῦ, ὅς ἐστιν ἄφθαρτός τε καὶ ἀναλλοίωτος καὶ ἀόρατος· αὐτὸς δὲ πάντα ὁρᾷ, καί, καθὼς βούλεται, ἀλλοιοῖ καὶ μεταβάλλει. τί οὖν λέγω περὶ τῶν στοιχείων;

Οἱ νομίζοντες τὸν οὐρανὸν εἶναι θεὸν πλανῶνται. ὁρῶμεν γὰρ αὐτὸν τρεπόμενον καὶ κατὰ ἀνάγκην κινούμενον, καὶ ἐκ πολλῶν συνεστῶτα· διὸ καὶ κόσμος καλεῖται. κόσμος δὲ κατασκευή ἐστί τινος τεχνίτου· τὸ κατασκευασθὲν δὲ ἀρχὴν καὶ τέλος ἔχει. κινεῖται δὲ ὁ οὐρανὸς κατὰ ἀνάγκην σὺν τοῖς αὐτοῦ φωστῆρσι· τὰ γὰρ ἄστρα τάξει καὶ διαστήματι φερόμενα ἀπὸ σημείου εἰς σημεῖον, οἱ μὲν δύουσιν, οἱ δὲ ἀνατέλλουσι, καὶ κατὰ καιροὺς πορείαν ποιοῦνται τοῦ ἀποτελεῖν θέρη καὶ χειμῶνας, καθὰ ἐπιτέτακται αὐτοῖς παρὰ τοῦ Θεοῦ, καὶ οὐ παραβαίνουσι τοὺς ἰδίους ὅρους, κατὰ ἀπαραίτητον φύσεως ἀνάγκην, σὺν τῷ οὐρανίῳ κόσμῳ. ὅθεν φανερόν ἐστι μὴ εἶναι τὸν οὐρανὸν θεὸν ἀλλ' ἔργον Θεοῦ.

Οἱ δὲ νομίζοντες τὴν γῆν εἶναι θεὰν ἐπλανήθησαν. ὁρῶμεν γὰρ αὐτὴν ὑπὸ τῶν ἀνθρώπων ὑβριζομένην καὶ κατακυριευομένην καὶ φυρομένην καὶ ἄχρηστον γινομένην. ἐὰν γὰρ ὀπτηθῇ, γίνεται νεκρά· ἐκ γὰρ τοῦ ὀστράκου φύεται οὐδέν. ἔτι

[1] ὄντος, Pemb. Coll. Camb. MS.

are not gods, how are the images, created to their honour, gods?

'Come we then, O king, to the elements themselves, that we may prove concerning them, that they are not gods, but corruptible and changeable things, brought out of non-existence by the command of him who is God indeed, who is incorruptible, and unchangeable, and invisible, but yet himself seeth all things, and, as he willeth, changeth and altereth the same. What then must I say about the elements?

'They, who ween that the Heaven is a god, are in error. For we see it turning and moving by law, and consisting of many parts, whence also it is called Cosmos![1] Now a "Cosmos" is the handiwork of some artificer: and that which is wrought by handiwork hath beginning and end. And the firmament is moved by law together with its luminaries. The stars are borne from Sign to Sign, each in his order and place: some rise, while others set: and they run their journey according to fixed seasons, to fulfil summer and winter, as it hath been ordained for them by God, nor do they transgress their proper bounds, according to the inexorable law of nature, in common with the heavenly firmament. Whence it is evident that the heaven is not a god, but only a work of God.

Nachor proveth that the elements are not gods,—neither Heaven,

'They again that think that the Earth is a goddess have gone astray. We behold it dishonoured, mastered, defiled and rendered useless by mankind. If it be baked by the sun, it becometh dead, for nothing groweth from a potsherd. And again, if it be soaked

nor Earth,

[1] A play on the Greek word *Kosmos* which means: (1) An orderly arrangement, (2) Universe.

δὲ καὶ ἐὰν ἐπὶ πλέον βραχῇ, φθείρεται καὶ αὐτὴ 242
καὶ οἱ καρποὶ αὐτῆς. καταπατεῖται δὲ ὑπό τε ἀνθρώπων καὶ τῶν λοιπῶν ζῴων, αἵμασι φονευομένων μιαίνεται, διορύσσεται, νεκρῶν θήκη γίνεται σωμάτων. τούτων οὕτως ὄντων, οὐκ ἐνδέχεται τὴν γῆν εἶναι θεὰν ἀλλ' ἔργον Θεοῦ εἰς χρῆσιν ἀνθρώπων.

Οἱ δὲ νομίζοντες τὸ ὕδωρ εἶναι θεὸν ἐπλανήθησαν. καὶ αὐτὸ γὰρ εἰς χρῆσιν τῶν ἀνθρώπων γέγονε, καὶ κατακυριεύεται ὑπ' αὐτῶν, μιαίνεται καὶ φθείρεται, καὶ ἀλλοιοῦται ἑψόμενον καὶ ἀλλασσόμενον χρώμασι, καὶ ὑπὸ τοῦ κρύους πηγνύμενον, καὶ εἰς πάντων τῶν ἀκαθάρτων πλύσιν ἀγόμενον. διὸ ἀδύνατον τὸ ὕδωρ εἶναι θεὸν ἀλλ' ἔργον Θεοῦ.

Οἱ δὲ νομίζοντες τὸ πῦρ εἶναι θεὸν πλανῶνται. καὶ αὐτὸ γὰρ εἰς χρῆσιν ἐγένετο ἀνθρώπων. καὶ κατακυριεύεται ὑπ' αὐτῶν, περιφερόμενον ἐκ τόπου εἰς τόπον εἰς ἕψησιν καὶ ὄπτησιν παντοδαπῶν κρεῶν, ἔτι δὲ καὶ νεκρῶν σωμάτων. φθείρεται δὲ καὶ κατὰ πολλοὺς τρόπους, ὑπὸ τῶν ἀνθρώπων σβεννύμενον. διὸ οὐκ ἐνδέχεται τὸ πῦρ εἶναι θεὸν ἀλλ' ἔργον Θεοῦ.

Οἱ δὲ νομίζοντες τὴν τῶν ἀνέμων πνοὴν εἶναι θεὰν πλανῶνται· φανερὸν γάρ ἐστιν ὅτι δουλεύει ἑτέρῳ, καὶ χάριν τῶν ἀνθρώπων κατεσκεύασται ὑπὸ τοῦ Θεοῦ πρὸς μεταγωγὴν πλοίων καὶ συγκομιδὰς τῶν σιτίων, καὶ εἰς λοιπὰς αὐτῶν χρείας αὔξει τε καὶ λήγει, κατ' ἐπιταγὴν Θεοῦ. διὸ οὐ νενόμισται τὴν τῶν ἀνέμων πνοὴν εἶναι θεὰν ἀλλ' ἔργον Θεοῦ.

Οἱ δὲ νομίζοντες τὸν ἥλιον εἶναι θεὸν πλανῶν-

overmuch, it rotteth, fruit and all. It is trodden under foot of men and the residue of the beasts: it is polluted with the blood of the murdered, it is digged and made a grave for dead bodies. This being so, Earth can in no wise be a goddess, but only the work of God for the use of men.

'They that think that Water is a god have gone astray. It also hath been made for the use of men. It is under their lordship: it is polluted, and perisheth: it is altered by boiling, by dyeing, by congealment, or by being brought to the cleansing of all defilements. Wherefore Water cannot be a god, but only the work of God. nor Water,

'They that think that Fire is a god are in error. It too was made for the use of men. It is subject to their lordship, being carried about from place to place, for the seething and roasting of all manner of meats, yea, and for the burning of dead corpses. Moreover, it perisheth in divers ways, when it is quenched by mankind. Wherefore Fire cannot be a god, but only the work of God. nor Fire,

'They that think that the breath of the Winds is a goddess are in error. This, as is evident, is subject to another, and hath been prepared by God, for the sake of mankind, for the carriage of ships, and the conveyance of victuals, and for other uses of men, it riseth and falleth according to the ordinance of God. Wherefore it is not to be supposed that the breath of the Winds is a goddess, but only the work of God. nor the breath of the Winds

'They that think that the Sun is a god are in Nor are the

ται. ὁρῶμεν γὰρ αὐτὸν κινούμενον κατὰ ἀνάγκην καὶ τρεπόμενον, καὶ μεταβαίνοντα ἀπὸ σημείου εἰς σημεῖον, δύνοντα καὶ ἀνατέλλοντα, 243
τοῦ θερμαίνειν τὰ φυτὰ καὶ βλαστὰ εἰς χρῆσιν τῶν ἀνθρώπων, ἔτι δὲ καὶ μερισμοὺς ἔχοντα μετὰ τῶν λοιπῶν ἀστέρων, καὶ ἐλάττονα ὄντα τοῦ οὐρανοῦ πολύ, καὶ ἐκλείποντα τοῦ φωτός, καὶ μηδεμίαν αὐτοκράτειαν ἔχοντα. διὸ οὐ νενόμισται τὸν ἥλιον εἶναι θεὸν ἀλλ' ἔργον Θεοῦ.

Οἱ δὲ νομίζοντες τὴν σελήνην εἶναι θεὰν πλανῶνται. ὁρῶμεν γὰρ αὐτὴν κινουμένην κατὰ ἀνάγκην καὶ τρεπομένην, καὶ μεταβαίνουσαν ἀπὸ σημείου εἰς σημεῖον, δύνουσάν τε καὶ ἀνατέλλουσαν εἰς χρείαν τῶν ἀνθρώπων, καὶ ἐλάττονα οὖσαν τοῦ ἡλίου, αὐξομένην τε καὶ μειουμένην, καὶ ἐκλείψεις ἔχουσαν. διὸ οὐ νενόμισται τὴν σελήνην εἶναι θεὰν ἀλλ' ἔργον Θεοῦ.

Οἱ δὲ νομίζοντες τὸν ἄνθρωπον εἶναι θεὸν πλανῶνται. ὁρῶμεν γὰρ αὐτὸν κινούμενον κατὰ ἀνάγκην, καὶ τρεφόμενον καὶ γηράσκοντα, καὶ μὴ θέλοντος αὐτοῦ. καί ποτε μὲν χαίρει, ποτὲ δὲ λυπεῖται, δεόμενος βρωμάτων καὶ ποτοῦ καὶ ἐσθῆτος. εἶναι δὲ αὐτὸν ὀργίλον καὶ ζηλωτὴν καὶ ἐπιθυμητήν, καὶ μεταμελόμενον, καὶ πολλὰ ἐλαττώματα ἔχοντα. φθείρεται δὲ κατὰ πολλοὺς τρόπους, ὑπὸ στοιχείων καὶ ζῴων, καὶ τοῦ ἐπικειμένου αὐτῷ θανάτου. οὐκ ἐνδέχεται οὖν εἶναι τὸν ἄνθρωπον θεὸν ἀλλ' ἔργον Θεοῦ. πλάνην οὖν μεγάλην ἐπλανήθησαν οἱ Χαλδαῖοι, ὀπίσω τῶν ἐπιθυμημάτων αὐτῶν. σέβονται γὰρ τὰ φθαρτὰ στοιχεῖα καὶ τὰ νεκρὰ ἀγάλματα, καὶ οὐκ αἰσθάνονται ταῦτα θεοποιούμενοι. 244

error. We see him moving and turning by law, and passing from Sign to Sign, setting and rising, to warm herbs and trees for the use of men, sharing power with the other stars, being much less than the heaven, and falling into eclipse and possessed of no sovranty of his own. Wherefore we may not consider that the Sun is a god, but only the work of God.

heavenly bodies gods —neither the Sun,

'They that think that the Moon is a goddess are in error. We behold her moving and turning by law, and passing from Sign to Sign, setting and rising for the use of men, lesser than the sun, waxing and waning, suffering eclipse. Wherefore we do not consider that the Moon is a goddess, but only the work of God.

nor the Moon

'They that think that Man is a god are in error. We see man moving by law, growing up, and waxing old, even against his will. Now he rejoiceth, now he grieveth, requiring meat and drink and raiment. Besides he is passionate, envious, lustful, fickle, and full of failings: and he perisheth in many a way, by the elements, by wild beasts, and by the death that ever awaiteth him. So Man cannot be a god, but only the work of God. Great then is the error that the Chaldeans have erred in following their own lusts; for they worship corruptible elements and dead images, neither do they perceive that they are making gods of these.

Nor again may Man himself be a god

Ἔλθωμεν οὖν ἐπὶ τοὺς Ἕλληνας, ἵνα ἴδωμεν εἴ τι φρονοῦσι περὶ Θεοῦ. οἱ οὖν Ἕλληνες
Cp. Rom. i. 22 σοφοὶ λέγοντες εἶναι ἐμωράνθησαν χεῖρον τῶν Χαλδαίων, παρεισάγοντες πολλοὺς θεοὺς γεγενῆσθαι, τοὺς μὲν ἄρρενας, τοὺς δὲ θηλείας, παντοίων παθῶν καὶ παντοδαπῶν δημιουργοὺς ἀνομημάτων. ὅθεν γελοῖα καὶ μωρὰ καὶ ἀσεβῆ παρεισήγαγον οἱ Ἕλληνες, βασιλεῦ, ῥήματα, τοὺς μὴ ὄντας προσαγορεύοντες θεούς, κατὰ τὰς ἐπιθυμίας αὐτῶν τὰς πονηράς, ἵνα, τούτους συνηγόρους ἔχοντες τῆς κακίας, μοιχεύωσιν, ἁρπάζωσι, φονεύωσι, καὶ τὰ πάνδεινα ποιῶσιν. εἰ γὰρ οἱ θεοὶ αὐτῶν τοιαῦτα ἐποίησαν, πῶς καὶ αὐτοὶ οὐ τοιαῦτα πράξουσιν; ἐκ τούτων οὖν τῶν ἐπιτηδευμάτων τῆς πλάνης συνέβη τοὺς ἀνθρώπους πολέμους ἔχειν συχνούς, καὶ σφαγὰς καὶ αἰχμαλωσίας πικράς. ἀλλὰ καὶ καθ' ἕκαστον τῶν θεῶν αὐτῶν εἰ θελήσομεν ἐλθεῖν τῷ λόγῳ, πολλὴν ὄψει τὴν ἀτοπίαν.

Ὁ πρῶτος παρεισάγεται αὐτοῖς πρὸ πάντων θεὸς ὁ λεγόμενος Κρόνος, καὶ τούτῳ θύουσι τὰ ἴδια τέκνα, ὃς ἔσχε παῖδας πολλοὺς ἐκ τῆς Ῥέας, καὶ μανεὶς ἤσθιε τὰ ἴδια τέκνα. φασὶ δὲ τὸν Δία κόψαι αὐτοῦ τὰ ἀναγκαῖα καὶ βαλεῖν εἰς τὴν
θάλασσαν, ὅθεν Ἀφροδίτην μυθεύεται γεννᾶσθαι. 245
δήσας οὖν τὸν ἴδιον πατέρα ὁ Ζεὺς ἔβαλεν εἰς τὸν Τάρταρον. ὁρᾷς τὴν πλάνην καὶ ἀσέλγειαν ἣν παρεισάγουσι κατὰ τοῦ θεοῦ αὐτῶν; ἐνδέχεται οὖν θεὸν εἶναι δέσμιον καὶ ἀπόκοπον; ὢ τῆς ἀνοίας· τίς τῶν νοῦν ἐχόντων ταῦτα φήσειεν;

Δεύτερος παρεισάγεται ὁ Ζεύς, ὅν φασι βασιλεῦσαι τῶν θεῶν αὐτῶν, καὶ μεταμορφοῦσθαι εἰς

'Now come we to the Greeks that we may see whether they have any understanding concerning God. The Greeks, then, professing themselves to be wise, fell into greater folly than the Chaldeans, alleging the existence of many gods, some male, others female, creators of all passions and sins of every kind. Wherefore the Greeks, O king, introduced an absurd, foolish and ungodly fashion of talk, calling them gods that were not, according to their own evil passions; that, having these gods for advocates of their wickedness, they might commit adultery, theft, murder and all manner of iniquity. For if their gods did so, how should they not themselves do the like? Therefore from these practices of error it came to pass that men suffered frequent wars and slaughters and cruel captivities. But if now we choose to pass in review each one of these gods, what a strange sight shalt thou see! Of the errors of the Greeks and of their strange gods

'First and foremost they introduce the god whom they call Kronos, and to him they sacrifice their own children, to him who had many sons by Rhea, and in a fit of madness ate his own children. And they say that Zeus cut off his privy parts, and cast them into the sea, whence, as fable telleth, was born Aphrodite. So Zeus bound his own father, and cast him into Tartarus. Dost thou mark the delusion and lasciviousness that they allege against their gods? Is it possible then that one who was prisoner and mutilated should be a god? What folly? What man in his senses could admit it? Of Kronos,

'Next they introduce Zeus, who, they say, became king of the gods, and would take the shape of animals, of Zeus,

ζῷα, ὅπως μοιχεύσῃ θνητὰς γυναῖκας. παρεισάγουσι γὰρ τοῦτον μεταμορφούμενον εἰς ταῦρον πρὸς Εὐρώπην, καὶ εἰς χρυσὸν πρὸς Δανάην, καὶ εἰς κύκνον πρὸς Λήδαν, καὶ εἰς σάτυρον πρὸς Ἀντιόπην, καὶ εἰς κεραυνὸν πρὸς Σεμέλην· εἶτα γενέσθαι ἐκ τούτων τέκνα πολλά, Διόνυσον, καὶ Ζῆθον καὶ Ἀμφίονα, καὶ Ἡρακλῆν, καὶ Ἀπόλλωνα καὶ Ἄρτεμιν, καὶ Περσέα, Κάστορά τε καὶ Ἑλένην καὶ Πολυδεύκην, καὶ Μίνωα, καὶ Ῥαδάμανθον, καὶ Σαρπηδόνα, καὶ τὰς ἐννέα θυγατέρας 246
ἃς προσηγόρευσαν Μούσας.

Εἶθ' οὕτως παρεισάγουσι τὰ κατὰ τὸν Γανυμήδην. συνέβη οὖν, βασιλεῦ, τοῖς ἀνθρώποις μιμεῖσθαι ταῦτα πάντα, καὶ γίνεσθαι μοιχοὺς καὶ ἀρρενομανεῖς, καὶ ἄλλων δεινῶν ἔργων ἐργάτας, κατὰ μίμησιν τοῦ θεοῦ αὐτῶν. πῶς οὖν ἐνδέχεται θεὸν εἶναι μοιχὸν ἢ ἀνδροβάτην ἢ πατροκτόνον;

Σὺν τούτῳ δὲ καὶ Ἥφαιστόν τινα παρεισάγουσι θεὸν εἶναι, καὶ τοῦτον χωλόν, καὶ κρατοῦντα σφῦραν καὶ πυρόλαβον, καὶ χαλκεύοντα χάριν τροφῆς. ἄρα ἐπιδεής ἐστιν· ὅπερ οὐκ ἐνδέχεται θεὸν εἶναι χωλὸν καὶ προσδεόμενον ἀνθρώπων.

Εἶτα τὸν Ἑρμῆν παρεισάγουσι θεὸν εἶναι ἐπιθυμητὴν καὶ κλέπτην καὶ πλεονέκτην καὶ μάγον, καὶ κυλλὸν καὶ λόγων ἑρμηνευτήν. ὅπερ οὐκ ἐνδέχεται θεὸν εἶναι τοιοῦτον.

Τὸν δὲ Ἀσκληπιὸν παρεισάγουσι θεὸν εἶναι, ἰατρὸν ὄντα καὶ κατασκευάζοντα φάρμακα καὶ σύνθεσιν ἐμπλάστρων, χάριν τροφῆς (ἐπενδεὴς γὰρ ἦν), ὕστερον δὲ κεραυνοῦσθαι αὐτὸν ὑπὸ τοῦ

that he might defile mortal women. They show him transformed into a bull, for Europa; into gold, for Danae; into a swan, for Leda; into a satyr, for Antiope; and into a thunder-bolt, for Semele. Then of these were born many children, Dionysus, Zethus, Amphion, Herakles, Apollo, Artemis, Perseus, Castor, Helen, Polydeukes, Minos, Rhadamanthos, Sarpedon, and the nine daughters whom they call the Muses.

'In like manner they introduce the story of Ganymede. And so befel it, O king, that men imitated all these things, and became adulterers, and defilers of themselves with mankind, and doers of other monstrous deeds, in imitation of their god. How then can an adulterer, one that defileth himself by unnatural lust, a slayer of his father be a god?

'With Zeus also they represent one Hephaestus as a god, and him lame, holding hammer and fire-tongs, and working as a copper-smith for hire. So it appeareth that he is needy. But it is impossible for one who is lame and wanteth men's aid to be a God. **of Hephaestus,**

'After him, they represent as a god Hermes, a lusty fellow, a thief, and a covetous, a sorcerer, bow-legged, and an interpreter of speech. It is impossible for such an one to be a God. **of Hermes,**

'They also exhibit Asklepius as god, a physician, a maker of medicines, a compounder of plasters for his livelihood (for he is a needy wight), and in the end, they say that he was struck by Zeus with a thunder- **of Asklepius,**

Διὸς διὰ Τυνδάρεων Λακεδαίμονος υἱόν, καὶ ἀποθανεῖν. εἰ δὲ Ἀσκληπιὸς θεὸς ὢν καὶ κεραυνωθεὶς οὐκ ἠδυνήθη ἑαυτῷ βοηθῆσαι, πῶς ἄλλοις βοηθήσει;

Ἄρης δὲ παρεισάγεται θεὸς εἶναι πολεμιστὴς καὶ ζηλωτής, καὶ ἐπιθυμητὴς θρεμμάτων καὶ 247
ἑτέρων τινῶν· ὕστερον δὲ αὐτὸν μοιχεύοντα τὴν Ἀφροδίτην δεθῆναι αὐτὸν ὑπὸ τοῦ νηπίου Ἔρωτος καὶ ὑπὸ Ἡφαίστου. πῶς οὖν θεός ἐστιν ὁ ἐπιθυμητὴς καὶ πολεμιστὴς καὶ δέσμιος καὶ μοιχός;

Τὸν δὲ Διόνυσον παρεισάγουσι θεὸν εἶναι, νυκτερινὰς ἄγοντα ἑορτὰς καὶ διδάσκαλον μέθης, καὶ ἀποσπῶντα τὰς τῶν πλησίον γυναῖκας, καὶ μαινόμενον καὶ φεύγοντα· ὕστερον δὲ αὐτὸν σφαγῆναι ὑπὸ τῶν Τιτάνων. εἰ οὖν Διόνυσος σφαγεὶς οὐκ ἠδυνήθη ἑαυτῷ βοηθῆσαι, ἀλλὰ καὶ μαινόμενος ἦν καὶ μέθυσος καὶ δραπέτης, πῶς ἂν εἴη θεός;

Τὸν δὲ Ἡρακλῆν παρεισάγουσι μεθυσθῆναι καὶ μανῆναι, καὶ τὰ ἴδια τέκνα σφάξαι, εἶτα πυρὶ ἀναλωθῆναι καὶ οὕτως ἀποθανεῖν. πῶς δ' ἂν εἴη θεός, μέθυσος καὶ τεκνοκτόνος, καὶ κατακαιόμενος; ἢ πῶς ἄλλοις βοηθήσει, ἑαυτῷ βοηθῆσαι μὴ δυνηθείς;

Τὸν δὲ Ἀπόλλωνα παρεισάγουσι θεὸν εἶναι ζηλωτήν, ἔτι δὲ καὶ τόξον καὶ φαρέτραν κρατοῦντα, ποτὲ δὲ καὶ κιθάραν καὶ ἐπαυθίδα,[1] καὶ μαντευόμενον τοῖς ἀνθρώποις χάριν μισθοῦ. ἄρα ἐπενδεής ἐστιν· ὅπερ οὐκ ἐνδέχεται θεὸν εἶναι ἐνδεῆ καὶ ζηλωτὴν καὶ κιθαρῳδόν.

[1] And so an eleventh cent. MS. at Wisbech; ἐπαυλίδα, Pemb. Coll. Camb.; λαβοῦτον (*i.e.* Laute or Lute?) Harl. 5619; Boissonade suggests πηκτίδα.

bolt, because of Tyndareus, son of Lakedaemon, and thus perished. Now if Asklepius, though a god, when struck by a thunder-bolt, could not help himself, how can he help others?

'Ares is represented as a warlike god, emulous, and covetous of sheep and other things. But in the end they say he was taken in adultery with Aphrodite by the child Eros and Hephaestus and was bound by them. How then can the covetous, the warrior, the bondman and adulterer be a god? of Ares,

'Dionysus they show as a god, who leadeth nightly orgies, and teacheth drunkenness, and carrieth off his neighbours' wives, a madman and an exile, finally slain by the Titans. If then Dionysus was slain and unable to help himself, nay, further was a madman, a drunkard, and vagabond, how could he be a god? of Dionysus,

'Herakles, too, is represented as drunken and mad, as slaying his own children, then consuming with fire and thus dying. How then could a drunkard and slayer of his own children, burnt to death by fire, be a god? Or how can he help others who could not help himself? of Herakles

'Apollo they represent as an emulous god, holding bow and quiver, and, at times, harp and flute, and prophesying to men for pay. Soothly he is needy: but one that is needy and emulous and a minstrel cannot be a god. of Apollo,

Ἄρτεμιν δὲ παρεισάγουσιν ἀδελφὴν αὐτοῦ εἶναι, κυνηγὸν οὖσαν, καὶ τόξον ἔχειν μετὰ φαρέτρας, καὶ ταύτην ῥέμβεσθαι κατὰ τῶν ὀρέων μόνην μετὰ τῶν κυνῶν, ὅπως θηρεύσει ἔλαφον ἢ 248
κάπρον. πῶς οὖν ἔσται θεὸς ἡ τοιαύτη γυνὴ καὶ κυνηγὸς καὶ ῥεμβομένη μετὰ τῶν κυνῶν;

Ἀφροδίτην δὲ λέγουσι καὶ αὐτὴν θεὰν εἶναι μοιχαλίδα. ποτὲ γὰρ ἔσχε μοιχὸν τὸν Ἄρην, ποτὲ δὲ Ἀγχίσην, ποτὲ δὲ Ἄδωνιν, οὗτινος καὶ τὸν θάνατον κλαίει, ζητοῦσα τὸν ἐραστὴν αὐτῆς· ἣν λέγουσιν καὶ εἰς Ἅδου καταβαίνειν, ὅπως ἐξαγοράσῃ τὸν Ἄδωνιν ἀπὸ τῆς Περσεφόνης. εἶδες, ὦ βασιλεῦ, μείζονα ταύτης ἀφροσύνην; θεὰν παρεισάγειν τὴν μοιχεύουσαν καὶ θρηνοῦσαν καὶ κλαίουσαν;

Ἄδωνιν δὲ παρεισάγουσι θεὸν εἶναι κυνηγόν, καὶ τοῦτον βιαίως ἀποθανεῖν πληγέντα ὑπὸ τοῦ ὑός, καὶ μὴ δυνηθέντα βοηθῆσαι τῇ ταλαιπωρίᾳ ἑαυτοῦ. Πῶς οὖν τῶν ἀνθρώπων φροντίδα ποιήσεται ὁ μοιχὸς καὶ κυνηγὸς καὶ βιοθάνατος;

Ταῦτα πάντα καὶ πολλὰ τοιαῦτα καὶ πολλῷ πλεῖον αἰσχρότερα καὶ πονηρὰ παρεισήγαγον οἱ Ἕλληνες, βασιλεῦ, περὶ τῶν θεῶν αὐτῶν, ἃ οὔτε λέγειν θέμις, οὔτ᾽ ἐπὶ μνήμης ὅλως φέρειν· ὅθεν λαμβάνοντες οἱ ἄνθρωποι ἀφορμὴν ἀπὸ τῶν θεῶν αὐτῶν ἔπραττον πᾶσαν ἀνομίαν καὶ ἀσέλγειαν καὶ ἀσέβειαν, καταμιαίνοντες γῆν τε καὶ ἀέρα ταῖς δειναῖς αὐτῶν πράξεσιν.

Αἰγύπτιοι δέ, ἀβελτερώτεροι καὶ ἀφρονέστεροι 249
τούτων ὄντες, χεῖρον πάντων τῶν ἐθνῶν ἐπλανήθησαν. οὐ γὰρ ἠρκέσθησαν τοῖς τῶν Χαλδαίων καὶ Ἑλλήνων σεβάσμασιν, ἀλλ᾽ ἔτι καὶ ἄλογα

'Artemis, his sister, they represent as an huntress, with bow and quiver, ranging the mountains alone, with her hounds, in chase of stag or boar. How can such an one, that is an huntress and a ranger with hounds, be a goddess? of Artemis,

'Of Aphrodite, adulteress though she be, they say that she is herself a goddess. Once she had for leman Ares, once Anchises, once Adonis, whose death she lamenteth, seeking her lost lover. They say that she even descended into Hades to ransom Adonis from Persephone. Didst thou, O king, ever see madness greater than this? They represent this weeping and wailing adulteress as a goddess. of Aphrodite,

'Adonis they show as an hunter-god, violently killed by a boar-tusk, and unable to help his own distress. How then shall he take thought for mankind, he the adulterer, the hunter who died a violent death? of Adonis

'All such tales, and many like them, and many wicked tales more shameful still, have the Greeks introduced, O king, concerning their gods; tales, whereof it is unlawful to speak, or even to have them in remembrance. Hence men, taking occasion from their gods, wrought all lawlessness, lasciviousness and ungodliness, polluting earth and air with their horrible deeds.

'But the Egyptians, more fatuous and foolish than they, have erred worse than any other nation. They were not satisfied with the idols worshipped by the Chaldeans and Greeks, but further introduced as gods brute beasts of land and water, and herbs Of the errors of the Egyptians,

ζῷα παρεισήγαγον θεοὺς εἶναι χερσαῖά τε καὶ ἔνυδρα, καὶ τὰ φυτὰ καὶ βλαστά, καὶ ἐμιάνθησαν ἐν πάσῃ μανίᾳ καὶ ἀσελγείᾳ χεῖρον πάντων τῶν ἐθνῶν ἐπὶ τῆς γῆς. ἀρχῆθεν γὰρ ἐσέβοντο τὴν Ἶσιν, ἔχουσαν ἀδελφὸν καὶ ἄνδρα τὸν Ὄσιριν, τὸν σφαγέντα ὑπὸ τοῦ ἀδελφοῦ αὐτοῦ Τύφωνος. καὶ διὰ τοῦτο φεύγει ἡ Ἶσις μετὰ Ὥρου τοῦ υἱοῦ αὐτῆς εἰς Βύβλον τῆς Συρίας, ζητοῦσα τὸν Ὄσιριν, πικρῶς θρηνοῦσα, ἕως ηὔξησεν ὁ Ὧρος καὶ ἀπέκτεινε τὸν Τύφωνα. οὔτε οὖν ἡ Ἶσις ἴσχυσε βοηθῆσαι τῷ ἰδίῳ ἀδελφῷ καὶ ἀνδρί· οὔτε ὁ Ὄσιρις σφαζόμενος ὑπὸ τοῦ Τύφωνος ἠδυνήθη ἀντιλαβέσθαι ἑαυτοῦ· οὔτε Τύφων ὁ ἀδελφοκτόνος, ἀπολλύμενος ὑπὸ τοῦ Ὥρου καὶ τῆς Ἴσιδος, εὐπόρησε ῥύσασθαι ἑαυτὸν τοῦ θανάτου. καὶ ἐπὶ τοιούτοις ἀτυχήμασι γνωρισθέντες αὐτοὶ θεοὶ ὑπὸ τῶν ἀσυνέτων Αἰγυπτίων ἐνομίσθησαν. 250

Οἵτινες, μηδ' ἐν τούτοις ἀρκεσθέντες ἢ τοῖς λοιποῖς σεβάσμασι τῶν ἐθνῶν, καὶ τὰ ἄλογα ζῷα παρεισήγαγον θεοὺς εἶναι. τινὲς γὰρ αὐτῶν ἐσεβάσθησαν πρόβατον, τινὲς δὲ τράγον, ἕτεροι δὲ μόσχον καὶ τὸν χοῖρον, ἄλλοι δὲ τὸν κόρακα καὶ τὸν ἱέρακα καὶ τὸν γῦπα καὶ τὸν ἀετόν, καὶ ἄλλοι τὸν κροκόδειλον, τινὲς δὲ τὸν αἴλουρον καὶ τὸν κύνα, καὶ τὸν λύκον καὶ τὸν πίθηκον, καὶ τὸν δράκοντα καὶ τὴν ἀσπίδα, καὶ ἄλλοι τὸ κρόμυον καὶ τὸ σκόροδον καὶ ἀκάνθας, καὶ τὰ λοιπὰ κτίσματα. καὶ οὐκ αἰσθάνονται οἱ ταλαίπωροι περὶ πάντων τούτων ὅτι οὐδὲν ἰσχύουσιν. ὁρῶντες γὰρ τοὺς θεοὺς αὐτῶν βιβρωσκομένους ὑπὸ ἑτέρων ἀνθρώπων καὶ καιομένους καὶ σφαττομένους καὶ

and trees, and were defiled in all madness and lasciviousness worse than all people upon earth. From the beginning they worshipped Isis, which had for her brother and husband that Osiris which was slain by his brother Typhon. And for this reason Isis fled with Horus her son to Byblos in Syria, seeking Osiris and bitterly wailing, until Horus was grown up and killed Typhon. Isis then was not able to help her own brother and husband; nor had Osiris, who was slain by Typhon, power to succour himself; nor had Typhon, who killed his brother and was himself destroyed by Horus and Isis, any resource to save himself from death. And yet, although famous for all these misadventures, these be they that were considered gods by the senseless Egyptians.

'The same people, not content therewith, nor with the rest of the idols of the heathen, also introduced brute beasts as gods. Some of them worshipped the sheep, some the goat, and others the calf and the hog; while certain of them worshipped the raven, the kite, the vulture, and the eagle. Others again worshipped the crocodile, and some the cat and dog, the wolf and ape, the dragon and serpent, and others the onion, garlic and thorns, and every other creature. And the poor fools do not perceive, concerning these things, that they have no power at all. Though they see their gods being devoured, burnt and killed by other men, and rotting

and of their animal gods

σηπομένους, οὐ συνῆκαν περὶ αὐτῶν ὅτι οὐκ εἰσὶ θεοί.

Πλάνην οὖν μεγάλην ἐπλανήθησαν οἵ τε Αἰγύπτιοι καὶ οἱ Χαλδαῖοι καὶ οἱ Ἕλληνες τοιούτους παρεισάγοντες θεούς, καὶ ἀγάλματα αὐτῶν ποιοῦντες, καὶ θεοποιούμενοι τὰ κωφὰ καὶ ἀναίσθητα εἴδωλα. καὶ θαυμάζω πῶς ὁρῶντες τοὺς θεοὺς αὐτῶν ὑπὸ τῶν δημιουργῶν πριζομένους καὶ πελεκωμένους, παλαιουμένους τε ὑπὸ τοῦ χρόνου καὶ ἀναλυομένους, καὶ χωνευομένους, οὐκ ἐφρόνησαν περὶ αὐτῶν ὅτι οὐκ εἰσὶ θεοί. ὅτε γὰρ περὶ τῆς ἰδίας σωτηρίας οὐδὲν ἰσχύουσι, πῶς τῶν ἀνθρώπων πρόνοιαν ποιήσονται; ἀλλ' οἱ ποιηταὶ αὐτῶν καὶ φιλόσοφοι, τῶν τε Χαλδαίων καὶ Ἑλλήνων καὶ Αἰγυπτίων, θελήσαντες τοῖς ποιήμασιν αὐτῶν καὶ συγγραφαῖς σεμνῦναι τοὺς παρ' αὐτοῖς θεούς, μειζόνως τὴν αἰσχύνην αὐτῶν ἐξεκάλυψαν καὶ γυμνὴν πᾶσι προὔθηκαν. εἰ γὰρ τὸ σῶμα τοῦ ἀνθρώπου πολυμερὲς ὂν οὐκ ἀποβάλλεταί τι τῶν 251
ἰδίων μελῶν, ἀλλὰ πρὸς πάντα τὰ μέλη ἀδιάρρηκτον ἕνωσιν ἔχον ἑαυτῷ ἐστι σύμφωνον, πῶς ἐν φύσει θεοῦ μάχη καὶ διαφωνία ἔσται τοσαύτη; εἰ γὰρ μία φύσις τῶν θεῶν ὑπῆρχεν, οὐκ ὤφειλεν θεὸς θεὸν διώκειν, οὔτε σφάζειν, οὔτε κακοποιεῖν· εἰ δὲ οἱ θεοὶ ὑπὸ θεῶν ἐδιώχθησαν καὶ ἐσφάγησαν, καὶ ἡρπάγησαν καὶ ἐκεραυνώθησαν, οὐκ ἔτι μία φύσις ἐστὶν ἀλλὰ γνῶμαι διῃρημέναι, πᾶσαι κακοποιοί, ὥστε οὐδεὶς ἐξ αὐτῶν ἐστι θεός. φανερὸν οὖν ἐστιν, ὦ βασιλεῦ, πλάνην εἶναι πᾶσαν τὴν περὶ τῶν θεῶν φυσιολογίαν.

Πῶς δὲ οὐ συνῆκαν οἱ σοφοὶ καὶ λόγιοι τῶν Ἑλλήνων ὅτι καὶ οἱ νόμους θέμενοι κρίνονται ὑπὸ

away, they cannot grasp the fact that they are no gods.

'Great, then, is the error that the Egyptians, the Chaldeans, and the Greeks have erred in introducing such gods as these, and making images thereof, and deifying dumb and senseless idols. I marvel how, when they behold their gods being sawn and chiselled by workmen's axes, growing old and dissolving through lapse of time, and molten in the pot, they never reflected concerning them that they are no gods. For when these skill not to work their own salvation, how can they take care of mankind? Nay, even the poets and philosophers among the Chaldeans, Greeks and Egyptians, although by their poems and histories they desired to glorify their people's gods, yet they rather revealed and exposed their shame before all men. If the body of a man, consisting of many parts, loseth not any of its proper members, but, having an unbroken union with all its members, is in harmony with itself, how in the nature of God shall there be such warfare and discord? For if the nature of the gods were one, then ought not one god to persecute, slay or injure another. But if the gods were persecuted by other gods, and slain and plundered and killed with thunder-stones, then is their nature no longer one, but their wills are divided, and are all mischievous, so that not one among them is God. So it is manifest, O king, that all this history of the nature of the gods is error.

Of the general folly of idolaters

'Furthermore, how do the wise and eloquent among the Greeks fail to perceive that law-givers themselves

He asketh how gods

Cp. Rom. vii. 12 τῶν ἰδίων νόμων; εἰ γὰρ οἱ νόμοι δίκαιοί εἰσιν,
ἄδικοι πάντως οἱ θεοὶ αὐτῶν εἰσι, παράνομα ποιήσαντες, ἀλληλοκτονίας καὶ φαρμακίας, καὶ μοι-
χείας καὶ κλοπὰς καὶ ἀρσενοκοισίας. εἰ δὲ καλῶς
ἔπραξαν ταῦτα, οἱ νόμοι ἄρα ἄδικοί εἰσι, κατὰ
τῶν θεῶν συντεθέντες. νυνὶ δὲ οἱ νόμοι καλοί εἰσι
καὶ δίκαιοι, τὰ καλὰ ἐπαινοῦντες καὶ τὰ κακὰ
ἀπαγορεύοντες· τὰ δὲ ἔργα τῶν θεῶν αὐτῶν
παράνομα· παράνομοι ἄρα οἱ θεοὶ αὐτῶν, καὶ
ἔνοχοι πάντες θανάτου καὶ ἀσεβεῖς οἱ τοιούτους
θεοὺς παρεισάγοντες. εἰ μὲν γὰρ μυθικαὶ αἱ περὶ
αὐτῶν ἱστορίαι, οὐδέν εἰσιν, εἰ μὴ μόνον λόγοι·
εἰ δὲ φυσικαί, οὐκ ἔτι θεοί εἰσιν οἱ ταῦτα ποιήσαντες καὶ παθόντες· εἰ δὲ ἀλληγορικαί, μῦθοί
εἰσι καὶ οὐκ ἄλλο τι. ἀποδέδεικται τοίνυν, ὦ βα- 252
σιλεῦ, ταῦτα πάντα τὰ πολύθεα σεβάσματα
πλάνης ἔργα καὶ ἀπωλείας ὑπάρχειν. οὐ χρὴ οὖν
θεοὺς ὀνομάζειν ὁρατοὺς καὶ μὴ ὁρῶντας· ἀλλὰ
τὸν ἀόρατον καὶ πάντας δημιουργήσαντα δεῖ
σέβεσθαι Θεόν.

Ἔλθωμεν οὖν, ὦ βασιλεῦ, καὶ ἐπὶ τοὺς Ἰουδαί-
ους, ὅπως ἴδωμεν τί φρονοῦσι καὶ αὐτοὶ περὶ
Luke xx. 37 Θεοῦ. οὗτοι γάρ, τοῦ Ἀβραὰμ ὄντες ἀπόγονοι
καὶ Ἰσαάκ τε καὶ Ἰακώβ, παρῴκησαν εἰς Αἴγυ-
Ps. cxxxvi. 12 πτον. ἐκεῖθεν δὲ ἐξήγαγεν αὐτοὺς ὁ Θεὸς ἐν χειρὶ
Acts xiii. 17 κραταιᾷ καὶ ἐν βραχίονι ὑψηλῷ διὰ Μωσέως τοῦ
νομοθέτου αὐτῶν καὶ τέρασι πολλοῖς καὶ σημείοις
ἐγνώρισεν αὐτοῖς τὴν ἑαυτοῦ δύναμιν. ἀλλ',
ἀγνώμονες καὶ αὐτοὶ φανέντες καὶ ἄχρηστοι, πολλάκις ἐλάτρευσαν τοῖς τῶν ἐθνῶν σεβάσμασι, καὶ
Mat. xxiii. 37 τοὺς ἀπεσταλμένους πρὸς αὐτοὺς προφήτας καὶ
δικαίους ἀπέκτειναν. εἶτα ὡς εὐδόκησεν ὁ Υἱὸς

are judged by their own laws? For if their laws are just, then are their gods assuredly unjust, in that they have offended against law by murders, sorceries, adulteries, thefts and unnatural crimes. But, if they did well in so doing, then are their laws unjust, seeing that they have been framed in condemnation of the gods. But now the laws are good and just, because they encourage good and forbid evil; whereas the deeds of their gods offend against law. Their gods then are offenders against law; and all that introduce such gods as these are worthy of death and are ungodly. If the stories of the gods be myths, then are the gods mere words: but if the stories be natural, then are they that wrought or endured such things no longer gods: if the stories be allegorical, then are the gods myths and nothing else. Therefore it hath been proven, O king, that all these idols, belonging to many gods, are works of error and destruction. So it is not meet to call those gods that are seen, but cannot see: but it is right to worship as God him who is unseen and is the Maker of all mankind.

can sin against their own laws

'Come we now, O king, to the Jews, that we may see what they also think concerning God. The Jews are the descendants of Abraham, Isaac and Jacob, and went once to sojourn in Egypt. From thence God brought them out with a mighty hand and stretched out arm by Moses their lawgiver; and with many miracles and signs made he known unto them his power. But, like the rest, these proved ungrateful and unprofitable, and often worshipped images of the heathen, and killed the prophets and righteous men that were sent unto them. Then, when it pleased

Of the Jews and their short-comings

τοῦ Θεοῦ ἐλθεῖν ἐπὶ τῆς γῆς, ἐμπαροινήσαντες εἰς
Mk. xv. 1 αὐτόν, προέδωκαν Πιλάτῳ τῷ ἡγεμόνι τῶν Ῥω-
μαίων καὶ σταυρῷ κατεδίκασαν, μὴ αἰδεσθέντες
τὰς εὐεργεσίας αὐτοῦ, καὶ τὰ ἀναρίθμητα θαύματα
ἅπερ ἐν αὐτοῖς εἰργάσατο. διὸ ἀπώλοντο τῇ ἰδίᾳ
παρανομίᾳ. σέβονται γὰρ καὶ νῦν Θεὸν τὸν
Rom. x. 2 μόνον παντοκράτορα, ἀλλ' οὐ κατ' ἐπίγνωσιν· τὸν
γὰρ Χριστὸν ἀρνοῦνται τὸν Υἱὸν τοῦ Θεοῦ, καί
εἰσι παρόμοιοι τοῖς ἔθνεσι, κἂν ἐγγίζειν πως τῇ
ἀληθείᾳ δοκῶσιν, ἧς ἑαυτοὺς ἐμάκρυναν. ταῦτα
περὶ τῶν Ἰουδαίων.

Οἱ δὲ Χριστιανοὶ γενεαλογοῦνται ἀπὸ τοῦ
Κυρίου Ἰησοῦ Χριστοῦ. οὗτος δὲ ὁ Υἱὸς τοῦ
Cp. Luke i. 32, 35 Θεοῦ τοῦ ὑψίστου ὁμολογεῖται, ἐν Πνεύματι
Mat. i. 21 Ἁγίῳ ἀπ' οὐρανοῦ καταβὰς διὰ τὴν σωτηρίαν 253
Is. vii. 14 τῶν ἀνθρώπων, καὶ ἐκ Παρθένου ἁγίας γεννηθεὶς
ἀσπόρως τε καὶ ἀφθόρως σάρκα ἀνέλαβε, καὶ
ἀνεφάνη ἀνθρώποις, ὅπως ἐκ τῆς πολυθέου
πλάνης αὐτοὺς ἀνακαλέσηται. καί, τελέσας
τὴν θαυμαστὴν αὐτοῦ οἰκονομίαν, διὰ σταυροῦ
Cp. John iii. 14 θανάτου ἐγεύσατο ἑκουσίᾳ βουλῇ κατ' οἰκονομίαν
1 Cor. xv. 4 μεγάλην· μετὰ δὲ τρεῖς ἡμέρας ἀνεβίω, καὶ εἰς
Acts i. 9, 10 οὐρανοὺς ἀνῆλθεν. οὗ τὸ κλέος τῆς παρουσίας
Cp. 1 Thess. iv. 15–17 ἐκ τῆς παρ' αὐτοῖς καλουμένης εὐαγγελικῆς
ἁγίας Γραφῆς ἔξεστί σοι γνῶναι, βασιλεῦ, ἐὰν
ἐντύχῃς. οὗτος δώδεκα ἔσχε μαθητάς, οἵ, μετὰ
τὴν ἐν οὐρανοῖς ἄνοδον αὐτοῦ, ἐξῆλθον εἰς τὰς
ἐπαρχίας τῆς οἰκουμένης, καὶ ἐδίδαξαν τὴν ἐκεί-
St. Thomas νου μεγαλωσύνην· καθάπερ εἷς ἐξ αὐτῶν τὰς
καθ' ἡμᾶς περιῆλθε χώρας, τὸ δόγμα κηρύττων
τῆς ἀληθείας. ὅθεν οἱ εἰσέτι διακονοῦντες τῇ
δικαιοσύνῃ τοῦ κηρύγματος αὐτῶν καλοῦνται

the Son of God to come on earth, they did shamefully entreat him and deliver him to Pilate the Roman governor, and condemn him to the Cross, regardless of his benefits and the countless miracles that he had worked amongst them. Wherefore by their own lawlessness they perished. For though to this day they worship the One Omnipotent God, yet it is not according unto knowledge; for they deny Christ the Son of God, and are like the heathen, although they seem to approach the truth from which they have estranged themselves. So much for the Jews.

'As for the Christians, they trace their line from the Lord Jesus Christ. He is confessed to be the Son of the most high God, who came down from heaven, by the Holy Ghost, for the salvation of mankind, and was born of a pure Virgin, without seed of man, and without defilement, and took flesh, and appeared among men, that he might recall them from the error of worshipping many gods. When he had accomplished his marvellous dispensation, of his own free will by a mighty dispensation he tasted of death upon the Cross. But after three days he came to life again, and ascended into the heavens,—the glory of whose coming thou mayest learn, O king, by the reading of the holy Scripture, which the Christians call the Gospel, shouldst thou meet therewith. This Jesus had twelve disciples, who, after his ascent into the heavens, went out into all the kingdoms of the world, telling of his greatness. Even so one of them visited our coasts, preaching the doctrine of truth; whence they who still serve the righteousness of his preaching are called Christians.

Of the Christians and of their Lord Jesus Christ,

Χριστιανοί. καὶ οὗτοί εἰσιν οἱ ὑπὲρ πάντα τὰ ἔθνη τῆς γῆς εὑρόντες τὴν ἀλήθειαν· γινώσκουσι γὰρ τὸν Θεόν, κτίστην καὶ δημιουργὸν τῶν ἁπάντων ἐν Υἱῷ μονογενεῖ καὶ Πνεύματι Ἁγίῳ, καὶ ἄλλον θεὸν πλὴν τούτου οὐ σέβονται. ἔχουσι τὰς ἐντολὰς αὐτοῦ τοῦ Κυρίου Ἰησοῦ Χριστοῦ ἐν ταῖς καρδίαις κεχαραγμένας, καὶ ταύτας φυλάττουσι, προσδοκῶντες ἀνάστασιν νεκρῶν καὶ ζωὴν τοῦ μέλλοντος αἰῶνος. οὐ μοιχεύουσιν, οὐ πορνεύουσιν, οὐ ψευδομαρτυροῦσιν, οὐκ ἐπιθυμοῦσι τὰ ἀλλότρια, τιμῶσι πατέρα καὶ μητέρα, καὶ τοὺς πλησίον φιλοῦσι, δίκαια κρίνουσιν, ὅσα οὐ θέλουσιν αὐτοῖς γίνεσθαι ἑτέρῳ οὐ ποιοῦσι, τοὺς ἀδικοῦντας αὐτοὺς παρακαλοῦσι καὶ προσφιλεῖς αὐτοὺς ἑαυτοῖς ποιοῦσι, τοὺς ἐχθροὺς εὐεργετεῖν σπουδάζουσι, πραεῖς εἰσι καὶ ἐπιεικεῖς, ἀπὸ πάσης συνουσίας ἀνόμου καὶ ἀπὸ πάσης ἀκαθαρσίας ἐγκρατεύονται, χήραν οὐχ ὑπερο- 254
ρῶσιν, ὀρφανὸν οὐ λυποῦσιν· ὁ ἔχων τῷ μὴ ἔχοντι ἀφθόνως ἐπιχορηγεῖ· ξένον ἐὰν ἴδωσιν, ὑπὸ στέγην εἰσάγουσι, καὶ χαίρουσιν ἐπ' αὐτῷ ὡς ἐπὶ ἀδελφῷ ἀληθινῷ· οὐ γὰρ κατὰ σάρκα ἀδελφοὺς ἑαυτοὺς καλοῦσιν, ἀλλὰ κατὰ πνεῦμα. ἕτοιμοί εἰσιν ὑπὲρ Χριστοῦ τὰς ψυχὰς αὐτῶν προέσθαι· τὰ γὰρ προστάγματα αὐτοῦ ἀσφαλῶς φυλάττουσιν, ὁσίως καὶ δικαίως ζῶντες, καθὼς Κύριος ὁ Θεὸς αὐτοῖς προσέταξεν, εὐχαριστοῦντες αὐτῷ κατὰ πᾶσαν ὥραν ἐν παντὶ βρώματι καὶ ποτῷ καὶ τοῖς λοιποῖς ἀγαθοῖς. ὄντως οὖν αὕτη ἐστὶν ἡ ὁδὸς τῆς ἀληθείας, ἥτις τοὺς

And these are they who, above all the nations of the earth, have found the truth: for they acknowledge God the Creator and Maker of all things in the only-begotten Son, and in the Holy Ghost, and other God than him they worship none. They have the commandments of the Lord Jesus Christ himself engraven on their hearts, and these they observe, looking for the resurrection of the dead and the life of the world to come. They neither commit adultery nor fornication; nor do they bear false witness, nor covet other men's goods: they honour father and mother, and love their neighbours: they give right judgement. They do not unto other that which they would not have done unto themselves. They comfort such as wrong them, and make friends of them: they labour to do good to their enemies: they are meek and gentle. They refrain themselves from all unlawful intercourse and all uncleanness. They despise not the widow, and grieve not the orphan. He that hath distributeth liberally to him that hath not. If they see a stranger, they bring him under their roof, and rejoice over him, as it were their own brother: for they call themselves brethren, not after the flesh, but after the spirit. For Christ his sake they are ready to lay down their lives: they keep his commandments faithfully, living righteous and holy lives, as the Lord their God commanded them, giving him thanks every hour, for meat and drink and every blessing. Verily, then, this is the way of truth

and of their holy and pure conversation

ὁδεύοντας αὐτὴν εἰς τὴν αἰώνιον χειραγωγεῖ βασιλείαν, τὴν ἐπηγγελμένην παρὰ Χριστοῦ ἐν τῇ μελλούσῃ ζωῇ.

Καὶ ἵνα γνῷς, βασιλεῦ, ὅτι οὐκ ἀπ' ἐμαυτοῦ ταῦτα λέγω, ταῖς Γραφαῖς ἐγκύψας τῶν Χριστιανῶν, εὑρήσεις οὐδὲν ἔξω τῆς ἀληθείας με λέγειν. καλῶς οὖν συνῆκεν ὁ υἱός σου, καὶ δικαίως ἐδιδάχθη λατρεύειν ζῶντι Θεῷ καὶ σωθῆναι εἰς τὸν μέλλοντα ἐπέρχεσθαι αἰῶνα. μεγάλα γὰρ καὶ θαυμαστὰ τὰ ὑπὸ τῶν Χριστιανῶν λεγόμενα καὶ πραττόμενα· οὐ γὰρ ἀνθρώπων ῥήματα λαλοῦσιν, ἀλλὰ τὰ τοῦ Θεοῦ. τὰ δὲ λοιπὰ ἔθνη πλανῶνται καὶ πλανῶσιν ἑαυτούς· ὁδεύοντες γὰρ ἐν σκότει προσρήσσονται ἑαυτοῖς ὡς μεθύοντες. ἕως ὧδε ὁ πρὸς σέ μου λόγος, βασιλεῦ, ὁ ὑπὸ τῆς ἀληθείας ἐν τῷ νοΐ μου ὑπαγορευθείς. διὸ παυσάσθωσαν οἱ ἀνόητοί σου σοφοὶ ματαιολογοῦντες κατὰ τοῦ Κυρίου· συμφέρει γὰρ ὑμῖν Θεὸν κτίστην σέβεσθαι καὶ 255
τὰ ἄφθαρτα αὐτοῦ ἐνωτίζεσθαι ῥήματα, ἵνα, κρίσιν ἐκφυγόντες καὶ τιμωρίαν, ζωῆς ἀνωλέθρου δειχθείητε κληρονόμοι.

XXVIII

Ταῦτα ὡς διεξῆλθεν ὁ Ναχώρ, ὁ μὲν βασιλεὺς τῷ θυμῷ ἠλλοιοῦτο· οἱ δὲ ῥήτορες αὐτοῦ καὶ νεωκόροι ἄφωνοι ἵσταντο, μὴ δυνάμενοι ἀντιλέγειν ἀλλ' ἢ σαθρά τινα καὶ οὐδαμινὰ λογίδια. ὁ δὲ τοῦ βασιλέως υἱὸς ἠγαλλιᾶτο τῷ πνεύματι, καὶ φαιδρῷ τῷ προσώπῳ ἐδόξαζε τὸν Κύριον,

which leadeth its wayfarers unto the eternal kingdom promised by Christ in the life to come.

'And that thou mayest know, O king, that I speak nought of myself,[1] look thou into the writings of the Christians, and thou shalt find that I speak nothing but the truth. Well, therefore, hath thy son understood it, and rightly hath he been taught to serve the living God, and to be saved for the world to come. Great and marvellous are the things spoken and wrought by the Christians, because they speak not the words of men but the words of God. But all other nations are deceived, and deceive themselves. Walking in darkness they stagger one against another like drunken men. This is the end of my speech spoken unto thee, O king, prompted by the truth that is in my mind. Wherefore let thy foolish wise-acres refrain from babbling idly against the Lord; for it is profitable to you to worship God the Creator, and hearken to his incorruptible sayings, in order that ye may escape judgement and punishment, and be found partakers of deathless life.'

The Christians alone hold the truth

XXVIII

When Nachor had fully delivered this oration, the king changed countenance for very anger, but his orators and temple-keepers stood speechless, having nothing but a few weak and rotten shreds of argument in reply. But the king's son rejoiced in spirit and with glad countenance magnified the Lord, who

Ioasaph rejoiceth at Nachor's speech

[1] It was the Apology of Aristides, written *circa* A.D. 125. See the Introduction.

τὸν ἐξ ἀπόρου πόρον διδόντα τοῖς πεποιθόσιν ἐπ᾽ αὐτόν, ὃς καὶ διὰ τοῦ πολεμίου καὶ ἐχθροῦ τὴν ἀλήθειαν ἐκράτυνε· καὶ ὁ τῆς πλάνης ἔξαρχος συνήγορος τοῦ ὀρθοῦ λόγου ἐδεικνυτο.

Ὁ μέντοι βασιλεύς, καίπερ δεινῶς ὀργιζόμενος τῷ Ναχώρ, οὐδὲν ὅμως ἐργάσασθαι κακὸν εἰς αὐτὸν ἠδύνατο, διὰ τὸ προλεχθὲν ἐπὶ πάντων θέσπισμα, ἀδεῶς αὐτὸν λέγειν ὑπὲρ τῶν Χριστιανῶν προτρεπόμενον· πολλὰ δὲ αὐτὸς ἀντιλέγων ὑπεμίμνησκε δι᾽ αἰνιγμάτων ὑπενδοῦναι τῆς ἐνστάσεως καὶ ἡττηθῆναι τῇ διαλέξει τῶν ῥητόρων. ὁ δὲ μειζόνως ὑπερίσχυε, διαλύων πάσας αὐτῶν τὰς προτάσεις καὶ συλλογισμούς, καὶ ἐλέγχων τὸ ἀπατηλὸν τῆς πλάνης. σχεδὸν δὲ μέχρις ἑσπέρας παραταθείσης τῆς διαλέξεως, ἐκέλευσεν ὁ βασιλεὺς διαλυθῆναι τὸ συνέδριον, ὡς τῇ ἐπιούσῃ βουλόμενος αὖθις περὶ τούτου διασκέψασθαι.

Ὁ δὲ υἱὸς ἔφη τῷ βασιλεῖ· Ὡς ἐν ἀρχῇ δικαίαν ἐκέλευσας κρίσιν γενέσθαι, δέσποτα, δικαιοσύνην καὶ τῷ τέλει ἐπίθες, τῶν δύο τὸ ἕτερον ποιῶν· ἢ τὸν ἐμὸν διδάσκαλον ἐπίτρεψον μεῖναι μετ᾽ ἐμοῦ τῇ νυκτὶ ταύτῃ, ὡς ὁμοῦ διασκε- 256
ψώμεθα περὶ ὧν χρὴ τὴν αὔριον λαλῆσαι τοῖς πολεμοῦσιν ἡμᾶς, τοὺς σοὺς δὲ πάλιν σὺ μεθ᾽ ἑαυτοῦ λαβὼν τὰ εἰκότα μελετήσατε καθὼς βούλεσθε· ἤ, τοὺς σοὺς ἐμοὶ παραχωρήσας τῇ νυκτὶ ταύτῃ, λάβε τὸν ἐμὸν πρὸς ἑαυτόν. εἰ δὲ ἀμφότεροι ὦσι παρὰ σοί, ὁ μὲν ἐμὸς ἐν θλίψει καὶ φόβῳ, οἱ δὲ σοὶ ἐν χαρᾷ καὶ ἀνέσει, οὔ μοι δοκεῖ δικαίαν εἶναι κρίσιν, ἀλλὰ δυναστείαν τῆς ἐξουσίας καὶ παράβασιν τῶν συνθηκῶν. ἡττηθεὶς

had made a path, where no path was, for them that trusted in him, who by the mouth of a foeman and enemy was establishing the truth; and the leader of error had proved a defender of the right cause.

But the king, although furiously enraged with Nachor, was nevertheless unable to do him any mischief, because of the proclamation already read before all, wherein he urged him to plead without fear in behalf of the Christians. So he himself made answer in many words, and by dark speeches hinted that Nachor should relax his resistance, and be worsted by the argument of the orators. But Nachor the more mightily prevailed, tearing to pieces all their propositions and conclusions and exposing the fallacy of their error. After the debate had been prolonged till well-nigh eventide, the king dismissed the assembly, making as though he would renew the discussion on the morrow.

Nachor triumpheth yet more over his adversaries

Then said Ioasaph to the king his father, 'As at the beginning, Sir, thou commandedst that the trial should be just, so too crown the end thereof with justice, by doing one or other of these two things. Either allow my teacher to tarry with me to-night, that we may take counsel together as touching those things which we must say unto our adversaries tomorrow: and do thou in turn take thine advisers unto thee, and duly practise yourselves as ye will. Or else deliver thy counsellors to me this night, and take mine to thyself. But if both sides be with thee, mine advocate in tribulation and fear, but thine in joy and refreshment, me thinketh it is not a fair trial, but a tyrannical misuse of power, and a breaking of the covenants.' The king, compelled to yield

Ioasaph outwitteth his father

δὲ ὁ βασιλεὺς τῷ ἀστείῳ τοῦ ῥήματος, τοὺς σοφοὺς αὐτοῦ καὶ ἱερεῖς πρὸς ἑαυτὸν λαβόμενος, τὸν Ναχὼρ παραχωρεῖ τῷ υἱῷ, ἐλπίδας ἔτι κεκτημένος ἐπ᾽ αὐτὸν καὶ φυλάττειν τὰ ὡμολογημένα δοκῶν.

᾿Απέρχεται τοίνυν ὁ τοῦ βασιλέως υἱὸς εἰς τὸ ἑαυτοῦ παλάτιον, ὥσπερ τις ᾿Ολυμπιονίκης τῶν ἀντιπάλων κρατήσας, ἔχων μεθ᾽ ἑαυτοῦ τὸν Ναχώρ. καὶ κατὰ μόνας καλέσας αὐτὸν ἔφη· Μὴ νομίσῃς λανθάνειν ἐμὲ τὰ κατὰ σέ· οἶδα γάρ σε ἀκριβῶς μὴ τὸν θειότατον εἶναι Βαρλαάμ, ἀλλὰ Ναχὼρ τὸν ἀστρολόγον. καὶ θαυμάζω πῶς ἔδοξεν ὑμῖν τοιαύτην ὑποκριθῆναι ὑπόκρισιν καὶ τοσαύτῃ ἀμβλυωπίᾳ νομίσαι περιβαλεῖν με μέσης ἡμέρας, ἵνα λύκον δέξωμαι ἀντὶ προβάτου.
Is. xxxii. 6 ἀλλὰ καλῶς ὁ λόγος ᾄδεται, ὅτι Καρδία μωροῦ μάταια νοήσει. τὸ μὲν οὖν ἐνθύμημα τοῦτο καὶ βούλευμα ὑμῶν ἕωλον ἦν καὶ πάντῃ ἀνόητον· τὸ δὲ ἔργον ὃ εἰργάσω πάσης ἐστὶ συνέσεως πεπληρωμένον. διὸ χαῖρε, Ναχώρ, καὶ ἀγαλλιῶ· πολλὰς γάρ σοι χάριτας ὁμολογῶ, ὅτι συνήγορος 257
σήμερον τῆς ἀληθείας γέγονας, καὶ οὐκ ἐμίανας τὰ χείλη σοι λόγοις μιαροῖς καὶ ὑποκρίσει δολίᾳ, ἀλλὰ τῶν πολλῶν μᾶλλον ἐξεκάθαρας μολυσμάτων, τὴν πλάνην τῶν ψευδωνύμων διελέγξας θεῶν καὶ τὴν ἀλήθειαν τῶν Χριστιανικῶν δογμάτων κρατύνας. ἐγὼ δὲ ἐσπούδασα ἀγαγεῖν σε μετ᾽ ἐμοῦ δυοῖν ἕνεκα· ἵνα μή κατὰ μόνας ὁ βασιλεὺς λαβών σε τιμωρήσηται ἐφ᾽ ᾧ οὐ τὰ καταθύμια αὐτῷ ἐφθέγξω, καὶ ἵνα τὴν χάριν ταύτην, ἣν σήμερον εἰργάσω, ἀνταμείψωμαι. τίς δὲ ἡ ἀντάμειψις; τὸ ὑποδεῖξαί σοι ἐκκλῖναι τῆς πο-

by the gracefulness of this speech took his wise men and priests to himself, and delivered Nachor to his son, still having hopes of him and thinking fit to keep his agreement.

The king's son, therefore, departed unto his own palace, like a conqueror in the Olympic games, and with him went Nachor. When alone, the prince called him and said, 'Think not that I am ignorant of thy tale, for I wot, of a surety, that thou art not saintly Barlaam, but Nachor the astrologer; and I marvel how it seemed thee good to act this play, and to think that thou couldst so dull my sight at mid-day, that I should mistake a wolf for a sheep. But well sung is the proverb, "The heart of a fool will conceive folly." So this your device and counsel was stale and utterly senseless; but the work that thou hast accomplished is full of wisdom. Wherefore, rejoice, Nachor, and be exceeding glad. I render thee many thanks, that thou hast been to-day advocate of the truth, and hast not polluted thy lips with foul words and crafty simulation, but hast rather cleansed them from many defilements, and thoroughly proven the error of the gods, as they be wrongly called, and hast established the truth of the Christian faith. I have been zealous to bring thee hither with me for two reasons; that the king might not privily seize and punish thee, because thou spakest not after his heart, and next that I might recompense thee for the favour that thou hast done me to-day. And what is my recompense for thee? To show

Ioasaph taketh Nachor to his own palace.

νηρᾶς ὁδοῦ καὶ ὀλισθηρᾶς ἣν ὥδευσας ἕως νῦν, πορευθῆναι δὲ τὴν εὐθεῖαν καὶ σωτήριον τρίβον, ἣν οὐκ ἀγνοῶν, ἀλλ' ἐθελοντὶ κακουργῶν, ἐξέφυγες, βαράθροις καὶ κρημνοῖς ἀνομίας σεαυτὸν κατακρημνίσας. σύνες οὖν, ὦ Ναχώρ, συνετὸς ὤν, καὶ προθυμήθητι τὸν Χριστὸν μόνον καὶ τὴν παρ' αὐτῷ κρυπτομένην ζωὴν κερδᾶναι, τῶν ῥεόντων τούτων καὶ φθειρομένων ὑπεριδών. οὐ γὰρ τὸν πάντα ζήσῃ αἰῶνα· ἀλλά, θνητὸς ὤν, ἀπελεύσῃ ὅσον οὔπω, καθὼς καὶ οἱ πρὸ σοῦ πάντες. Καὶ οὐαί σοι, εἰ τὸν βαρὺν φόρτον τῆς ἁμαρτίας ἐπιφερόμενος ἀπελεύσῃ ἐκεῖ ὅπου κρίσις δικαία καὶ ἀνταπόδοσις τῶν ἔργων ἐστί, καὶ μὴ ἀπορρίψῃς τοῦτον, ῥᾳδίας οὔσης τῆς ἀποθέσεως.

Ὁ Ναχὼρ τοίνυν, κατανυγεὶς τὴν ψυχὴν ἐπὶ τοῖς λόγοις τούτοις, ἔφη· Καλῶς εἶπας, ὦ βασιλεῦ, καλῶς. οἶδα γὰρ κἀγὼ τὸν ἀληθινὸν καὶ ἀψευδῆ Θεόν, δι' οὗ τὰ πάντα γέγονε, καὶ τὴν μέλλουσαν κρίσιν ἐπίσταμαι, ἀπὸ πολλῶν Γραφικῶν ῥημάτων ταύτην ἀκηκοώς· ἀλλ' ἡ πονηρὰ συνήθεια καὶ ἡ τοῦ παλαιοῦ ἐπήρεια πτερνιστοῦ 258
τοὺς ὀφθαλμοὺς ἐτύφλωσε τῆς καρδίας μου, καὶ σκότος βαθὺ περιέχυσέ μου τῷ λογισμῷ· νυνὶ δὲ ἐπὶ τῷ ῥήματί σου, τὸ κάλυμμα τὸ ζοφῶδες ἀπορρίψας, τῷ φωτὶ προσδραμοῦμαι τοῦ προσώπου Κυρίου. ἴσως ἐλεήσει με, καὶ θύραν ἀνοίξει μετανοίας τῷ πονηρῷ δούλῳ καὶ ἀποστάτῃ, εἰ καὶ ἀδύνατον δοκεῖ μοι ἄφεσιν γενέσθαι τῶν ψάμμου βαρυτέρων μου πταισμάτων, ὧν ἐν γνώσει καὶ ἀγνοίᾳ ἥμαρτον νηπιόθεν καὶ μέχρι ταύτης μου τῆς ἡλικίας καὶ πολιᾶς.

Ταῦτα ὡς ἤκουσεν ὁ τοῦ βασιλέως υἱός, εὐθὺς

thee how to turn from the evil and slippery road which thou hast trodden until now, and to journey along the straight and saving pathway which thou hast avoided, not in ignorance, but by wilful wrong-doing, throwing thyself into depths and precipices of iniquity. Understand then, Nachor, man of understanding as thou art, and be thou zealous to gain Christ only, and the life that is hid with him, and despise this fleeting and corruptible world. Thou shalt not live for ever, but, being mortal, shalt depart hence ere long, even as all that have been before thee. And wo betide thee, if, with the heavy load of sin on thy shoulders, thou depart thither where there is righteous judgement and recompense for thy works, and cast it not off, while it is easy to rid thyself thereof!'

and blameth him for his deceit, but praiseth him for his true speech

Pricked at heart by these words, spake Nachor, 'Well said! Sir prince, well said! I do know the true and very God, by whom all things were made, and I wot of the judgement to come, having heard thereof from many texts of the Scriptures. But evil habit and the insolence of the ancient supplanter hath blinded the eyes of my heart, and shed a thick darkness over my reason. But now, at thy word, I will cast away the veil of gloom, and run unto the light of the countenance of the Lord. May be, he will have mercy on me, and will open a door of repentance to his wicked and rebellious servant, even if it seem impossible to me that my sins, which are heavier than the sand, be forgiven; sins, which, wittingly or unwittingly, I have sinned from childhood upwards to this my hoary age.'

Nachor is pricked at heart and repenteth him of his sins

When the king's son heard these words, im-

Ioasaph biddeth

διανίσταται καὶ θερμότερος τὴν ψυχὴν γίνεται.
καὶ τὸν λογισμὸν τοῦ Ναχὼρ πρὸς ἀπόγνωσιν
συγκύπτοντα ἀναλαμβάνειν ἄρχεται, καὶ στερρό-
τερον περὶ τὴν Χριστοῦ πίστιν διατιθέναι, Μη-
δείς, ὦ Ναχώρ, λέγων, μηδεὶς ἔστω σοι περὶ
Mat. iii. 9 τούτου δισταγμός. γέγραπται γὰρ δυνατὸν εἶναι
τῷ Θεῷ καὶ ἐκ τῶν λίθων τούτων ἐγεῖραι τέκνα τῷ
Ἀβραάμ· ὅπερ τί ἄλλο ἢ τοῦτό ἐστιν, ὡς ὁ
πατὴρ ἔφη Βαρλαάμ, τὸ ἐξ ἀνελπίστων καὶ
πάσαις κατακρανθέντων ἀνομίαις δύνασθαι σωθῆναι, καὶ δούλους γενέσθαι Χριστοῦ, ὃς δι'
ἄκραν φιλανθρωπίας ὑπερβολὴν πᾶσι τοῖς ἐπιστρέφουσι τὰς οὐρανίους διήνοιξε πύλας, οὐδενὶ
τῶν πάντων τὴν τῆς σωτηρίας ἀποκλείσας ὁδόν,
ἀλλὰ συμπαθῶς τοὺς μετανοοῦντας δεχόμενος;
διὰ ταῦτα γὰρ καὶ τοῖς περὶ πρώτην καὶ τρίτην,
ἕκτην τε καὶ ἐννάτην καὶ ἑνδεκάτην ὥραν προσ-
ελθοῦσι τῷ ἀμπελῶνι κατ' ἴσον ἀφορίζεται ὁ
Mat. xx. 9 μισθός, ὡς τὸ ἅγιόν φησιν Εὐαγγέλιον· ὥστε,
κἂν μέχρι τοῦ νῦν ἐν ἁμαρτίαις κατεγήρασας, 259
ἐὰν θερμῶς προσέλθῃς, τῶν αὐτῶν τοῖς ἐκ νεότητος ἀγωνισαμένοις ἀξιωθήσῃ γερῶν.

Πολλὰ δὲ καὶ ἕτερα περὶ μετανοίας λαλήσας ὁ
θειότατος νεανίας τῷ παλαιωθέντι ἐν κακοῖς Ναχώρ, καὶ ἵλεων γενέσθαι τὸν Χριστὸν ὑποσχό-
μενος καὶ ἐγγυησάμενος τὴν ἄφεσιν, καὶ πληρο-
φορήσας αὐτὸν ὡς ἕτοιμός ἐστιν ὁ ἀγαθὸς ἀεὶ τοῦ
δέχεσθαι τὴν μετάνοιαν, τὴν νενοσηκυῖαν ψυχὴν
αὐτοῦ οἷά τισι φαρμάκοις καταμαλάξας, καθαρὰν
ἐχαρίσατο τὴν ὑγίειαν. ἔφη γὰρ εὐθὺς ὁ Ναχὼρ
πρὸς αὐτόν· Σὺ μέν, ὦ εὐγενέστατε τὴν ψυχὴν
μᾶλλον ἢ τὸ σῶμα, καλῶς μεμνημένος τὰ θαυ-

mediately he arose, and his heart waxed warm, and he began to try to raise Nachor's courage which was drooping to despair, and to confirm it in the faith of Christ, saying, 'Let no doubt about this, Nachor, find place in thy mind. For it is written, God is able of these very stones to raise up children unto Abraham. What meaneth this (as father Barlaam said) except that men beyond hope, stained with all manner of wickedness, can be saved, and become servants of Christ, who, in the exceeding greatness of his love toward mankind, hath opened the gates of heaven to all that turn, barring the way of salvation to none, and receiving with compassion them that repent? Wherefore to all that have entered the vineyard at the first, third, sixth, ninth or eleventh hour there is apportioned equal pay, as saith the holy Gospel: so that even if, until this present time, thou hast waxen old in thy sins, yet if thou draw nigh with a fervent heart, thou shalt gain the same rewards as they who have laboured from their youth upwards.'

Nachor be of good courage

With these and many other words did that saintly youth speak of repentance to that aged sinner Nachor, promising him that Christ was merciful, and pledging him forgiveness, and satisfying him that the good God is alway ready to receive the penitent, and with these words, as it were with ointments, did he mollify that ailing soul and give it perfect health. Nachor at once said unto him, 'O prince, more noble in soul even than in outward show, well instructed in these marvellous mysteries, mayst thou con-

Nachor departeth to seek out his salvation,

μαστὰ μυστήρια ταῦτα, μένοις ἐν τῇ καλῇ ὁμολογίᾳ μέχρι τέλους, καὶ μηδεὶς ταύτην χρόνος ἢ τρόπος τῆς σῆς ἐκτέμοι καρδίας· ἐγὼ δὲ πορεύσομαι ἐξ αὐτῆς τὴν ἐμὴν ζητῶν σωτηρίαν, καὶ διὰ μετανοίας τὸν Θεὸν ἐξιλεωσόμενος ὃν παρώργισα. οὐκ ἔτι γὰρ τὸ τοῦ βασιλέως ὄψομαι πρόσωπον, εἰ σὺ μόνον θελήσειας. περιχαρὴς δὲ γενόμενος ὁ τοῦ βασιλέως υἱὸς καὶ ἀσμένως τὸν λόγον δεξάμενος, περιλαβὼν αὐτὸν κατεφίλει, καὶ ἐντενῶς πρὸς τὸν Θεὸν εὐξάμενος ἐκπέμπει τοῦ παλατίου.

Ἐξελθὼν δὲ ὁ Ναχὼρ κατανενυγμένος τὴν ψυχὴν ἐπὶ τὴν βαθυτάτην ἅλλεται ὡς ἔλαφος ἔρημον, καὶ μοναχοῦ τινος, ἱερωσύνης περικειμένου ἀξίαν, καταλαμβάνει σπήλαιον, ἔνθα ἐκέκρυπτο ἐκεῖνος διὰ τὸν ἐπικείμενον φόβον.
Luke vii. 37, 38 τούτῳ δὲ θερμότατα προσπίπτει, πλύνει τοὺς πόδας δάκρυσι, τήν ποτε μιμούμενος πόρνην, καὶ τὸ θεῖον ἐξαιτεῖται βάπτισμα. ὁ τοίνυν ἱερεύς, θείας ὢν χάριτος πεπληρωμένος, ἥσθη τε λίαν, καὶ παραχρῆμα, ὥσπερ ἔθος, κατηχήσας αὐτόν, δι' ἡμερῶν οὐκ ὀλίγων τελειοῖ τῷ βαπτίσματι εἰς ὄνομα τοῦ Πατρὸς καὶ τοῦ Υἱοῦ καὶ τοῦ Ἁγίου Πνεύματος. ἔμεινε δὲ Ναχὼρ μετ' αὐτοῦ μετανοῶν ἀεὶ ἐφ' οἷς ἥμαρτε, καὶ εὐλογῶν
Ez. xviii. 23 τὸν Θεὸν τὸν μὴ βουλόμενον ἀπολέσθαι τινά, ἀλλὰ πάντων τὴν ἐπιστροφὴν ἐκδεχόμενον καὶ μετανοοῦντας φιλανθρώπως δεχόμενον.

Ἕωθεν δὲ μαθὼν τὰ κατὰ τὸν Ναχὼρ ὁ βασιλεύς, καὶ ἀπογνοὺς ἧς εἶχεν ἐλπίδος ἐπ' αὐτῷ, ἰδὼν δὲ καὶ τοὺς σοφοὺς αὐτοῦ καὶ παράφρονας ῥήτορας οὕτως ἀνὰ κράτος ἡττη-

tinue in thy good confession until the end, and may neither time nor tide ever pluck it out of thine heart! For myself, I will depart straightway in search of my salvation, and will by penance pacify that God whom I have angered: for, except thou will it, I shall see the king's face no more.' Then was the prince exceeding glad, and joyfully heard his saying. And he embraced and kissed him affectionately; and, when he had prayed earnestly to God, he sent him forth from the palace.

and is baptized by an holy monk in the desert

So Nachor stepped forth with a contrite heart, and went bounding into the depths of the desert, like as doth an hart, and came to a den belonging to a monk that had attained to the dignity of the priesthood, and was hiding there for fear of the pressing danger. With a right warm heart knelt Nachor down before him, and washed his feet with his tears, like the harlot of old, and craved holy Baptism. The priest, full of heavenly grace, was passing glad, and did at once begin to instruct him, as the custom is, and after many days, perfected him with baptism in the name of the Father, and of the Son, and of the Holy Ghost. And Nachor abode with him, always repentant of his sins, and blessing that God who never willeth that any should perish, but receiveth all that turn again unto him, and lovingly accepteth the penitent.

The king dismisseth his spokesmen with scorn and contumely,

Now on the morrow when the king heard what had befallen Nachor, he despaired of the hopes that he once had in him: and, seeing those wise and foolish orators of his mightily discomfited, he was at his

θέντας, ἐν ἀμηχανίᾳ ἦν. καὶ ἐκείνους μὲν ὕβρεσι
δειναῖς καὶ ἀτιμίαις βαλών, οὓς δὲ καὶ βουνεύροις
σφοδρῶς μαστιγώσας καὶ ἀσβόλῃ τὰς ὄψεις
περιχρίσας, ἐξέβαλε τοῦ ἰδίου προσώπου· αὐτὸς
δὲ καταγινώσκειν ἤρξατο τῆς τῶν ψευδωνύμων
θεῶν ἀσθενείας, εἰ καὶ μὴ τελείως τῷ φωτὶ
Χριστοῦ προσβλέψαι τέως ἠθέλησε. τὸ γὰρ
τῆς περικειμένης αὐτῷ ἀχλύος παχὺ νέφος
κατεῖχεν ἔτι τὰς ὁράσεις αὐτοῦ τῆς καρδίας.
ἀλλ' οὖν οὐκ ἔτι τοὺς νεωκόρους ἐτίμα, οὔτε μὴν
ἑορτὰς ἦγε καὶ σπονδὰς ἐπετέλει τοῖς εἰδώλοις·
ἀλλὰ σαλευομένην εἶχε τὴν διάνοιαν ἀμφοτέ-
ρωθεν, ἔνθεν μὲν τῆς ἀσθενείας καταγινώσκων
τῶν θεῶν αὐτοῦ, ἐκεῖθεν δὲ τὴν ἀκρίβειαν
δεδοικὼς τῆς εὐαγγελικῆς πολιτείας καὶ δυσαποσπάστως τῶν πονηρῶν ἔχων ἐθῶν.[1] πάνυ 261
γὰρ ταῖς ἡδοναῖς κατεδουλοῦτο τοῦ σώματος,
καὶ ὅλος ἦν πρὸς τὰ πάθη αἰχμαλώτου δίκην
Is. li. 21 ἀγόμενος, καὶ μεθύων, ὅ φησιν Ἠσαΐας, ἄνευ
οἴνου, καὶ ὥσπερ ὑπὸ κημοῦ τῆς πονηρᾶς συνηθείας ἑλκόμενος.

Οὕτως οὖν τοῦ βασιλέως δυσὶ παλαίοντος λογισμοῖς, ὁ εὐγενέστατος αὐτοῦ υἱός, καὶ τῷ ὄντι βασιλικωτάτην κεκτημένος ψυχήν, ἠρεμῶν ἦν ἐν τῷ παλατίῳ αὐτοῦ, τὸ τῆς φύσεως αὐτοῦ γενναῖον κόσμιόν τε καὶ βεβηκὸς διὰ τῶν ἔργων πᾶσι παριστῶν. θέατρα γὰρ καὶ ἀγῶνες ἵππων καὶ κυνηγεσίων μελέτη, καὶ πᾶσαι αἱ τῆς νεότητος κεναὶ σχολαὶ καὶ ἀπάται, τὰ τῶν ἀφρόνων ψυχῶν δελεάσματα, παρ' οὐδὲν ἐλογίζοντο αὐτῷ· ἀλλ' ὅλος τῶν τοῦ Χριστοῦ ἐξήρτητο ἐντολῶν,

[1] v.l. θεῶν, "gods."

wits' end. Them he visited with terrible outrage and dishonour, scourging some severely with whips of ox-hide, besmearing their eyes with soot, and casting them away from his presence. He himself began to condemn the impotence of the gods falsely so called, although as yet he refused to look fully at the light of Christ, for the dense cloud of darkness, that enveloped him, still bound the eyes of his heart. Howbeit he no longer honoured his temple-keepers, nor would he keep feasts, nor make drink-offerings to his idols, but his mind was tossed between two opinions. On the one hand, he poured scorn on the impotence of his gods; on the other, he dreaded the strictness of the profession of the Gospel, and was hardly to be torn from his evil ways, being completely in slavery to the pleasures of the body, and like a captive drawn towards sinful lusts, and being drunken, as saith Esay, but not with wine, and led as it were with the bridle of evil habit.

and doubteth of his own gods

While the king was thus wrestling with two opinions, his noble and truly royal-hearted son dwelt at peace in his palace, proving to all men by his deeds the nobility, order and steadfastness of his nature. Theatres, horse-races, riding to hounds, and all the vain pleasures of youth, the baits that take foolish souls, were reckoned by him as nothing worth. But he hung wholly on the commands of Christ for whom he yearned, his heart being

Of the noble conversation of the prince

καὶ αὐτὸν ἐπόθει τρωθεὶς τὴν ψυχὴν ἔρωτι θείῳ·
Cant. v. 16 αὐτὸν ἐπόθει τὸν ὄντως ποθητόν, ὅς ἐστιν ὅλος
γλυκασμὸς καὶ ἐπιθυμία, καὶ ἀκόρεστος ἔφεσις.

Εἰς μνήμην δὲ ἐρχόμενος τοῦ διδασκάλου
Βαρλαάμ, καὶ τὸν ἐκείνου ἐνοπτριζόμενος βίον,
ἔρωτι τὴν ψυχὴν ἐθέλγετο, καὶ ὅπως αὐτὸν ἴδοι
ἐφρόντιζεν ἐπιμελέστατα, καί, τοὺς λόγους αὐτοῦ
Ps. i. 3 ἐν τῇ καρδίᾳ περιφέρων ἀλήστως, οἱονεὶ ξύλον
ἦν πεφυτευμένον παρὰ τοῖς ψαλμικοῖς ὕδασιν,
ἀρδευόμενον ἀδιαλείπτως καὶ ὡραίους προσάγον
καρποὺς τῷ Κυρίῳ. πολλὰς γὰρ ψυχὰς τῶν
τοῦ διαβόλου ἐρρύσατο ἀρκύων καὶ τῷ Χριστῷ 262
προσήγαγε σεσωσμένας· πολλοὶ γὰρ εἰς αὐτὸν
φοιτῶντες λόγων ἀπήλαυον σωτηρίων, ἐξ ὧν
οὐκ ὀλίγοι, τὴν πλάνην φυγόντες, τῷ σωτηρίῳ
προσέδραμον λόγῳ· ἄλλοι δέ, μακρὰν τοῖς τοῦ
βίου χαίρειν εἰπόντες, τὴν ἀσκητικὴν ὑπεισῆλθον
παλαίστραν. αὐτὸς δὲ εὐχαῖς ἐσχόλαζε καὶ
νηστείαις, καὶ συχνῶς ταύτην ἀνέπεμπε τὴν
φωνήν, Ὦ Κύριε, λέγων, Κύριέ μου καὶ Βασιλεῦ,
ᾧ ἐγὼ ἐπίστευσα, ἐφ' ὃν ἐγὼ κατέφυγον καὶ
τῆς πλάνης ἐρρύσθην, ἀπόδος μισθὸν ἄξιον
τῷ θεράποντί σου Βαρλαάμ, ἀνθ' ὧν μοι τῷ
πλανηθέντι σὲ ὑπέδειξε, τὴν ὁδὸν τῆς ἀληθείας
καὶ τῆς ζωῆς· καὶ μὴ στερήσῃς με αὖθις ἰδεῖν
τὸν ἐν σώματι ἄγγελον ἐκεῖνον, οὗ οὐκ ἔστιν
Heb. xi. 38 ὁ κόσμος ἐπάξιος, καὶ σὺν αὐτῷ τελέσαι τὸ
λοιπὸν τῆς ζωῆς μου, ἵνα, κατ' ἴχνος τῆς αὐτοῦ
πολιτείας περιπατήσας, εὐαρεστήσω σοι τῷ Θεῷ
καὶ Δεσπότῃ.

wounded with love divine. For him he longed, who alone is to be longed for, who is all sweetness and desire and aspiration insatiable.

Now, when he came to think upon his teacher Barlaam, and as in a mirror saw his life, his soul was enchanted with love, and he much occupied himself a-thinking how he might see him; and ever carrying his sayings in his heart, he was like the tree in the Psalms planted by the river side, unceasingly watered, and bringing forth unto the Lords his fruits in due season. Many were the souls that he delivered from the snares of the devil, and brought safely unto Christ; for many resorted unto him, and profited by his wholesome words. And not a few left the way of error, and ran toward the word of salvation; while others bade a long farewell to the concerns of the world, and came to the wrestling-school of the monastic life. He himself spent his time in prayers and fastings, and would often offer up this prayer, 'O Lord, my Lord and King, in whom I have trusted, to whom I have fled and been delivered from my error, render thou due recompense to Barlaam thy servant, because when I was in error he pointed thee to me, who art the way of truth and life. Forbid me not to behold once more that angel in bodily shape, of whom the world is not worthy, but grant me in his company to finish the residue of my life, that, treading in the footsteps of his conversation, I may be well-pleasing to thee my God and Lord.'

Of his desire once more to behold Barlaam

XXIX

Κατ' ἐκεῖνο δὲ καιροῦ πανήγυρις ἦν τῶν ψευδωνύμων θεῶν δημοτελὴς ἐν τῇ πόλει ἐκείνῃ· ἔδει δὲ τὸν βασιλέα παρεῖναι τῇ ἑορτῇ καὶ θυσιῶν δαψιλείᾳ ταύτην κοσμῆσαι. ἀλλ' ἐδεδίεσαν οἱ νεωκόροι, ὁρῶντες αὐτὸν ἀμελῶς περὶ τὸ σέβας αὐτῶν καὶ χλιαρῶς διακείμενον, μή ποτε ἀμελήσειε τῆς ἐν τῷ ναῷ παρουσίας, καὶ στερηθεῖεν αὐτοὶ τῆς διδομένης αὐτοῖς βασιλικῆς δωρεᾶς καὶ τῶν λοιπῶν προσόδων. ἀναστάντες 263
οὖν καταλαμβάνουσιν ἄντρον ἐν βαθυτάτῃ διακείμενον τῇ ἐρήμῳ, ἔνθα κατῴκει ἀνήρ τις μαγικαῖς σχολάζων τέχναις, καὶ τῆς εἰδωλικῆς πλάνης θερμότατος ὑπάρχων προασπιστής· Θευδᾶς ὄνομα αὐτῷ· ὃν καὶ ὁ βασιλεὺς ἐτίμα διαφερόντως, καὶ φίλον ἡγεῖτο καὶ διδάσκαλον, διὰ τῆς αὐτοῦ λέγων μαντείας εὐθενουμένην προκόπτειν τὴν αὐτοῦ βασιλείαν· ὡς εἰς αὐτὸν τοίνυν οἱ μὴ ἱερεῖς τῶν εἰδώλων ἀφικόμενοι τοῦτον εἰς βοήθειαν προσεκαλοῦντο, καὶ τὴν ἐγγινομένην τῷ βασιλεῖ τῶν θεῶν κατάγνωσιν δήλην ἐποίουν, οἷά τε ὁ τοῦ βασιλέως πεποιήκει υἱός, οἷα δὲ κατ' αὐτῶν ὁ Ναχὼρ δεδημηγορήκει, καὶ ὡς, Εἰ μὴ αὐτός, φασίν, ἐλεύσῃ βοηθήσων ἡμῖν, πᾶσα ἐξέλιπεν ἐλπίς, πάντα ἀπόλωλε τὰ τῶν θεῶν σεβάσματα· σὺ γὰρ μόνος ἡμῖν ὑπελείφθης τῆς συμφορᾶς παραμύθιον, καὶ ἐπὶ σοὶ τὰς ἐλπίδας ἐθέμεθα.

XXIX

Now about the same time there was in that city a public assembly in honour of the false gods, and the king must needs be present at the feast, and grace it with lavish sacrifices. But the temple-keepers, seeing that he was careless and lukewarm with regard to their worship, feared that he might neglect to be present in their temple, and that they might lose the royal largess, and the rest of their revenues. So they arose, and withdrew to a cavern situate in the depth of the desert, where dwelt a man who busied himself with magical arts, and was a fervent champion of the error of idolatry: Theudas was his name. Him the king honoured exceedingly, and counted him his friend and teacher, because, he said, it was by the guidance of his prophecies that his kingdom ever prospered. So these idol-priests, that were no priests, came to him, and appealed to him for help, and made known to him the evil opinion of their gods which was growing on their king, and all that the king's son had done, and all the eloquent discourse that Nachor had held against them. And they said, 'Except thou come thyself to our succour, gone is all hope! and lost is all the reverence of the gods. Thou only art left to be our comfort in this misfortune, and upon thee we fix our hopes.'

The idol priests resort to Theudas the magician

Ἐκστρατεύει τοίνυν ὁ Θευδᾶς μετὰ τῆς συμπαρούσης αὐτῷ σατανικῆς στρατιᾶς, καὶ κατὰ τῆς ἀληθείας ὁπλίζεται, πολλὰ τῶν πονηρῶν πνευμάτων καλέσας, ἃ πρὸς τὰ φαῦλα συνεργεῖν οἶδε προθύμως, καὶ οἷς ἐκεῖνος ἀεὶ διακόνοις ἐχρῆτο· μεθ' ὧν παραγίνεται πρὸς τὸν βασιλέα.

Ὡς δὲ ἐμηνύθη τῷ βασιλεῖ ἡ ἄφιξις αὐτοῦ, καὶ εἰσῆλθε, ῥάβδον μὲν κατέχων βαϊνήν, μηλωταρίον δὲ περιεζωσμένος, ἀνέστη ὁ βασιλεὺς τοῦ θρόνου, καὶ τοῦτον προσυπαντήσας ἠσπάσατο, καὶ θρόνον 264
ἐνεγκὼν πλησίον αὐτοῦ συνεδριάζειν πεποίηκεν. εἶτα λέγει Θευδᾶς τῷ βασιλεῖ· Βασιλεῦ, εἰς τοὺς αἰῶνας ζῆθι, τῇ τῶν μεγίστων θεῶν εὐμενείᾳ σκεπόμενος. ἤκουσα γὰρ ἀγῶνά σε μέγαν ἀγωνίσασθαι κατὰ τῶν Γαλιλαίων καὶ λαμπροτάτοις διαδήμασι νίκης καταστεφθῆναι. διὸ ἐλήλυθα, ἵνα εὐχαριστήριον ἑορτὴν ὁμοῦ τελέσωμεν, νεανίσκους τε ὡραίους καὶ κόρας εὐόπτους τοῖς ἀθανάτοις θεοῖς καταθύσωμεν, ταύρους τε ἑκατὸν καὶ ζῷα τούτοις πλεῖστα προσενέγκωμεν, ὡς ἂν ἔχοιμεν αὐτοὺς καὶ εἰς τὸ ἑξῆς συμμάχους ἀηττήτους, ὅλον ἡμῖν τὸν βίον ἐξομαλίζοντας.

Πρὸς ταῦτα ὁ βασιλεύς, Οὐ νενικήκαμεν, ἔφη, ὦ πρεσβῦτα· οὐ νενικήκαμεν, ἀλλ' ἀνὰ κράτος μᾶλλον ἡττήμεθα. οἱ γὰρ ὑπὲρ ἡμῶν καθ' ἡμῶν ἐξαίφνης γεγόνασι. παράβακχόν τε καὶ μανικὴν καὶ ἀσθενῆ τὴν ἡμετέραν εὑρόντες παράταξιν, τέλεον ταύτην κατέβαλον. νυνὶ δέ, εἴ τίς σοι δύναμις πρόσεστι καὶ ἰσχὺς εἰς τὸ βοηθῆσαι τῇ κάτω κειμένῃ θρησκείᾳ ἡμῶν καὶ ταύτην αὖθις ἀνορθῶσαι, ἀνάγγειλόν μοι.

Ὁ δὲ Θευδᾶς τοιαύτας ἐδίδου τὰς ἀποκρίσεις

So forth marched Theudas, in company with his Satanic host; and he armed himself against the truth, invoking many of his evil spirits, who knew how to lend ready aid for evil ends, and whom he alway used for his ministers; and with these allies he came to the king.

He taketh the field for them

When his arrival had been announced to the king, and he had entered in, with a palm-staff in his hand and a sheep-skin girt about his loins, the king arose from his throne, and met and welcomed him; and, fetching a seat, he made him to sit down beside him. Then spake Theudas unto the king, 'O king, live for ever under the shelter of the favour of the most puissant gods! I have heard that thou hast foughten a mighty fight with the Galileans, and hast been crowned with right glorious diadems of victory. Wherefore I am come, that we may celebrate together a feast of thanksgiving, and sacrifice to the immortal gods young men in the bloom of youth and well-favoured damsels, and eke offer them an hecatomb of bullocks and herds of beasts, that we may have them from henceforth for our allies invincible, making plain our path of life before us.'

Theudas wisheth the king joy of his signal victory

Hereto the king made answer, 'We have not conquered, aged sir, we have not conquered: nay, rather have we been defeated in open fight. They that were for us turned suddenly against us. They found our host a wild, half-drunken, feeble folk, and utterly overthrew it. But now, if there be with thee any power and strength to help our fallen religion and set it up again, declare it.'

The king showeth how it was no victory but foul defeat

Theudas replied in this wise, 'Dread not, O king,

Theudas

τῷ βασιλεῖ· Τὰς μὲν τῶν Γαλιλαίων ἐνστάσεις
καὶ ματαιολογίας μὴ φοβοῦ, βασιλεῦ· τίνα γάρ
εἰσι τὰ παρ᾽ αὐτῶν λεγόμενα πρὸς ἄνδρας λο-
γικοὺς καὶ ἐχέφρονας; ἅτινα, ἐμοὶ δόξαν, ῥᾳδίως
καταβληθήσεται μᾶλλον ἢ φύλλον ἀνέμῳ κατα-
σεισθέν. οὐδὲ γὰρ κατὰ πρόσωπόν μου ἐλθεῖν
ὑπομενοῦσι μὴ ὅτι γε καὶ λόγον συνᾶραι καὶ εἰς
προτάσεις μοι καὶ ἀντιθέσεις χωρῆσαι. ἀλλ᾽,
ἵνα τοῦτό τε τὸ προκείμενον ἀγώνισμα καὶ πᾶν
ὁτιοῦν ἂν βουληθείημεν ἐπ᾽ εὐθείας ἡμῖν γένοιτο 265
καὶ κατὰ ῥοῦν τὰ πράγματα χωρήσειε, τὴν ἑορτὴν
κόσμησον ταύτην τὴν δημοτελῆ, καὶ τὴν εὐμέ-
νειαν τῶν θεῶν ὥσπερ τι κραταιὸν περιβαλοῦ
ὅπλον· καὶ εὖ σοι γένηται.

Ps. lii. 1 Οὕτω καυχησάμενος ὁ ἐν κακίᾳ δυνατὸς εἶναι
ἀνομίαν τε ὅλην τὴν ἡμέραν μελετήσας (συμφθεγ-
Hab. ii. 15 γέσθω γὰρ ἡμῖν ὁ Δαυΐδ), ἀνατροπὴν δὲ θολεράν,
καθά φησιν Ἡσαΐας, τῷ πλησίον ποτίσας, συνεργίᾳ τῶν συμπαρομαρτούντων αὐτῷ πονηρῶν
πνευμάτων ἐπιλαθέσθαι τὸν βασιλέα παντάπασι
τῶν πρὸς σωτηρίαν ὑπομιμνησκόντων λογισμῶν
πεποίηκε καὶ τῶν συνήθων πάλιν ἐπιμελῶς
ἔχεσθαι. ἔνθεν τοὶ καὶ γραμμάτων βασιλικῶν
πανταχοῦ διαπεφοιτηκότων τοῦ συνελθεῖν πάντας
ἐν τῇ μυσαρᾷ πανηγύρει αὐτῶν, ἦν ἰδεῖν συρ-
ρέοντα τὰ πλήθη, πρόβατά τε καὶ βόας καὶ
διάφορα γένη ζῴων ἀγόμενα.

Πάντων τοίνυν συνεληλυθότων, ἀναστὰς ὁ
βασιλεὺς μετὰ τοῦ ἀπατεῶνος Θευδᾶ πρὸς τὸν
ναὸν ἐχώρει, ταύρους καταθῦσαι φέρων ἑκατὸν
εἴκοσι καὶ ζῷα πολλά. καὶ ἐτέλουν τὴν ἐπάρατον
αὐτῶν ἑορτήν, ὡς περιηχεῖσθαι μὲν τὴν πόλιν ὑπὸ

the oppositions and vain babblings of the Galileans: for of what worth against reasonable and sensible men are the arguments that they use? These methinks shall be more easily overthrown than a leaf shaken with the wind. They shall not endure to face me, far less join argument, or come to propositions and oppositions with me. But, in order that the coming contest and all our wishes may prosper, and that our matters may run smoothly with the stream, adorn thou with thy presence this public festival, and gird on for thy strong sword the favour of the gods, and well befall thee!'

promiseth the king a sure triumph

When the mighty in wickedness had thus boasted himself and thought of mischief all the day long (let David bear his part in our chorus), and when, as saith Esay,[1] he had given his neighbour a drink of turbid dregs, by the help of the evil spirits his comrades he made the king utterly to forget the thoughts that inclined him to salvation, and caused him again to cleave to his wonted ways. Then the king despatched letters hither and thither, that all men should gather together to this loathsome assembly. Then mightest thou have seen multitudes streaming in, and bringing with them sheep and oxen and divers kinds of beasts.

So when all were assembled, the king arose, with that deceiver Theudas, and proceeded to the temple, bringing one hundred and twenty bullocks and many animals for sacrifice. And they celebrated their accursed feast till the city resounded with the cry of

The king maketh a great feast in honour of his idols

[1] It should be Habakkuk.

τῆς τῶν ἀλόγων ζῴων φωνῆς, τῇ δὲ τῶν θυσιῶν κνίσῃ καὶ αὐτὸν μολύνεσθαι τὸν ἀέρα. τούτων οὕτω τελεσθέντων, καὶ τῶν τῆς πονηρίας πνευμάτων λίαν ἐγκαυχησαμένων ἐπὶ τῇ νίκῃ τοῦ Θευδᾶ, καὶ χάριτας αὐτῷ ὁμολογησάντων τῶν νεωκόρων, εἰς τὸ παλάτιον αὖθις ἐπανῆκεν ὁ βασιλεύς. καί φησι τῷ Θευδᾷ· Ἰδοὺ δή, καθὰ 266
ἐκέλευσας, οὐδεμίαν ἐνελίπομεν σπουδὴν ἐπὶ τῇ λαμπροφορίᾳ τῆς πανηγύρεως καὶ δαψιλείᾳ τῶν θυσιῶν. καιρὸς οὖν ἤδη τὰ ἐπηγγελμένα πληρῶσαι καὶ τὸν ἀποστατήσαντα τῶν ἡμετέρων σεβασμάτων υἱόν μου τῆς πλάνης ἀναρρύσασθαι τῶν Χριστιανῶν, καὶ τοῖς εὐμενέσι καταλλάξαι θεοῖς. ἐγὼ γὰρ τέχνην πᾶσαν καὶ χεῖρα κινήσας οὐδεμίαν εὗρον τοῦ κακοῦ θεραπείαν· ἀλλὰ πάντων κρείττονα τὴν αὐτοῦ γνώμην ἐθεασάμην. εἰ πράως αὐτῷ ἐνέτυχον καὶ ἠπίως, οὐδὲ τὸν νοῦν μοι προσέχοντα ὅλως εὕρισκον· εἰ αὐστηρῶς ἐχρησάμην καὶ ἐμβριθῶς, εἰς ἀπόνοιαν μᾶλλον αἰρόμενον ἐθεώρουν. τῇ σῇ λοιπὸν σοφίᾳ τὰ τῆς ἐπελθούσης μοι συμφορᾶς ἀνατίθημι. εἰ οὖν, ταύτης ἀπαλλαγεὶς διὰ σοῦ, τὸν ἐμὸν αὖθις ὄψομαι υἱὸν σὺν ἐμοὶ τοῖς θεοῖς μου λατρεύοντα καὶ τῶν ἐπιθυμιῶν τῆς ἐνηδόνου ζωῆς ταύτης καὶ βασιλείας ἀπολαύοντα, στήλην σοι ἀνεγείρας χρυσῆν, ἴσα θεοῖς θήσομαι παρὰ πάντων τιμᾶσθαι εἰς τὸν ἐπιόντα ἀτελεύτητον χρόνον.

Ὁ Θευδᾶς τοίνυν οὖς εὐήκοον ὑποκλίνας τῷ πονηρῷ, καὶ παρ᾽ ἐκείνου μυηθεὶς βουλὴν πονηρὰν καὶ ὀλέθριον, γλῶσσά τε καὶ στόμα αὐτῷ γενόμενος, φησὶ πρὸς τὸν βασιλέα· Εἰ χειρώσα- 267

the brute beasts and the very air was polluted with the reek of sacrifice. This done, when the spirits of wickedness had greatly vaunted them over Theudas' victory, and when the temple-keepers had rendered him thanks, the king went up again unto his palace, and said unto Theudas, 'Behold now, as thou badest us, we have spared no pains over the splendour of this gathering and the lavishness of the sacrifice Now, therefore, it is time for thee to fulfil thy promises, and to deliver from the error of the Christians my son that hath rebelled against our religion, and to reconcile him to our gracious gods. For, though I have left no device and deed untried, yet have I found no remedy for the mischief, but I perceive that his will is stronger than all. When I have dealt gently and kindly with him, I have found that he payeth me no regard whatsoever. When I have treated him harshly and severely, I have seen him driven the quicker to desperation. To thy wisdom for the future I leave the care of this calamity that hath befallen me. If then I be delivered from this trouble by thy means, and once more behold my son worshipping my gods with me, and enjoying the gratification of this life of pleasure, and this royal estate, I will set up unto thee a golden statue, and make thee to receive divine honours from all men for all time to come.'

Hereupon Theudas, bowing an attentive ear to the evil one, and learning from him the secret of his evil and deadly counsel, became himself the devil's tongue and mouthpiece, and spake unto the king, 'If

Theudas prepareth a deadly snare to entrap the prince

σθαι τὸν σὸν βούλει υἱόν, καὶ κενὴν αὐτῷ τὴν
ἔνστασιν θεῖναι, εὕρηταί μοι τέχνη πρὸς ἣν οὐδὲ
ἀντέχειν δυνατὸς ἔσται, ἀλλὰ ῥᾷον μαλαχθήσεται
ὁ ἀτεράμων καὶ ἀμείλικτος αὐτοῦ λογισμὸς ἢ
κηρὸς πυρκαϊᾷ σφοδροτάτῃ ὁμιλήσας. ὁ δὲ βασιλεύς, τὸν μάταιον οὕτω διακενῆς φυσῶντα
ἰδών, πρὸς ἡδονὴν εὐθὺς καὶ φαιδρότητα μετε-
βάλλετο, ἐλπίσας τὴν ἀκόλαστον ἐκείνην καὶ
θρασεῖαν γλῶσσαν τῆς θεοδιδάκτου καὶ φιλοσοφίας γεμούσης περιγενέσθαι ψυχῆς. Καὶ τίς ἡ
Ps. lii. 8 τέχνη μαθεῖν ἤρετο. τότε Θευδᾶς ὡσεὶ ξυρὸν
ἠκονημένον ὑφαίνει τὸ κακούργημα καὶ δεινῶς ἀρτύει τὰ φάρμακα. καὶ ὅρα σόφισμα κακότεχνον
καὶ ὑποβολὴν τοῦ πονηροῦ. Πάντας, φησίν, ὦ βασιλεῦ, τοὺς παρισταμένους τῷ υἱῷ σου καὶ ὑπηρε-
τοῦντας μακρύνας ἀπ' αὐτοῦ, γυναῖκας εὐειδεῖς
καὶ λίαν περικαλλεῖς, καὶ κεκοσμημένας εἰς τὸ
ἐπαγωγότερον, συνεῖναι αὐτῷ διηνεκῶς καὶ καθυπηρετεῖν, συνδιαιτᾶσθαί τε καὶ συναυλίζεσθαι,
πρόσταξον. ἐγὼ δέ, τῶν πνευμάτων ἓν τῶν εἰς
τὰ τοιαῦτά μοι τεταγμένων ἐπαποστείλας αὐτῷ,
βιαιότερον τὸ τῆς ἡδονῆς πῦρ ἀνάψω. καὶ ἅμα
τῷ συγγενέσθαι αὐτὸν μιᾷ καὶ μόνῃ τῶν τοιούτων
γυναικῶν, εἰ μὴ πάντα ἕξει σοι κατὰ γνώμην,
παροπτέος ἐγὼ τὸ λοιπόν σοι καὶ ἄχρηστος, καὶ
Cp. Numb. τιμωριῶν μεγίστων, οὐ τιμῶν, ἄξιος. οὐδὲν γὰρ 268
xxxi. 15, 16; ὡς ὄψις γυναικῶν ἐπάγεσθαι καὶ θέλγειν τοὺς
xxv. 1, 2 ἀρρένων λογισμοὺς πέφυκε. καὶ ἄκουσον διη-
γήσεως τῷ ἐμῷ συμμαρτυρούσης ῥήματι.

thou wilt get the better of thy son, and make his opposition vain, I have discovered a plan, which he shall in no wise be able to resist, but his hard and obdurate mind shall melt quicker than wax before the hottest fire.' The king, seeing this foolish fellow swelling with empty pride, immediately grew merry and joyful, hoping that the unbridled and boastful tongue would get the mastery of that divinely instructed and philosophic soul. 'And what is the plan?' he asked. Then began Theudas to weave his web. He made his villainy sharp as any razor and did cunningly prepare his drugs. Now behold this malicious device and suggestion of the evil one. 'Remove, O king,' said he, 'all thy son's waiting men and servants far from him, and order that comely damsels, of exceeding beauty, and bedizened to be the more winsome, be continually with him and minister to him, and be his companions day and night. For myself, I will send him one of the spirits told off for such duties, and I will thus kindle all the more fiercely the coals of sensual desire. After that he hath once only had intercourse with but one of these women, if all go not as thou wilt, then disdain me for ever, as unprofitable, and worthy not of honour but of dire punishment. For there is nothing like the sight of women to allure and enchant the minds of men. Listen to a story that beareth witness to my word.'

which he telleth to the king

XXX

Βασιλεύς τις παιδὸς ἀμοιρῶν ἄρρενος ἠνιᾶτο λίαν τὴν ψυχὴν ἀχθόμενος, καὶ ἀτύχημα τοῦτο οὐ μικρὸν λογιζόμενος. ἐν τούτοις οὖν αὐτῷ ὄντι γεννᾶται υἱός· καὶ χαρᾶς ἐπὶ τούτῳ τὴν καρδίαν ἐπεπλήρωτο ὁ βασιλεύς. εἶπον δὲ αὐτῷ οἱ τῶν ἰατρῶν ἐπιστήμονες, ὡς, εἰ ἐντὸς τῶν δώδεκα χρόνων ἥλιον ἢ πῦρ τὸ παιδίον τοῦτο ἴδοι, στερηθήσεται παντάπασι τοῦ φωτός· τοῦτο γὰρ ἡ τῶν ὀμμάτων αὐτοῦ θέσις δηλοῖ. ταῦτα τὸν βασιλέα ἀκούσαντα λέγεται οἰκίσκον ἀντρῶδες ἐκ πέτρας τινὸς λαξεῦσαι, κἀκεῖσε τὸν παῖδα μετὰ τῶν τιθηνούντων αὐτὸν κατακλείσαντα, μηδόλως, μέχρι συμπληρώσεως τῶν δώδεκα ἐνιαυτῶν, φωτὸς ὑποδεῖξαι μαρμαρυγὴν τὸ παράπαν. μετὰ δὲ τὴν συμπλήρωσιν τῶν δώδεκα ἐτῶν ἐξάγει τοῦ οἰκίσκου τὸν παῖδα μηδὲν ὅλως τοῦ κόσμου θεασάμενον, καὶ κελεύει ὁ βασιλεὺς πάντα κατὰ γένος παραστήσαντας ὑποδεῖξαι αὐτῷ, ἄνδρας μὲν ἐν ἑνὶ τόπῳ, ἀλλαχοῦ δὲ γυναῖκας, ἑτέρωθι χρυσόν, ἄργυρον, ἀλλαχόθεν μαργαρίτας τε καὶ λίθους πολυτελεῖς, ἱμάτια λαμπρὰ καὶ κόσμια, ἅρματα περικαλλῆ μετὰ ἵππων βασιλικῶν χρυσοχαλίνων σὺν τάπησιν ἁλουργοῖς, καὶ ἀναβάτας ἐπ᾽ αὐτοῖς ὁπλοφόρους, βουκόλιά τε βοῶν καὶ ποίμνια προβάτων. καί, ἁπλῶς εἰπεῖν, πάντα στοιχηδὸν ὑπεδείκνυον τῷ παιδί. πυνθανομένου δὲ αὐτοῦ
τί τούτων ἕκαστον καλεῖται, οἱ τοῦ βασιλέως 269
ὑπασπισταὶ καὶ δορυφόροι τὴν ἑκάστου κλῆσιν ἐδήλουν. ὡς δὲ τὴν κλῆσιν τῶν γυναικῶν ἤρετο

XXX

'A CERTAIN king was grieved and exceeding sad at heart, because that he had no male issue, deeming this no small misfortune. While he was in this condition, there was born to him a son, and the king's soul was filled with joy thereat. Then they that were learned amongst his physicians told him that, if for the first twelve years the boy saw the sun or fire, he should entirely lose his sight, for this was proved by the condition of his eyes. Hearing this, the king, they say, caused a little house, full of dark chambers, to be hewn out of the rock, and therein enclosed his child together with the men that nursed him, and, until the twelve years were past, never suffered him to see the least ray of light. After the fulfilment of the twelve years, the king brought forth from his little house his son that had never seen a single object, and ordered his waiting men to show the boy everything after his kind; men in one place, women in another; elsewhere gold and silver; in another place, pearls and precious stones, fine and ornamental vestments, splendid chariots with horses from the royal stables, with golden bridles and purple caparisons, mounted by armed soldiers; also droves of oxen and flocks of sheep. In brief, row after row, they showed the boy everything. Now, as he asked what each of these was called, the king's esquires and guards made known unto him each by name: but, when he

Theudas telleth the tale of the prince and the 'devils that deceive men'

APOLOGUE X

μαθεῖν, τὸν σπαθάριον τοῦ βασιλέως χαριέντως εἰπεῖν, δαίμονας αὐτὰς καλεῖσθαι, αἳ τοὺς ἀνθρώπους πλανῶσιν. ἡ δὲ τοῦ παιδὸς καρδία τῷ ἐκείνων πόθῳ πλέον τῶν λοιπῶν ἐθέλχθη. ὡς οὖν, πάντα περιελθόντες, πρὸς τὸν βασιλέα ἐπανήγαγον αὐτόν, ἐπηρώτα ὁ βασιλεὺς τί ἀρεστὸν αὐτῷ τῶν ὁραθέντων ἐφάνη. Τί, φησὶν ὁ παῖς, ἀλλ' ἢ οἱ δαίμονες ἐκεῖνοι, οἱ τοὺς ἀνθρώπους πλανῶντες; οὐδενὸς γὰρ τῶν ὀφθέντων μοι σήμερον, ἢ τῇ ἐκείνων φιλίᾳ ἐξεκαύθη μου ἡ ψυχή. καὶ ἐθαύμασεν ὁ βασιλεὺς ἐκεῖνος ἐπὶ τῷ ῥήματι τοῦ παιδός, καὶ οἷόν ἐστι τυραννικὸν χρῆμα γυναικῶν ἔρως. καὶ σὺ τοίνυν μὴ ἄλλως οἴου ὑποτάξαι σου τὸν υἱόν, ἢ τούτῳ δὴ τῷ τρόπῳ.

Δέχεται τὸν λόγον ἀσμένως ὁ βασιλεύς. καὶ παράγονται αὐτῷ ἐξ ἐπιλογῆς κόραι ὡραῖαι καὶ περικαλλεῖς, ἃς καὶ κόσμῳ λαμπρύνας διαυγεῖ καὶ ὅλως πρὸς τὸ ἐπαγωγὸν εὐτρεπίσας, τοὺς μὲν θεράποντας καὶ ὑπηρέτας τοῦ υἱοῦ πάντας ἐκβάλλει τοῦ παλατίου, ἐκείνας δὲ ἀντικαθίστησιν. αὗται οὖν περιεφύοντο αὐτῷ, συνεπλέκοντο, πρὸς τὴν μυσαρὰν αὐτὸν συνουσίαν ἠρέθιζον, διὰ πάντων σχημάτων τε καὶ ῥημάτων ἐκκαλούμεναι πρὸς ἡδονήν. οὐκ εἶχεν ἑτέρῳ τινὶ προσβλέψαι ἢ ὁμιλῆσαι, ἢ συναριστῆσαι· αὗται γὰρ ἦσαν αὐτῷ πάντα. καὶ ταῦτα μὲν ὁ βασιλεὺς ἐποίει. Θευδᾶς 270
δὲ πάλιν τὸ πονηρὸν ἐκεῖνο καταλαβὼν σπήλαιον, καὶ εἰς τὰς βίβλους ἐγκύψας τὰς ταῦτα ἐνεργεῖν δυναμένας, καὶ ἓν τῶν πονηρῶν πνευμάτων καλέσας, εἰς πόλεμον ἐκπέμπει τοῦ στρατιώτου τῆς Χριστοῦ παρατάξεως· οὐκ εἰδὼς ὁ ἄθλιος οἷον ἔμελλε γέλωτα ὑποστῆναι καὶ αἰσχύνης πληρου-

desired to learn what women were called, the king's spearman, they say, wittily replied that they were called, "Devils that deceive men." But the boy's heart was smitten with the love of these above all the rest. So, when they had gone round everywhere, and brought him again unto the king, the king asked, which of all these sights had pleased him most. "What," answered the boy, "but the Devils that deceive men? Nothing that I have seen to-day hath fired my heart with such love as these." The king was astonished at the saying of the boy, to think how masterful a thing the love of women is. Therefore think not to subdue thy son in any other way than this.'

The king heard this tale gladly; and there were brought before him some chosen damsels, young and exceeding beautiful. These he bedizened with dazzling ornaments and trained in all winsome ways: and then he turned out of the palace all his son's squires and serving men, and set these women in their stead. These flocked around the prince, embraced him, and provoked him to filthy wantonness, by their walk and talk inviting him to dalliaunce. Besides these, he had no man at whom to look, or with whom to converse or break his fast: for these damsels were his all. Thus did the king. But Theudas went home to his evil den, and, dipping into his books that had virtue to work such magic, he called up one of his wicked spirits and sent him forth, for to battle with the soldier of the army of Christ. But the wretch little knew what laughter he should create against

The king setteth fair damsels to wait on his son

σθαι σὺν πάσῃ τῇ ὑπ' αὐτὸν δαιμονικῇ φάλαγγι.
Luke xi. 26 τὸ δὲ πονηρὸν πνεῦμα, ἄλλα τε πονηρότερα συμ-
παραλαβὸν πνεύματα, τὸν κοιτῶνα καταλαμβάνει
τοῦ γενναίου παιδός, καὶ ἐπιπίπτει αὐτῷ λαβρό-
τατον ἀνάψαν τῆς σαρκὸς τὴν κάμινον. καὶ ὁ
μὲν πονηρὸς ἔνδον ἀνέφλεγεν· αἱ δὲ τὴν ὄψιν
εὐπρεπεῖς, τὴν δὲ ψυχὴν καὶ λίαν δυσειδεῖς, κόραι
ἔξωθεν τὴν πονηρὰν ἐχορήγουν ὕλην.

Ἡ δὲ καθαρὰ ἐκείνη ψυχὴ τῆς προσβολῆς αἰ- 271
σθομένη τοῦ πονηροῦ, καὶ τὸν πόλεμον ὁρῶσα τῶν
ἀτόπων λογισμῶν ἐπ' αὐτὴν σφοδρῶς ἐρχόμενον,
διεταράττετο· καὶ λύσιν εὑρεῖν τοῦ τοσούτου
κακοῦ ἐπεζήτει, καθαρόν τε ἑαυτὸν παραστῆσαι
τῷ Χριστῷ, καὶ μὴ τῷ βορβόρῳ τῶν παθῶν
καταχρᾶναι τὴν ἁγίαν ἐκείνην στολήν, ἣν αὐτὸν ἡ
τοῦ ἁγίου βαπτίσματος ἠμφιάσατο χάρις. εὐθὺς
οὖν ἔρωτι ἀνθίστησιν ἔρωτα, τῷ ἀκολάστῳ τὸν
θεϊκόν, καὶ εἰς μνήμην ἄγει ἑαυτὸν τῆς ὡραιότητος ἐκείνης καὶ ἀνεκλαλήτου δόξης Χριστοῦ
τοῦ ἀθανάτου νυμφίου τῶν καθαρωτάτων ψυχῶν,
Mat. xxii. 1–14 καὶ τοῦ νυμφῶνος ἐκείνου καὶ γάμου, οὗπερ
ἐλεεινῶς ἐκβάλλονται οἱ τὸν νυμφικὸν σπιλώ-
σαντες χιτῶνα, δεδεμένοι χεῖρας καὶ πόδας, εἰς
τὸ ἐξώτερον σκότος. ταῦτα λογισάμενος καὶ
σύνδακρυς γενόμενος, ἔτυπτε τὸ στῆθος, οἷα
κακοὺς κηφῆνας τοὺς πονηροὺς ἐκεῖθεν λογισμοὺς
φυγαδεύων. εἶτα διαναστὰς καὶ χεῖρας εἰς οὐρανὸν διάρας, θερμοῖς δάκρυσι καὶ στεναγμοῖς
τὸν Θεὸν ἐπεκαλεῖτο πρὸς συμμαχίαν, καὶ ἔλεγε·
Κύριε παντοκράτορ, ὁ μόνος δυνατὸς καὶ οἰκτίρμων, ἡ ἐλπὶς τῶν ἀπηλπισμένων, ἡ τῶν ἀβοη-
Luke xvii. 10 θήτων βοήθεια, μνήσθητί μου τοῦ ἀχρείου σου

himself, and to what shame he should be put, with the whole devilish troop under him. So the evil spirit, taking to him other spirits more wicked than himself, entered the bed-chamber of this noble youth, and attacked him by kindling right furiously the furnace of his flesh. The evil one plied the bellows from within: while the damsels, fair of face, but uncomely of soul, supplied the evil fuel from without.

Ioasaph, being sore tempted to sin, prayeth fervently to God for succour,

But Ioasaph's pure soul was disturbed to feel the touch of evil, and to see the warlike host of strange thoughts that was charging down upon him. And he sought to find deliverance from this great mischief, and to present himself pure unto Christ, and not defile in the mire of sinful lust that holy apparel, wherein the grace of holy Baptism had clothed him. Immediately he set love against love, the divine against the lascivious; and he called to remembrance the beauty and unspeakable glory of Christ, the immortal bridegroom of virgin souls, and of that bride chamber and marriage, from whence they that have stained their wedding-garment are piteously cast out, bound hand and foot, into outer darkness. When he had thought thereon, and shed bitter tears, he smote upon his breast, driving out evil thoughts, as good-for-nothing drones from the hive. Then he rose, and spread out his hands unto heaven, with fervent tears and groans calling upon God to help him, and he said, 'Lord Almighty, who alone art powerful and merciful, the hope of the hopeless, and the help of the helpless, remember me thine un-

δούλου ἐν τῇ ὥρᾳ ταύτῃ, καὶ ἱλέῳ μοι ἐπίβλεψον
Ps. xxii. 20 ὄμματι, καὶ ῥῦσαι ἀπὸ ῥομφαίας δαιμονικῆς τὴν
ψυχήν μου καὶ ἐκ χειρὸς κυνὸς τὴν μονογενῆ
μου· καὶ μὴ ἐάσῃς ἐμπεσεῖν με εἰς χεῖρας ἐχθρῶν
Ps. xxxv. 19 μου, μηδὲ ἐπιχαρείησάν μοι οἱ μισοῦντές με· καὶ
μὴ ἐγκαταλίπῃς με καταφθαρῆναι ἐν ἀνομίαις, 272
καὶ καθυβρίσαι μου τὸ σῶμα ὅπερ ἁγνόν σοι
παραστῆσαι ἐπηγγειλάμην. σὲ γὰρ ποθῶ, καὶ
σοὶ προσκυνῶ τῷ Πατρὶ καὶ τῷ Υἱῷ καὶ τῷ
Ἁγίῳ Πνεύματι νῦν καὶ ἀεὶ καὶ εἰς τοὺς αἰῶνας.
καὶ ἐπειπὼν τὸ ἀμήν, θείας ᾔσθετο παρακλήσεως
οὐρανόθεν αὐτῷ ἐπιφοιτησάσης, καὶ οἱ πονηροὶ
ὑπεχώρουν λογισμοί· αὐτὸς δὲ μέχρι πρωΐας
εὐχόμενος διετέλεσε. καὶ γνοὺς τὰ μηχανήματα
τοῦ δολίου, ἤρξατο ἐπὶ πλεῖον πιέζειν τὸ σῶμα
τροφῆς ἐνδείᾳ καὶ δίψῃ, καὶ τῇ ἄλλῃ ταλαιπωρίᾳ, ὁλονύκτους μὲν ἐπιτελῶν στάσεις, ἑαυτὸν
δὲ ἀναμιμνήσκων τῶν πρὸς τὸν Θεὸν ὁμολογιῶν,
καὶ ὑπογράφων τῷ λογισμῷ τὴν ἐκεῖθεν τῶν
δικαίων λαμπρότητα, τὴν ἠπειλημένην τε τοῖς
φαύλοις γέενναν ἀνιστορῶν ἐναργέστατα· ὅπως
μή, ἀργὴν καὶ ἄνετον ὁ ἐχθρὸς εὑρὼν τὴν ψυχήν,
λογισμοὺς αὐτῇ πονηροὺς ῥᾳδίως ὑποσπείρῃ, καὶ
τὸ καθαρὸν ἐπιθολώσῃ τῆς διανοίας. πάντοθεν 273
τοίνυν ὁ ἐχθρὸς ἐξαπορηθείς, καὶ παντελῶς
ἀπαγορεύσας ἑλεῖν τὸν γενναῖον, ἑτέραν ἔρχεται
ὁ δεινὸς ἀπάτην ποικιλωτέραν, ὁ ἀεί ποτε πονηρὸς
ὢν καὶ τὸ τεχνάζεσθαι καὶ βλάπτειν οὐδαμῶς
ἀπολείπων. εἰς ἔργον γὰρ ἀγαγεῖν τὰ ἐντεταλ-
μένα αὐτῷ παρὰ τοῦ Θευδᾶ μυρία γέγονε
σπουδή. καὶ οὕτω πάλιν τὰ φάρμακα ἀρτύει.

Μίαν γὰρ ὑπεισελθὼν τῶν νεανίδων ἐκείνων,

profitable servant at this hour, and look upon me with a gracious countenance, and deliver my soul from the sword of the devil, and my darling from the paw of the dog : suffer me not to fall into the hands of mine enemies, and let not them that hate me triumph over me. Leave me not to be destroyed in iniquities, and to dishonour my body which I swore to present unto thee chaste. For for thee I yearn; thee I worship, the Father, and the Son, and the Holy Ghost, now and for evermore, and world without end.' When he had added the *Amen*, he felt heavenly comfort stealing over him from above, and the evil thoughts withdrew, and he continued in prayer until early morn. Being ware of the devices of the crafty foe, he began more and more to afflict his body by abstinence from meat and drink, and by other severities, standing in prayer all the night long, and reminding himself of his covenants made with God, and picturing in his mind the glory of the righteous yonder, and recounting to himself the full terrors of the Gehenna wherewith the wicked are threatened; all this, that the enemy might not find his soul lying fallow and untilled, and thus easily sow therein the seeds of evil thoughts, and befoul the cleanness of his mind. So, when the enemy was in great straits on every side, and altogether in despair of taking this noble youth, like a cunning knave, he proceeded to another more subtil device, he that is for ever wicked, and never stinteth to contrive mischief and hurt. For he made furious endeavour to carry out the orders that Theudas had given him, and once more prepared his drugs, and on this wise.

and mortifieth his flesh by fasts and vigils

The devil entered into the heart of one of the

The devil

ἥτις πασῶν ἦν εὐμορφοτάτη, θυγάτηρ οὖσα βασιλέως, καὶ αἰχμάλωτος τῆς ἰδίας ἀλλοτριωθεῖσα πατρίδος, τῷ βασιλεῖ δὲ Ἀβενὴρ ὡς μέγιστόν τι προσαχθεῖσα δῶρον, ἥν, ὡς πάνυ ὡραιοτάτην οὖσαν, εἰς ὄλισθον καὶ ὑποσκελισμὸν τοῦ υἱοῦ ὁ πατὴρ ἦν ἀποστείλας, ταύτην ὁ ἀπατεὼν ὑπεισέρχεται, καὶ λόγους αὐτῇ ὑποτίθησι, πάνυ τὸ σοφὸν καὶ συνετὸν ἐμφαίνοντας τοῦ ταύτης λογισμοῦ. πάντα γὰρ τὰ πρὸς κακίαν μηχανήματα ῥᾳδίως ὁ πονηρὸς μετέρχε-
Zech. iii. 1; Ps. cix. 6 ται. εἶτα, τῷ τοῦ βασιλέως υἱῷ ἐκ δεξιᾶς
προσπεσών, φίλτρον ἐντίθησιν αὐτῷ τῆς κόρης, διὰ τὸ νουνεχὲς δῆθεν αὐτῆς καὶ κόσμιον, καὶ
διὰ τὸ εὐγενῆ οὕτω καὶ βασιλικῆς οὖσαν σειρᾶς 274
τῆς πατρίδος ἅμα καὶ δόξης ἐστερῆσθαι. πρὸς τούτοις καὶ λογισμοὺς ὑποσπείρει τοῦ ἀπαλλάξαι αὐτὴν τῆς εἰδωλομανίας καὶ Χριστιανὴν ποιῆσαι.

Ταῦτα δὲ πάντα μηχαναὶ ἦσαν τοῦ δολίου δράκοντος. οὕτω γὰρ τὴν ψυχὴν διατεθεὶς ὁ τοῦ βασιλέως υἱὸς καὶ μηδένα λογισμὸν ῥυπαρὸν ἢ ἔρωτα ἐμπαθῆ βλέπων ἐν ἑαυτῷ πρὸς τὴν κόρην σαλευόμενον, ἀλλ' ἢ μόνον συμπάθειαν καὶ ἔλεος τῆς τε συμφορᾶς καὶ τῆς ψυχικῆς ἀπωλείας, οὐκ ᾔδει δαιμονικὴν εἶναι μηχανὴν
2 Cor. xi. 14 τὸ πρᾶγμα· ὄντως γὰρ σκότος ἐστὶν ἐκεῖνος καὶ
τὸ φῶς ὑποκρίνεται. ὡς γὰρ ὁμιλεῖν ἤρξατο τῇ κόρῃ ὁ τοῦ βασιλέως υἱὸς καὶ τὰ τῆς θεογνωσίας αὐτῇ προσλαλεῖν λόγια, Σύνες, λέγων, ὦ γύναι, τὸν ζῶντα εἰς τοὺς αἰῶνας Θεόν, καὶ μὴ τῇ πλάνῃ ταύτῃ τῶν εἰδώλων καταφθαρῇς, ἀλλὰ τὸν Δεσπότην ἐπίγνωθι καὶ δημιουργὸν τοῦδε

young damsels. Of all she was the most seemly, a king's daughter, carried away captive from her own country, given to king Abenner as a great prize, and sent by him, being of ripe beauty, to his own son, for to cause him to slip or to trip. Of her the deceiver took possession, and whispered in her ear suggestions that plainly showed the wisdom and understanding of her mind; for the evil one easily pursueth all devices that make for wickedness. Then the evil spirit attacked the king's son on the right hand, and gave him a potion to make him love the maiden, by reason—so he pretended—of her prudence and discretion and of her nobility and royal blood that yet had not saved her from banishment and loss of glory. Moreover the devil secretly sowed in Ioasaph's heart thoughts that he might recover her from idolatry, and make her a Christian.

entereth into one of the damsels

But these were all stratagems of the wily serpent. For the king's son, being in this frame of mind, could see in himself no unclean thought or passionate affection for the damsel, but only sympathy and pity for her misfortune, and the ruin of her soul, and knew not that this matter was a device of the devil; for verily he is darkness, and feigneth to be light. So he began to commune with the damsel, and talk with her over the oracles of the knowledge of God, and said, 'Lady, be thou acquainted with the ever-living God, and perish not in the error of these idols; but know thy Lord, and the Maker of

Ioasaph, unconscious of his passion, pleadeth with her to become a Christian

τοῦ παντός, καὶ μακαρία ἔσῃ νυμφευθεῖσα τῷ
ἀθανάτῳ νυμφίῳ· πολλὰ δὲ τοιαῦτα νουθετοῦντος
αὐτοῦ, εὐθὺς τὸ πονηρὸν πνεῦμα ὑπαγορεύει τῇ
γυναικὶ τὰ τῆς ἀπάτης ὑφαπλῶσαι θήρατρα καὶ 275
πρὸς τὸν τῆς ἐμπαθείας κατασῦραι βόθρον τὴν
θεοφιλῆ ψυχὴν ἐκείνην, καθά ποτε καὶ τῷ
Gen. iii. 6 γενάρχῃ πεποίηκε διὰ τῆς Εὔας, τοῦ παραδείσου
καὶ τοῦ Θεοῦ ταλαιπώρως φεῦ ἐξορίσας, καὶ
θανάτῳ ὑπόδικον αὐτὸν ἀντὶ τῆς μακαρίας καὶ
ἀθανάτου ζωῆς γενέσθαι παρασκευάσας.

Ὡς γὰρ ἤκουσεν ἡ κόρη τὰ ῥήματα ἐκεῖνα τὰ
πάσης πεπληρωμένα σοφίας, ἀσύνετος οὖσα οὐ
συνῆκεν· ἀλλὰ τοιαύτας ἐδίδου τὰς ἀποκρίσεις,
ὡς ἅτε γλῶσσα καὶ στόμα τῷ πονηρῷ γενομένη,
καί φησιν· Εἰ τῆς ἐμῆς, ὦ δέσποτα, σωτηρίας
φροντίζεις, καὶ προθυμῇ τῷ Θεῷ σου προσαγαγεῖν με καὶ τὴν ταπεινὴν ψυχήν μου σῶσαι,
ποίησον καὶ αὐτὸς μίαν μου αἴτησιν, καί, πᾶσιν
εὐθὺς τοῖς πατρῴοις μου θεοῖς ἀποταξαμένη, τῷ
σῷ συντάξομαι Θεῷ, μέχρι τελευταίας αὐτῷ
λατρεύουσα ἀναπνοῆς, καὶ μισθὸν λήψῃ τῆς
ἐμῆς σωτηρίας καὶ πρὸς τὸν Θεὸν ἐπιστροφῆς.

Τοῦ δέ, Τίς ἡ ἀξίωσις, ὦ γύναι; εἰπόντος, 276
ἐκείνη καὶ σχῆμα καὶ βλέμμα καὶ φθέγμα καὶ
ὅλην ἑαυτὴν πρὸς τὸ θέλγειν καταστήσασα,
Συνάφθητί μοι, ἔφη, γάμου κοινωνίᾳ, κἀγώ σου
τοῖς προστάγμασι χαίρουσα ἐξακολουθήσω.

Ὁ δέ, Μάτην, φησίν, ὦ γύναι, τοιαύτην μοι
προέτεινας σκληρὰν ἀξίωσιν· τῆς μὲν γὰρ σῆς
ἰσχυρῶς κήδομαι σωτηρίας, καὶ τοῦ βυθοῦ τῆς
ἀπωλείας ποθῶ σε ἀνελκῦσαι· μολῦναι δὲ τὸ

all this world, and thou shalt be happy, the bride of the immortal bridegroom.' While he exhorted her with many such-like words, immediately the evil spirit whispered to the girl that she should spread under his feet the nets of deceit to drag his blessed soul into the pit of lust, as he once did to our first parent by means of Eve, thus miserably banishing him, alas! from Paradise and God, and making him to become subject to death in lieu of bliss and everlasting life.

When the damsel heard Ioasaph's words fulfilled with all wisdom, being without understanding, she understood them not, but made answer thus, becoming the tongue and mouth-piece of the evil one: 'If, sir, thou takest thought for my salvation, and desirest to bring me to thy God, and to save my poor soul, do thou also thyself grant me one request, and straightway I will bid good-bye to my fathers' gods, and join thy God, serving him until my last breath; and thou shalt receive recompense for my salvation, and for my turning to God-ward.'

'Lady, and what is thy request?' said he. But she, setting her whole self, figure, look and voice in a fashion to charm him, answered, 'Be thou joined with me in the bonds of wedlock, and I will joyfully follow out thy behests.'

She prayeth him to wed her,

'In vain, O Lady,' said he, 'hast thou made this hard request. For though I earnestly care for thy salvation, and long to heave thee from the depth of

σῶμά μου δι' αἰσχρᾶς μίξεως βαρύ μοι καὶ πάντη ἀδύνατον.

Ἡ δέ, ὅλην ὁμαλίζουσα τὴν ὁδὸν αὐτῷ καὶ διαλεαίνουσα, Ἱνατί, φησί, τοιαῦτα φθέγγῃ σύ, ὁ πάσης πεπληρωμένος σοφίας; ἱνατί μολυσμὸν τὸ πρᾶγμα καὶ αἰσχρὰν ἐκάλεσας μῖξιν; οὐκ ἀμύητος γάρ εἰμι κἀγὼ τῶν Χριστιανικῶν βιβλίων· ἀλλὰ πολλαῖς μὲν δέλτοις ἐν τῇ πατρίδι μου ἐνέτυχον, πολλῶν δὲ ὁμιλούντων μοι Χριστιανῶν ἀκήκοα. οὐ γέγραπται τοίνυν ἔν τινι
Heb. xiii. 4 τῶν καθ' ὑμᾶς βιβλίων, Τίμιος ὁ γάμος καὶ ἡ
1 Cor. vii. 9 κοίτη ἀμίαντος; καί, Κρεῖσσον γαμεῖν ἢ πυροῦ-
Mat. xix. 6 σθαι; καί, Ἃ ὁ Θεὸς συνέζευξεν ἄνθρωπος μὴ
χωριζέτω; οὐ πάντας τοὺς πάλαι δικαίους,
πατριάρχας τε καὶ προφήτας, γάμῳ συναφθῆναι
Mat. viii. 14 αἱ Γραφαὶ διδάσκουσιν ὑμῶν; οὐ Πέτρον ἐκεῖ- 277
νον, ὃν καὶ κορυφαῖον τῶν ἀποστόλων φατὲ γεγο-
1 Cor. ix. 5 νέναι, γαμετὴν γέγραπται ἐσχηκέναι; τίσιν οὖν
αὐτὸς πειθόμενος μολυσμὸν τοῦτο καλεῖς; πάνυ μοι δοκεῖς, δέσποτα, τῆς ἀληθείας τῶν δογμάτων ὑμῶν ἀποπλανᾶσθαι.

Ὁ δέ, Ναί, φησίν, ὦ γύναι· οὕτως ἔχει ταῦτα πάντα καθὼς εἴρηκας. ἐφεῖται γὰρ τοῖς βουλομένοις γάμῳ κοινωνεῖν· ἀλλ' οὐ τοῖς ἅπαξ ἐπαγγελλομένοις τῷ Χριστῷ παρθενεύειν. ἐγὼ γάρ, ἐξότε τῷ λουτρῷ ἐκαθαρίσθην τοῦ θείου βαπτίσματος, τῶν τῆς νεότητος καὶ ἀγνοίας μου πταισμάτων καθαρὸν ἐμαυτὸν παραστῆσαι τῷ Χριστῷ συνεταξάμην· καὶ πῶς τὰ ὡμολογημένα Θεῷ διαλῦσαι τολμήσω;

Ἔφη δὲ αὖθις ἡ γυνή· Ἔστω καὶ τοῦτό σου τὸ θέλημα, καθὼς βούλοιο. ἄλλην δὲ μικράν τινα

perdition, yet to pollute my body through unclean union is grievous for me, and utterly impossible.'

She, seeking to make the way straight and smooth for him, cried, 'Why dost thou, who are so wise, talk thus? Wherefore speakest thou of it as of defilement and shameful intercourse? I am not unacquainted with the Christian books: nay, I have met with many volumes in mine own country, and have heard the discourses of many Christians. What, is it not written in one of your books, "Marriage is honourable, and the bed undefiled"? and, "It is better to marry than to burn"? and again, "What God hath joined together, let not man put asunder"? Do not your Scriptures teach that all the righteous men of old, patriarchs and prophets, were wedded? Is it not written that the mighty Peter, whom ye call Prince of the Apostles, was a married man? Who, then, hath persuaded thee to call this defilement? Methink, sir, thou strayest utterly away from the truth of your doctrines.'

proving to him, from the Scriptures, the holiness of wedlock

'Yea, Lady,' said he, 'all this is even as thou sayest. It is permitted to all who will to live in wedlock, but not to them that have once made promise to Christ to be virgins. For myself, ever since I was cleansed in the laver of Holy Baptism from the sins of my youth and ignorance, I have resolved to present myself pure to Christ, and how shall I dare break my covenants with God?'

Ioasaph telleth her of his own vow of chastity

Again quoth the damsel, 'Let this also be thy pleasure, as thou wilt. But fulfil me one other small

The damsel would have him for her leman,

καὶ οὐδαμινὴν πλήρωσον ἐπιθυμίαν μου, εἴπερ
ὄντως ἐν ἀληθείᾳ τὴν ψυχήν μου θέλεις σῶσαι.
συγγενοῦ μοι ταύτῃ τῇ νυκτὶ καὶ μόνον, καὶ τοῦ
σοῦ κατατρυφῆσαί με κάλλους ποίησον, τῆς ἐμῆς
τε αὐτὸς ἐμπλήσθητι ὡραιότητος. καὶ λόγον σοι
δίδωμι, ἅμα πρωῒ Χριστιανὴν γενέσθαι καὶ πᾶσαν ἐκφυγεῖν τὴν τῶν θεῶν μου λατρείαν. καὶ
ἔσται σοι οὐ μόνον συγγνώμη ἕνεκεν τῆς οἰκονομίας ταύτης, ἀλλὰ καὶ δωρεῶν ἀντάμειψις παρὰ
τῷ Θεῷ σου ἕνεκα τῆς ἐμῆς σωτηρίας· Χαρὰ
Luke xv. 7 γάρ, φησὶν ἡ Γραφή σου, γίνεται ἐν οὐρανῷ 278
ἐφ' ἑνὶ ἁμαρτωλῷ μετανοοῦντι. εἰ οὖν χαρὰ
γίνεται ἐν οὐρανῷ δι' ἐπιστροφὴν ἁμαρτωλοῦ,
τῷ προξένῳ τῆς ἐπιστροφῆς οὐ μέγας ἐπο-
φείλεται μισθός; ναί, οὕτως ἔχει, καὶ μὴ ἀμφί-
βαλλε. οὐ πολλὰ δὲ καὶ οἱ ἀρχηγοὶ τῆς θρησκείας ὑμῶν ἀπόστολοι κατ' οἰκονομίαν ἐποίουν,
παραβαίνοντες ἔσθ' ὅτε ἐντολήν ἕνεκα μείζονος
Acts xvi. 3 ἐντολῆς; οὐ τὸν Παῦλον λέγεται περιτεμεῖν τὸν
Τιμόθεον, ἕνεκα κρείττονος οἰκονομίας; καίτοι
παράνομον Χριστιανοῖς ἡ περιτομὴ λελόγισται·
ἀλλ' ὅμως ἐκεῖνος οὐ παρῃτήσατο τοῦτο ποιῆσαι.
καὶ πολλὰ τοιαῦτα ἐν ταῖς Γραφαῖς σου εὑρήσεις.
εἰ οὖν κατὰ ἀλήθειαν, καθὼς λέγεις, σῶσαί μου
τὴν ψυχὴν ζητεῖς, τὴν μικράν μου ταύτην ἐπιθυμίαν πλήρωσον. καὶ ἐγὼ μὲν τελείᾳ σοι
κοινωνίᾳ γάμου συναφθῆναι ζητοῦσα, ἐπεί σοι
οὐ καταθύμιόν ἐστι τοῦτο, οὐκ ἔτι σε καταναγ-
κάζω, τὰ ἀρεστά σοι πάντα ποιοῦσα· λοιπὸν καὶ
αὐτὸς μὴ πάντη βδελύξῃ· ἀλλ', ὑπακούσας μου
τὸ ἅπαξ τοῦτο, σώσεις με, τῆς δεισιδαίμονος

and trivial desire of mine, if thou art in very truth minded for to save my soul. Keep company with me this one night only, and grant me to revel in thy beauty, and do thou in turn take thy fill of my comeliness. And I give thee my word, that, with daybreak, I will become a Christian, and forsake all the worship of my gods. Not only shalt thou be pardoned for this dealing, but thou shalt receive recompense from thy God because of my salvation, for thy Scripture saith, "There is joy in heaven over one sinner that repenteth." If, therefore, there is joy in heaven over the conversion of a sinner, shall not great recompense be due to the causer of that conversion? Yea, so it is: and dispute it not. Did not even the Apostles, the leaders of your religion, do many a thing by dispensation, at times transgressing a commandment on account of a greater one? Is not Paul said to have circumcised Timothy on account of a greater dispensation? And yet circumcision hath been reckoned by Christians as unlawful, but yet he did not decline so to do. And many other such things shalt thou find in thy Scriptures. If then in very sooth, as thou sayest, thou seekest to save my soul, fulfil me this my small desire. And although I seek to be joined with thee in the full estate of matrimony, yet, sith this is contrary to thy mind, I will never constrain thee again, but will do everything that liketh thee. For the rest, do not thou utterly abhor me; but hearken to me for the nonce, and thou shalt deliver me from superstitious error, and thou shalt do whatever

if he will not be her husband

πλάνης ῥυσάμενος, τὰ δεδογμένα δέ σοι εἰς τὸ ἑξῆς ποιήσεις διὰ βίου παντός.

Οὕτω λέγουσα (καὶ γὰρ εἶχε τὸν εἰσηγούμενον,
Greg. Naz. Orat. xl. 10 ᾧ καὶ τὰ ὦτα ὑπεῖχεν αὕτη κρυφίως· καὶ Γραφῶν ἔμπειρος ὁ ληστὴς ἦν, ὁ τῆς κακίας ὄντως δημιουργὸς καὶ διδάσκαλος), τοιαῦτα τοιγαροῦν λέγουσα καὶ ὑποσαίνουσα, δίκτυά τε καὶ παγίδας ἐκ δεξιῶν τε καὶ ἐξ εὐωνύμων αὐτῷ περιπλέκουσα, τὸν πύργον αὐτοῦ τῆς ψυχῆς διασαλεύειν ἤρχετο, τὸν τόνον τε ὑποχαλᾶν αὐτοῦ τῆς προθέσεως, καὶ τὴν γνώμην μαλακωτέραν ποιεῖν. ὁ 279
δὲ σπορεὺς τῆς κακίας καὶ τῶν δικαίων ἐχθρός, σαλευομένην αὐτοῦ τὴν καρδίαν ἰδὼν χαρᾶς ἔμπλεως γεγονὼς φωνεῖ παρευθὺ τὰ σὺν αὐτῷ παραγενόμενα τῆς πονηρίας πνεύματα, Ὁρᾶτε, κράζων, ὅπως ἡ κόρη αὕτη διανῦσαι ἐπείγεται ἃ οὐκ ἠδυνήθημεν ἡμεῖς ἀνῦσαι. δεῦτε οὖν, ἰσχυρῶς νῦν ἐπιπέσωμεν αὐτῷ· οὐχ εὑρήσομεν γὰρ ἄλλον καιρὸν οὑτωσὶ ἐπιτήδειον τὸ θέλημα πληρῶσαι τοῦ πέμψαντος ἡμᾶς. ταῦτα συλλαλήσας ὁ δολιόφρων τοῖς ἑαυτοῦ κυσίν, ἐπεμβαίνουσι τῷ Χριστοῦ στρατιώτῃ, πάσας αὐτοῦ τῆς ψυχῆς τὰς δυνάμεις ταράξαντες, καὶ δεινὸν ἔρωτα τῆς κόρης ὑποθέμενοι, πῦρ τε σφοδρότατον ἐπιθυμίας ἐκκαύσαντες ἐν αὐτῷ.

Ὁρῶν δὲ ἑαυτὸν ἐκεῖνος ἰσχυρῶς φλεγόμενον καὶ πρὸς τὴν ἁμαρτίαν αἰχμαλωτιζόμενον, καὶ τοὺς λογισμοὺς αὐτοῦ τὴν σωτηρίαν τῆς κόρης καὶ πρὸς Θεὸν ἐπιστροφήν, ὡς ἀγκίστρῳ δέλεαρ, τῇ προκειμένῃ πράξει περιτιθεμένους, καὶ ὀχλοῦντας αὐτῷ τῇ τοῦ ἐχθροῦ ὑποβολῇ μὴ ἁμαρτίαν εἶναι τὸ ἐπὶ σωτηρίᾳ ψυχῆς ἅπαξ γυναικὶ

seemeth thee good hereafter all the days of thy life.'

Thus spake she; for indeed she had, for her adviser, one to whom she lent a privy ear, and the pirate was well versed in Scripture, being verily the creator and teacher of iniquity. Thus then she spake with fawning words entangling him, right and left, around with her toils and meshes, and she began to shake the citadel of his soul, and to slacken his tension of purpose, and to soften the temper of his mind. Then the sower of these evil tares, and enemy of the righteous, when he saw the young man's heart wavering, was full of joy, and straightway called to the evil spirits that were with him, crying, 'Look you how yond damsel hasteth to bring to pass all that we were unable to accomplish! Hither! fall we now furiously upon him: for we shall find none other season so favourable to perform the will of him that sent us.' Thus spake this crafty spirit to his hounds: and straightway they lept on that soldier of Christ, disquieting all the powers of his soul, inspiring him with vehement love for the damsel, and kindling within him the fiercest fire of lust.

Ioasaph, spurred on to sin by the evil spirits, is like to fall,

When Ioasaph saw that he was greatly inflamed, and was being led captive into sin, and perceived that his thoughts about the salvation of the damsel and her conversion to God had been set like bait on hook to hide the deed which she purposed, and were troubling him with the suggestion of the enemy, that, for the salvation of a soul, it was not sin for once to lie with a

but, viewing the pit before his feet, prayeth for deliverance

συγγενέσθαι, στενάξας ἐν ἀπορίᾳ ψυχῆς βύθιον
τι καὶ τετηκός, ἑαυτὸν εὐθὺς πρὸς εὐχὴν συντεί-
νει, καὶ ὀχετοὺς δακρύων ἐξ ὀφθαλμῶν δαψιλῶς
προχέων ἐβόα πρὸς τὸν δυνάμενον σώζειν τοὺς
Ps. xxxi. 1 ἐπ' αὐτῷ πεποιθότας· Ἐπὶ σοί, Κύριε, ἤλπισα·
Ps. xxv. 2 μὴ καταισχυνθείην εἰς τὸν αἰῶνα, μηδὲ κατα-
γελασάτωσάν με οἱ ἐχθροί μου, τὸν τῆς σῆς
ἐχόμενον δεξιᾶς· ἀλλὰ παράστηθί μοι ἐν τῇ
Ps. v. 8 ὥρᾳ ταύτῃ, καὶ κατὰ τὸ σὸν θέλημα εὔθυνον τὰς
ὁδούς μου, ἵνα δοξασθῇ τὸ ὄνομά σου τὸ ἔνδοξον
καὶ φοβερὸν ἐπ' ἐμοὶ τῷ οἰκέτῃ σου, ὅτι εὐλογητὸς εἶ εἰς τοὺς αἰῶνας. ἀμήν.

Ἐφ' ἱκανὰς δὲ ὥρας μετὰ δακρύων εὐξάμενος καὶ πολλὰ γονυκλιτήσας, καθῆκεν ἑαυτὸν ἐπὶ τοῦ ἐδάφους. καὶ ὑπνώσας μικρόν, ὁρᾷ ἑαυτὸν ὑπό τινων φοβερῶν ἁρπαγέντα, καὶ τόπους οὓς οὐδέποτε ἑωράκει διελθόντα, καὶ ἔν τινι γενόμενον μεγίστῃ πεδιάδι ὡραίοις ἄνθεσι καὶ λίαν εὐώδεσι κομώσῃ, ἔνθα φυτὰ μὲν ἑώρα παντοδαπὰ καὶ ποικίλα, καρποῖς ξένοις τισὶ καὶ θαυμασίοις βρίθοντα, ἰδεῖν τε ἡδίστοις καὶ ἅψασθαι ποθεινοῖς. τά τε φύλλα τῶν δένδρων λιγυρὸν ὑπήχει αὔρᾳ τινὶ λεπτοτάτῃ, καὶ ἀκόρεστον καὶ χαριεστάτην ἐκπέμποντα εὐωδίαν κινούμενα, θρόνοι τε ἀνέκειντο ἐκ καθαρωτάτου χρυσίου καὶ λίθων τιμίων κατεσκευασμένοι, λαμπρὰν οἵαν αἴγλην ἀφιέντες, καὶ κλῖναι ἐν ἐξάλλοις τισὶ στρωμναῖς καὶ τῷ κάλλει τὴν διήγησιν νικώσαις κατηγλαϊσμέναι. ὕδατά τε παρέρρει διαυγῆ λίαν καὶ αὐτὰς εὐφραίνοντα τὰς ὁράσεις. τὴν δὲ θαυμαστὴν ταύτην καὶ μεγάλην πεδιάδα οἱ φοβεροὶ ἐκεῖνοι διαγαγόντες αὐτὸν εἰς πόλιν εἰσήγαγον

woman, then in the agony of his soul he drew a deep and lamentable groan, and nerved himself to pray, and, with streams of tears running down his cheeks, he cried aloud to him that is able to save them that trust in him, saying, 'On thee, O Lord, have I set my trust: let me not be confounded for ever; neither let mine enemies triumph over me, that hold by thy right hand. But stand thou by me at this hour, and according to thy will make straight my path, that thy glorious and dreadful name may be glorified in me thy servant, because thou art blessed for ever. Amen.'

Ioasaph falling asleep, beholdeth in a vision the joy of the righteous,

Now when he had prayed in tears for many hours, and often bent the knee, he sunk down upon the pavement. After he had slumbered awhile, he saw himself carried off by certain dread men, and passing through places which he had never heretofore beheld. He stood in a mighty plain, all a-bloom with fresh and fragrant flowers, where he descried all manner of plants of divers colours, charged with strange and marvellous fruits, pleasant to the eye and inviting to the touch. The leaves of the trees rustled clearly in a gentle breeze, and, as they shook, sent forth a gracious perfume that cloyed not the sense. Thrones were set there, fashioned of the purest gold and costly stones, throwing out never so bright a lustre, and radiant settles among wondrous couches too beautiful to be described. And beside them there were running waters exceeding clear, and delightful to the eye. When these dread men had led him through this great and wondrous plain, they brought him to a city that

ἀρρήτῳ τινὶ λαμπρότητι ἀποστίλβουσαν, ἐκ χρυσίου μὲν διαυγοῦς τὰ τείχη, λίθων δὲ ὧν οὐδεὶς πώποτε ἑώρακε τὰς ἐπάλξεις ἔχουσαν ἀνεγηγερμένας. ὢ τίς ἂν ἐκείνης εἴποι τὸ κάλλος τῆς πόλεως καὶ τὴν φαιδρότητα; φῶς ἄνωθεν 281
πυκνὰ ταῖς ἀκτῖσι διᾳττον πάσας αὐτῆς τὰς πλατείας ἐπλήρου· καὶ ὑπόπτεροί τινες στρατιαί, αὐτὴ ἑκάστη φῶς οὖσαι, ταύτῃ ἐπεδήμουν, μέλος ᾄδουσαι ἀκοῇ βροτείᾳ μηδέποτε ἀκουσθέν. καὶ φωνῆς ἤκουσε λεγούσης· Αὕτη ἡ ἀνάπαυσις τῶν δικαίων· αὕτη ἡ εὐφροσύνη τῶν εὐαρεστησάντων τῷ Κυρίῳ. ἐκεῖθεν οὖν ἐξαγαγόντες οἱ φρικωδέστατοι ἄνδρες ἐκεῖνοι, εἰς τοὐπίσω ἄγειν ἔλεγον. ὁ δέ, τῆς τερπνότητος ἐκείνης καὶ θυμηδίας ὅλος γενόμενος, Μὴ στερήσητέ με, ἔλεγε, μὴ στερήσητε, δυσωπῶ, τῆς ἀρρήτου χαρᾶς ταύτης· ἀλλὰ δότε κἀμοὶ ἐν μιᾷ τῆς μεγίστης ταύτης πόλεως γωνίᾳ διαιτᾶσθαι. οἱ δέ, Ἀδύνατόν ἐστι νῦν, ἔλεγον, εἶναί σε ἐνταῦθα. ἀλλὰ κόπῳ πολλῷ καὶ ἱδρῶτι ἐλεύσῃ ὧδε, εἴπερ ἑαυτὸν βιάσῃ.

Ταῦτα εἶπον· καί, τὴν μεγίστην αὖθις πεδιάδα διελθόντες, εἰς τόπους ἀπήνεγκαν σκοτεινοὺς καὶ πάσης ἀηδίας πεπληρωμένους, ἰσόρροπον τῆς ὁραθείσης φαιδρότητος τὸ λυπηρὸν κεκτη-
Mat. viii. 12; xxii. 13 μένους. σκότος γὰρ ἦν ἀφεγγὲς καὶ ζοφερὸν
παντελῶς· θλίψεως δὲ καὶ ταραχῆς τὸ πᾶν
Is. lxvi. 24; ἐπεπλήρωτο. ἔνθα κάμινος ἐξῆπτε πυρὸς ἀνα-
Mk. ix. 43–46, 48 φλεγομένη· καὶ σκωλήκων γένος ἦν κολαστικῶν ἕρπον ἐκεῖσε. δυνάμεις δὲ τιμωρητικαὶ ἐφεστῶσαι τῇ καμίνῳ, καί τινες ἐλεεινῶς τῷ πυρὶ 282
κατακαιόμενοι. καὶ φωνὴ ἠκούετο λέγουσα· Οὗτος ὁ τόπος τῶν ἁμαρτωλῶν· αὕτη ἡ κόλασις

glistered with light unspeakable, whose walls were of dazzling gold, with high uprear'd parapets, built of gems such as man hath never seen. Ah! who could describe the beauty and brightness of that city? Light, ever shooting from above, filled all her streets with bright rays; and wingèd squadrons, each of them itself a light, dwelt in this city, making such melody as mortal ear ne'er heard. And Ioasaph heard a voice crying, 'This is the rest of the righteous: this the gladness of them that have pleased the Lord.' When these dread men had carried him out from thence, they spake of taking him back to earth. But he, that had lost his heart to that scene of joyaunce and heartsease, exclaimed, 'Reave me not, reave me not, I pray you, of this unspeakable joy, but grant me also to dwell in one corner of this mighty city.' But they said, 'It is impossible for thee to be there now; but, with much toil and sweat, thou shalt come hither, if thou constrain thyself.'

and the torment of sinners

Thus spake they; and again they crossed that mighty plain, and bare him to regions of darkness and utter woe, where sorrow matched the brightness which he had seen above. There was darkness without a ray of light, and utter gloom, and the whole place was full of tribulation and trouble. There blazed a glowing furnace of fire, and there crept the worm of torment. Revengeful powers were set over the furnace, and there were some that were burning piteously in the fire, and a voice was heard, saying, 'This is the place of sinners; this the punishment for

τῶν πράξεσιν αἰσχραῖς ἑαυτοὺς μολυνάντων·
ἐπὶ τούτοις ἐξήγαγον αὐτὸν ἐκεῖθεν οἱ καὶ εἰσαγαγόντες. καὶ εἰς ἑαυτὸν εὐθὺς ἐλθὼν ἔντρομος
ἦν ὅλος· δάκρυα δὲ ποταμηδὸν κατέδυον οἱ
ὀφθαλμοὶ αὐτοῦ. πᾶσα δὲ ἡ ὡραιότης τῆς ἀκο-
λάστου κόρης ἐκείνης καὶ τῶν λοιπῶν δυσωδεσ-
τέρα βορβόρου καὶ σαπρίας αὐτῷ λελόγιστο.
στρέφων δὲ ἐν τῇ ψυχῇ τῶν ὁραθέντων τὴν
μνήμην, τῷ πόθῳ τῶν ἀγαθῶν καὶ τῷ φόβῳ
τῶν ἀνιαρῶν ἐκείνων ἐπὶ τῆς κλίνης κατέκειτο
ἥκιστα ἐγερθῆναι δυνάμενος.

Ἀνηγγέλθη δὲ τῷ βασιλεῖ ἡ τοῦ υἱοῦ ἀρρω-
στία. καὶ ὃς ἐλθὼν ἐπηρώτα τί τὸ συμβάν.
ὁ δὲ τὰ ὁραθέντα αὐτῷ διηγεῖται, καί φησιν·
Ps. lvii. 7 Ἱνατί παγίδα ἡτοίμασας τοῖς ποσί μου, καὶ
Ps. xciv. 17 κατέκαμψας τὴν ψυχήν μου; εἰ μὴ γὰρ Κύριος
ἐβοήθησέ μοι, παραβραχὺ παρῴκησεν ἂν τῷ
Ps. lxxiii. 1 ᾅδῃ ἡ ψυχή μου. ἀλλ᾿ ὡς ἀγαθὸς ὁ Θεὸς τῷ
Ἰσραήλ, τοῖς εὐθέσι τῇ καρδίᾳ· ὃς καὶ τὴν ἐμὴν ἐρ-
Cp. Ps. lvii. 4 ρύσατο ταπείνωσιν ἐκ μέσου σκύμνων. ἐκοιμήθην
γὰρ τεταραγμένος. ἀλλ᾿ ἐπεσκέψατό με ἐξ ὕψους
ὁ Θεός μου καὶ Σωτήρ μου, καὶ ἔδειξέ μοι οἵων
ἀγαθῶν ἀπεστέρησαν ἑαυτοὺς οἱ παροργίζοντες
αὐτόν, οἵων δὲ κολάσεων ὑπευθύνους εἰργάσαντο.
καὶ νῦν, ὦ πάτερ, ἐπεί σου τὰ ὦτα ἔβυσας
τοῦ μὴ ἀκοῦσαί μου τῆς φωνῆς τῆς τὰ ἀγαθά
σοι ἐπᾳδούσης, κἂν ἐμὲ μὴ κώλυε τὴν εὐθεῖαν 283
βαδίσαι ὁδόν. τοῦτο γὰρ ποθῶ, τούτου ἐφίεμαι,
τοῦ πάντων ἀπαλλαγῆναι, καὶ τόπους καταλαβεῖν ἔνθα Βαρλαὰμ ὁ τοῦ Χριστοῦ θεράπων
τὰς οἰκήσεις ἔχει, καὶ σὺν αὐτῷ τὸ λοιπὸν τῆς
παρούσης μου διανῦσαι ζωῆς. εἰ δὲ βίᾳ κατα-

them that have defiled themselves by foul practices.' Hereupon Ioasaph was carried thence by his guides; and, when he came to himself, immediately he trembled from head to foot, and, like a river, his eyes dropped tears, and all the comeliness of that wanton damsel and her fellows was grown more loathsome to him than filth and rottenness. And as he mused in his heart on the memory of the visions, in longing for the good and in terror of the evil, he lay on his bed utterly unable to arise.

Ioasaph falleth sick and the king visiteth him

Then was the king informed of his son's sickness; and he came and asked what ailed him. And Ioasaph told him his vision, and said, 'Wherefore hast thou laid a net for my feet, and bowed down my soul? If the Lord had not helped me, my soul had well nigh dwelt in hell. But how loving is God unto Israel, even unto such as are of a true heart! He hath delivered me that am lowly from the midst of the dogs. For I was sore troubled and I fell on sleep: but God my Saviour from on high hath visited me, and showed me what joy they lose that provoke him and to what punishments they subject themselves. And now, O my father, since thou hast stopped thine ears not to hear the voice that will charm thee to good, at least forbid me not to walk the straight road. For this I desire, this I long for, to forsake all, and reach that place, where Barlaam the servant of Christ hath his dwelling, and with him to finish what remaineth of my life. But if thou keep me back by

σχεῖν με θελήσειας, ὄψει με θᾶττον τῇ λύπῃ καὶ ἀδημονίᾳ νεκρόν· καὶ οὔτε σὺ τὸ λοιπὸν πατὴρ κληθήσῃ, οὔτε υἱόν με ἔτι ἕξεις.

XXXI

Πάλιν οὖν ἀθυμία κατεσχε τὸν βασιλέα·
πάλιν ἀπελέγετο ὅλην αὐτοῦ τὴν ζωήν, καὶ
δεινὰ στρέφων ἐν ἑαυτῷ εἰς τὸ ἴδιον ἀπῄει παλάτιον. τὰ δὲ παρὰ τοῦ Θευδᾶ ἀποσταλέντα
τῆς πονηρίας πνεύματα κατὰ τοῦ θείου παιδός,
ἐπανελθόντα πρὸς αὐτόν, κατῃσχυμμένα τὴν
ἧτταν ἀνωμολόγει, καίτοι φιλοψευδῆ ὄντα· σύμ-
βολα γὰρ σαφῆ τῆς ἥττης ἔφερον ἐπὶ τῆς
πονηρᾶς αὐτῶν ὄψεως. ὁ δέ, Καὶ οὕτω, φησίν,
ἀσθενεῖς ὑμεῖς καὶ ταλαίπωροι, ὡς ἑνὸς μειρα-
κίου μὴ περιγενέσθαι; τότε τὰ πονηρὰ πνεύ-
Cyril, Cat. xiii. 140 ματα, θείᾳ δυνάμει τιμωρούμενα, εἰς φῶς ἄκοντα
τὴν ἀλήθειαν ἦγεν, Οὐχ ὑπομένομεν, λέγοντα,
οὐδὲ ἀντοφθαλμῆσαι ὅλως τῇ τοῦ Χριστοῦ
δυνάμει καὶ τῷ συμβόλῳ τοῦ πάθους αὐτοῦ, ὃν
σταυρὸν καλοῦσιν. ἐκείνου γὰρ τυπουμένου,
φθάνομεν ἀνακράτος φεύγοντές τε καὶ διωθού-
Eph. vi. 12 μενοι πάντες οἱ τοῦ ἀέρος ἄρχοντες καὶ κοσμο- 284
κράτορες τοῦ σκότους, πρὶν ἢ τελείως αὐτὸ
τυπωθῆναι. ὅθεν καὶ τῷ νεανίσκῳ τούτῳ ἐπιπε-
Prudentius, Cathem. 134 ff. σόντες δεινῶς ἐταράξαμεν· ὁ δέ, τὸν Χριστὸν
ἐπικαλεσάμενος εἰς συμμαχίαν καὶ τῷ σημείῳ
τοῦ σταυροῦ καθοπλίσας ἑαυτόν, ἡμᾶς τε διώ-
σατο μετ᾽ ὀργῆς καὶ ἀσφάλειαν ἑαυτῷ ἔθετο.
μὴ μελλήσαντες οὖν εὕρομεν ὄργανον, δι᾽ οὗ καὶ

force, thou shalt quickly see me die of grief and despair, and thou shalt be no more called father, nor have me to thy son.'

XXXI

Again therefore the king was seized with despondency, and again he was like to abjure his whole way of life; and with strange thoughts he went again unto his own palace. But the evil spirits, that had been sent out by Theudas for to attack the young saint, returned to him, and, lovers of leasing though they were, confessed their shameful defeat, for they bare visible tokens of their defeat, upon their evil countenance. Said Theudas, 'And be ye so weak and puny that ye cannot get the better of one young stripling?' Then did the evil spirits, constrained, to their sorrow, by the might of God, bring to light the truth, saying, 'We cannot abide even the sight of the might of Christ, and the symbol of his Passion, which they call the Cross. For, when that sign is made, immediately all we, the princes of the air, and the rulers of the darkness of the world, are utterly routed and discomfited, even before the sign is completed. When we first fell upon this youth, we vexed him sore; but when he called on Christ for help, and armed him with the sign of the Cross, he routed us in angry wise, and stablished himself in safety. So incontinent we found a weapon, wherewith our chief

The foul fiends report to Theudas their own defeat

τῷ πρωτοπλάστῳ ὁμιλήσας ποτὲ ὁ ἄρχων ἡμῶν τοῦτον ἐχειρώσατο. καὶ δὴ παρ' οὐδὲν ἐθέμεθα ἂν καὶ ἡμεῖς κενὴν τὴν ἐλπίδα τοῦ νέου, ἀλλ' ἐπικληθεὶς αὖθις ὁ Χριστὸς εἰς συμμαχίαν, πυρὶ τῆς ἄνωθεν ὀργῆς ἡμᾶς καταφλέξας, φυγάδας εἰργάσατο. καὶ ἔγνωμεν μηκέτι πλησιάσαι αὐτῷ. οὕτω μὲν οὖν τὰ πονηρὰ πνεύματα σαφῶς ἐγνώρισε τῷ Θευδᾷ τὰ γεγενημένα.

Ὁ δὲ βασιλεύς, πάντοθεν ἀπορούμενος, τὸν Θευδᾶν αὖθις προσκαλεῖται, καί φησι· Τὰ μὲν δεδογμένα σοι, σοφώτατε, πάντα πληρώσαντες, οὐδεμίαν τὴν ὠφέλειαν εὕρομεν· νυνὶ δέ, εἴ τίς σοι ἑτέρα ὑπολέλειπται ἐπίνοια, κἀκείνης πεῖραν 285
ληψόμεθα· ἴσως εὕρω τινὰ τοῦ κακοῦ λύσιν.

Αἰτησαμένου δὲ τοῦ Θευδᾶ εἰς ὁμιλίαν ἐλθεῖν τοῦ υἱοῦ, ἕωθεν συμπαραλαβὼν αὐτόν, ὁ βασιλεὺς εἰς ἐπίσκεψιν ἀπέρχεται τοῦ υἱοῦ. καὶ καθίσας λόγους ἐκίνησεν ὁ βασιλεύς, ὀνειδίζων αὐτὸν καὶ μεμφόμενος ἐπὶ τῇ ἀνηκοΐᾳ αὐτοῦ καὶ ἀνενδότῳ γνώμῃ. ἐκείνου δὲ τὰ αὐτὰ αὖθις βεβαιοῦντος καὶ μηδὲν προτιμᾶν τῆς Χριστοῦ ἀγάπης βοῶντος, παρελθὼν εἰς μέσον, ὁ Θευδᾶς ἔφη· Τί κατέγνως, ὦ Ἰωάσαφ, τῶν ἀθανάτων ἡμῶν θεῶν, ὅτι τῆς αὐτῶν ἀπέστης λατρείας, καί, τὸν σὸν πατέρα καὶ βασιλέα οὕτως παροργίζων, μισητὸς παντὶ γέγονας τῷ λαῷ; οὐχὶ παρ' αὐτῶν σοι τὸ ζῆν; οὐκ αὐτοὶ παρέσχον σε τῷ πατρί, τῆς αὐτοῦ ἀκούσαντες εὐχῆς καὶ τῶν τῆς ἀτεκνίας δεσμῶν λυτρωσάμενοι; πολλὰς δὲ ματαιολογίας καὶ ἀνωφελεῖς προτάσεις ὁ ἐν κακοῖς γηράσας προβαλλόμενος, καὶ συλλογισμοὺς ῥάπτων περὶ τοῦ κηρύγματος τοῦ

did once confront the first-made man and prevailed against him. And verily we should have made this young man's hope vain; but again Christ was called on for help, and he consumed us in the fire of his wrath from above, and put us to flight. We have determined to approach the prince no more.' Thus, then, did the evil spirits plainly make known unto Theudas all that was come to pass.

Theudas, again besought by the king, visiteth Ioasaph and argueth with him

But the king, perplexed on every side, again summoned Theudas, and said, 'Most wisest of men, all that seemed good to thee have we fulfilled, but have found no help therein. But now, if thou hast any device left, we will make trial thereof. Peradventure I shall find some escape from this evil.'

Then did Theudas ask for a meeting with his son; and on the morrow the king took him and went forth to visit the prince. The king sat down and provoked debate, upbraiding and chiding him for his disobedience and stubbornness of mind. When Ioasaph again maintained his case, and loudly declared that he valued nothing so much as the love of Christ, Theudas came forward and said, 'Wherefore, Ioasaph, dost thou despise our immortal gods, that thou hast departed from their worship, and, thus incensing thy father the king, art become hateful to all the people? Dost thou not owe thy life to the gods? And did they not present thee to the king in answer to his prayer, thus redeeming him from the bondage of childlessness?' While this Theudas, waxen old in wickedness, was putting forth these many vain arguments and useless propositions, and weaving words about the preaching of the Gospel,

Εὐαγγελίου, βουλόμενος τοῦτο μὲν χλευάζειν,
τὰ δὲ τῶν εἰδώλων κρατύνειν, ὀλίγον ἐπισχὼν
Heb. viii. 2 ὁ τῆς ἄνω βασιλείας υἱός, καὶ τῆς πόλεως
ἐκείνης πολίτης ἣν ἔπηξεν ὁ Κύριος καὶ οὐκ
ἄνθρωπος, φησὶ πρὸς τὸν Θευδᾶν.
Exod. x. 21 Ἄκουσον, ὦ πλάνης βυθὲ καὶ ψηλαφητοῦ
σκότους ζοφωδέστερε, τὸ Βαβυλώνιον σπέρμα,
τὸ τῆς Χαλανικῆς[1] πυργοποιΐας ἔκγονον, δι' ἧς
ὁ κόσμος συνεχύθη, ματαιόφρον καὶ ἄθλιε γέ-
Gen. xix. 24 ρον, οὗπερ καὶ ἡ πυρὶ καὶ θείῳ κατακαυθεῖσα 286
Jude 7 πεντάπολις ἐλαφροτέρα τοῖς ἁμαρτήμασι γέγονε. τί χλευάζειν ἐπιχειρεῖς τὸ τῆς σωτηρίας
κήρυγμα, δι' ἧς τὰ ἐσκοτισμένα ἐφωτίσθη, δι'
ἧς οἱ πεπλανημένοι τὴν ὁδὸν εὗρον, δι' ἧς οἱ
ἀπολωλότες καὶ δεινῶς αἰχμαλωτισθέντες ἀνε-
κλήθησαν; τί κρεῖττον, εἰπέ μοι, Θεῷ λατρεύειν
παντοκράτορι σὺν Υἱῷ μονογενεῖ καὶ Πνεύματι
Ἁγίῳ, Θεῷ ἀκτίστῳ καὶ ἀθανάτῳ, τῇ ἀρχῇ καὶ
πηγῇ τῶν ἀγαθῶν, οὗ τὸ κράτος ἀνείκαστον
Dan. vii. 10 καὶ ἡ δόξα ἀκατάληπτος, ᾧ παρειστήκεισαν
χίλιαι χιλιάδες καὶ μύριαι μυριάδες ἀγγελικῶν
ταγμάτων καὶ οὐρανίων, καὶ πλήρης ὁ οὐρανὸς
καὶ ἡ γῆ τῆς δόξης αὐτοῦ, δι' οὗ τὰ πάντα ἐκ
τοῦ μὴ ὄντος παρήχθη, δι' οὗ κρατεῖται τὸ πᾶν
καὶ συνέχεται καὶ τῇ προνοίᾳ αὐτοῦ διοικεῖται,
τούτῳ βέλτιον λατρεύειν, ἢ δαίμοσι ὀλεθρίοις
καὶ ἀψύχοις εἰδώλοις, ὧν ἡ δόξα καὶ ὁ ἔπαινος
μοιχεία ἐστὶ καὶ παιδοφθορία καὶ τὰ λοιπὰ τῆς
ἀνομίας ἔργα, ἃ περὶ τῶν ὑμετέρων ἀναγέγρα-
πται θεῶν ἐν τοῖς συντάγμασι τῆς δεισιδαιμο-

[1] Οὐκ ἔλαβον τὴν χώραν τὴν ἐπάνω Βαβυλῶνος καὶ Χαλαννή, οὗ ὁ πύργος ᾠκοδομήθη; Is. x. 9 (Sept.) and Gen. xi. 9.

desiring to turn it into mockery, and magnify idolatry, Ioasaph, the son of the heavenly king, and citizen of that city which the Lord hath builded and not man, waited a while and then said unto him,

'Give ear, thou abyss of error, blacker than the darkness that may be felt, thou seed of Babylon, child of the building of the tower of Chalané, whereby the world was confounded, foolish and pitiable dotard, whose sins out-weigh the iniquity of the five cities that were destroyed by fire and brimstone. Why wouldest thou mock at the preaching of salvation, whereby darkness hath been made light, the wanderers have found the way, they that were lost in dire captivity have been recalled. Tell me whether is better? To worship God Almighty, with the only-begotten Son and the Holy Ghost, God increate and immortal, the beginning and well-spring of good, whose power is beyond compare, and his glory incomprehensible, before whom stand thousand thousands, and ten thousand times ten thousand of Angels and heavenly hosts, and heaven and earth are full of his glory, by whom all things were brought into being out of nothing, by whom everything is upheld and sustained and ordered by his providence; or to serve deadly devils and lifeless idols, whose glory and boast is in adultery and the corrupting of boys, and other works of iniquity that have been recorded concerning your gods in the books of your superstition? Have ye no

Ioasaph denounceth the wickedness of Theudas, convicting

νίας ὑμῶν; οὐκ αἰδεῖσθε, ταλαίπωροι, πυρὸς
ἀκοιμήτου βορά, ὁμοίωμα γένους Χαλδαϊκοῦ,
Cp. Is. xliv. 8-20 οὐκ αἰσχύνεσθε νεκρὰ ξόανα προσκυνοῦντες, χει- 287
ρὸς ἀνθρωπίνης ἔργα; λίθον γὰρ λαξεύσαντες
ἢ ξύλον τεκτονεύσαντες, θεὸν προσηγορεύσατε·
εἶτα τὸν κάλλιστον ἐκ βουκολίων ταῦρον λαβόν-
τες, ἢ ἄλλο τυχὸν τῶν εὐπρεπεστάτων ζῴων,
νεκρῷ σεβάσματι θύετε ἀνόητοι. τιμιώτερόν
ἐστί σου τοῦ σεβάσματος τὸ θῦμα· τὸ μὲν γὰρ
ξόανον ἄνθρωπος ἐποίησε, τὸ δὲ ζῷον ὁ Θεὸς
ἐδημιούργησε. καὶ πόσον σοῦ μᾶλλον τοῦ λογι-
κοῦ συνετώτερόν ἐστι τὸ ἄλογον ζῷον; τὸ μὲν
Is. i. 3 γὰρ οἶδε τὸν τρέφοντα· σὺ δὲ τὸν Θεὸν ἠγνόησας,
δι' οὗ ἐκ τοῦ μὴ ὄντος παρήχθης, δι' οὗ ζῇς καὶ
συντετήρησαι, καὶ καλεῖς θεόν, ὃν πρὸ μικροῦ
ἔβλεπες σιδήρῳ τυπτόμενον καὶ πυρὶ καιόμενόν
τε καὶ χωνευόμενον, καὶ σφύραις ἐλαυνόμενον, ὃν
ἄργυρον καὶ χρυσὸν περιέθηκας καὶ χαμόθεν
ὑψώσας ἐφ' ὑψηλοῦ μετεώρισας· εἶτα, πεσὼν
ἐπὶ τῆς γῆς, τοῦ ταπεινοῦ λίθου κεῖσαι ταπεινό-
τερος, προσκυνῶν οὐ Θεὸν ἀλλὰ τὰ ἔργα τῶν
χειρῶν σου τὰ νεκρὰ καὶ ἄψυχα. μᾶλλον δὲ 288
οὐδὲ νεκρὸν ἂν εἴη δίκαιον καλεῖσθαι τὸ εἴδωλον.
πῶς γὰρ ἂν νεκρὸν εἴη τὸ μηδέποτε ζῆσαν; ἀλλά
τι καινὸν ἔδει ἐφευρεῖν αὐτῷ ὄνομα καὶ τῆς τοσαύτης παραφροσύνης ἐπάξιον. ὁ μὲν γὰρ λίθινος
θρύπτεται, ὁ δὲ ὀστράκινος κατάγνυται, ὁ χαλ-
κοῦς ἰοῦται, ὁ χρυσοῦς καὶ ὁ ἀργυροῦς χωνεύεται.
ἀλλὰ καὶ πιπράσκονται οἱ θεοί σου, οἱ μὲν
εὐώνως, οἱ δὲ τιμῆς ὅτι πλείστης. οὐχ ἡ θεότης
γὰρ αὐτοῖς, ἀλλ' ἡ ὕλη τὴν πολυτέλειαν δίδωσι.
Θεὸν δὲ τίς ἀγοράζει; Θεὸν τίς πωλεῖ; θεὸς δὲ

modesty, ye miserable men, fuel for unquenchable fire, true copy of the Chaldean race, have ye no shame to worship dead images, the works of men's hands? Ye have carvèd stone and graven wood and called it God. Next ye take the best bullock out of your folds, or (may be) some other of your fairest beasts, and in your folly make sacrifice to your dead divinity. Your sacrifice is of more value than your idol; for the image was fashioned by man, but the beast was created by God. How much wiser is the unreasonable beast than thou the reasonable man? For it knoweth the hand that feedeth it, but thou knowest not that God by whom thou wast created out of nothing, by whom thou livest, and art preserved; and thou callest God that which thou sawest, but now, smitten by steel, and burnt and moulded in the fire, and beaten with hammers, which thou hast covered around with silver and gold, and raised from the ground, and set on high. Then, falling upon the earth, thou liest baser than the base stone, worshipping not God but thine own dead and lifeless handiwork. Or rather, the idol hath no right to be called even dead, for how can that have died which never lived? Thou shouldest invent some new name worthy of such madness. Thy stone god is broken asunder; thy potsherd god shattered; thy brazen god rusteth; thy gold or silver god is melted down. Aye, and thy gods are sold, some for a paltry, others for a great price. Not their divinity but their material giveth them value. But who buyeth God? Who offereth God for sale? And

him of all the follies of idolatry.

ἀκίνητος πῶς ὀνομάζεται θεός; ἢ οὐχ ὁρᾷς ὅτι ὁ μὲν ἑστὼς οὐδέποτε καθέζεται, ὁ δὲ καθεζόμενος οὐδέποτε ἀνίσταται;

Αἰσχύνθητι, ἀνόητε, χεῖρα θὲς ἐπὶ στόματι σῷ, μεμωραμένε, τὰ τοιαῦτα ἐπαινῶν. τῆς ἀληθείας γὰρ ἀλλοτριωθείς, ψευδέσι τύποις ἐπλανήθης, ἀγάλματα πλάττων, καὶ τοῖς ἔργοις τῶν χειρῶν σου Θεοῦ περιτιθεὶς ὄνομα. ἀνάνηψον, ἄθλιε, καὶ σύνες ὅτι πρεσβύτερος εἶ τοῦ ὑπὸ σοῦ γενομένου θεοῦ. ταῦτα πολλῆς ἐστι μανίας. πέπεικας δὲ σαυτόν, ἄνθρωπος ὤν, Θεὸν δύνασθαι ποιεῖν. καὶ πῶς ἐνδέχεται τοῦτο γενέσθαι; ὥστε οὐ Θεὸν ποιεῖς, ἀλλὰ μόρφωμα ἀνθρώπου ἢ ζῴου τινός, μὴ γλῶσσαν ἔχον, μὴ λάρυγγα, μὴ ἐγκέφαλον, μήτε τῶν ἐντός τι· ὥστε οὔτε ἀνθρώπου ἐστὶν ὁμοίωμα, οὔτε ζῴου, ἀλλ' ἄχρηστον πάντη καὶ ματαιότητος πλῆρες. τί οὖν τὰ ἀναίσθητα κολακεύεις; τί τοῖς ἀκινήτοις καὶ ἀνωφελέσι προσκάθησαι; εἰ μὴ τέχνη παρῆν τοῦ λιθοξόου ἢ τοῦ τέκτονος ἢ τοῦ σφυροκόπου, θεὸν οὐκ ἂν εἶχες. εἰ μὴ φύλακες παρεκάθηντο, ἀπώλεσας ἂν τὸν θεόν σου. ᾧ γὰρ
πολλάκις πόλις πολυάνθρωπος ἀφρόνων εὔχεται 289
ὡς θεῷ διαφυλαχθῆναι, τούτῳ ὀλίγοι παραμένουσι φύλακες ἵνα μὴ κλαπῇ. καὶ εἰ μὲν ἀργυροῦς ἢ χρυσοῦς ἔσται, ἐπιμελῶς φυλάσσεται· ἐὰν δὲ ᾖ λίθινος ἢ πήλινος, ἢ ἄλλης τινὸς τοιαύτης εὐτελεστέρας ὕλης, ἑαυτὸν φυλάσσει· ἰσχυρότερος γὰρ ἴσως ἐστὶν ὁ πήλινος τοῦ χρυσοῦ καθ' ὑμᾶς.

Οὐκ εἰκότως ἐστὶν ὑμᾶς τοὺς ἄφρονας, τυφλοὺς καὶ ἀσυνέτους, δικαίως καταγελᾶσθαι, μᾶλλον δὲ πενθεῖσθαι; μανίας γὰρ τὰ ἔργα ὑμῶν, οὐκ εὐσε-

how is that god that cannot move called God? Seest thou not that the god that standeth cannot sit, and the god that sitteth cannot stand?

'Be ashamed, thou fool, and lay thine hand upon thy mouth, thou victim of folly, that commendest such things as these. Estranged from the truth, thou hast been led astray by false images, fashioning statues and attaching to the works of thine own hands the name of God. O wretched man, return to thy senses, and learn that thou art older than the god made by thee. This is downright madness. Being a man, thou hast persuaded thyself that thou canst make God. How can this be? Thou makest not God, but the likeness of a man, or of some beast, sans tongue, sans throat, sans brains, sans inwards, so that it is the similitude neither of a man, nor of a beast, but only a thing of no use and sheer vanity. Why therefore flatterest thou things that cannot feel? Why sittest thou at the feet of things that cannot move and help thee? But for the skill of the mason, or timber-wright, or hammer-smith, thou hadst not had a god. Had there been no warders nigh at hand, thou hadst lost thy god. He, to whom many a populous city of fools prayeth as God to guard it, the same hath suite of guards at hand to save him from being stolen. And if he be of silver or gold, he is carefully guarded; but if of stone or clay or any other less costly ware, he guardeth himself, for with you, no doubt, a god of clay is stronger than one of gold.

and of worshipping lifeless and helpless images

'Do we not, then, well to laugh you to scorn, or rather to weep over you, as men blind and without understanding? Your deeds are deeds of madness

Ioasaph showeth that idols are naught

βείας ἐστίν. ὁ μὲν γὰρ πόλεμον ἀσκήσας, στρατιωτικῆς ἀντίμιμον ἰδέας ξόανον ἱδρύσας, ἐκάλεσεν Ἄρην· ὁ δὲ γυναικομανοῦς ἐπιθυμίας τὴν ψυχὴν ἀνατυπωσάμενος, ἐθεοποίησε τὸ πάθος, Ἀφροδίτην προσαγορεύσας. ἄλλος, τῆς ἑαυτοῦ φιλοινίας ἕνεκεν, ἔπλασεν εἴδωλον, ὅπερ ἐκάλεσε Διόνυσον. ὁμοίως δὲ καὶ τῶν ἄλλων κακῶν ἐπιθυμηταὶ τῶν ἰδίων παθῶν ἔστησαν εἴδωλα· τὰ πάθη γὰρ αὐτῶν θεοὺς ὠνόμασαν. καὶ διὰ τοῦτο παρὰ τοῖς αὐτῶν βωμοῖς ἡδυπαθεῖς εἰσιν ὀρχήσεις, πορνικῶν ᾀσμάτων ἦχοι καὶ μανιώδεις ὁρμαί. τίς δὲ αὐτῶν καθεξῆς τὴν βδελυρὰν ἐξείποι πρᾶξιν; τίς ἀνέξεται, τὰς ἐκείνων αἰσχρολογίας καταλέγων, τὸ ἑαυτοῦ μολῦναι στόμα; ἀλλὰ πᾶσι δῆλα, κἂν ἡμεῖς σιωπῶμεν. ταῦτά σου τὰ σεβάσματα, Θευδᾶ τῶν ξοάνων σου ἀναισθητότερε, τούτοις με ἐπιτρέπεις προσκυνεῖν, ταῦτα σέβεσθαι. τῆς σῆς ὄντως κακουργίας καὶ
Ps. cxiv. 8 ἀσυνέτου γνώμης ἡ βουλή· ἀλλ' ὅμοιος αὐτῶν γένοιο, σύ τε καὶ πάντες οἱ πεποιθότες ἐπ' αὐτοῖς.

Ἐγὼ δὲ τῷ Θεῷ μου λατρεύσω, καὶ αὐτῷ 290
θύσω ὅλον ἐμαυτόν, τῷ Θεῷ τῷ κτίστῃ καὶ
προνοητῇ τῶν ἁπάντων διὰ τοῦ Κυρίου ἡμῶν
1 Tim. i. 1 Ἰησοῦ Χριστοῦ τῆς ἐλπίδος ἡμῶν, δι' οὗ τὴν
Eph. ii. 18 προσαγωγὴν ἐσχήκαμεν πρὸς τὸν Πατέρα τῶν
Jas. i. 17 φώτων ἐν Πνεύματι Ἁγίῳ, δι' οὗ ἐξηγοράσθημεν
τῆς πικρᾶς δουλείας ἐν τῷ αἵματι αὐτοῦ. εἰ μὴ
Phil. ii. 7, 8 γὰρ ἐταπείνωσεν ἑαυτὸν μέχρι καὶ δούλου μορφῆς,
Gal. iv. 4 οὐκ ἂν ἡμεῖς τῆς υἱοθεσίας ἠξιώθημεν. ἐτα-
Phil. ii. 6 πεινώθη γοῦν δι' ἡμᾶς, οὐχ ἁρπαγμὸν ἡγούμενος
τὴν θεότητα,[1] ἀλλ' ὃ ἦν διέμεινε, καὶ ὃ οὐκ ἦν

[1] Τουτέστιν οὐκ ἀπηξίωσεν ὡς ἄνθρωπος ὑπακοῦσαι, *Max. Conf.* Schol. 57D.

and not of piety. Your man of war maketh to himself an image after the similitude of a warrior, and calleth it Ares. And the lecher, making a symbol of his own soul, deifieth his vice and calleth it Aphrodite. Another, in honour of his own love of wine, fashioneth an idol which he calleth Dionysus. Likewise lovers of all other evil things set up idols of their own lusts; for they name their lusts their gods. And therefore, before their altars, there are lascivious dances, and strains of lewd songs and mad revelries. Who could recount in order their abominable doings? Who could endure to defile his lips by the repeating of their filthy communications? But these are manifest to all, even if we hold our peace. These be thine objects of worship, O Theudas, who art more senseless than thine idols. Before these thou biddest me fall down and worship. This verily is the counsel of thine iniquity and senseless mind. But thou thyself shalt be like unto them, and all such as put their trust in them.

but the images of men's vices

'As for me, I will serve my God, and to him will I wholly sacrifice myself, to God, the Creator and protector of all things through our Lord Jesus Christ, my hope, by whom we have access unto the Father of lights, in the Holy Ghost: by whom we have been redeemed from bitter slavery by his blood. For if he had not humbled himself so far as to take the form of a servant, we had not received the adoption of sons. But he humbled himself for our sake, not considering the Godhead a thing to be grasped, but he remained that which he was, and took

He rebuffeth the attacks made by Theudas on the Faith.

Cp. Baruch. iii. 28 προσέλαβεν, ὡμίλησε τοῖς ἀνθρώποις, ἀνῆλθεν
Mat. xii. 40 ἐν τῷ σταυρῷ τῇ σαρκὶ αὐτοῦ, ἐτέθη τάφῳ
1 Pet. iii. 18–20 ἐπὶ τρισὶν ἡμέραις, κατῆλθεν ἐν τῷ ᾅδῃ, καὶ
Eph. iv. 8 ἐξήγαγεν οὓς κατεῖχε δεσμίους ὁ δεινὸς κοσμο-
κράτωρ πεπραμένους ὑπὸ τῆς ἁμαρτίας. τίς
Cp. Greg. Naz. Orat. xxxviii. p. 672 οὖν ἐγένετο βλάβη αὐτῷ ἐκ τούτων, ὅ τι χλευάζειν δοκεῖς; οὐχ ὁρᾷς τὸν ἥλιον τοῦτον, πό-
σοις καταπέμπει τὴν ἀκτῖνα τόποις ἀχρήστοις
καὶ ῥυπαροῖς; πόσα ἐπιβλέπει σώματα νεκρῶν
ὀδωδότα; μή τις αὐτῷ προστρίβεται μῶμος; οὐ 291
τὰ ῥυπαρὰ μὲν καὶ σεσηπότα ξηραίνει καὶ συ-
σφίγγει, τὰ ἐσκοτισμένα δὲ φωτίζει, καὶ αὐτὸς
ἀσινὴς πάντη καὶ ἀνεπίδεκτος παντὸς ὑπάρχει
ῥύπου; τί δὲ τὸ πῦρ; οὐ τὸν σίδηρον μέλανα
λαβὼν ἐν ἑαυτῷ καὶ ψυχρόν, φλογοειδῆ ὅλον καὶ
πεπυρακτωμένον ἐργάζεται; μή τι μετέλαβε τῶν
ἰδιωμάτων τοῦ σιδήρου; μή, τυπτομένου τοῦ
σιδήρου σφύραις καὶ μαστιζομένου, πάσχει τι τὸ
πῦρ ἢ βλάβην ὅλως ὑφίσταται;

Εἰ οὖν τὰ κτιστὰ ταῦτα καὶ φθαρτὰ οὐδὲν ἀπὸ τῆς κοινωνίας τῶν εὐτελεστέρων πάσχειν πέφυκε, τίνι λόγῳ, ἀνόητε σὺ καὶ λιθοκάρδιε, χλευάζειν με τολμᾷς λέγοντα ὅτι ὁ υἱὸς καὶ λόγος τοῦ Θεοῦ, οὐδόλως ἐκστὰς τῆς πατρικῆς δόξης, ἀλλ' ὁ αὐτὸς ὢν Θεός, ἐπὶ σωτηρίᾳ τῶν ἀνθρώπων ἀνείληφε σῶμα ἀνθρώπινον, ἵνα τοὺς ἀνθρώπους κοινωνοὺς ποιήσῃ τῆς θείας καὶ νοερᾶς φύσεως, καὶ ἐκ τῶν καταχθονίων τοῦ ᾅδου ἐξ-αγαγὼν τὴν ἡμῶν οὐσίαν, τῇ οὐρανίῳ τιμήσῃ δόξῃ ἵνα τὸν ἄρχοντα τοῦ σκότους τοῦ αἰῶνος τούτου, τῇ προσλήψει τῆς σαρκὸς δελεάσας, χειρώσηται, καὶ τὸ γένος ἡμῶν τῆς αὐτοῦ τυραννίδος ἐλευθερώσειεν. ἔνθεν τοι καὶ ἀπαθῶς προσ-

on himself that which he was not, and conversed with men, and mounted the Cross in his flesh, and was laid in the sepulchre by the space of three days; he descended into hell, and brought out from thence them whom the fierce prince of this world held prisoners, sold into bondage by sin. What harm then befell him thereby that thou thinkest to make mock of him? Seest thou not yonder sun, into how many a barren and filthy place he darteth his rays? Upon how many a stinking corpse doth he cast his eye? Hath he therefore any stain of reproach? Doth he not dry and shrivel up filth and rottenness, and give light to dark places, himself the while unharmed and incapable of receiving any defilement? And what of fire? Doth it not take iron, which is black and cold in itself, and work it into white heat and harden it? Doth it receive any of the properties of the iron? When the iron is smitten and beaten with hammers is the fire any the worse, or doth it in any way suffer harm?

'If, then, these created and corruptible things take no hurt from contact with things commoner than themselves, with what reason dost thou, O foolish and stony-hearted man, presume to mock at me for saying that the Son, the Word of God, never departing from the Father's glory, but remaining the same God, for the salvation of men hath taken upon him the flesh of man, to the end that he may make men partakers of his divine and intelligent nature and may lead our substance out of the nether parts of hell, and honour it with heavenly glory; to the end that by taking of our flesh he may ensnare and defeat the ruler of the darkness of this world, and free our race from his tyranny. Wherefore, I tell thee, without suffering

and asserteth the glory of Jesus Christ

ομιλεῖ τῷ πάθει τοῦ σταυροῦ, τὰς δύο παριστῶν φύσεις αὐτοῦ· ὡς μὲν γὰρ ἄνθρωπος σταυροῦται,
Mat xxvii. 45 ff. ὡς θεὸς δὲ σκοτίζει τὸν ἥλιον, κλονεῖ τὴν γῆν, καὶ πολλὰ κεκοιμημένα ἐγείρει σώματα ἐκ τῶν μνημάτων· πάλιν ὡς ἄνθρωπος θνήσκει, ὡς δὲ 292
θεὸς ἐξανίσταται σκυλεύσας τὸν ᾅδην. διὸ καὶ
Is. xiv. 9 κέκραγεν ὁ προφήτης· Ὁ ᾅδης ἐπικράνθη συναντήσας σοι κάτω. ἐπικράνθη γὰρ καὶ ἐνεπαίχθη ἄνθρωπον δοκῶν λαβεῖν ψιλόν, τῷ Θεῷ δὲ περιτυχών, καὶ κενὸς ἐξαίφνης γεγονὼς καὶ αἰχμάλωτος. ἐγείρεται τοιγαροῦν ὡς Θεός, καὶ ἀνέρχεται εἰς οὐρανούς, ὅθεν οὐδαμῶς ἐχωρίσθη. καὶ τὴν φύσιν ἡμῶν τὴν εὐτελῆ, τὴν πάντων ἀσυνετωτέραν, τὴν ἀγνώμονα καὶ ἠτιμωμένην, τῶν πάντων ἀνωτέραν πεποίηκε, καὶ ἐπὶ θρόνου δόξης ἐνίδρυσε, δόξης ἀποστίλβουσαν ἀθανάτου. τίς οὖν αὐτῷ τῷ Θεῷ καὶ λόγῳ προσεγένετο ἐντεῦθεν βλάβη, ὅτι βλασφημεῖν οὐκ ἐρυθριᾷς; τί δέ; βέλτιον ταῦτα ὁμολογεῖν, καὶ τοιοῦτον σέβεσθαι Θεόν, ἀγαθὸν καὶ φιλάνθρωπον, ὃς ἐντέλλεται δικαιοσύνην, ἐγκράτειαν ἐπιτάσσει, καθαρότητα νομοθετεῖ, ἐλεεῖν διδάσκει, πίστιν παρέχει, εἰρήνην κηρύσσει, αὐτοαλήθεια ὀνομάζεται καὶ ἔστιν, αὐτοαγάπη, αὐτοαγαθότης· τοῦτον βέλτιον σέβεσθαι ἢ τοὺς θεούς σου, τοὺς πολυπαθεῖς καὶ κακούς, τοὺς αἰσχροὺς καὶ τοῖς πράγμασι καὶ τοῖς ὀνόμασιν; οὐαὶ ὑμῖν, τῶν λίθων λιθωδέστεροι καὶ τῶν ἀλόγων ἀλογώτεροι, τῆς ἀπωλείας υἱοί, τοῦ σκότους κληρονόμοι· μακάριος δὲ ἐγὼ καὶ πάντες οἱ Χριστιανοί, Θεὸν ἔχοντες ἀγαθὸν καὶ φιλάνθρωπον. οἱ γὰρ αὐτῷ λατρεύοντες, κἂν ὀλίγον χρόνον ἐν τῷ νῦν βίῳ κακο-

he met the suffering of the Cross, presenting therein his two natures. For, as man, he was crucified; but, as God, he darkened the sun, shook the earth, and raised from their graves many bodies that had fallen asleep. Again, as man, he died; but, as God, after that he had harried hell, he rose again. Wherefore also the prophet cried, Hell is in bitterness at having met thee below: for it was put to bitter derision, supposing that it had received a mere man, but finding God, and being made suddenly empty and led captive. Therefore, as God, he rose again, and ascended into heaven, from whence he was never parted. And our nature, so worthless and senseless beyond everything, so graceless and dishonoured, hath he made higher than all things, and established it upon a throne of honour, with immortal honour shining round. What harm therefore came to God, the Word, that thou blasphemest without a blush? Go to! Better were it to make this confession, and to worship such a God, who is good and a lover of mankind, who commandeth righteousness, enjoineth continency, ordaineth chastity, teacheth mercy, giveth faith, preacheth peace; who is called and is himself the very truth, the very love, the very goodness. Him were it not better to worship than thy gods of many evil passions, of shameful names and shameful lives? Woe unto you that are more stony-hearted than the stones, and more senseless than the senseless, sons of perdition, inheritors of darkness! But blessed am I, and all Christian folk, having a good God and a lover of mankind! They that serve him, though, for a season in this life they endure evil,

Ioasaph glorieth in his Faith

παθήσωσιν, ἀλλὰ τὸν ἀθάνατον τῆς ἀνταποδόσεως καρπὸν τρυγήσουσιν ἐν τῇ βασιλείᾳ τῆς 293
ἀτελευτήτου καὶ θείας μακαριότητος.

XXXII

Ἔφη δὲ πρὸς αὐτὸν ὁ Θευδᾶς· Ἰδοὺ φανερόν ἐστιν, ὅτι τὴν καθ' ἡμᾶς θρησκείαν πολλοὶ καὶ μεγάλοι σοφοί, καὶ ἐξηγηταί, καὶ θαυμαστοὶ τὴν ἀρετὴν καὶ ἐπιστήμην, ἐνομοθέτησαν, καὶ πάντες οἱ βασιλεῖς τῆς γῆς καὶ δυνάσται ὡς καλὴν καὶ μηδὲν σφαλερὸν ἔχουσαν ἐδέξαντο, τὴν δὲ τῶν Γαλιλαίων ἄγροικοί τινες, πτωχοί τε καὶ εὐτελεῖς ἐκήρυξαν ἄνδρες, καὶ αὐτοὶ εὐαρίθμητοι καὶ μὴ τῶν δώδεκα τὸ μέτρον ὑπερβαίνοντες. πῶς οὖν τῶν ὀλίγων, ἀσήμων τε καὶ ἀγροίκων, τὸ κήρυγμα προτιμητέον τῆς τῶν πολλῶν καὶ μεγάλων καὶ σοφίᾳ τοσαύτῃ λαμψάντων νομοθεσίας; τίς δὲ ἡ ἀπόδειξις τούτους ἀληθεύειν, κἀκείνους ψεύδεσθαι;

Αὖθις οὖν ὁ τοῦ βασιλέως υἱὸς ἀπεκρίνατο·
Τάχα, Θευδᾶ, ὄνος εἶ,[1] τὸ τοῦ λόγου, λύρας
Ps. lviii. 4 ἀκούων καὶ ἀσύνετος μένων, μᾶλλον δὲ ἀσπὶς
βύων τὰ ὦτα τοῦ μὴ ἀκοῦσαι φωνῆς ἐπᾳδόντων.
Jer. xiii. 23 καλῶς οὖν ὁ προφήτης εἶπε περὶ σοῦ· εἰ ἀλλά-
ξεται Αἰθίοψ τὸ δέρμα αὐτοῦ καὶ πάρδαλις τὰ
ποικίλματα αὐτῆς, καὶ σὺ δυνήσῃ εὖ ποιῆσαι
μεμαθηκὼς κακά. μωρὲ καὶ τυφλέ, πῶς οὐκ
ἄγει σε εἰς αἴσθησιν ἡ τῆς ἀληθείας ἰσχύς; 294
τοῦτο γὰρ αὐτὸ τὸ παρὰ πολλῶν μὲν ἐπὶ σοφίᾳ
θαυμαζομένων ἐπαινεῖσθαι τὰ μιαρά σου σεβά-

[1] ὄνος λύρας ἤκουσε καὶ σάλπιγγος ὗς.

yet shall they reap the immortal harvest of recompense in the kingdom of unending and divine felicity.'

XXXII

Theudas claimeth the mighty and wise for his supporters

THEUDAS said unto him, 'Behold, it is evident that our religion was instituted by many mighty wise men, and interpreters, marvellous in virtue and learning; and all the kings and rulers of the earth have received it as good and sure in every point. But that of the Galileans was preached by some country peasants, poor and common men, a mere handful, not exceeding twelve in number. How then should one prefer the preaching of these few obscure countrymen to the ordinance of the many that are mighty and brilliantly wise? What is the proof that your teachers be right and the others wrong?'

Ioasaph proveth in this very point the might of the Gospel,

Again the king's son made answer, 'Belike, Theudas, thou art the ass of the proverb, that heard but heeded not the harp; or rather the adder that stoppeth her ears, that she may not hear the voice of the charmers. Well, therefore, spake the prophet concerning thee. If the Ethiopian can change his skin, or the leopard his spots, then mayest thou also do good, that hast been taught to do evil. Thou fool and blind, why doth not the force of truth bring thee to thy senses? The very fact that your foul idols are commended by many men of marvellous

σματα, παρὰ πολλῶν δὲ βασιλέων κρατύνεσθαι, τὸ δὲ κήρυγμα τοῦ Εὐαγγελίου παρ' ὀλίγων καὶ ἀσήμων ἀνδρῶν κηρυχθῆναι, δεικνύει τῆς ἡμῶν θεοσεβείας τὴν ἰσχὺν καὶ τῶν ὑμετέρων πονηρῶν δογμάτων τὸ ἀσθενὲς καὶ ὀλέθριον· ὅτι τὰ μὲν ὑμέτερα, καὶ συνηγόρους ἔχοντα σοφοὺς καὶ ἀντιλήπτορας ἰσχυρούς, ὅμως σβέννυται καὶ ἀσθενεῖ, τὰ δὲ τῆς θεοσεβείας, μηδεμίαν ἀνθρωπίνην κεκτημένα βοήθειαν, λάμπει τηλαυγέστερον ἡλίου καὶ τοῦ κόσμου κατέσχε τὰ πληρώματα. εἰ μὲν γὰρ παρὰ ῥητόρων τε καὶ φιλοσόφων ἐξετέθη, βασιλεῖς δὲ καὶ δυνάστας εἶχε συνεργοῦντας, εὗρες ἂν σὺ ὁ πονηρὸς εἰπεῖν ἀνθρωπίνης δυνάμεως τὸ πᾶν γεγενῆσθαι· νυνὶ δέ, ὁρῶν παρὰ ἁλιέων μὲν εὐτελῶν τὸ ἅγιον συντεθὲν Εὐαγγέλιον, παρὰ πάντων δὲ τυράννων διωχθέν, καὶ μετὰ τοῦτο τὴν οἰκουμένην κατα-
Ps. xix. 4 σχὸν (εἰς πᾶσαν γὰρ τὴν γῆν ἐξῆλθεν ὁ φθόγγος 295
αὐτοῦ καὶ εἰς τὰ πέρατα τῆς οἰκουμένης τὰ ῥήματα αὐτοῦ), τί ἂν εἴποις, ἢ θείαν εἶναι καὶ ἄμαχον δύναμιν ἐπὶ σωτηρίᾳ τῶν ἀνθρώπων τὰ ἑαυτῆς βεβαιοῦσαν; τίνα δὲ ἀπόδειξιν ζητεῖς, ἀνόητε, τοῦ ψεύδεσθαι μὲν τοὺς σούς, ἀληθεύειν δὲ τοὺς ἡμετέρους, κρείττονα τῶν εἰρημένων; εἰ μὴ γὰρ λῆρος ἦν καὶ ψεῦδος πάντα τὰ σά, οὐκ ἄν, τοσαύτην ἔχοντα παρὰ ἀνθρώπων ἰσχύν,
Ps. xxxvii. 35 ἠλαττοῦτο καὶ ἐξησθένει. Εἶδον γάρ, φησί, τὸν ἀσεβῆ ὑπερυψούμενον καὶ ἐπαιρόμενον ὡς τὰς κέδρους τοῦ Λιβάνου· καὶ παρῆλθον, καὶ ἰδοὺ οὐκ ἦν, καὶ ἐζήτησα αὐτόν, καὶ οὐχ εὑρέθη ὁ τόπος αὐτοῦ.

Περὶ ὑμῶν ταῦτα εἴρηκεν ὁ Προφήτης τῶν

wisdom, and established by kings, while the Gospel is preached by a few men of no mark, sheweth the might of our religion and the weakness and deadliness of your wicked doctrines. Because your side, despite its having wise advocates and mighty champions, is dying down, and waxing weak, whilst our religion, though possessed of no human help, shineth from afar brighter than the sun, and hath won the fulness of the world. If it had been set up by orators and philosophers, and had had kings for its succour, thou that art evil wouldst have found occasion to declare that it was wholly of human power. But now, seeing, as thou dost, that the holy Gospel, though composed but by common fishermen, and persecuted by every tyrant, hath after this won the whole world—for its sound hath gone out into all lands, and its words into the ends of the world—what canst thou say but that it is a divine and unconquerable power establishing its own cause for the salvation of mankind? But what proof seekest thou, O fool, that thy prophets are liars and ours true, better than the truths I have told thee? Except thy cause had been vain talk and falsehood, it could not, possessing such human support as it did, have suffered loss and decline. For he saith, "I have seen the ungodly in great power, and exalted like the cedars of Libanus: and I went by and lo, he was gone: and I sought him but his place could nowhere be found."

that it waxeth great without aid of man

'Concerning you, the defenders of idolatry, were

He proclaimeth

ὑπασπιστῶν τῆς εἰδωλομανίας. μικρὸν γὰρ ὅσον
ὅσον καὶ οὐ μὴ εὑρεθῇ ὁ τόπος ὑμῶν, ἀλλ', ὡς
Ps. lxviii. 2 ἐκλείπει καπνός, ἐκλείψετε, καὶ ὡς τήκεται
κηρὸς ἀπὸ προσώπου πυρός. περὶ δὲ τῆς Εὐαγ-
Mat. xxiv. 35 γελικῆς θεογνωσίας εἶπεν ὁ Κύριος· Ὁ οὐρανὸς
καὶ ἡ γῆ παρελεύσονται, οἱ δὲ λόγοι μου οὐ μὴ
Ps. cii. 25 παρέλθωσι. καί· Σὺ κατ' ἀρχάς, Κύριε, φησὶν
αὖθις ὁ ψαλμῳδός, τὴν γῆν ἐθεμελίωσας, καὶ 296
Heb. i. 10 ἔργα τῶν χειρῶν σού εἰσιν οἱ οὐρανοί· αὐτοὶ
ἀπολοῦνται· σὺ δὲ διαμένεις· καὶ πάντες ὡσεὶ
ἱμάτιον παλαιωθήσονται, καὶ ὡσεὶ περιβόλαιον
ἑλίξεις αὐτοὺς καὶ ἀλλαγήσονται, σὺ δὲ ὁ αὐτὸς
εἶ, καὶ τὰ ἔτη σου οὐκ ἐκλείψουσι. καὶ οἱ μὲν
θεῖοι κήρυκες τῆς τοῦ Χριστοῦ παρουσίας, οἱ
Mark i. 17 σοφοὶ τῆς οἰκουμένης ἁλιεῖς, οἱ πάντας ἑλκύ-
σαντες τοῦ βυθοῦ τῆς ἀπάτης, οὓς ὁ εὐτελὴς
σύ, καὶ δοῦλος ὄντως τῆς ἁμαρτίας, ἐξευτελίζεις,
Acts v. 12 ἔλαμψαν σημείοις καὶ τέρασι καὶ ποικίλαις
δυνάμεσιν ὡς ἥλιος ἐν τῷ κόσμῳ, τυφλοῖς τὸ
Acts iii. 1-10 φῶς δωρούμενοι, κωφοῖς τὸ ἀκούειν, χωλοῖς τὸ
Acts v. 12 περιπατεῖν, νεκροῖς τὸ ζῆν χαριζόμενοι. αἱ σκιαὶ
γὰρ αὐτῶν μόναι πάντα τὰ πάθη τῶν ἀνθρώπων
ἐθεράπευον. δαίμονας, οὓς ὑμεῖς φοβεῖσθε ὡς
θεούς, οὐ μόνον τῶν ἀνθρωπίνων ἀπήλαυνον
σωμάτων, ἀλλὰ καὶ αὐτῆς ἐδίωκον τῆς οἰκουμένης, τῷ τοῦ σταυροῦ σημείῳ, δι' οὗ πᾶσαν
μὲν ἠφάνισαν μαγείαν πᾶσαν δὲ φαρμακείαν
ἀνενέργητον ἔδειξαν. καὶ ἐκεῖνοι μέν, οὕτως τὴν
ἀνθρωπίνην ἰασάμενοι ἀσθένειαν τῇ τοῦ Χριστοῦ
δυνάμει καὶ τὴν κτίσιν πᾶσαν καινουργήσαντες,
ὡς τῆς ἀληθείας κήρυκες θαυμάζονται παρὰ
πάντων εἰκότως τῶν εὖ φρονούντων. τί δὲ ὁ

these words spoken by the prophet. For a very, very little while and your place shall not be found: but, like as the smoke vanisheth, and like as wax melteth in face of the fire, so shall ye fail. But, as touching the divine wisdom of the Gospel, thus saith the Lord, "Heaven and earth shall pass away, but my words shall not pass away." And again the Psalmist saith, "Thou, Lord, in the beginning hast laid the foundation of the earth; and the heavens are the work of thy hands. They shall perish, but thou endurest; and they all shall wax old as doth a garment, and as a vesture shalt thou fold them up, and they shall be changed, but thou art the same, and thy years shall not fail!" And those divine preachers of the coming of Christ, those wise fishers of the world, whose nets drew all men from the depths of deceit, whom thou, in thy vileness and bondage to sin, dost vilify, did by signs and wonders and manifold powers shine as the sun in the world, giving sight to the blind, hearing to the deaf, motion to the lame, and life to the dead. Their shadows alone healed all the ailments of men. The devils, whom ye dread as gods, they not only cast forth from men's bodies, but even drave out of the world itself by the sign of the cross, whereby they destroyed all sorcery, and rendered witchcraft powerless. And these men, by curing every disease of man by the power of Christ, and renewing all creation, are rightly admired as preachers of truth by all men of sound mind. But what hast thou thyself to say of thy wise

the might of the preachers of the Gospel

Cp. 1 Cor. i. 17–29 αὐτὸς ἔχεις εἰπεῖν περὶ τῶν σοφῶν σου καὶ 297
ῥητόρων, ὧν ἐμώρανεν ὁ Θεὸς τὴν σοφίαν, τῶν
συνηγόρων τοῦ διαβόλου; τί μνήμης ἄξιον κατέ-
λιπον τῷ βίῳ; εἰπέ. τί δ' ἂν εἴποις περὶ αὐτῶν,
ἢ ἀλογίαν καὶ αἰσχρότητα, καὶ τέχνην ματαίαν,
τῇ καλλιεπείᾳ τῶν λόγων τὸν βόρβορον συγκα-
λύπτουσαν τῆς δυσώδους αὐτῶν θρησκείας;

Ἀλλὰ καὶ αὐτῶν τῶν ποιητῶν ὅσοι μικρόν
τι δεδύνηνται τῆς πολλῆς ἀνανεῦσαι μανίας,
εἶπον τὸ ἀληθέστερον, ὅτι οἱ λεγόμενοι θεοὶ
ἄνθρωποι ἦσαν, καί, διὰ τό τινας μὲν αὐτῶν
ἄρξαι χωρῶν τε καὶ πόλεων, τινὰς δὲ ἄλλο τι
οὐδαμινὸν κατὰ τὸν βίον ποιῆσαι, πλανηθέντας
Eustathius in Hexaem. p. 56 τοὺς ἀνθρώπους θεοὺς αὐτοὺς καλέσαι. καταρχὰς
μὲν γὰρ ὁ Σεροὺχ ἐκεῖνος ἱστόρηται τὰ τῶν 298
ἀγαλμάτων ἐξευρεῖν. τοὺς γὰρ ἐν τοῖς πάλαι χρόνοις ἢ ἀνδρείας ἢ φιλίας, ἤ τινος ἑτέρας ἀνδραγαθίας ἔργον μνήμης ἄξιον ἐπιδειξαμένους ἀνδριάσι λέγεται καὶ στήλαις τιμῆσαι. οἱ δὲ μετὰ ταῦτα τὴν τῶν προγόνων ἀγνοήσαντες γνώμην, καὶ ὅτι, μνήμης ἕνεκα μόνον, τοῖς ἐπαινετόν τι ποιήσασιν ἀνδριάντας καὶ στήλας ἀνέστησαν, κατὰ μικρὸν πλανώμενοι τῇ τοῦ ἀρχεκάκου δαίμονος ἐνεργείᾳ, ὡς ἀθανάτοις θεοῖς τοῖς ὁμοιοπαθέσι καὶ φθαρτοῖς ἀνθρώποις προσετέθησαν, καὶ θυσίας αὐτοῖς καὶ σπονδὰς ἐπενοήσαντο, τῶν δαιμόνων δηλονότι τοῖς ξοάνοις ἐνοικησάντων, καὶ πρὸς ἑαυτοὺς τὴν τιμὴν καὶ τὰς θυσίας μεθελκυσάντων. ἐκεῖνοι τοίνυν τοὺς μὴ δοκιμάζοντας τὸν Θεὸν ἔχειν ἐν ἐπιγνώσει πείθουσι θεοὺς αὐτοὺς ἡγεῖσθαι, δυοῖν χάριν·

men and orators, whose wisdom God hath made foolish, the advocates of the devil? What worthy memorial have they bequeathed to the world? Tell me. And what canst thou tell of them but unreason and shamefulness, and vain craft that with glosing words concealeth the mire of their unsavoury worship?

'Moreover such of your poets as have been able to soar a little above this great madness have said, with more truth, that they, which are called gods, were men; and because certain of them had been rulers of regions and cities, and others had done something of no great account in their lifetime, men were so deceived as to call them gods. It standeth on record that the man Seruch[1] was the first to bring in the use of images. For it is said that in the old times he honoured those who had achieved some memorable deed of courage, friendship, or any other such virtue with statues and pillars. But after generations forgat the intention of their ancestors: and, whereas it was only for remembrance sake that they had set up statues and pillars to the doers of noble deeds, now they were, little by little, led astray through the working of the prince of evil, the devil, and treated as immortal gods men of like passions and corruptible as themselves and further devised sacrifices and drink-offerings for them,—the devils, thou mayest know, taking up their abode in these images and diverting to themselves these honours and sacrifices. Accordingly these devils persuade men, who refuse to have God in their knowledge, to consider them as gods for two reasons: first,

He showeth the origin of idolatry

[1] Serug, Gen. xi. 20; Luke iii. 35.

ἵν᾽ αὐτοὶ μὲν τῇ προσηγορίᾳ δοξάζοιντο ταύτῃ
(ἥδονται γάρ, ἅτε πλήρεις ἀλαζονείας ὄντες,
ὡς θεοὶ τιμᾶσθαι), αὐτοὺς δὲ οὓς ἠπατήκασιν
Mat. xxv. 41 εἰς τὸ ἡτοιμασμένον αὐτοῖς ἄσβεστον ἑλκύσωσι
πῦρ. ὅθεν πᾶσαν αὐτοὺς ἐδίδαξαν παρανομίαν
καὶ αἰσχρότητα, ὡς ἅπαξ ὑποταγέντας τῇ
ἐκείνων ἀπάτῃ. ἐπὶ τοῦτον οὖν τὸν κολοφῶνα
τῶν κακῶν ἐλθόντες οἱ ἄνθρωποι, ἐσκοτισμένοι
ὄντες, ἕκαστος τοῦ ἰδίου πάθους καὶ τῆς ἰδίας
ἐπιθυμίας ἔστησε στήλην, καὶ θεὸν ὠνόμασε, 299
βδελυκτοὶ τῆς πλάνης, βδελυκτότεροι τῆς ἀτο-
πίας τῶν προσκυνουμένων γενόμενοι, ἕως ἐλθὼν
Luke i. 78 ὁ Κύριος διὰ σπλάγχνα ἐλέους αὐτοῦ ἐλυτρώ-
σατο ἡμᾶς τοὺς πιστεύοντας αὐτῷ τῆς πονηρᾶς
ταύτης καὶ ὀλεθρίου πλάνης, καὶ ἐδίδαξε τὴν
Cp. Acts iv. 12 ἀληθῆ θεογνωσίαν. οὐκ ἔστι γὰρ σωτηρία, εἰ
μὴ ἐν αὐτῷ, καὶ οὐκ ἔστιν ἄλλος θεὸς οὔτε ἐν
οὐρανῷ, οὔτε ἐπὶ γῆς, εἰ μὴ αὐτὸς μόνος ὁ τοῦ
Heb. i. 3 παντὸς ποιητής, ὁ πάντα φέρων τῷ ῥήματι τῆς
Ps. xxxiii. 6 δυνάμεως αὐτοῦ. Τῷ λόγῳ γάρ, φησί, Κυρίου
οἱ οὐρανοὶ ἐστερεώθησαν, καὶ τῷ πνεύματι τοῦ
στόματος αὐτοῦ πᾶσα ἡ δύναμις αὐτῶν· καί,
John i. 3 πάντα δι᾽ αὐτοῦ ἐγένετο, καὶ χωρὶς αὐτοῦ ἐγένετο
οὐδὲ ἓν ὃ γέγονεν.

Ὁ δὲ Θευδᾶς, τούτων ἀκούσας τῶν ῥημάτων, καὶ ὅτι πλήρης ὁ λόγος θεοδιδάκτου σοφίας ἐτύγχανεν, οἷα βροντῆς ἤχῳ καταπλαγείς, ἀφωνίᾳ συνείχετο. ὀψὲ δὲ καὶ μόλις εἰς αἴσθησιν ἐλθὼν τῆς ἑαυτοῦ ἀθλιότητος (ἥψατο γὰρ τῶν ἐσκοτισμένων ὀφθαλμῶν τῆς καρδίας αὐτοῦ ὁ σωτήριος λόγος, καὶ πολὺς τῶν προτέρων αὐτοῦ εἰσῄει μεταμελος), καὶ τῆς τῶν εἰδώλων πλάνης κατα-

that they may be glorified by this title (for they are puffed up with arrogance, and delight to be honoured as gods) next, that they may drag their poor dupes into the unquenchable fire prepared for themselves. Hence they teach men all iniquity and filthiness, seeing that they have once subjected themselves to their deceit. So when men had arrived at this pinnacle of evil, they, being darkened, set up every man an idol of his own vice and his own lust, and call it a god. They were abominable in their error, more abominable in the absurdity of the objects that they chose to worship, until the Lord came, and of his tender mercy redeemed us that trust in him from this wicked and deadly error, and taught men the true knowledge of God. For there is no salvation except in him, and there is none other God, neither in heaven, nor in earth, except him only, the Maker of all, who moveth all things by the word of his power: for he saith, "By the word of the Lord were the heavens made stedfast, and all the power of them by the breath of his mouth," and, "All things were made by him, and without him was not anything made that was made."'

How men came to worship devils as gods

When Theudas had heard these sayings, and seen that the word was full of divine wisdom, like one thunder-struck, he was smitten dumb. Now late in time, and with difficulty, came he to understand his own misery, for the word of salvation had touched the darkened vision of his heart, and there fell upon him deep remorse for his past sins. He renounced the error of his idols, and ran towards the light of godli-

Theudas is convicted of error and acknowledgeth defeat

γνούς, τῷ φέγγει τῆς εὐσεβείας προσέδραμε. καὶ
τὸ ἀπ' ἐκείνου οὕτω τῆς μοχθηρᾶς ἀγωγῆς ἀπέστη καὶ τοσοῦτον ἑαυτὸν τοῖς ἀτίμοις ἐξεπολέμωσε
πάθεσι καὶ μαγείαις, ὅσην ἄρα πρὸ τούτου τὴν
πρὸς αὐτὰ φιλίαν ἐσπείσατο. τότε μὲν γὰρ ἐν
μέσῳ τοῦ συνεδρίου ἑστώς, τοῦ βασιλέως προ-
καθεζομένου, μεγάλῃ τῇ φωνῇ ἐβόησεν· Ἀληθῶς, 300
Rom. viii. 9, 11 ὦ βασιλεῦ, πνεῦμα Θεοῦ οἰκεῖ ἐν τῷ υἱῷ σου·
ἀληθῶς ἡττήμεθα, καὶ οὐδεμίαν ἔτι ἀπολογίαν
ἔχομεν, οὔτε ἀντοφθαλμῆσαι πρὸς τὰ παρ' αὐτοῦ
λεγόμενα ἰσχύομεν. μέγας οὖν τῷ ὄντι ὁ τῶν
Χριστιανῶν Θεός, μεγάλη ἡ πίστις αὐτῶν, μεγάλα
τὰ μυστήρια.

Ἐπιστραφεὶς δὲ πρὸς τὸν υἱὸν ἔφη τοῦ βασι-
λέως· Λέγε μοι τοίνυν, ὦ πεφωτισμένε τὴν
ψυχήν· δέχεταί με ὁ Χριστός, εἰ, ἐκ τῶν πονηρῶν μου πράξεων ἀποστάς, ἐπιστρέψω πρὸς
αὐτόν; Ναί, φησὶν ὁ τῆς ἀληθείας κῆρυξ, ναί,
δέχεται καὶ σὲ καὶ πάντας τοὺς εἰς αὐτὸν ἐπιστρέ-
Luke xv. 20 ff. φοντας. δέχεται δὲ οὐχ ἁπλῶς, ἀλλ', ὡς υἱῷ ἀπὸ
μακρᾶς ἐπιδημήσαντι χώρας, προσυπαντᾷ τῷ ἐκ
τῆς ὁδοῦ τῶν ἀνομιῶν ἐπιστρέφοντι· καὶ τοῦτον
περιλαβὼν κατασπάζεται, καὶ τὸ τῆς ἁμαρτίας
αἶσχος περιελὼν αὐτίκα ἱμάτιον περιτίθησι
σωτηρίου, καὶ στολὴν λαμπροτάτης περιβαλὼν
δόξης, μυστικὴν ταῖς ἄνω δυνάμεσιν ἐπιτελεῖ
εὐφροσύνην, τὴν ἐπιστροφὴν ἑορτάζων τοῦ ἀπο-
Luke xv. 4 λωλότος προβάτου. αὐτὸς γὰρ ἔφη ὁ Κύριος
Luke xv. 7 χαρὰν γίνεσθαι ἐν οὐρανῷ μεγίστην ἐπὶ ἑνὶ ἁμαρ-
Luke v. 32 τωλῷ μετανοοῦντι. καὶ πάλιν, Οὐκ ἦλθον, φησί,
καλέσαι δικαίους, ἀλλὰ ἁμαρτωλοὺς εἰς μετά-

ness, and from henceforth departed from his miserable life, and made himself as bitter an enemy of vile affections and sorceries as he before had pledged himself their devoted friend, For at this season he stood up in the midst of the assembly,[1] and cried with a loud voice, saying, 'Verily, O king, the Spirit of God dwelleth in thy son. Verily, we are defeated, and have no further apology, and have no strength to face the words that he hath uttered. Mighty therefore, in sooth, is the God of the Christians: mighty is their faith : mighty are their mysteries.'

Then he turned him round toward the king's son and said, 'Tell me now, thou man, whose soul is enlightened, will Christ accept me, if I forsake my evil deeds and turn to him?' 'Yea,' said that preacher of truth; 'Yea, he receiveth thee and all that turn to him. And he not only receiveth thee, but he goeth out to meet thee returning out of the way of iniquity, as though it were a son returning from a far country. And he falleth on his neck and kisseth him, and he strippeth him of the shameful robe of sin, and putteth on him a cloak of brightest glory, making mystic gladness for the powers on high, keeping feast for the return of the lost sheep. The Lord himself saith, "There is exceeding great joy in heaven over one sinner that repenteth": and again, "I am not come to call the righteous but

Theudas asketh if he may yet obtain pardon

[1] This reference to an assembly suggests a variant version of this episode: for above (p. 477) Theudas is closeted with Ioasaph and the king.

Ez. xxxiii. 11 ff. νοιαν. φησὶ δὲ καὶ διὰ τοῦ προφήτου· Ζῶ ἐγώ,
λέγει Κύριος· οὐ βούλομαι τὸν θάνατον τοῦ 301
ἁμαρτωλοῦ καὶ ἀσεβοῦς, ὡς τὸ ἐπιστρέψαι ἀπὸ
τῆς ὁδοῦ αὐτοῦ καὶ ζῆν αὐτόν· ἀποστροφῇ ἀπο-
στρέψατε ἀπὸ τῆς ὁδοῦ ὑμῶν τῆς πονηρᾶς· καὶ
ἱνατί ἀποθνήσκετε, οἶκος Ἰσραήλ; ἀνομία γὰρ
ἀνόμου οὐ μὴ κακώσῃ αὐτόν· ἐν ᾗ ἂν ἡμέρᾳ ἀπο-
στρέψῃ ἀπὸ τῆς ἀνομίας αὐτοῦ καὶ ποιήσῃ δικαιοσύνην, καὶ ἐν προστάγματι ζωῆς διαπορεύσηται,
ζωῇ ζήσεται καὶ οὐ μὴ ἀποθάνῃ· πᾶσαι αἱ
ἁμαρτίαι αὐτοῦ ἃς ἥμαρτεν οὐ μὴ μνησθῶσιν·
ὅτι κρῖμα δικαιοσύνης ἐποίησεν, ἐν αὐτῇ ζήσεται.
Is. i. 16–18 καὶ αὖθις, Λούσασθε, δι' ἑτέρου βοᾷ προφήτου,
καθαροὶ γένεσθε, ἀφέλετε τὰς πονηρίας ἀπὸ τῶν
ψυχῶν ὑμῶν ἀπέναντι τῶν ὀφθαλμῶν μου· παύ-
σασθε ἀπὸ τῶν πονηριῶν ὑμῶν· μάθετε καλὸν
ποιεῖν· καὶ δεῦτε καὶ διαλεχθῶμεν· καὶ ἐὰν ὦσιν
αἱ ἁμαρτίαι ὑμῶν ὡς φοινικοῦν, ὡς χιόνα λευκανῶ,
ἐὰν δὲ ὦσιν ὡς κόκκινον, ὡσεὶ ἔριον λευκανῶ.
τοιούτων οὖν προκειμένων ἐπαγγελιῶν παρὰ τοῦ
Θεοῦ τοῖς ἐπιστρέφουσι, μὴ μέλλε, ὦ ἄνθρωπε,
μηδὲ ἀναβάλλου· ἀλλὰ πρόσελθε πρὸς Χριστὸν
τὸν φιλάνθρωπον Θεὸν ἡμῶν, καὶ φωτίσθητι, καὶ
Ps. xxxiv. 5 τὸ πρόσωπόν σου οὐ μὴ καταισχυνθῇ. ἅμα γὰρ
τῷ καταδῦναί σε τῇ κολυμβήθρᾳ τοῦ θείου βαπτίσματος, ὅλον τὸ αἶσχος τοῦ παλαιοῦ ἀνθρώπου
καὶ ὅλος ὁ φόρτος τῶν πολλῶν ἁμαρτημάτων
Greg. Naz. Orat. xl. p. 638 ἐνθάπτεται τῷ ὕδατι καὶ εἰς τὸ μὴ ὂν χωρεῖ, νέος
δὲ σὺ ἐκεῖθεν καὶ παντὸς ῥύπου καθαρὸς ἀνέρχῃ, 302
μηδένα σπῖλον ἢ ῥυτίδα ἁμαρτίας ἐπιφερόμενος,
καὶ λοιπὸν ἐπὶ σοί ἐστι τὸ διαφυλάξαι ἑαυτῷ

sinners to repentance." And he saith also by the prophet, "As I live, saith the Lord, I have no pleasure in the death of the sinner, and the ungodly, but that he should turn from his way and live. Turn ye, turn ye from your evil way. And why will ye die, O house of Israel?" For the wickedness of the wicked shall not hurt him in the day that he turneth from his wickedness, if he do righteousness and walk in the statutes of life, he shall surely live; he shall not die. None of his sins which he hath committed shall be remembered against him. Because he hath done the decree of righteousness, he shall live thereby. And again he crieth by the mouth of another prophet, "Wash you, make you clean; put away the evil of your doings from before mine eyes; cease to do evil: learn to do well. Come now, and let us reason together: though your sins be as scarlet, I will make them white as snow; though they be red like crimson, I will make them white as wool." Such therefore being the promises made by God to them that turn to him, tarry not, O thou man, nor make delay: but draw nigh to Christ, our loving God, and be enlightened, and thy face shall not be ashamed. For as soon as thou goest down into the laver of Holy Baptism, all the defilement of the old man, and all the burden of thy many sins, is buried in the water, and passeth into nothingness, and thou comest up from thence a new man, pure from all pollution, with no spot or wrinkle of sin upon thee; and thenceforward it is in thy power

Ioasaph showeth him fair hopes

τὴν ἐκεῖθέν σοι προσγινομένην κάθαρσιν διὰ
Luke i. 78 σπλάγχνα ἐλέους Θεοῦ ἡμῶν.

Ὁ μὲν οὖν Θευδᾶς, τούτοις κατηχηθεὶς τοῖς ῥήμασιν, ἔξεισιν εὐθέως, καὶ τὸ πονηρὸν ἐκεῖνο
Cp. Acts. xix. 19 καταλαβὼν ἄντρον, καὶ τὰς ἑαυτοῦ λαβὼν μαγικὰς βίβλους, ὡς κακίας πάσης ἀπαρχάς, ὡς ὀργίων δαιμονικῶν θησαυρούς, πυρὶ κατέκαυσεν. αὐτὸς δὲ τὸ σπήλαιον καταλαμβάνει τοῦ ἱεροῦ ἀνδρὸς ἐκείνου, πρὸς ὃν καὶ ὁ Ναχὼρ ἀπεληλύθει, καὶ τὰ κατ' αὐτὸν διηγεῖται πάντα, κόνιν μὲν ἐπὶ κεφαλῆς καταχεάμενος, βαρεῖς τε ἀναφέρων στεναγμοὺς καὶ λούων τοῖς δάκρυσιν ἑαυτόν, καθεξῆς δὲ τῷ γέροντι τὰς μυσαρὰς αὐτοῦ διηγούμενος πράξεις. ἐκεῖνος δέ, περὶ τὸ σῶσαι ψυχὴν καὶ τῆς τοῦ δολίου δράκοντος ἐξαρπάσαι φάρυγγος εὐτεχνότατος ὤν, κατεπᾴδει αὐτὸν ῥήμασι σωτηρίοις, ἐγγυᾶται τὴν ἄφεσιν, ἵλεων ὑπισχνεῖται τὸν δικαστήν. εἶτα κατηχήσας καὶ νηστεύειν ἐπὶ πολλὰς ἐντειλάμενος ἡμέρας, τῷ θείῳ καθαίρει βαπτίσματι. καὶ ἦν ὁ ἄνθρωπος μετανοῶν γνησίως πάσας αὐτοῦ τὰς ἡμέρας, ἐφ' οἷς ἐπλημμέλησε, δάκρυσί τε καὶ στεναγμοῖς τὸν Θεὸν ἐξιλεούμενος.

XXXIII

Ὁ δέ γε βασιλεύς, τούτων οὕτως ἀποβάντων, πάντοθεν ἐξαπορηθείς, δῆλος ἦν ἰσχυρῶς ἀνιώμενος καὶ πολὺν τὸν σάλον φέρων ἐν τῇ ψυχῇ. συγκαλέσας δὲ αὖθις ὅσοι τῆς συγκλήτου βουλῆς
ἐτύγχανον, ἐσκέπτετο τί λοιπὸν τῷ ἰδίῳ ποιή- 303

ever to keep for thyself the purity that thou gainest hereby through the tender mercy of our God.'

When Theudas had been thus instructed, he went out immediately and gat him to his evil den, and took his magical books, and, because they were the beginnings of all evil, and the store-houses of devilish mysteries, burnt them with fire. And he betook himself to the cave of that same holy man, to whom Nachor also had resorted, and told him that which had befallen him, casting dust upon his head, and groaning deeply, and watering himself with his tears, and telling the aged man the full tale of his loathly deeds. He, well skilled in the saving of a soul and the snatching it from the jaw of the wily serpent, charmed away his sorrow with words of salvation, and pledged him forgiveness and promised him a merciful Judge. Then, after he had instructed and charged him to fast many days, he cleansed him in Holy Baptism. And all the days of his life Theudas heartily repented him of his misdeeds, with tears and sighs seeking the favour of God.

Theudas burneth his magic books and is baptized

XXXIII

As for the king, when things fortuned thus, he was completely bewildered, and plainly showed his sore vexation and tumult of soul. So again he called all his senators together, and considered what means were still his to deal with his son. Many men put

The king debateth again over the prince

σειεν υἱῷ. πολλὰς δὲ βουλὰς τῶν πολλῶν ὑποθεμένων, ὁ ἀνωτέρω μνημονευθεὶς Ἀραχὴς ἐκεῖνος, ἐπιφανέστερος τὴν ἡγεμονίαν καὶ πρῶτος τῆς βουλῆς ὑπάρχων, ἔφη τῷ βασιλεῖ· Τί ἔδει, βασιλεῦ, ποιῆσαι τῷ υἱῷ σου καὶ οὐ πεποιήκαμεν, τοῦ πεῖσαι αὐτὸν τοῖς ἡμετέροις ἕπεσθαι δόγμασι καὶ τοῖς θεοῖς ἡμῶν λατρεύειν; ἀλλ', ὡς ὁρῶ, ἀνηνύτοις ἐπιχειροῦμεν· ἐκ φύσεως γὰρ αὐτῷ, ἢ τῆς τύχης ἴσως, τὸ φιλόνεικόν τε καὶ ἀμείλικτον. εἰ μὲν οὖν βασάνοις αὐτὸν ἐκδοῦναι θελήσειας καὶ τιμωρίαις, σύ τε πολέμιος ἔσῃ τῆς φύσεως καὶ οὐ πατὴρ ἔτι κληθήσῃ, κἀκεῖνον ζημιωθήσῃ ἑτοίμως ἔχοντα ὑπὲρ Χριστοῦ ἀποθανεῖν. λείπεται γοῦν τοῦτο μόνον ποιῆσαι· διελεῖν αὐτῷ τὴν βασιλείαν, καὶ εἰς τὸ ἐπιβάλλον αὐτῷ μέρος βασιλεύειν ἐπιτρέψαι. καί, εἰ μὲν ἡ τῶν πραγμάτων φύσις καὶ ἡ μέριμνα τῶν βιωτικῶν ἑλκύσωσιν αὐτὸν τὸν ἡμέτερον ἀσπάσασθαι σκοπόν τε καὶ βίον, ἔσται ἡμῖν κατὰ σκοπὸν τὸ πρᾶγμα· τὰ γὰρ ἰσχυρῶς βεβαιωθέντα τῇ ψυχῇ ἔθη δυσεξάλειπτά εἰσι καὶ πειθοῖ μᾶλλον ἢ βίᾳ μεταβάλλεται. εἰ δὲ τῇ θρησκείᾳ παραμενεῖ τῶν Χριστιανῶν, αὐτὸ δὴ τοῦτο, τὸ μὴ ζημιωθῆναί σε τὸν υἱόν, ἔσται σοι τῆς ἀθυμίας ποσῶς παραμύθιον. ταῦτα τοῦ Ἀραχῆ εἰπόντος, πάντες συνεμαρτύρουν ἀποδεχόμενοι τὴν γνώμην. συντίθεται τοίνυν καὶ ὁ βασιλεὺς οὕτω ταῦτα διατεθῆναι.

Καὶ δὴ προσκαλεσάμενος ἕωθεν ἔφη τῷ υἱῷ·
Οὗτός μοι τελευταῖος ἤδη πρὸς σὲ λόγος, υἱέ· 304
οὗπερ εἰ μὴ εὐθὺς κατήκοος γένῃ καὶ κἂν ἐν τούτῳ τὴν ἐμὴν θεραπεύσῃς καρδίαν, οὐκ ἔτι σου, εὖ ἴσθι, φείσομαι. τοῦ δὲ υἱοῦ πυθομένου τίς ἡ

forward many counsels, but that Araches, of whom we have spoken, the most famous in his office, and first of his councillors, spake unto the king, saying, 'What was there to be done with thy son, O king, that we have not done, to induce him to follow our doctrines and serve our gods? But, as I perceive, we aim at the impossible. By nature, or, it may be, by chance, he is contentious and implacable. Now, if it be thy purpose to deliver him to torture and punishment, thou shalt do contrary to nature, and be no more called a father; and thou shalt lose thy son, willing, as he is, to lay down his life for Christ his sake. This, then, alone remaineth: to divide thy kingdom with him, and entrust him with the dominion of that part which falleth to his lot; and if the course of events, and the care of the business of life, draw him to embrace our aim and way, then the thing shall be according to our purpose; for habits, firmly established in the soul, are difficult to obliterate, and yield quicker to persuasion than to violence. But if he shall continue in the Christian religion, yet shall it be some solace to thee in thy distress, that thou hast not lost thy son.' Thus spake Araches, and all bare witness that they welcomed his proposal. Therefore also the king agreed that this matter should thus be settled.

He adopteth the counsel of Araches

So at day-break he called his son, and said unto him, 'This is now my latest word with thee, my son. Unless thou be obedient thereto, and in this way heal my heart, know thou well, that I shall no longer spare thee.' When his son enquired the

τοῦ λόγου δύναμις, Ἐπείπερ, φησί, πολλὰ μογήσας, ἀνένδοτόν σε πρὸς πάντα εὗρον τοῦ πεισθῆναί μου τοῖς λόγοις, δεῦρο δὴ λοιπόν, τὴν βασιλείαν διελών, ἀνὰ μέρος εἶναί σε καὶ βασιλεύειν ποιήσω· καὶ ἔσται σοι λοιπὸν ἐπ᾽ ἀδείας ἣν ἂν ποθῇς ἰέναι ὁδόν. γνοῦσα δὲ ἡ θεία ψυχὴ ἐκείνη καὶ τοῦτο ἐπ᾽ ὀλίσθῳ τῆς αὐτοῦ προαιρέσεως προβαλεῖν τὸν βασιλέα, ὅμως ἐπακοῦσαι συνεῖδεν, ἵνα, τὰς αὐτοῦ διαδρὰς χεῖρας, τὴν ἐπιθυμουμένην αὐτῷ πορεύσηται ὁδόν. ὑπολαβὼν οὖν, τῷ βασιλεῖ ἔφη· Ἐγὼ μὲν ἐπόθουν τὸν θεῖον ἐκεῖνον ζητῆσαι ἄνδρα, τὸν ὑποδείξαντά μοι τὴν ὁδὸν τῆς σωτηρίας, καὶ πᾶσι χαίρειν εἰπόντα μετ᾽ αὐτοῦ τὸ λοιπὸν τῆς ζωῆς μου διανύσαι· ἀλλ᾽ ἐπεί με, πάτερ, οὐ συγχωρεῖς τὰ καταθύμια πράττειν, πείθομαί σοι ἐν τούτῳ. ἐν οἷς γὰρ οὐ πρόκειται προφανὴς ἀπώλεια καὶ Θεοῦ ἀλλοτρίωσις, καλὸν τῷ πατρὶ πείθεσθαι.

Χαρᾶς οὖν ὅτι πλείστης ὁ βασιλεὺς πλησθεὶς διαιρεῖ μὲν τὴν ὑποτελῆ αὐτῷ χώραν πᾶσαν εἰς δύο, χειροτονεῖ δὲ τὸν υἱὸν βασιλέα, κοσμεῖ τῷ διαδήματι, καὶ πάσῃ τοῦτον βασιλικῇ καταλαμπρύνας δόξῃ εἰς τὴν ἀφορισθεῖσαν αὐτῷ ἐκπέμπει βασιλείαν μετὰ λαμπρᾶς δορυφορίας. τοῖς ἄρχουσι δὲ καὶ ἡγεμόσι, στρατηγοῖς τε καὶ σατράπαις κελεύει, παντὶ τῷ βουλομένῳ, ἀπελθεῖν μετὰ τοῦ υἱοῦ αὐτοῦ καὶ βασιλέως. καὶ πόλιν τινὰ μεγάλην καὶ πολυάνθρωπον ἀφορίζει αὐτοῦ 305
τῇ βασιλείᾳ, καὶ πάντα δίδωσι τὰ πρέποντα βασιλεῦσιν. τότε δὴ τότε τὴν ἐξουσίαν παραλαβὼν ὁ Ἰωάσαφ τῆς βασιλείας, ἡνίκα τὴν πόλιν κατέλαβεν ἔνθα τὰ τῆς βασιλείας ηὐτρέπιστο

meaning of his word, he said, 'Since, after all my labours, I find thee in all points unyielding to the persuasion of my words, come now; I will divide with thee my kingdom, and make thee king over the half-part thereof; and thou shalt be free, from now, to go whatsoever way thou wilt without fear.' He, though his saintly soul perceived that the king was casting yet another snare to trip his purpose, resolved to obey, in order that he might escape his hands, and take the journey that he desired. So he answered and said, 'I have indeed been longing to go in quest of that man of God that pointed out to me the way of salvation, and, bidding farewell to everything, to pass the rest of my life in his company. But, father, since thou sufferest me not to fulfil my heart's desire, I will obey thee herein: for where there is no clear danger of perdition and estrangement from God, it is right to obey one's father.'

The king was filled with exceeding great joy, and divided all the country under his sovranty into two parts, and appointed his son king, and adorned him with the diadem, and arrayed him in all the splendour of kingship, and sent him forth with a magnificent body-guard into the kingdom set apart for him. And he bade his rulers and governors and satraps, every one that would, to depart together with his son the king. And he set apart a mighty and populous city for his kingdom, and gave him everything that befitted a king. Thus then did Ioasaph receive the power of kingship; and when he had reached that city, where royal state had been

and divideth his realm with Ioasaph

αὐτῷ, τὸ τοῦ δεσποτικοῦ μὲν πάθους σημεῖον, τὸν σεβάσμιον σταυρὸν τοῦ Χριστοῦ, ἑκάστῳ ἐφίστησι τῆς πόλεως πύργῳ· τοὺς δὲ εἰδωλικοὺς ναοὺς καὶ βωμοὺς περιστὰς ἐπολιόρκει, κατέσειεν ἀνώρυττε τὸ ἔδαφος, ἐξεκάλυπτε τοὺς θεμελίους, μηδὲν λείψανον τῆς ἀσεβείας καταλιπών.

Κατὰ δὲ μέσης τῆς πόλεως ναὸν μέγαν τε καὶ περικαλλῆ τῷ Δεσπότῃ ἀνεγείρει Χριστῷ. καὶ κελεύει τὸ πλῆθος ἐκεῖ συνεχὲς ἐπιχωριάζοντας
Cp. De fide orth. Bk. IV., Ch. II. προσάγειν τῷ Θεῷ τὸ σέβας διὰ τῆς τοῦ σταυροῦ προσκυνήσεως, εἰς μέσον πρὸ πάντων αὐτὸς παρελθὼν καὶ ἐκτενεστάτῃ διδοὺς ἑαυτὸν δεήσει. πάντας δὲ τοὺς ὑπὸ τὴν αὐτοῦ χεῖρα γενομένους ἐνουθέτει, παρεκάλει, πάντα ἐποίει τοῦ ἀποσπάσαι τῆς δεισιδαίμονος πλάνης καὶ τῷ Χριστῷ οἰκειῶσαι· τὴν ἀπάτην δὲ ὑπεδείκνυ τῆς εἰδωλομανίας καὶ τὸ κήρυγμα κατήγγελλε τοῦ Εὐαγγελίου, τὰ περὶ τῆς τοῦ Θεοῦ Λόγου διεξῄει συγκαταβάσεως, τὰ θαυμάσια ἐκήρυττε τῆς αὐτοῦ παρουσίας, τὸ πάθος ἐγνώριζε τοῦ σταυροῦ δι' οὗ σεσώσμεθα, τὴν τῆς ἀναστάσεως δύναμιν καὶ τὴν πρὸς οὐρανοὺς ἄνοδον, τὴν φοβερὰν ἐπὶ τούτοις διήγγελλεν ἡμέραν τῆς φρικτῆς αὐτοῦ δευτέρας παρουσίας, τά τε ἀποκείμενα τοῖς πιστοῖς ἀγαθὰ καὶ τὰ ἐκδεχόμενα τοὺς ἁμαρτωλοὺς κολαστήρια. ταῦτα πάντα ἤθει χρηστῷ καὶ μειλιχίοις διεξῄει ῥήμασιν· οὐ τοσοῦτον γὰρ ἀπὸ τοῦ ὄγκου τῆς ἐξουσίας καὶ τῆς βασιλικῆς μεγαλο- 306
πρεπείας ἤθελεν αἰδέσιμος εἶναι καὶ φοβερός, ὅσον ἀπὸ τῆς ταπεινοφροσύνης καὶ πραότητος· ᾧ καὶ μᾶλλον εἷλκε πάντας πρὸς ἑαυτόν, τῷ εἶναι τοῖς ἔργοις μὲν θαυμάσιος, ἐπιεικὴς δὲ καὶ

prepared for him, on every tower of his city he set up the sign of his Lord's passion, the venerable Cross of Christ. And in person he besieged the idolatrous temples and altars, and razed them to the ground, and uncovered their foundations, leaving no trace of their ungodliness.

And in the middle of the city he upreared for Christ, his Lord, a temple mighty and passing fair, and he bade the people there often to resort thither, and offer their worship to God by the veneration of the Cross, himself standing in the midst in the presence of all, and earnestly giving himself unto prayer. And as many as were under his hand he admonished and exhorted, and did everything to tear them away from superstitious error, and to unite them to Christ; and he pointed out the deceits of idolatry, and proclaimed the preaching of the Gospel, and recounted the things concerning the condescension of God, the Word, and preached the marvels of his coming, and made known his sufferings on the Cross whereby we were saved, and the power of his Resurrection, and his Ascension into heaven. Moreover he declared the terrible day of his dreadful second coming, and the bliss laid up for the righteous, and the punishments awaiting sinners. All these truths he expounded with kindly mien and gentle words. For he was not minded to be reverenced and feared for the grandeur of his power and kingly magnificence, but rather for his humility and meekness. Hereby also he more easily drew all men unto himself, being verily marvellous in his acts, and equitable and modest in

Ioasaph buildeth a Christian temple in his chief city,

μέτριος τῷ φρονήματι. ὅθεν ἡ ἐξουσία, τὴν μετριοφροσύνην καὶ ἐπιείκειαν μέγαν συνεργὸν λαβοῦσα, πάντας εἴκειν αὐτοῦ τοῖς λόγοις πεποίηκεν.

Ἀμέλει οὕτως ἐν ὀλίγῳ χρόνῳ πᾶς ὁ ὑποτελὴς αὐτῷ λαὸς πολίτης τε καὶ ἐγχώριος τοῖς θεοφθόγγοις αὐτοῦ ἐμυσταγωγήθη λόγοις, ὡς ἐξαρνήσασθαι μὲν τὴν πολύθεον πλάνην καὶ ἀπορραγῆναι τῶν εἰδωλικῶν σπονδῶν τε καὶ βδελυγμάτων, τῇ ἀπλανεῖ δὲ προστεθῆναι πίστει, καὶ ταῖς 307
αὐτοῦ μεταπλασθέντας διδασκαλίαις τῷ Χριστῷ οἰκειωθῆναι. πάντες δέ, οἱ ἐν ὄρεσι καὶ σπηλαίοις διὰ τὸν φόβον τοῦ πατρὸς αὐτοῦ ἐγκεκλεισμένοι, ἱερεῖς τε καὶ μονάζοντες καὶ τῶν ἐπισκόπων ὀλίγοι, ἐξελθόντες τῶν καταδύσεων, πρὸς αὐτὸν χαίροντες ἐχώρουν. αὐτὸς δὲ τοὺς διὰ Χριστὸν ἐν τοιούτοις περιπεσόντας ἀνιαροῖς καὶ οὕτω ταλαιπωρήσαντας προσυπαντῶν ἐντίμως ἐδέχετο, καὶ εἰς τὸ ἑαυτοῦ εἰσῆγε παλάτιον,
Cp. John xiii. 14 πόδας ῥύπτων, κόμην ῥυπῶσαν ἀποπλύνων, καὶ παντοίως αὐτοὺς θεραπεύων. εἶτα τὴν νεουργηθεῖσαν αὐτῷ ἐνθρονίζει ἐκκλησίαν, καί τινα τῶν ἐπισκόπων, πολλὰ διὰ τὴν εἰς Χριστὸν πίστιν κακοπαθήσαντα καὶ τὸν ἴδιον ἀπολέσαντα τῆς ἐπισκοπῆς θρόνον, ἀρχιερέα ἐν ταύτῃ καθίστησιν, ἄνδρα ἅγιον καὶ τῶν ἐκκλησιαστικῶν κανόνων ἐπιστήμονα, ζήλου τε θείου τὴν ψυχὴν πεπληρωμένον. κολυμβήθραν δὲ εὐθὺς σχεδιάσας, βαπτίζειν τοὺς πρὸς Χριστὸν ἐπιστρέφοντας κελεύει. καὶ δὴ βαπτίζονται οἱ ἄρχοντες πρῶτον καὶ ὅσοι ἐν τέλει, οἱ ἐν στρατείᾳ τε αὖθις καὶ

spirit. Wherefore his power, being strongly reinforced by his gentleness and equity, caused all men to yield themselves to his words.

What wonder, then, if, in a little while, all his subjects, in city or country, were so well initiated into his inspired teachings, that they renounced the errors of their many gods, and broke away from idolatrous drink-offerings and abominations, and were joined to the true faith and were created anew by his doctrine, and added to the household of Christ? And all, who for fear of Ioasaph's father had been shut up in mountains and dens, priests and monks, and some few bishops, came forth from their hiding places and resorted to him gladly. He himself would meet and receive with honour those who had fallen upon such tribulation and distress, for Christ his sake, and bring them to his own palace, washing their feet, and cleansing their matted hair, and ministering to them in every way. Then he dedicated his newly built church, and therein appointed for chief-priest one of the bishops that had suffered much, and had lost his own see, on account of his faith in Christ, an holy man, and learned in the canons of the Church, whose heart was fulfilled with heavenly zeal. And forthwith, when he had made ready a rude font,[1] he bade baptize them that were turning to Christ. And so they were baptized, first the rulers and the men in authority; next, the soldiers on service and the rest

and leadeth his people to the Christian Faith

[1] Strictly a swimming-bath. Then, in Ecclesiastical Greek, a font.

ὁ λοιπὸς ὄχλος. καὶ οἱ βαπτιζόμενοι οὐ μόνον τὴν ψυχικὴν ἀπελάμβανον ὑγίειαν, ἀλλὰ δὴ καὶ ὅσοι νόσοις ἦσαν σωματικαῖς καὶ πηρώσεσι πιεζόμενοι, πάντα ἀποθέμενοι, καθαροὶ τὰς ψυχάς, ἄρτιοι δὲ τὰ σώματα, τῆς θείας ἀνήρχοντο 308
κολυμβήθρας, θεραπείαν τρυγήσαντες ψυχῶν τε ὁμοῦ καὶ σωμάτων.

Ἔνθεν τοι καὶ συνέρρει πρὸς τὸν βασιλέα Ἰωάσαφ πανταχόθεν τὰ πλήθη, μυηθῆναι τὴν εὐσέβειαν ὑπ' αὐτοῦ ζητοῦντες. καὶ πάντα μὲν κατεσκάπτετο εἰδωλικὰ σεβάσματα, ἀφῄρητο δὲ πᾶς ὁ πλοῦτος καὶ τὰ ἀποκείμενα τοῖς εἰδωλείοις χρήματα· καὶ ἱερὰ τεμένη τῷ Θεῷ ἀντῳκοδομεῖτο. καὶ τὸν ἐκεῖνον πλοῦτον αὐτοῖς καὶ τὰς πολυτελεῖς ἐσθῆτας ὁ βασιλεὺς Ἰωάσαφ καὶ τοὺς θησαυροὺς ἀνετίθει, τὴν ἄτιμον ἐκείνην καὶ περιττὴν ὕλην ἐνεργὸν ἐντεῦθεν ποιῶν καὶ
Minucius Felix, Ch. 27 ὠφέλιμον. οἱ δὲ τοῖς βωμοῖς ἐκείνοις καὶ ναοῖς διατρίβοντες μιαροὶ δαίμονες διωγμῷ χαλεπωτάτῳ ἠλαύνοντο, καὶ τὴν ἐπελθοῦσαν αὐτοῖς συμφορὰν εἰς πολλῶν ἐπήκοον ἀνεβόων. καὶ ἠλευθεροῦτο ἡ περίχωρος πᾶσα ἐκείνη τῆς ζοφερᾶς αὐτῶν ἀπάτης, τῷ φωτί τε περιελάμπετο τῆς ἀμωμήτου τῶν Χριστιανῶν πίστεως.

Ἀμέλει καὶ βασιλεὺς ἀγαθὸν πᾶσιν ὑπόδειγμα ἦν, καὶ πολλοὺς ἐπὶ τὴν ὁμοίαν γνώμην ἀνέφλεγε καὶ ἐξῆπτε. τοιοῦτον γὰρ ἡ ἐξουσία· συμμορφοῦται ταύτῃ ἀεὶ τὸ ὑποχείριον, τῶν αὐτῶν τε φιλεῖ ἐρᾶν, κἀκεῖνα ἐπιτηδεύειν οἷσπερ ἂν τὸν ἄρχοντα αἴσθηται χαίροντα. ἐντεῦθεν, τοῦ Θεοῦ συνερ- 309
γοῦντος, ἡ εὐσέβεια ηὐξάνετο ἐν αὐτοῖς καὶ ἐπεδίδου. καὶ ὅλως ἦν τῶν τοῦ Χριστοῦ ἐντολῶν

of the multitude. And they that were baptized not only received health in their souls, but indeed as many as were afflicted with bodily ailments and imperfections cast off all their trouble, and came up from the holy font pure in soul, and sound in body, reaping an harvest of health for soul and body alike.

Multitudes flock for to hear his teaching

Wherefore also from all quarters multitudes flocked to King Ioasaph, desirous to be instructed by him in godliness. And all idolatrous images were utterly demolished, and all their wealth and temple treasure was taken from them, and in their stead holy courts were built for God. For these King Ioasaph dedicated the riches and costly vestments and treasures of the idolatrous temples, thereby making this worthless and superfluous material fit for service, and profitable. And the foul fiends that dwelt in their altars and temples were rigorously chased away and put to flight; and these, in the hearing of many, loudly lamented the misfortune that had overtaken them. And all the region round about was freed from their dark deceit, and illuminated with the light of the blameless Christian faith.

The perfect pattern of his rule,

And, soothly, the king was a good example to all; and he inflamed and kindled the hearts of many to be of the same mind with himself. For such is the nature of authority. Its subjects alway conform to its likeness, and are wont to love the same objects, and to practise the pursuits which they perceive to be pleasing to their governor. Hence, God helping, religion grew and increased amongst them. The

καὶ τῆς αὐτοῦ ἀγάπης ἐξηρτημένος ὁ βασιλεύς,
οἰκονόμος τε τοῦ λόγου τῆς χάριτος, καὶ ψυχῶν
κυβερνήτης πολλῶν, εἰς τὸν λιμένα τοῦ Θεοῦ
Agapetus, Ch. 1-2 ταύτας καθορμίζων. ᾔδει γὰρ τοῦτο εἶναι πρὸ
πάντων βασιλέως ἔργον, ἵνα τοὺς ἀνθρώπους
διδάξῃ τὸν Θεὸν φοβεῖσθαι καὶ τὸ δίκαιον τηρεῖν.
ὃ δὴ καὶ ἐποίει· ἑαυτόν τε εἰς τὸ βασιλεῦσαι
τῶν παθῶν καταρτίζων, καὶ τοῖς ὑπ' αὐτὸν ὡς
κυβερνήτης ἄριστος διακατέχων ἀκριβῶς τῆς
εὐνομίας τοὺς οἴακας. τοῦτο γὰρ ὅρος ἀληθινῆς
βασιλείας, τὸ βασιλεύειν καὶ κρατεῖν τῶν ἡδο-
Id. Ch. νῶν· ὅπερ ἐκεῖνος ἐποίει. ἐπὶ προγόνων μέντοι
εὐγενείᾳ καὶ τῇ περὶ αὐτὸν οὔσῃ βασιλικῇ δόξῃ
μηδόλως ἐναβρυνόμενος, εἰδὼς ὅτι πήλινον ἔχομεν
πάντες τοῦ γένους προπάτορα, καὶ τοῦ αὐτοῦ
φυράματος ἐσμὲν πλούσιοί τε καὶ πένητες, ἐν
ἀβύσσῳ δὲ ταπεινοφροσύνης ἀεὶ τὸν νοῦν ἐμβάλ-
λων, καὶ τῆς ἐκεῖθεν μακαριότητος μεμνημένος,
πάροικον μὲν ἑαυτὸν τῶν ἐνταῦθα ἐλογίζετο,
ἐκεῖνα δὲ ἐγίνωσκεν ἴδια εἶναι ὧν ἂν μετὰ τὴν
ἐνθένδε τύχοι ἐκδημίαν. ἐπεὶ δὲ πάντα καλῶς
εἶχεν αὐτῷ, καί, πάντας τοὺς ὑπὸ χεῖρα τῆς 310
παλαιᾶς ἀπαλλάξας πλάνης πατροπαραδότου,
1 Pet. i. 18 δούλους εἰργάσατο τοῦ ἐξαγοράσαντος ἡμᾶς τῆς
πονηρᾶς δουλείας τῷ τιμίῳ αὐτοῦ αἵματι, δεύτε-
ρον ἐννοεῖ ἔργον, τὴν τῆς εὐποιΐας ἀρετήν. σωφροσύνη γὰρ καὶ δικαιοσύνη ἤδη προκατώρθωτο
αὐτῷ, ὡς τὸν στέφανον τῆς σωφροσύνης ἀναδη-
σαμένῳ καὶ τὴν πορφύραν τῆς δικαιοσύνης ἀμ-
Agapetus, Ch. 7 φιασαμένῳ. ἐνενόει οὖν τοῦ ἐπιγείου πλούτου τὸ
ἄστατον ποταμίων ὑδάτων μιμεῖσθαι τὸν δρόμον.
Mat. vi. 19-21 ἐκεῖ τοίνυν ἔσπευδε τοῦτον ἀποθέσθαι, ὅπου οὔτε

king was wholly dependent on the commandments of Christ and on his love, being a steward of the word of grace, and pilot to the souls of many, bringing them to safe anchorage in the haven of God. For he knew that this, afore all things, is the work of a king, to teach men to fear God and keep righteousness. Thus did he, training himself to be king over his own passions, and, like a good pilot, keeping a firm hold of the helm of good government for his subjects. For this is the end of good kingship, to be king and lord over pleasure—which end also he achieved. Of the nobility of his ancestors, or the royal splendour around him, he was in no wise proud, knowing that we all have one common forefather, made of clay, and that, whether rich or poor, we are all of the same moulding. He ever abased his soul in deepest humility, and thought on the blessedness of the world to come, and considered himself a stranger and pilgrim in this world, but realised that that was his real treasure which he should win after his departure hence. Now, since all went well with him, and since he had delivered all the people from their ancient and ancestral error, and made them servants of him who redeemed us from evil servitude by his own precious blood, he turned his thoughts to his next task, the virtue of almsgiving. Temperance and righteousness he had already attained; he wore on his brow the crown of temperance, and wrapped about him the purple of righteousness. He called to mind the uncertainty of earthly riches, how they resemble the running of river waters. Therefore made he

his charity and alms

σὴς οὔτε βρῶσις ἀφανίζει, καὶ ὅπου κλέπται οὐ
διορύσσουσιν οὐδὲ κλέπτουσι. καὶ δὴ ἤρξατο
πάντα τοῖς πένησι διανέμειν τὰ χρήματα, μηδόλως
αὐτῶν φειδόμενος. ᾔδει γὰρ ὡς ὁ μεγάλης ἐξουσίας ἐπιλαβόμενος τὸν δοτῆρα τῆς ἐξουσίας
ὀφείλει μιμεῖσθαι κατὰ δύναμιν, ἐν τούτῳ δὲ μά-
Cp. Cic. pro Marc. 8 λιστα τὸν Θεὸν μιμήσεται, ἐν τῷ μηδὲν ἡγεῖσθαι
τοῦ ἐλεεῖν προτιμότερον. ὑπὲρ χρυσίον οὖν καὶ
λίθον τίμιον τῆς εὐποιΐας τὸν πλοῦτον ἑαυτῷ
συναθροίζων ἦν, τὸν καὶ ὧδε κατευφραίνοντα τῇ
ἐλπίδι τῆς μελλούσης ἀπολαύσεως, κἀκεῖ κατα-
γλυκαίνοντα τῇ πείρᾳ τῆς ἐλπισθείσης μακαριότητος. ἐντεῦθεν ἠρευνῶντο αὐτῷ φυλακαί, οἱ ἐν
μετάλλοις κατακεκλεισμένοι, οἱ ὑπὸ δανειστῶν
συμπνιγόμενοι· καί, πᾶσιν ἀφθόνως ἐπιχορηγῶν
Cp. Ps. lxviii. 5 πάντα, πατὴρ ἦν ἁπάντων τῶν ὀρφανῶν τε καὶ
χηρῶν καὶ πενήτων, πατὴρ φιλόστοργος καὶ ἀγα- 311
θός, ἑαυτὸν δοκῶν εὐεργετεῖν ἐκ τῆς εἰς αὐτοὺς
γενομένης εὐεργεσίας. πλουσιόδωρος γὰρ ὢν τὴν
ψυχὴν καὶ τῷ ὄντι βασιλικώτατος, πᾶσιν ἐδίδου
δαψιλῶς τοῖς χρῄζουσιν· ἀπειροπλασίους γὰρ
ἤλπιζεν ὑπὲρ τούτων ἀμοιβὰς κομίσασθαι ὅταν
ἔλθῃ ὁ καιρὸς τῆς τῶν ἔργων ἀνταποδόσεως.

Πανταχοῦ δὲ τῆς τοιαύτης αὐτοῦ φήμης ἐν
ὀλίγῳ διαβαινούσης, πάντες πρὸς αὐτόν, ὥσπερ
ὑπό τινος ὀσμῆς μύρου κεκινημένοι, καθ' ἑκάστην
συνέρρεον, σωμάτων τε ὁμοῦ καὶ ψυχῶν πενίαν
ἀποτιθέμενοι, καὶ ἐν τοῖς ἁπάντων στόμασιν ἦν.
οὐχ ὁ φόβος γὰρ καὶ ἡ τυραννὶς εἷλκε τὸν λαόν,
ἀλλ' ὁ πόθος καὶ ἡ πρὸς αὐτὸν ἐκ καρδίας ἀγάπη.
ἥτις ἐκ Θεοῦ καὶ τῆς αὐτοῦ καλλίστης πολιτείας
ἐνεφυτεύθη ταῖς πάντων ψυχαῖς. τότε δὴ τότε

haste to lay up his treasure where neither 'moth nor rust doth corrupt and where thieves do not break through nor steal.' So he began to distribute all his money to the poor, sparing naught thereof. He knew that the possessor of great authority is bound to imitate the giver of that authority, according to his ability; and herein he shall best imitate God, if he hold nothing in higher honour than mercy. Before all gold and precious stone he stored up for himself the treasure of almsgiving; treasure, which here gladdeneth the heart by the hope of enjoyment to come, and there delighteth it with the taste of the hoped-for bliss. After this he searched the prisons, and sought out the captives in mines, or debtors in the grip of their creditors; and by generous largesses to all he proved a father to all, orphans, and widows, and beggars, a loving and good father, for he deemed that by bestowing blessings on these he won a blessing for himself. Being endowed with spiritual riches, and, in sooth, a perfect king, he gave liberally to all that were in need, for he hoped to receive infinitely more, when the time should come for the recompense of his works.

The fame of Ioasaph outshineth the fame of Abenner

Now, in little while, the fame of Ioasaph was blazoned abroad; and led, as it were by the scent of sweet ointment, all men flocked to him daily, casting off their poverty of soul and body: and his name was on every man's lips. It was not fear and oppression that drew the people to him, but desire and heart-felt love, which by God's blessing and the king's fair life had been planted in their hearts.

καὶ οἱ τῷ πατρὶ αὐτοῦ ὑποκείμενοι αὐτῷ μᾶλλον
προσετίθεντο, καί, τὴν πλάνην πᾶσαν ἀποτιθέμενοι, τὴν ἀλήθειαν εὐηγγελίζοντο. καὶ ὁ μὲν
Luke i. 80 οἶκος τοῦ Ἰωάσαφ ηὔξανε καὶ ἐκραταιοῦτο, ὁ δὲ
οἶκος τοῦ Ἀβεννὴρ ἠλαττονοῦτο καὶ ἠσθένει, καθάπερ δὴ περὶ τοῦ Δαυὶδ καὶ τοῦ Σαοὺλ ἡ τῶν 312
2 Sam. iii. 1 Βασιλειῶν διαγορεύει βίβλος.

XXXIV

Ταῦτα ὁρῶν ὁ βασιλεὺς Ἀβεννὴρ, ὀψὲ καὶ μόλις
εἰς συναίσθησιν ἐλθών, τῶν ἑαυτοῦ κατεγίνωσκε
ψευδωνύμων θεῶν τῆς ἀσθενείας καὶ κενῆς ἀπάτης.
καὶ ἐκκλησιάσας αὖθις τοὺς πρώτους τῆς βουλῆς
τὰ μελετώμενα αὐτῷ εἰς φῶς ἐξῆγε. πάντων δὲ
Luke i. 78 τὰ αὐτὰ βεβαιούντων (ἐπεσκέψατο γὰρ αὐτοὺς
ἀνατολὴ ἐξ ὕψους, ὁ Σωτὴρ τῆς δεήσεως ἀκούσας
τοῦ θεράποντος αὐτοῦ Ἰωάσαφ), ἔδοξε τῷ βασιλεῖ
δῆλα ταῦτα τῷ υἱῷ ποιῆσαι. γράφει οὖν τῇ ἑξῆς
ἐπιστολὴν τῷ Ἰωάσαφ περιέχουσαν οὕτως·

Βασιλεὺς Ἀβεννὴρ τῷ ποθεινοτάτῳ υἱῷ Ἰωάσαφ, χαίρειν. Λογισμοὶ πολλοί, εἰς τὴν ἐμὴν ὑπεισερχόμενοι ψυχήν, δεινῶς, φίλτατε, τυραννοῦσιν, υἱέ. τὰ γὰρ ἡμέτερα πάντα ἐκλείποντα ὁρῶν, ὃν τρόπον καπνὸς ἐκλείπει, τὰ τῆς σῆς δὲ θρησκείας λάμποντα ὑπὲρ ἥλιον, εἰς αἴσθησιν δὲ ἐλθών, ἀληθῆ τὰ παρὰ σοῦ μοὶ ἀεὶ λεγόμενα ἔγνωκα εἶναι, καὶ ὅτι σκότος ἡμᾶς βαθὺ τῶν ἁμαρτιῶν καὶ τῆς ἀσεβείας ἐκάλυπτεν, ὡς ἐντεῦθεν οὐδὲ πρὸς τὴν ἀλήθειαν διαβλέψαι καὶ τὸν ἁπάντων Δημιουργὸν

Then, too, did his father's subjects begin to come to him, and, laying aside all error, received the Gospel of truth. And the house of Ioasaph grew and waxed strong, but the house of Abenner waned and grew weak, even as the Book of the Kings declareth concerning David and Saul.

XXXIV

When king Abenner saw this, though late and loth, he came to his senses, and renounced his false gods with all their impotence and vain deceit. Again he called an assembly of his chief counsellors, and brought to light the thoughts of his heart. As they confirmed his words (for the day-spring from on high had visited them, the Saviour who had heard the prayer of his servant Ioasaph), it pleased the king to signify the same to his son. Therefore on the morrow he wrote a letter to Ioasaph, running thus:

Abenner again taketh counsel,

'King Abenner to his well-beloved son Ioasaph, greeting. Dearest son, many thoughts have been stealing into my soul, and rule it with a rod of iron. I see our state vanishing, like as smoke vanisheth, but thy religion shining brighter than the sun; and I have come to my senses, and know that the words which thou hast ever spoken unto me are true, and that a thick cloud of sin and wickedness did then cover us, so that we were unable to discern the truth,

and writeth a letter to Ioasaph, renouncing his idolatry

καταμαθεῖν ἠδυνάμεθα· ἀλλὰ καὶ φῶς οὕτω τηλαυγέστερον διὰ σοῦ ἀναδειχθὲν ἡμῖν, τοὺς ὀφθαλμοὺς μύσαντες, ἡμεῖς ὁρᾶν οὐκ ἠθελήσαμεν, πολλὰ μέν σοι κακὰ ἐνδειξάμενοι, ἐλεεινῶς δὲ 313
φεῦ καὶ τῶν Χριστιανῶν οὐκ ὀλίγους ἀνελόντες, οἵτινες, τῇ συνεργούσῃ αὐτοῖς ἀμάχῳ δυνάμει κραταιούμενοι, διὰ τέλους πρὸς τὴν ἡμετέραν ὠμότητα ὑπερέσχον. νυνὶ δέ, τὴν παχεῖαν ἐκείνην ἀχλὺν τῶν ἡμετέρων ὀμμάτων περιελόντες, αὐγήν τινα μικρὰν τῆς ἀληθείας ὁρῶμεν, καὶ τῶν προτέρων μεταμέλεια εἰσέρχεται κακῶν. ἀλλὰ καὶ ταύτην τὴν αὐγὴν νέφος ἄλλο δεινῆς ἀπογνώσεως ἐπιπολάζον σκοτίζειν πειρᾶται, τὸ πλῆθος προβαλλόμενον τῶν ἐμῶν κακῶν, καὶ ὅτι βδελυκτὸς ἤδη ἐγὼ τῷ Χριστῷ καὶ ἀπρόσδεκτός εἰμι, ὡς ἀποστάτης καὶ πολέμιος αὐτοῦ γεγονώς. τί οὖν πρὸς ταῦτα, τέκνον γλυκύτατον, λέγεις αὐτός, δῆλά μοι τάχιστα ποίησον, καὶ τί δεῖ ποιεῖν με τὸν σὸν πατέρα δίδαξον, καὶ πρὸς ἐπίγνωσιν χειραγώγησον τοῦ συμφέροντος.

Ταύτην τὴν ἐπιστολὴν ὁ Ἰωάσαφ δεξάμενος, καὶ τὰ ἐμφερόμενα ἐπελθών, ἡδονῆς ὁμοῦ καὶ θαύματος τὴν ψυχὴν ἐπληροῦτο. εἰς τὸ ἑαυτοῦ δὲ ταμιεῖον εἰσελθὼν εὐθὺς καὶ ἐπὶ πρόσωπον πεσὼν ἐνώπιον τοῦ Δεσποτικοῦ χαρακτῆρος, δάκρυσι τὴν γῆν κατέβρεχεν, εὐχαριστῶν ὁμοῦ τῷ δεσπότῃ καὶ ἐξομολογούμενος, καὶ χείλη ἀγαλλιάσεως κινῶν πρὸς ὑμνῳδίαν·

Ps. cxlv. 1, 3 Ὑψώσω σε, λέγων, ὁ Θεός μου καὶ βασιλεύς μου, καὶ εὐλογήσω τὸ ὄνομά σου εἰς τὸν αἰῶνα καὶ εἰς τὸν αἰῶνα τοῦ αἰῶνος· μέγας εἶ, Κύριε, καὶ αἰνετὸς σφόδρα, καὶ τῆς μεγαλωσύνης σου

and recognize the Creator of all. Nay, but we shut our eyes, and would not behold the light which thou didst enkindle more brightly for us. Much evil did we do unto thee, and many of the Christians, alas! did we destroy; who, strengthened by the power that aided them, finally triumphed over our cruelty. But now we have removed that dense mist from our eyes, and see some small ray of truth, and there cometh on us repentance of our misdeeds. But a new cloud of despair would overshadow it; despair at the multitude of mine offences, because I am now abominable and unacceptable to Christ, being a rebel and a foeman unto him. What, then, sayest thou, dearest son, hereto? Make known to me thine answer, and teach me that am thy father what I should do, and lead me to the knowledge of my true weal.'

When Ioasaph had received this letter, and read the words therein, his soul was filled with mingled joy and amazement. Forthwith he entered his closet, and falling on his face before the image of his Master, watered the ground with his tears, giving thanks to his Lord and confessing him, and tuning lips of exultation to sing an hymn of praise, saying: **Ioasaph receiveth the letter,**

'I will magnify thee, O God, my King, and I will praise thy name for ever and ever. Great art thou O Lord, and marvellous-worthy to be praised, and of **and singeth a hymn of praise to God,**

Ps. cvi. 2 οὐκ ἔστι πέρας. καὶ τίς λαλήσει τὰς δυναστείας
σου, ἀκουστὰς ποιήσει πάσας τὰς αἰνέσεις σου,
Ps. cxiv. 8 τοῦ στρέψαντος τὴν πέτραν εἰς λίμνας ὑδάτων
καὶ τὴν ἀκρότομον εἰς πηγὰς ὑδάτων; ἰδοὺ γὰρ 314
ἡ ἀκρότομος αὕτη καὶ πέτρας σκληροτέρα καρδία
τοῦ ἐμοῦ πατρός, σοῦ θελήσαντος, ὡσεὶ κηρὸς
Mat. iii. 9 ἐμαλάχθη. δυνατὸν γάρ σοι καὶ ἐκ τῶν λίθων
τούτων ἐγεῖραι τέκνα τῷ Ἀβραάμ. εὐχαριστῶ
σοι, Δέσποτα φιλάνθρωπε, Θεὲ τοῦ ἐλέους,
ὅτι ἐμακροθύμησας καὶ μακροθυμεῖς τοῖς παραπτώμασιν ἡμῶν, καὶ ἕως τοῦ νῦν ἀτιμωρήτους
ἡμᾶς εἴασας εἶναι. ἡμεῖς μὲν γὰρ ἄξιοι ἦμεν
πάλαι ἀπορριφθῆναι ἀπὸ τοῦ προσώπου σου καὶ
παραδειγματισθῆναι ἐν τῷ βίῳ τούτῳ, ὡς οἱ
Gen. xix. 24 τὴν Πεντάπολιν οἰκοῦντες παράνομοι, πυρὶ καὶ
θείῳ κατακαυθέντες· ἡ δὲ ἀνείκαστός σου μακροθυμία ἐφιλανθρωπεύσατο εἰς ἡμᾶς. εὐχαριστῶ
σοι ὁ εὐτελὴς ἐγὼ καὶ ἀνάξιος, εἰ καὶ μὴ ὑπάρχω
αὐτάρκης πρὸς δοξολογίαν τῆς σῆς ἀγαθότητος.
καὶ δέομαι τῶν ἀμετρήτων σου οἰκτιρμῶν, Κύριε
Ἰησοῦ Χριστέ, Υἱὲ καὶ Λόγε τοῦ ἀοράτου
Πατρός, ὁ πάντα λόγῳ παραγαγὼν καὶ θελήματι τῷ σῷ συνέχων, ὁ ῥυσάμενος ἡμᾶς τοὺς
ἀναξίους δούλους σου τῆς τοῦ ἀρχεκάκου ἐχθροῦ
Mat. xii. 29 δουλείας, ὁ ταθεὶς ἐπὶ ξύλου καὶ δήσας τὸν
ἰσχυρόν, καὶ τοῖς ὑπ᾽ ἐκείνου δεθεῖσιν αἰώνιον
ἐπιβραβεύσας ἐλευθερίαν· αὐτὸς καὶ τὰ νῦν
ἔκτεινόν σου τὴν ἀόρατον χεῖρα καὶ παντουργόν,
καὶ εἰς τέλος ἐλευθέρωσον τὸν δοῦλόν σου καὶ
πατέρα μου τῆς χαλεπῆς ἐκείνης αἰχμαλωσίας
τοῦ διαβόλου· καὶ ὑπόδειξον αὐτῷ ἐναργέστατα,
ὅτι σὺ εἶ ὁ ἀεὶ ζῶν Θεὸς ἀψευδὴς καὶ βασιλεὺς

thy greatness there is no end. Who can express thy noble acts, or show forth all thy praise, who hast turned the hard rock into a standing water and the flint-stone into a springing well? For behold this my father's flinty and more than granite heart is at thy will melted as wax; because thou art able of these stones to raise up children unto Abraham. I thank thee, Lord, thou lover of men, and God of pity, that thou hast been, and art, long-suffering towards our offences, and hast suffered us until now to go unpunished. Long have we deserved to be cast away from thy face, and made a by-word on earth, as were the sinful inhabiters of the five cities, consumed with fire and brimstone; but thy marvellous long-suffering hath dealt graciously with us. I give thanks unto thee, vile and unworthy though I be, and insufficient of myself to glorify thy greatness. And, by thine infinite compassions, I pray thee, Lord Jesu Christ, Son and Word of the invisible Father, who madest all things by thy word, and sustainest them by thy will; who hast delivered us thine unworthy servants from the bondage of the arch-fiend our foe: thou that wast stretched upon the Rood, and didst bind the strong man, and award everlasting freedom to them that lay bound in his fetters: do thou now also stretch forth thine invisible and almighty hand, and, at the last, free thy servant my father from that cruel bondage of the devil. Show him full clearly that thou art the ever living true God, and only King, eternal and

and prayeth for his aid

μόνος αἰώνιος καὶ ἀθάνατος. ἴδε μου, Δέσποτα,
τὴν συντριβὴν τῆς καρδίας ἵλεῳ καὶ εὐμενεῖ 315
ὄμματι· καὶ κατὰ τὴν ἀψευδῆ σου ἐπαγγελίαν
γενοῦ μετ᾽ ἐμοῦ τοῦ γινώσκοντος καὶ ὁμολο-
γοῦντός σε ποιητὴν καὶ προνοητὴν πάσης κτί-
John iv. 14 σεως. πηγασάτω ἐν ἐμοὶ τὸ σὸν ἁλλόμενον
Eph. vi. 19 ὕδωρ· καὶ δοθήτω μοι λόγος ἐν ἀνοίξει τοῦ
στόματος, καὶ νοῦς καλῶς ἡδρασμένος ἐν σοὶ
Cp. Is. xxviii. 16 τῷ ἀκρογωνιαίῳ λίθῳ, ἵνα δυνήσομαι ὁ ἀχρεῖος
οἰκέτης σου καταγγεῖλαι τῷ ἐμῷ γεννήτορι,
ὡς δεῖ, τὸ μυστήριον τῆς σῆς οἰκονομίας, καὶ
ἀποστῆσαι αὐτὸν τῇ σῇ δυνάμει τῆς ματαίας
πλάνης τῶν πονηρῶν δαιμόνων, καὶ προσαγαγεῖν
Ez. xviii. 23 σοι τῷ Θεῷ καὶ δεσπότῃ, τῷ μὴ βουλομένῳ
τὸν θάνατον ἡμῶν τῶν ἁμαρτωλῶν, ἀλλ᾽ ἀνα-
μένοντι τὴν ἐπιστροφὴν καὶ τὴν μετάνοιαν, ὅτι
δεδοξασμένος εἶ εἰς τοὺς αἰῶνας. ἀμήν.

Οὕτως εὐξάμενος καὶ πληροφορίαν λαβὼν μὴ
διαμαρτεῖν τοῦ ποθουμένου, τῇ εὐσπλαγχνίᾳ τοῦ
Χριστοῦ θαρρήσας, ἐξάρας ἐκεῖθεν μετὰ τῆς
βασιλικῆς δορυφορίας, τὰ βασίλεια καταλαμβάνει τοῦ ἰδίου πατρός. ὡς δὲ τῷ πατρὶ ἀνηγ-
γέλη ἡ ἄφιξις τοῦ υἱοῦ, ἐξέρχεται εὐθὺς εἰς
συνάντησιν αὐτῷ, περιπλέκεται, καταφιλεῖ, μεγίστην ποιεῖται χαρὰν καὶ δημοτελῆ ἑορτὴν ἐπὶ
τῇ παρουσίᾳ τοῦ υἱοῦ αὐτοῦ.

Τί δὲ τὸ μετὰ ταῦτα; συγκαθέζονται καταμόνας
ἀλλήλοις. καὶ τί ἄν τις εἴποι ἅπερ διείλεκται τότε
τῷ βασιλεῖ ὁ υἱὸς καὶ μεθ᾽ ὅσης τῆς φιλοσοφίας;
Τί δὲ ἄλλο γε ἢ τὰ τῷ θείῳ Πνεύματι αὐτῷ
Mk. i. 17 ὑπηχούμενα, δι᾽ οὗ οἱ ἁλιεῖς σαγηνεύουσι τῷ 316
Χριστῷ τὸν κόσμον ὅλον, καὶ οἱ ἀγράμματοι τῶν

immortal. Behold, O Lord, with favourable and kindly eye, the contrition of my heart; and, according to thine unerring promise, be with me that acknowledge and confess thee the Maker and protector of all creation. Let there be a well of water within me springing up, and let utterance be given unto me that I may open my mouth, and a mind well fixed in thee, the chief corner-stone, that I, thine unprofitable servant, may be enabled to preach to my father, as is right, the mystery of thine Incarnation, and by thy power deliver him from the vain deceit of wicked devils, and bring him unto thee his God and Lord, who willest not the death of us sinners, but waitest for us to return and repent, because thou art glorified for ever and ever. Amen.'

Ioasaph visiteth his father,

When he had thus prayed, and received fulness of assurance that he should not miscarry in his desire, he took courage by the tender mercy of Christ, and arose thence, with his royal body-guard, and arrived at his father's palace. When it was told unto his father, 'Thy son is come,' he went forth straightway for to meet him, and embraced and kissed him lovingly, and made exceeding great joy, and held a general feast in honour of the coming of his son. And afterward, they two were closeted together.

and preacheth the Gospel to him

But how tell of all that the son spake with his father, and of all the wisdom of his speech? And what was that speech but the words put into his mouth by the Holy Ghost, by whom the fishermen enclosed the whole world in their nets for Christ and the unlearned are found wiser than

σοφῶν σοφώτεροι δείκνυνται. τῇ τούτου χάριτι καὶ αὐτὸς σοφισθεὶς ἐλάλει τῷ βασιλεῖ καὶ πατρί, φωτίζων αὐτὸν φῶς γνώσεως. καὶ πρότερον γάρ, πολλὰ κοπιάσας τοῦ ἑλκῦσαι τῆς δεισιδαίμονος πλάνης τὸν πατέρα, τί μὲν οὐ λέγων, τί δὲ οὐ ποιῶν, ὥστε τοῦτον ἐπαναγαγέσθαι, κενὴν ψάλλειν ἐῴκει, καὶ εἰς ὦτα λέγειν μὴ ἀκουόντων· ὅτε δὲ ἐπέβλεψεν ὁ Κύριος ἐπὶ τὴν ταπείνωσιν τοῦ δούλου αὐτοῦ Ἰωάσαφ, καί, τῆς δεήσεως αὐτοῦ ὑπακούσας, τὰς κεκλεισμένας πύλας τῆς καρδίας τοῦ πατρὸς αὐτοῦ διήνοιξε
Ps. cxlv. 19 (θέλημα γάρ, φησί, τῶν φοβουμένων αὐτὸν ποιήσει, καὶ τῆς δεήσεως αὐτῶν εἰσακούσεται), ῥᾳδίως τὰ λεγόμενα συνίει ὁ βασιλεύς· ὥστε, καιροῦ εὐθέτου τυχόντα, τὸν υἱὸν τῇ τοῦ Χριστοῦ χάριτι κατὰ τῶν πονηρῶν ἆραι νίκην πνευμάτων τῶν κυριευσάντων τῆς ψυχῆς τοῦ πατρὸς αὐτοῦ, καὶ τῆς τούτων πλάνης τέλεον ἐλευθερῶσαι αὐτόν, τὸν σωτήριον δὲ τρανῶς γνωρίσαι λόγον καὶ τῷ ἐν οὐρανοῖς οἰκειῶσαι ζῶντι Θεῷ.

Ἐξ ἀρχῆς γὰρ τὸν λόγον ἀναλαβών, ἀνήγγειλεν αὐτῷ ἃ οὐκ ᾔδει μεγάλα καὶ θαυμαστά, ἃ τοῖς ὠσὶ τῆς καρδίας οὐκ ἀκηκόει, πολλὰ μὲν αὐτῷ περὶ Θεοῦ φθεγξάμενος καὶ τὴν εὐσέ- 317
βειαν παραδεικνύς, ὡς οὐκ ἔστιν ἄλλος Θεὸς ἐν οὐρανῷ ἄνω, οὔτε ἐπὶ γῆς κάτω, εἰ μὴ ὁ ἐν Πατρὶ καὶ Υἱῷ καὶ Ἁγίῳ Πνεύματι γνωριζόμενος εἷς Θεός· πολλὰ δὲ μυστήρια γνωρίσας τῆς θεολογίας, ἐφ᾽ οἷς καὶ τὰ περὶ τῆς ἀοράτου τε καὶ ὁρατῆς διήγγειλε κτίσεως, ὅπως ἐκ μὴ ὄντων
Heb. xi. 3 τὰ πάντα παραγαγὼν ὁ Δημιουργός, κατ᾽ εἰκόνα
Gen. i. 26 καὶ ὁμοίωσιν αὐτοῦ πλάσας τὸν ἄνθρωπον καὶ

the wise. This Holy Spirit's grace and wisdom taught Ioasaph to speak with the king his father, enlightening him with the light of knowledge. Before now he had bestowed much labour to drag his father from superstitious error, leaving nothing unsaid and nothing undone to win him over, but he seemed to be twanging on a broken string, and speaking to deaf ears. But when the Lord looked upon the lowliness of his servant Ioasaph, and, in answer to his prayer, opened the closed gates of his father's heart (for it is said, he will fulfil the desire of them that fear him, and will hear their cry), then the king easily understood the things that were spoken; so that, when a convenient season came, through the grace of Christ, this son triumphed over those evil spirits that had lorded it over the soul of his father, and clean freed him from their error, and made the word of salvation clearly known unto him, and joined him to the living God on high.

Ioasaph took up his tale from the beginning, and expounded to his father great and marvellous things which he knew not, which he had never heard with the ears of his heart; and he told him many weighty sayings concerning God, and showed him righteousness: to wit that there is no other God in heaven above, nor in the earth beneath, except the one God, revealed in the Father, the Son, and the Holy Ghost. And he made known unto him many mysteries of divine knowledge; and amongst them he told him the history of creation, visible and invisible, how the Creator brought every thing out of nothing, and how he formed man after his own image and likeness

He telleth of the Creation and the Fall

τοῦτον τῷ αὐτεξουσίῳ τιμήσας, τῶν ἐν παραδείσῳ καλῶν μετέχειν πεποίηκεν, ἀπέχεσθαι
Gen. ii. 17 τούτου μόνου κελεύσας ὅπερ ἦν τὸ ξύλον τῆς
γνώσεως, ἠθετηκότα δὲ τὴν ἐντολὴν τοῦ παραδείσου ἐξώρισεν· ὅθεν, τῆς πρὸς αὐτὸν οἰκειό-
τητος ὀλισθῆσαν, εἰς τὰς πολλὰς ταύτας περιπέπτωκε πλάνας τὸ ἀνθρώπινον γένος, δουλωθὲν
ταῖς ἁμαρτίαις καὶ ὑποπεσὸν τῷ θανάτῳ διὰ
τῆς τυραννίδος τοῦ διαβόλου· ὅς, ὑποχειρίους
ἅπαξ τοὺς ἀνθρώπους λαβών, παντελῶς ἐπιλαθέσθαι πεποίηκε τοῦ Θεοῦ καὶ δεσπότου, καὶ
αὐτῷ ἀνέπεισε λατρεύειν διὰ τῆς τῶν εἰδώλων
Mat. i. 18–20; Luke i. 43; John xix. 26; Acts ii. 14 μυσαρᾶς προσκυνήσεως. σπλαγχνισθεὶς οὖν ὁ
πλάσας ἡμᾶς Θεός, εὐδοκίᾳ τοῦ Πατρὸς καὶ
συνεργίᾳ τοῦ Ἁγίου Πνεύματος, εὐδόκησεν ἐκ
Παρθένου ἁγίας, τῆς Θεοτόκου Μαρίας, καθ᾿
ἡμᾶς τεχθῆναι· καί, πάθεσιν ὁμιλήσας ὁ ἀπαθής,
διὰ τρίτης τε ἡμέρας ἐκ νεκρῶν ἀναστάς, ἐλυτρώ-
σατο ἡμᾶς τοῦ προτέρου ἐπιτιμίου καὶ κλέους
τοῦ προτέρου ἠξίωσε. συνανήγαγε γὰρ ἡμᾶς
εἰς οὐρανοὺς ἀνερχόμενος, ὅθεν ἐτύγχανε κατα-
βεβηκώς· ὃν καὶ αὖθις ἥξειν πιστεύομεν, ἵνα τὸ 318
Rom. ii. 6 πλάσμα τὸ ἑαυτοῦ ἀναστήσῃ. ἀποδώσει δὲ
ἑκάστῳ κατὰ τὰ ἔργα αὐτοῦ. ἐπὶ τούτοις τὴν
ἐκδεχομένην τοὺς ἀξίους τῶν οὐρανῶν ἐμυστα-
γώγει βασιλείαν καὶ τὰ ἀπόρρητα ἀγαθά. τὴν
ἀποκειμένην τοῖς φαύλοις προσετίθει βάσανον,
Mat. xxv. 30; Mk. ix. 44 τὸ ἄσβεστον πῦρ, τὸ ἐξώτερον σκότος, τὸν
ἀτελεύτητον σκώληκα, καὶ ὅσην ἄλλην οἱ τῆς
ἁμαρτίας δοῦλοι κόλασιν ἑαυτοῖς ἐθησαύρισαν.

Ταῦτα πάντα λόγοις πλείστοις, καὶ δαψιλῶς
αὐτῷ ἐνυπάρχουσαν τὴν τοῦ Πνεύματος μαρτυ-

and endowed him with power of free-will, and gave him Paradise to his enjoyment, charging him only to abstain from one thing, the tree of knowledge; and how, when man had broken his commandment, he banished him out of Paradise; and how man, fallen from union with God, stumbled into these manifold errors, becoming the slave of sins, and subject unto death through the tyranny of the devil, who, having once taken men captive, hath made them utterly forget their Lord and God, and hath persuaded them to serve him instead, by the abominable worshipping of idols. So our Maker, moved with compassion, through the good-will of the Father, and the co-operation of the Holy Ghost, was pleased, for our sakes,[1] to be born of an holy Virgin, Mary, the mother of God, and he, that cannot suffer, was acquainted with sufferings. On the third day he rose again from the dead, and redeemed us from our first penalty, and restored to us our first glory. When he ascended into the heavens, from whence he had descended, he raised us up together with him; and thence, we believe that he shall come again, to raise up his own handiwork; and he will recompense every man according to his works. Moreover Ioasaph instructed his father concerning the kingdom of heaven that awaiteth them that are worthy thereof, and the joy unspeakable. Thereto he added the torment in store for the wicked, the unquenchable fire, the outer darkness, the undying worm and whatsoever other punishment the servants of sin have laid up in store for themselves.

of the Incarnation and the Redemption,

All these things set he forth in many words, which bore witness that the grace of the Spirit was

[1] Or 'like one of us' (?).

Cp. pp. 94, 95 ροῦσι χάριν, διεξελθών, εἶτα καὶ τὸ ἀνεξιχνίαστον πέλαγος τῆς τοῦ Θεοῦ διηγούμενος φιλανθρωπίας καὶ οἷός ἐστιν ἕτοιμος δέχεσθαι τὴν μετάνοιαν τῶν πρὸς αὐτὸν ἐπιστρεφόντων, καὶ ὡς οὐκ ἔστιν ἁμαρτία νικῶσα τὴν αὐτοῦ εὐσπλαγχνίαν, εἴπερ θελήσομεν μετανοῆσαι, ἐκ πολλῶν δὲ τοῦτο παραδειγμάτων καὶ γραφικῶν παραστήσας μαρτυριῶν, ὁ μὲν τέλος ἐπέθηκε τῷ λόγῳ.

XXXV

Κατανυγεὶς δὲ ὁ βασιλεὺς Ἀβεννὴρ ἐπὶ τῇ θεοδιδάκτῳ σοφίᾳ ταύτῃ, φωνῇ μεγάλῃ καὶ θερμοτάτῃ ψυχῇ τὸν σωτῆρα Χριστὸν ὡμολόγει, πάσης ἀποστὰς δεισιδαίμονος πλάνης.[1]
τὸ σημεῖόν τε προσκυνεῖ τοῦ ζωοποιοῦ σταυροῦ 319
ὑπὸ τῇ πάντων ὄψει καὶ εἰς ἐπήκοον ἁπάντων Θεὸν κηρύττει ἀληθινὸν τὸν Κύριον ἡμῶν Ἰησοῦν Χριστόν· τήν τε προτέραν ἀσέβειαν διεξελθών, τὴν οἰκείαν τε κατὰ τῶν Χριστιανῶν ὠμότητα καὶ μιαιφονίαν ἐλέγξας, μέγα μέρος πρὸς τὴν εὐσέβειαν γίνεται· ὡς ἐντεῦθεν ἔργῳ τὸ εἰρημένον
Rom. v. 20 τῷ Παύλῳ γνωσθῆναι, καὶ ὅπου ὁ τῆς ἀσεβείας ὑπῆρχε πλεονασμός, ἐκεῖ καὶ τὴν περισσείαν γενέσθαι τῆς χάριτος.

Πολλὰ τοίνυν καὶ τοῦ σοφωτάτου Ἰωάσαφ τοῖς συνελθοῦσι τότε στρατηγοῖς τε καὶ σατράπαις καὶ παντὶ τῷ λαῷ περὶ Θεοῦ καὶ τῆς εἰς αὐτὸν εὐσεβείας διαλεγομένου, καὶ οἱονεὶ

[1] A good iambic line ends here with 'πλάνης.'

dwelling richly within him. Then he described the uncharted sea of the love of God towards mankind, and how he is ready to accept the repentance of them that turn to him; and how there is no sin too great for his tender mercy, if we will but repent. And when he had confirmed these truths by many an example, and testimony of Scripture, he made an end of speaking.

and of the infinite love of God to man

XXXV

King Abenner was pricked to the heart by this inspired wisdom and with loud voice and fervent heart confessed Christ his Saviour, and forthwith forsook all superstitious error. He venerated the sign of the life-giving Cross in the sight of all and, in the hearing of all, proclaimed our Lord Jesus Christ to be God. By telling in full the tale of his former ungodliness, and of his own cruelty and blood-thirstiness toward the Christians, he proved himself a great power for religion. So here was proved in fact, the saying of Paul; that where sin abounded, there did grace much more abound.

King Abenner renounceth idolatry and becometh a Christian

While then the learned Ioasaph was speaking of God, and of piety towards him, to the dukes and satraps and all the people there assembled, and was

The whole multitude giveth praise to God

Cp. Acts ii. 3 πυρίνῃ γλώσσῃ καλόν τι καὶ ᾠδικὸν τερετίζοντος,
ἡ τοῦ Ἁγίου Πνεύματος χάρις ἐπιφοιτήσασα
πάντας εἰς δοξολογίαν ἐκίνει Θεοῦ, ὡς ἐκ μιᾶς
φωνῆς πάντων βοησάντων τῶν ὄχλων· Μέγας
ὁ Θεὸς τῶν Χριστιανῶν· οὐκ ἔστιν ἄλλος θεὸς
πλὴν τοῦ Κυρίου ἡμῶν Ἰησοῦ Χριστοῦ σὺν
Πατρὶ καὶ Ἁγίῳ Πνεύματι δοξαζομένου.

Ζήλου δὲ θείου κατάπλεως γενόμενος, ὁ βασιλεὺς
Ἀβεννὴρ ἐφάλλεται στερρῶς τοῖς εἰδώλοις
ἃ ἦσαν ἐν τῷ παλατίῳ αὐτοῦ ἐκ χρυσοῦ καὶ
ἀργύρου πεποιημένα, καὶ εἰς ἔδαφος ταῦτα κατασπᾷ.
εἶτα, εἰς λεπτὰ διελών, πένησι διανέμει,
ὠφέλιμα οὕτω τὰ ἀνωφελῆ θέμενος· ἀμέλει καὶ 320
μετὰ τοῦ υἱοῦ τοὺς εἰδώλων ναοὺς καὶ βωμοὺς
περιστάντες μέχρις αὐτῶν κατηδάφουν τῶν θεμελίων·
ἱερὰ δὲ τῷ Θεῷ τεμένη ἀντῳκοδόμουν.
οὐ μόνον δὲ ἐν τῇ πόλει, ἀλλὰ καὶ ἀνὰ πᾶσαν
τὴν χώραν σπουδῇ ταῦτα ἐποίουν. τὰ δὲ πονηρὰ
πνεύματα τὰ τοῖς βωμοῖς ἐνοικοῦντα ὀλολύζοντα
ἠλαύνοντο, καὶ τὴν ἄμαχον τοῦ Θεοῦ ἡμῶν
δύναμιν ὑποτρέμοντα ἐβόων. πᾶσα δὲ ἡ περίχωρος
καὶ τὰ τῶν προσοίκων ἐθνῶν πλεῖστα
πρὸς τὴν εὐσεβῆ πίστιν ἐχειραγωγοῦντο. τότε
δὴ τοῦ ἀνωτέρω ῥηθέντος θειοτάτου ἐπισκόπου
παραγενομένου, κατηχεῖται ὁ βασιλεὺς Ἀβεννήρ,
Mat. xxviii. 19 καὶ τῷ θείῳ τελειοῦται βαπτίσματι εἰς τὸ ὄνομα
τοῦ Πατρός, τοῦ Υἱοῦ καὶ τοῦ Ἁγίου Πνεύματος. 321
καὶ Ἰωάσαφ τοῦτον ἐκ τῆς θείας κολυμβήθρας
ἀναδέχεται, τοῦτο δὴ τὸ καινότατον γεννήτωρ τοῦ
πατρὸς ἀναδειχθείς, καὶ τῷ σαρκικῶς γεννήσαντι
τῆς πνευματικῆς ἀναγεννήσεως πρόξενος γενόμενος.
υἱὸς γὰρ ἦν τοῦ οὐρανίου Πατρὸς καὶ

as it were with a tongue of fire piping unto them a goodly ode, the grace of the Holy Spirit descended upon them, and moved them to give glory to God, so that all the multitude cried aloud with one voice, 'Great is the God of the Christians, and there is none other God but our Lord Jesus Christ, who, together with the Father and Holy Ghost, is glorified.'

The temples of the idols are razed to the ground

Waxen full of heavenly zeal, King Abenner made a sturdy assault on the idols, wrought of silver and gold, that were within his palace, and tore them down to the ground. Then he brake them into small pieces, and distributed them to the poor, thus making that which had been useless useful. Furthermore he and his son besieged the idols' temples and altars and levelled them even to the ground, and in their stead, and to the honour of God, built holy courts. And not only in the city but throughout all the country also, thus did they in their zeal. And the evil spirits that dwelt in those altars were driven forth with shrieks, and cried out in terror at the invincible power of our God. And all the region round about, and the greater part of the neighbour nations, were led, as by the hand, to the true Faith.

The king is baptized

Then came the holy Bishop, of whom we have spoken, and King Abenner was instructed, and made perfect with Holy Baptism, in the name of the Father, and of the Son, and of the Holy Ghost. And Ioasaph received him as he came up from the Holy Font, in this strange way appearing as the begetter of his own father, and proving the spiritual father to him that begat him in the flesh: for he was the son of

καρπὸς ὄντως τῆς θείας ῥίζης θειότατος, ῥίζης
John xv. 5 ἐκείνης τῆς βοώσης· Ἐγώ εἰμι ἡ ἄμπελος, ὑμεῖς
τὰ κλήματα.
John iii. 5 Οὕτως ἀναγεννηθεὶς ὁ βασιλεὺς Ἀβεννὴρ δι'
1 Pet. i. 8 ὕδατος καὶ Πνεύματος ἔχαιρε χαρᾷ ἀνεκλαλήτῳ·
σὺν αὐτῷ δὲ καὶ πᾶσα ἡ πόλις καὶ ἡ περίχωρος
1 Thess. v. 5 τοῦ θείου ἠξιοῦτο βαπτίσματος, καὶ φωτὸς υἱοὶ
ἀνεδείκνυντο οἱ πρὶν ἐσκοτισμένοι. πᾶσα δὲ νόσος
καὶ πᾶσα δαιμονικὴ ἐπιφορὰ πόρρω τῶν πιστευόν-
των ἠλαύνετο· ἄρτιοι δὲ καὶ ὑγιεῖς πάντες τὰς
ψυχὰς καὶ τὰ σώματα ἦσαν. καὶ πολλὰ ἕτερα
θαυμάσια εἰς βεβαίωσιν τῆς πίστεως ἐτελοῦντο.
ἐκκλησίαι τε ἀνῳκοδομοῦντο, καὶ ἐπίσκοποι, οἵ
τε κεκρυμμένοι διὰ τὸν φόβον ἐφανεροῦντο καὶ
τὰς ἰδίας ἀπελάμβανον ἐκκλησίας, καὶ ἄλλοι ἔκ 322
τε τῶν ἱερέων καὶ τῶν μοναζόντων προεχειρίζοντο
εἰς τὸ ποιμαίνειν τὸ τοῦ Χριστοῦ ποίμνιον. ὁ
μέντοι βασιλεὺς Ἀβεννήρ, οὕτω τῆς προτέρας
ἐκείνης μοχθηρᾶς ἀγωγῆς ἀποστὰς καὶ μετάμελος
ὢν ἐφ' οἷς ἔπραξε, πᾶσαν μὲν τὴν βασίλειον
ἀρχὴν τῷ υἱῷ παραδίδωσιν· αὐτὸς δὲ καθ' ἑαυτὸν
ἠρεμῶν, κόνιν ἀεὶ τῆς κεφαλῆς καταχέων, βαρεῖς
τε ἀναφέρων στεναγμοὺς καὶ λούων τοῖς δάκρυσιν
ἑαυτόν, μόνος μόνῳ τῷ πανταχοῦ παρόντι ὡμίλει,
συγγνώμην αὐτῷ τῶν οἰκείων πταισμάτων ἐξαι-
τούμενος. εἰς τοσαύτην δὲ κατανύξεως καὶ ταπεινοφροσύνης ἄβυσσον ἑαυτὸν καθῆκεν ὡς
παραιτεῖσθαι καὶ τὸ τοῦ Θεοῦ ὄνομα τοῖς ἑαυτοῦ
ὀνομάζειν χείλεσι, μόλις δὲ τούτου τῇ τοῦ υἱοῦ
νουθεσίᾳ κατατολμῆσαι. οὕτω δὲ τὴν καλὴν
ἀλλοίωσιν ἠλλοιώθη καὶ τὴν πρὸς ἀρετὴν ἀπάγουσαν ὥδευσε τρίβον ὡς ὑπερβῆναι αὐτὸν τῇ εὐσε-

his heavenly Father, and verily divine fruit of that divine Branch, which saith, 'I am the vine, ye are the branches.'

Thus King Abenner, being born again of water and of the spirit, rejoiced with joy unspeakable, and with him all the city and the region round about received Holy Baptism, and they that were before darkness now became children of light. And every disease, and every assault of evil spirits was driven far from the believers, and all were sane and sound in body and in soul. And many other miracles were wrought for the confirmation of the Faith. Churches too were built, and the bishops, that had been hiding for fear, discovered themselves, and received again their own churches, whilst others were chosen from the priests and monks, to shepherd the flock of Christ. But King Abenner, having thus forsaken his former disgraceful life, and repented of his evil deeds, handed over to his son the rule of all his kingdom. He himself dwelt in solitude, continually casting dust on his head, and groaning for very heaviness, and watering his face with his tears, being alone, communing with him who is everywhere present and imploring him to forgive his sins. And he abased himself to such a depth of contrition and humility, that he refused to name the name of God with his own lips, and was scarce brought by his son's admonitions to make so bold. Thus the king passed through the good change and entered the road that leadeth to virtue, so that his righteousness now surpassed his former sins of ignorance.

The Christian Faith prospereth greatly in his kingdom

Of the king's repentance and holy life

βείᾳ τῶν προτέρων ἀνομιῶν τὸ ἀγνόημα. ἐπὶ τέσσαρας δὲ χρόνους οὕτω βιοὺς ἐν μετανοίᾳ καὶ
δάκρυσι καὶ ἀρετῇ πάσῃ, ἀρρωστίᾳ περιέπεσεν,
ἐν ᾗ καὶ τελευτᾷ. ὅτε δὲ τὸ τέλος ἤγγισεν, ἤρξατο
φοβεῖσθαι καὶ ἀδημονεῖν, μνείαν ποιούμενος τῶν
αὐτῷ πεπραγμένων κακῶν. ὁ δὲ Ἰωάσαφ ῥήμασι
παρακλητικοῖς τὸ ἐπιπεσὸν αὐτῷ διεκούφιζεν
Ps. xlii. 6, 7 ἄχθος, Ἱνατί περίλυπος εἶ, λέγων, ὦ πάτερ, καὶ
ἱνατί συνταράττεις ἑαυτόν; ἔλπισον ἐπὶ τὸν Θεὸν
Ps. lxv. 5 καὶ ἐξομολόγει αὐτῷ, ὅς ἐστιν ἐλπὶς πάντων τῶν
περάτων τῆς γῆς καὶ τῶν ἐν θαλάσσῃ μακράν, ὃς
Is. i. 16 ff. κέκραγε διὰ τοῦ προφήτου βοῶν· Λούσασθε, 323
καθαροὶ γένεσθε· ἀφέλετε τὰς πονηρίας ἀπὸ
τῶν ψυχῶν ὑμῶν ἀπέναντι τῶν ὀφθαλμῶν μου·
μάθετε καλὸν ποιεῖν· καί, Ἐὰν ὦσιν αἱ ἁμαρτίαι
ὑμῶν ὡς φοινικοῦν, ὡς χιόνα λευκανῶ· ἐὰν δὲ
ὦσιν ὡς κόκκινον, ὡσεὶ ἔριον λευκανῶ. μὴ φοβοῦ
τοίνυν, ὦ πάτερ, μηδὲ δίσταζε· οὐ νικῶσι γὰρ αἱ
ἁμαρτίαι τῶν ἐπιστρεφόντων πρὸς Θεὸν τὴν ἄπειρον αὐτοῦ ἀγαθότητα. αὗται γὰρ ὑπὸ μέτρον εἰσὶ
καὶ ἀριθμὸν, ὅσαι ἂν ὦσιν· ἐκείνη δὲ ἀμέτρητός
ἐστι καὶ ἀναρίθμητος. οὐκ ἐνδέχεται τοίνυν τὸ
ὑποκείμενον μέτρῳ τοῦ ἀμετρήτου περιγενέσθαι.

Τοιούτοις παρακλητικοῖς ῥήμασι κατεπᾴδων
αὐτοῦ τὴν ψυχήν, εὔελπιν ἀπειργάσατο. εἶτα
ἐκτείνας ὁ πατὴρ τὰς χεῖρας, εὐχαριστῶν αὐτῷ
ὑπερηύχετο, καὶ τὴν ἡμέραν εὐλόγει ἐν ᾗ
αὐτὸς ἐγγεννήθη, Τέκνον, λέγων, γλυκύτατον,
τέκνον οὐκ ἐμόν, ἀλλὰ τοῦ οὐρανίου Πατρός, ποίαν
ἀποδώσω σοι χάριν; ποίαις εὐλογήσω σε εὐλογίαις; τίνα δὲ εὐχαριστίαν ἀναπέμψω τῷ Θεῷ
Cf. Luke xv. 6, 24, 32 περὶ σοῦ; ἀπολωλὼς γὰρ ἤμην, καὶ εὑρέθην διὰ

For four years did he live thus in repentance and tears and virtuous acts, and then fell into the sickness whereof he died. But when the end drew nigh, he began to fear and to be dismayed, calling to remembrance the evil that he had wrought. But with comfortable words Ioasaph sought to ease the distress that had fallen on him, saying, 'Why art thou so full of heaviness, O my father, and why art thou so disquieted within thee? Set thy hope on God, and give him thanks, who is the hope of all the ends of the earth, and of them that remain in the sea afar, who crieth by the mouth of his prophet, "Wash you, make you clean: put away from before mine eyes the wickedness of your souls; learn to do well"; and "Though your sins be as scarlet, I will make them white as snow; though they be red like crimson, I will make them as wool." Fear not, therefore, O my father, neither be of doubtful mind: for the sins of them that turn to God prevail not against his infinite goodness. For these, however many, are subject to measure and number: but measure and number cannot limit his goodness. It is impossible then for that which is subject to measure to exceed the unmeasurable.'

How the king was sick unto death

Ioasaph comforteth his despondency

With such comfortable words did Ioasaph cheer his soul, and bring him to a good courage. Then his father stretched out his hands, and gave him thanks and prayed for him, blessing the day whereon Ioasaph was born, and said 'Dearest child, yet not child of me, but of mine heavenly Father, with what gratitude can I repay thee? With what words of blessings may I bless thee? What thanks shall I offer God for thee? I was lost, and was found through thee:

The king maketh a good end

σοῦ· νεκρὸς ἤμην τῇ ἁμαρτίᾳ, καὶ ἀνέζησα·
ἐχθρὸς καὶ ἀποστάτης Θεοῦ, καὶ κατηλλάγην.
τί οὖν ἀνταποδώσω σοι ὑπὲρ τούτων ἁπάντων;
Θεός ἐστιν ὁ ἀξίας σοι παρέχων τὰς ἀμοιβάς. 324
οὕτω λέγων, πυκνὰ κατεφίλει τὸν φίλτατον παῖδα.
Cp. Ps. xxxi. 6 εἶτα εὐξάμενος, καί, Εἰς χεῖράς σου, φιλάνθρωπε
Θεέ, παρατίθημι τὸ πνεῦμά μου, εἰπών, ἐν μετα-
νοίᾳ τὴν ψυχὴν καὶ εἰρήνῃ παρέθετο τῷ Κυρίῳ.

Ὁ δὲ Ἰωάσαφ δάκρυσι τιμήσας τελευτήσαντα
τὸν πατέρα, καὶ κηδεύσας αὐτοῦ τὸ λείψανον
ἐντίμως, κατέθετο ἐν μνήματι ἀνδρῶν εὐσεβῶν, οὐ
μέντοι βασιλικῇ περιβαλὼν ἐσθῆτι, ἀλλὰ μετανοίας κοσμήσας ἀμφίοις. στὰς δὲ ἐπὶ τῷ μνήματι,
χεῖράς τε εἰς οὐρανὸν διάρας, καὶ δάκρυα ποταμηδὸν τῶν ὀμμάτων καταδύσας, ἐβόησε πρὸς τὸν
Θεόν, λέγων·

Ὁ Θεός, εὐχαριστῶ σε, Βασιλεῦ τῆς δόξης,
μόνε κραταιὲ καὶ ἀθάνατε, ὅτι οὐ παρεῖδες τὴν
Ps. xxxix. 13 δέησίν μου καὶ τῶν δακρύων μου οὐ παρεσιώπη-
σας, ἀλλ᾿ εὐδόκησας τὸν δοῦλόν σου τοῦτον καὶ
πατέρα μου τῆς ὁδοῦ ἐπιστρέψαι τῶν ἀνομιῶν καὶ
πρὸς ἑαυτὸν ἑλκύσαι τὸν σωτῆρα τῶν ἁπάντων,
ἀποστήσας μὲν τῆς ἀπάτης τῶν εἰδώλων, καταξιώσας δὲ γνωρίσαι σε τὸν ἀληθινὸν Θεὸν καὶ
φιλάνθρωπον. καὶ νῦν, ὦ Κύριέ μου καὶ Θεέ, ὁ
ἀνεξιχνίαστον ἔχων τὸ τῆς ἀγαθότητος πέλαγος,
τάξον αὐτὸν ἐν τόπῳ χλοερῷ, ἐν τόπῳ ἀναπαύσεως, ὅπου τὸ φῶς λάμπει τοῦ προσώπου σου· 325
καὶ μὴ μνησθῇς ἀνομιῶν αὐτοῦ ἀρχαίων, ἀλλὰ
Col. ii. 14 κατὰ τὸ πολὺ ἔλεός σου ἐξάλειψον τὸ χειρόγρα-
φον τῶν αὐτοῦ πταισμάτων, καὶ τὰ γραμματεῖα
διάρρηξον τῶν αὐτοῦ ὀφλημάτων, καὶ τοὺς ἁγίους

I was dead in sin and am alive again: an enemy, and rebel against God, and am reconciled with him. What reward therefore shall I give thee for all these benefits? God is he that shall make the due recompense.' Thus saying, he pressed many kisses on his beloved son; then, when he had prayed, and said, 'Into thy hands, O God, thou lover of men, do I commit my spirit,' he committed his soul unto the Lord in penitence and peace.

Now, when Ioasaph had honoured with his tears his father that was dead, and had reverently cared for his body, he buried him in a sepulchre wherein devout men lay; not indeed clad in royal raiment, but robed in the garment of penitence. Standing on the sepulchre, and lifting up his hands to heaven, the tears streaming in floods from his eyes, he cried aloud unto God saying, **Ioasaph burieth his father,**

'O God, I thank thee, King of glory, alone mighty and immortal, that thou hast not despised my petition, and hast not held thy peace at my tears, but hast been pleased to turn this thy servant, my father, from the way of wickedness, and to draw him to thyself, the Saviour of all, departing him from the deceitfulness of idolatry, and granting him to acknowledge thee, who art the very God and lover of souls. And now, O my Lord and God, whose ocean of goodness is uncharted, set him in that place where much grass is, in a place of refreshment, where shineth the light of thy countenance. Remember not his old offences; but, according to the multitude of thy mercies, blot out the hand-writing of his sins, and destroy the tablets of his debts, and **and thanketh God for his salvation**

σου κατάλλαξον αὐτῷ οὓς πυρί τε καὶ ξίφει ἀνεῖ-
λεν· ἐπίταξον αὐτοὺς μὴ κατ' αὐτοῦ ὀργίζεσθαι.
πάντα γὰρ δυνατά σοι τῷ πάντων Δεσπότῃ, ἀλλ'
ἢ μόνον τὸ μὴ ἐλεεῖν τοὺς μὴ ἐπιστρέφοντας πρὸς
σέ· τοῦτο ἀδύνατον. τὸ γὰρ ἔλεός σου ἐκκέχυ-
ται ἐπὶ πάντας, καὶ σώζεις τοὺς ἐπικαλουμένους
σε, Κύριε Ἰησοῦ Χριστέ, ὅτι πρέπει σοι δόξα εἰς
τοὺς αἰῶνας. ἀμήν.

Τοιαύτας εὐχὰς καὶ δεήσεις προσέφερε τῷ Θεῷ
ἐν ὅλαις ἑπτὰ ἡμέραις, μηδόλως τοῦ μνήματος
Cp. Ps. cii. 4 ἀποστάς, μὴ βρώσεως ἢ πόσεως τοπαράπαν μνη-
σθείς, μήτε μὴν ἀναπαύσεως ὕπνου μετασχών·
ἀλλὰ δάκρυσι μὲν τὸ ἔδαφος ἔβρεχε, στεναγμοῖς δὲ ἀσιγήτοις εὐχόμενος διετέλει. τῇ ὀγδόῃ
δὲ εἰς τὸ παλάτιον ἐπανελθών, πάντα τὸν πλοῦτον καὶ τὰ χρήματα τοῖς πένησι διένειμεν, ὡς
μηκέτι ὑπολειφθῆναί τινα τῶν χρείαν ἐχόντων.

XXXVI

Εν ὀλίγαις δὲ ἡμέραις τὴν τοιαύτην τελέσας
διακονίαν καὶ πάντας τοὺς θησαυροὺς κατα-
Mat. vii. 13 κενώσας, ὅπως μέλλοντι τὴν στενὴν εἰσιέναι πύ-
Luke xiii. 24 λην μηδὲν αὐτῷ ἐμποδίσειεν ὁ τῶν χρημάτων
ὄγκος, τῇ τεσσαρακοστῇ ἡμέρᾳ τῆς τοῦ πατρὸς
τελευτῆς, μνήμην αὐτῷ τελῶν, συγκαλεῖ πάντας
τοὺς ἐν τέλει καὶ τοὺς στρατιωτικὰ περιεζω-
σμένους καὶ τοῦ πολιτικοῦ λαοῦ οὐκ ὀλίγους. 326
καὶ προκαθίσας, ὡς ἔθος, φησὶν εἰς ἐπήκοον
πάντων· Ἰδού, καθὼς ὁρᾶτε, Ἀβεννὴρ πατήρ
μου καὶ βασιλεὺς τέθνηκεν ὡς εἷς τῶν πενήτων,

set him at peace with thy Saints whom he slew with fire and sword. Charge them not to be bitter against him. For all things are possible with thee, the Lord of all, save only to withhold pity from them that turn not unto thee; this is impossible. For thy pity is poured out upon all men, and thou savest them that call upon thee, Lord Jesu Christ, because glory becometh thee for ever and ever. Amen.'

Ioasaph mourneth for his father

Such were the prayers and intercessions that he made unto God, by the space of seven full days, never leaving the grave, and never thinking of meat or drink, and taking no refreshment of sleep: but he watered the ground with his tears, and continued praying and moaning unceasingly. But, on the eighth day, he went back to his palace and distributed amongst the poor all his wealth and riches, so that not one person was left in want.

XXXVI

Ioasaph summoneth an assembly,

In a few days, after he had ended this ministry, and emptied all his coffers, in order that the burden of his money might not hinder him from entering in at the narrow gate, on the fortieth day after his father's decease, and in remembrance of him, he called together all his officers, and those who wore soldiers' attire, and of the citizens not a few. Sitting in the front, according to custom, in the audience of all he said, 'Lo, as ye see, Abenner, my father the king, hath died like any beggar. Neither wealth, nor kingly

καὶ οὐδὲν αὐτῷ οὔτε ὁ πλοῦτος οὔτε ἡ βασιλικὴ δόξα, οὔτε μὴν ἐγὼ ὁ φιλοπάτωρ υἱός, οὔτε τις τῶν λοιπῶν αὐτοῦ φίλων καὶ συγγενῶν, βοηθῆσαι ἴσχυσεν αὐτῷ καὶ τῆς ἀπαραιτήτου ψήφου ἐξελέσθαι. ἀλλ' ὑπάγει πρὸς τὰ ἐκεῖθεν δικαιωτήρια, λόγον ὑφέξων τῆς πολιτείας τοῦ παρόντος βίου, μηδένα τῶν ἁπάντων συνεργὸν ἐπαγόμενος, ἀλλ' ἢ μόνα τὰ αὐτῷ πεπραγμένα ὁποῖα ἂν ᾖ. τὸ αὐτὸ δὲ τοῦτο καὶ πᾶσι τοῖς τὴν βρότειον λαχοῦσι φύσιν συμβαίνειν πέφυκε, καὶ ἄλλως οὐκ ἔστι. νῦν οὖν ἀκούσατέ μου, φίλοι καὶ ἀδελφοί, λαὸς Κυρίου καὶ κλῆρος ἅγιος, οὓς ἐξηγόρασε Χριστὸς ὁ Θεὸς ἡμῶν τῷ τιμίῳ αὐτοῦ αἵματι καὶ ἐρρύσατο τῆς παλαιᾶς πλάνης καὶ δουλείας τοῦ ἀντικειμένου. αὐτοὶ οἴδατε τὴν ἐν ὑμῖν ἀναστροφήν μου, ὡς ἐξότε τὸν Χριστὸν ἔγνων καὶ δοῦλος αὐτοῦ ἠξιώθην γενέσθαι, πάντα μισήσας, αὐτὸν ἐπεπόθησα μόνον, καὶ τοῦτό μοι ἦν καταθύμιον, τῆς ζάλης τοῦ βίου καὶ ματαίας τύρβης ὑπεξελθόντα, μόνον μόνῳ αὐτῷ συνεῖναι καὶ ἐν ἀταράχῳ γαλήνῃ ψυχῆς δουλεῦσαι τῷ Θεῷ μου καὶ δεσπότῃ. ἀλλά με
Exod. xx. 12 κατέσχεν ἡ τοῦ πατρός μου ἔνστασις, καὶ ἐντολὴ ἡ τιμᾶν τοὺς γεννήτορας κελεύουσα. ὅθεν, Θεοῦ χάριτι καὶ συνεργείᾳ, οὐκ εἰς μάτην ἐκοπίασα, οὐδ' εἰς κενὸν τὰς τοιαύτας ἀνηλωσά ἡμέρας· ἀλλ' ἐκεῖνόν τε ᾠκείωσα Χριστῷ καὶ πάντας 327
ὑμᾶς τοῦτον μόνον γινώσκειν Θεὸν ἀληθινὸν καὶ
1 Cor. xv. 10 Κύριον τοῦ παντὸς ἐδίδαξα, οὐκ ἐγὼ τοῦτο ποιήσας, ἀλλ' ἡ χάρις αὐτοῦ ἡ σὺν ἐμοί, ἥτις κἀμὲ τῆς δεισιδαίμονος πλάνης καὶ λατρείας τῶν εἰδώλων ἐξείλετο, καὶ ὑμᾶς, λαός μου, τῆς χαλεπῆς

glory, nor I his loving son, nor any of his kith and kindred, has availed to help him, or to save him from the sentence without reprieve. But he is gone to yonder judgement seat, to give account of his life in this world, carrying with him no advocate whatsoever, except his deeds, good or bad. And the same law is ordained by nature for every man born of woman, and there is no escape. Now, therefore, hearken unto me, friends and brethren, people and holy heritage of the Lord, whom Christ our God hath purchased with his own precious blood, and delivered from the ancient error, and bondage of the adversary. Ye yourselves know my manner of life among you; that ever since I knew Christ, and was counted worthy to become his servant, I have hated all things, and loved him only, and how this was my desire, to escape from the tempest and vain tumult of the world, and commune alone with him, and in undisturbed peace of soul serve my God and Master. But my father's opposition held me back, and the command that biddeth us to honour our fathers. So, by the grace and help of God, I have not laboured in vain, nor spent these days for naught, I have brought my father nigh to Christ, and have taught you all to know the one true God, the Lord of all; and yet not I, but the grace of God which was with me, which rescued me also from superstitious error, and from the worship of idols, and freed you, O my

and maketh known to all his desire to lay aside his royal estate

ἠλευθέρωσεν αἰχμαλωσίας. καιρὸς οὖν ἤδη
λοιπὸν τὰ ἐπηγγελμένα τῷ Θεῷ ἔργα πληρῶσαι·
καιρὸς ἀπελθεῖν ὅπου ἂν αὐτὸς ὁδηγήσῃ με καὶ
ἀποδοῦναι τὰς εὐχάς μου ἃς ηὐξάμην αὐτῷ. νῦν
οὖν σκέψασθε ὑμεῖς ὃν ἂν βούλοισθε ἀφηγεῖσθαι
ὑμῶν καὶ βασιλεύειν· ἤδη γὰρ κατηρτισμένοι
ἐστὲ εἰς τὸ θέλημα τοῦ Κυρίου, καὶ οὐδὲν ἀποκέ-
κρυπται ὑμῖν τῶν αὐτοῦ προσταγμάτων· ἐν τούτοις πορεύεσθε· μὴ ἐκκλίνητε δεξιὰ ἢ ἀριστερά·
Rom. xv. 33 καὶ ὁ Θεὸς τῆς εἰρήνης εἴη μετὰ πάντων ὑμῶν.

Ταῦτα ὡς ἤκουσεν ὁ λαὸς ἐκεῖνος καὶ δῆμος,
θόρυβος εὐθὺς καὶ πάταγος καὶ βοὴ πλείστη
καὶ σύγχυσις ἦν, κλαιόντων πάντων καὶ ὀδυ-
ρομένων τὴν ὀρφανίαν. τοιαῦτα θρηνοῦντες,
πρὸς τοῖς θρήνοις καὶ ὅρκοις ἐβεβαίουν μὴ
μεθήσειν ὅλως, ἀλλ' ἀνθέξεσθαι, καὶ τὴν ὑποχώ-
ρησιν αὐτῷ μὴ τοπαράπαν παραχωρῆσαι. οὕτω
βοῶντος τοῦ δήμου καὶ τῶν ἐν τέλει πάντων,
Acts xxi. 40 ὑπολαβὼν ὁ βασιλεὺς κατασείει τὸν ὄχλον, καὶ
σιγᾶν αὐτοῖς διακελεύεται. καὶ εἴκειν τῇ ἐκείνων
ἐνστάσει εἰπών, λυπουμένους ὅμως καὶ τὰ τῆς
οἰμωγῆς σημεῖα ἐπὶ τῶν παρειῶν φέροντας οἴκαδε ἐκπέμπει. αὐτὸς δὲ ἕνα τῶν ἀρχόντων, ὃς
ἦν πρόκριτος αὐτῷ, ἐπ' εὐσεβείᾳ καὶ σεμνότητι 328
βίου θαυμαζόμενος, Βαραχίας τοὔνομα (ὅνπερ
p. 388 καὶ ἀνωτέρω ἐδήλωσεν ὁ λόγος, ἡνίκα Ναχὼρ
τὸν Βαρλαὰμ ὑποκρινόμενος φιλοσόφοις διελέγετο,
καὶ μόνος ὁ Βαραχίας ἡτοιμάσθη συμπαραστῆναι
αὐτῷ καὶ συναγωνίσασθαι, ζήλῳ θείῳ ἐκκαυθεὶς
τὴν καρδίαν, τοῦτον καταμόνας λαβὼν ὁ βασιλεύς, προσηνῶς διελέγετο, καὶ θερμότατα ἐδεῖτο
παραλαβεῖν τὴν βασιλείαν, καὶ ἐν φόβῳ Θεοῦ

people, from cruel captivity. So now it is high time to fulfil the service that I promised to God; high time to depart thitherward, where he himself shall lead me, where I may perform my vows which I made unto him. Now, therefore, look you out a man whom ye will, to be your leader and king; for by this time ye have been conformed to the will of the Lord, and of his commandments nothing hath been hidden from you. Walk ye therein; turn not aside, neither to the right hand, nor to the left, and the God of peace be with you all!'

The people cry out for sorrow and will not let him go

When all that company and the common people heard thereof, anon there arose a clamour, an uproar, and a mighty cry and confusion, all weeping like orphans and bewailing their loss. Lamenting bitterly, they protested with oaths and with tears, that they would never let him go, but would restrain him and not suffer in any wise his departure. While the common people, and they in authority, were thus crying aloud, the king broke in, and beckoned with his hand to the multitude and charged them to keep silence. He declared that he gave in to their instancy, and dismissed them still grieving, and bearing on their cheeks the signs of sorrow. And Ioasaph did thus. There was one of the senators first in favour with Ioasaph, a man honoured for his godliness and dignity, Barachias by name, who, as hath been already told, when Nachor, feigning to be Barlaam, was disputing with the philosophers, alone was ready to stand by Nachor and fight for him, for his heart was fired with heavenly love. Him the king took apart, and spake gently with him, and earnestly besought him to receive the kingdom, and, in the fear of God, to shepherd his people; in order

τὸν λαὸν αὐτοῦ ποιμᾶναι, ὡς ἂν αὐτὸς τὴν ποθουμένην αὐτῷ πορεύσηται ὁδόν.

Ὡς δὲ αὐτὸν ἀπαναινόμενον εἶδε καὶ πάντη ἀπαγορεύοντα, καί, Ὦ βασιλεῦ, λέγοντα, ὡς ἄδικός σου ἡ κρίσις· ὡς οὐ κατ' ἐντολὴν σοῦ ὁ
Lev. xix. 18; Mat. xxii. 39 λόγος· εἰ γὰρ ἀγαπῆσαι τὸν πλησίον ὡς ἑαυτὸν ἐδιδάχθης, τίνι λόγῳ ὅπερ αὐτὸς ἀπορρίψαι βάρος σπουδάζεις, ἐμοὶ ἐπιθεῖναι ἐπείγῃ; εἰ μὲν γὰρ καλὸν τὸ βασιλεύειν, αὐτὸς τὸ καλὸν κάτεχε· εἰ δὲ πρόσκομμα τοῦτο ψυχῆς καὶ σκάνδαλον, τί μοι προτίθης καὶ ὑποσκελίζειν βούλει; ὡς οὖν τοιαῦτα λέγοντα καὶ διαβεβαιούμενον εἶδεν, ἐπαύσατο τῆς ὁμιλίας. καὶ δὴ ὑπὸ νύκτα βα- 329
θεῖαν ἐπιστολὴν μὲν διαχαράττει πρὸς τὸν λαόν, πολλῆς γέμουσαν φιλοσοφίας καὶ πᾶσαν ὑπαγορεύουσαν τὴν εὐσέβειαν, ὁποίαν τε ὀφείλουσι περὶ Θεοῦ δόξαν ἔχειν, οἷον δὲ βίον αὐτῷ προσφέρειν, οἵους δὲ ὕμνους, οἵας εὐχαριστίας· εἶτα μὴ ἄλλον ἢ τὸν Βαραχίαν δέξασθαι εἰς τὴν βασίλειον κελεύει ἀρχήν. καί, εἰς τὸν ἑαυτοῦ κοιτῶνα τὸν χάρτην ἐν ᾧ ἡ ἐπιστολὴ καταλιπών, λαθὼν ἅπαντας ἐξέρχεται τοῦ παλατίου. ἀλλ' οὐκ ἠδυνήθη λαθεῖν εἰς τέλος. ἅμα γὰρ πρωῒ τοῦτο ἀκουσθὲν τάραχον εὐθὺς καὶ ὀδυρμὸν τῷ λαῷ ἐνεποίησε· καὶ πάντες τάχει πολλῷ εἰς ζήτησιν αὐτοῦ ἐξέρχονται, προκαταλαβεῖν αὐτῷ τὴν φυγὴν ἐκ παντὸς τρόπου διανοούμενοι· ὅθεν οὐδὲ εἰς μάτην αὐτοῖς ἐχώρησεν ἡ σπουδή. ὡς γὰρ πάσας προκατελάμβανον τὰς ὁδούς, ὄρη δὲ πάντα περιεκύκλουν καὶ ἀτριβεῖς περιήρχοντο φάραγγας, ἐν χειμάρρῳ τινὶ τοῦτον εὑρίσκουσι,

that he himself might take the journey that he desired.

But Barachias would put aside and reject his offer, saying, 'O king, how wrongful is thy judgement, and thy word contrary to divine command! If thou hast learned to love thy neighbour as thyself, with what right art thou eager to shift the burden off thy back and lay it upon mine? If it be good to be king, keep the good to thy self: but, if it be a stone of stumbling and rock of offence to thy soul, why put it in my pathway and seek to trip me up?' When Ioasaph perceived that he spake thus, and that his purpose was fixed, he ceased from communing with him. And now, at about the dead of night, he wrote his people a letter, full of much wisdom, expounding to them all godliness; telling them what they should think concerning God, what life, what hymns and what thanksgiving they should offer unto him. Next, he charged them to receive none other than Barachias to be ruler of the kingdom. Then left he in his bed-chamber the roll containing his letter, and, unobserved of all, went forth from his palace. But he might not win through undetected: for, early on the morrow, the tidings, that he was departed, anon made commotion and mourning among the people, and, in much haste, forth went every man for to seek him; they being minded by all means to cut off his flight. And their zeal was not spent in vain; for, when they had occupied all the high-ways, and encompassed all the mountains, and surrounded the pathless ravines, they discovered him in a water-

Barachias refuseth the kingdom proffered him by Ioasaph

Ioasaph seeketh to escape by stealth

χεῖρας εἰς οὐρανὸν ἐκτεταμένας ἔχοντα, καὶ τὴν εὐχὴν τῆς ἕκτης ἐπιτελοῦντα ὥρας.

Ἰδόντες δὲ αὐτὸν περιεχύθησαν δάκρυσι δυσωποῦντες καὶ τὴν ἀποδημίαν ὀνειδίζοντες. ὁ δέ· Τί, φησί, μάτην κοπιᾶτε; μηκέτι γὰρ ἐμὲ βασιλέα ἔχειν ἐλπίζετε. τῇ πολλῇ δὲ αὐτῶν ὑπενδοὺς ἐνστάσει, ὑποστρέφει αὖθις εἰς τὸ παλάτιον. καί, συναγαγὼν ἅπαντας, τὴν ἑαυτοῦ ἐφανέρωσε βουλήν. εἶτα καὶ ὅρκοις ἐμπεδοῖ τὸν λόγον, ὡς οὐδεμίαν αὐτοῖς τοῦ λοιποῦ συνέσται ἡμέραν. Ἐγὼ γάρ, φησί, τὴν πρὸς ὑμᾶς διακονίαν μου
Acts xx. 20 ἐπληροφόρησα καὶ οὐδὲν ἐνέλιπον, οὐδὲ ὑπεστειλάμην τῶν συμφερόντων, τοῦ μὴ ἀναγγεῖλαι ὑμῖν καὶ διδάξαι διαμαρτυρόμενος πᾶσι τὴν εἰς τὸν Κύριον ἡμῶν Ἰησοῦν Χριστὸν πίστιν, καὶ μετανοίας ὁδοὺς ὑποδεικνύων. καὶ νῦν ἰδοὺ ἐγὼ πορεύομαι τὴν ὁδὸν ἣν ἔκπαλαι ἐπόθουν· καὶ οὐκ
Acts xx. 26, 27 ἔτι ὄψεσθε τὸ πρόσωπόν μου ὑμεῖς πάντες. διὸ μαρτύρομαι ὑμῖν τῇ σήμερον ἡμέρᾳ, κατὰ τὸν θεῖον Ἀπόστολον, ὅτι καθαρὸς ἐγώ εἰμι ἀπὸ τοῦ αἵματος πάντων ὑμῶν. οὐ γὰρ ὑπεστειλάμην τοῦ μὴ ἀναγγεῖλαι ὑμῖν πᾶσαν τὴν βουλὴν τοῦ Θεοῦ.

Ταῦτα ἀκούσαντες, καὶ τὸ τῆς γνώμης αὐτοῦ στερρὸν ἐπιστάμενοι, ὡς οὐδὲν τῆς προθέσεως κωλῦσαι δύναται, ὠδύροντο μὲν τὴν ὀρφανίαν, οὐκ εἶχον δὲ ὅλως αὐτὸν πειθόμενον. τότε ὁ βασιλεὺς τὸν Βαραχίαν ἐκεῖνον, ὃν καὶ φθάσας ὁ λόγος ἐδήλωσε, κατασχών, Τοῦτον, εἶπεν, ἀδελφοί, ὑμῖν προχειρίζομαι βασιλέα. τοῦ δὲ ἰσχυρῶς πρὸς τὸ πρᾶγμα ἀπειθοῦντος, ἄκοντα καὶ μὴ βουλόμενον τῇ βασιλικῇ ἀρχῇ ἐγκαθ-

course, his hands uplifted to heaven, saying the prayer proper of the Sixth Hour.

When they beheld him, they surrounded him, and besought him with tears, upbraiding him for departing from them. 'But,' said he, 'why labour ye in vain? No longer hope to have me to your king.' Yet gave he way to their much opposition, and turned again to his palace. And, when he had assembled all the folk, he signified his will. Then with oath he confirmed his word, that he would dwell with them not one day more. 'For,' said he, 'I have fulfilled my ministry toward you, and have omitted naught, neither have I kept back anything that was profitable unto you, in failing to show or teach you, testifying to all the faith in our Lord Jesus Christ, and pointing out the paths of repentance. And now behold I go the road that I have long time desired, and all ye shall see my face no more. Wherefore I take you to record this day, as saith the holy Apostle, that I am pure from the blood of you all, for I have not shunned to declare unto you all the counsel of God.'

The people pursue and overtake him

When they heard this, and perceived the steadfastness of his purpose, that nothing could hinder him from his resolve, they wept like orphans over their bereavement, but could in no wise over-persuade him. Then did the king take that Barachias, of whom we have already spoken, saying, 'This is he, brethren, whom I appoint to be your king.' And though Barachias stoutly resisted, yet he established

Ioasaph, holding to his purpose, maketh Barachias king,

ἵστησι, καὶ τῇ κεφαλῇ αὐτοῦ τὸ διάδημα περιτίθησι, τὸν βασιλικόν τε δακτύλιον δίδωσιν εἰς
See De fide orth. Bk. iv. Ch. 12 τὴν χεῖρα. καὶ στὰς κατὰ ἀνατολὰς ηὔξατο
εὐχὴν τῷ βασιλεῖ Βαραχίᾳ· ἀπερίτρεπτον αὐτῷ
τὴν εἰς Θεὸν φυλαχθῆναι πίστιν καὶ ἀκλινῆ τὴν 331
κατὰ τὰς ἐντολὰς τοῦ Χριστοῦ εὑρεῖν πορείαν.
σὺν τούτῳ δὲ ὑπερηύχετο τοῦ κλήρου καὶ τοῦ ποιμ-
νίου παντός, αἰτούμενος ἀντίληψιν αὐτοῖς παρὰ
Κυρίου καὶ σωτηρίαν, καὶ πᾶν ὅτιπερ ἂν αὐτοῖς
εἰς αἴτησιν ᾖ πρὸς τὸ συμφέρον οἰκονομούμενον.

Οὕτως εὐξάμενος ἐπιστραφεὶς λέγει τῷ Βαρα-
χίᾳ· Ἰδού σοι, ἀδελφέ, ἐντέλλομαι καθώς ποτε ὁ
Acts xx. 28 Ἀπόστολος διεμαρτύρατο· Πρόσεχε σεαυτῷ καὶ
παντὶ τῷ ποιμνίῳ, ἐν ᾧ σε τὸ Πνεῦμα τὸ Ἅγιον
ἔθετο βασιλέα, ποιμαίνειν τὸν λαὸν τοῦ Κυρίου
ὃν περιεποιήσατο διὰ τοῦ αἵματος τοῦ ἰδίου.
καὶ καθὼς πρὸ ἐμοῦ ἔγνως τὸν Θεὸν καὶ ἐλάτρευσας αὐτῷ ἐν καθαρῷ συνειδότι, οὕτω καὶ
νῦν πλείονα σπουδὴν ἐνδείκνυσο εὐαρεστῆσαι
αὐτῷ. ὡς γὰρ καὶ μεγάλης ἠξιώθης παρὰ τοῦ
Θεοῦ ἀρχῆς, τοσούτῳ μείζονος ἀμοιβῆς ὀφειλέτης
ὑπάρχεις. οὐκοῦν ἀπόδος τῷ εὐεργέτῃ τὸ χρέος
τῆς εὐχαριστίας, τὰς ἁγίας αὐτοῦ φυλάσσων
ἐντολὰς καὶ πάσης ἐκκλίνων ὁδοῦ εἰς ἀπώλειαν
Agapet. c. 10 φερούσης. ὥσπερ γὰρ ἐπὶ τῶν πλεόντων, ὅταν
μὲν ναύτης σφαλῇ, μικρὰν φέρει τοῖς πλέουσι
βλάβην· ὅταν δὲ ὁ κυβερνήτης, παντὸς ἐργάζεται τοῦ πλοίου ἀπώλειαν· οὕτω καὶ ἐν βασιλείοις, ἂν μέν τις τῶν ἀρχομένων ἁμάρτῃ, οὐ
τοσοῦτον τὸ κοινὸν ὅσον ἑαυτὸν ἀδικεῖ, ἂν δὲ 332
αὐτὸς ὁ βασιλεύς, πάσης ἐργάζεται τῆς πολιτείας βλάβην. ὡς μεγάλας οὖν ὑφέξων εὐθύνας,

him, unwilling and reluctant, upon the royal throne, and placed the diadem on his head, and gave the kingly ring into his hand. Then he stood facing the East and made prayer for King Barachias, that his faith toward God might be preserved unwavering, and that he might keep without faltering the path of Christ's commandments. Therewith he prayed for the clergy and all the flock, asking of God succour for them and salvation, and all that might fitly be asked for their welfare.

and chargeth him to administer his trust as in God's sight,

Thus he prayed, and then turning said unto Barachias, 'Behold, brother, I charge thee, as the Apostle once adjured his people, "Take heed unto thyself, and to all the flock, over the which the Holy Ghost hath made thee king, to feed the Lord's people, whom he hath purchased with his own blood." And even as thou wast before me in the knowledge of God, and didst serve him with a pure conscience, so now also show the more zeal in pleasing him. For, as thou hast received of God a mighty sovereignty, thou owest him the greater repayment. Render therefore to thy Benefactor the debt of thanksgiving, by the keeping of his holy commandments and by turning aside from every path whose end is destruction. For it is with kingdoms as with ships. If one of the sailors blunder it bringeth but small damage to the crew. But if the steersman err, he causeth the whole ship to perish. Even so it is with sovranty: if a subject err, he harmeth himself more than the state. But if the king err, he causeth injury to the whole realm. Therefore, as one that shall render strict account, if

εἴ τι παρίδοις τῶν δεόντων, μετὰ πολλῆς ἀκριβείας φύλαττε σεαυτὸν ἐν τῷ ἀγαθῷ. μίσησον
πᾶσαν ἡδονὴν πρὸς ἁμαρτίαν ἕλκουσαν· φησὶ
Heb. xii. 14 γὰρ ὁ Ἀπόστολος· Εἰρήνην διώκετε μετὰ πάντων,
καὶ τὸν ἁγιασμὸν οὗ χωρὶς οὐδεὶς ὄψεται τὸν
Agapet. c. 11 Κύριον. τὸν κύκλον πρόσεχε ὅστις περιτρέχει
τῶν ἀνθρωπίνων πραγμάτων, ἄλλοτε ἄλλως φέ-
ρων αὐτὰ καὶ περιφέρων· καὶ ἐν τῇ τούτων
ἀγχιστρόφῳ μεταβολῇ ἀμετάβλητον ἔχε τὸν
εὐσεβῆ λογισμόν. τὸ γὰρ συμμεταβάλλεσθαι
ταῖς τῶν πραγμάτων μεταβολαῖς διανοίας ἀβε-
Agapet. c. 13 βαίου τεκμήριον. σὺ δὲ πάγιος ἔσο, ἐν τῷ
ἀγαθῷ ὅλως ἐρηρεισμένος. μὴ ἐπαίρου διὰ τῆς
Agapet. c. 14 προσκαίρου δόξης πρὸς μάταιον φύσημα· ἀλλὰ
κεκαθαρμένῳ λογισμῷ τὸ οὐτιδανὸν τῆς ἑαυτοῦ
νόει φύσεως, τὸ βραχύ τε καὶ ὠκύμορον τῆς
ἐνταῦθα ζωῆς καὶ τὸν συνεζευγμένον τῇ σαρκὶ
θάνατον. καὶ ταῦτα λογιζόμενος εἰς τὸν τῆς
ὑπεροψίας οὐ βληθήσῃ βόθρον, ἀλλὰ φοβηθήσῃ
τὸν Θεόν, τὸν ἀληθινὸν καὶ ἐπουράνιον βασιλέα,
Ps. cxxviii. 1 καὶ ὄντως μακάριος ἔσῃ. Μακάριοι γάρ, φησί,
πάντες οἱ φοβούμενοι τὸν Κύριον, οἱ πορευόμενοι
Ps. cxii. 1 ἐν ταῖς ὁδοῖς αὐτοῦ· καί· Μακάριος ἀνὴρ ὁ
φοβούμενος τὸν Κύριον· ἐν ταῖς ἐντολαῖς αὐτοῦ
θελήσει σφόδρα. ποίας δὲ πρὸ πάντων ὀφείλεις
Mat. v. 7 τηρεῖν ἐντολάς; Μακάριοι οἱ ἐλεήμονες, ὅτι 333
Luke vi. 36 αὐτοὶ ἐλεηθήσονται· καί· Γίνεσθε οἰκτίρμονες, ὡς ὁ
Πατὴρ ὑμῶν ὁ οὐράνιος οἰκτίρμων ἐστί. ταύτην
γὰρ τὴν ἐντολὴν πρὸ πάντων ἀπαιτοῦνται οἱ ἐν
Agapet. c. 37 μεγίστῃ ὄντες ἀρχῇ. καὶ ἀληθῶς ὁ μεγάλης
ἐξουσίας ἐπιλαβόμενος τὸν δοτῆρα τῆς ἐξουσίας
ὀφείλει μιμεῖσθαι κατὰ δύναμιν· ἐν τούτῳ δὲ

thou neglect aught of thy duty, guard thyself with all diligence in that which is good. Hate all pleasure that draweth into sin: for, saith the Apostle, "Follow peace with all men, and holiness, without which no man shall see the Lord." Consider the wheel of men's affairs, how it runneth round and round, turning and whirling them now up, now down: and amid all its sudden changes, keep thou unchanged a pious mind. To change with every change of affairs betokeneth an unstable heart. But be thou steadfast, wholly established upon that which is good. Be not lifted and vainly puffed up because of temporal honour; but, with purified reason, understand the nothingness of thine own nature, and the span-length and swift flight of life here, and death the yoke-fellow of the flesh. If thou consider these things, thou shalt not be cast into the pit of arrogance, but shalt fear God, the true and heavenly King, and verily thou shalt be blessed. For he saith, "Blessed are all they that fear the Lord, and walk in his ways," and "Blessed is the man that feareth the Lord: he shall have great delight in his commandments." And which commandments above all shouldest thou observe? "Blessed are the merciful, for they shall obtain mercy," and "Be ye merciful, as your heavenly Father is merciful." For the fulfilment of this commandment, above all, is required of them that are in high authority. And, soothly, the holder of great authority ought to imitate the giver of that authority, to the best of his ability. And herein shall he best

to show mercy to all men,

μάλιστα τὸν Θεὸν μιμήσεται, ἐν τῷ μηδὲν ἡγεῖσθαι τοῦ ἐλεεῖν προτιμότερον. ἀλλὰ καὶ τὸ ὑπήκοον οὐδὲν οὕτως εἰς εὔνοιαν ἐφέλκεται, ὡς εὐποιΐας χάρις διδομένη τοῖς χρῄζουσιν· ἡ γὰρ διὰ φόβον γινομένη θεραπεία κατεσχηματισμένη ἐστὶ θωπεία, πεπλασμένῳ τιμῆς ὀνόματι φενακί-
Agapet. c. 35 ζουσα τοὺς αὐτῇ προσέχοντας· καὶ τὸ ἀκουσίως ὑποτεταγμένον στασιάζει καιροῦ λαβόμενον· τὸ δὲ τοῖς δεσμοῖς τῆς εὐνοίας κρατούμενον βεβαίαν
Agapet. c. 8 ἔχει πρὸς τὸ κρατοῦν τὴν εὐπείθειαν. διὸ εὐπρόσιτος ἔσο τοῖς δεομένοις, καὶ ἄνοιγε τὰ ὦτα τοῖς πενομένοις, ἵνα εὕρῃς τὴν τοῦ Θεοῦ ἀκοὴν ἀνεῳγμένην· οἷοι γὰρ τοῖς ἡμετέροις γινόμεθα συνδούλοις, τοιοῦτον περὶ ἡμᾶς εὑρήσομεν τὸν δεσπότην,
Agapet. c. 23 καὶ ὡς ἀκούομεν ἀκουσθησόμεθα, ὡς ὁρῶμεν ὁραθησόμεθα ὑπὸ τοῦ θείου καὶ παντεφόρου βλέμματος. προεισενέγκωμεν οὖν τοῦ ἐλέου τὸν ἔλεον, ἵνα τῷ ὁμοίῳ τὸ ὅμοιον ἀντιλάβωμεν.

Ἀλλὰ καὶ ἑτέραν ἄκουε ἐντολὴν σύζυγον τῆς
Cp. Mat. vi. 15 προτέρας· Ἄφετε, καὶ ἀφεθήσεται ὑμῖν· καί,
Mk. xi. 26 Ἐὰν οὐκ ἀφῆτε τοῖς ἀνθρώποις τὰ παραπτώματα 334
αὐτῶν, οὐδὲ ὑμῖν ἀφήσει ὁ Πατὴρ ὑμῶν ὁ οὐράνιος τὰ παραπτώματα ὑμῶν. διὸ μὴ μνησικακήσῃς τοῖς πταίουσιν· ἀλλά, συγγνώμην αἰτούμενος ἁμαρτημάτων, συγγίνωσκε καὶ αὐτὸς τοῖς εἰς σὲ πλημμελοῦσιν, ὅτι ἀφέσει ἀντιδίδοται ἄφεσις, καὶ τῇ πρὸς τοὺς ὁμοδούλους ἡμῶν καταλλαγῇ τῆς δεσποτικῆς ὀργῆς γίνεται ἀπαλλαγή. καὶ αὖθις τὸ ἀσυμπαθὲς ἡμῶν πρὸς τοὺς πταίοντας ἀσύγγνωστα ποιεῖ ἡμῖν τὰ ἡμέτερα πταί-
Mat. xviii. 24 σματα· καθάπερ ἀκούεις τί ὁ τῶν μυρίων πέπονθεν ὀφειλέτης ταλάντων, τῇ πρὸς τὸν σύν-

imitate God, by considering that nothing is to be preferred before showing mercy. Nay, further, nothing so surely draweth the subject to loyalty toward his Sovereign as the grace of charity bestowed on such as need it. For the service that cometh from fear is flattery in disguise, with the pretence of respect cozening them that pay heed to it; and the unwilling subject rebelleth when he findeth occasion. Whereas he that is held by the ties of loyalty is steadfast in his obedience to the ruling power. Wherefore be thou easy of access to all, and open thine ears unto the poor, that thou mayest find the ear of God open unto thee. For as we are to our fellow-servants, such shall we find our Master to us-ward. And, like as we do hear others, so shall we be heard ourselves: and, as we see, so shall we be seen by the divine all-seeing eye. Therefore pay we first mercy for mercy, that we may obtain like for like.

'But hear yet another commandment, the fellow of the former; "Forgive, and it shall be forgiven unto you;" and "If ye forgive not men their trespasses, neither will your heavenly father forgive you your trespasses." Wherefore bear no malice against them that offend against thee; but, when thou askest forgiveness of thy sins, forgive thyself also them that injure thee, because forgiveness is repaid by forgiveness, and by making peace with our fellow-servants we are ourselves delivered from the wrath of our Master. Again, a lack of compassion towards them that trespass against us maketh our own trespasses unpardonable, even as thou hast heard what befell the man that owed ten thousand talents, how, through his want of pity on his fellow-

and to forgive all men their trespasses against him

δοῦλον ἀσπλαγχνίᾳ ἑαυτῷ τὴν εἴσπραξιν ἀνα-
νεώσας τοῦ τοσούτου χρέους. διὸ προσεκτέον
ἀκριβῶς, μὴ καὶ ἡμεῖς τὰ ὅμοια πάθοιμεν· ἀλλ'
ἀφήσωμεν πᾶσαν ὀφειλήν, καὶ πᾶσαν μῆνιν ἐκ
καρδίας ἐκβάλλωμεν, ἵνα καὶ ἡμῖν ἀφεθῇ τὰ
πολλὰ ἡμῶν ὀφλήματα. ἐπὶ πᾶσι δὲ καὶ πρὸ
2 Tim. i. 14 πάντων τὴν καλὴν φύλαττε παρακαταθήκην, τὸν
εὐσεβῆ τῆς πίστεως λόγον, ὃν ἔμαθες καὶ ἐδιδά-
χθης· καὶ πᾶν ζιζάνιον αἱρέσεως μὴ ἐκφυέσθω ἐν
ὑμῖν· ἀλλὰ καθαρὸν καὶ ἄδολον τὸν θεῖον διατή-
ρησον σπόρον, ἵνα πολύχουν τὸν καρπὸν ὑποδείξῃς τῷ δεσπότῃ, ἡνίκα ἔλθῃ λόγον ἀπαιτῶν
ἑκάστῳ τῶν βεβιωμένων καὶ ἀποδιδοὺς καθὰ
Mat. xiii. 43 ἐπράξαμεν, ὅταν οἱ μὲν δίκαιοι λάμψωσιν ὡς ὁ
Dan. xii. 2 ἥλιος, τοὺς ἁμαρτωλοὺς δὲ τὸ σκότος καλύψῃ
Acts xx. 32 καὶ αἰσχύνη αἰώνιος. καὶ τὰ νῦν, ἀδελφοί, 335
παρατίθεμαι ὑμᾶς τῷ Θεῷ, καὶ τῷ Λόγῳ τῆς
χάριτος αὐτοῦ, τῷ δυναμένῳ ὑμᾶς ἐποικοδομῆσαι
καὶ δοῦναι ὑμῖν κληρονομίαν ἐν τοῖς ἡγιασμένοις
πᾶσι.

Acts xx. 36 Καὶ ταῦτα εἰπών, θεὶς τὰ γόνατα αὐτοῦ, καθὼς γέγραπται, μετὰ δακρύων αὖθις προσηύξατο.
καὶ ἐπιστραφεὶς κατεφίλησε τὸν Βαραχίαν ὃν
βασιλέα προεχειρίσατο, καὶ πάντας τοὺς ἐν
τέλει. τότε δὴ γίνεται πρᾶγμα δακρύων ὡς
ἀληθῶς ἄξιον. περιστάντες γὰρ αὐτὸν ἅπαντες,
ὥσπερ τῷ ἐκείνῳ συνεῖναι ζῶντες καὶ τῇ διαιρέσει
μέλλοντες συναφαιρεῖσθαι καὶ τὰς ψυχάς, τί μὴ
πρὸς οἶκτον ἔλεγον; ποίαν θρήνων ὑπερβολὴν
ἀπελίμπανον; κατεφίλουν αὐτόν, περιέβαλλον·
παραφρονεῖν αὐτοὺς ἐποίει τὸ πάθος. Οὐαὶ ἡμῖν,
ἐβόων, τῆς χαλεπῆς ταύτης δυστυχίας· δεσ- 336

servant, he was again required to pay all that mighty debt. So we must take good heed lest a like fate betide us. But let us forgive every debt, and cast all anger out of our hearts, in order that our many debts, too, may be forgiven. Beside this, and before all things, keep thou that good thing which is committed to thy trust, the holy Word of faith wherein thou hast been taught and instructed. And let no tare of heresy grow up amongst you, but preserve the heavenly seed pure and sincere, that it may yield a manifold harvest to the master, when he cometh to demand account of our lives, and to reward us according to our deeds, when the righteous shall shine forth as the sun, but darkness and everlasting shame shall cover the sinners. And now, brethren, I commend you to God, and to the word of his grace, which is able to build you up, and to give you an inheritance among all them which are sanctified.'

Ioasaph departeth from his grief-stricken people

And when he had thus spoken, he kneeled down, as it is written, and prayed again in tears. And he turned him round, and kissed Barachias, whom he had chosen to their king, and all the officers. Then came a scene fit, belike, to make one weep. They all crowded around him, as though his presence meant life to them, and his departure would reave them of their very souls; and what piteous pleading, what extravagance of grief did they omit? They kissed him; they hung about him; they were beside themselves for anguish of heart. 'Wo is us,' cried they, 'for this grievous calamity!' They called him,

πότην αὐτὸν ἀνεκαλοῦντο, πατέρα, σωτῆρα, εὐεργέτην· Διά σου, φησί, τὸν Θεὸν ἔγνωμεν· τῆς πλάνης λελυτρώμεθα· τῶν κακῶν πάντων ἀνάπαυσιν εὕρομεν. τί λοιπὸν ἔσται ἡμῖν μετὰ τὸν σὸν χωρισμόν; ποῖα οὐ καταλήψεται κακά; τοιαῦτα λέγοντες, τὰ στήθη ἔπαιον, καὶ τὴν κατασχοῦσαν αὐτοὺς ἀνωλοφύροντο συμφοράν. ὁ δὲ λόγοις αὐτοὺς παρακλήσεως τῶν πολλῶν κατασιγήσας οἰμωγῶν, καὶ συνεῖναι τῷ πνεύματι ἐπαγγειλάμενος, ὡς τῷ γε σώματι ἀδύνατον ἤδη τοῦτο γενέσθαι, τοιαῦτα εἰπών, πάντων ὁρώντων ἐξέρχεται τοῦ παλατίου. καὶ εὐθὺς πάντες συνείποντο. τὴν ὑποστροφὴν ἀπηγόρευον· τὴν πόλιν, ὡς μηκέτι δυνατὸν ὄμμασιν ὀφθῆναι τοῖς ἑαυτῶν, ἀπεδίδρασκον. ὡς δὲ τῆς πόλεως ἔξω γεγόνασι, μόλις ποτέ, τῇ τομῇ τοῦ λόγου παραινοῦντος αὐτοῦ καὶ δριμυτέραν που τὴν ἐπιτίμησιν ἐπιφέροντος, ἀπ' αὐτοῦ διερράγησαν, καὶ ἄκοντες ἐπανήρχοντο, πυκνῶς αὐτοῖς τῶν ὀφθαλμῶν ἐπιστρεφομένων, καὶ τὴν πορείαν τοῖς ποσὶν ἐγκοπτόντων. τινὲς δὲ τῶν θερμοτέρων καὶ ὀδυρόμενοι
μακρόθεν ἠκολούθουν αὐτῷ, ἕως ἡ νὺξ ἐπελθοῦσα 337
διέστησεν αὐτοὺς ἀπ' ἀλλήλων.

XXXVII

Ἐξῆλθεν οὖν τῶν βασιλείων ὁ γενναῖος ἐκεῖνος χαίρων, ὡς ὅταν ἐκ μακρᾶς ἐξορίας εἰς τὴν ἰδίαν τις ἐπανερχόμενος γηθοσύνως πορεύοιτο. καὶ ἦν ἐνδεδυμένος, ἔξωθεν μὲν τὰ ἐξ ἔθους ἱμάτια, ἔσωθεν δὲ τὸ τρίχινον ῥάκος ἐκεῖνο ὅπερ ὁ Βαρλαὰμ

Master, Father, Saviour, Benefactor. 'Through thee,' said they, 'we learned to know God, and were redeemed from error, and found rest from every ill. What remaineth us after thou art gone? What evils shall not befall us?' Thus saying, they smote upon their breasts, and bewailed the misfortune that had overtaken them. But he with words of comfort hushed their sobs, and promised to be with them still in the spirit though he might no longer abide with them in the body. And when he had thus spoken, in the sight of all he went forth from the palace. And immediately all the people followed him. They despaired of his return; they ran from the city, as from a sight that they could no longer endure. But when they were outside the city, Ioasaph addressed them with sharp words, and chode with them harshly; and so they were parted from him, and unwillingly went home, often turning round to look on him, and stumbling on their road. And some of the hotter spirits also followed afar off weeping, until the shades of night parted them one from another.

XXXVII

Ioasaph goeth forth into the desert, smitten by the love of Christ,

Thus this noble man went forth from his palace rejoicing, as when after long exile a man returneth with joy to his own country. Outwardly he wore the robes that he was wont to wear, but beneath was the hair-shirt which Barlaam had given him.

αὐτῷ δεδώκει. τῇ δὲ νυκτὶ ἐκείνῃ εἰς οἰκίσκον
πένητός τινος καταντήσας, τὰ περικείμενα αὐτῷ
ἄμφια ἐκβαλών, τελευταίαν ταύτην εὐποιΐαν τῷ
πένητι δίδωσι· καὶ οὕτω ταῖς ἐκείνου τε καὶ πολλῶν ἑτέρων πενήτων εὐχαῖς ἐπίκουρον ἑαυτοῦ τὸν
Θεὸν θέμενος, καὶ τὴν αὐτοῦ χάριν καὶ βοήθειαν
ὡς ἱμάτιον σωτηρίου καὶ χιτῶνα εὐφροσύνης
ἑαυτῷ περιβαλλόμενος, ἐπὶ τὸν ἐρημικὸν ἐξῆλθε
βίον, μὴ ἄρτον ἐπιφερόμενος, μὴ ὕδωρ, μηδ' ἄλλο
τι τῶν πρὸς τροφὴν ἐπιτηδείων, μὴ ἱμάτιον ἐνδεδυμένος, ἀλλ' ἢ τὸ σκληρὸν ἐκεῖνο ῥάκος μόνον,
οὗπερ πρὸ μικροῦ ἐμνήσθημεν. πόθῳ γάρ τινι
ὑπερφυεῖ καὶ ἔρωτι θείῳ τρωθεὶς τὴν ψυχὴν τοῦ
ἀθανάτου βασιλέως Χριστοῦ, ὅλως ἦν τοῦ ποθουμένου ἐξεστηκώς, ὅλως ἠλλοιωμένος Θεῷ, κάτοχος
Cp. Cant. viii. 6 τῇ τούτου ἀγάπῃ· Κραταιὰ γάρ, φησίν, ὡς πῦρ
ἀγάπη· τοιαύτην αὐτὸς ἀπὸ τῆς θείας ἀγάπης
ἐδέξατο μέθην, καὶ οὕτως ἐξεκαύθη τῷ δίψει, κατὰ 338
Ps. xlii. 1 τὸν εἰπόντα· Ὃν τρόπον ἐπιποθεῖ ἡ ἔλαφος ἐπὶ
τὰς πηγὰς τῶν ὑδάτων, οὕτως ἐπιποθεῖ ἡ ψυχή
μου πρὸς σέ, ὁ Θεός· ἐδίψησεν ἡ ψυχή μου πρὸς
τὸν Θεὸν τὸν ἰσχυρόν, τὸν ζῶντα· καὶ καθὼς ἡ
Cant. ii. 5; iv. 9; ii. 14 τετρωμένη τῆς τοιαύτης ἀγάπης ψυχὴ βοᾷ ἐν τῷ
Ἄισματι τῶν ᾀσμάτων· Ἐκαρδίωσας ἡμᾶς τῷ
πόθῳ σου, ἐκαρδίωσας ἡμᾶς· καί· Δεῖξόν μοι
τὴν ὄψιν σου, καὶ ἀκούτισόν μοι τὴν φωνήν σου·
ἡ γὰρ φωνή σου φωνὴ ἡδεῖα καὶ ἡ ὄψις σου
ὡραία.

Ταύτης τῆς ἀνεκλαλήτου ὡραιότητος Χριστοῦ
τὸν πόθον ἐν καρδίᾳ δεξάμενος ὁ τῶν ἀποστόλων
χορὸς καὶ τῶν μαρτύρων οἱ δῆμοι πάντων ὑπερεῖ-
δον τῶν ὁρωμένων, πάσης δὲ ζωῆς τῆς προσκαίρου,

That night he halted at a poor man's cabin, and stripped himself of his outer raiment, which, as his last alms, he bestowed upon his poor host, and thus by the prayers of that poor man, as well as of so many others, he made God his ally, and put on his grace and help as a garment of salvation; and, clad in a coat of gladness, thus went he off to his hermit-life, carrying with him neither bread, nor water, nor any necessary food, with no garment upon him save the aforesaid rough shirt. For his heart was wounded with a marvellous longing and divine love for Christ the immortal King; he was beside himself with longing, mad for God, possessed by love of him; 'For love,' he saith, 'is strong as fire.' So drunken was he with this heavenly love, so parched with thirst, according to him that saith, 'Like as the hart desireth the water-brooks, so longeth my soul after thee, O God. My soul is athirst for the mighty and living God'; or, as the soul that is sick of love crieth in the Song of Songs, 'Thou hast ravished us, ravished us with the desire of thee'; and, 'Let me see thy countenance, and let me hear thy voice, for thy voice is a sweet voice, and thy countenance is comely.'

the same love that fired the Apostles and the Martyrs

It was the desire for this unspeakable comeliness of Christ that fired the hearts of the Apostolic Quire and of the Martyr folk to despise the things that are seen, and all this temporal life, and the rather to

καὶ τὰ μυρία τῶν βασάνων καὶ θανάτων εἴδη
προείλοντο, ἐρασθέντες τοῦ θείου κάλλους καὶ τὸ
περὶ ἡμᾶς τοῦ θείου Λόγου λογισάμενοι φίλτρον.
τοῦτο τὸ πῦρ καὶ ὁ καλὸς οὗτος καὶ εὐγενὴς μὲν
τῷ σώματι, εὐγενέστατος δὲ μᾶλλον καὶ βασιλικώτατος τὴν ψυχήν, ἐν ἑαυτῷ δεξάμενος, πάντων ὁμοῦ τῶν γηΐνων καταφρονεῖ, πατεῖ πάσας
τὰς τοῦ σώματος ἡδονάς, ὑπερορᾷ πλούτου καὶ
δόξης καὶ τῆς παρὰ ἀνθρώπων τιμῆς, ἀποτίθεται
διάδημα καὶ ἁλουργίδα, τῶν ἀραχνίων ὑφασμά-
των εὐτελέστερα ταῦτα λογισάμενος, πρὸς πάντα
δὲ τὰ ἐπίπονα καὶ λυπηρὰ τοῦ ἀσκητικοῦ βίου
Ps. lxiii. 9 προθύμως ἑαυτὸν ἐκδίδωσιν, Ἐκολλήθη, βοῶν, ὦ
Χριστέ μου, ἐκολλήθη ἡ ψυχή μου ὀπίσω σου·
ἐμοῦ δὲ ἀντελάβετο ἡ δεξιά σου. 339

Καὶ οὕτως ἀμεταστρεπτὶ χωρήσας εἰς τὸ τῆς
ἐρήμου βάθος, καὶ ὡς ἄχθος τι καὶ κλοιὸν βαρύ-
τατον ἀποθέμενος τῶν προσκαίρων τὴν σύγχυσιν,
εὐφράνθη τῷ πνεύματι, καὶ τῷ ποθουμένῳ ἀτενίσας Χριστῷ, ἐβόα πρὸς αὐτόν, ὡς παρόντι καὶ τῆς
φωνῆς ἐπαΐοντι διαλεγόμενος· Μὴ τὰ ἀγαθά,
φησί, τοῦ κόσμου τούτου ἴδοι ὁ ὀφθαλμός μου ἔτι,
Κύριε· μὴ μετεωρισθείην ἀπὸ τῆς δεῦρο τὸν νοῦν
ὑπὸ τῆς παρούσης ματαιότητος· ἀλλ᾿ ἔμπλησον
τοὺς ὀφθαλμούς μου, Κύριε, δακρύων πνευματικῶν
Ps. xl. 2 καὶ κατεύθυνον τὰ διαβήματά μου, καὶ ὑπόδειξόν
μοι τὸν σὸν θεράποντα Βαρλαάμ. ὑπόδειξόν μοι
τὸν ἐμοὶ σωτηρίας γενόμενον πρόξενον, ἵνα καὶ
τοῦ ἐρημικοῦ βίου τούτου καὶ ἀσκητικοῦ δι᾿ αὐτοῦ
τὴν ἀκρίβειαν μάθοιμι καὶ μὴ τῇ ἀπειρίᾳ τῶν
πολέμων τοῦ ἐχθροῦ ὑποσκελισθῶ. δός μοι,
Κύριε, τὴν ὁδὸν εὑρεῖν δι᾿ ἧς ἐπιτύχω σου, ὅτι

choose ten thousand forms of death and torture, being enamoured of his heavenly beauty, and bearing in mind the charm that the divine Word used for to win our love. Such was the fire that was kindled in the soul of this fair youth also, noble in body, but most noble and kingly in soul, that led him to despise all earthly things alike, to trample on all bodily pleasures, and to contemn riches and glory and the praise of men, to lay aside diadem and purple, as of less worth than cobwebs, and to surrender himself to all the hard and irksome toils of the ascetic life, crying, 'O my Christ, my soul is fixed upon thee, and thy right hand hath upholden me.'

Ioasaph prayeth that he may find Barlaam

Thus, without looking back, he passed into the depth of the desert; and, laying aside, like a heavy burden and clog, the stress of transitory things, he rejoiced in the Spirit, and looked steadfastly on Christ, whom he longed for, and cried aloud to him, as though he were there present to hear his voice, saying, 'Lord, let mine eyes never again see the good things of this present world. Never, from this moment, let my soul be excited by these present vanities, but fill mine eyes with spiritual tears; direct my goings in thy way, and show me thy servant Barlaam. Show me him that was the means of my salvation, that I may learn of him the exact rule of this lonely and austere life, and may not be tripped up through ignorance of the wiles of the enemy. Grant me, O Lord, to discover the way whereby to attain unto

τέτρωται ἡ ψυχή μου τῷ πόθῳ σου, καὶ σὲ διψῶ
τὴν πηγὴν τῆς σωτηρίας.
Ταῦτα ἔστρεφε καθ' ἑαυτὸν ἀεί, καὶ τῷ Θεῷ διελέγετο, διὰ προσευχῆς αὐτῷ καὶ θεωρίας ὑψηλοτάτης ἑνούμενος. καὶ οὕτω συντόνως τὴν
ὁδοιπορίαν διήνυε, τὸν χῶρον σπεύδων καταλαβεῖν, ἔνθα Βαρλαὰμ διῆγεν. ἐτρέφετο δὲ ταῖς
φυομέναις βοτάναις κατὰ τὴν ἔρημον· οὐδὲν γὰρ
p. 562 ἄλλο ἐπεφέρετο, καθάπερ ἔφθην εἰπών, εἰ μὴ
μόνον τὸ σῶμα τὸ ἴδιον καὶ τὸ ῥάκος ὃ περιεβέβλητο.
Ἀλλὰ τροφὴν μὲν μετρίαν καὶ οὐδαμινὴν ἐκ
τῶν βοτανῶν ποριζόμενος, ὕδατος παντελῶς
ἠπόρει, ἀνύδρου καὶ ξηρᾶς οὔσης τῆς ἐρήμου 340
ἐκείνης. ἤδη τοίνυν περὶ τὰς μεσημβρίας, τοῦ
ἡλίου σφοδρὸν φλέγοντος, τῆς ὁδοιπορίας ἐχό-
μενος, σφοδρότερον αὐτὸς ἐφλέγετο ἐν δίψει
καύματος ἐν ἀνύδρῳ, καὶ τὴν ἐσχάτην ἐτα-
λαιπωρεῖτο ταλαιπωρίαν· ἀλλ' ἐνίκα ὁ πόθος
τὴν φύσιν, καὶ ἡ δίψα, ἣν πρὸς τὸν Θεὸν ἐδίψα,
τὴν φλόγα ἐδρόσιζε τῆς τοῦ ὕδατος δίψης.
Athanas. Vita Antonii § 5 Ὁ δὲ μισόκαλος καὶ φθονερὸς διάβολος, μὴ
ὑποφέρων ἐν αὐτῷ τὴν τοιαύτην ὁρᾶν πρόθεσιν
καὶ οὕτω θερμοτάτην πρὸς τὸν Θεὸν ἀγάπην,
πολλοὺς αὐτῷ κατὰ τὴν ἔρημον ἐξήγειρε πειρα-
σμούς, ὑποβάλλων αὐτῷ μνήμην τῆς βασιλικῆς
αὐτοῦ δόξης καὶ τῆς παρισταμένης αὐτῷ λαμπροτάτης δορυφορίας, φίλων τε καὶ συγγενῶν καὶ
ὁμηλίκων, καὶ ὡς αἱ πάντων ψυχαὶ τῆς αὐτοῦ
ἐξήρτηντο ψυχῆς, καὶ τὰς ἄλλας ἀνέσεις τοῦ
βίου· εἶτα τὸ τραχὺ τῆς ἀρετῆς προεβάλλετο
καὶ τοὺς πολλοὺς αὐτῆς ἱδρῶτας, τοῦ σώματός

thee, for my soul is sick of love for thee, and I am athirst for thee, the well of salvation.'

These were the thoughts of his heart continually, and he communed with God, being made one with him by prayer and sublime meditation. And thus eagerly he pursued the road, hoping to arrive at the place where Barlaam dwelt. His meat was the herbs that grow in the desert; for he carried nothing with him, as I have already said, save his own bones, and the ragged garment that was around him.

He pusheth on his journey,

But whilst he found some food, though scanty and insufficient, from the herbs, of water he was quite destitute in that waterless and dry desert. And so at noon-tide, as he held on his way under the fierce blaze of the sun, he was parched with thirst in the hot drought of that desert place, and he suffered the extreme of anguish. But desire of Christ conquered nature, and the thirst wherewith he thirsted for God bedewed the heat of thirst for water.

tormented by thirst,

Now the devil, being envious and full of hate for that which is beautiful, unable to endure the sight of such steadfastness of purpose, and glowing love towards God, raised up against Ioasaph many temptations in the wilderness. He called to his remembrance his kingly glory, and his magnificent body-guard, his friends, kinsfolk and companions, and how the lives of all had depended on his life, and he minded him of the other solaces of life. Then he would confront him with the hardness of virtue, and the many sweats that she requireth,

and tempted of the devil

τε τὴν ἀσθένειαν καὶ τὸ ἀσύνηθες αὐτοῦ ἐν τῇ τοιαύτῃ ταλαιπωρίᾳ, καὶ τοῦ χρόνου τὸ μῆκος, τὴν ἐν χερσίν τε ἀνάγκην τῆς δίψης, καὶ τὸ μηδαμόθεν ἐκδέχεσθαι παράκλησιν ἢ τέλος τοῦ τοσούτου κόπου· καὶ ὅλως πολὺν αὐτῷ ἤγειρε
Athanas. Vita Antonii § 5 κονιορτὸν τῶν λογισμῶν ἐν τῇ διανοίᾳ, καθά που
καὶ περὶ τοῦ μεγάλου γέγραπται Ἀντωνίου. 341

Ὡς δὲ εἶδεν ἑαυτὸν ὁ ἐχθρὸς ἀσθενοῦντα πρὸς τὴν ἐκείνου πρόθεσιν (τὸν Χριστὸν γὰρ αὐτὸς ἐνθυμούμενος καὶ τῷ ἐκείνου πόθῳ φλεγόμενος, ῥωννύμενός τε καλῶς τῇ ἐλπίδι καὶ τῇ πίστει στηριζόμενος, εἰς οὐδὲν τὰς ἐκείνου ὑπερβολὰς ἐλογίζετο), κατῃσχύνθη ὁ πολέμιος ἐκ πρώτης, ὃ λέγεται, προσβολῆς πεσών. ἑτέραν οὖν ἔρχεται ὁδόν (πολλαὶ γὰρ αὐτῷ αἱ τῆς κακίας τρίβοι), καὶ φαντάσμασι ποικίλοις ἀνατρέπειν αὐτὸν ἐπειρᾶτο καὶ εἰς δειλίαν ἐμβαλεῖν, ποτὲ μὲν μέλας αὐτῷ φαινόμενος, οἷός ἐστι· ποτὲ δέ, ῥομφαίαν ἐσπασμένην κατέχων, ἐπεπήδα αὐτῷ, καὶ πατάξαι ἠπείλει, εἰ μὴ θᾶττον εἰς τὰ ὀπίσω στραφῇ· ἄλλοτε θηρίων ὑπήρχετο παντοδαπῶν μορφάς, βρυχῶν κατ᾽ αὐτοῦ καὶ δεινότατον ἀπο-
Ps. xci. 13 τελῶν μυκηθμὸν καὶ ψόφον· εἶτα καὶ εἰς δράκοντα μετεμορφοῦτο καὶ ἀσπίδα καὶ βασιλίσκον. ὁ δὲ καλὸς ἐκεῖνος καὶ γενναιότατος ἀθλητὴς
Ps. xci. 9 ἀτρέμας ἦν τὴν ψυχήν, ἅτε δὴ τὸν ὕψιστον ἑαυτοῦ καταφυγὴν θέμενος. νήφων δὲ τῇ διανοίᾳ καὶ κατεγγελῶν τοῦ πονηροῦ, ἔλεγεν· Οὐκ ἔλαθές με, ὦ ἀπατεών, ὅστις εἶ, ὁ ταῦτά μοι ἐγείρων, ὁ ἐξ ἀρχῆς κακὰ τεκταινόμενος τῶν ἀνθρώπων τῷ γένει, καὶ ἀεί ποτε πονηρὸς ὢν καὶ τὸ βλάπτειν οὐδαμῶς ἀπολείπων. ἀλλ᾽ ὡς

with the weakness of his flesh, with his lack of practice in such rigours, the long years to come, this present distress from thirst, his want of any comfort, and the unendingness of his toils. In a word, he raised a great dust-cloud of reasonings in his mind, exactly, I ween, as it hath been recorded of the mighty Antony.

The fiend, in the likeness of divers beasts, seeketh to terrify Ioasaph

But, when the enemy saw himself too weak to shake that purpose (for Ioasaph set Christ before his mind, and glowed with love of him, and was well strengthened by hope, and steadfast in faith, and recked nothing of the devil and his suggestions), then was the adversary ashamed of having fallen in the first assault. So he came by another road (for many are his paths of wickedness), and endeavoured to overthrow and terrify Ioasaph by means of divers apparitions. Sometimes he appeared to him in black, and such indeed he is: sometimes with a drawn sword he leapt upon him, and threatened to strike, unless he speedily turned back. At other times he assumed the shapes of all manner of beasts, roaring and making a terrible din and bellowing; or again he became a dragon, adder, or basilisk. But that fair and right noble athlete kept his soul in quietness, for he had made the Most High his refuge: and, being sober in mind, he laughed the evil one to scorn, and said, 'I know thee, deceiver, who thou art, which stirrest up this trouble for me; which from the beginning didst devise mischief against mankind, and art ever wicked, and never stintest to do hurt. How becoming and right proper is thy

προσῆκόν σοι τὸ σχῆμα καὶ οἰκειότατον, αὐτῷ δὴ
τούτῳ τῷ θηρίοις καὶ ἑρπετοῖς ὁμοιοῦσθαι, τὸ 342
θηριῶδές σου τῆς γνώμης καὶ σκολιόν, ἰοβόλον
τε καὶ βλαπτικὸν τῆς προαιρέσεως ἐνδεικνυμένῳ.
τί οὖν ἀνηνύτοις ἐπιχειρεῖς, ἄθλιε; ἐξότε γὰρ
ἔγνων τῆς σῆς εἶναι κακίας τὰ μηχανήματα ταῦτα
καὶ φόβητρα, οὐδεμία μοι λοιπὸν ἔτι ἐστὶ φροντὶς
Ps.cxviii.6.7 περὶ σοῦ. Κύριος ἐμοὶ βοηθός, κἀγὼ ἐπόψομαι
Ps. xci. 13 τοὺς ἐχθρούς μου, καὶ ἐπὶ ἀσπίδα καὶ βασιλίσκον
σε ἐπιβήσομαι οἷς ὁμοιοῦσαι, καὶ καταπατήσω
σε τὸν λέοντα καὶ δράκοντα, τῇ δυνάμει τοῦ
Χριστοῦ κραταιούμενος. αἰσχυνθείησαν καὶ ἐν-
Ps. vi. 10 τραπείησαν πάντες οἱ ἐχθροί μου· ἀποστρα-
Ps. lxx. 2 φείησαν καὶ καταισχυνθείησαν σφόδρα διὰ
τάχους.

Ταῦτα λέγων, καὶ τὸ σημεῖον τοῦ σταυροῦ
ἑαυτῷ περιβαλὼν ὅπλον ἀκαταγώνιστον, πάσας
τὰς τοῦ διαβόλου φαντασίας κατήργησεν. εὐθὺς
γὰρ τά τε θηρία καὶ τὰ ἑρπετά, ὡς ἐκλείπει
καπνός, ἐξέλιπον, καὶ ὡς τήκεται κηρὸς ἀπὸ προσώπου πυρός· αὐτὸς δέ, τῇ τοῦ Χριστοῦ δυνάμει
ἰσχύων, ἐπορεύετο χαίρων καὶ εὐχαριστῶν τῷ
Cp. Mark i. 13 Κυρίῳ. ἀλλὰ καὶ θηρία πολλὰ καὶ ποικίλα καὶ
ὄφεων παντοδαπὰ καὶ δρακοντόμορφα γένη ἡ
ἔρημος ἐκείνη τρέφει, ἅτινα συναντῶντα αὐτῷ οὐκ
ἔτι φαντασίᾳ, ἀλλ' ἀληθείᾳ ἐδείκνυτο, ὡς ἐντεῦθεν φόβου μὲν ἦν πλήρης ἡ ὁδὸς καὶ πόνου·
αὐτὸς δὲ ἀμφοτέρων ὑπερίπτατο τῷ λογισμῷ, 343
1 John iv. 18 τὸν μὲν φόβον τῆς ἀγάπης, ὥς φησιν ἡ Γραφή,
ἔξω βαλλούσης, τὸν πόνον δὲ τοῦ πόθου ἐπικου-
φίζοντος. οὕτως οὖν πολλαῖς καὶ ποικίλαις
συμφοραῖς καὶ ταλαιπωρίαις πυκτεύσας, δι'

habit, that thou shouldest take the shape of beasts and of creeping things, and thus display thy bestial and crooked nature, and thy venomous and hurtful purpose! Wherefore, wretch, attempt the impossible? For ever since I discovered that these be the contrivances and bug-bears of thy malice, I have now no more anxiety concerning thee. The Lord is on my side, and I shall see my desire upon mine enemies. I shall go upon the adder and basilisk, the which thou dost resemble; thee, the lion and dragon I shall tread under my feet; for I am strengthened with the might of Christ. Let mine enemies be ashamed and turned backward: let them be driven and put to shame suddenly.'

Ioasaph journeyeth on triumphant through the desert

Thus speaking, and girding on that invincible weapon, the sign of the Cross, he made vain the devil's shows For straightway all the beasts and creeping things disappeared, like as the smoke vanisheth, and like as wax melteth at the fire. And he, strong in the might of Christ, went on his way rejoicing and giving thanks unto the Lord. But there dwelt in that desert many divers beasts, and all kinds of serpents, and dragon-shaped monsters, and these met him, not now as apparitions but in sober sooth, so that his path was beset by fear and toil. But he overcame both, for love, as saith the scripture, cast out fear, and longing made toil light. Thus he wrestled with many sundry misfortunes and hardships until, after many

ἡμερῶν οὐκ ὀλίγων κατέλαβε τὴν ἔρημον ἐκείνην τῆς Σενααρίτιδος γῆς, ἐν ᾗ ὁ Βαρλαὰμ ᾤκει· ἔνθα καὶ ὕδατος τυχὼν τὴν φλόγα κατέσβεσε τῆς δίψης.

XXXVIII

Ἔμεινε δὲ Ἰωάσαφ διετίαν ὅλην κατὰ τὸ πέλαγος τῆς ἐρήμου ταύτης ἀλώμενος καὶ μὴ εὑρίσκων τὸν Βαρλαάμ, τοῦ Θεοῦ κἀνταῦθα τὸ στερρὸν τοῦ λογισμοῦ αὐτοῦ καὶ τὸ τῆς ψυχῆς γενναῖον δοκιμάζοντος. καὶ ἦν οὕτως αἴθριος συγκαιόμενος τῷ καύσωνι καὶ τῷ κρύει πηγνύμενος καὶ ἀπαύστως ζητῶν ὥσπερ τινὰ θησαυρὸν πολύτιμον τὸν τιμιώτατον γέροντα. πολλοὺς δὲ ὑπέμεινε πειρασμοὺς καὶ πολέμους τῶν πονηρῶν πνευμάτων, καὶ πολλοὺς ὑπήνεγκε πόνους τῆς τῶν βοτανῶν ἐνδείας, ἃς εἰς τροφὴν ἐκέχρητο, ὅτι καὶ ταύτας ξηρὰ οὖσα ἡ ἔρημος ἐνδεῶς ἐβλά- 344
στανεν. ἀλλὰ τῷ πόθῳ τοῦ Δεσπότου φλεγομένη ἡ ἀδαμαντίνη ψυχὴ ἐκείνη καὶ ἀήττητος ῥᾷον ἤνεγκε τὰ λυπηρὰ ταῦτα ἢ τὰς ἡδονὰς ἕτεροι. διὸ τῆς ἄνωθεν οὐ διήμαρτε συμμαχίας, ἀλλά, κατὰ τὸ πλῆθος τῶν ὀδυνῶν αὐτοῦ καὶ πόνων, αἱ παρὰ τοῦ ποθουμένου Χριστοῦ ἐγγινόμεναι παρακλήσεις καθ' ὕπνους τε καὶ καθ' ὕπαρ
Ps. xciv. 19 εὔφραναν τὴν ψυχὴν αὐτοῦ. συμπληρουμένης δὲ τῆς διετίας, Ἰωάσαφ μὲν ἀπαύστως περιῄει ζητῶν τὸν ποθούμενον, καὶ ἐποτνιᾶτο πρὸς τὸν Θεὸν δάκρυα ποταμηδὸν τῶν ὀφθαλμῶν προχεόμενος, καί, Δεῖξόν μοι, Δέσποτα, βοῶν, δεῖξόν μοι τὸν αἴτιόν μοι τῆς σῆς ἐπιγνώσεως καὶ τῶν τοσούτων

days, he arrived at that desert of the land of Senaar, wherein Barlaam dwelt. There also he found water and quenched the burning of his thirst.

XXXVIII

Ioasaph dwelleth for two years alone in the waste places

Now two full years spent Ioasaph wandering about the ocean of that desert, without finding Barlaam; for here also God was proving the steadfastness of his purpose, and the nobility of his soul. He lived thus in the open air, scorched with heat or frozen with cold, and, as one in search of precious treasure, continually looking everywhere for his treasured friend, the aged Barlaam. Frequent were the temptations and assaults of the evil spirits that he encountered, and many the hardships that he endured through the lack of herbs that he needed for meat, because the desert, being dry, yielded even these in but scant supply. But, being kindled by love of her Master, this adamantine and indomitable soul bore these annoyances more easily than other men bear their pleasures. Wherefore he failed not of the succour that is from above, but, many as were the sorrows and toils that he endured, comfort came to him from Christ, and, asleep or awake, refreshed his soul. By the space of those two years Ioasaph went about continually, seeking him for whom he yearned, and rivers of waters ran from his eyes, as he implored God, crying aloud and saying, 'Show me O Lord, show me the man that was the means of my knowledge of thee,

ἀγαθῶν γενόμενόν μοι πρόξενον· καὶ μή, διὰ τὸ πλῆθος τῶν ἀνομιῶν μου, καλοῦ με τοσούτου στερήσῃς. ἀλλ' ἀξίωσόν με ἰδεῖν τε αὐτὸν καὶ ἴσον αὐτῷ τὸν ἀγῶνα τῆς ἀσκήσεως θέσθαι.

Εὑρίσκει δὲ Θεοῦ χάριτι σπήλαιον, ἰχνηλατήσας τῶν ἐκεῖσε πορευομένων τὴν τρίβον. καὶ μοναχῷ τινι ἐντυγχάνει τὸν ἐρημικὸν μετιόντι 345
βίον. καὶ τούτῳ θερμότατα περιχυθεὶς καὶ ἀσπασάμενος, τοῦ Βαρλαὰμ ἠρώτα τὸ σκήνωμα εὑρεῖν, καὶ τὰ καθ' ἑαυτὸν διεξῄει, δῆλα τῷ ἀνδρὶ θέμενος. δι' αὐτοῦ τοίνυν τὸν τόπον διδαχθεὶς τῆς τοῦ ζητουμένου οἰκήσεως, καταλαμβάνει τάχιστα, ὡς ὅταν θηρευτὴς ἐμπειρότατος ἴχνεσιν ἐπιτύχῃ τοῦ θηράματος. καὶ φθάσας τινὰ σημεῖα τὰ παρὰ τοῦ ἄλλου γέροντος διδαχθέντα αὐτῷ, ἐπορεύετο χαίρων καὶ τῇ ἐλπίδι ῥωννύμενος, ὡς νήπιος ἐκ μακροῦ χρόνου τὸν πατέρα ἐλπίζων θεάσασθαι. ὅταν γὰρ ὁ κατὰ Θεὸν πόθος εἰς ψυχὴν ῥαγῇ, πολλῷ τοῦ φυσικοῦ δείκνυται θερμότερός τε καὶ βιαιότερος.

Ἐφίσταται τοίνυν τῇ θύρᾳ τοῦ σπηλαιου, καὶ κρούσας, Εὐλόγησον, εἶπε, Πάτερ, εὐλόγησον. ὡς δὲ τῆς φωνῆς ἀκούσας ἐξῆλθεν ὁ Βαρλαὰμ τοῦ σπηλαίου, ἐγνώρισε τῷ πνεύματι τόν, κατά γε τὴν ἔξω θέαν, οὐκ εὐχερῶς γνωρισθῆναι δυνάμενον, διὰ τὴν θαυμαστὴν ἐκείνην μεταβολὴν καὶ ἀλλοίωσιν ἣν ἠλλοίωτο καὶ μετεβέβλητο τῆς ὄψεως ἐκείνης τῆς προτέρας
Cp. Job xxx. 30; Cant i. 6 καὶ τῆς ὡραῖον ἀνθούσης νεότητος, μεμελανωμένος μὲν ἐκ τῆς ἡλιακῆς καύσεως, κατάκομος δὲ ταῖς θριξίν, ἐκτετηκυίας δὲ τὰς παρειὰς καὶ τοὺς ὀφθαλμοὺς ἔσω που εἰς βάθος δεδυκότας

and the cause of my many blessings. Because of the multitude of mine offences, deprive me not of this good thing; but grant me to see him, and fight with him the ascetic fight.'

By the grace of God, he found a cave, by following footsteps that led thither. There he met a monk pursuing a hermit life. Him he embraced and saluted tenderly. He asked where to find Barlaam's dwelling, and told him his own tale, laying all bare. Of him then he learned the abode of the man whom he sought, and thither went foot-hot, as when a cunning hunter happeneth on the tracks of his game. And when he had met with certain signs, pointed out to him by this other old hermit, he went on rejoicing, strong in hope, like a child hoping after long absence to see his father. For when divine love hath broken into a soul, it proveth hotter and stronger than the natural.

Ioasaph findeth a hermit who directeth him to Barlaam's abode

So he stood before the door of the cave, and knocked, saying '*Benedicite,* father, *benedicite*!' When Barlaam heard his voice, he came forth from the cave, and by the spirit knew him, who by outward appearance could not easily be known, because of the marvellous change and alteration that had changed and altered his face from its former bloom of youth; for Ioasaph was black with the sun's heat, and overgrown with hair, and his cheeks were fallen

Ioasaph and Barlaam meet again

καὶ τὰ βλέφαρα περιπεφλεγμένα ἔχων ταῖς ῥοαῖς
τῶν δακρύων καὶ τῇ πολλῇ τῆς ἐνδείας ταλαιπωρίᾳ. ἔγνω δὲ καὶ Ἰωάσαφ τὸν πνευματικὸν
πατέρα, τοὺς χαρακτῆρας μάλιστα τῆς ὄψεως
ἔχοντα τοὺς αὐτούς. στὰς οὖν εὐθὺς κατὰ ἀνα-
τολάς, ὁ γέρων εὐχὴν ἀνέπεμψε τῷ Θεῷ εὐχαριστήριον. καὶ μετὰ τὴν εὐχὴν ἐπειπόντες τὸ 346
ἀμήν, περιλαβόντες τε καὶ περιπτυξάμενοι θερμο-
τάταις ἠμείβοντο ἀλλήλους περιπλοκαῖς, χρονίου
πόθου ἐμφορούμενοι ἀκορέστως.

Ἐπεὶ δὲ ἀρκούντως περιέλαβον καὶ προσηγόρευσαν, καθίσαντες διωμίλουν. λόγου δὲ ἀρξά-
μενος ὁ Βαρλαάμ, Καλῶς ἦλθες, ἔλεγε, τέκνον
ἠγαπημένον, τέκνον Θεοῦ καὶ κληρονόμε τῆς
ἐπουρανίου βασιλείας διὰ τοῦ Κυρίου ἡμῶν
Ἰησοῦ Χριστοῦ, ὃν ἠγάπησας, ὃν ἐπόθησας
δικαίως ὑπὲρ τὰ πρόσκαιρα καὶ φθαρτά· καί,
Mat. xiii. 44–46 ὡς ἐχέφρων ἔμπορος καὶ σοφός, πάντα πωλήσας,
τὸν ἀτίμητον ἐξωνήσω μαργαρίτην, καὶ τῷ ἀσύλῳ
ἐντυχὼν θησαυρῷ κεκρυμμένῳ ἐν τῷ ἀγρῷ τῶν
ἐντολῶν τοῦ Κυρίου, πάντα δέδωκας μηδενὸς 347
φεισάμενος τῶν ὅσον οὔπω παρερχομένων, ἵνα
τὸν ἀγρὸν ἐκεῖνον ἀγοράσῃς ἑαυτῷ. δῴη σοι
Κύριος ἀντὶ τῶν προσκαίρων τὰ αἰώνια, ἀντὶ τῶν
φθαρτῶν τὰ ἄφθαρτα καὶ μὴ παλαιούμενα.

Εἰπὲ γοῦν μοι, φίλτατε, πῶς ἐνταῦθα παρε-
γένου, πῶς μετὰ τὴν ἐμὴν ἄφιξιν γέγονε τὰ κατὰ
σέ, καὶ εἰ ἔγνω τὸν Θεὸν ὁ σὸς πατήρ, ἢ καὶ
εἰσέτι, τῇ προτέρᾳ φερόμενος ἀφροσύνῃ, ὑπὸ τῆς
τῶν δαιμόνων ἀπάτης αἰχμαλωτίζεται.

Ταῦτα τοῦ Βαρλαὰμ ἐρομένου, ἀναλαβὼν ὁ
Ἰωάσαφ τὸν λόγον, ὅσα μετὰ τὴν ἐκείνου ἀποδη-

in, and his eyes deep sunken, and his eyelids seared with floods of tears, and much distress of hunger. And Ioasaph recognised his spiritual father, for his features were, for the more part, the same. So the old man stood, and, facing the East, offered up to God a prayer of thanksgiving; and, after the prayer, when they had said the Amen, they embraced and kissed each other affectionately, taking their full fill of long deferred desire.

Barlaam greeteth Ioasaph with exceeding great joy,

But, when they had done with embracing and greeting, they sat them down and conversed. Barlaam began, saying, 'Welcome art thou, son well-beloved, son of God, and inheritor of the heavenly kingdom through Jesus Christ our Lord, whom thou lovest, whom thou rightly desirest above the things that are temporal and corruptible! Like a prudent and wise merchant, thou hast sold all, and bought the pearl that is beyond price, and hast found the treasure that cannot be stolen, hidden in the field of the commandments of the Lord; thou hast parted with all, and spared naught of the things that so soon pass away, that thou mightest purchase that field for thyself. The Lord give thee the eternal for the temporal, the things that are incorruptible and wax not old for the corruptible!

and asketh after his fortunes

'But tell me, dearly beloved, how thou camest hither? How did thy matters speed after my departure? And hath thy father learned to know God, or is he still carried away with his former foolishness, still under the bondage of devilish deceits?'

Thus questioned Barlaam, and Ioasaph answered, telling him piece by piece all that had befallen him

μιαν γέγονεν αὐτῷ, καὶ ὅσα Κύριος εὐώδωσε
μέχρι τῆς αὖθις συνελεύσεως αὐτῶν, πάντα κατὰ
μέρος διῄει.

Ὁ δὲ γέρων, ἀκούων σὺν ἡδονῇ καὶ θαύματι,
θερμῶς δακρύων, ἔλεγε· Δόξα σοι, ὁ Θεὸς ἡμῶν,
ὁ ἀεὶ παριστάμενος καὶ βοηθῶν τοῖς ἀγαπῶσί σε.
δόξα σοι, Χριστέ, Βασιλεῦ τῶν ἁπάντων καὶ Θεὲ
πανάγαθε, ὅτι εὐδόκησας τὸν σπόρον, ὃν ἐν τῇ
ψυχῇ κατέβαλον τοῦ δούλου σου Ἰωάσαφ, οὕτως
Mat. xiii. 23 ἑκατοστεύοντα καρπὸν ἐνεγκεῖν, ἐπάξιον σοῦ τοῦ
γεωργοῦ καὶ Δεσπότου τῶν ἡμετέρων ψυχῶν.
δόξα σοι, Παράκλητε ἀγαθέ, τὸ πανάγιον Πνεῦμα, ὅτι ἧς ἔδωκας χάριτος τοῖς ἁγίοις σου
ἀποστόλοις, ταύτης μετασχεῖν κατηξίωσας τοῦτον, καὶ πολυάνθρωπα πλήθη τῆς δεισιδαίμονος
δι' αὐτοῦ ἠλευθέρωσας πλάνης καὶ τῇ ἀληθινῇ
ἐφώτισας θεογνωσίᾳ.

Οὕτω παρ' ἀμφοτέρων ηὐχαριστεῖτο ὁ Θεός.
καὶ τοιαῦτα ὁμιλούντων καὶ τῇ τοῦ Θεοῦ ἀγαλ-
λιωμένων χάριτι, κατελάμβανεν ἡ ἑσπέρα. καὶ 348
δὴ πρὸς εὐχὴν ἀναστάντες τὰς συνήθεις ἐτέλουν
λειτουργίας. εἶτα καὶ τροφῆς μνησθέντες, παρε-
τίθει πολυτελῆ ὁ Βαρλαὰμ τράπεζαν, τῆς πνευματικῆς πεπληρωμένην καρυκείας, αἰσθητῆς δὲ
ἥκιστα μετέχουσαν παρακλήσεως. λάχανα γὰρ
ἦσαν ὠμά, ὧν αὐτουργὸς καὶ γεωργὸς ἦν ὁ γέρων,
καὶ φοίνικες ὀλίγοι ἐν τῇ αὐτῇ εὑρισκόμενοι ἐρήμῳ,
καὶ ἄγριαι βοτάναι. εὐχαριστήσαντες οὖν, καὶ
τῶν παρατιθεμένων μεταλαβόντες, καὶ ὕδωρ ἐκ
Ps. cxlv. 16 τῆς παρατυγχανούσης πηγῆς πιόντες, τῷ ἀνοί-
γοντι χεῖρα καὶ ἐμπιπλῶντι πᾶν ζῷον αὖθις
ηὐχαρίστουν Θεῷ. ἀναστάντες δὲ πάλιν, καὶ τὰς

since he went away; and in how many ways the Lord had prospered him, until they were come together again.

The old man listened with pleasure and amazement, and with hot tears said, 'Glory to thee, our God, that ever standest by and succourest them that love thee! Glory to thee, O Christ, King of all and God all-good, that it was thy pleasure that the seed, which I sowed in the heart of Ioasaph, thy servant, should thus bring forth fruit an hundred-fold worthy of the husbandman and Master of our souls! Glory to thee, good Paraclete, the all-holy Spirit, because thou didst vouchsafe unto this man to partake of that grace which thou gavest thine holy Apostles, and by his hand hast delivered multitudes of people from superstitious error, and enlightened them with the true knowledge of God!'

Barlaam, hearing his tale, giveth thanks unto God

Thus was God blessed by both, and thus were they conversing and rejoicing in the grace of God until evenfall. Then stood they up for to pray and to perform the sacred services. Then also remembered they that it was meal-time, and Barlaam spread his lavish table, laden with spiritual dainties, but with little to attract the palate of sense. These were uncooked worts, and a few dates, planted and tended by Barlaam's own hands, such as are found in the same desert, and wild herbs. So they gave thanks and partook of the victuals set before them, and drank water from the neighbour springing well, and again gave thanks to God, who openeth his hand and filleth all things living. Then they arose

They spend the night in holy conversation

νυκτερινὰς πληρώσαντες εὐχάς, τῆς πνευματικῆς πάλιν μετὰ τὴν εὐχὴν ἥπτοντο ὁμιλίας, λόγους σωτηρίους καὶ τῆς οὐρανίου πεπληρωμένους φιλοσοφίας παρ' ὅλην διεξερχόμενοι τὴν νύκτα, ἕως αὐτοὺς ὄρθρος τῶν συνήθων αὖθις μνησθῆναι εὐχῶν πεποίηκεν.

Ἔμεινε δὲ Ἰωάσαφ μετὰ τοῦ Βαρλαὰμ ἱκανοὺς
οὑτωσὶ χρόνους, τὴν θαυμαστὴν ταύτην καὶ ὑπὲρ
ἄνθρωπον μετερχόμενος πολιτείαν, καὶ ὡς πατρὶ
τούτῳ καὶ παιδευτῇ μεθ' ὅσης συμπαρομαρτῶν
αὐτῷ ὑποταγῆς καὶ ταπεινώσεως, καὶ πρὸς πᾶσαν
ἰδέαν γυμναζόμενος ἀρετῆς, ἄριστά τε παιδευό-
Cp. Eph. vi. 12 μενος τὴν πάλην τῶν πονηρῶν καὶ ἀοράτων πνευμάτων. ἐντεῦθεν τὰ μὲν πάθη ἐθανάτωσε πάντα·
τὸ φρόνημα δὲ τῆς σαρκὸς οὕτω καθυπέταξε τῷ 349
πνεύματι, ὡς δοῦλον δεσπότῃ, τρυφῆς καὶ ἀναπαύσεως ἐπιλαθόμενος πάντῃ, τῷ ὕπνῳ δὲ ὡς κακῷ προστάσσων οἰκέτῃ. καί, ἁπλῶς εἰπεῖν, τοσοῦτος ἦν αὐτῷ ὁ ἀγὼν τῆς ἀσκήσεως, ὡς καὶ αὐτὸν θαυμάζειν τὸν πολλοὺς ἐν ταύτῃ χρόνους διενεγκόντα Βαρλαάμ, καὶ τῆς καρτερᾶς αὐτῷ ἡττᾶσθαι ἐνστάσεως. τοσοῦτον μὲν γὰρ τῆς σκληρᾶς ἐκείνης καὶ ἀπαρακλήτου μετελάμβανε βρώσεως, ὅσον ἀποζῆν μόνον, καὶ μὴ βιαίως θανόντα τοὺς μισθοὺς ζημιωθῆναι τῆς τῶν καλῶν ἐργασίας. οὕτω δὲ εἰς τὸ ἀγρυπνεῖν τὴν φύσιν ὑπέταξεν, ὡς ἄσαρκός τις καὶ ἀσώματος. εὐχῆς δὲ αὐτῷ καὶ τῆς νοερᾶς ἐργασίας ἄληκτον τὸ ἔργον ἦν, καὶ ἅπας ὁ τῆς ζωῆς χρόνος εἰς θεωρίας ἀνηλίσκετο πνευματικάς τε καὶ οὐρανίους, ὡς μὴ ὥραν, μὴ στιγμὴν αὐτὸν τοπαράπαν ζημιωθῆναι, ἀφ' οὗπερ τὴν ἔρημον ᾤκησε ταύτην.

again, and, when they had ended their Night Hours, after prayer, they joined in spiritual converse again, discoursing wholesome words, and full of heavenly wisdom, all the night long until day-break bade them once more remember the hour of prayer.

Ioasaph dwelleth many years with Barlaam, in all the rigours of the ascetic life

So Ioasaph abode with Barlaam for some many years, pursuing this marvellous and more than human life, dwelling with him as with a father and tutor, in all obedience and lowliness, exercising himself in every kind of virtue, and learning well from practice how to wrestle with the invisible spirits of evil. From that time forward he mortified all his sinful passions, and made the will of the flesh as subject to the spirit as slave is to his master. He was altogether forgetful of comforts or repose, and tyrannized over sleep as over a wicked servant. And, in brief, such was his practice of the religious life, that Barlaam, who had spent many years therein, marvelled at him, and failed to equal the earnestness of his life. For he took only so much of that coarse and cheerless food as would keep him alive; else had he died afore his time, and forfeited the reward of his well-doing. He subdued himself to watchings, as though he were without flesh and body. In prayer and mental exercise his work was unceasing, and all the time of his life was spent in spiritual and heavenly contemplation, so that not an hour, nor even a single moment was wasted, from the day that he came to dwell in the desert. For this is the end of

τοῦτο γὰρ ἔργον μοναχικῆς τάξεως, τὸ μηδέποτε ἀργὸν τῆς πνευματικῆς ἐργασίας εὑρεθῆναι· ὃ δὴ καλῶς κατώρθωσεν ὁ γενναῖος καὶ εὐσταλὴς σταδιοδρόμος τῆς οὐρανίου πορείας. καὶ ἄσβεστον αὐτοῦ τὴν θέρμην ἐφύλαξεν ἀπ' ἀρχῆς μέχρι
Cp. Ps. lxxxiv. 6 τέλους, ἀναβάσεις ἀεὶ ἐν καρδίᾳ τιθέμενος, καὶ ἐκ δυνάμεως εἰς ὑψηλοτέραν μεταβαίνων δύναμιν, πόθῳ πόθον καὶ σπουδὴν σπουδῇ διηνεκῶς προστιθείς, ἕως ἔφθασεν εἰς τὴν ἐλπιζομένην καὶ ποθουμένην μακαριότητα.

XXXIX

Οὕτως οὖν ἀλλήλοις συνόντες Βαρλααμ τε καὶ 350
Ἰωάσαφ, καὶ τὴν καλὴν ἅμιλλαν ἁμιλλώμενοι, ἐκτὸς πάσης μερίμνης καὶ πάσης βιωτικῆς ὄντες ταραχῆς, ἀνεπιθόλωτόν τε τὸν νοῦν κεκτημένοι καὶ ἀμιγῆ πάσης συγχύσεως, μετὰ τοὺς πολλοὺς δὲ αὐτῶν ὑπὲρ εὐσεβείας καμάτους, ἐν μιᾷ τῶν ἡμερῶν προσκαλεσάμενος τὸν πνευματικὸν υἱόν,
1 Cor. iv. 15 ὃν διὰ τοῦ Εὐαγγελίου ἐγέννησε, λόγου ἥπτετο καὶ ὁμιλίας πνευματικῆς, Πάλαι, λέγων, ὦ φίλτατε Ἰωάσαφ, ἐν ταύτῃ σε τῇ ἐρήμῳ κατοικεῖν ἔδει· καὶ τοῦτό μοι ὁ Χριστὸς προσευχομένῳ περὶ σοῦ ἐπηγγείλατο πρὸ τῆς τοῦ βίου τελευτῆς ὄψεσθαι. εἶδον οὖν ὡς ἐπεθύμουν· εἶδόν σε ἀπορραγέντα μὲν κόσμου καὶ τῶν ἐν κόσμῳ, συναφθέντα δὲ τῷ Χριστῷ ἀδιστάκτῳ τῇ γνώμῃ, καὶ
Cp. Eph. iv. 13 εἰς μέτρον ἐλθόντα τελειότητος τοῦ πληρώματος αὐτοῦ. νῦν οὖν ἐπειδή μοι ὁ τῆς ἀναλύσεως καιρὸς ἐπὶ θύραις, καὶ ἡ σύντροφος καὶ ἡλικιῶτις

monastic life, never to be found idle in spiritual employment: and well herein did this noble and active runner of the heavenly race order his way. And he kept his ardour unquenched from beginning to end, ever ascending in his heart, and going from strength to strength, and continually adding desire to desire, and zeal to zeal, until he arrived at the bliss that he had hoped and longed for.

XXXIX.

Barlaam feeling that his hour is at hand, giveth Ioasaph his last admonition,

Thus did Barlaam and Ioasaph dwell together, rivals in the good rivalry, apart from all anxious care and all the turmoils of life, possessing their minds undisturbed and clear of all confusion. After their many labours after godliness, one day Barlaam called to him his spiritual son, whom he had begotten through the Gospel, and opened his mouth to discourse of spiritual things, saying, 'Long ago, dearly beloved Ioasaph, was it destined that thou shouldest dwell in this wilderness; and, in answer to my prayer for thee, Christ promised me that I should see it before the ending of my life. I have seen my desire: I have seen thee severed from the world and the concerns of the world, united to Christ, thy mind never wavering, and come to the measure of the perfection of his fulness. Now therefore as the time of my departure is at the door, and seeing that my desire, that hath grown with my growth and aged with

ἐπιθυμία τοῦ συνεῖναι τῷ Χριστῷ διὰ παντὸς ἤδη
πληροῦται, σὲ μὲν δεῖ καλῦψαί μου τὸ σῶμα τῇ
γῇ καὶ τὸν χοῦν ἀποδοῦναι τῷ χοΐ, μεῖναι δὲ τοῦ
λοιποῦ ἐν τῷδε τῷ τόπῳ τῆς πνευματικῆς ἐχόμενον πολιτείας καὶ τῆς ἐμῆς μνείαν ποιούμενον
μετριότητος. δέδοικα γὰρ μή ποτε ἡ ζοφερὰ τῶν
δαιμόνων πληθὺς τῇ ψυχῇ μου ἐμποδὼν καταστῇ
διὰ τὸ πλῆθος τῶν ἐμῶν ἀγνοημάτων.

Σὺ οὖν, τέκνον, μὴ ὀλιγωρήσῃς τὸ ἐπίπονον τῆς
Athanas. Vita Antonii § 5 ἀσκήσεως, μηδὲ δειλιάσῃς τὸ μῆκος τοῦ χρόνου
καὶ τὰς ἐπιβουλὰς τῶν δαιμόνων· ἀλλὰ τούτων
μὲν τῆς ἀσθενείας, τῇ τοῦ Χριστοῦ ῥωννύμενος
χάριτι, τολμηρῶς καταγέλα, πρὸς δὲ τὴν σκληρότητα τῶν πόνων καὶ τὸ τοῦ χρόνου διάστημα 351
οὕτως ἔσο, ὡς καθ' ἡμέραν τὴν ἐντεῦθεν ἀνάλυσιν
προσδοκῶν, καὶ ὡς ἀρχὴν εἶναί σοι τῆς ἀσκήσεως
τὴν αὐτὴν ἡμέραν καὶ τέλος. οὕτως ἀεὶ τῶν μὲν
ὀπίσω ἐπιλανθανόμενος, πρὸς τοῖς δὲ ἔμπροσθεν
ἐπεκτεινόμενος, κατασκοπῶν δίωκε τὸ βραβεῖον
τῆς ἄνω κλήσεως τοῦ Θεοῦ ἐν Χριστῷ Ἰησοῦ,
Phil. iii. 13, 14 καθάπερ ὁ θεῖος Ἀπόστολος παρακελεύεται, Μὴ
ἐκκακῶμεν, λέγων· ἀλλ' εἰ καὶ ὁ ἔξω ἡμῶν ἄνθρωπος διαφθείρεται, ἀλλ' ὁ ἔσω ἀνακαινοῦται
ἡμέρᾳ καὶ ἡμέρᾳ· τὸ γὰρ παραυτίκα ἐλαφρὸν τῆς
θλίψεως ἡμῶν καθ' ὑπερβολὴν εἰς ὑπερβολὴν
αἰώνιον βάρος δόξης κατεργάζεται ἡμῖν, μὴ σκο-
πούντων ἡμῶν τὰ βλεπόμενα, ἀλλὰ τὰ μὴ βλε-
2 Cor. iv. 16–18 πόμενα· τὰ γὰρ βλεπόμενα πρόσκαιρα, τὰ δὲ
μὴ βλεπόμενα αἰώνια.

Ταῦτα λογιζόμενος, ἀγαπητέ, ἀνδρίζου καὶ
2 Tim. ii. 3 ἴσχυε, καὶ ὡς καλὸς στρατιώτης σπούδαζε τῷ
στρατολογήσαντι ἀρέσαι. κἂν λογισμούς σοι

my years, to be for ever with Christ, is even now being fulfilled, thou must bury my body in the earth and restore dust to dust, but thyself abide for the time to come in this place, holding fast to thy spiritual life, and making remembrance of me, poor as I am. For I fear lest perchance the darksome army of fiends may stand in the way of my soul, by reason of the multitude of mine ignorances.

'So do thou, my son, think no scorn of the laboriousness of thy religious life, neither dread the length of the time, nor the tricks of devils. But, strong in the grace of Christ, confidently laugh at the weakness of these thy foes; and, as for the hardness of thy toils, and the long duration of the time, be as one that daily expecteth his departure hence, and as if the same day were the beginning and the end of thy religious life. Thus, always forgetting the things which are behind, and reaching forth unto those things which are before, press toward the mark for the prize of the high calling of God in Christ Jesus, according to the exhortation of the holy Apostle, who saith, "Let us not faint; but though our outward man perish, yet the inward man is renewed day by day. For our light affliction, which is but for a moment, worketh for us a far more exceeding eternal weight of glory; while we look not at the things which are seen, but at the things which are not seen: for the things which are seen are temporal; but the things which are not seen are eternal."

charging him to endure and faint not,

'Ponder thou over these things, beloved: quit thee like a man; yea, be strong; and, as a good soldier, do thy diligence to please him who hath called thee to be a soldier. And, even if the evil one stir in thee

but to quit him like a man and be strong,

ὀλιγωρίας ὁ πονηρὸς φέρῃ καὶ τὸν τόνον ὑποχαλᾷν
τῆς προθέσεως σπεύδῃ, μὴ φοβοῦ αὐτοῦ τὰς ἐπι-
John xvi. 33 βουλάς, τὸ Δεσποτικὸν ἐννοῶν πρόσταγμα, Ἐν
τῷ κόσμῳ θλῖψιν ἕξετε, λέγοντος· ἀλλὰ θαρ-
Phil. iv. 4, 6 σεῖτε· ἐγὼ νενίκηκα τὸν κόσμον. διὸ χαῖρε ἐν
Κυρίῳ πάντοτε, ὅτι ἐξελέξατό σε καὶ διεχώρισεν
ἐκ τοῦ κόσμου, καὶ ἔθετο ὡς ἐν προσώπῳ αὐτοῦ.
αὐτὸς δέ, ὁ καλέσας σε κλήσει ἁγίᾳ, ἐγγύς ἐστιν
Phil. iv. 6 ἀεί. μηδὲν μερίμνα· ἀλλ' ἐν παντὶ τῇ προσευχῇ καὶ τῇ δεήσει μετὰ εὐχαριστίας τὰ αἰτή- 352
ματά σου γνωριζέσθω πρὸς τὸν Θεόν. αὐτὸς γὰρ
Heb. iv. 5 εἴρηκεν· Οὐ μή σε ἀνῶ, οὐδ' οὐ μή σε ἐγκαταλίπω.
οὕτως μὲν οὖν ἐν τῇ σκληρότητι τῆς ἀγωγῆς καὶ
τῇ ὀλιγωρίᾳ τῆς ἀσκήσεως τοιούτους κτώμενος
λογισμούς, εὐφραίνου, μεμνημένος Κυρίου τοῦ
Ps. lxxvii. 3 Θεοῦ ἡμῶν· Ἐμνήσθην γάρ, φησί, τοῦ Θεοῦ, καὶ
εὐφράνθην.

Ὅταν δὲ πάλιν ὁ ἐξ ἐναντίας ἄλλον σοι τρόπον
ἐπινοῇ πολέμων, ὑψηλόφρονας προβάλλων λογισμούς, καὶ τὴν δόξαν ὑποδεικνύων τῆς τοῦ
κόσμου βασιλείας ἧς κατέλιπες, καὶ τὰ λοιπὰ
τὰ ἐν τῷ κόσμῳ, τὸν σωτήριον προβαλοῦ λόγον,
Eph. vi. 16 ὡς θυρεόν, τὸν φάσκοντα· Ὅταν ποιήσητε πάντα
Luke xviii. 10 τὰ διαταχθέντα ὑμῖν, λέγετε, ὅτι Ἀχρεῖοι δοῦλοί
ἐσμεν, ὅτι ὃ ὀφείλομεν ποιῆσαι πεποιήκαμεν.
ἀλλὰ καὶ τίς ἐξ ἡμῶν δύναται τὴν ὀφειλὴν ἐκτῖ-
2 Cor. viii. 9 σαι ἣν ὀφείλομεν τῷ Δεσπότῃ, ὑπὲρ ὧν δι' ἡμᾶς
ἐπτώχευσε πλούσιος ὤν, ἵνα ἡμεῖς τῇ ἐκείνου
πτωχείᾳ πλουτήσωμεν, καὶ ἔπαθεν ὁ ἀπαθὴς ἵνα
τῶν παθῶν ἡμᾶς ἐλευθερώσῃ; ποία γὰρ χάρις
δούλῳ ὅμοια τῷ Δεσπότῃ παθεῖν; ἡμεῖς δὲ πολλὰ
τῶν αὐτοῦ ὑστερούμεθα παθημάτων. ταῦτα ἐν- 353

thoughts of neglecting duty, and thou art minded to slacken the string of thy purpose, fear not his devices, but remember the Lord's command, which saith, "In the world ye shall have tribulation: but be of good cheer; I have overcome the world." Wherefore, rejoice in the Lord alway; for he hath chosen and separated thee out of the world, and set thee, as it were before his countenance. The Master, who hath called thee with a holy calling, is alway near. Be careful for nothing, but in everything, by prayer and supplication with thanksgiving let thy requests be made known unto God. For he himself hath said, "I will never leave thee, nor forsake thee." So, by the hardness of thy life, and by scorn of its rigours, win such thoughts as these, and rejoice, remembering our Lord God, for he saith, "I remembered God and was glad."

and to keep himself from all arrogance and pride

'But when the adversary, seeking another fashion of war, proposeth high and arrogant thoughts, and suggesteth the glory of the kingdom of this world, which thou hast forsaken, and all its lures, hold out, as a shield before thee, the saving word that saith, "When ye shall have done all those things which are commanded you, say, 'We are unprofitable servants, for we have done that which was our duty to do.'" And, indeed, which of us is able to repay the debt that we owe our Master, for that he, though he was rich, yet for our sakes became poor, that we through his poverty might become rich, and, being without suffering, yet suffered, that we might be delivered from suffering? What thanks hath the servant if he suffer like as his Master? But *we* fall far short of his sufferings. Meditate

2 Cor. x. 5 νόει, λογισμοὺς καθαίρων καὶ πᾶν ὕψωμα ἐπαιρόμενον κατὰ τῆς γνώσεως τοῦ Θεοῦ, καὶ αἰχμα-
λωτίζων πᾶν νόημα εἰς τὴν ὑπακοὴν τοῦ Χριστοῦ·
Phil. iv. 7 καί ἡ εἰρήνη τοῦ Θεοῦ, ἡ ὑπερέχουσα πάντα
νοῦν, φρουρήσει τὴν καρδίαν καὶ τὰ νοήματά σου
ἐν Χριστῷ Ἰησοῦ.

Τούτων ὑπὸ τοῦ μακαρίου Βαρλαὰμ λεχθέντων, ἡ ῥοὴ τῶν δακρύων τοῦ Ἰωάσαφ μέτρον
οὐκ εἶχεν, ἀλλ', ὡς ἐκ πηγῆς πολυχεύμονος
βρύουσα, ὅλον αὐτὸν καὶ τὴν γῆν ἐν ᾗ ἐκάθητο
κατέβρεχεν. ὀδυρόμενος δὲ τὸν χωρισμόν, ἠξίου
μάλα θερμῶς συνοδοιπόρος αὐτῷ τῆς τελευταίας
πορείας γενέσθαι, καὶ μηκέτι παραμεῖναι τῷ
βίῳ μετὰ τὴν ἐκείνου ἐκδημίαν, Διὰ τί, λέγων,
τὸ σεαυτοῦ ζητεῖς μόνον, ὦ Πάτερ, καὶ μὴ καὶ
τὸ τοῦ πλησίου; πῶς δὲ τὴν τελείαν ἐν τούτῳ
Mat. xxii. 39 πληροῖς ἀγάπην κατὰ τὸν εἰπόντα, Ἀγαπήσεις
τὸν πλησίον σου ὡς σεαυτόν, πρὸς ἀνάπαυσιν
μὲν καὶ ζωὴν αὐτὸς ἀπαίρων, εἰς θλῖψιν δὲ καὶ
ταλαιπωρίαν ἐμὲ καταλιμπάνων, καί, πρὶν καλῶς
ἐγγυμνασθῆναι τοῖς ἄθλοις τῆς ἀσκήσεως καὶ
τῶν πολεμίων μαθεῖν τὰς πολυτρόπους ἐφόδους,
πρὸς μονομαχίαν με τῆς αὐτῶν παρατάξεως προβαλλόμενος; ἵνα τί γένηται ἄλλο, εἰ μὴ βληθῆ-
ναί με ταῖς κακοτρόποις αὐτῶν μηχαναῖς, καὶ
ἀποθανεῖν οἴμοι τὸν ψυχικὸν ὄντως καὶ αἰώνιον
θάνατον; ὅπερ τοῖς ἀπείροις καὶ δειλοῖς συμβαίνειν πέφυκε μοναχοῖς.[1] ἀλλὰ δεήθητι τοῦ
Κυρίου, δυσωπῶ, συνέκδημον κἀμὲ τοῦ βίου 354
λαβεῖν. ναὶ πρὸς αὐτῆς τῆς ἐλπίδος ἧς ἔχεις
ἀπολαβεῖν τοῦ καμάτου τὸν μισθόν, δεήθητι

[1] *v. l.* μονομάχοις.

upon these things, casting down imaginations, and every high thing that exalteth itself against the knowledge of God, and bringing into captivity every thought to the obedience of Christ. And the peace of God which passeth all understanding shall keep thy heart and thoughts in Christ Jesus.'

Ioasaph would fain die with Barlaam

When blessèd Barlaam had so said, Ioasaph's tears knew no measure, but, like water from the brimming fountain, bedewed him and the ground whereon he sat. He mourned over the parting, and earnestly implored that he might be his companion on his last journey, and might remain no longer in this world after Barlaam's decease, saying, 'Wherefore, father, seekest thou only thine own, and not thy neighbour's welfare? How fulfillest thou perfect love in this, according to him that said, "Thou shalt love thy neighbour as thyself," in departing thyself to rest and life, and leaving me to tribulation and distress? And, before I have been well exercised in the conflicts of the religious life, before I have learned the wily attacks of the enemy, why expose me to fight single-handed against their marshalled host? And for what purpose but to see me overthrown by their mischievous machinations, and to see me die, alas! the true spiritual and eternal death? That is the fate which must befall inexperienced and cowardly monks. But, I beseech thee, pray the Lord to take me also together with thee from life. Yea, by the very hope that thou hast of receiving the reward of

μηδεμίαν ἡμέραν μετὰ τὸν σὸν χωρισμὸν παροικεῖν τῷ βίῳ, καὶ εἰς τὸ πέλαγος ταύτης πλανᾶσθαι τῆς ἐρήμου.

Ταῦτα τοῦ Ἰωάσαφ σὺν δάκρυσι λέγοντος, ὁ γέρων πράως ἀνακόπτων καὶ ὁμαλῶς, Οὐκ ὀφείλομεν, τέκνον, ἔφη, τοῖς ἀνεφίκτοις κρίμασι τοῦ Θεοῦ ἀνθίστασθαι. ἐγὼ γὰρ πολλὰ δεηθεὶς περὶ τούτου, καὶ τὸν ἀβίαστον Δεσπότην βιασάμενος τοῦ μὴ χωρισθῆναι ἡμᾶς ἀπ' ἀλλήλων, ἐδιδάχθην παρὰ τῆς αὐτοῦ ἀγαθότητος ὡς οὐκ ἔστι συμφέρον σὲ νῦν τὸ ἄχθος τῆς σαρκὸς ἀποθέσθαι· ἀλλὰ παραμεῖναι δεῖ τῇ ἀσκήσει, ἕως λαμπρότερον ἑαυτῷ τὸν στέφανον πλέξῃς. οὐ γὰρ ἀρκούντως ἀκμὴν ἠγωνίσω πρὸς τὴν ἡτοιμασμένην σοι μισθαποδοσίαν· ἀλλὰ δεῖ σε
Mat. xxv. 23 κοπιάσαι μικρὸν ἵνα χαίρων εἰσέλθῃς εἰς τὴν χαρὰν τοῦ Κυρίου σου. ἐγὼ γὰρ ἐγγύς που τῶν ἑκατὸν λοιπόν εἰμι χρόνων, διατελέσας ἐν τῇ ἐρήμῳ ταύτῃ ἐνιαυτοὺς ἤδη πέντε καὶ ἑβδομήκοντα· σοὶ δέ, εἰ καὶ τοσοῦτον οὐκ ἐκταθήσεται ὁ χρόνος, ἀλλὰ πλησίον που γενέσθαι δεῖ, καθὼς κελεύει ὁ Κύριος, ἵν' ἐφάμιλλος ἀναδειχθῇς, καὶ
Mat. xx. 12 μηδὲν ὅλως ὑστερούμενος τῶν βαστασάντων τὸ βάρος τῆς ἡμέρας καὶ τὸν καύσωνα. δέχου τοίνυν, ὦ φιλότης, τὰ τῷ Θεῷ δεδογμένα ἀσμένως. ἃ γὰρ αὐτὸς βεβούλευται, τίς ἱκανὸς ἀνθρώπων διασκεδάσαι; καὶ καρτέρει τῇ ἐκείνου φυλαττόμενος χάριτι.

Νῆφε δὲ ἀεὶ πρὸς τοὺς ἐναντίους λογισμούς, 355
καὶ τὴν καθαρότητα τοῦ νοὸς ὥσπερ τινὰ θησαυρὸν πολύτιμον ἄσυλον διατήρει, πρὸς ὑψηλοτέραν ἐργασίαν καὶ θεωρίαν ἐμβιβάζων ἑαυτὸν

thy labour, pray that, after thy departure, I may not live one day more in the world, nor wander into the ocean depths of this desert.'

While Ioasaph spake thus in tears, the old man checked him gently and calmly, saying, 'Son, we ought not to resist the judgements of God, which are beyond our reach. For though I have oftentimes prayed concerning this matter, and constrained the Master, that cannot be constrained, not to part us one from the other, yet have I been taught by his goodness that it is not expedient for thee now to lay aside the burden of the flesh: but thou must remain behind in the practice of virtue, until the crown, which thou art weaving, be more glorious. As yet, thou hast not striven enough after the recompense in store for thee, but must toil yet a little longer, that thou mayest joyfully enter into the joy of thy Lord. For myself, I am, as I reckon, well-nigh an hundred winters old, and have now spent seventy and five years in this desert place. But for thee, even if thy days be not so far lengthened as mine, yet must thou approach thereto, as the Lord ordereth, that thou mayest prove no unworthy match for them that have borne the burden and heat of the day. Therefore, beloved, gladly accept the decrees of God. What God hath ordered, who, of men, can scatter? Endure, then, under the protection of his grace.

Barlaam chideth him gently and maketh known to him the will of God

'But be thou ever sober against thoughts other than these; and, like a right precious treasure, keep safely from robbers thy purity of heart, stepping up day by day to higher work and contemplation, that

ἡμέραν καθ' ἡμέραν, ἵνα πληρωθῇ ἐπὶ σοὶ ὃ τοῖς
John xiv. 23 φίλοις αὐτοῦ ὁ Σωτὴρ ἐπηγγείλατο, Ἐάν τις
ἀγαπᾷ με, λέγων, τὸν λόγον μου τηρήσει, καὶ
ὁ Πατήρ μου ἀγαπήσει αὐτόν, καὶ πρὸς αὐτὸν
ἐλευσόμεθα, καὶ μονὴν παρ' αὐτῷ ποιήσομεν.

Ταῦτα εἰπὼν ὁ γέρων, καὶ πολλῷ πλείονα τῆς ἡγιασμένης αὐτοῦ ψυχῆς καὶ θεολόγου γλώττης ἐπάξια, τὴν ἀνιωμένην τοῦ Ἰωάσαφ ψυχὴν παρεμυθεῖτο. εἶτα πρός τινας ἐκπέμπει αὐτὸν ἀδελφούς, ἐκ πολλοῦ διαστήματος τὴν οἴκησιν ἔχοντας, τοῦ ἀγαγεῖν τὰ πρὸς τὴν ἱερὰν θυσίαν ἁρμόδια. καὶ δὴ ἀναζωσάμενος ὁ Ἰωάσαφ λίαν τάχιστα τὴν διακονίαν πληροῖ· ἐδεδίει γὰρ μή πως ἀπόντος αὐτοῦ τὴν ὀφειλὴν ὁ Βαρλαὰμ τῆς φύσεως ἀποδῷ, καί, τὸ πνεῦμα παραθεὶς τῷ Κυρίῳ, ζημίαν αὐτῷ τὴν χαλεπὴν ἐπενέγκοι, μὴ ῥημάτων, μὴ προσφθεγμάτων ἐξοδίων, μὴ εὐχῶν, μὴ εὐλογιῶν τῶν ἐκείνου τυγχάνοντι.

Οὕτω δὲ ἀνδρικώτατα διελθόντος αὐτοῦ τὴν
μακρὰν ὁδὸν ἐκείνην καὶ τὰ τῆς ἱερᾶς θυσίας
ἐνεγκόντος, προσφέρει τῷ Θεῷ τὴν ἀναίμακτον
θυσίαν ὁ θειότατος Βαρλαάμ. καὶ κοινωνήσας
αὐτός, μεταδοὺς δὲ καὶ τῷ Ἰωάσαφ τῶν ἀχράν- 356
των τοῦ Χριστοῦ μυστηρίων, ἠγαλλιάσατο τῷ
Πνεύματι. καὶ τῆς συνήθους μεταλαβόντες τροφῆς, ψυχωφελέσι λόγοις τὴν ψυχὴν αὖθις ἔτρεφε τοῦ Ἰωάσαφ, Οὐκ ἔτι, λέγων, ἡμᾶς, ὦ φίλτατε υἱέ, συναγάγῃ ἐν τῷ βίῳ τούτῳ εἰς ἓν ἑστία καὶ τράπεζα· πορεύομαι γὰρ ἤδη τὴν τελευταίαν ὁδὸν τῶν πατέρων μου. χρὴ οὖν σε τὸ πρὸς ἐμὲ φίλτρον διὰ τῆς φυλακῆς τῶν τοῦ Θεοῦ ἐντολῶν, καὶ τῆς ἐν τῷδε τῷ τόπῳ μέχρι τέλους καρτερίας,

that may be fulfilled in thee, which the Saviour promised to his friends, when he said, "If any man love me, he will keep my word: and my father will love him, and we will come unto him, and make our abode with him."'

Ioasaph is sent by Barlaam on an errand

With these words, and many others, full worthy of that sanctified soul and inspired tongue, did the old man comfort Ioasaph's anguished soul. Then he sent him unto certain brethren, which abode a long way off, for to fetch the things fitting for the Holy Sacrifice. And Ioasaph girded up his loins, and with all speed fulfilled his errand: for he dreaded lest peradventure, in his absence, Barlaam might pay the debt of nature, and, yielding up the ghost to God, might inflict on him the loss of missing his departing words and utterances, his last orisons and blessings.

Barlaam taketh his last farewell of Ioasaph

So when Ioasaph had manfully finished his long journey, and had brought the things required for the Holy Sacrifice, saintly Barlaam offered up to God the unbloody Sacrifice. When he had communicated himself, and also given to Ioasaph of the undefiled Mysteries of Christ, he rejoiced in the Spirit. And when they had taken together of their ordinary food, Barlaam again fed Ioasaph's soul with edifying words, saying, 'Well-beloved son, no longer in this world shall we share one common hearth and board; for now I go my last journey, even the way of my fathers. Needs must thou, therefore, prove thy loving affection for me by thy keeping of God's commandments, and by thy continuance in this place even to the end, living as thou hast

ἐπιδείξασθαι, πολιτευόμενος καθὼς ἔμαθες καὶ ἐδιδάχθης, καὶ μεμνημένος διὰ παντὸς τῆς ταπεινῆς καὶ ῥαθύμου μου ψυχῆς. χαρᾷ οὖν χαῖρε, καὶ τῇ ἐν Χριστῷ ἀγαλλιάσει εὐφραίνου, ὅτι τῶν ἐπιγείων καὶ φθαρτῶν ἀντηλλάξω τὰ αἰώνιά τε
καὶ ἄφθαρτα, καὶ ὅτι ἐγγίζει ὁ μισθὸς τῶν ἔργων 357
σου, καὶ ὁ μισθαποδότης ἤδη πάρεστιν, ὃς ἥξει
Mat. xx. 1–16 τὸν ἀμπελῶνα ἰδεῖν ὃν ἐγεώργησας καὶ πλουσίως
2 Tim. ii. 11 σοι τὸν μισθὸν τῆς γεωργίας παρέξει. Πιστὸς γὰρ ὁ λόγος καὶ πάσης ἀποδοχῆς ἄξιος, καθὼς ὁ θεσπέσιος βοᾷ Παῦλος· Εἰ γὰρ συναπεθάνομεν, καὶ συζήσομεν· εἰ ὑπομένομεν, καὶ συμβασιλεύσομεν βασιλείαν τὴν αἰώνιον καὶ ἀτελεύτητον, τῷ
1 Tim. vi. 15 φωτὶ καταλαμπόμενοι τῷ ἀπροσίτῳ, καὶ τῆς ἐλλάμψεως καταξιούμενοι τῆς μακαρίας ὄντως καὶ ζωαρχικῆς Τριάδος.

Τοιαῦτα μὲν ὁ Βαρλαὰμ ἕως ἑσπέρας καὶ παρ' ὅλην τὴν νύκτα τῷ Ἰωάσαφ ὡμίλει, ἀκατασχέτοις δάκρυσιν ὀδυρομένῳ καὶ τὸν χωρισμὸν μὴ φέροντι. ἄρτι δὲ τῆς ἡμέρας διαφανούσης, τὴν πρὸς αὐτὸν ὁμιλίαν διαπεράνας, ἦρεν εἰς οὐρανὸν χεῖράς τε καὶ ὄμματα, καὶ εὐχαριστίαν ἀναπέμψας τῷ Θεῷ, ἔφη.

Κύριε, ὁ Θεός μου, ὁ πανταχοῦ παρὼν καὶ τὰ πάντα πληρῶν, εὐχαριστῶ σοι, ὅτι ἐπεῖδες τὴν ταπείνωσίν μου καὶ ἐν τῇ ὀρθοδόξῳ σου ὁμολογίᾳ καὶ ἐν ὁδῷ τῶν ἐντολῶν σου ἠξίωσας τὸν δρόμον τελέσαι με τῆς ἐνθάδε παροικίας μου. καὶ νῦν, φιλάγαθε Δέσποτα καὶ πανοικτίρμον, δέξαι με
Luke xvi. 9 εἰς τὰς αἰωνίους σου σκηνάς, καὶ μὴ μνησθῇς ὅσα σοι ἥμαρτον ἐν γνώσει τε καὶ ἀγνοίᾳ. φύλαξον δὲ καὶ τὸν πιστόν σου δοῦλον τοῦτον, οὗπερ προ-

learned and been instructed, and alway remembering my poor and slothful soul. Rejoice, therefore, with great joy, and make merry with the gladness that is in Christ, because thou hast exchanged the earthly and corruptible for the eternal and incorruptible; and because there draweth nigh the reward of thy works, and thy rewarder is already at hand, who shall come to see the vineyard which thou hast dressed, and shall richly pay thee the wages of thine husbandry. "Faithful is the saying, and worthy of all acceptation," as proclaimed by Paul the divine, "For if we be dead with him, we shall also live with him; if we endure, we shall also reign with him in his eternal and everlasting kingdom, being illuminated with the light unapproachable, and guerdoned with the effulgence of the blessed and life-giving Trinity."'

Barlaam's last prayer and thanksgiving

Thus until even-tide and all night long did Barlaam converse with Ioasaph, who wept tears that could not be stayed, and could not bear the parting. But just as day began to dawn, Barlaam ended his discourse, lifted up his hands and eyes to heaven, and offered his thanks to God, thus saying, 'O Lord, my God, who art everywhere present, and fillest all things, I thank thee, for that thou hast looked upon my lowliness, and hast granted me to fulfil the course of this mine earthly pilgrimage in thy true Faith, and in the way of thy commandments. And now, thou lover of good, all-merciful Master, receive me into thine everlasting habitations; and remember not all the sins that I have committed against thee, in knowledge or in ignorance. Defend also this thy faithful servant, before whom

στῆναί με τὸν ἀχρεῖόν σου ἠξίωσας οἰκέτην·
ῥῦσαι αὐτὸν ἀπὸ πάσης ματαιότητος καὶ ἐπη- 358
ρείας τοῦ ἀντικειμένου, καὶ ὑψηλότερον αὐτὸν
ποίησον τῶν πολυπλόκων παγίδων, ὧν εἰς σκάνδαλον ἥπλωσεν ὁ πονηρὸς πάντων τῶν θελόντων
σωθῆναι. ἀφάνισον, παντοδύναμε, πᾶσαν τὴν
δύναμιν τοῦ ἀπατεῶνος ἀπὸ προσώπου τοῦ δούλου σου, καὶ δὸς αὐτῷ ἐξουσίαν πατεῖν τὴν
ὀλεθροτόκον κάραν τοῦ πολεμίου τῶν ἡμετέρων
ψυχῶν. κατάπεμψον ἐξ ὕψους τὴν χάριν τοῦ
Ἁγίου σου Πνεύματος. καὶ ἐνίσχυσον αὐτὸν
πρὸς τὰς ἀοράτους παρατάξεις, ἵνα τὸν τῆς νίκης
ἀξιωθῇ παρὰ σοῦ στέφανον δέξασθαι, καὶ δοξασθῇ ἐν αὐτῷ τὸ ὄνομά σου, τοῦ Πατρός, καὶ
τοῦ Υἱοῦ, καὶ τοῦ Ἁγίου Πνεύματος, ὅτι σοὶ
πρέπει δόξα καὶ αἴνεσις εἰς τοὺς αἰῶνας. ἀμήν.

Ταῦτα εὐξάμενος, καὶ τὸν Ἰωάσαφ πατρικῶς
Rom. xvi. 6 περιπτυξάμενος, καὶ ἀσπασμὸν αὐτῷ δοὺς ἐν
Ez. ix. 4, 6 φιλήματι ἁγίῳ, τῷ τύπῳ τε τοῦ σταυροῦ ἑαυτὸν
Gen. xlix. 33 ἐπισφραγισάμενος, καὶ τοὺς πόδας ἐξάρας, καὶ
Athanas. Vita λίαν περιχαρὴς γενόμενος, ὥσπερ τινῶν ἐπιδη-
Antonii § 92 μησάντων φίλων, πρὸς τὴν μακαρίαν ἀπῆλθε
πορείαν, πρὸς τὴν ἐκεῖθεν διελθὼν γεροδοσίαν,
πρεσβύτης ὢν καὶ πλήρης ἡμερῶν τῶν τοῦ
πνεύματος.

XL

Ὁ δὲ Ἰωάσαφ, περιχυθεὶς τῷ πατρὶ μεθ' ὅσης
ἂν εἴποις τῆς εὐλαβείας καὶ οἰμωγῆς, δάκρυσί τε
p. 312 τὸ λείψανον λούσας, καὶ τῷ τριχίνῳ ῥακίῳ, ὅπερ

thou hast granted to me, thine unprofitable servant, to stand. Deliver him from all vanity, and all despiteful treatment of the adversary, and set him clear of the many-meshed nets which the wicked one spreadeth abroad for to trip all them that would full fain be saved. Destroy, Almighty Lord, all the might of the deceiver from before the face of thy servant, and grant him authority to trample on the baneful head of the enemy of our souls. Send down from on high the grace of thy Holy Spirit; and strengthen him against the invisible hosts, that he may receive at thy hands the crown of victory, and that in him thy name may be glorified, the Father, the Son, and the Holy Ghost, for to thee belongeth glory and praise for ever and ever. Amen.'

Barlaam giveth up the ghost

Thus prayed he, and in fatherly wise embraced Ioasaph, and saluted him with an holy kiss. Then he sealed himself with the sign of the Cross, and gathered up his feet, and, with exceeding great joy, as at the home-coming of friends, departed on that blessed journey, to receive his reward yonder, an old man and full of days in the Spirit.

XL

Ioasaph burieth the body of Barlaam

Then did Ioasaph embrace the good father, with all the devotion and sorrow that can be told, and washed his corpse with his tears. Then he wrapped

αὐτὸς ἐν τῷ παλατίῳ παρέσχεν, περιελίξας, τοὺς
νενομισμένους ἐπιλέγει ψαλμούς, διὰ πάσης τῆς
ἡμέρας καὶ τῆς νυκτὸς ὅλης ψάλλων ἅμα καὶ δάκρυσι τὸ τίμιον τοῦ μάκαρος βρέχων σῶμα. τῇ δὲ
ἐπιούσῃ ἡμέρᾳ, τάφον ποιήσας ἐχόμενον τοῦ σπηλαίου, καὶ εὐλαβῶς ἄγαν τὸ ἱερὸν λείψανον δια- 359
βαστάσας, ἐν τῷ μνήματι κατέθετο τὸν πνευματικὸν πατέρα ὁ καλὸς υἱὸς καὶ τιμιώτατος. καὶ
θερμότερον ἐκκαυθεὶς τὴν ψυχήν, εἰς ἐκτενεστέραν
τε συντείνας εὐχὴν ἑαυτόν, ἔφη·

Ps. xxvii. 7–11 Κύριε, ὁ Θεός μου, εἰσάκουσον τῆς φωνῆς μου
ἧς ἐκέκραξα· ἐλέησόν με καὶ εἰσάκουσόν μου, ὅτι
σε ἐκ καρδίας μου ζητῶ. ἐξεζήτησέ σε ἡ ψυχή
μου· μὴ ἀποστρέψῃς τὸ πρόσωπόν σου ἀπ᾿ ἐμοῦ,
καὶ μὴ ἐκκλίνῃς ἐν ὀργῇ ἀπὸ τοῦ δούλου σου.
βοηθός μου γενοῦ· μὴ ἀποσκορακίσῃς με, καὶ μὴ
ἐγκαταλίπῃς με, ὁ Θεὸς ὁ Σωτήρ μου, ὅτι ὁ πατήρ
μου καὶ ἡ μήτηρ μου ἐγκατέλιπόν με· σὺ δέ,
Κύριε, προσλαβοῦ με. νομοθέτησόν με, Κύριε,
ἐν τῇ ὁδῷ σου, καὶ ὁδήγησόν με ἐν τρίβῳ εὐθείᾳ,
ἕνεκα τῶν ἐχθρῶν μου. μὴ παραδῷς με εἰς
Ps. xxii. 4 ψυχὰς θλιβόντων με, ὅτι ἐπὶ σὲ ἐπερρίφην ἐκ
μήτρας, ἀπὸ γαστρὸς μητρός μου Θεός μου εἶ
σύ· μὴ ἀποστῇς ἀπ᾿ ἐμοῦ, ὅτι πλὴν σοῦ οὐκ
ἔστιν ὁ βοηθῶν μοι. ἰδοὺ γὰρ εἰς τὸ πέλαγος
τῶν οἰκτιρμῶν σου τὴν ἐλπίδα ἐθέμην τῆς ψυχῆς
μου· κυβέρνησόν μου τὴν ζωήν, ὁ πᾶσαν τὴν
κτῆσιν ἀρρήτῳ σοφίας προνοίᾳ κυβερνῶν, καὶ
Ps. cxliii. 8 γνώρισόν μοι ὁδὸν ἐν ᾗ πορεύσομαι. καὶ σῶσόν
με, ὡς ἀγαθὸς Θεὸς καὶ φιλάνθρωπος, εὐχαῖς
καὶ πρεσβείαις τοῦ θεράποντός σου Βαρλαάμ,
ὅτι σὺ εἶ ὁ Θεός μου, καὶ σὲ δοξάζω τὸν Πατέρα, 360

it in the hair-shirt, which Barlaam had given him in his palace; and over him he recited the proper psalms, chanting all the day long, and throughout the night, and watering the venerable body of the Saint with his tears. On the morrow, he made a grave hard by the cave, and thither reverently bore the sacred body, and there, like a good and honourable son, laid his spiritual father in his sepulchre. And then, the fire of grief kindling all the hotter within his soul, he set himself to pray the more earnestly, saying:

Ioasaph prayeth God to be his helper

'O Lord my God, hearken unto my voice, when I cry unto thee. Have mercy upon me, and hear me, for I seek thee with all my heart. My soul hath sought for thee: O hide not thy face from me, and turn not away in anger from thy servant. Be thou my helper; cast me not utterly away, and forsake me not, O God my Saviour, because my father and mother forsake me; but do thou, O Lord, take me up. Teach me thy way, O Lord, and lead me in the right way because of mine enemies. Deliver me not over unto the souls of them that afflict me; for I have been cast upon thee ever since I was born; thou art my God even from my mother's womb. O go not from me, because, except thee, there is none to help me. For lo, I set the hope of my soul upon the ocean of thy mercies. Be thou the pilot of my soul, thou that steerest all creation with the unspeakable forethought of thy wisdom; and shew thou me the way that I should walk in; and, as thou art a good God and a lover of men, save me by the prayers and intercessions of Barlaam thy servant, for thou art my

καὶ τὸν Υἱὸν καὶ τὸ Ἅγιον Πνεῦμα εἰς τοὺς αἰῶνας
τῶν αἰώνων. ἀμήν.
Ταῦτα εὐξάμενος, πλησίον τοῦ μνήματος
ἐκάθισε κλαίων. καὶ καθεζόμενος ὕπνωσε. καὶ
p. 280 ὁρᾷ τοὺς φοβεροὺς ἄνδρας ἐκείνους, οὓς καὶ
πρότερον ἑωράκει, ἐλθόντας πρὸς αὐτόν, καὶ
ἀπαγαγόντας αὐτὸν εἰς τὴν μεγίστην καὶ θαυμαστὴν ἐκείνην πεδιάδα, καὶ πρὸς τὴν δεδοξα-
σμένην καὶ ὑπέρλαμπρον εἰσαγαγόντες πόλιν.
εἰσερχομένῳ δὲ αὐτῷ τὴν πύλην ἕτεροι ὑπήντουν
πολλῷ κατηγλαϊσμένοι φωτί, στεφάνους ἔχοντες
ἐν χερσὶν ἀρρήτῳ διαλάμποντας κάλλει καὶ οἵους
ὀφθαλμοὶ οὐδέποτε βρότειοι ἐθεάσαντο. ἐρομένου δὲ τοῦ Ἰωάσαφ, Τίνος οἱ στέφανοι τῆς δόξης
οἱ ὑπέρλαμπροι, οὓς ὁρῶ; Σὸς μὲν ὁ εἷς, ἔφησαν,
Cp. Dan. xii. 3 ὑπὲρ τῶν πολλῶν σοι ψυχῶν ὧν ἔσωσας κατα-
σκευασθείς, κοσμηθεὶς δὲ νυνὶ πλέον ὑπὲρ τῆς
ἀσκήσεως ᾗ μετέρχῃ, εἴπερ ἀνδρείως ταύτην ἕως
τέλους διέλθῃς· ὁ δὲ ἕτερος σὸς μὲν καὶ αὐτός·
ἀλλὰ τῷ πατρί σου δεῖ σε τοῦτον παρασχεῖν, τῷ
διὰ σοῦ τῆς ὁδοῦ ἐκκλίναντι τῆς πονηρᾶς καὶ
μετανοήσαντι γνησίως τῷ Κυρίῳ. ὁ δὲ Ἰωάσαφ
δυσχεραίνοντι ἐῴκει· καί, Πῶς δυνατόν, φησίν,
ἴσων ἐμοῦ, τοῦ τοσαῦτα κοπιάσαντος, τυχεῖν
τὸν πατέρα μου δωρεῶν ὑπὲρ μόνης τῆς μετανοίας; εἶπε ταῦτα, καὶ τὸν Βαρλαὰμ εὐθὺς
ἐδόκει βλέπειν ὀνειδίζοντα οἱονεὶ καὶ λέγοντα·
Οὗτοι οἱ λόγοι μου, Ἰωάσαφ, οὕς ποτέ σοι,
p. 266 Ὅταν ὑπερπλουτήσῃς, ἔλεγον, οὐκ εὐμετάδοτος
ἔσῃ· καὶ αὐτὸς ἠπόρεις ἐπὶ τῷ ῥήματι. νυνὶ
δὲ πῶς ἐδυσχέρανας ἐπὶ τῇ ἰσοτιμίᾳ τοῦ πατρός
σου, καὶ οὐ μᾶλλον εὐφράνθης τὴν ψυχὴν ὅτι 361

God, and thee I glorify, the Father, the Son, and the Holy Ghost, world without end. Amen.'

Ioasaph, in a vision, vieweth the glorious city and the crown laid up in store for the righteous

Thus prayed he, and sat him down nigh the sepulchre, a-weeping. And as he sat, he fell asleep, and saw those dread men, whom he had seen before, coming to him, and carrying him away to the great and marvellous plain, and bringing him to that glorious and exceeding bright city. When he had passed within the gate, there met him others, gloriously apparelled with much light, having in their hands crowns radiant with unspeakable beauty, such as mortal eye hath never seen. And, when Ioasaph enquired, 'Whose are these exceeding bright crowns of glory, which I see?' 'Thine,' said they, 'is the one, prepared for thee, because of the many souls which thou hast saved, and now made still more beautiful because of the religious life that thou leadest, if thou continue therein bravely until the end. And this other crown is thine also; but it must thou give unto thy father, who, by thy means, turned from his evil way unto the Lord, and was truly penitent.' But Ioasaph was as one sore vexed, and said, 'How is it possible that, for his repentance alone, my father should receive reward equal to mine, that have laboured so much? Thus spake he, and straightway thought that he saw Barlaam, as it were, chiding him and saying, 'These are my words, Ioasaph, which I once spake unto thee, saying, "When thou waxest passing rich, thou wilt not be glad to distribute," and thou understoodest not my saying. But now, why art thou displeased at thy father's equality with thee in honour, and art not rather glad at heart that thine orisons in

εἰσηκούσθη σου ἡ πολλὴ περὶ αὐτοῦ δέησις; ὁ δὲ Ἰωάσαφ, ὡς εἴθιστο ἀεὶ λέγειν αὐτῷ, Συγχώρησον, ἔφη, Πάτερ, συγχώρησον. ποῦ δὲ αὐτὸς οἰκεῖς γνώρισόν μοι. Ἐν ταύτῃ, φησί, τῇ μεγάλῃ καὶ περικαλλεῖ πόλει· οἰκεῖν ἔλαχον ἐν μεσαιτάτῃ τῆς πόλεως πλατείᾳ φωτὶ καταστραπτομένῃ ἀπλέτῳ. ἀξιοῦν δὲ αὖθις ὁ Ἰωάσαφ ἐδόκει τὸν Βαρλαὰμ εἰς τὸ ἑαυτοῦ ἀπαγαγεῖν αὐτὸν σκήνωμα καὶ φιλοφρόνως ξεναγῆσαι. ἀλλ' οὔπω τὸν καιρὸν ἥκειν, ἔλεγεν ἐκεῖνος, πρὸς ἐκεῖνά σε τὰ σκηνώματα ἐλθεῖν, ἔτι τῷ φορτίῳ τοῦ σώματος ὑποκείμενον. Εἴπερ οὖν ἀνδρείως καρτερήσεις, καθάπερ σοι ἐνετειλάμην, ἥξεις μικρὸν ὕστερον, καὶ τῶν αὐτῶν ἀξιωθήσῃ σκηνωμάτων, τῆς αὐτῆς τεύξῃ χαρᾶς τε καὶ δόξης, καὶ συνδιαιωνίζων ἔσῃ μοι. ἔξυπνος δὲ ἐπὶ τούτοις γενόμενος, ὁ Ἰωάσαφ τοῦ φωτὸς ἐκείνου καὶ τῆς ἀρρήτου δόξης εἶχε τὴν ψυχὴν ἔτι πεπληρωμένην, καὶ σὺν πολλῷ τῷ θαύματι τῷ Δεσπότῃ χαριστήριον ἀνέπεμπεν ὕμνον.

Ἔμεινε δὲ μέχρι τέλους τὴν ἀγγελικὴν ἀληθῶς ἐπὶ γῆς ἀνύων διαγωγήν, καὶ σκληροτέρᾳ ἀσκήσει μετὰ τὴν παρέλευσιν τοῦ γέροντος χρώμενος· πέμπτῳ μὲν καὶ εἰκοστῷ τῆς ἡλικίας ἔτει τὴν ἐπίγειον καταλιπὼν βασιλείαν καὶ τὸν ἀσκητικὸν ὑπελθὼν ἀγῶνα, πέντε δὲ καὶ τριάκοντα χρόνους ἐν τῇ πανερήμῳ ταύτῃ ἀσκήσας, ὥσπερ τις ἄσαρκος, τὴν ὑπὲρ ἄνθρωπον ἄσκησιν, πολλὰς 362
μὲν πρότερον ψυχὰς ἀνθρώπων τοῦ ψυχοφθόρου δράκοντος ἀποσπάσας καὶ τῷ Θεῷ προσαγαγὼν σεσωσμένας, καὶ ἀποστολικῆς ἐν τούτῳ χάριτος ἀξιωθείς, μάρτυς δὲ τῇ προαιρέσει γενόμενος, καὶ

his behalf have been heard?' Then Ioasaph said unto him, as he was ever wont to say, 'Pardon! father, pardon! But shew me where thou dwellest?' Barlaam answered, 'In this mighty and exceeding fair city. It is my lot to dwell in the mid-most street of the city: a street that flasheth with light supernal.' Again Ioasaph thought he asked Barlaam to bring him to his own habitation, and, in friendly wise, to shew him the sights thereof. But Barlaam said that his time was not yet come to win those habitations, while he was under the burden of the flesh. 'But,' said he, 'if thou persevere bravely, even as I charged thee, in a little while thou shalt come hither, and gain the same habitations, and obtain the same joy and glory, and be my companion for ever.' Hereupon Ioasaph awoke out of sleep, but his soul was still full of that light and ineffable glory; and greatly wondering, he raised to his Lord a song of thanksgiving.

and speaketh with holy Barlaam

And he continued to the end, verily leading on earth the life of an angel, and after the death of his aged friend using himself to severer austerity. Twenty and five years old was he when he left his earthly kingdom, and adopted the monastic life; and thirty and five years in this vast desert did he, like one dis-fleshed, endure rigours above the endurance of man, but not before he had delivered the souls of many men from the soul-devouring dragon, and presented them to God, saved for aye; winning herewith the Apostolic grace. In will he had proved a martyr, and had with boldness

Of Ioasaph's holy life in the desert

παρρησίᾳ τὸν Χριστὸν ἐνώπιον βασιλέων ὁμολο-
γήσας καὶ τυράννων, καὶ κήρυξ μεγαλοφωνότατος
τῆς αὐτοῦ μεγαλειότητος ἀναφανείς, πολλὰ δ' αὖ
πάλιν πνεύματα πονηρίας ἐν τῇ ἐρήμῳ καταπα-
λαίσας, καὶ πάντων τῇ τοῦ Χριστοῦ περιγε-
νόμενος δυνάμει, καὶ τῆς ἄνωθεν πλουσίως μετα-
σχὼν δωρεᾶς τε καὶ χάριτος, ἐντεῦθεν κεκα-
θαρμένον τὸ τῆς ψυχῆς ὄμμα πάσης περιγείου
ἀχλύος εἶχεν, ὡς παρόντα δὲ τὰ μέλλοντα προ-
εθεώρει, καὶ Χριστὸς ἦν αὐτῷ ἀντὶ πάντων,
Χριστὸν ἐπόθει, Χριστὸν ὡς παρόντα ἑώρα,
Χριστοῦ τὸ κάλλος διὰ παντὸς ἐνωπτρίζετο,
Ps. xvi. 8 κατὰ τὸν Προφήτην τὸν λέγοντα· Προωρώμην
τὸν Κύριον ἐνώπιόν μου διὰ παντός, ὅτι ἐκ δεξιῶν
Ps. lxiii. 9 μοῦ ἐστιν ἵνα μὴ σαλευθῶ· καὶ αὖθις· Ἐκολλήθη
ἡ ψυχή μου ὀπίσω σου· ἐμοῦ δὲ ἀντελάβετο ἡ
δεξιά σου. ἐκολλήθη γὰρ ὄντως ἡ ψυχὴ αὐτοῦ
ὀπίσω τοῦ Χριστοῦ, συναρμοσθεῖσα αὐτῷ ἀρ-
ραγεῖ συναφείᾳ. οὐ μετετράπη τῆς θαυμαστῆς
ταύτης ἐργασίας, οὐκ ἠλλοίωσε τὸν κανόνα τῆς
ἀσκήσεως ἑαυτοῦ, ἀπ' ἀρχῆς μέχρι τέλους, ἴσην
τηρήσας τὴν προθυμίαν ἐκ νεωτέρας μέχρι τῆς
τοσαύτης ἡλικίας, μᾶλλον δὲ καὶ εἰς ὑψηλοτέραν
ὁσημέραι προκόπτων τὴν ἀρετὴν καὶ καθαρωτέρας ἀξιούμενος θεωρίας.

Ἀμέλει τοιαύτην πολιτευσάμενος πολιτείαν καὶ
οὕτως ἀξίαν τῆς ἑαυτοῦ κλήσεως ἐργασίαν ἀπο-
Gal. vi. 14 δεδωκὼς τῷ καλέσαντι, σταυρώσας τὸν κόσμον 363
ἑαυτῷ καὶ ἑαυτὸν τῷ κόσμῳ, ἐν εἰρήνῃ πρὸς τὸν
τῆς εἰρήνης ἀναλύει Θεόν, καὶ πρὸς τὸν ἀεὶ
ποθούμενον ἐκδημεῖ Δεσπότην, καὶ τῷ προσώπῳ
Κυρίου ἀμέσως καὶ καθαρῶς ἐμφανίζεται, τῷ τῆς

confessed Christ before kings and tyrants, and had proved himself the mighty-voiced preacher of his greatness, and had overthrown many spirits of wickedness in the desert, and had overcome all in the strength of Christ. Partaking richly of the gift of grace from above, he kept his mind's eye purified from every earth-born cloud, and looked forward to the things that are to come, as though they were already come. Christ was his recompense for all: Christ was his desire: Christ he ever saw as present with him: Christ and his fair beauty everywhere met his sight, according to the saying of the prophet, 'I have set God always before me; for he is on my right hand, therefore I shall not fall.' And again, 'My soul cleaveth to thee; thy right hand hath upholden me.' For verily Ioasaph's soul clave to Christ, being knit to him in indissoluble union. From this marvellous work he never swerved, never altered the rule of his ascetic life, from beginning to end, but maintained his zeal from his youth even until old age; or rather, he daily advanced higher in virtue, and daily gained purer power of vision.

Ioasaph departeth this life

Thus did Ioasaph spend his days, and render unto him that called him labour worthy of his calling, having crucified the world to himself, and himself unto the world, and, at the last, departed in peace unto the God of peace, and passed to that Master whom he had alway longed for. There he appeared in the immediate presence of the Lord, and was crowned with the crown of glory already prepared

ἐκεῖθέν τε δόξης ἤδη προητρεπισμένῳ αὐτῷ
στεφάνῳ κοσμεῖται, καὶ Χριστὸν βλέπειν κατ-
αξιοῦται, Χριστῷ συνεῖναι, Χριστοῦ τῷ κάλλει
διὰ παντὸς ἐναγάλλεσθαι, οὗπερ εἰς χεῖρας τὴν
Ps. cxvi. 9 ἑαυτοῦ ψυχὴν παραθέμενος, ἐν τῇ τῶν ζώντων
Cp. Ps. lxxxvii. 7 μετεφοίτησε χώρᾳ, ἔνθα ἦχος ἑορταζόντων, ἔνθα
τῶν εὐφραινομένων ἡ κατοικία.

Τὸ δέ γε τίμιον αὐτοῦ σῶμα ἐκ γειτόνων αὐτῷ
τὰς οἰκήσεις ποιούμενός τις ἀνὴρ ἅγιος, ὃς καὶ τὴν
πρὸς Βαρλαὰμ πορείαν ἐκείνῳ ποτὲ ὑπέδειξε, θείᾳ
τινὶ μυηθεὶς ἀποκαλύψει κατ' αὐτὴν τὴν ὥραν τῆς
τελειώσεως αὐτοῦ παραγίνεται, καὶ ὕμνοις ἱεροῖς
τιμήσας, δάκρυά τε κατασπείσας, σύμβολον τοῦ
πρὸς αὐτὸν πόθου, τἄλλα δὴ τὰ νενομισμένα
Χριστιανοῖς πάντα τελέσας, ἐν τῷ τοῦ πατρὸς
ἔθετο Βαρλαὰμ μνήματι. συνεῖναι γὰρ ἔδει τὰ
σώματα ὧν αἱ ψυχαὶ συνδιαιωνίζειν ἔμελλον
ἀλλήλαις.

Προστάγματι δέ τινος φοβερωτάτου κατ' ὄναρ
κραταιῶς ἐπισκήπτοντος πεισθείς, ὁ τοῦτον 364
κηδεύσας ἀναχωρητὴς τὰ βασίλεια καταλαμβάνει Ἰνδῶν, καὶ τῷ βασιλεῖ Βαραχίᾳ προσελθὼν
πάντα αὐτῷ δῆλα τὰ περὶ τοῦ Βαρλαὰμ καὶ τοῦ
μακαρίου τούτου τίθησιν Ἰωάσαφ. ὁ δέ, μηδὲν
μελλήσας, ἀπέρχεται αὐτὸς μετὰ δυνάμεως ὄχλου,
καὶ τῷ σπηλαίῳ ἐφίσταται, τὸ μνῆμά τε θεωρεῖ,
καί, τούτῳ θερμότατα ἐπιδακρύσας, αἴρει τὸ
κάλυμμα. καὶ ὁρᾷ τόν τε Βαρλαὰμ καὶ τὸν
Ἰωάσαφ ἔχοντας τὰ μέλη κατὰ σχῆμα κείμενα,
καὶ τὰ σώματα οὐδὲν τοῦ προτέρου χρωτὸς
παραλλάττοντα, ὁλόκληρα δὲ καὶ ἀκριβῶς ὑγιῆ
σὺν τοῖς ἐνδύμασι. ταῦτα τοίνυν τὰ ἱερὰ τῶν

for him: there it is granted to him to behold Christ, to be with Christ, to rejoice for ever in the fair beauty of Christ, into whose hands he commended his spirit, when he departed to walk in the land of the living, where is the song of them that feast, the dwelling-place of them that rejoice.

As for his venerable body, it befell thus; about the very hour of Ioasaph's death, there came by divine revelation, from one of the neighbouring cells, a certain holy man. It was the same that once pointed out to Ioasaph his way to Barlaam. This man honoured the corpse with sacred hymns, and shed tears, the token of affection, over him, and performed all the last Christian rites, and laid him in the sepulchre of his father Barlaam; for it was only meet that their bodies should rest side by side, since their souls were to dwell through eternity together.

An holy man burieth the body of Ioasaph in the tomb of Barlaam

In obedience to the strict command of a dread Angel that appeared to him in a dream, this hermit, who had performed the last rites, journeyed to the kingdom of India, and, entering in to King Barachias, made known unto him all that had befallen Barlaam, and this blessed Ioasaph. Barachias, making no delay, set forth with a mighty host, and arrived at the cave, and beheld their sepulchre, and wept bitterly over it, and raised the gravestone. There he descried Barlaam and Ioasaph lying, as they had been in life. Their bodies had not lost their former hue, but were whole and uncorrupt, together with their garments. These, the consecrated tabernacles

Barachias, learning all from the holy man, carrieth the bodies of the saints to his kingdom

ἁγίων ψυχῶν σκηνώματα, πολλὴν ἐκπέμποντα τὴν εὐωδίαν καὶ οὐδὲν ὅλως ἀηδὲς ἐπιδεικνύμενα, θήκαις ἐνθεὶς ὁ βασιλεὺς τιμίαις, εἰς τὴν ἑαυτοῦ πατρίδα μετακομίζει.

Ὡς δὲ εἰς τὰς ἀκοὰς ἔπιπτε τοῦ λαοῦ τὸ γεγονός, πλῆθος ἀριθμοῦ κρεῖττον ἔκ πάντων τε τῶν πόλεων καὶ τῶν περιχώρων εἰς προσκύνησιν καὶ θέαν συνέρρεον τῶν μακαρίων σωμάτων ἐκείνων. ἔνθεν τοι καὶ ὕμνους ἐπ' αὐτοῖς τοὺς ἱεροὺς ᾄσαντες, καὶ λαμπάδας φιλοτίμως ἀνάψαντες (ἀκολούθως, ἄν τις εἶπεν, ἐκεῖ καὶ λίαν οἰκείως τὰ φῶτα περὶ τοὺς τοῦ φωτὸς υἱούς τε καὶ κληρονόμους), λαμπρῶς δὲ ὁμοῦ καὶ μεγαλοπρεπῶς ἐν τῇ ἐξ αὐτῶν κρηπίδων παρὰ τοῦ Ἰωάσαφ ἀνεγηγερμένῃ κατέθεντο ἐκκλησίᾳ. πολλὰ δὲ θαύματα καὶ ἰάσεις ἔν τε τῇ μετακομιδῇ, ἔν τε τῇ καταθέσει, καὶ ἐν τοῖς ἑξῆς χρόνοις διὰ τῶν ὁσίων 365
αὐτοῦ θεραπόντων ἐποίησε Κύριος. καὶ εἶδεν ὁ βασιλεύς τε Βαραχίας καὶ πᾶς ὁ ὄχλος τὰς δι' αὐτῶν γενομένας δυνάμεις, καὶ πολλοὶ τῶν πέριξ ἐθνῶν, ἀπιστίαν νοσοῦντες καὶ τοῦ Θεοῦ ἄγνοιαν, διὰ τῶν γινομένων ἐν τῷ μνήματι σημείων ἐπίστευσαν. καὶ πάντες οἱ ὁρῶντές τε καὶ ἀκούοντες τὴν ἀγγελομίμητον τοῦ Ἰωάσαφ πολιτείαν καὶ τὸν ἐξ ἁπαλῶν ὀνύχων διάπυρον αὐτοῦ πρὸς τὸν Θεὸν πόθον, ἐθαύμαζον δοξάζοντες ἐν πᾶσι τὸν Θεόν, τὸν ἀεὶ συνεργοῦντα τοῖς ἀγαπῶσιν αὐτὸν καὶ μεγίσταις τούτους ἀμειβόμενον δωρεαῖς.

Ἕως ὧδε τὸ πέρας τοῦ παρόντος λόγου, ὃν κατὰ δύναμιν ἐμὴν γεγράφηκα, καθὼς ἀκήκοα παρὰ τῶν ἀψευδῶς παραδεδωκότων μοι τιμίων

of two holy souls, that sent forth full sweet savour, and showed naught distressful, were placed by King Barachias in costly tombs and conveyed by him into his own country.

Of the miracles wrought by these holy relics

Now when the people heard tell of that which had come to pass, there assembled a countless multitude out of all the cities and regions round about, to venerate and view the bodies of these Saints. Thereupon, sooth to say, they chanted the sacred hymns over them, and vied one with another to light lamps lavishly, and rightly and fitly, might one say, in honour of these children and inheritors of light. And with splendour and much solemnity they laid their bodies in the Church which Ioasaph had built from the very foundation. And many miracles and cures, during the translation and deposition of their relics, as also in later times, did the Lord work by his holy servants. And King Barachias and all the people beheld the mighty virtues that were shown by them; and many of the nations round about, that were sick of unbelief and ignorance of God, believed through the miracles that were wrought at their sepulchre. And all they that saw and heard of the Angelic life of Ioasaph, and of his love of God from his childhood upward, marvelled, and in all things glorified God that alway worketh together with them that love him, and granteth them exceeding great reward.

The author prayeth that he and his readers, by the inter-

Here endeth this history, which I have written, to the best of my ability, even as I heard it from the truthful lips of worthy men who delivered it

ἀνδρῶν. γένοιτο δὲ ἡμᾶς, τοὺς ἀναγινώσκοντάς τε καὶ ἀκούοντας τὴν ψυχωφελῆ διήγησιν ταύτην, τῆς μερίδος ἀξιωθῆναι τῶν εὐαρεστησάντων τῷ Κυρίῳ, εὐχαῖς καὶ πρεσβείαις Βαρλαάμ τε καὶ Ἰωάσαφ τῶν μακαρίων, περὶ ὧν ἡ διήγησις, ἐν Χριστῷ Ἰησοῦ τῷ Κυρίῳ ἡμῶν, ᾧ πρέπει τιμή, κράτος, μεγαλωσύνη τε καὶ μεγαλοπρέπεια, σὺν τῷ Πατρὶ καὶ τῷ Ἁγίῳ Πνεύματι νῦν καὶ ἀεί, καὶ εἰς τοὺς αἰῶνας τῶν αἰώνων. ἀμήν.

unto me. And may God grant that all we that read or hear this edifying story may obtain the heritage of such as have pleased the Lord, by the prayers and intercessions of blessed Barlaam and Ioasaph, of whom this story telleth, in Christ Jesu our Lord; to whom belongeth worship, might, majesty and glory, with the Father and the Holy Ghost, now and for evermore, world without end. Amen.

cession of Barlaam and Ioasaph, may attain to everlasting felicity

GENERAL INDEX

GENERAL INDEX

GENERAL INDEX

GENERAL INDEX

GREEK INDEX

GREEK INDEX

GREEK INDEX

GREEK INDEX

BIBLE INDEX

BIBLE INDEX

BIBLE INDEX